ROYAL CAPTIVE

PRAISE FOR HEATHER FROST

"Royal Captive is a standout in its genre!
Full of heart-pounding romance, high-stakes action, and
intricate court politicking, this book lives up to its title...
it holds you captive from start to finish!"
- Author Renee Dugan on *Royal Captive*

"A new powerful addition to a remarkable series I strongly
suggest you read. Once you start, you won't be able to stop, and
you'll thank ~~the fates~~ Frost for creating this captivating world!"
- Darkest Sins (Silvia) on *Royal Captive*

"Heather Frost is fabulous at telling enthralling tales!
From the very beginning, you are swept into the world of
Eyrinthia and may never want to leave."
- The Reading Pantry (Anna) on *Royal Captive*

"Eyrinthia has never been more dangerous — or enticing. The
irresistible characters draw you in and steal your breath, and the
unexpected turns will keep you glued to the pages right to the
end. Once again, Frost displays her mastery of the genre,
weaving a story so compelling it's impossible to put down."
- Author Rebecca McKinnon on *Royal Captive*

"Royal Spy is a gripping story with strong, powerful characters.
Excitement, betrayal, love with every turn of the page in this
heart pounding adventure. I couldn't put it down!"
- Min Reads and Reviews (Mindy) on *Royal Spy*

"Royal Spy is a breathtaking page turner that leaves you wanting more! Frost has outdone herself with her irresistible characters and fascinating backdrop of Eyrinthia.
This is a must-read for any fantasy lover!"
- Author Ashley I. Hansen on *Royal Spy*

"Heather Frost is a force to be reckoned with! This is quite honestly my favorite Indie author series. Hands down, the best. ...So many twists, turns and puzzle pieces, it truly makes Frost one of my favorite authors!"
- Author Sarah Hill on *Royal Spy*

"Heather Frost can write complex characters like nobody's business! ...[This] series is a hidden gem that I want to shout from the rooftops. If you are a fan of fantasy, this is a series that you need in your life."
-Book Briefs on *Royal Spy*

"Frost has written a magnificent young adult fantasy romance that readers will absolutely love. The turn of every page is jam packed with fast paced, thrilling and adventurous twists..."
- Singing Librarian Books (Sydney) on *Royal Decoy*

"This book has just about everything! ... The intrigue is fantastic. This is a series that is worth reading. I will anxiously await the next installment to see what happens next."
- Bookworm Lisa on *Royal Decoy*

"This book was superb. Heather Frost will be an author that I keep on my radar from now on."
- A Court of Coffee and Books (Stacy) on *Royal Decoy*

"An amazing first book in a series! The premise of this novel was so interesting! It's something that I'm fairly certain I haven't read before in other books."
- Chapters and Pages (Caitlin) on *Royal Decoy*

"If you are looking for a good read with royalty, mystery, intrigue, spies, war, and romance, this book has it all."
- Why Not? Because I Said So (Sheila) on *Royal Decoy*

"Super unique ... The story flowed and [...] was well-paced and didn't end off in a cliffhanger. I totally recommend this book to everyone especially those who want a fresh royalty read."
- Thindbooks on *Royal Decoy*

"This is a story that completely captured my attention from the very beginning and didn't let go the whole way through ... I've been craving a book like this."
- Getting Your Read On (Aimee) on *Royal Decoy*

"*Seers* is a really good paranormal read mixed with a great romance, and a some really fun characters."
- Mundie Moms Blog on *Seers*

"Heather does an amazing job of keeping the story rolling, fast paced and full of intrigue and suspense."
- Author Cindy C. Bennett on *Demons*

"As soon as I finished the final pages of *Demons* I was on a countdown until I had *Guardians* in my hands. And it did not disappoint!"
- FicTalk Review on *Guardians*

Also by Heather Frost:

Fate of Eyrinthia Series
Royal Decoy
Royal Spy

Fate of Eyrinthia Novellas
Fire & Ash

Seers Trilogy
Seers
Demons
Guardians

Asides: A Short Story Collection

ROYAL CAPTIVE

FATE OF EYRINTHIA · BOOK 3

HEATHER FROST

To my grandparents–
Thank you for the love, the stories, and the legacy.

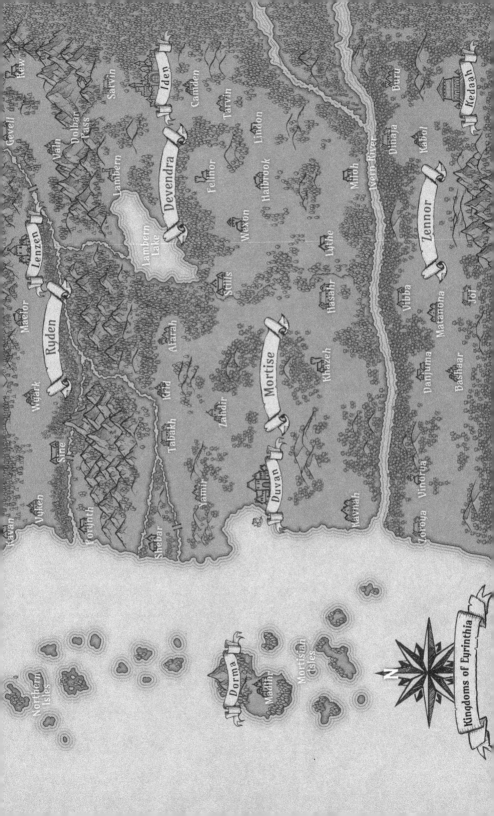

Rew

Gevell

Dolbar Pass

Vain

Sarvin

Iden

Camden

Tarvin

Lindon

Burn

Miloh

Dihaya

Kabol

Kedaah

Lambern

Devendra

Fellnor

Hafbrook

Zennor

Lambern Lake

Wexon

Vibba

Jor

Maelor

Lenzen

Stills

Lythe

Hasahr

Matanona

Wdark

Ruden

Alarah

Khazeh

Danjuma

Bashaar

Reld

Mortise

Vinoria

Sine

Tabakh

Zahdir

Navnah

Toroja

Vuken

Portinth

Jamil

Duvan

Kavan

Shebar

Northern Isles

Dorma

Madihn

Mortisian Isles

Ivern River

N

Kingdoms of Eyrinthia

CHAPTER I

BENNICK

"BE STILL," WILF BARKED.

Agony engulfed Bennick. He sucked in air, his fists digging into the ground, his body on fire. The blade had pierced his back and ripped through his body, coming out somewhere on his lower left side.

The pain was excruciating, but that wasn't what mattered.

"Go," he gasped. "Go after her."

Wilf ignored him. His fearsome expression was marked by old pox scars and deep lines, his jaw locked in a frown as he tore Bennick's bloody shirt, exposing the injury. His hard mouth became harder, his eyes going flat.

Bennick didn't have to see the wound to know the stabbing was fatal. His eyes pinched closed for a moment, sweat beading on his forehead. Everything inside him was screaming, but he forced words through his constricted throat. "Wilf, go. *Please*."

Wilf didn't respond, only leaned close. "It's clean," he grunted. "The smell, and the color of the blood. Perhaps nothing vital was hit. Hold still."

Bennick clenched his jaw as Wilf pressed a hand to his abdomen. His other hand slid beneath Bennick's back to find the entrance wound. He squeezed, attempting to staunch the blood flow with his bare hands. Bennick snarled through gritted teeth, his fingers clawing the ground to keep from tearing at Wilf's crushing grip.

"Dirk!" Wilf boomed. "We need a fire. Now!"

Sweat and blood drenched Bennick's shivering body. He knew his skin was flushed, and the shaking grew worse with every fractured breath. "Wilf," he croaked. "Stop. I'm already—dead."

Wilf's eyes didn't lift from his bloody hands, still pressed against Bennick's wounds. "You certainly talk a lot for a dead man."

"Please," Bennick rasped. "Go. Clare . . ."

"She'd never forgive me if I left you now," Wilf snapped. The pressure of his hands increased. "You're going to be fine."

Time was difficult to judge through the fog of pain.

Suddenly, Dirk knelt beside him, a few other guards huddled around them. When Dirk passed a heated dagger to Wilf, dread and panic punched through Bennick's chest. The guards leaned in, holding him down, giving him nowhere to retreat as Wilf pressed the red-hot blade against his skin.

A shattering scream tore through his throat. His head kicked back. His limbs jerked. Fingers tightened their bruising hold on his wrists and shoulders, keeping him pinned to the ground. He still thrashed against them, an involuntary response, his lungs nearly bursting with his anguished cries.

The blistering heat was unlike anything he had ever felt. Wilf was sealing the wound—the logical part of him knew that. They were giving him his best chance. But this was excruciating torture. The smell of burning flesh—*his* flesh—charred the air as the blade seared his skin. His stomach rolled—clenched—heaved. Someone turned his head to the side so he wouldn't choke on his vomit.

"This won't work," Dirk said, his voice low and tight.

Wilf's words were encased in steel. "It will."

The sizzle of scalding skin finally stopped, but the burning was relentless, even after the knife was lifted.

"Turn him over," Wilf ordered.

As they did, Bennick felt his awareness slipping. Darkness blotted out his sight, coming to claim him.

A blessing, considering what Wilf was about to do again.

As his cheek pressed into the dirt, Bennick struggled to gasp out his last request. "Save—her."

"I will," Wilf vowed, his voice rough. "Just as soon as I'm done saving you."

The fiery dagger touched his skin again, and Bennick was gone.

His last thought—the last image in his head—was of Clare.

CHAPTER 2

WILF

BENNICK'S SCREAMS RANG IN WILF'S EARS, even after unconsciousness had cut them off. A darting look assured him that his captain was still breathing, his chest lifting and falling, his pulse thrumming in his neck. The scent of charred flesh made Wilf's stomach lurch, and he swallowed down a wave of bile. He did not allow his hands to shake as he continued to press the heated blade to Bennick's flesh.

"Searing the wounds won't help if something vital was hit," Dirk said, his voice low and tense. He was terrified, too.

Wilf gritted his teeth. "He'll be fine."

He had to be.

Dirk didn't argue. He released his hold on Bennick, as it was no longer necessary to restrain him. He pushed to his feet, twist-

4

ing to look around them.

Wilf knew what he would see.

The carriage, sitting empty on the road, door ajar. Bodies of men and horses strewn over the ground. Arrows stuck in the trees, the carriage—and in the bodies that littered the area. Remnants of an ambush that had taken them all by surprise. Even now, the moans and sobs of the still-dying threaded the air.

"Cardon got away with Serene," Dirk said, his voice too level. Wilf had served with the man for years—he knew when Dirk was trying to reassure himself. "Imara's guards got her away as well. They'll all return to Serai Nadir's home to regroup."

"Good." It was a relief that both princesses were safe, but Clare was in the hands of bloodthirsty Mortisians who thought she was the princess. They hadn't killed her outright, and Wilf had to believe that was a good sign. They needed her alive. But for how long? And what would happen if they discovered she *wasn't* the princess?

"Where is Venn?"

Wilf stiffened at Dirk's sudden question. "I lost sight of him in the fight."

The older bodyguard was already striding away, searching the bodies on the ground.

Wilf's heart hammered in his chest. Fates, he couldn't lose anyone else . . .

Dirk wandered several paces before he froze. He muttered a curse and fell to his knees as he rolled a body over. "Venn? Venn!"

There was an answering groan, which loosened the knot in Wilf's throat. He set aside the still-hot dagger and forced himself to focus on Bennick. He'd stopped the bleeding, but that was only part of his captain's battle. Bennick needed a physician. *Now.*

"Vera," Venn slurred, pain riding his voice hard.

Dirk shook his head, the silver hairs among his otherwise dark head catching in the sunlight. "I don't know where she is."

"Gone," Venn said, the word ending on a groan as he struggled to rise. "They took her." Instead of forcing him back down, Dirk grabbed the young man's arm and helped him sit—a good sign that Venn wasn't too badly injured.

A growl vibrated through Wilf's chest. "They took Clare, too."

Venn's head swiveled toward him, blood tracking down the right side of his face from a blow to his temple. The young man's eyes dipped, and his dark skin visibly paled. "Bennick?"

"He's alive." Determination lived in Wilf's voice.

Dirk's gaze swept the surrounding area. "Ser Zephan is dead. He escaped his guards, but not the arrows of the attackers."

Wilf didn't have the capacity to feel anything about the Mortisian's death. Ser Zephan had tried to kill Serene more than once, and he had only been their prisoner so they could take him to Serjah Desfan to be tried for his treason. The irony that Zephan had been killed by other Mortisians, however, did not escape Wilf's notice.

Venn's shoulders tensed. "The Rose?"

"We have him," a new voice rang out, and Wilf felt a flash of relief to see a couple of soldiers dragging the infamous assassin—hands still bound—between them. The guard spoke again, his voice rigid. "He was attempting to get away."

The Rose lifted one shoulder. "You can't blame me for trying." His eyes fell on Bennick and his head tipped to the side, brown locks falling over his forehead. "Is he dead?" He didn't sound concerned, or even excited—merely curious.

"No." Wilf pushed to his feet. He ignored the fact that, as senior bodyguard, Dirk was technically in charge. "I'm going after them. Dirk, take Bennick and Venn to Serai Nadir's estate."

Venn's head jerked up. "No. I'm going after Vera and Clare."

"You're injured," Wilf argued.

The young bodyguard shoved to his feet, only swaying a little. His bloody face was set in stone. "I'm the best tracker here. I'm going with you."

Fates blast it . . . "Fine," Wilf bit out. "But if you fall over, I'm not picking you up. And we move now. If we hurry, we can find them before dark."

"It's charming you think so," the Rose drawled.

Wilf shot him a glare. "Dirk, take him with you."

"I would be far more useful with you," the Rose countered. "Those were mercenaries. And not just any mercenaries, but Salim's men. They're far more clever than you think." He nodded to the treeline. "They'll ride in a large group for a while, but then they'll split off in the forest, taking a few riders in every direction. You'll have dozens of trails to follow, and only one will lead to Clare. What are the chances you'll pick the right one?"

"How do you know this Salim?" Venn demanded.

"I've hired him before. He's cunning, greedy, and sadistic. Since he thinks he's abducted a princess, he's going to want to deal with her personally." The corner of the Rose's mouth lifted. "And I happen to know exactly which path through the forest he favors, so I can help you bypass the false trails. I could lead you right to him— to her."

A growl rumbled in Wilf's chest. "What do you want in return?"

"My freedom. The moment I lead you to Clare, you let me walk away."

"No," Wilf said. "The only freedom I'll ever give you is the kind found in death."

The Rose shrugged. "Fine. But by the time you manage to find the right trail, you'll be lucky to find Clare's corpse."

Bennick groaned behind him. A quick look assured Wilf that

7

he was still unconscious, but even unaware of the world, deep lines cut into his face, clearly showing his pain.

They were wasting time.

Dirk cleared his throat. "Clare was on my horse. That will make her easier to track." All royal horses were marked, which made their hoof prints distinct.

"Salim will check for that," the Rose said. "He'll put her on another horse and use the marked one to deliberately steer you away."

Wilf ignored the assassin. "Venn, gather any soldier able to walk."

The young man stalked away, every line of his body showing absolute focus on his mission.

Dirk frowned. "There were a great many of them, Wilf. You need more men."

"There's no time." The nearest place to get Devendran reinforcements was in Stills, and that small town wouldn't have many soldiers. The nearest military out-post was even further.

They would have to do this on their own.

Wilf dragged a hand over his stiff jaw. "Help me get him into the carriage."

Dirk and Wilf lifted Bennick as gently as possible, using infinite care as they set him on the carriage floor; it would be the most stable place for him on the journey back to Serai Nadir's estate.

Bennick flinched, but didn't wake.

"I've saved men like this before," Wilf said quickly to Dirk. "It's a battlefield technique. A fever may follow, and if there's any sign of bloating or discoloration, the physician may need to reopen the wounds—"

"I know." Dirk laid a hand on Wilf's shoulder, his grip firm. "I'll look after him. You focus on saving Clare and Vera." His dark eyebrows pulled together. "Do you want to take the Rose with you?"

"No," he said, his voice firm. "I don't need him." He turned on his heel and strode away, not bothering to glance at the assassin he knew watched him.

He had done all he could to save Bennick. Now it was time to save Clare.

I'm coming, my little defender.

He would destroy anyone who harmed her.

CHAPTER 3

SERENE

SERENE STOOD IN TAMAR NADIR'S COLORFUL drawing room, facing the large window that viewed the sunny courtyard. She would be able to see the others the moment they arrived.

They *would* arrive.

She kept repeating the words, a mantra that barely managed to ground her. Scenes of the chaotic ambush flashed through her memory, and her fingernails dug into her palms. Residual adrenaline still spiked through her hours later, making her heart stutter and pound in her chest. Standing in such a highly decorated room with towering bookshelves, overstuffed chairs, and brightly painted walls done in blue and gold, all made the attack on the road seem even more violent. The fists at her sides hadn't loosened.

Where were they?

The door behind her opened and Cardon entered. She could tell it was him without looking.

She had always been able to tell.

"Serai Nadir thought you might like some tea," he said, his smooth voice filling the room.

Serene snorted, not turning away from the window. "I don't think that will help."

A tray clattered lightly as it was set on the low table behind her, near the long settee. The smell of tea drifted to her. It was a familiar blend; Serai Nadir must keep some Devendran teas on hand. When china rattled, Serene twisted around.

Cardon stood over the tray, arranging cups on saucers. His large hands should not be able to handle the delicate items so deftly, but every motion was perfectly controlled.

Everything about him was familiar to her. He was thirty years old, and his brown hair was silvering in a few select places. He was taller than her, though not by much. He had broad shoulders and strong arms—byproducts of years spent on a training field. The thin scar on his right cheek didn't detract from his features, but somehow enhanced them. Though she couldn't see them right now, she could easily imagine the intensity in his brown eyes. He dedicated himself completely to every task—even something as simple as pouring tea.

She got a little lost watching him.

When he finished, she straightened sharply. He crossed the bright yellow rug with two filled cups and stopped directly in front of her. The scent of him—leather and spice—triggered a flutter low in her stomach, and her heart skipped at his nearness.

She forced herself to meet his gaze. "I don't want tea."

The corner of his mouth lifted slightly, his eyes knowing. "You always want tea."

The strong fragrance drifted up, carried on the steam that billowed in twisting, curling tendrils. Ghosting—there, then gone.

She could feel the weight of Cardon's stare as he waited.

Fates blast it . . .

She reached for the cup and he eased it into her hands. His callused fingertips grazed her fingers, making her breath hitch.

Her voice came out a little too heavy as she said, "I do not *always* want tea, Sir Brinhurst."

He raised a brow. "I know I've irritated you when you start calling me that."

"It is your name."

"I rather hate it."

"I know."

His lips twitched.

She cleared her throat. "Is Imara still with Hanna?" Her cousin's maid had been shot during their retreat.

"Yes," Cardon said. "The physician Serai Nadir sent for is with her."

"Good." Serene blew lightly on her scalding drink as she turned back toward the window. "They should have made it back by now."

From her periphery, she caught the long scar on Cardon's cheek jump as his jaw clenched. "I'm sure they'll be here soon." The unspoken anxiety that threaded through his words perfectly matched her own. His next words surprised her. "We could return to Iden."

Serene exhaled shortly. "My father would love that."

"Your safety is more important than anything. Even the king's treaty."

"That edges on treason."

The skin around Cardon's eyes tightened. "It's my job to protect you. There is no treason in that."

But there was, in a way. Because Serene had been a traitor since she was sixteen years old. She hid the truth from her father by exaggerating a role of petulance and harmless rebellion, knowing he became too frustrated with her to ever look closer. He had never suspected that she was the leader of a rebellion, because all she complained about were dress-fittings and irritable nobles. He never knew that marrying Desfan was a part of *her* plan, because she complained so strenuously about the betrothal. He didn't know that she would not rest until she'd destroyed him and her younger brother, Grandeur.

King Newlan was a terrible monarch who took advantage of his people and ruled with fear and threats. He had also murdered his wife—a crime he had never been held accountable for. Grandeur had known about the slow poisoning of the queen, and he had done nothing. That made him just as much to blame, in Serene's eyes.

Neither of them deserved the throne, and she would take it from them by any means necessary. Even if that meant marrying a stranger. She needed strong allies if she was going to overthrow her father and brother. It was why she couldn't go back to Iden, no matter how dangerous things became.

"I should thank you," Serene said suddenly.

"For the tea?" Cardon asked mildly.

She rolled her eyes. "No." Although she had to admit, just holding the warm cup and smelling the comforting fragrance helped her breathe easier. He knew her too well. "You saved my life yet again. How many times is that?"

He gave her a sidelong look. "It's not as though I keep track."

"You sound a little smug."

"Perhaps I'm simply glad you're alive."

"I suppose your employment *does* depend on my survival."

His gaze trailed the side of her face. "There are other reasons, Princess." Her heart clenched in her chest. "You're right, though," he continued. "It would end my career. Not even a half-rate merchant would hire me after learning I failed to protect my last charge."

She arched a brow, and ordered her heart to stop pounding. "I hate to think my death would cause such troubles for you. You might have to take up another occupation altogether."

Cardon huffed, bringing his cup to his lips. He took a lingering sip, his throat flexing as he swallowed. "I think, Princess," he finally said, his voice deeper than before. "If I failed to preserve your life, I would become a drunk."

The image of Cardon hunched over a mug, mourning her death, perhaps being broken by it—

No. *No.*

She refused to do this. See things that weren't there. Read too deeply into every word and look. Imposing feelings on him that he had already denied—emphatically.

She steeled her spine. "You would miss me, then?" she said, almost blithely.

His knuckles whitened around his cup. His lips parted, but the door was pushed open, ending the moment.

Imara swept in, tendrils of black hair falling loose from her bun, exhaustion etched on her round face.

Serene faced her cousin, her cheeks feeling too warm. "How is Hanna?"

"She'll be fine, thank the fates." Imara rubbed her temple. "The arrow pierced the fleshy part of her arm, so there won't be any lasting damage. Have the others returned?"

"Not yet."

Her cousin dropped into a cushioned chair, her shoulders falling. "There were so many of them. What if . . .?"

The unspoken question was one Serene could not bear to think.

A muted thundering spun them all toward the window, where a dozen mounted soldiers surrounded the royal carriage as it rolled into the courtyard.

"Thank the fates," Serene breathed.

Cardon was already moving for the door, setting his teacup on the tray as he passed. Serene was right behind him, Imara striding alongside her.

They exited the manor's front door and rushed down the stone steps where the carriage jerked to a stop.

The small door swung open and Dirk climbed out, looking horribly grim. His face was as familiar as any in Serene's life; he had been her bodyguard since her birth. And he had only ever looked so grave once before.

When he had brought the news that her mother had died.

Serene's stomach instinctively dropped. When Dirk shifted and she glimpsed Bennick lying on the carriage floor, a hand flew to her mouth.

"Is he dead?" Imara asked, trembling beside her.

"No." Dirk's throat flexed as he swallowed. "But he needs immediate assistance. He was stabbed."

Cardon rushed forward and Imara murmured about getting the physician as she darted back inside the manor.

"Wilf seared the wounds," Dirk told Cardon as the two of them carefully lifted Bennick out. "He hasn't awoken, and he's feverish. He may not survive."

"He will," Cardon said firmly.

Serene's heart clenched. She looked around, noticing for the first time that Clare wasn't in the yard. Or Vera. She froze. "Where are Clare and Vera?"

"They're not dead," Dirk said quickly. "They were taken by the mercenaries who attacked us. Venn and Wilf took six men and are tracking them now into the forest."

"They won't find them," sang out a horribly cheerful voice.

Serene faced the Rose—*Zilas*, as she preferred to call him. Using his real name stole some of his threat and mystery, and she was sure it would irritate him as well. He was still shackled, a guard on each arm pulling him toward the manor.

Strange, how seeing an enemy could help her focus. Her superior mask slipped into place and she regarded him with an edge of haughtiness. "You seem quite sure of that, Zilas."

The assassin smiled, his eyes dancing. As if he knew why she had used his name, and he found it amusing. "Oh, I'm dead certain of it, Princess."

Serene dismissed him by turning on her heel and following Cardon and Dirk inside. Bennick was carried between them. The blood on his uniform alone had her fighting a gag, but as they climbed the stairs, the folds of his shirt fell aside and she saw the wound. It was low on the left side of his abdomen, the skin terribly burned and blistered. Serene swallowed quickly to keep acidic bile from rising up her throat.

Bennick was pale, his skin slick with sweat. Even his breathing was pained.

They reached the first available room and Serene dodged around them to open the door. As they lowered him onto the bed, Bennick's agonized groan scraped her ears, clawing at her heart.

16

Then Cardon swore. "He was run through?"

Dirk straightened stiffly. "Yes."

A tremble shook through Serene. With an injury like that, it was a fates-blasted miracle Bennick was still breathing.

The physician ran in, Imara right behind him. The Mortisian man was older, but his eyes were clear and sharp as he took in his newest patient. "The two soldiers can stay," he said. "I'll need you to hold him down if he wakes. The rest of you—out."

Serene's feet were stuck to the floor. It was Imara's hand slipping around hers, tugging her toward the door, that finally made her move.

They remained in the corridor just outside, listening to the indistinct murmur of voices. Time passed. Servants ducked in and out, bringing water, towels, and other supplies. Horrible, gut-wrenching screams pierced through the closed door, and Serene had to tell herself it was a good sign—it meant Bennick was still alive.

Serene paced the hall, chewing the edge of her thumbnail, aware of Imara's sharp eyes on her. They hadn't spoken much, just waited together with bated breath for news.

Finally, the door eased open and Dirk ducked out. He looked exhausted, but his eyes found Serene easily enough. "He's sleeping now," he said, pulling the door closed until it clicked shut. "Cardon and the physician will remain with him."

"Will he survive?" Serene asked.

"The physician has done what he can, but the fever is a concern." Dirk gripped the back of his neck, his expression grim. "Time will tell."

Bennick had to live. And Clare and Vera had to be found.

Serene could not bear any other alternative.

CHAPTER 4

CLARE

CLARE WAS THROWN TO THE GROUND. The impact jarred her shoulder and she grunted, fingers digging into the gritty soil of the forest floor. After hours of riding with an enemy, she finally had something solid to lean on, even if it was only the hard ground.

Everything was raw. Her body, from hours of riding. Her throat, from screaming; her eyes, swollen from crying. Every part of her trembled with pain. It hurt to breathe. It even hurt to blink, for every time she closed her eyes, even for a fraction of a second, she saw that sword tear through Bennick.

The truth stared her in the face, yet it had never felt more like a lie.

Bennick was dead. There was no way he could have survived that.

Her entire soul screamed.

"You got her?"

"We did." The man who had tossed Clare from the horse dismounted, landing on his feet beside her. "Meet the princess of Devendra."

"You didn't kill her, did you?"

"Does she look dead?"

"She isn't moving."

"She's in shock." A boot nudged against her back and Clare flinched away from him. "See? She's alive."

Clare scanned the clearing. Their group of about twenty men had joined a camp of a dozen more. Their sheer numbers raked a chill through her body.

"Got a bonus, too!" a new voice hooted, gaining cheers from the raucous group.

Clare gasped when she saw Vera lying on the ground nearby. The seventeen-year-old maid was shaking, her blonde hair hanging in loose strands around her pale face. Her terror was obvious in her light green eyes as the men crowded closer.

Clare had seen Vera get taken, but she'd been so distracted by Bennick's fate that she hadn't called out to her friend. Then they'd been riding, and Clare had lost sight of her.

She scrambled to her feet, but before she could step toward Vera, the man who'd captured her snagged her with his arms. "Hey there, Princess. Easy."

Clare struggled, though his grip was like iron. "Leave her alone," she gasped, her throat burning.

The man standing near Clare—the one her current captor had been talking to—followed her gaze. "Tariq! Leave her."

The man closest to Vera scowled, but he took a step back and the others followed suit.

Vera's frantic gaze met Clare's, fear and desperation lining her face. The young maid had been through too much. Her sister had been murdered by the Rose a mere week ago, and now she had been abducted by these Mortisians. Clare couldn't let anything else happen to her.

A thickly-built man stepped in front of Clare, blocking her view. His eyes scanned her face, noting the salty tracks left by her tears, the firm set of her jaw. A slow smile spread across his lips, but there was nothing human in his gaze; it was dark and cold. "You really are beautiful, Princess," he said, his voice a low rumble as he spoke the trade language. "Just like the rumors say." His fingers moved for her cheek and she jerked back, though there was nowhere to retreat; the man holding her from behind was a solid wall at her back, trapping her.

Callused fingertips ghosted over her skin, the light touch making her shudder.

The man's grin hiked as he pulled back his hand. "I am Salim. One thing you need to know about me is that I keep my word. If I say I'm going to kill you, I'm going to kill you. If I say I'm *not* going to kill you, then I won't. Do you understand?"

Clare stared at him, forcing her spine to remain rigid, her knees locked. She would not give him the satisfaction of getting another reaction from her. "Yes," she managed to say.

"Good. It's important you know I'm a man of my word." Salim rocked back on his heels, his hands going to his hips. "Now, we're going to be traveling quite a distance together. We've been offered a great deal of coin, and I'm itching to get paid, so we'll move light and fast." He glanced toward Vera, and his mere acknowledgement of her had Clare's gut dropping. "Is she your maid?"

"Yes."

"You care about her?"

The tears in her eyes were unwanted, but she couldn't blink them away. "Yes."

"All right, no need to get emotional. Now, I mentioned how keen I am to move quickly? Well, if you do anything to slow us down, I will kill your maid. You do anything I don't like, I'll kill her. You try to escape? I'll kill her."

Clare's fingers clenched, rolling to fists at her sides. "Threats are unnecessary. You can let her go. I won't try to escape."

Salim clicked his tongue. "But I'm sure you're used to having servants, and I wouldn't want to make things uncomfortable for you."

Around them, men snickered, the sound menacing. Fates, there were so many of them.

She tried to ignore them, keeping her gaze focused on Salim. "I promise I'll do everything you say if you let her go."

"You know," the man said, tapping a finger to his bearded chin. "I think you'll do everything I say if I *keep* her here." His head angled to the side as he studied her. "I've heard you have defensive training, but I would urge you not to use it. Best not to risk your maid. And I'll be asking now for any weapons you might have."

His eyes bit into her, and he wasn't the only one watching. Waiting. Completely surrounded, Clare knew there was nothing she could do with the blade strapped to her calf. So when the man holding her dropped his arms, she didn't hesitate to turn it over, still in its sheath.

Salim passed it to one of his men, and then he lifted a dark eyebrow. "Is that all?"

Clare nodded, though her heart pounded and the silver bracelet on her wrist burned. The hidden garrote was an exact copy of a bracelet Serene had; Bennick had given it to her, and it could prove useful later. She would not give it up.

Salim, it seemed, was not a man who trusted easily. He looked to the man standing behind her. "Search her."

Large hands brushed over her, and it took every bit of restraint Clare had not to strike out at him. His palms swept over her arms, waist, hips, and dragged down each leg. Her entire body trembled from fear, revulsion, and anger. When his fingertips strayed over her bracelet, she fought to keep her body from tensing. Especially when he hesitated, looking to Salim.

He merely shrugged. "Let her keep her pretty things for now." His smile turned mocking. "I would hate to upset a princess."

The man's search continued, and he dipped a hand into her pockets.

Clare stiffened when he drew out the small tin soldier she always kept with her. It was dented, the blue paint scratched. Mark, her youngest brother, had given it to her when she left home, to protect her. Her heart ached to see a Mortisian criminal hold something so precious.

"An odd thing for a princess to carry." Salim held out a hand, and Clare took an involuntary step forward as the toy soldier was dropped into his palm.

One of his men grabbed Clare's shoulder, halting her.

Salim grinned, inspecting the tin soldier. "Interesting. A battered children's toy is worth more to you than your dagger, or even that fancy silver bracelet." He stepped forward, and Clare tensed as he leaned in until their noses almost touched. "I won't kill you, Princess. I wasn't hired to do that. But there are ways I can punish you, if you defy me." Clare felt him slip the tin soldier back into her pocket, and it took all her willpower not to shiver as his head shifted, placing his mouth at her ear. His breath was hot and foul against her skin. "Never forget—I hold everything. You have nothing."

He drew back, the corner of his mouth twitching. "Take a moment to see to your needs. You'll forgive me, but I think we'll bind your hands afterward, just to be safe. Then we'll be on our way. We're riding through the night." He glanced over the group at large. "Lay your best trails to deceive any followers."

Men nodded, and some immediately broke away—tending to horses, or digging out some food to eat. The clearing was suddenly bustling, and Clare felt the moment the man behind her moved away. Salim watched her, as if waiting for her to realize that even if she wasn't being physically held, she was still their prisoner.

Clare stared at him, attempting to crush her rising panic. These despicable men would kill her and Vera the moment they realized she wasn't the princess. All the lessons in etiquette, dancing, how to hold a teacup—none of those things had prepared her to be Serene's decoy here. She was surrounded by enemies, trapped in a hostile kingdom, and Bennick was not coming for her. The thought was a knife in her chest, and she knew if she did not have Vera to take care of, his death would have crippled her. She had just lost Eliot. Her brother's death had broken something inside of her, but Bennick . . . She wanted to sink into her grief, but she couldn't. For Vera's sake, she needed to bury her emotions. She needed to become Serene completely. The cool, untouchable version of the princess that Clare had first known.

It was the only way to survive.

She straightened her shoulders and lifted her chin, adopting the now-familiar mannerisms like they were a shield—a weapon. "Where are you taking me?" She was prepared for him to threaten her or refuse to answer. She was not prepared for the amusement that crossed his face.

"I'm taking you to the man who bought you, Princess," Salim said with a smile. "I'm afraid he wants to kill you himself."

CHAPTER 5

GRAYSON

GRAYSON STARED AT THE BOOK SPREAD IN front of him, one hand buried in his dark hair, the other fisted on the table. The open page revealed a simple registry of noble families written in a decorative Mortisian script.

Ul and Mari Sifa

Children:

Vari Sifa

Kema Sifa

Mia Sifa

Grayson had lost track of how many hours he'd spent in the small records room of the royal Mortisian library. Ever since his older brother, Liam, had shared what he'd learned about the Sifa family, Grayson hadn't been able to stop looking at this book. Fates, had it only been two days? It felt much longer.

Mia Sifa.

Everything about the first name was familiar. *Mia* meant home. Warmth. Peace. It belonged to his only friend—the young woman he loved.

Sifa was foreign. Angry. Hateful. It was the name of a Mortisian on the ruling council who despised everything to do with Ryden—including Grayson.

With good reason, he reminded himself.

Abeil Sifa blamed Ryden for slaughtering his brother's family nine years ago at their home near the border, but there was something Abeil did not know about that night. The youngest daughter, Mia, hadn't been killed with the rest of her family. She had been kidnapped and brought to Lenzen.

Grayson was still reeling with the ramifications of Liam's revelation.

Mia Sifa had been born sixteen years ago—so had *his* Mia. The date of Mia Sifa's death matched the date *his* Mia had arrived in Lenzen.

Mia Sifa *was* his Mia, even if that felt like a cruel trick of the fates.

His thoughts spiraled back to a question that made his stomach clench: Was Mia really *his* anymore?

Yes, a voice in his head snarled.

His fingers dug into his scalp and he pinched his eyes closed. He wished she'd told him the truth, though he knew that wasn't fair. Mia had been a child, traumatized and beaten until she couldn't even think about her past without flinching. He had found her after she'd been in that cell for a year, and he had quickly learned not to ask questions. Still, if he'd known . . .

What would it have changed?

Nothing, he decided. He still would have loved her. Protected her. Come here, to Mortise, for her sake.

And yet, now it changed everything. Liam's words had triggered something inside him. Finally, he'd realized there was no point in hovering between choices.

Liam wanted to destroy the Kaelin family, and Grayson was ready to help him. With his spymaster brother's resources, he believed it was actually possible—not that Liam had shared any details of his plan yet. But he had promised Grayson that he would help get Mia out of Ryden, and while the rest of the Kaelin family burned, they would retreat to Zennor.

In taking Mia away from her uncle—her only surviving family—are you any different from your father?

Another question that flashed into Grayson's mind too often, filling him with guilt. He might be the Black Hand, but he *refused* to be his father. He would let Mia choose what she wanted. After all these years, her uncle would be a virtual stranger—she may not want to live with him, even though they were family. And Grayson couldn't deny that Mia loved him. As impossible as that seemed sometimes, he knew it was true. She would choose to come to Zennor with him.

But what if she chooses Sifa?

The thought gutted him. Losing Mia would destroy him—he knew that. But he would let her go, if that was what she chose.

Fates, let me be strong enough to let her go . . .

He needed to stop. These thoughts were endless, the questions

27

unanswerable. He closed the book, his gloved hand lingering on the leather cover for a final moment. He would not come back, he vowed. He would not spend another hour here. He would find Liam—wherever his brother had disappeared to today—and demand to know the plan for destroying their father and rescuing Mia. *That* was what deserved his attention. He'd been wasting precious time staring at this book and letting his heart bleed.

It was time for action.

Grayson carried the book back to its place on the overloaded shelf, sliding it in among the other ancestral lines and family histories housed in this small room. Then he strode for the door.

With every step he missed the familiar weight of his belted sword. In Ryden, wearing weapons around the castle was normal. In Mortise, it was considered barbaric, unless you were a guard. Liam had told him to wear nothing larger than a dagger on his belt, so Grayson compromised by having one obvious dagger, and then several concealed throwing knives strapped to various parts of his body.

Perhaps he should go to the training yard today. At least there, he was allowed to carry his sword.

Grayson pushed out of the records room, entering the main part of the library. It was much larger than the library in Ryden, with shelves sprawling in every direction, the vaulted ceiling, the varied nooks and crannies that held collections of tables and chairs. One long wall was made entirely of windows and open spaces between wide columns that led to balconies overlooking the sea. The Mortisian library managed to be both vast and intimate. And, perhaps best of all, rarely anyone spoke to him when he was here.

As he came around a corner, Grayson took in the group of five young men clustered around a long table. They were talking and chuckling, passing around a bottle of wine. The laughter died the moment they spotted Grayson.

A familiar prickle ran over his skin as they stared. Even though he was around their same age at seventeen—almost eighteen, now—he didn't see himself reflected in them. His parents had never deemed it needful for him to socialize with others. He had grown up in a castle surrounded by nobles, servants, and guards, but he had always been apart from them. And though his lack of friends didn't bother him, he did, in these moments, envy Liam's ability to say the right thing, wear the right expression. If nothing else, it might get them to stop staring.

One of the young men was seated on the table, his feet planted on the wooden bench. He held the bottle of wine, and as his eyes dragged over Grayson, his smile sharpened. "I didn't realize the Black Hand was such a literal term." The condescension in his voice, the arrogant tilt of his chin, and the quality of his clothing all screamed entitled noble.

Every noble in Mortise had been wise enough to keep their distance from him.

Until now.

The young man smirked. "Apologies, Prince Grayson," he said in Rydenic, his brown eyes edged with mockery. "I forgot you don't speak Mortisian."

Snickers broke out, but Grayson ignored them, his focus on the obvious leader of this pack. He didn't bother to correct the boy and tell him he understood Mortisian well enough, even if he wasn't as practiced in speaking it. "You have me at a disadvantage," he said in Rydenic.

The boy's mouth quirked. "Yes, I suppose I do."

His friends grinned, but Grayson kept his expression neutral, giving no sign that he'd perceived the slight. It hadn't escaped his notice that none of the boys had bowed, either—something he didn't care about, but in the Mortisian culture was certainly meant as an insult.

The young man cleared his throat. "In Mortise, we value culture and education, so I speak several languages, including three Zennorian dialects," he bragged, still speaking Rydenic, though not well. His superior tone indicated he didn't realize his errors. "But I've heard you're pretty good with a sword, so I suppose that makes up for it."

More sniggers from his friends.

"A blade *can* be universally understood," Grayson said, his voice too tight. He didn't have the patience for this.

He moved to leave, but drew to a stop when the boy jumped off the table and stepped in front of him. "I'm Arav Anoush," he said. "My father was just sworn in on the council."

"There were quite a few open seats, weren't there?" Grayson allowed a thin bite of sarcasm to color the words.

Arav's eyes darkened slightly. "My father was one of the first the serjah appointed."

Grayson just stared at him. The flatness of his expression—and his growing silence—seemed to ruffle Arav.

The boy's jaw tightened. "I was merely trying to be a friend. It's obvious you have few acquaintances here. Perhaps we could spar sometime?"

The thought was laughable. Grayson would annihilate this boy in an instant. "No."

Arav's gaze narrowed, making his angular features even sharper. "I've seen you practice in the yard. Only your own soldiers will spar with you, and that must become boring."

"No," he said again.

"You—"

"I believe Prince Grayson said no," a new voice said.

Grayson's eyes flicked past Arav to take in yet another noble-man who had just stepped around a towering bookshelf. He was taller than Arav, his frame thin, though not without some muscle. He looked to be seventeen—around the same age as the rest of them—and his warm brown skin and dark brown hair indicated his Mortisian heritage. Grayson noticed a pale scar on his cheekbone, but no other signs marked him as a threat. A slim book was held in a long-fingered hand as he walked toward them, and he didn't stop until he was positioned slightly forward of Arav.

He offered a half-smile. "I would think you'd recognize the word, as it's one the young ladies have said to you—repeatedly."

Arav's nostrils flared as he switched to Mortisian. "This isn't your concern, Ranon."

"Oh, I'm not concerned," Ranon said easily in Rydenic, ignor-ing Arav's pointed shift in language. "But as much as I enjoy watch-ing you make a fool of yourself, I wouldn't wish your odiousness on anyone. Let alone Serjah Desfan's special guest." His eyes slid meaningfully to Grayson, and he gave a deep bow. "Prince Gray-son, it's a pleasure to meet you."

Unsure of how to reply, Grayson merely inclined his head.

Ranon straightened and turned back to Arav, his voice lower-ing as he switched to Mortisian. "You're trying to intimidate the Black Hand of Ryden. You can't be so drunk as to not realize how insane that is. If something happens here, your father will kill you, because Serjah Desfan will blame him. There is no way this plays out favorably for you, so back away."

Arav's eyes cut over Grayson before he shot a look to his watching friends. His jaw flexed, then he aimed a thin smile at Grayson. "I meant no offense, Prince Grayson. My sincerest apologies."

Grayson didn't respond and, after a slight hesitation, Arav rejoined his friends at the table. His friends immediately started whispering while Arav tipped back the bottle of wine.

Grayson strode away, a little surprised when Ranon fell into step beside him. When they turned the corner, the Mortisian spoke Rydenic in a low voice. "I would apologize for Arav, but I don't want to take any responsibility for him, so I'll simply ask that you don't judge us all to be the same."

"Unfortunately, I know people like Arav exist in other kingdoms, too."

Ranon grunted. "I've had the displeasure of growing up in the same circle as Arav. We attended the same academy, have gone to all the same parties and dinners our entire lives. I'm afraid he will attempt to corner you again."

"Why?"

He shrugged his narrow shoulders. "Because he's a *srik*."

Grayson was unfamiliar with the Mortisian word, but he thought he understood the meaning. The corner of his mouth lifted. "Thank you for dismissing him. I'm afraid in my current mood, I might have hurt him."

"Perhaps I should have stood back, then," Ranon chuckled. "Your Highness," he belatedly added.

"Please, call me Grayson."

"You honor me." He held out a hand, which Grayson slowly took. The boy's grip was surprisingly firm. "I'm Ranon, of course," he said. "Ranon Sifa."

Everything inside Grayson froze. "Sifa?"

"Yes," Ranon said, oblivious to his sudden tension. "I don't particularly like having things in common with Arav, but my father was also just sworn onto the council. He'd been serving in a temporary capacity before that. Perhaps you've had a chance to meet him?"

Grayson just stared at him.

Fates. Ranon was Mia's *cousin.*

The young man's forehead creased, his brown eyes searching Grayson's face. "I didn't mean to cause any distress. I'm sure if you haven't met my father, you will soon enough."

It took every bit of will Grayson had to summon the ability to speak. "We've met."

"Oh." Ranon frowned. "I take it the meeting wasn't favorable?"

"He doesn't seem to want me here." He'd want Grayson around even less if he knew the truth.

"Ah." Ranon winced, shoving a hand into his thick curls. "I'm afraid he does have some reservations when it comes to Rydenic relations."

That was a mild way of labeling Ser Sifa's loathing.

Grayson eyed him. "And how do you feel about Ryden?"

"I have some complicated feelings as well. But I don't know you, so I can't judge you. And I can't hold you accountable for the sins of others." He cracked a smile. "I wouldn't make a good politician, I'm afraid. I'm far too blunt. But I'll be living at the palace for the next year, same as Arav. We're expected to take part in the celebrations and support our fathers in their new roles." He snorted. "Clearly, Arav is intent on making his mark. He probably hopes he'll befriend the serjah while we're here. Or at least catch the eye of a young serai from a prominent family."

"Poor girl," Grayson muttered.

"Indeed. Luckily, Mortisian women are uncommonly smart,

so they'll probably avoid him easily enough."

They reached the entrance of the library and Grayson halted when he saw Liam leaning against the wide desk of a librarian. The young woman blushed as she stared up at the Rydenic prince, raptly listening to every softly-spoken word he offered.

Liam was undeniably handsome. He was the middle Kaelin, and King Henri's spymaster. He was tall, sun-bronzed, and managed to fit in anywhere. He knew multiple languages—including the spy language, which was made up of subtle hand gestures—and he had several established identities throughout all four kingdoms of Eyrinthia. His light-brown hair was combed back from his face, and a light beard traced over his angular jaw. A charming smile was usually in place, making him even more approachable—the exact opposite of Grayson.

People shrank back when Grayson entered a room. He was the Black Hand, the deadliest of the Kaelin princes. From the dark hair that fell over his brow to the black clothes he wore, everything about him screamed a warning. His gray eyes were a chilling echo of his mother's, and his father's influence was in every rigid line of muscle Grayson had earned through years of agonizing train- ing. His skin was still pale compared to the Mortisians, despite gaining a slight tan from his travels. Dark gloves covered the scars that traced over his hands, and he always wore long sleeves, even in summer. But there was no hiding the marks on his face. All of his brothers had scars, but, as the youngest, Grayson carried more. He'd been smaller. Weaker. Easy to trap and abuse.

That had changed.

Now, his brothers feared him. He was a weapon—one feared throughout all of Eyrinthia. He may resent what his family had made him become, but he would happily use his skills to destroy them.

Liam spotted Grayson and Ranon. He straightened, giving a few last whispered words to the pretty librarian before striding toward them. The leather bracelet he always wore was stamped with a pattern of twisting vines, and he slowly spun it around his right wrist as he walked forward.

"I had no idea you were here, brother," Liam said in perfect Mortisian, his eyes sliding to Ranon. "And with a friend, no less."

Grayson gestured to the young man beside him, who was currently bowing to Liam. "This is Ranon Sifa. Ranon, my brother, Prince Liam."

Liam's features lifted in surprise, though Grayson wasn't sure if the expression was feigned. He often knew more than he let on. "Sifa," he repeated. "Your father was just appointed officially to the council, wasn't he?"

"Yes, Your Highness. You have a good memory."

"I make an effort to remember those I meet." Liam angled toward Grayson. "I hate to pull you away, but I'd like a word with you, if you have a moment."

"Of course."

As Ranon dismissed himself and walked away, Grayson caught an odd flash in Liam's eyes. Frowning, Grayson lifted his fingers and flicked them in the signed spy language as they left the library: *Is something wrong?*

Liam's fingers flashed. *No, but we need to discuss the political shift in Mortise.*

Grayson assumed Liam referred to the fact that half the ruling council had been recently arrested for treason. *Does it impact your plan?* he signed.

Yes. Liam's hand fell back to his side, and Grayson knew their conversation had been put on hold until they could speak freely.

Liam led them easily through the halls of the palace. Their trailing bodyguards took up positions in the hall as Liam unlocked the door to his suite and pushed inside. Grayson followed, nudging the door closed with the heel of his boot as his eyes scanned the room. It was an ingrained habit; check every new space carefully. Never feel totally at ease—especially in the areas that were familiar, and thus more relaxing. His parents had taught him these lessons early on, and had reinforced them through the years with the help of his brothers. He didn't know how many times he'd found Peter or some poisonous trap hidden in his bedroom.

Liam checked the room with a practiced routine, glancing under the bed while Grayson checked the closet. After Liam had flicked the curtains back into place, he gestured for Grayson to take a seat in a cushioned chair as he took the one opposite.

"The ruling council of Mortise is powerful," his brother said, speaking in Rydenic now that they were alone, his voice pitched carefully so it would not carry from the room. "Desfan is appointing people to the council as soon as he arrests the previous members, but his investigations are ongoing. Until we know who will be on the council, my plan cannot be enacted."

"Why?" Politics had never been Grayson's focus, so he didn't really understand the particulars of court—especially a foreign one like Mortise.

"I'm playing an intricate game," Liam said. "I can work with some variables, but I need to know who the final council members will be before I take any steps forward. I need to be able to predict the outcome of any vote the council might take."

"What *is* your plan?"

"I already told you—to start a war."

"That's exactly what Father ordered us to do."

"But we're going to give him a different war. One he won't expect."

Grayson's gloved hands fisted. "You've said that before, but I want to know everything. What exactly are you planning?"

"Forgive my caution, but there are some things best left quiet for now."

He wasn't surprised by his brother's guarded reply, but it made the muscles along the back of his neck tense. "I don't like being in the dark."

"I know. And I'm sorry." Liam leaned forward, sitting on the edge of his chair. "I can tell you this. Our mission was to assassinate Princess Serene and make it look like Mortise was to blame, so Devendra would retaliate against them. But my plan will instead bring war to Ryden—something Father isn't prepared for."

Grayson's spine stiffened. "What about Mia?"

"She'll be out of Ryden before war breaks out, you have my word. But we can't smuggle her out yet. It would reveal our treason too soon, and we don't have a safe place to retreat to yet."

Liam's words made sense, but that didn't diffuse the tension in Grayson's shoulders. "I can't just sit here and do nothing."

"First lesson of being a spy, little brother—you must have patience." Liam stood, crossing to a side table that held an assortment of drinks. He lifted one of the bottles, amber liquid rippling inside. "Impatience will get you killed in this sort of work. You have to be cautious." He removed the lid on the decanter, sniffed, and then inspected two short glasses before pouring a splash of the liquid inside. He handed one to Grayson, then took a swallow from his glass. "Did you seek Ranon Sifa out?"

Grayson frowned at the unexpected question. "No."

"Interesting." Liam sat back in his chair, the glass dangling from his long fingers. "I don't know much about him, but I assumed he would hate us just like his father does."

"With good reason," Grayson muttered.

Liam tipped his head. "The Sifas have much to blame Ryden for."

"It was strange," he admitted. "Talking with Ranon. Knowing that Mia is his cousin."

"I can only imagine." His brother took another drink from his glass, and Grayson sipped from his own. The liquid scorched his throat, but he managed not to spit it out. Liam chuckled. "Sorry, it's quite potent."

"Another acquired taste?" Grayson asked, coughing slightly from the burn.

"Indeed."

Grayson eyed his glass, wondering *why* he'd want to acquire a taste for something so vile.

When Liam spoke again, his voice was surprisingly quiet. "Do you miss her?"

Grayson's fingers tightened around the glass. "Every moment."

His brother's jaw hardened, his eyes going distant. "There is no greater pain than being separated from the one you love."

His words hung in the air, and Grayson wanted to say something; ask who Liam had lost, or even just release more of his own fears about Mia. He'd been away from her nearly a month and a half, now. But the words wouldn't come. Being vulnerable was not something Kaelins did, and it made this moment intensely uncomfortable.

Finally, Liam cleared his throat. "It might work to our benefit to have some friends in high places. If you have an opportunity to befriend Ranon, take it. His father may be the one on the council, but Ranon could reveal something that might help us."

Grayson nodded. The more help he gave his brother, the sooner he could be reunited with Mia.

For however long that lasts, a voice taunted in his head.

CHAPTER 6

DESFAN

DESFAN CLAIMED A SEAT AT THE SIMPLE WOODEN table, his nerves tight as he viewed the closed prison door. The air in the upper dungeon of the palace was cool, and torches cast flickering light over the stone walls of the interrogation room. Karim stood behind him, and Desfan was grateful for his presence. Not just as his bodyguard, but as his friend.

Desfan's jaw still ached from the blow it had taken two days ago in the royal library. The fight had left several throbbing bruises, but the deepest pain came from the betrayal of men and women who were supposed to have stood with him, but instead had conspired against him. Half of the ruling council of Mortise had been arrested, including Serai Yahri—the most senior member of the council, and a woman who had fought to obscure the truth about Desfan's father's illness.

After dealing with the fallout of the past couple of days, it was finally time for answers.

The door pushed open and Desfan's head lifted. Serai Yahri limped inside, her cane clacking against the stone floor. The silver-haired woman was bent slightly with age and she relied heavily on that cane. She had not been shackled, though the guards surrounding her made it clear she was a prisoner. The wrinkles deepened around her eyes when she met Desfan's gaze. The woman was old enough to be his grandmother, but she wasn't the matronly sort. She had been a leading figure in Mortisian politics for Desfan's entire life, which made her powerful and intelligent. Someone he would do well not to underestimate.

She eased into the chair on the opposite side of the table, bony fingers clutching the top of her cane. "Thank you for finally agreeing to see me."

His eyes narrowed. "You didn't call this meeting."

"True," she said primly. "If I had, you would have been down here much sooner."

Desfan lifted one eyebrow. Her time in prison had not dampened her superior air. "Yes, well, I've been busy arresting seven council members and interrogating Jamal."

As the leader of the treasonous bunch—and a drug master who had been smuggling olcain into Duvan—Jamal had been Desfan's first priority. Jamal had blackmailed most of the council as well as some key nobles and officials in the city, and Desfan was obligated to untangle that mess, even though he'd wanted to move right to questioning Yahri.

The woman shrugged one thin shoulder. "Busy or not, I wish

you would have deigned to see me sooner. There are things I wish to explain."

"I'm glad you're in a forthcoming mood, because I have a lot of questions." Desfan nodded to the guards, a silent order for them to leave.

"Did you find the box in my room?" Yahri asked. "The one I told you about, with all the letters?"

"We did." Desfan's mouth tugged into a frown as he focused on her. "I know from what I overheard in the library that Jamal was blackmailing you, and according to your claims at the time of your arrest, you didn't know the identity of your blackmailer. You were attempting to gather more information about him, which is why you didn't make a report—but you should have come forward at once."

"Perhaps. But it all worked out in the end."

Her flippant tone grated. "None of this changes the fact that I discovered a treasonous letter in your room. It stated clearly that you hired the Rose to kill Princess Serene, and that you committed treason against the serjan. The letter also said you took powerful steps to ensure no one learned the truth about what happened to him the night of his collapse."

The woman looked completely unruffled, despite his darkening tone. "As you are well aware, Jamal wrote that letter. It was a planted lie so you would think I was guilty of hiring the Rose. It was part of his plan to keep suspicions away from himself."

"That might be true, but you *were* with the serjan the night he collapsed."

Yahri's lips pursed. "I was."

Desfan's eyes narrowed. "You lied to me. To everyone. Why?"

She breathed out slowly, her shoulders dropping. "It's complicated."

42

"You coerced the royal physician to lie. You made guards disappear, and you stole the rotation ledger so no one would even know who was on duty that night."

She rolled her eyes. "I didn't have them killed, for fates' sake. I offered them an early and generous retirement, begged for their discretion, and they obliged."

"Why? What were you hiding? The fact that you poisoned him?"

The lines around her eyes tightened—her first sign of stress. "I did not poison the serjan. The physician can confirm no poison was used."

"It's rather hard to believe him after his lies."

"You make it sound so insidious. He was omitting some details, but they were not relevant to the serjan's health."

"I had a right to know you were with my father when he collapsed," Desfan countered.

The old woman sighed. "You may have trouble believing this, but every action I took was to protect your father, and the crown."

"How? How could these lies have possibly been for the good of Mortise, or for his benefit?"

"Because some things should never come to light."

Desfan set his hands on the table and leaned in, his voice low. "Tell me exactly what happened that day, Yahri. All of it."

Her chin lifted, her gaze steady. "The morning of the serjan's collapse, I received notice that a sailor named Gamble was rather insistently begging for a private audience with the serjan."

Desfan wasn't sure what he'd expected, but it certainly wasn't this. "What did this man want to discuss?"

"He wouldn't say. He only insisted that he had to meet with the serjan privately." Yahri sighed. "As I'm sure the physician told you, your father's health was in a steep decline. He was under a great deal of stress, and had sunk into depression. He was tired all the time, but he couldn't sleep—even with the aid of powders. Admittedly, he was drinking too much, and he was barely eating."

Guilt needled Desfan, and he couldn't hide his wince. If he hadn't been at sea, if he had been at the castle, shouldering responsibility as he should have . . .

But there was no changing the past, no matter how desperately he wished he could.

"Naturally, as the head of the council, I tried to assist the serjan in every way possible. So, I offered Gamble a private audience." She shifted in her chair, the grip on her cane tightening. "We met that afternoon, and he told me he had information about the shipwreck that killed your mother and sisters."

Desfan's chest tightened. "What kind of information?"

"Exactly what I asked him. He refused to say. He was nervous. Licking his lips, eyeing the door. He looked ready to bolt at the slightest provocation. He said he was risking his life by coming to the palace, and he needed to see the serjan—only him."

"You arranged the meeting?"

Her pointy chin jutted out. "I didn't want to. I worried about the serjan's reaction to what could only be difficult news. The tragedy of the seraijan's death, the loss of those little girls . . ." She shook her head. "I didn't want to bring further pain to the serjan, but I knew I couldn't keep this from him."

Desfan's pulse kicked faster. "Did Gamble attack the serjan?"

"No." Her eyebrows drew together. "Gamble wanted to meet alone with the serjan, but I refused to leave his office. Your father did dismiss the guards, though."

"It was only the three of you, then?"

"Yes."

There was a short silence, and Desfan could barely breathe around the pit yawning in his gut. "What happened? What did Gamble say?"

Yahri was clearly reluctant to continue her story, but she did so. "The man claimed to have been in a tavern weeks ago when he overheard a group of men that he suspected were pirates. They were talking about the shipwreck from nine years ago. They said they'd come across the wreckage . . ." Yahri met Desfan's eye. "They claimed one of the seraijahs survived—that they pulled her from the water."

Everything inside Desfan froze. His thoughts, his breath—all of it.

Behind him, Karim's voice was a low growl. "Impossible."

"I agree," Yahri said easily. "And I said as much. But Gamble was insistent."

"It makes no sense," Karim said. "There was no ransom demand—nothing."

"Who?" The word strangled in Desfan's throat. "Did he say who survived? Tahlyah or Meerah?"

Yahri's gaze softened with pity. "No. They never said a name."

Something crushed his chest, compressing his lungs—despair and hope? Grief and longing? Somehow, it was all of those things.

Karim stepped closer, planting his hands on the table beside Desfan. Anger thrummed from him as he faced Yahri. "This Gamble—he was clearly lying. I assume he demanded coin for what he knew?"

"That was the strange thing," the woman said. "He didn't demand anything. He said he came across the rumor and it troubled him greatly. He couldn't get it out of his mind, so he knew he needed to share it with the serjan directly."

Desfan heard their words through a strange echo. His mind was whirling, his heart beating too quickly. "What exactly did the rumor say?" he finally managed to ask. "Is she still alive? Did the pirates claim to still have her?"

"There is no truth to this, Desfan," Yahri said gently. "I've made thorough investigations, and I've found nothing to corroborate Gamble's story."

"But why would he have come to share the story if he didn't believe it?" Desfan argued.

"I think he *did* believe it. But he could supply no proof, nor could I find any." Yahri leaned back in her chair, shaking her head slowly. "The serjan was stricken by the news. He nearly went to his knees when Gamble said one of the seraijahs had survived."

Desfan could fully understand that—he was reeling at the possibility. One of his sisters, still alive? How was such a thing possible? *How could he have not known?*

Every muscle in Desfan's body turned to steel. Once, he'd believed that his family had been stolen by the work of pirates. Evil men—not the fates. But what if this rumor was true? What if the fates weren't to blame?

His voice came out low and dark. "Did Gamble know the names of the pirates claiming to have her?"

"No." Yahri's brow furrowed. "I told you before—there's no truth to this rumor."

He ignored that. "What did my father say?"

She sighed. "He demanded answers Gamble didn't have. I tried to calm the serjan, tried to speak reason, but he wouldn't hear me. He was so agitated. He ordered me to make arrangements for him to sail to your last known position. He wanted you to begin a search for your sister."

46

"Why didn't you tell me?" The pain and fury in his voice didn't seem to surprise the old woman. If anything, she looked . . . sad.

"I knew you would react exactly as he did," she said quietly. "For all your differences, you and the serjan are, at the core, exactly alike. You would want to leave everything behind and search for her."

Desfan shot to his feet, a muscle in his aching jaw pulsing. "One of my sisters might be alive. Of course I'm going to search for her!"

"You would be chasing a ghost," Yahri said. "I have already ivestigated—"

"You didn't do enough," he bit out.

"I sent a team of men to discreetly—"

"You didn't send *me.*"

Yahri drew back a little. There was a short silence, then, "I'm sorry, Desfan. Truly. But your mother and sisters are dead."

Desfan shoved away from the table and began to pace, a dull roar in his ears. "I want to see Gamble. I want to question the men you hired. I'll personally question every pirate we have in custody, and I'll chase down every other one who has sailed in the last nine years. I'll offer a reward for any information—"

"You'll create panic," Yahri cut in. "If you give credence to this rumor—if you publicize it—you will send the message that the pirates are stronger than the crown. You will inspire greedy men to sell you lies, and can you imagine how many young women will rush forward, claiming to be a long-lost Cassian?" She shook her gray head. "I implore you, Desfan, do not do this. No good will come from announcing this rumor to the world."

Desfan's hands fisted at his sides. He hated that Yahri's words made sense.

That didn't mean he was giving up.

"I want to speak with Gamble," he repeated.

"Unfortunately, he disappeared," Yahri said grimly. "I've attempted to find him several times since, and always failed."

"What exactly happened that night?" Karim asked. "Why did the serjan collapse?"

"He was so overwhelmed by the news, he worked himself into a frenzy," Yahri said. "In the midst of making plans, he suddenly grabbed his chest and fell, his body seizing. I called for the guards, the physician . . . but as you know, he has never been fully alert since. I knew there would be questions about the strange man who had come to see him, and the last thing Mortise needed was to fear an assassin had been sent to kill the serjan. So, I made arrangements to keep things quiet. I persuaded the guards it was in Mortise's best interest, and they quietly retired. As for Gamble . . . I asked him to keep quiet about the rumor, and everything that had happened with the serjan. I paid him handsomely for his trouble, and I assured him I would look into the claims. When I tried to locate him later, I learned he had fled Duvan that very night." Her eyes narrowed. "He may have claimed he didn't want any coin, but he certainly took it and ran."

"And you found no trace of Tahlyah or Meerah?" Desfan demanded. "No indication that Gamble's rumor was true?"

"None." Yahri's face sharpened. "I beg you not to pursue this, Desfan."

He gritted his teeth. "You lied to me, Yahri. What you have admitted borders on treason."

"No. My actions have preserved the stability of Mortise. You're simply annoyed with me."

That was undeniable.

"I know you're upset," she said quietly. "I don't blame you for that. But please see things from my point of view. I was trying to protect the Cassian name. The crown. Mortise itself. I was also trying to preserve the dignity and innocence of our beloved seraijahs. And—whether you believe me or not—I was trying to protect you. I saw no cause to distress you, when I had the investigation in hand. And, though I had my doubts about you taking over as regent, I knew Mortise would be in chaos if you abandoned the throne for this wild search."

Desfan heard the sincerity in her words, and even though he hated that she'd lied . . . fates, he understood. More than that, he knew her fears about him were merited. If he'd returned home to learn one of his sisters might be alive, he would have marched right back to his ship. He wouldn't have spared a second thought for the fates-blasted throne.

He supposed it spoke volumes that he hadn't already walked out the door now.

He crossed his arms over his chest. "I won't forget that you kept secrets from me. Information I deserved to know. But you have cooperated in this interrogation, and because I heard it from Jamal myself, I know you had nothing to do with hiring the Rose, or the treason so many others on the council are guilty of. Without any further evidence, I can't accuse you of any crime."

Yahri's eyebrows lifted. "I'm pleased to hear you reach that conclusion. It tells me you're thinking like a true monarch."

"You once asked me to abdicate. I haven't forgotten that."

"I merely suggested a course that would have potentially brought you the most happiness, and subsequently be best for Mortise." She tilted her head to the side. "Will I be reinstated to the council?"

"Yes." He wasn't allowed to dismiss anyone his father had appointed, unless they were guilty of a crime. And while Yahri's actions certainly rode the line, there was nothing he could truly convict her of. And—even if he didn't personally like her most of the time—she was unflinchingly loyal to Mortise. That was something he needed from the council, especially now.

"Thank you, Serjah." Yahri's head canted to the side. "I must ask . . . Do you mean to investigate this rumor of Gamble's?"

"Yes." He hated that he couldn't take up the search himself, but Mortise needed him here. And—despite his raised hopes—it was only an unconfirmed rumor. "I'll be discreet," he said, "but I'll learn the truth. And if it's only a rumor, I'll find the one who started it." His chin dipped, his voice deepening with promise. "And he will hang."

CHAPTER 7

WILF

THE ROSE HAD BEEN RIGHT.

The thought grated every nerve Wilf had, but it was undeniable. The trail left by the mercenaries had been easy to follow at first. The tracks were so plentiful, they hardly had to stop to inspect the ground. Even when darkness fell, their torches lit the way easily. But everything changed at the large clearing.

The mercenaries had met up with others here, and there was evidence of twenty to thirty men now. Panic dug fierce claws into Wilf's lungs, stopping his breath, but he and Venn had searched every part of the clearing; there were no bodies, no freshly dug graves. No sign that Clare and Vera had been killed, or greatly harmed.

51

The mercenaries probably hadn't met with the one who'd hired them. This clearing had merely been a gathering point for them, and then they'd ridden on, splitting up in all directions to confuse anyone who might follow. A few soldiers had followed two of the trails and reported that even those split after a while.

Clare could be anywhere in this fates-blasted forest. Venn had scouted carefully and found signs of Dirk's horse, which they'd followed to no avail. The mercenaries had known the horse was marked, and they were leading them in circles.

Just like the Rose had said.

It was in this clearing that Wilf faced Venn, and the two came to a decision they both clearly hated.

They needed the Rose.

Everything inside Wilf rebelled. Turning to the assassin for help, making a deal to set him free . . . it went against every instinct he had. But time was something they didn't have. Clare and Vera had already been gone too long.

Wilf had been drowning in grief since losing his wife five years ago. He had fought to find purpose, mostly because Bennick kept ordering him to. Clare, with her kindness and gentle smiles despite his gruffness, had burrowed deep under Wilf's skin. He didn't know when she had become so important to him. It had happened slowly. Gradually. But there was no denying it had happened. She was his friend. In many ways, she was the daughter he had never been able to have. He would protect her with everything he had.

No matter what deals he had to make with the Rose, one thing was certain—that assassin was not walking away from this. Wilf was not as honorable as the men he served with. Cardon, Dirk, Bennick, Venn . . . they would make a deal with a killer like the Rose, and they would keep it.

Wilf felt no such compulsion.

They rode back to Serai Nadir's estate, hardly slowing their pace, even though exhaustion gripped them all. Fear and frustration twisted in Wilf's gut as they finally rode into the familiar yard just as the sun was rising.

Clare had been gone nearly two days, now.

Venn dismounted first. The nineteen-year-old typically irritated Wilf with his constant need to grin and make others do the same, but there was nothing light about Venn now. The young man's dark face was inscrutable. His eyes were sharp, tension running along every hard line of his body. A muscle ticked continuously in his jaw. He'd scrubbed most of the blood off his face, but Wilf still caught dried streaks of it along his hairline. The blow to his temple had been serious, but his determined pace had not lagged.

Dirk stepped out to meet them. His eyes roved the group as he descended the manor's front steps, disappointment cutting into his face when he didn't see Clare or Vera.

"They're not dead," Wilf said firmly. Until he found their bodies, he would believe they were alive.

"You're here to make that deal with the Rose, then?" Dirk asked.

"Yes." Wilf swung down from his mount.

Dirk's forehead creased. "He said he'd only help in exchange for his freedom."

"I don't care," Venn said. "If I have to make a deal with a demon to get Vera and Clare back, I'll do it."

Dirk glanced at Wilf, but he found no help there. "Once he's free, he'll come after Serene again."

"He probably will," Venn said. "But this time we won't make the mistake of capturing him—we'll kill him." His voice thinned.

"How is Bennick?"

It was the question Wilf had been too afraid to ask.

"He's still alive," Dirk said, though his expression was grim. "He hasn't regained consciousness. He's battling a fever, but the physician is watching him carefully."

"And the princess?" Wilf asked.

"Safe, though worried about Clare and Vera. I told her everything the Rose said back at the ambush site, and she was ready to send him to you with guards. Cardon and I convinced her to wait." He paused, his shoulders falling a little. "Are you sure this is worth the risk?"

"No," Wilf said. "But he's the best chance we have right now of finding them."

Dirk exhaled slowly. "I'll tell the princess."

"We'll need more men," Venn said. "And fresh horses."

"I'll see it done. In the meantime, you both should have some food, maybe get an hour of rest."

"Later," Venn said. "I want to see Bennick." He moved for the manor, one hand pressed against his temple.

Dirk frowned as he watched the younger man go. "Is he all right?"

"No," Wilf answered honestly. "But I need him, so he's coming with me." Frankly, he didn't think he'd be able to keep Venn at the estate, even if he'd wanted to.

"I wish I could go with you."

Wilf shook his head. "You and Cardon need to remain with Serene."

"I know." Dirk scrubbed a hand over the back of his neck, his dark hair sprinkled liberally with silver that caught in the early sunlight. He was the oldest bodyguard of their group. At fifty, he was five years older than Wilf, and he had been the princess's guard all her life. But despite his seniority, he had never wanted to lead them. He was quiet, fiercely loyal, and extremely good at what he did. That was why Wilf wasn't surprised when Dirk asked the question that had been haunting Wilf since Clare had been taken. "What will they do if they realize she's not the princess?"

Wilf's shoulders tensed. "Pray to the fates they don't."

Serene and Cardon met Wilf and Dirk in a large drawing room a half hour later. Venn was still with Bennick. Wilf wanted to visit him, too, but he didn't feel ready. He'd failed to find Clare; until he could do that, he was reluctant to see his captain.

Sunlight streamed through the room's row of windows, and though there were cushioned chairs and settees set atop vibrantly colored rugs, no one was sitting. There was too much tension in the air.

Serene folded her arms. "I don't know if Zilas can be trusted, but I agree with you—the Rose is our best chance at finding Clare and Vera."

A needle of guilt pricked Wilf. "We brought him to Mortise so your path could be secure. He knows which nobles to avoid."

She shook her head. "That is far less important right now. But if he tries to double-cross you—kill him."

"With pleasure."

"Serai Nadir suggested that you should travel as refugees, rather than as soldiers," the princess added. "It will help you draw less attention."

Wilf nodded. It was a good suggestion.

Dirk, who stood beside the princess, exchanged a quick look with Cardon. "Princess, there is something else we must discuss. With Bennick unable to lead us, the mantle falls to me." Dirk set his hands on his hips. "I know you won't want to hear this, but we need to leave for Duvan tomorrow morning."

Serene drew back. "No. What about Bennick? Clare and Vera?"

"I understand it feels like we're abandoning them, but I've discussed the situation with Cardon. We both feel that keeping you here would be a mistake."

Cardon cleared his throat. "If the mercenaries who abducted Clare realize she's not you, they may come here looking for you. They know this was our nearest place of safety, and that you stayed here before. Remaining at the estate is simply a risk we can't take."

Dirk jumped in once more. "We'll leave men to guard Bennick, and the physician will remain to help heal him. But he needs time to recover—time we don't have."

Serene frowned. "You waited to tell me this until Wilf and Venn could be here, so you could all vote against me."

Cardon's voice was quiet. "There are times you give us orders, Princess, and there are times you must listen to us. This is one of those times. Your safety is more important than anything else."

Her jaw firmed. "How can we leave Bennick here, not even knowing if . . .?"

Dirk took a step closer to her, his head ducking so he could meet her gaze. "He's not going to die. Don't even think it. But he would agree with me. We need to get you to Duvan."

"We'll make a rush to the city," Cardon said. "No unnecessary stops. Dirk and Serai Nadir discussed a plan last night."

Dirk glanced at Wilf, including him in his words. "We'll travel in her carriage, disguised as part of her entourage. We'll bypass any of the places we were supposed to stay. By the time any of the Mortisian nobles can complain to Desfan that we never arrived, we will have arrived in Duvan. Serai Nadir believes we can make the journey in two weeks."

Serene let out a slow breath. "My father won't be pleased if I slight the Mortisian nobles who planned to host me."

"King Newlan can reprimand us all he wants," Cardon said. "We won't endanger you by parading you around anymore. We are too weakened, and the political gains are no longer worth the risk."

"It's a good plan," Wilf admitted. "Bennick will have time to heal here, and then he can make his way to Duvan. That's where I'll bring Clare and Vera."

Because he *would* find them.

Serene pursed her lips. "I'll have to announce my presence in Duvan as soon as we arrive at the palace. To delay longer would risk rumors spreading that I was killed or abducted. But if word reaches the mercenaries that have Clare . . ."

"We'll secure her before then," Wilf vowed.

Serene nodded, but the worry in her eyes was genuine. Seeing that, Wilf was struck by the fact that most people did not know who Serene really was. They saw her different personas—a kind, generous princess; a rebellious, irritable daughter; an elegant, skilled diplomat. But few ever saw her as a person. And virtually no one saw her vulnerable.

"Find them, Wilf," she said quietly.

He bowed his head. "I will."

There was a knock on the door, and then two guards shuffled in with the Rose shackled between them. Chains bound him, ankle and wrist, and though he was a prisoner, the smile on his face was relaxed. When he saw Wilf, his grin widened. "Decided you needed me after all?"

"Zilas." Serene commanded his attention with one word, authority resonating in her voice.

The assassin looked at her. "Yes, Princess?"

Wilf didn't miss the way the scar on Cardon's cheek jumped. Even Dirk, the calmest of them all, tensed at the Rose's sardonic tone.

Serene's carefully arranged features revealed nothing. "You will help us find Clare and Vera. If your information leads us to them, you will be allowed your freedom. If you cannot guide us to them, then your life is in the hands of Sir Lines." She indicated Wilf with a subtle tilt of her head. "As you stabbed him once, I wouldn't count on receiving any mercy."

The assassin didn't even glance at Wilf. His eyes were trained on the princess. Unmoving. Unnerving. And yet, Serene met his focus with an unfaltering calm.

"I have your word, Princess?" the Rose asked. "My freedom will be granted?"

"If you guide us to Clare and Vera, yes."

"Deal." He lifted his chained hands.

"Oh, no, those stay on unless Wilf deems them necessary to remove." Serene deliberately kept control of the room by taking a seat in a comfortable-looking armchair. She crossed one leg imperiously over the other, her arms resting on the chair arms. One eyebrow arched. "I know what you told my guards, Zilas. The men who took Clare are led by a mercenary named Salim. Do you know who may have hired him?"

"No." The Rose shifted his weight, the chains connecting his wrists clinking. "Salim's talents are well-known. He could have been hired by nearly anyone. Coin is his only allegiance."

"Do you know where he might go?"

His lips curled. "Are you feeling a little guilty, Princess? That Clare is suffering now because of you?"

"Answer the princess's question," Cardon said, his voice hard.

The Rose's smile lingered, but he obeyed. "Considering where he struck, and his retreat into the northern forest . . . I suspect his destination is Krid. It's a large city to the northwest of here, and rather lawless. Salim favors it for business transactions. Unless the one who hired him dictated another meeting place, Salim will have chosen Krid."

Serene raised an eyebrow. "You seem quite confident."

"I am. I make it a point to know anyone I hire, and I've used Salim's varied talents before. I know his habits."

The princess turned to Wilf. "I want you to take Zilas, Venn, and however many guards we can spare. Follow Salim's trail through the forest."

"It would be smarter for us to go directly to Krid," the assassin said. "By road, we can be there in a week. It will take Salim a few extra days by his favorite, more secluded route through the forest. We can get ahead of him, rather than follow behind."

"No." Wilf's rumbling growl was final, but he looked to Serene to make his case. "We don't know for certain that Krid is their destination, and we can't risk losing Salim's trail." Or the chance to recover Clare and Vera sooner.

Serene's head dipped. "I agree. Follow the trail we have. As a precaution, I'll send men straight to Krid, to intercept Salim—if that is indeed his destination." She turned to Zilas. "I want a list of any places in Krid we might find him."

The corner of the assassin's mouth lifted. "I'll need some paper and ink."

CHAPTER 8

SERENE

SERENE SAT IN A CHAIR BESIDE BENNICK, who had yet to regain full consciousness. He had thrashed in the throes of his fever for several hours, but now things were tempering, and he breathed a little easier as he slept.

The physician visited often, tending to the still-vivid burns on his back and stomach, working to diminish Bennick's fever and offering what pain relief he could. The powders—which dissolved slowly on Bennick's tongue—helped to keep him asleep. "Sleep is what he needs," the middle-aged Mortisian had said. "As much as we can give him. It will help his body heal."

With every hour Bennick still breathed, the physician said his chances of survival grew.

Serene clung to that assurance.

Dirk sat in a chair beside her. He gently cleared his throat. "Morning will come quickly. You should retire to your room."

"I know," she whispered, her eyes on Bennick. "I just hate to leave him."

Not only now, but in the morning. How could she leave him, still so broken, when it was her fault he was fighting for his life?

"This is not your fault," Dirk said quietly.

Serene shot him a look. "You always manage to read my mind."

"Not always."

She sighed. "After the prisoner exchange . . . I was the one who insisted we continue to Mortise."

"You didn't know what would happen," Dirk said softly. "You don't control the fates, Serene."

If only she could. She shook her head slowly. "I just hate to leave him behind."

"Bennick will understand." Dirk leaned forward, his arms slung over his knees. His voice was a little lighter as he said, "Did I ever tell you how I became your bodyguard?"

"Which version?"

The corner of his mouth twitched. "I did tell you some wild stories, didn't I?"

Since Dirk had been her bodyguard since her birth, she had grown up hearing several different tales. When she was four or five, he had insisted that he'd won the honor by slaying an evil dragon who had abducted her as an infant. She remembered begging him to reenact the battle, and he—incredibly long-suffering person he was—had done so, with an enthusiasm that had made her shriek with laughter.

"I was appointed to guard your mother when she first arrived in Devendra," Dirk said, spinning a silver ring on his forefinger, his eyes distant. "She had Zennorian guards, of course, but your father wanted her to have Devendran guards as well. She was very gracious to me. I remember the first time I met her, she wanted to know all about me. She was genuine and kind."

Her heart ached, as it always did whenever anyone talked about her mother. But she was also desperate for every word, every detail.

"Serving as Queen Aren's guard was a great honor," Dirk continued. "I saw her through many stages. Her introduction to the Devendran court, her marriage to your father. Her ascension as queen of Devendra, and all the responsibilities she took so seriously. Her charitable endeavors. Her pregnancy with you." He stopped fiddling with his ring and gave her a somewhat rueful smile. "When she asked to speak with me after your birth, I remember thinking she was going to promote me to serve as the captain of her guard. My captain was an aging man, ready to retire, so it made sense. What I did *not* expect was for her to drag me into the nursery and introduce me to you—my new charge. I'll admit, I was disappointed. I can remember staring at you; a tiny infant, sleeping quietly under your blanket. All I could think about were the boring days ahead of me, watching you sleep, listening to you cry. It felt like such a demotion. A punishment, even.

"Your mother must have sensed my feelings, because she squeezed my arm and whispered, *I need the guard I trust most to protect the one I love most.*"

Tears clouded Serene's eyes, her throat pinching with a surge of emotion.

Dirk set a steadying hand on her arm. "I have never regretted it. Every long nap I supervised, every scraped knee I tended. Every sinister shadow you asked me to check for monsters, and every tea party you invited me to. Even when you began to grow up and started smiling at boys, I loved being the one standing behind you, pinning them with a glare. I have loved every part of being your bodyguard. I never needed a captaincy to feel like I had the highest honor."

A tear escaped to roll down her cheek. "Fates, where is this coming from?"

"I didn't mean to make you cry. I only wanted to share something I've come to learn. Sometimes in life, the things that happen to us might seem like a blow, but I believe any setback can be a gateway to something better. When your mother first asked me to become your guard, I thought I'd failed her somehow. But she was rewarding me with a gift far more precious than anything I could have imagined."

Serene sniffed, brushing the tears from her face. "Are you secretly a philosopher or poet?"

He chuckled. "No. Just an old soldier who makes attempts at wisdom from time to time." He straightened in his chair, his soft eyes serious. "I know leaving Bennick feels wrong, just as continuing on to Duvan without Clare and Vera feels wrong. I also know the prospect of marrying Serjah Desfan must be frightening. But in all of this, I believe the fates have a plan. I know you're meant to find happiness, Serene."

She gave him a wavering smile, her eyes still stinging with tears. "Sometimes it's hard to believe that."

"I know." He stood, offering her a hand. "Come. You need your rest."

Serene took his hand and stood, then she wrapped her arms around his waist. It had been a long time since she'd embraced

him—probably not since her mother's funeral. He seemed startled, but then his arms came around her, a familiar and comforting hold.

"Thank you," she whispered into his chest. "For everything."

And, just like he used to do when she was young, he placed a
kiss on top of her head. "Always, my princess."

When they pulled back, Serene was shocked to see Bennick's
head turned toward them, his eyes blinking blearily.

"Bennick!" Serene sat gently on the bed beside him, taking hold
of his hand as Dirk darted from the room to fetch the physician.

Bennick's throat constricted as he struggled to swallow. His fingers wrapped weakly around hers. "Clare," he croaked. "Where . . .
is . . .?"

Serene squeezed his hand. "She was taken by Mortisian mercenaries, along with Vera. We haven't recovered them yet."

His eyes pinched shut, pain slashing across his face as he shifted
on the bed.

She pressed a hand to his shoulder. "Don't move. You have to
lie still."

His breathing hitched, his body taut as a bowstring as he visibly struggled with the pain.

The door opened and the physician hurried in with Dirk and
Cardon at his heels.

Bennick's head rolled toward them and pain slashed across his
face. His fingers clamped down on Serene's, making her wince.

"Easy," the physician said, stepping up to the bed. "You need
to remain as still as possible."

"Clare," he gritted out. It sounded like an order.

Serene knew Bennick had become good friends with Clare, but
she was surprised by his desperate intensity. Curiosity pricked her.

In her time traveling apart from them, had their relationship deepened?

Cardon crouched beside the bed, putting them at eye level. His voice was low and steady. "Wilf and Venn went after her and Vera. The Rose went with them. He claims to know the leader of the mercenaries who abducted them—a man named Salim. He believes Krid may be their destination, but they're following them through the forest to be sure."

Bennick swallowed hard. "How soon can . . . I go?"

The physician whistled lowly. "You do realize you were run through? You're lucky to still be breathing."

"You aren't going anywhere until you're healed," Serene insisted. "That could take weeks."

Bennick closed his eyes, exhaling hard through his nose. His frustration was palpable.

Dirk stepped closer. "We're taking the princess to Duvan in the morning. We'll travel in Serai Nadir's carriage and avoid every planned stop. You'll remain here with a few men. Once you're well, you can join us in Duvan."

"No," Bennick said, argument stiffening his voice as his eyes peeled open. "As soon as . . . I can stand . . . I'm going to Krid."

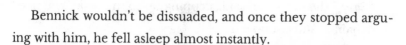

Bennick wouldn't be dissuaded, and once they stopped arguing with him, he fell asleep almost instantly.

The physician spoke with them for a few minutes, promising to stay in the room with him tonight. Serene thanked him, then slipped into the hall, Cardon and Dirk following her.

Tamar Nadir was in the corridor. The Mortisian noblewoman was beautiful, her frame willowy and her hair dark and full even though she was nearing fifty. She was a widow who had lost her husband soon after their marriage in the border skirmishes. As a result, she was a strong supporter of the al-liance.

"How is Captain Markam?" she asked, her Mortisian accent rolling thickly as she spoke Devendran.

Serene did not miss how the woman's eyes lingered on Dirk. She smiled a little. "He woke for a moment."

Some of the tension in Tamar's shoulders dropped. "Thank the fates. That's a good sign."

Dirk took a step toward her. "It's late. Why are you still awake?"

Tamar sighed. "I've been seeing to the freed prisoners. Not all of them are ready to travel home just yet."

Serene easily recalled the weariness in the Mortisian prisoners that had been under Commander Markam's less-than-attentive care. Turning those men over to Tamar Nadir had been the only good thing about the disastrous prisoner exchange.

Tamar folded her arms. "I'm also trying to prepare the estate for our departure. I still need to speak with the guards I'm leaving behind to watch the manor. If those mercenaries do come here, I want my men focused on a safe retreat, rather than a last stand."

Dirk's brow furrowed. "I should come with you. In case they have any questions about the mercenaries."

"Of course," Tamar said quickly. "Your help would be much appreciated, if the princess can spare you."

Dirk glanced to Serene, who was already waving him off. "Go. I'm sure Cardon can walk me safely down the corridor."

Cardon snorted.

"Thank you." Dirk offered his arm to Tamar, who took hold with an appreciative smile. As they walked toward the staircase, Serene fought her own smile.

"That's unexpected," Cardon murmured, watching the couple disappear.

"I think it's romantic."

It was also proof that a Mortisian and a Devendran could overlook their differences, and even have fond feelings for each other. That was reassuring to see, as marrying a Mortisian was in Serene's future.

She started walking down the shadowed hall, and Cardon fell into step beside her.

"Of course," he said, "it could also be a distraction."

Serene rolled her eyes. "And you never find yourself distracted?" The question was out before she could consider the wisdom of it.

The last thing she wanted to know was that Cardon had a woman who distracted him.

The skin around his eyes tightened as he looked at her. "No," he finally said. "Never."

She wasn't sure how she felt about his answer. Relieved, of course, but there was a twinge of disappointment as well. What would it feel like to be the woman who distracted Cardon Brinhurst?

Clearly she would never know.

They reached her room, which was guarded by two men. Cardon leaned around her to open the door, and his arm brushed hers.

Serene stilled, her cheeks warming at the incidental touch.

As Cardon drew back, she twisted to face him—perfectly aware that the guards were watching. "Goodnight, Sir Brinhurst."

He inclined his head, the scar on his cheek catching in the soft light. "Goodnight, Princess."

She slipped into her room and closed the door, pinching her eyes closed. After a few measured breaths that did little to still the erratic beating of her heart, she peeled away from the door. She was exhausted, but she bypassed the bed and headed for the small desk in the corner.

She needed to write to James. Her rebel network wasn't strong in Mortise, but if there was anything they could do for Clare and Vera, she knew James—one of the key leaders in the rebellion— would do it.

Writing coded messages had always helped take her mind off things, and at the moment, she had far too many things clambering around inside her head.

And her heart.

It was a good distraction.

When she finished her message to James—telling him not only about Clare and Vera's abduction, but also the new plan to rush to Duvan without predictable stops—she eyed a clean sheet of paper and considered writing a letter to Desfan, her future husband.

This marriage alliance was something she needed. It had become a vital part of her plan. Something that would strengthen her rebellion and give her more resources to fight against her father and brother. If she could create peace between Mortise and Devendra along the way, so much the better. But that didn't mean she wasn't afraid to marry Desfan. She was fates-blasted terrified. Which was probably why she abandoned the desk without writing anything else and moved for her bedroom.

Marrying a stranger was enough to make anyone nervous. But this was a man who had more stories told about him than any other royal she knew—with the exception of the Kaelin princes.

69

Maybe.

Desfan was a thrill-seeker. A gambler. An addict, many claimed, though some said that was only in his past. He was a man who had shirked his responsibilities in court for years to sail the sea as a reckless pirate-hunter. A man who had no interest in ruling a kingdom or improving the lives of his subjects.

Desfan Saernon Cassian did not seem like her perfect match.

But then, if life had taught Serene anything, it was that nothing was ever perfect.

CHAPTER 9

MIA

MIA STOOD NEAR THE WINDOW, FINGERING her pebble necklace as she eyed the thick curtain that blocked the morning light. She knew the sun was shining, because the warm glow peeked around the edges of the heavy drapes.

The curtains had been pulled back each day she'd been here, usually by Devon, as the physician came to check on her, or even by Tyrell. But after five days of other people giving her sunlight, she was ready to do it herself.

Her fingers trembled as she grasped the edge of the curtain, and then she tugged it aside.

The sunlight was blinding. She blinked quickly, trying to get her

71

eyes to adjust. It took a few moments to see the hazy outline of the castle walls. And, beyond, the rooftops of Lenzen, the city that nestled lower on the hill. In the far distance were towering mountains sheathed in pines and tipped with snow, even as summer waxed on.

The outside world was beautiful and terrifying. It didn't look real. It was vast, the sky never-ending. And it could be ripped away from her at any time.

The door to the room opened, and Mia looked over her shoulder to see Tyrell step in.

He wore black leathers and a white shirt that was molded to his chest due to the sweat coating his body. He breathed deeply, clearly fresh from the training grounds. His dark hair curled over his forehead and ears, his face clean-shaven. He was two years older than her sixteen years, and not so long ago she had been absolutely terrified of him.

The uneasiness she felt in this moment was purely because he had not brought up the things he'd said to her the other night.

He had feelings for her—feelings she did not return. She loved his brother, Grayson. Tyrell had been her enemy, but now he was her friend. That still felt tentative though, because she knew he wanted more.

Tyrell stalled when he saw her at the window. "Should you be out of bed?"

"Devon said it would be good to stretch my legs."

Tyrell frowned, his dark brows tugging together. "Surely he didn't mean for you to try such a thing on your own."

Mia shrugged one shoulder. The movement rippled across her stomach, stretching her still-healing wound. She grimaced, and Tyrell stalked forward.

She held up a hand. "I'm fine."

He still grabbed her arm, his fingers warm and strong, yet surprisingly gentle. His chin lowered along with his voice. "You were stabbed. You need to be careful so your body can heal."

"I'm sick of being in bed."

"I can get you a chair, then. I'll even open the window."

"Really?"

"Of course." His hand flexed carefully around her arm, and then he released her. He dragged a heavy armchair across the stone floor, making a terrible noise. When she protested that she could use the wooden stool by the fireplace instead, he rolled his eyes but otherwise ignored her.

Once the chair was angled in front of the window, Mia gratefully sank onto the soft cushion, one hand rubbing gently over her bandaged middle.

Tyrell worked the latch on the window, then pushed it open.

Fresh air, birdsong, and the smell of earth and summer wafted inside. Mia closed her eyes, absorbing the distant sounds of voices in the courtyard, the barking of dogs, and the baying of goats and sheep. She wasn't a part of the outside world—not really—but she was closer to it than she had been in years.

"You're so beautiful."

Her cheeks flushed. She opened her eyes to see the prince staring at her. Her heart lurched. "Tyrell . . ."

He pushed off from the window. "I'm going to wash up. We can have breakfast together when I'm done."

Mia squirmed in her chair, following him with her eyes as he trekked to his closet and rifled for a clean shirt. "I really don't need to stay in your room," she finally said. "Devon offered a private room in the physician's ward until I recover." At which point, she would no doubt be returned to her prison cell.

"No," Tyrell said without turning.

She frowned. "I'd be closer to Devon and less of an inconvenience to you."

"It will be more inconvenient if you make me trek up to Devon's drafty tower every time I want to see you." He twisted, clutching clean clothes in his fist. He lifted an eyebrow at her. "Besides, my window offers a better view than any in the physician's ward."

That was probably true; it *was* quite spectacular.

"At least let me move into the adjoining room," she said. "You can't be comfortable there." It was a servant's room, and far smaller than this one.

"I don't mind."

"I don't feel right taking your room."

He shrugged. "I rather like seeing you in my bed."

She blushed, even as she scowled. "Be serious."

He lifted one dark brow. "Oh, I'm completely serious."

Mia shook her head. "I've displaced you enough. I'm only trying to—"

"Mia." He suddenly looked serious, and that more than anything made her listen. "I want you to stay here. You're close enough to Devon, and this way you're close to me. This suite is well defended, this room even more so. Anyone who tries to get to you will have to get through me first. You're safe."

Safe. It was an ironic word. She had often felt safe with Grayson, and oddly enough, she did feel safe with Tyrell. But neither of them could change the fact that she was the king's prisoner. Neither had been able to always protect her.

Still, she was grateful for all Tyrell had done. Even for the fact that he had killed Papa. Knowing she no longer had to fear the man who had terrorized her for so many years . . . it was freeing.

"Thank you," she whispered.

Tyrell scrubbed a hand over the back of his neck, his ears reddening as he glanced away. "I'll be back soon." He hurried from the room, closing the door behind him.

Mia turned her gaze back to the window. The light breeze was cool against her skin, and she closed her eyes to concentrate better on the smells. Some flowers she thought she recognized—lilac, roses; wildflowers the Poison Queen hadn't ordered ripped out, because surely she didn't ask the groundskeepers to maintain something as trivial as a flower garden. Grayson had once told her of his mother's infamous poison garden. The thought of something so unpleasant made her shudder.

There was a fresh scent on the air, a crisp smell she found most pleasant. She would need to ask Tyrell what it was. She swore it was something she'd smelled on Grayson's skin before, after he'd returned from the mountains.

Fates, she missed him. He had been her only friend for years; a light when she had needed one most. She had fallen in love with him, and that love had only grown deeper as they'd grown older.

He was in Mortise, now. In the city of Duvan, which meant beaches, cliffs, colorful homes, and spices on the air. An entirely different world.

Mia's heartbeat quickened, and at first she thought it had been the turn of her thoughts that had caused the reaction. Then her scalp prickled.

She wasn't alone in the room.

She knew it wasn't Tyrell—he would have announced himself. As would Devon or Fletcher, her guard.

No, this was someone new. A stranger.

Her eyes snapped open and she twisted in her chair, ignoring the painful pinch in her belly as her injury strained.

A man stood in the doorway. He was shorter than Tyrell or Grayson and his shoulders were less broad, but he was older—maybe in his mid-twenties. And though his hair was a lighter brown and his face rounder, she knew he was a Kaelin prince. He was well-dressed, his hair neatly combed, and his light-brown eyes were riveted on Mia. "Well, well," he murmured, a slow grin twisting his expression. "I didn't realize Tyrell had a new mistress."

Mia swallowed hard, one hand going to the base of her throat. She wore a nightgown—something she had grown used to in her convalescence, and she hadn't felt uncomfortable in it until this moment.

The man cocked his head to the side. "You're Mortisian." He switched languages seamlessly. "I didn't realize Tyrell spoke Mortisian, but I suppose being with one as beautiful as you doesn't require much talking."

"I'm not Tyrell's mistress," she said in Rydenic.

His eyebrows lifted, his eyes sparking with interest. "Oh?"

Her gut twisted. Perhaps she should have let him believe such a thing. But it was too late now. She lifted her chin. "I'm his friend."

"Ah. Forgive me, I didn't know Tyrell had friends." He stepped fully into the room. She caught the glint of a signet ring on his finger as he shifted his hands behind his back. His smile was cordial, but edged with a cruelty he could not disguise. And suddenly, she knew exactly who this was.

Peter, Grayson's oldest brother. She had never met him, but from the few stories Grayson had told, she would bet anything that this was the oldest Kaelin brother.

"What is your name?" he asked.

It was an order, but she ignored it. "I don't think Tyrell would want you in here."

"I'm sure he wouldn't. Yet here I am."

Her eyes darted to the door behind him. Hadn't Tyrell heard his brother slip past? Washing couldn't be that distracting. Had he left the suite without telling her?

"Your name?" Peter repeated, his tone a little harder than before.

Mia's eyes flicked back to him as he took another step forward. She pushed to her feet, one hand braced on the chair's back so she wouldn't sway. "Mia. And you are Peter."

The corner of his mouth twitched higher. "Yes, Mia. *Prince* Peter."

Hatred flashed at the confirmation. Grayson did not often share specifics of the tortures he'd suffered at the hands of his family, but she knew Peter was exceptionally cruel and ruthless. She should probably be more afraid of him, but the crown prince of Ryden infused her with such revulsion, she couldn't cower. She *wouldn't*.

She had found new strength over the last several weeks, and she refused to lose it now. "I would like you to leave."

"But we're just getting acquainted." Peter stepped closer, and Mia's fingers dug into the wing of the chair. "You intrigue me. You are not his usual type of . . . *friend*."

The word was pure insult, but she kept his unnerving gaze. "Do you have a message for Tyrell? I can give it to him if you wish."

Peter was only three paces from her now, and her legs trembled. She locked her knees.

Calculation filled his gaze as he viewed her. "I think you could help deliver many good messages. But none we have to resort to today." He held out his hand, palm up. It was an invitation, and she nearly refused it. But a voice in her head whispered it would be worse for her if she did—that showing fear would be a fatal mistake.

She set her cold fingers against his, and Peter drew her hand to his mouth, forcing her to take a step closer. His dry lips brushed her knuckles.

She nearly shivered, and his smile curved higher.

"Peter."

Mia startled at Tyrell's voice. Peter dropped her hand and twisted to face the door.

Tyrell stood in the doorway, the ends of his hair wet and clinging to his neck. He clearly hadn't bothered to dry himself. He looked relaxed, his expression indifferent, but Mia could see the tension in his shoulders. "My guards didn't announce you."

"I asked them not to." Peter once more clasped his hands behind his back as he cast a sideways look at Mia. "Besides, your short absence gave me valuable time with your new friend. She's lovely." His eyes trailed pointedly over Mia's body, making her stomach curdle. "Do let me know if you ever want to share."

Tyrell folded his arms across his chest. "Did you come for some purpose?"

Peter straightened. "I want you to intensify the grappling routines. I visited the field yesterday, and the new recruits seem to be struggling. I thought maybe you could starve them for a couple of days, then promise a meal to the winners. That might incentivize them."

Tyrell dipped his head. "A good suggestion. I'll see it done."

Mia stiffened, bile climbing her throat.

Peter smiled. "Good. Do tell me when the matches will be. I know Jazarah would enjoy the sport as well." He glanced at Mia and dipped his head. "It's been a pleasure, Mia."

She said nothing as she watched him stride from the room. Tyrell tracked his brother's retreat, and he didn't look away until the door had closed. Then he pivoted to face Mia.

All indifference was gone, concern and something alarmingly like fear in his eyes. "Are you all right?"

Her stomach still rolled unpleasantly. "He's completely repellent."

Tyrell crossed the room quickly, and though his hands twitched, he didn't touch her. "I had no idea he would come in. My family rarely visits. But now that Peter knows about you . . ."

Mia paled. She hadn't thought of that. If he told others, they might come to see her. Carter. The Poison Queen.

King Henri.

She knew the king had visited while she was in and out of unconsciousness, fighting for her life after Papa had stabbed her. But while she thought she'd heard him speak, she hadn't seen the king since she was a child. Not since the day he had discovered her and Grayson playing together, and he'd ordered Grayson to burn the doll he'd made for her.

"I'll bring in more guards," Tyrell said firmly.

His words were meant to comfort her, but they didn't. She knew even if she had a hundred guards, it wouldn't matter.

Guards couldn't stop a member of the royal family, as Peter had just proven.

CHAPTER 10

GRAYSON

GRAYSON ROLLED THE SWORD IN HIS HAND, eyes locked on his opponent. The Rydenic guard slowly circled him, sweat dripping over his brow. The Mortisian sun was insufferably hot, but Grayson refused to let the heat keep him from training. He needed the outlet. The distraction.

Be patient, Liam had told him. The only problem was, Grayson hadn't been raised as a spy, so all of this waiting just made him feel trapped.

Desfan had yet to appoint a noble to the final seat on the council. According to Liam, Mortisian law dictated that a position on the council could only be vacant for three weeks, so Desfan would have to make a decision soon. But until he did, Liam said they had no choice but to wait.

Grayson hated inaction.

The guard charged him, and Grayson met the blows easily, the clang of their swords echoing in the practice yard. The spacious grounds were enclosed in a courtyard, sandstone columns lining the square. Most of the ground was packed dirt, but there was a corner laid out with sand. Grayson didn't like the way it shifted underfoot, but he forced himself to practice on it every day in order to get used to it. At the moment, he was on solid earth, and it helped him fall into a familiar rhythm.

Whenever he trained with his guards, the Mortisians always backed away, giving them plenty of space. But they watched. They hovered on the edge of the dirt field, or peered from the shadowed archways that encircled the grounds. He even caught men and women standing at the windows that overlooked the yard. If he paid too much attention, his skin prickled under their watchful gazes. It was yet another reason he had not given into the urge to train with his shirt off, like most of the Mortisians did. He didn't want people staring at his scars.

Grayson ducked the swinging blade and it arced over him, slicing through air with an audible sweep. Two quick blows later, and his opponent's sword was on the ground.

Hands flashed up in surrender, the Rydenic man's chest rising and falling rapidly.

"Well done," a deep voice called out.

Grayson turned, aware of movement rippling across the yard as men abandoned their mock battles and bowed.

Serjah Desfan strode through the crowd toward Grayson, his bodyguard Karim right behind him. He carried two swords, the blades thin and slightly curved. Intrigue flickered through Grayson. He'd never seen blades like that.

Desfan seemed to read his mind. When he reached Grayson, he held out one of the swords, the blade aimed down. "They're short and lightweight, perfect for delivering cuts and slices. Not so great at stabbing, but I like a little finesse."

"I didn't see much finesse during the fight in the library," Grayson said.

Desfan flashed a grin. "Yes, well, I *like* finesse, but it's not always practical."

Grayson tested the blade, swinging it out, then slicing it straight up; it whistled easily through the air. "I like it," he said, passing it back. "I haven't ever seen dual blades like that."

The serjah rolled his wrist, smoothly flipping the blade around. "They're not common, except on the southern isles of Zennor. I picked up the skill years ago. A patrol ship captain taught me."

"Ah, yes. You spent years at sea."

"I did." He leaned in, lowering his voice. "Truthfully, I prefer swimming with real sharks rather than those who walk the palace halls."

Grayson frowned. "Didn't you arrest all of your enemies?"

"Fates, I doubt it. I have too many." The serjah drew back. "I came to lose myself in a match. Care to join me?"

Karim choked.

Grayson blinked. "You . . . want to spar with me?"

Desfan smiled. "Yes, please."

Karim grabbed the serjah's arm and hauled him back a step, whispering low and fierce. Desfan responded quietly, winked, and stepped back to Grayson. "Well?"

Grayson eyed Karim, who was glaring behind the serjah. He should probably say no. But something—boredom? Desfan's eagerness?—had him tipping his head. "All right."

Desfan's grin split wide. "Excellent." He handed Karim his swords, then grasped the back of his shirt and jerked it over his head. The serjah was clearly not one to sit idle on his throne; his broad shoulders and strong arms revealed years spent in hard work, and his torso was ridged with muscle. Grayson noticed the women in the yard edge closer.

Desfan nodded to Grayson's black shirt. "Aren't you dying in that?"

Sweat rolled down his body, but he forced himself to shrug. "It pays to train with distractions." His father had often said that. Once, when Grayson was eleven years old, he'd ordered a dog to attack Grayson while he fought Tyrell. He still had scars from some of the deeper bites on his legs, and he'd had a silent fear of dogs ever since.

Desfan chuckled. "I suppose that's true."

They stepped into the open space, spectators forming a ring around them. Whispers cut through the afternoon air, and even though Grayson's back was to Karim, he could feel the bodyguard's dagger-like stare. A lethal promise was there, unspoken but clear.

If Desfan was harmed, Grayson would be on Karim's to-murder-slowly list.

Desfan faced Grayson, idly rotating both blades. Grayson stood motionless, his longsword in hand.

Desfan struck.

The serjah was surprisingly fast, but his darting eyes and the shifting of his body a blink before he moved betrayed him. Grayson knew exactly where Desfan intended to strike, even with two blades. Grayson's sword was in place to parry the blows perfectly; he didn't wait for Desfan to move. He moved *with* him.

Desfan's blade whispered along Grayson's, a steel rattle that cut off when Desfan drew back.

The serjah's eyes danced. "This will be fun."

Their blades spun as he lunged, and Grayson enjoyed the uniqueness of the fight. Desfan's two blades operated together perfectly, yet could move with autonomy. It kept Grayson alert. Focused. He had to adjust his fighting style to meet Desfan's, and while it wasn't exactly a challenge, it was exhilarating.

Men and women cheered for their serjah. Grayson's bodyguards lingered on the edge of the crowd, but remained silent. They knew he wasn't really trying to fight back—or perhaps they had no desire to favor him as a champion. Grayson could believe either option.

After exchanging a few blows, Desfan took a step back, blades spinning at his sides. His smile was a little crooked. "You don't need to hold back. I promise Karim won't kill you."

Grayson saw something in Desfan's gaze that he recognized; the serjah wanted to lose himself in this match. Grayson had turned to fighting for similar relief often enough—that's what he'd been doing here today.

He tipped his head. "As you wish." This time, he struck the first blow.

Desfan blocked it with crossed blades, his grin broad.

Grayson didn't release his full skill into the fight, but he did make an effort to test Desfan, which he thought the serjah appreciated. Karim certainly didn't, but Grayson mostly ignored everyone around them, even the flinching bodyguard. Desfan was good. Better than most of the Rydenic soldiers Grayson had been training with.

As they fought, Grayson occasionally paused and remarked on something Desfan could improve. Loosening his elbow. Driving a blow with more of his weight. Lifting the blades a fraction higher when he blocked an enemy sword, for better control. Desfan even gave him a little advice when it came to deflecting dual swords, and the hazards of the curved blades.

When they finally stopped, Grayson realized almost an hour had passed. The Mortisian spectators had grown bored and wandered off, though Karim was still there, his teeth actually bared. Sweat dripped from his temples, and his body was so rigid it looked as if *he'd* been the one in the fight.

Desfan stepped back, breathing heavily. "Thank you." The corner of his mouth lifted, a full smile he was obviously trying to suppress. It was an expression he'd seen on Mia's face—the sort of expression exchanged between friends. The thought shocked him. Surely Desfan wasn't interested in becoming his friend?

"And thank you for the advice," Desfan added.

Grayson cleared his throat. "Of course."

"We'll have to do it again soon," the serjah said.

Karim muttered under his breath, but Grayson found—quite surprisingly—that he looked forward to it.

"Here."

Grayson tensed as Liam threw a book at his head. He caught it with one hand, a scowl on his face. "Do you ever knock?"

"Rarely." Liam flashed a smile as he crossed Grayson's room. "Spy, remember?"

Grayson snorted. "Right."

Liam folded his arms over his chest. "I heard you and Desfan sparred this morning."

"And?"

His brother shrugged. "The serjah seems to like you. That's good. Did you ask him about the final council seat?"

"No." The thought hadn't even crossed his mind.

"Oh. Perhaps next time you can learn something from him."

For some reason, the thought of using Desfan for information bothered him. It shouldn't, of course. The sooner Liam knew the name of the last council member, the sooner he would tell Grayson the details of his plan.

He looked down at the book in his hand. "What's this?"

"A bit of history." Liam sat on the edge of the bed. "What were you working on?"

Grayson twisted in his hardback chair, putting the desk behind him. "Practicing my Mortisian." Fates knew he needed something to do.

"Well, I think I can bring you a more interesting diversion." He reclined on the bed, elbows propping him up. "I find history quite fascinating. It's taught as fact, and yet it's so changeable. Every kingdom can remember the same event differently. Every generation can rewrite the past. It's fascinating. I like to read the histories of other kingdoms and make comparisons; it's a hobby of mine." He tipped his chin toward the book in Grayson's hand. "That particular book is a copy of a journal penned by a Devendran foot soldier, Kent Sowell. He became a bit of a poet—not bad, though not to my taste. In any case, his fame ensured the survival of his journal after he died, and I thought you might find it interesting."

Grayson eyed the leather spine. "Why would I find that interesting?"

"Because he was there when father's brother was killed."

His words made no sense. Grayson frowned. "Father doesn't have a brother."

"Well, not anymore. He died."

Grayson shot his brother a bland look and thumbed the book open. Unsurprisingly, it was written in Devendran, which he could read a little of, since Mia had loved several Devendran texts. A bookmark helped him find the passage Liam must have been referencing. The entry was titled, *The Battle of Dolbar Pass*. He eyed his brother. "Father was an only child."

"Except he wasn't. Henri was the second-born son of King Ezra. Of course, Father tried to destroy all records of his brother when he became king—and he largely succeeded, at least in Ryden."

"Why?"

Liam nodded to the book. "It's all in there."

Grayson snapped it closed. "I can read it later. I want you to stop being so cryptic and just tell me what you know."

His brother cracked a grin. "I'm growing on you, aren't I?"

"Liam . . ."

"Very well." His brother sat up. "To defeat an enemy, you have to first understand that enemy. So, I set about learning everything I could about Father. I didn't realize his full history until leaving Ryden, because he'd erased his older brother from our records. But I've pieced together the story. You know that King Ezra, our grandfather, died before Peter was born. What you don't know is that Ezra had an entirely different family before our father was born." Liam fiddled with the leather bracelet on his wrist, his eyes animated with his storytelling. "Ezra was crowned when he was just sixteen, after his father was trampled by a horse. Soon after taking the throne, Ezra married a noblewoman named Valene."

Grayson frowned. "But—"

"Not our grandmother, no. Now, I'm not convinced Ezra knew anything about love, but he obsessed over Valene and their son, Farrell. When Farrell was twenty years old, he joined his father on a battlefield near Dolbar Pass. They were invading Devendra, because Ezra wanted to expand Ryden's borders. Farrell was killed, and the battle was lost. When Valene heard that her son was dead, she took her own life before Ezra could return to the castle. In one battle, he had lost the majority of his army—which cost him most of the Kaelin fortune—as well as his son and heir, and his wife. Naturally, he blamed Devendra for all of it.

"He remarried almost immediately—Valene's youngest sister Oslynn, who was barely eighteen—and they had a child within the year. Ezra named him Henri, and he raised him with the sole purpose of revenge. He instilled in his son a hatred for Devendra, and all the other kingdoms who had stood by while Ezra's life was stolen from him. He raised a monster." A muscle in Liam's jaw ticked. "It makes some sense of our childhoods, doesn't it? Our father was bred for a single purpose: to seek revenge for a brother he never knew. A brother with whom he was locked in some sick sort of competition with. That's how he made us. We only have meaning in what we can do for him, which was exactly how his father made him."

Grayson didn't feel pity for his father. None. And yet, for a brief moment, he tried to picture his father as a child. A little boy, raised with such focused vengeance.

He shifted in his chair, resting the book on his leg. "If he was raised to avenge his older brother, why did he erase Farrell from our history?"

Liam quirked a mirthless smile. "Why indeed? A question I

asked myself while piecing together the past. The answer I've concluded? Father rebelled against his father. I wouldn't be surprised if Henri murdered Ezra before Peter was born, simply so he could mold his own children into whatever he wanted them to be. The fact that he scrubbed out all mentions of Farrell and Valene from our history tells me that he feels resentful and jealous of Ezra's first family—Farrell in particular. Henri had never been wanted by his father. Not really. Our father's entire existence was about avenging the son Ezra had *actually* wanted. I think he has such grand plans to conquer Devendra and Mortise because he wants to prove that he's better than Farrell ever would have been."

Grayson tried to think like Liam. "Father is ruled more by emotion than we thought. He has jealousies and weaknesses."

"Yes. He's not an untouchable monster. He *can* be outsmarted. He can be killed."

"So, our family history—full of violence and death—is supposed to make me feel better?"

Liam shrugged. "Did it work?"

Grayson snorted despite himself.

His brother's mouth twitched. "I think there is also merit in viewing this story as proof that there are multiple sides to every story, which is a good reminder." He pushed up from the bed. "I'll leave you to your studies."

He moved for the door, but before he made it there, Grayson voiced one of the questions that bothered him. "You say Father feels emotion, and I suppose I can see that now. But . . . do you think he loves Mother?"

Liam lifted a single eyebrow. "If you want to hear the story of how they met and married, I can tell you. But I warn you, you'll probably have nightmares forever."

Grayson huffed a dry laugh. "Never mind, then."

"I think he loves her," Liam allowed. "In his own way. If we ever laid a blade against her throat, he *would* hesitate. But if the blade was flipped? If Father was threatened and Mother had to choose whether to save him or let him die, I have no doubt she would simply watch him bleed."

Imagining the Poison Queen's cold gray eyes, Grayson fought a shiver. "I think you're right."

"What a thing to be right about." He shook his head. "It's a wonder any of us have any sanity, coming from such evil parents." He reached for the door, but Grayson's voice stopped him once more.

"What happened to Oslynn? Our grandmother? I know her name, but I don't know how or when she died."

Liam stared back at him. "The story I heard came from a castle maid who was in the room when Father was born. According to her, Oslynn looked at her newborn son as he lay in her arms and said, 'He looks just like his father.' Then she tried to snap his neck."

Everything inside Grayson went cold.

Liam's eyes went flat. "Our father's first glimpse of the world was to nearly die at his mother's hand, only to watch his father kill his mother in retribution. A dagger through her heart, even as she held him."

The silence in the room was heavy, but Liam didn't have to say anything. Grayson knew exactly what his brother was thinking, because the same thought burned in his mind.

This is our family. We are their legacy.

No wonder we are so broken.

CHAPTER II

DESFAN

'WHAT BY ALL THE FATES WERE YOU THINKING, sparring with Prince Grayson?" Karim growled as they walked the darkened streets of Duvan. Their boots clipped rapidly over the cobblestones, and the smell of the harbor grew stronger the closer they came to the docks.

"Your faith in my skill is inspiring," Desfan quipped.

Karim was not amused. "He could have killed you—feigned an accident so we couldn't outright blame Ryden. It would have been a disaster."

"And I would have been dead," Desfan added.

Karim punched his arm, making him stumble.

He cursed under his breath. "That hurt," he complained.

"Too bad it won't knock any sense into you," his bodyguard muttered.

Desfan sighed. "I'm sorry I worried you. I just . . . needed a challenge."

"Your habit of jumping off the nearest cliff when you need to feel alive is going to be the death of me."

He cracked a smile. "It could be the death of me, too."

"Not funny, Des."

He slung an arm around his friend's stiff shoulders. "Let me buy you a drink."

"It won't do much to relax me, since we're having drinks with the most infamous pirate who ever lived."

"Fair. But you have to admit, Syed Zadir is more amusing than you expected."

Karim rolled his eyes. "You should have let me bring his payment for uncovering the truth about Jamal. You didn't need to come."

"I needed to get out of the palace."

His bodyguard huffed out a breath, carefully eyeing the shadows as they walked. "Have you chosen your last council member yet?"

Desfan dropped his arm with a groan. "Not you, too. Yahri won't stop pestering me."

"You appointed the others quickly. What's different about this last one?"

"The others were in Duvan—that made things efficient."

"You have someone in mind, then?"

"Yes, but I don't know if she'll accept the role, since politics aren't her passion. I haven't received a reply yet."

Karim grunted. "That might be a nice change, actually. Someone in politics who doesn't want to be there."

"I thought that was my role?"

That received a snorting laugh. They walked in silence for a minute, and when Karim spoke, his voice was quieter. "We haven't really talked about what Yahri said. About what happened to your father, and that rumor."

Desfan tensed. "I'm not sure what there is to say. It's obvious you agree with Yahri."

Karim's brow furrowed, his eyes narrowing as a group of staggering drunks passed them, bellowing a rather out-of-tune rendition of a popular sea shanty. "There's no proof Gamble was telling the truth. Yahri investigated the matter."

"And you trust her?"

"I do, at least in this." Karim shook his head. "Think about it, Des. Pirates who just happened to sail by the scene of the shipwreck before anyone else, and somehow one of your sisters is still alive, even though there were no other survivors—not even among the strongest sailors on the ship? And then these pirates don't even try to ransom her to a grieving father who would have given his entire kingdom for his daughter's return, but they keep her? It makes no sense."

"I know. But I can't ignore this."

There was a beat of silence. Then, "We're not just meeting Zadir to pay him for investigating the olcain. You're going to hire him to find Gamble."

"Yes. And before you get upset about it, don't worry—I'm not going to tell him why. Yahri was right about that. If we start asking questions, people will come forward with lies in an effort to gain something from me. It will only muddy the waters and make it harder to find the truth."

"I know how desperate you are for this to be real, Des. I know all those years at sea, all those people we saved . . . in your mind, you were saving your family." He let out a thin breath. "I just don't want to see you hurt."

"I know." And he was grateful for his friend, who had been with him through some of his darkest days. "I just need to know for sure."

Karim didn't say anything, but he remained beside him. They were nearly to the tavern when his bodyguard finally spoke. "I've been thinking about Princess Serene and the fact the Rose was hired by the council. Do you think she'll immediately go home when she finds out?"

"I don't know." The thought of her rejecting their betrothal filled Desfan with several different emotions. Relief and excitement were there, undeniably, but there was also fear and apprehension. "We can't afford a war with Devendra. Or Ryden."

Karim grunted. "We could stand a *little* war with Ryden."

"You can't kill Grayson. Or Liam."

"I will if they hurt you."

"They've been nothing but polite guests."

"Liam is far too agreeable. I don't trust him at all. And Grayson is the fates-blasted Black Hand. If they're truly here for peace talks, I'll drop dead."

"A dangerous bet."

"I learned from the most reckless gambler I know."

Desfan smiled. "So you did."

They reached the tavern and slipped inside, moving to the back corner table. Syed Zadir was already there with a handful of his men. Ori, the small boy Desfan had once saved from smugglers, was perched on one of the chairs. He waved eagerly when he saw them.

Desfan grinned and waved back.

"Exciting times at your palace lately," Zadir drawled.

The pirate reclined in his seat, looking perfectly at ease talking with the future serjan of Mortise. The man was in his middle years, his beard thick and black. He was built a little stocky, and a grin twisted in his beard more often than not. For a criminal, he was quite decent. He had a moral code, such as it was, and Desfan was perfectly content to work with the infamous pirate.

He could always arrest him later.

Desfan pulled out a chair across from the pirate captain and sat, Karim following suit beside him. "My life is generally more exciting than I'd like," he said.

"And yet you claim to bore easily."

"True."

"An enigma is our serjah."

The men chuckled, and Desfan ordered two drinks. As the serving maid walked away, he pulled out a heavy purse and dropped it onto the table. "For your services to the crown."

"Not a phrase I've heard before." Zadir lifted the purse and tossed it to the man beside him. "Count it, Whistler."

Desfan quirked a brow. "You don't trust me?"

"I don't trust anyone. It's how I'm still alive." Zadir folded his arms across his broad chest. "I admit, I was sorry to hear my findings reached you too late."

"Jamal was stopped. That's what matters."

"Him and half your council, it sounds like."

"Various crimes." Desfan shrugged. "Politics."

"Nasty business."

"And pirating isn't?" Karim asked.

Zadir smiled. "At least pirating is fun."

95

Their drinks arrived, and Desfan took a generous swallow before squaring his shoulders. "I have another job for you, if you're interested."

"I don't think my skills are the best fit to track Sahvi," Zadir said, naming the Zennorian drug master who had sold the olcain to Jamal. "He's far inland."

"With Jamal in prison, it will take Sahvi a while to find another buyer in Duvan." Hopefully. "I can coordinate with King Zaire Buhari to take care of Sahvi in Zennor."

"So, this job has nothing to do with the olcain?"

"No. I want you to find someone for me. A sailor."

"Name?"

"Gamble."

The pirate frowned. "Sounds like a nickname. Common among those who call the sea home, but blasted hard to get to the bottom of. What ship does he sail on?"

"I don't know. And there's a chance he's not sailing anymore."

"Do you have a description?"

"Mortisian. Brown hair. Middle-aged."

Zadir blinked. "You're joking, right?"

Karim snorted into his tankard. "If only."

Desfan leaned in, focused on Zadir. "Gamble has some information I need. I want you to find him as quickly and discreetly as possible."

The captain reached over the table and grabbed Desfan's mug, taking a healthy swallow. When he set it down, he was shaking his head. "I hate to suck the air from your sails, but you're a blasted fool if you think even *I* can find a man with so little to go on."

"I've been called worse."

"He has," Karim attested.

"You have boys like Ori in every port," Desfan said. "I'm sure you can use that network to locate Gamble."

"I probably shouldn't have told you about that," Zadir muttered.

"I rather like knowing how you operate." Desfan flashed a smile. "It will make it easier to catch you someday."

Zadir chuckled. "Good luck, Serjah." He shook his head again, blowing out a breath. "When was the last anyone saw Gamble?"

"A year ago. Here in Duvan."

"He may not even be alive. Sailors can have an alarmingly short lifespan."

"Maybe," Desfan allowed. "But if he is alive, I know you can find him." He deposited another pouch onto the table. "Consider this an incentive. Your actual payment will be triple, and I'll cover any costs you incur related to the search."

"Generous." Zadir glanced at his men, then back to Desfan. "Do you want me to abduct him?"

"If he can't be persuaded to come willingly, yes. It's vital that I talk to him."

"I don't mind a little abduction."

Desfan stiffened. What if Zadir had been the pirate to abduct his sister? The man was notorious, and he had been active for decades.

Just as quickly, he shoved away the doubting thought. Zadir didn't seem the type to kidnap a child. Desfan had seen how the pirate cared for Ori. Though he was tempted to ask Zadir about the rumors, it would be a mistake to give air to the story. Not only for the reasons Yahri had cited, but because if the rumor *was* true and the kidnappers learned the serjah was looking for his sister, they might kill her in order to avoid getting caught.

He would not risk that.

"You know," Zadir said, "you could consider letting some

things go."

"Not this. I need to speak with Gamble."

The pirate scratched at his beard. "Did you know I'm part noble?"

Desfan blinked, thrown by the unexpected question. "Ah, no."

"It's true. Noble blood flows through this pirate's veins. But you don't know it, because it doesn't matter. Blood is blood; if it leaves your body, it's not good. That's about the end of it."

Desfan's brow furrowed. "Does this have a point?"

"Indeed it does." Zadir settled back in his chair. "My father was cast from his family for falling in love with a common girl. They rejected him, and he didn't fight it when they insisted he change his name. He let it go." A grin split his bearded face. "Of course, he only dropped one letter from his name. I came by most of my best traits honestly, I'm proud to say."

Desfan fitted the puzzle together, and his eyes rounded. "You're one of the *Zahdirs?*"

They were a powerful family in Mortise, and had been for centuries. They didn't hold political power in Duvan, but they had raised an empire in the city of Zahdir, making it one of the largest and most profitable trade cities in the country.

Zadir didn't seem as impressed. "I'm not one of them anymore. My father let it all go for love. His inheritance, his family—all of it."

"Not all of us have that luxury," Desfan said, thoughts flashing to Serene and his future with her.

"Perhaps not," Zadir allowed. "But my father was much happier being Zadir the fisherman, than Zahdir the nobleman. It's a freeing thing, really—learning that you don't need everything to be happy."

"And so you took this lesson to heart and became a pirate who steals compulsively?" Karim asked flatly.

Zadir threw back his head and laughed. "Ah, I like you, tense bodyguard. You *do* have a sense of humor, even if it's as dry as the desert."

Whistler—who had finished carefully counting the coins in the first purse—gestured to Zadir, nodding to assure him they hadn't been swindled.

Zadir pocketed the newest pouch of gold Desfan had offered. "Very well, Serjah. If you insist on finding Gamble, I'll conduct a search. If we're able to find him, we'll bring him to you." He cracked a smile. "Look at you, making a habit of hiring pirates."

"And look at you, making a habit of working for me. It's a strange world."

The pirate laughed. "It is that."

CHAPTER 12

CLARE

CLARE SLUMPED BESIDE VERA ON THE GROUND, their backs against a thick tree. Her body trembled with fatigue and pain. She was covered in bruises from sharing a saddle, and the ropes around her wrists were stained with blood. The painful chafing almost distracted her from the gnawing in her stomach. They had been riding relentlessly with Salim's men since their capture five days ago. They'd been given food and water, but never enough to relieve the hunger pangs, and not nearly often enough.

Clare had done everything Salim ordered. Resistance was not worth the risk to Vera. Staying alive—keeping her friend alive— was Clare's only focus.

Even so, the blade in her heart could twist without warning. A shocking, gut-wrenching reminder that Bennick was gone. Whenever that pain came, she pushed it away, buried it deep. She needed to be Serene, not Clare. In some ways, that made the grief easier to deal with.

The sun was setting as they made camp by a small creek. The mercenaries divided their chores; some built a fire, others tended the horses, and a couple readied food. There were eight men, including Salim. Clare knew their names and had memorized their faces.

She couldn't stop looking at them.

The flames of the sputtering campfire painted their cruel grins in violent slashes of orange flame and black shadow. She hadn't really seen the face of Bennick's killer. She'd been too focused on Bennick. On the cracking of her heart. It was possible the murderer had gone with one of the other groups, but that didn't stop her from searching the faces around her. Looking at their swords, and wondering.

If she ever found the man who had taken Bennick from her, she would rip him apart.

Beside her, Vera shifted her position, trying to settle more comfortably against the hard ground. Her bound wrists were just as bloody and swollen as Clare's, and she balanced them gingerly on her lap. "Our pace was slower today," Vera whispered. "Did you notice?"

The man standing closest to them was Tariq, and he was far enough away that Clare didn't worry about him overhearing if they spoke quietly.

"Salim doesn't think anyone can track him," Clare said softly.

Unfortunately, that could very well be true. The mercenary leader was clearly comfortable in the dense forest, and he had laid so many false trails.

Vera's lips pursed. "Venn could track him."

Clare knew Venn was renowned for his tracking skills, but still . . . No. She shoved the doubt aside and met Vera's gaze. "I'm sure they're coming." It had become a reassurance they gave each other in hopeful whispers.

The attack on the road had been brutal. Clare had seen Ser Zephan's dead body, and she'd wondered more than once if the Rose had also been killed. She knew Serene had escaped with Cardon. She'd seen Imara get away, too. And while she hadn't seen Venn recover from his injury, she repeatedly told herself that he had lived. That Wilf and Dirk were alive, too. Any other alternative was too painful to contemplate. But she knew they couldn't rely on a rescue.

"If we have a chance to escape," Clare said softly, "we need to take it."

Vera's jaw tightened, but she nodded.

Tariq glanced over at them, though nothing on his face showed he might have overheard their words. He was chatting with another man who had come up to him.

Clare's bound hands fisted on her lap.

Tariq often watched Vera with open desire. Salim had made it clear that the men weren't to touch Clare or Vera more than necessary, but Tariq had been subtly testing that. If he helped Vera dismount, his hands lingered at her waist. He found excuses to touch her shoulder, her bound hands—even her cheek, or hair.

Clare wanted to claw out his eyes.

Vera's soft voice cut into her violent thoughts. "I lied to him."

Clare frowned. "Who?"

"Venn," Vera breathed. Her pale cheeks were smeared with dirt from their days of travel, and it was easy to see the trails her tears made. "I told him I didn't love him. That I could *never* love him. I told him that, if he'd done his job and caught the Rose sooner, Ivonne wouldn't have died." She pulled in a sharp breath. "I was so angry. Not even at him, just—everything. And I felt so guilty."

Clare leaned closer, until their shoulders touched. Fates knew she still felt guilt about Eliot's death, even though she knew she wasn't to blame. Not really. But she remembered the harsh way Michael Byers had yelled at her—how he'd thrown his knife at her. Her brother's best friend had clearly blamed her for Eliot's death.

She swallowed hard. "It's natural to feel guilty, I think. I feel like I should have done more to help Eliot."

Vera was silent for a long time, her shoulder still braced against Clare's. When she did speak, her voice was barely audible. "It could have been me. If I'd stayed at the inn and she'd gone for the physician, I would have been the one on that bed with a rose in my mouth and a dagger in my heart. And when I saw her body . . . I was *relieved.*" Her voice cracked. "I still breathed while my sister was dead, and I felt *relief.* I can't—I can't believe I felt that, even for a moment. What kind of monster am I? To be relieved that my sister died, and I lived?"

"Oh, Vera." Clare gently took Vera's bound hand with her own, wishing she could embrace her friend as she trembled.

"I didn't want my sister to die," Vera said through her tears. "But I was glad it wasn't me. How could I think that? I should have *wanted* it to be me. I wish that, now, but I didn't in the beginning, and I can never take that back."

"And so you punished yourself by pushing Venn away?"

"I had to," she said brokenly. "I couldn't have his comfort. I couldn't have *him.* I didn't deserve him, and Ivonne never approved and . . . I just couldn't be with him. Not after everything."

She sucked in a pained breath. "I lied to him. I told him I blamed him and that I didn't want him. I hurt him, and if we die out here, that's the last memory he'll have of me."

Clare started to answer, but a shadow fell over them.

Salim stood there, a bag in hand and a mocking smile on his face. "I hope I'm not interrupting this emotional moment."

Vera pulled back her hands and wiped her wet cheeks, her eyes downcast.

Clare met Salim's gaze firmly. "What do you want?"

"Always the princess, aren't you?" Salim said, sounding amused.

Despite her underlying fear, Clare felt a flash of vicious pride for fooling him. To play the part of the princess, she was usually clothed in the finest dresses, had her hair perfectly arranged, and had dye applied to her visible skin to make her a shade darker. Now, her dress was dirty and rumpled, her hair unkempt, and the faded dye had been replaced by layers of grime. But still he thought she was Serene Aren Demoi.

Salim reached into his bag and pulled out a piece of salted meat. Clare's stomach instantly cramped, and her mouth watered.

"I thought I'd offer you something more than the hard biscuits you had earlier," Salim said. "Of course, I think it's only fair you repay me with a kiss." His eyes glinted with cruel mirth. "I've always wanted a kiss from a princess."

The men behind him chuckled as they crowded closer.

Clare glared up at Salim. "I'd rather starve."

He snorted. "That's only because you haven't ever known true hunger, Princess."

Clare nearly laughed. The man had no idea how often she'd gone hungry as a child after her parents had died. Her father had been executed for standing with the losing side in the civil war and her mother had died soon after. Clare and Eliot had done everything to keep Thomas and Mark fed, and that often meant there wasn't enough left over for them. Hunger was something she could easily endure.

Salim took a large bite from the dried meat, chewing loudly in front of her.

When her expression didn't alter, his smile grew. "It seems all the rumors about you are true. You're beautiful *and* stubborn. If you change your mind, let me know. One kiss, and this is yours." He lifted the dried meat, then twisted away.

Vera's shoulders stiffened. "If you were paying attention, you would notice the princess is falling ill."

Clare's head snapped toward Vera, surprised by the edge in the usually shy girl's voice.

Salim turned back to face the maid. "What are you talking about?"

Vera didn't cower under his attention. "The princess has a slight fever. Probably from the open wounds left by these infernal ropes. You should untie her and let me treat her wrists, and give her a real meal."

Salim lifted one eyebrow. "Fates, the maid can speak."

Men sniggered.

Vera didn't blink as she stared up at Salim. "If you want her alive by the time we get to wherever we're going, you need to take better care of her."

The leader of the mercenaries looked between them, and Clare couldn't read the expression on his face. It was flat, but not remote. Contemplative, maybe.

She knew what Vera was trying to do—get the ropes removed, in case an opportunity to escape arrived, and get some food so they'd have the strength to run. Perhaps she was even just trying to get Salim to torment her, instead of Clare. Regardless, wariness pierced her as Salim crouched in front of Clare.

He reached for her brow and she cringed back instinctively, but her retreat was stopped by the tree behind her. The back of Salim's hand coasted over her skin, testing her forehead and temple. "Perhaps you are a little warm. How thoughtless of me. We should clean your wounds."

He grabbed the ropes that bound her wrists and hauled her to her feet. Pain flared as the rope grated against her torn skin. Clare sucked in a breath, only partially smothering a cry as she was pulled toward the glowing fire.

Vera let out a scream of protest, but Tariq shot past Clare and seized her before the maid could throw herself after Clare.

Salim brought her so close to the flames that the heat licked her arms and face. Then, still holding her by her bound hands, he jerked her against him.

The feel of their bodies colliding, the heat of his breath fanning her cheek as he ducked toward her—it was all too much. Instinct took over. Clare shifted her weight and kneed him between his legs.

He doubled over with a curse, his hand still wrapped around the rope. The rough fibers dug into her split wrists, but she ignored the sparking agony and brought her knee up again, this time catching his chin. This time, he released her, and as his head snapped back and he staggered, she kicked him between his legs once more.

Salim crashed to the ground, curled into a ball. Clare dove for the knife belted at his side. Her palm grazed the cold hilt, but she didn't get a chance to draw it.

Painful hands grabbed her, hauling her back from Salim. Clare screamed, kicked, and twisted. Her elbow connected with flesh a few times before she was wrestled into submission. Several men ran to kneel by Salim, and Clare could hear the group's shocked muttering.

Adrenaline rushed through her veins, tightening her muscles and heating her skin. Her fatigued body didn't feel weak in this moment, despite being restrained. Her heart pounded and her pulse roared. A hard chest made an unforgiving wall at her back and arms crushed around her, trapping her arms at her sides. Her chest rose and fell quickly, her breaths stuttering and sharp. She wanted to attack all of them—put them through the pain they'd put her through.

She wanted to kill them for stealing Bennick from her.

Salim slowly uncurled from his tensed position on the ground. He thrust away an assisting hand and shoved to his feet. His face was flushed, his eyes dark with fury.

Tension stiffened Clare's spine, but she didn't drop her glare.

"That was very foolish of you, Princess," Salim said, anger threading every word. He limped slightly as he came to stand in front of her. Seeing him struggle to walk flooded her with a perverse joy.

His voice was deathly quiet. "I told you I'm a man of my word. And I told you I would kill your maid if you did anything I didn't like."

Clare's blood turned to ice. She shot a look to Vera.

Tariq stood behind her friend, an arm wrapped around her middle, a blade at her throat.

Terror locked Clare's lungs, stealing her breath. "Don't," she gasped. "Don't do this."

"Giving orders, Princess?"

The title—however false—made Clare stiffen. *Be Serene. Not you.* She pushed back her fear. "You don't need to kill her. Punish me instead. Wouldn't that be more gratifying for you? To strike a princess?"

Salim's eyes narrowed as he studied her face, and she almost let herself believe her words would be enough to tempt him—persuade him. Then he looked over his shoulder at Tariq. "Bring her."

Vera cried out and Clare bucked against the arms that held her. "No!"

Tariq dragged Vera forward, but Salim's eyes were on Clare. "I won't kill her," he said.

The relief hardly penetrated. All Clare could hear were Vera's sobs.

Salim tipped his head closer to Clare. "I won't kill her, but I want to make sure you learn your lesson." He looked to Tariq. "Cut her free."

Tariq's smile was chilling as he quickly complied, sawing through the bloodied rope that bound Vera's hands.

Clare's heart thudded so hard in her chest, it was all she could hear.

Salim moved over to some saddlebags on the ground. He rifled through one briefly before pulling out a clear bottle. He strode back to them, uncorking the bottle as he went. "Seawater," he said, answering the question in Clare's eyes. "Helps clean a wound better than anything else I know." His lip curled, and he jerked his chin at Tariq, who gripped Vera's forearms, exposing her raw and oozing wrists. Vera squirmed against the man at her back, her wide eyes on Salim as he stalked toward her.

Clare sucked in a breath, but nothing could have prepared her for Vera's scream. The piercing sound shattered the night as Salim poured seawater onto her bleeding wrists. His body blocked Clare's view, but Vera's agony burned her soul. Especially as Salim started scrubbing the saltwater into her wounds with a cloth, sharpening Vera's screams.

Clare's entire body shook with rage, guilt, and the force of her tears.

The torture lasted an eternity. Vera's cries were never-ending, and each one stabbed Clare like a blade. Her ears rang, and every part of her ached when Salim finally stepped back.

Vera sagged in Tariq's arms, pale and trembling, tears soaking her face. Seawater and blood dripped down from her freshly abused wrists. Tariq's cheek rested against Vera's, his chin on her shoulder. There was a sickening look of pleasure on his face as he cradled her, but Vera was so exhausted that she did nothing but groan when he scooped her into his arms and carried her back to the tree. As he laid her on the ground and brushed a strand of blonde hair off her face, Salim stepped in front of Clare.

"I think your maid was right," he said, holding up the bottle of saltwater and bloodstained rag. "We better tend your wounds, Princess."

Her gut dropped as the ropes were cut from her wrists. Panic and fear clawed at her throat, but she refused to beg.

That resolve didn't stop her from screaming when the saltwater burned into her open wounds.

CHAPTER 13

BENNICK

BENNICK GRITTED HIS TEETH, SWEAT BEADING on his forehead as he slowly forced his body to shift on the bed. His fists dug into the mattress and the pillows behind him bunched as he pushed back, struggling to sit. His lower left side flared with pain, but he didn't stop moving until his shoulders were braced against the wooden headboard. He wasn't sitting fully, but it was a start.

He hated how weak his body was. His limbs trembled from the simple exertion, his chest rising and falling too quickly.

Nearly a week he'd been in this bed. He needed to get out of it.

Bennick flinched at a stab of pain in his side. His shaking hand coasted over the thick bandages that encircled his middle. He'd glimpsed his seared flesh when the physician—a Mortisian man named Jibar—had changed his bandages last. The burn was ugly and uneven, angry red and horribly blistered. He didn't want to see it again, or the matching one on his back. They were ugly, and they made any position agony.

The physician called him fates-blessed, and Bennick knew that was true. He should be dead after such an injury. It was easily the most pain he'd ever felt, but it wasn't what caused him the most torture.

The first few days of his recovery, he'd been locked in a feverish sleep, mostly oblivious to the world around him. Now he was perfectly aware of the passage of time. It was even worse when Jibar made him drink the medicines that forced him to sleep, though. There, only nightmares waited. Images that would haunt him forever. Clare, alone. Hurt. Bleeding. Crying out for him.

Dying.

When he finally woke, it was to find more time gone. The realization made his gut churn.

Clare was slipping away from him. *That* was the thing killing him.

Serene and the others had left with Serai Nadir four days ago, which meant time was running out for Clare. If the mercenaries received word that Serene was alive and well in Duvan, they would realize Clare was a decoy. They would kill her.

If they hadn't already.

The thought was a knife in his heart.

There had been no news from Wilf or Venn. The Rose was with them—something Bennick didn't know how to feel about.

Zilas. His half-brother.

Zilas was the commander's illegitimate son. Clare, Venn, and Bennick's father were among the only ones to know that truth.

Bennick had only learned it recently, while interrogating the Rose. It had been a shock, but it explained so much. Why the assassin's stalking and attacks had become so personal—especially after Zilas had discovered Bennick's feelings for Clare.

And yet, the older brother who hated him might be the one person who could help save Clare now. Though, if he helped them, he would be given his freedom.

He'd be free to come after Clare and Serene again.

The door pushed open, and Jibar halted as he took in Bennick's half-seated position. "Are you *trying* to kill yourself?" he asked, his Devendran heavily accented.

The Mortisian physician was in his forties, Bennick guessed. He had a short dark beard and hair that reached his shoulders. He had a wife and five children, and lived near the Nadir estate. He was a personal friend to Serai Nadir, and he seemed to have un-relenting stamina. Jibar also talked a lot, which was how Bennick knew so much about him.

"I need to get out of this bed," Bennick said, a low growl vi-brating in his chest.

"If you push yourself prematurely, you'll be exchanging this bed for eternal rest."

Bennick scowled at the physician. "I can't just lie here."

"That's exactly what you'll do, if you want to live." The man nudged the door closed and took a seat in the wooden chair beside the bed. He met Bennick's gaze without blinking. "You were run through, Captain. That's not something a body simply shrugs off. You need to let yourself heal."

"How long?"

"If I had my way, you'd be here for four to six weeks." He lifted a hand, forestalling Bennick's protest. "I know there's no chance of you following that advice; I've mended many a soldier, so I know what a stubborn lot you are. But I will insist on two weeks."

Bennick shook his head. "I can't do that. I need to leave now."

Jibar leaned back, quirking a bushy eyebrow. "If it didn't go against my principles as a healer, I'd like to see you try and make it down those stairs and mount a horse."

Frustration clawed his throat and sharpened his gaze.

"I know," Jibar said. "You feel useless because everyone else left for Duvan and the woman you love was abducted."

Bennick blinked, his heart thudding hard. "I never said—"

"Boy, you didn't have to. It's obvious you love that Clare." He snorted. "I've never even met the girl, but I know you're desperately in love with her."

Bennick stared. He and Clare had been keeping the secret for so long, it didn't seem real that a stranger had picked it out so effortlessly.

Jibar rolled his eyes. "And now you're worried your secret is revealed. I suppose having a bodyguard in love with the princess's maid wouldn't exactly be encouraged."

He didn't know the half of it. Bennick's eyes narrowed. "I don't—"

"Don't insult me with a lie. Now, this Clare—you want to see her again?"

He ground his teeth. "Of course."

"Then you need to listen to me and stay in this bed."

Bennick's hands fisted on the quilt. "I'm stronger every day. I can feel it."

"I'm not denying that, but your body isn't ready. If you push yourself now, you'll only succeed in killing yourself."

Bennick looked away, a muscle in his jaw throbbing.

Not knowing where Clare was right now, not being with her

when she needed him most . . . it was agony.

He never should have let her come to Mortise. He should have insisted that she return to Iden. He'd relived that last morning they'd spent together, on a balcony in the same house he was trapped in now. They had watched the sunrise, and he'd told her she could go home. He would make that happen, if she chose. But she'd wanted to stay with him, and he'd been selfish enough that he hadn't pressured her to take the safer path. He had thought he could protect her from anything.

He'd been wrong. And now the woman he loved was in the hands of ruthless men.

If they hurt her, he would tear them apart with his bare hands.

Jibar silently watched him, waiting.

"You're right," he said, his voice thick and heavy. "I do love her. It's not something I've said out loud to anyone but her, but I love her more than anything in this fates-blasted world. And I can't just lay here, completely and utterly useless, while she's out there. I *have* to go after her. Please. My fever is gone, and I can manage the pain."

Jibar stared at him, his expression unreadable. When he did speak, his voice was low. "You're very persistent."

Bennick's brow furrowed. "Does that mean you're considering it?"

The man studied him a little longer before he sighed. "One week. That's all I'm willing to compromise, and you must promise to do everything I say. No sitting up without me, and certainly no walking around yet." He nodded toward the powder on the bedside table. "And I want you to take that, which I know you've been avoiding."

Bennick's forehead creased. "I'll do everything you say if you let me walk out of here in a week."

"Very well. But if you can't walk out of here on your own, then you'll remain in this bed for two more weeks."

Bennick nodded, easily agreeing to the man's terms because he *would* walk out of here in a week—no matter what.

If getting on a horse took all of his strength, he could always tie himself to the saddle.

Hold on, Clare. I'm coming.

CHAPTER 14

WILF

VENN CROUCHED, HIS DARK FINGERS RUNNING over the length of frayed rope in his hands. It was stained with dried blood. He'd found two lengths of rope deserted by the burnt-out fire.

"Their bonds were cut," Venn said. "I'm not sure why. There's no evidence that another group joined them."

Wilf knelt beside the younger man, studying the rope he held. "That's a lot of blood."

Venn nodded, his hard eyes on the ground. His fingertips brushed over some dark specks in the dirt. "More blood," he murmured. "They're hurt. I don't know how badly—it could have been from the ropes alone." His knuckles whitened as he clutched the rope. "Their wrists must be raw to have soaked the rope so thoroughly."

Wilf shoved to his feet, his gaze cutting over the deserted camp-site once more. "But there's no sign of bodies or graves."

"No. They're still alive." Venn uncoiled from the ground, still clutching the rope—like it was a lifeline. "The fire is at least two days old. We're still too far behind."

"You could always take my advice," the Rose called out. He stood on the other side of the clearing, chains still shackling his hands before him, two guards on either side of him at all times.

Wilf scowled. "Shut up."

The Rose rolled his eyes, looking far too relaxed in his chains. "If you refuse to listen to me, then why am I here?"

Wilf's hands fisted at his sides. "We're following the trail you helped point out."

"If you want to catch up to Salim, you need to stop following the clues he leaves behind and head him off."

"We're not leaving the forest for Krid." That might be Salim's final destination, but what if the Rose was wrong? Wilf didn't want to risk everything on a guess. Besides, reinforcements had been sent to Krid—they might reach the city before Salim, and they would keep an eye out.

The Rose shrugged. "Fine, forget Krid for now. But Salim's trail is leading north. He's going to pass by Sedah. It's a small town he favors along this route. If we ride hard, we could possibly reach the village while he's still there."

Wilf glanced at Venn and jerked his chin toward the nearby treeline. The younger man crossed to him without question. They stepped over a small creek, finally far enough away from the Rose that Wilf dared speak. "What do you think?"

Venn clenched his jaw, his long dark ponytail caught in the

light wind that swept through the trees. "He's right. If we keep stopping to follow the trail, we're always going to be behind them." His eyebrows drew in tight. "I don't want to find their bodies, Wilf. I need to find them alive."

"Ignoring the trail feels like we're abandoning them."

"We could always split up. Some of us could stay with the trail while the others go to Sedah."

He considered it. "You said there's evidence of six or eight mercenaries traveling with them, and there are eight of us. I hate to separate and lose that advantage. And what if he's lying about this village?"

"He picked out the right trail." Venn fisted the rope. "These ropes, the smaller footprints we found—we know we're on the right path. If the Rose is right again, we can move quickly enough to maybe intercept them at Sedah. That's a risk worth taking."

Wilf weighed the options. "It's still a gamble. I don't trust him enough to risk losing the trail. We'll send two men to Sedah, and we'll keep following the trail." They'd wasted enough time when they'd had to double back to Serai Nadir's estate to get the Rose; he couldn't afford to lose another precious hour, let alone a couple of days.

Clare and Vera needed them *now*.

"Send the fastest men we have," Venn said, his jaw hard. "If Clare and Vera are in Sedah, one of the men needs to shadow them while the other comes back to us. Engaging Salim and his men will only get them killed; we're all needed for the attack."

"Agreed."

Venn nodded, and the decision was made.

CHAPTER 15

MIA

IT HAD BEEN THREE DAYS SINCE PETER'S VISIT, and Mia had yet to see him again or any other Kaelins. Perhaps she and Tyrell had worried over nothing, and Peter hadn't told anyone about her.

Devon said she was healing well, though she tired easily and any quick movements were painful. Tyrell had brought in several dresses for her, as well as paints and canvases, along with her sketchbook and pencils. She spent much of her days with her art, working in the sunlight that poured through the window. With fresh air brushing her skin, and the scents from outside filling her lungs, it was an exquisite experience. She had asked Tyrell about the clean, sharp smell, and he'd told her it was pine. It made her think of Grayson, and the pinecone he'd brought her so long ago. She painted that from memory, as well as landscapes of mountains covered in pines—like those she saw through her window. She wondered idly if she'd ever see one up close.

Tyrell left only when he had to. When he was with her, he would watch her paint or sketch, or he would work on reports at his desk. Sometimes they would play card games, or talk about nothing in particular, and other times he asked her to read to him.

The days were falling into a comfortable routine. Every night when she went to bed, Mia felt a stab of fear that this might be the last night she would fall asleep seeing the stars. The last time she'd see the glow of the moon. But the days passed, and no one ordered her back into her cell.

Finally, while she and Tyrell played a new game called Stratagem, she asked, "When do I have to go back?"

He didn't look up as he studied the beautifully carved pieces of wood that dotted the brown and black checkered board. "Back where?"

"You know where."

Eyes focused on the board, his forehead creased. "You don't have to go back."

She blinked. "I don't?"

"No."

"But . . ."

He finally glanced up. "I made a deal with my father. As long as I keep my side of the bargain, you don't have to go back to that cell."

Her stomach twisted unpleasantly. "What did you promise him?"

"It doesn't matter." Tyrell moved one of his soldiers to a new space on the board.

"Please tell me what's going on. I don't want to be kept in the dark."

He leaned back in his chair. "I didn't mean to keep anything from you. It's just not important."

"It's my life, Tyrell. I deserve to know."

He thought about that, then dipped his head. "I asked him to let you stay here, and in return I promised that no harm would come to you. That you wouldn't try to escape, and that I would take over Grayson's duties and be at my father's disposal for any mission he requires." He shrugged one shoulder. "As he is my king, I must always be at his disposal, so it's really nothing."

That seemed far too easy. Mia folded her arms across her chest. "What if I *do* try to escape?"

He lifted an eyebrow. "Would you?"

She didn't have an immediate response. Even if she could get out of the castle, past the soldiers in the yard, through the gate and into Lenzen . . . what then? She had no coin. No experience with the world. Nowhere to go.

Mortise.

She could go to Duvan. To Grayson.

She doubted she could make the journey on her own. She hadn't stepped foot outside in nearly a decade. The mere thought made her chest tighten—the familiar press of a building panic.

Tyrell's voice quieted. "If you were to try, I would be forced to bring you back. And it would not be just you that my father punished. I've tied our fates together."

Mia's eyes dropped to the board. She moved a piece without thought, her voice a low murmur as she said, "I'm still a prisoner, then."

"Aren't we all?" he muttered. He moved a general, taking one of her soldiers. He tossed the piece into the tray beside them.

She winced at the clatter. "You should be careful with them. A replacement for a piece that exquisitely carved would be expensive."

"You do remember I'm a prince, right?"

She snorted. "You seem to remind me often enough."

The corner of his mouth twitched. He tapped a finger against his king—the most powerful piece on the board. "As it happens, a replacement wouldn't be too difficult. It's the time, more than anything."

It took a moment for his words to process. "You made these?"

"Years ago. The first set I made was awful. It was probably for the best when my mother burned it."

"She burned it?"

He jutted his chin toward the board. "It's your turn."

She made a clumsy move, and he snared another soldier. She couldn't care less about the game. "How old were you when you made your first set?"

"Eight, I think. I'd seen some of the soldiers play in the barracks and I wanted to learn. I didn't want to risk purchasing a board, however—my mother watched us all very closely as children, and I knew she would disapprove."

He eyed her, prompting her to move a piece. He instantly retaliated.

She fingered her black queen, contemplating her next move as Tyrell continued his story. "I'd been playing the game against myself for weeks, but I got careless. She walked in and grew livid. Called it a waste of my time. She threw it all in the fire. Well, except for one piece."

He nodded to the queen Mia touched. "That was in my hand.

I swear, my fist carried the indentation for days after I finally let it go. It took a year or two before I was ready to try carving a new set. I needed a distraction after a . . . particularly difficult mission. I embellished the old queen, and made a whole new set."

Mia lifted the queen, rolling the smooth piece over her palm. "It's beautiful. You're very talented."

He scoffed. "It's not a useful skill."

"It's art."

"No, what you do . . . *that's* art."

"So is this. Have you made anything else?"

"Little things. I burned most of them."

That broke her heart. "You shouldn't destroy the things you create."

"Better by my hand than wait for my mother to do it." He smiled faintly. "Are you going to take your turn?"

She lowered the queen to the board. "I'm quite certain winning is impossible at this point."

"Not entirely. You have your queen still, and she's well-guarded."

Mia frowned. "I still don't understand why the game ends if the queen dies. The king is the most powerful player on the board— you said that yourself."

"The king has more moves and tactical advantages," Tyrell allowed, looking directly at her. "But if the queen dies, the king forfeits the game. There's no purpose without her. That's why she's the most powerful."

Her heart thumped louder in her chest. "He shouldn't give up if he loses her. I don't think she would want him to."

"He didn't make the rules. It's just the way it is." Tyrell tilted his head to the side, his dark eyes fixed on her. "Your move, Mia."

She was saved from having to respond when Devon walked in. She had never been so eager to see the physician, and she was quick to escape Tyrell's weighted gaze.

"That's a well-done sketch," Devon said.

Mia stepped from behind the dressing screen, one hand rubbing over her freshly bandaged middle.

The physician held the drawing she'd made of the black queen from Tyrell's Stratagem set. The black king was slightly behind the queen, it's design a little neater, more intricate. Mia had studied the queen closely in order to sketch her, and the piece was a little plainer than the others, despite a younger Tyrell's efforts to add detail. She had found a few mistakes in the carving, and she loved it all the more for the imperfections. She had taken care to represent them in her drawing.

The carved piece was an echo of Tyrell, and she had come to learn that the Rydenic prince was, in a word, complicated.

"Such simple objects, but there are so many emotions. The shadow work is impressive." Devon shot her a smile as he lowered the paper back to Tyrell's desk, where other loose sketches sat. "You're very talented, Mia."

Heat bloomed in her cheeks. "Thank you. And thank you for taking such excellent care of me."

"It's no trouble." The middle-aged physician had always been exceedingly kind to her over the years. He was one of the few people she felt comfortable with. He scooped up an unused bandage from the bed and spooled it around his hand. "You'll let me know if the pain becomes worse?"

She nodded.

There was a light knock on the door, and Fletcher poked his gray head in. The man was tall and thin, and several years older than Devon. He had been Mia's primary guard from the start of her imprisonment. He didn't speak often, and he never said much, but his small kindnesses over the years had not gone unnoticed. He had been a familiar face when all she had was cruelty at the hands of Mama and Papa. Fletcher had been there when her panics came, and he'd been the one to fetch Devon that first, terrifying time. He had allowed Grayson into her life—not just once, but repeatedly. And he had been especially attentive since Grayson had left.

Fletcher's cautious expression as he scanned the room made Mia smile. "It's all right, we're done. You can come in."

The older man's cheeks reddened a little, but he stepped into the room. "How are you?" he asked.

"Healing." She nodded to Devon. "He's very good."

"Our Mia is a fighter," the physician said.

Warmth spread through her chest at the compliment. So often in her life, she hadn't felt like a fighter. She was the girl in the cell. Quiet. Broken. Forgotten. But Grayson had changed all of that. He saw her. He taught her to fight. Taught her to live. The fact that Devon and Fletcher also cared for her meant she truly wasn't alone.

Devon closed his bag and shouldered it. "Send for me if there's any need, but I think as long as you avoid anything strenuous for the time being, it would be good for you to walk around a little more. Take in some fresh air."

"I will, thank you." Even now, the windows were open. She

intended to enjoy every bit of summer air she could, because it still seemed impossible that she wouldn't have to return to her windowless cell.

Devon left, and Fletcher faced her. "Prince Tyrell mentioned you'll be staying here."

"You're not leaving?" The words bolted from her in a rush, dread twisting her gut.

"No." Fletcher's eyebrows pulled together. "Unless you would feel more comfortable with another guard."

"Not at all." She set her hands on the back of a cushioned chair, her heart still racing. "Fates, I thought you might have to go back to the prison."

"Tyrell has said I can continue to guard you. Along with his men, of course."

Mia had only glimpsed the soldiers who stood guard in the hall. While she had regained her mobility, she still had not dared ask if she could wander out of Tyrell's suite of rooms. "I want you to be my guard," she assured Fletcher.

The corner of his mouth twitched, though his boots shuffled as if uncomfortable. "Very well. Now, for what I came to say. Since you'll be staying up here in the castle, Tyrell mentioned you'll need a personal maid."

Mia's eyes widened. Since coming upstairs, she'd been tended by several different servants as needed. But now that she was healing, she didn't think she would need the extra care.

"Tyrell said you can pick anyone," Fletcher continued. "I thought I might suggest my wife. She currently works in the castle laundry, but she's been a maid to visiting nobles and has the necessary skills."

"Of course," Mia said. "I would love that."

His shoulders relaxed a little. "Truly?"

"Yes. I can't wait to meet her."

"I'll bring her by later this evening." The man glanced at the partially open door to the sitting room, his voice lowering carefully. "I also wanted to make sure you're . . . safe here."

Mia felt her face soften. "I'm safe with Tyrell," she assured him. As for the rest of his family . . . that remained to be seen.

CHAPTER 16

DESFAN

DESFAN SANK INTO THE CHAIR BESIDE HIS father's bedside, ignoring the quiet shuffling of the physician and attendants as they filed from the room. He heard the door click as Karim tugged it closed, and Desfan allowed his shoulders to slump. He was alone with his father, no one to witness his weariness after a long day of meetings.

"I'm sorry I haven't been around to visit," he whispered.

His father, of course, did not respond.

Serjan Saernon Jaron Cassian had collapsed nearly a year ago, and had not regained full consciousness since. His skin was pale, his cheeks hollow. Below his closed lids, his eyes occasionally rolled, bespeaking a restlessness that his otherwise prone body contradicted. While his body had at times twitched or seized, even that had stopped recently. His lungs filled and emptied in shallow breaths. He managed to swallow a little water and broth with aid, but his skin sagged over his bones. His frailness was accentuated by the large bed. He looked so small tucked under the covers. So fragile.

He had once been the biggest, strongest man in Desfan's life. A man capable of fixing any problem.

Fates, he could use that man now.

"I've mostly rebuilt the council," he said quietly, watching his father's unresponsive face. "And for better or worse, I reinstated Yahri. I'm not sure if that makes me a fool. Time will tell, I suppose." He scrubbed a hand over his forehead. "I'm not sure what's going to happen when Princess Serene arrives. She'll learn the Rose was hired by men and women on the council, and I really wouldn't blame her if she left."

And what a problem that would cause. The fragile truce between Mortise and Devendra would shatter. War would come. Would Desfan ally with Ryden, then? He may not have a choice, if King Henri offered. Mortise was strong, but he wasn't foolish enough to think they could stand against Devendra and Zennor if it came to war.

Desfan sighed. "The marriage alliance was a wise choice." The only choice, really. His father had been a good ruler, even if he had not always been the best father.

Guilt sliced through him at the thought, making him cringe. His relationship with his father had deteriorated after losing his mother and sisters. His father had lost himself in work and drink, and Desfan had buried himself as well. In trouble, mostly. Any conversation between him and his father had become curt. Argumentative.

At fifteen, Desfan had been thrown onto a patrol ship because his father hadn't known what else to do with him. That had been a rough time, but eventually Desfan had found a freedom he'd never thought possible. He and his father hadn't exactly made amends, but some forgiveness had been exchanged. There were a couple of letters he'd received from his father over the years that he still had today, folded up in his desk.

Words were so much easier to put on paper than they were to speak in person.

When his father had first invited him home, Desfan had declined. He'd chosen to finish his year at sea. But he remembered everything about his eventual homecoming—however short-lived it had been.

His heart had pounded against his ribs as the *Phoenix* had docked. He and Karim had made their way to the palace, and so many words burned inside him, things he needed to say to his father.

I'm sorry for everything I did to hurt you.

He'd never said that, though.

Walking the halls of the palace, his steps had lagged. Everything was strangely cold. Empty. He'd felt a little like a ghost, drifting through the halls. Panic pulsed through him, and suddenly—in this place that used to be home—he couldn't breathe.

People had stared at him with apprehension, concern, or wariness. No sign of welcome. He had changed after a year at sea, but everything here felt exactly the same. The people still viewed him as the rebellious, self-destructive boy he'd been a year ago.

When he entered the throne room, a hundred eyes were on him. His father had stood to greet him, but it was painfully formal. Stilted and awkward. Sentiments that had been expressed in letters over the course of the last year were glaringly absent. There was no embrace. No tear-filled eyes. No, *I'm sorry I sent you away.*

When his father asked if he'd enjoyed his time at sea, Desfan had spoken without thought. "Yes, and I'm going back. I'm only here for a brief visit."

His father's eyes had rounded, and he remembered Serai Yahri's intake of breath as she and the rest of the court played witness to this strained moment between father and son.

The serjan's throat had flexed. "Very well," he finally said. "If that is what you wish."

Desfan was aware of Karim's confusion, but he ignored his friend as he nodded. "Yes, that's exactly what I want."

The lie had burned his tongue, but what he wanted was irrelevant in the face of his reality. His mother was dead, along with his sisters. His father—though standing before him—was not the man he'd known for the first eleven years of his life.

Sitting at his father's bedside now, Desfan pinched his eyes closed, shoulders heavy with a deep sense of loss. His father's illness was not death, but it was a near-complete abandonment all the same. So much left unspoken between them—resolution he may never get.

"I wonder what would have happened if I'd stayed," he whispered. "Perhaps you and I would have regained a relationship."

He would have learned how to rule, so he wouldn't have to fumble things now. He would have gained allies in the court, rather than be an outsider. He would have helped his father, so his health would not have declined so drastically. He would have been there when Gamble had come and shocked Saernon Cassian with the rumor that one of his daughters might be alive.

Desfan's hands fisted on his knees. "I'm sorry," he whispered, his voice low but thick. "I know I've failed you, but I *will* find the truth. If Tahlyah or Meerah live, I will find out. I'll find her." He swallowed hard, then reached out and placed a hand against his father's. Lying atop the blankets, his hand was cold. Desfan squeezed gently. "I swear it," he vowed.

Beneath his hand, his father's fingers twitched.

Desfan froze.

He'd imagined it, surely. The serjan hadn't moved except during his seizures for nearly a year now.

Pulse hammering, Desfan leaned in, his fingers tightening their hold. "Father?"

A pause. Then one of the serjan's finger's jumped against Desfan's hand again.

His gaze raked over the man's sunken face. There was no change in his expression. Nothing, but—

Another twitch of a finger.

Desfan shoved to his feet, still clutching his father's hand as he called out for the physician.

The door swung open, and it wasn't a surprise to see Karim stalk inside first. "What is it?" his bodyguard demanded, his hand on the hilt of his sword, his eyes slicing over the room.

"My father—his hand—it moved." Desfan shot a look to the physician who was just sweeping into the room. "I squeezed his hand, and I felt his fingers move."

The physician frowned. "Perhaps you were mistaken—"

"It happened three times," Desfan snapped.

The physician leaned over the serjan, his frown deepening. "It's possible it was a muscle spasm, or a prelude to a seizure."

"I know what I felt. He was responding." Whether to his touch or his voice, Desfan wasn't sure. But his father *had* been aware of him. Relief and joy washed through him, and he couldn't stop his smile. "He's improving."

The physician pursed his lips, still scanning the serjan's body. "Intentional movement would indeed be an improvement. But I caution you to—" His words choked off, his eyes flying wide.

Desfan grinned, tears stinging his eyes as his father's fingers curled ever so slightly around his.

"Fates," the physician breathed, clearly stunned.

Desfan gripped his father's hand. "Father? Can you hear me?"

There was no response. No change on the serjan's face.

But there was still life in his father, which meant there was still hope.

Desfan strode briskly down the hall, Karim beside him. A few other guards trailed behind, hurrying to match Desfan's pace. He was going to be late for the council meeting. His morning had been spent wading through countless letters. Nobles from the far reaches of Mortise had been writing to him constantly. They didn't have much to say, they just wanted him to see their names.

They wanted to be chosen for the final council seat.

The person he'd asked, of course, had not responded. Desfan was beginning to think he might need to consider someone else, though he didn't relish that task. It would require too much focus, and all of his thoughts remained with his father.

It had only been yesterday that Saernon Cassian's fingers had moved, but the physician had already logged several positive changes in the serjan. His fingers had twitched several more times, and the right side of his mouth had even turned down in a partial grimace.

Desfan had asked the physician to keep all of these changes private. Irrationally, he worried that if anyone else found out, the improvement might end.

They were nearing the council chamber when Ser Amil Havim stepped out of an intersecting hallway.

The young man's eyes widened slightly, but he bowed at once. "Serjah."

"Ser Havim. It's good to see you." Desfan spoke with sincerity. Amil had been sequestered in his room at the palace for weeks. He and his father, Bahri Havim, had been sent to Devendra as emissaries to help broker peace. They had helped negotiate the betrothal agreement between Desfan and Serene, which would be signed into legality at summer's end, after Serene arrived in Duvan. But Bahri had been killed in an unfortunate attack in Devendra, and Amil blamed King Newlan, even though the story Desfan had gathered proved the Devendran king was not at fault.

Amil had wanted war with Devendra. Desfan had said no.

They hadn't really spoken since.

Amil gripped his hands together, and Desfan saw the flash of a gold ring. It was large, and engraved with the symbol of the Havim family—a lion. Desfan assumed it had belonged to Amil's father. It's presence on his hand was a harsh reminder of Bahri's death, spoken without words.

"Have you had any word from Princess Serene?" Amil asked.

"Not recently," Desfan admitted. "She should arrive in Duvan in a few more weeks, though."

The nobleman's expression was difficult to read. "I'm sure you'll be relieved to have her here. Her journey has proven perilous."

"Indeed." Desfan took a step closer. "Amil, I wondered if you would like to hold a memorial for your father? His pyre was conducted in Devendra, but we could honor him with a ceremony here."

"No. Thank you." Amil's throat worked on a tense swallow. "I would like to request keeping the Havim rooms a little longer. I'm afraid my father had many things, and it's taking me longer than expected to go through them and pack."

"You don't have to leave. Your father's sacrifice will long be remembered."

Amil's jaw tightened fractionally. "He was a great man." He shifted back a step and bowed at the waist. "Good day, Serjah." He stepped away, his footsteps echoing off the stone walls of the corridor.

"He seems to be doing better," Karim murmured.

"Then why are you frowning?"

Karim lifted a single shoulder, his frown still in place as he watched Amil disappear.

Before Desfan could press, footsteps sounded from the opposite direction, and two people strode into view.

Prince Liam Kaelin was always smiling, his expression relaxed and open. His features were warm; his skin bronzed by the sun, his hair light-brown, his brown eyes bright.

Prince Grayson Kaelin, however, was his opposite. His mouth was usually set in a straight line, though the corners tended to tilt down. His dark hair was almost black, like the clothing he chose to wear and the gloves that encased his hands. His uncommon gray eyes were sharp, seeming to miss nothing. *Guarded* was the word that came to mind. *Lethal* was another.

Liam's smile widened. "Serjah Desfan, I'm so glad we caught you."

"Do you need something?" Desfan asked, not impolitely, even

though he knew he needed to hurry. The council had many new members, and he didn't want to make a bad impression with tardiness.

Liam gestured to Grayson. "We were just commenting on how intriguing we find the Mortisian political structure. Your council is quite unique in Eyrinthia. Would it be possible for us to join you in this meeting?"

Desfan glanced between them, perfectly aware of Karim's tension. "They can be quite boring," he warned.

"We don't mind," Liam said. "We'll sit among the other spectators. This is an open meeting, yes?"

Sometimes the council met in private, and other times they allowed an audience. Desfan just hadn't expected a Rydenic presence.

So much for good impressions with the new council.

He forced a smile. "Of course. Please join us."

Karim's displeasure was obvious, and Desfan avoided the looks he knew his friend was shooting at him.

They arrived at the council chamber, and the guards swept open the wide double doors. Desfan marched in—and promptly stalled.

A young woman stood in the center of the room, chatting with Ser Anoush. She turned at their entrance and Desfan heard Karim's sharp intake of breath.

Serai Razan Krayt was beautiful. Her long dark hair trailed down her back, just like it had five years ago. Her bearing was graceful, her form tall and lithe. She smiled a little at Desfan, dropping into a curtsy. "Serjah. I hope you don't mind, but I thought I would answer your request in person." She smoothed down her bright purple sari and lifted her chin. "I would be honored to fill the final seat on the council."

Beside him, Karim stared, his shock palpable.

Desfan should have warned his friend, but he hadn't thought Razan would arrive without writing first. He'd assumed he would have plenty of time to prepare Karim—if she accepted the position at all.

Five years ago, Razan had proven a friend to Desfan, and he needed those. Unfortunately, she had also broken Karim's heart, and now—for the first time since then—they stood face-to-face.

Karim tensed beside Desfan, and anger spiked in his gaze as he muttered a curse. "I'm going to kill you, Des."

Fates, this morning was not going well.

CHAPTER 17

GRAYSON

GRAYSON AND LIAM SAT IN THE BACK OF THE council chambers. Desfan's throne was at the front of the room, as well as the assigned seats for the council. The rest of the vast space was filled with rows of tiered benches that encircled the back and sides of the room, allowing enough seating for hundreds to witness the open meetings. It was a strange thing to see, since an audience hall like this didn't exist in Ryden. King Henri did not rule with input from his subjects.

Most of the front seats were taken by nobles, businessmen, and even some slightly worn looking peasants. Liam had picked a more shadowed spot at the back of the room, and no one sat around them. Guards stood near the three exits, and Grayson kept track of each

138

closed door. Just in case.

Liam tapped Grayson's leg, his fingers twisting in the subtle spy sign language as the Mortisian council discussed matters in the city. *Are you watching the dynamics between Karim, Desfan, and Serai Krayt?*

It was difficult not to. Karim's jaw was hard as rock, and his intense gaze bored a hole in the wall across from him.

Desfan kept shooting his bodyguard worried looks.

Serai Razan Krayt—the newest member on the council—sat primly in her seat, speaking fluidly and confidently when it was her turn. But she kept casting glances at Karim, who did not look in her direction once.

There's a history there, Liam signed, his fingers jumping, curling, tapping to form the silent words. *It clearly involved a romantic relationship gone wrong. I have to admit, I'm curious.*

Grayson was uncomfortable. He didn't want to be here, though Liam had insisted they join the first meeting of the new council; he wanted to observe the council members, get to know them.

Grayson's attention kept trailing back to Sifa.

Mia's uncle had glared at them when they first entered the room, and he had watched them take their seats. He was not the only councilman to have stared at them, but he was pointedly ignoring them now.

I was half convinced Karim was made of stone, Liam continued with a practiced flick of his fingers. *But he may have a weakness.*

Grayson's spine stiffened. *You sound like Father,* he signed, keeping his hand low so no one would see. Not that anyone here would understand the silent language; it was a heavily guarded secret that only spies in Ryden used. And, according to Liam, many of the signs the brothers currently used had been invented by Liam so no other Rydenic spy would be able to understand them, even if they knew the sign language.

His brother's paranoia was intense, but understandable. They had been raised not to trust anyone.

Forgive the vocabulary of my youth, Liam signed to Grayson. *I simply meant, we may have found what makes Karim human. I thought he only cared for Desfan.*

Do you see Karim right now? I don't think he cares for Serai Krayt. It took Grayson's gloved fingers a moment to spell out the newest councilwoman's name. The spy language was still new enough that he was clumsy at times.

Liam was patient, reading each careful sign. His mouth twitched. *He's clearly angry with her, but there are subtleties.* He tipped his head toward Karim, his fingers flying. *See how he's standing? Feet aimed straight ahead. But look at the slight tilt to his head. He's angled toward her, if only slightly. He can see her in the corner of his eye. His ear is toward her. And his fists—he keeps clenching and unclenching them. If he felt pure rage, they would not unclench. He's conflicted. And see the lines on his forehead? The way his eyebrows pull together and down? The way his eyes dart occasionally? He's sorting through memories. He's remembering how much she hurt him—how much she meant to him.*

Fates, his brother was terrifying sometimes. *Is there anything you don't notice?*

Not much. Just like I've noticed you can't look away from Sifa. That man's hatred of Ryden is almost impressive. Every time his eyes start to move this way, he scowls and looks pointedly away.

Can you blame him? Considering everything Sifa had lost to Ryden—even though King Henri had never been outright blamed—Grayson could understand why the man loathed him and Liam. They were the embodiment of the evil kingdom that had slaughtered his brother's family.

How much more would Sifa hate them if he knew the truth? That Mia, his niece, had been a prisoner all these years?

Liam eyed him. *What's wrong? You just tensed.*

Grayson rolled his stiff shoulders. *I don't see the resemblance,* he finally signed. *Mia is nothing like him.*

Thank the fates we can be different from our relatives, his brother signed back.

I know, but part of me feels like I should talk to him.

Why?

Grayson shrugged. *He's Mia's uncle. When this is over . . . Mia may want to stay with him.*

Liam frowned. *I didn't think of that.*

Grayson snorted. *I can't stop thinking about it.*

Liam leaned in, his whisper lost amid the other whispers of the spectators and Desfan's projected voice as he addressed the council. "She'll want to stay with you, Grayson. Don't doubt that."

The words loosened a knot that had been lodged in his chest for days. *Thank you,* he signed.

Liam merely smiled.

The hair on the back of Grayson's neck lifted, and his eyes cut over the crowd.

Seated about halfway up the left side of the room, Arav and the other young nobles from the library whispered and shot smirks at Grayson and Liam.

"More friends of yours?" Liam asked under his breath. "Between the Sifas and the serjah, I don't know how you keep up."

Grayson's brow furrowed as he twisted back to Liam. "Desfan isn't my friend," he whispered.

"With a little effort, he could be." Liam's fingers took up the rest of his reply. *It could put us in a powerful position. You should seek him out. Ask him to spar with you.*

Grayson was saved from answering when Arav's father, Ser Anoush, spoke so loudly his voice boomed around the spacious room. "I think I speak for us all when I say we're relieved the olcain problem in Duvan has diminished greatly with the imprisonment of Omar Jamal. Are any investigations into the origin of the olcain being conducted?"

Desfan straightened on his throne. "We have the name of the man suspected of selling the olcain to Jamal, and I am coordinating an investigation with King Zaire."

"It was a Zennorian issue, then?" Ser Anoush asked.

"A Zennorian man sold the olcain to Jamal, yes."

"Is it possible this was a strategically planned attack by Zennor?" Anoush pressed.

"Interesting," Liam murmured.

Grayson shot his brother a look, even as Desfan spoke. "We have no evidence to suggest anything of the kind."

"But it's possible?"

"It's highly unlikely," Desfan said. "We have good trade relations with Zennor."

"But they are allies with Devendra."

"And Devendra will become our ally," Desfan countered. "Zennor has nothing to gain by sabotaging us."

Anoush tipped his head, but his lips were tight.

Grayson's fingers flashed. *What makes Anoush's bias against Zennor so interesting?*

Liam glanced at him. *I want to make note of any prejudices on the council. I think Anoush is the only one who has a distaste for Zennor. Probably because trade with Zennor has made most of these men and women wealthy, and no one wants to disrupt that.*

"Are there any other questions from the council?" Serai Yahri asked.

Grayson was grateful to see the old Mortisian woman looking well. The last he'd seen her had been in the library, when Jamal had tried to kill her. Grayson and Liam had joined Desfan's fight that day, and Grayson had respected the spine of steel Yahri had shown, despite the frailties of her age.

"I have a question about Princess Serene," Serai Krayt said. "I've heard some of the dangers she's faced on her journey. Have we sent aid?"

"I've sent messages, and aid has been declined," Desfan answered. "Now that she is in Mortise, I'm sure she'll experience a safe journey to Duvan."

Liam snorted.

Grayson sent him a questioning look, but his brother just waved his hand, his attention on Desfan and the council.

Sifa had the next question. "I'm curious to know what talks have begun with Ryden." His gaze shifted to Grayson, and he felt the man's hatred like a blow. "We have among us two princes of Ryden, ambassadors for potential peace, yet the council has not been involved in any such conversations."

Grayson's fingers flicked. *His prejudice is no surprise.*

Liam's mouth twitched. *That doesn't mean we can't find a way to use it to our advantage.*

Grayson didn't see anything useful in Sifa's hatred, but he didn't ask for clarification. He watched for Desfan's response.

"Discussions have not officially begun," the serjah said diplomatically. "For now, Prince Liam and Prince Grayson are our honored guests, and we look forward to opening talks once Princess

Serene is here as well."

The meeting continued, long enough that Grayson's body ached from sitting, and nervous energy kept his heel jumping. Finally, the meeting concluded, and everyone rose.

"You should talk to Desfan," Liam said. "It doesn't matter about what."

"Why?"

"Make a friend. I'm going to engage an enemy." Liam wiggled his eyebrows. "Wish me luck." He darted off to intercept Sifa.

Grayson muttered a curse and stepped down the stone steps, making his way through the dispersing crowd and crossing the floor to Desfan's throne.

He saw Desfan turn to Karim, but the bodyguard lifted a hand and took a step back. Grayson was just close enough that he heard Karim's quick words to the serjah. "Keep the guards with you. Don't follow me." Then he stalked away, leaving Desfan behind.

The serjah's entire face fell. Then he spotted Grayson, and he forced a strained smile. "Prince Grayson. I hope you enjoyed the meeting."

"It was . . . interesting."

"*Exhausting*, I think is the word you're looking for." Desfan straightened, which made Grayson glance over his shoulder.

Serai Krayt approached, and the newest councilwoman looked a lot less confident as her fingers twisted into a knot in front of her. "Desfan, I'm sorry to interrupt."

"Not at all. I'd like to introduce you to Prince Grayson Kaelin. Your Highness, may I introduce Serai Razan Krayt?"

"A pleasure," Grayson said, as politely as Liam had drilled into him.

The young woman smiled a little as she dropped into a curtsy.

"Prince Grayson, the pleasure is mine." Her eyes flashed back to Desfan. "I'm sorry I surprised you as I did."

"It's all right."

Her brow furrowed. "Karim didn't look all right."

"He was just surprised. He'll be fine."

"The council seat is permanent, Desfan. You just sentenced him to a life with me in it." She shook her head. "When I received your letter, I thought you might both want me here. If I'd known . . ."

Desfan clasped her hand. "Razan, I want you on the council. I need someone I can trust."

She raised an eyebrow. "With our history, I make that list?"

"Yes."

She huffed a laugh. "You certainly haven't changed."

Grayson shifted awkwardly beside them, and Serai Krayt's attention darted to him. Color touched her cheeks and she tugged her hand free of Desfan's. "I'm rather tired after my journey," she said. "I think I'll retire."

"Any of the servants can escort you to your room," Desfan said. "And we'll find a time soon to meet and talk more."

"Thank you." Her eyes were serious and her voice grew thinner as she said, "Really, Desfan. Thank you for this chance. I won't let you down."

"I know." Desfan watched her turn away, and then he surprised Grayson by grabbing his arm and tugging him toward the nearest door. "Let's get out of here before some new disaster hits."

Desfan's guards followed them into the corridor, and the serjah steered them to a nearby room Grayson had never entered. By the look of things, it was Desfan's office. A desk, littered with papers, dominated the room. Colorful carpets, tapestries, and some paintings covered the walls, and a window brightened the space with warm light.

Desfan looked to his guards. "That will be all for now, but send someone after Karim. I want to know where he is. No need to interrupt him, though."

The men bowed and retreated, delivering a few pointed looks at Grayson before shutting the door.

Desfan let out a long groan as he sank into the cushioned chair behind his desk, the heels of his hands digging into his eyes. "I'm the worst friend in Eyrinthia."

"I doubt that." Grayson was still standing. A portrait on the wall had captured his attention. The painting depicted a regal, severe-looking man with a golden crown, and a young boy with dark, curling hair. The boy's eyes were too wide. Sad. His small hand looked even smaller, braced as it was on his father's large shoulder.

"I was eleven," Desfan said.

Grayson twisted around to see Desfan eyeing the portrait. "My father and I sat for this soon after we received word that my mother and sisters were dead. I remember every agonizing second of posing. It was horrific. Trying to hold myself together, when all I could think about was the last family portrait I'd sat for."

"I'm sorry." The words were insufficient, but he meant them.

"Thank you." Desfan gestured to a chair across from him. "Please, sit."

Grayson did, nudging the chair just enough that he could keep a partial view of the closed door.

"I'm sorry I herded you out so quickly," Desfan said. "I was anxious to escape, and I thought if I brought you with me, people would be less likely to follow."

Ah. He knew people were hesitant to approach the Black Hand. It hadn't been about Desfan wanting to actually spend time with

Grayson.

Strange, but he felt a ripple of disappointment.

"I understand," he said.

The serjah reclined in his chair. "I'm sorry if anything Sifa said made you or Liam uncomfortable."

"I barely noticed what he said," he lied.

Desfan snorted. "I suppose there was enough discomfort in there with Razan and Karim, eh?"

Grayson shifted in his chair. "If I can ask . . ." And yet, he couldn't put it into words. He knew Liam wouldn't hesitate, but he hated to pry.

"Not many know this," Desfan said quietly, "but I didn't choose to go to sea. My father sent me away on my fifteenth birthday. I wasn't exactly making wise choices, so he forced me to go on a patrol ship for a year. Karim became my bodyguard, and I rather hated him at first. He was sixteen, but acted like he had all the wisdom of an ancient." He cracked a rueful smile. "None of that really matters. But it was during this time that we met Razan. I won't bore you with the details, but she became a friend. And between her and Karim . . . well, it was more than friendship. Razan wasn't honest about a lot of things, though, and she nearly got us killed." He leveled a look at Grayson. "I forgave her a long time ago. Karim still hasn't—obviously. I should have told him . . ." He expelled a heavy breath. "Life is complicated."

Grayson grunted. He understood complicated.

His father had sent him to Mortise under the guise of a peacemaker, when he was really supposed to assassinate Princess Serene and start a war. His mother had sent him with a bottle of poison, ordering him to murder Liam. Peter and Carter wanted him to kidnap Princess Imara of Zennor, who would supposedly be arriving in Duvan to support her cousin, Serene. Grayson planned to commit treason with his other brother, Liam, who had yet to disclose his actual plan. Not to mention he was in love with a girl who was imprisoned by his father, and who was also related to a Mortisian man who hated everything about Grayson.

Yes, life was complicated.

Desfan rubbed a hand over his forehead. "Sorry. You didn't ask for any of that."

"It's all right. I understand how life can feel out of control sometimes."

"Out of control." Desfan nodded. "Yes, that's exactly how it feels. And I'm stuck here, when all I want to do is be out there, looking for . . ." He shook his head. "Never sit on a throne, Grayson."

"Trust me when I say that will never happen."

Desfan eased out a smile. "I can't imagine what it's like, having four older brothers."

Hell, Grayson wanted to say. At least with his brothers.

"I always knew I was destined for the crown." Desfan thumbed the edge of his desk, his gaze distant. "I never thought much about it growing up. It was inevitable. A fact. As sure as I breathed, I knew I would one day rule Mortise." His hand fell. "And then the fates took away my family, and it was just my father and me, and the crown suddenly terrified me."

"And now?"

"Oh, it still terrifies me." He flashed a small smile. "But when my father fell ill, I had no choice but to return."

Grayson hesitated. "How is the serjan?"

"There have been some subtle improvements recently, but time will tell." Desfan looked to Grayson. "I don't know what else you had planned today, but I could really use a good sparring match."

His lips twitched. "I *am* better with a blade than I am with words."

Desfan chuckled. "Me too, Grayson. Me too."

CHAPTER 18

DESFAN

AFTER SPARRING WITH GRAYSON, DESFAN FELT marginally better. The youngest prince of Ryden was not talkative, but he was an intent listener. And when he did speak, his words were honest. Desfan also felt relaxed around him, which was probably something Karim would lecture him about. But Grayson didn't feel like an enemy. He felt like a friend.

When Desfan returned to his room he learned from one of the guards that Karim was down at the royal beach. Drinking, apparently.

Desfan's stomach growled, but he ignored that as he walked past the banquet hall, where the new council was indulging in a celebratory dinner. He trekked out the door that led him to the familiar switchback trail.

The sun was setting, the sky awash in pink, orange, purple, and blue. Sunlight glanced off the sea as rolling waves battered the shore, white foam scattering over the sand. He reached the private stretch of beach and waved back his guards, who stopped at the foot of the trail. Desfan walked through the sand alone and dropped to sit beside Karim.

His friend had set aside his boots and rolled up his trousers, though his sandencrusted feet weren't currently in the water. He sat just outside the reach of the lapping waves, one hand wrapped loosely around a bottle of wine.

Another bottle—empty—lay discarded in the sand nearby.

Desfan yanked off his own boots, tossing them aside with less care than Karim had shown his footwear.

"I don't particularly want you here," Karim said, his words barely slurring.

"I can understand that." Desfan rolled up the cuffs of his pants, then stretched out his legs, letting the incoming wave roll over his feet. The water was warm and perfect, the sun heating his body as it sank lower in the sky.

"Please leave," Karim said.

"No. Not when you need me."

He snorted, drawing up one knee and tossing his arm over it. "I don't need you."

"Yes you do. I used to push everyone away too, remember? I know the signs. I gave you space all day. It's time to talk." He eyed the bottle of wine. "Anything left in there?"

Karim shoved the bottle at Desfan without looking at him.

He took it, taking a quick swallow before setting the bottle in the sand on his other side. Goal one accomplished—the wine was out of Karim's reach.

Now for goal two.

"I'm sorry," he said. "I should have told you that I offered the council seat to Razan. I didn't know if she would accept the offer, and I didn't want to distress you if she turned me down. I certainly didn't think she'd arrive without notice. I thought I'd have time to tell you."

Karim's hand fisted, his gaze squinted toward the setting sun. "You still made the decision without me."

"I know. I'm sor—"

"I know. You're sorry. You said as much." He shook his head and dropped his chin, breathing out slowly through his mouth. His words were still tight as he said, "You're the regent of Mortise. You can make any decision you want. You don't need to apologize to me, or consult with me. I'm only your bodyguard."

"You're my friend. And considering your history with Razan, I should have talked to you first."

"*My* history? She nearly killed you, too."

Desfan scoffed. "That makes it sound like she held a knife to us. If it wasn't for her, we would have died."

"If it wasn't for her, we wouldn't have been in danger to begin with." Karim's eyes narrowed. "She used me to hurt you. I can't forgive that, Des. I won't."

"My history with Razan is different from yours," Desfan said. "She didn't love me."

"Well, she certainly didn't love me."

"She did. And I know you loved her."

"We were sixteen. It wasn't real."

Desfan scrubbed the back of his neck. "I trust her, Karim."

He shook his head, his jaw hard. "You're too good."

Desfan choked on a rough laugh. "*I'm* too good? You're a fates-blasted saint. And you know my sins all too well."

"You're not without flaws," his friend allowed. "But you're still too good. You trust too easily. You hire a pirate when it would be easier to simply order a patrol ship to do what you want. You invite enemy princes to the palace—and befriend the Black Hand, for fates' sake. You release Yahri from prison and reinstate her on the council—"

"I had to do that," Desfan argued. "It was the law."

Karim leveled him with a look. "You could have kept her in prison. No one would have challenged you. And now you appoint Razan Krayt, a woman who once betrayed you, to one of the most powerful positions in Mortise."

Desfan lifted a single shoulder. "I'm optimistic."

"You're a fool."

"A *royal* fool."

Karim frowned. "That makes it sound like you're an even *worse* fool."

A fair point. Desfan ran his hand through the sand, letting the coarse grains sift between his long fingers. "I don't know how to explain it. I trust Zadir, Yahri, and Grayson. And I trust Razan."

"A royal fool indeed," Karim muttered. Then he scowled. "Where's the wine?"

"I finished it."

His forehead creased. "I'm not that drunk. That was a fresh bottle, and you only had one sip."

"Forget the wine. You've had enough."

"Not nearly. I'm still able to see her." Karim dragged his hands over his face, groaning. "Fates blast it. Why is it always her face I see? I hate her."

"I don't think you do."

Karim kicked Desfan's outstretched leg, looking a little petulant. "I don't care what you think."

Desfan stared at his leg, which throbbed dully. "You know, for a bodyguard, you certainly hit me a lot."

Karim huffed. "You deserve it."

"Probably. But still."

"Do you want my resignation?"

"Never." His shoulders dropped. "You won't leave over this, will you?"

Karim's voice was quiet, but resolute. "No. You're my best friend. My brother, in all ways that matter. I might kick you from time to time, but you're stuck with me."

"And what about Razan?"

Karim glanced away, his voice roughening. "What about her?"

"She'll be living at the palace. You'll have to speak to her eventually. You can't ignore her forever."

"Watch me."

Challenge rang in his words, and Desfan bit back a sigh.

One victory at a time. At least he still had his best friend.

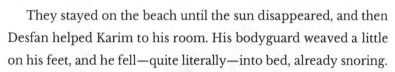

They stayed on the beach until the sun disappeared, and then Desfan helped Karim to his room. His bodyguard weaved a little on his feet, and he fell—quite literally—into bed, already snoring.

Once Karim was settled, Desfan made his way to the banquet

hall. He thought about eating alone in his room, but he knew it was important for people in the palace to see him. For once, he was thanking the fates that Mortisian feasts often lasted for hours, because there was still food to be had. He nodded to a few members of court who called out to him, but he made it to his chair with most of the conversations in the room going unbroken. Lutes and flutes played in the corner as Desfan shoveled food into his mouth, hardly tasting it.

"You used to always eat that way," Yahri said, cane in hand as she sank into the empty chair beside his.

With his mouth full of lemon pepper fish, he was unable to reply.

The old councilwoman cracked a thin smile, her silver hair catching the lamplight. "You and your sisters would always eat in a frenzy. I remember your mother was constantly patting your head, telling you to slow down and savor it. Your father always laughed and said you all had too many important things to do to waste time eating."

Desfan swallowed. "I finally listened to her—after choking."

Yahri chuckled. "I remember."

He eyed the woman, caught off guard by the nostalgia in her expression. He was a little unsure of how to interact with her, it was so different from their usual conversations. "Is there something you needed?" he finally asked.

"I wanted to thank you again for reinstating me."

He grunted, cutting another bite of fish. "I was upholding the law."

"Hmm." Yahri's chin lowered a fraction. "You had an opportunity few in the royal line get—a chance to shape nearly an entire council. A lesser man would have appointed only his friends. You didn't do that. You listened to the advice of the council, accepting names they offered. And you put me back in my position, even though you dislike me."

"I don't dislike you."

She gave him a loaded stare.

He almost smiled. "There have been *times* I disliked you," he admitted. "And I don't always agree with you. But in the end, that's why I reinstated you."

Her brow furrowed. "You reinstated me because I disagree with you?"

"Yes. The council is designed to offer me perspectives. Alternatives. What use would they be if they always agreed with me?"

She blinked. "That was surprisingly wise, Serjah."

"It was bound to happen at some point."

She sat beside him in silence as he ate. When his hunger pangs eased, he took a drink of wine.

That's when Yahri cleared her throat. "Have you begun any investigations?" She didn't have to specify what she meant.

His fingers tightened around his glass. "Yes."

Fates, if Tahlyah or Meerah had really survived, they would be so grown up now. No longer the little sisters he had known.

If one of them lived, he *would* find her.

"I hope you'll keep me apprised," Yahri murmured.

"I will."

"Good." She straightened. "I spoke with Serai Krayt tonight. I'm probably one of the only ones who knows about her less-than-savory history with you, and it would be best to keep it that way. But I wanted you to know that I like her."

Desfan cracked a smile. "Should that worry me?"

"I don't think so." Yahri pushed to her feet, arching one thin eyebrow. "After all, I like you." She tipped her head, then limped away, relying heavily on her cane.

Desfan watched her go, shaking his head a little.

A strange and complicated world indeed.

CHAPTER 19

MIA

"I WANT TO SHOW YOU SOMETHING," TYRELL said, striding into the sitting room.

Mia lowered her book. "What is it?"

"Not here." He took her hand and pulled her up from the settee, his head tipping toward the main door. "It's in another room."

Anxiety slid through her veins, and she tugged her hand from his. Nerves danced in her stomach. The thought of leaving the comfort of this room—her sanctuary—was overwhelming. So many fears bombarded her. She hadn't stepped foot outside her cell in years, and though Tyrell's room had given her light and a sense of freedom, she still hadn't left his suite as she healed from her injury. What would it feel like to walk the halls of the castle? To see other people? To be seen?

"I don't think I can," Mia said.

Tyrell frowned at the stiffness in her voice. "Why not?"

She looked toward the closed door, her scalp prickling. "Would the king want me to wander the halls? What if someone sees me?" She glanced down at her simple green dress. "I don't think I'm wearing the right thing." Since Rena Fletcher had become her maid, Mia had been wearing new styles and colors, and the dresses fit better than anything she'd worn since her imprisonment. But still . . .

"Your dress is perfect," Tyrell assured her. "And my father has given you permission to go about the palace and even the grounds. I just thought we'd start with something simple."

Her throat pinched. Every day she looked out the open windows of Tyrell's room and smelled the fresh air. She wanted to be a part of the world again, but it had been so long . . . The fact that Tyrell knew this, and wanted to ease her into this new freedom, made her eyes sting. "Thank you," she whispered.

He inclined his head slightly, then gestured to the door. "Shall we?"

Slowly, she nodded.

Tyrell moved for the door. His fingers curled over the handle and he shot her a last look. "Ready?"

Mia's lungs tightened.

For years, she had dreamed about leaving her prison. That Grayson would take her hand and they would walk out of her cell together. She had never envisioned this moment without him. It would be so easy to balk. To give in to the fears that swirled inside her and stay in this room forever.

Grayson's face flashed in her mind. His gentle smile, his warm gray eyes. He had always seen strength in her, even when she felt weak. He called her courageous, even when she was afraid.

She did not want to be afraid anymore.

Her shoulders lifted, and though she trembled, she pulled in a long breath. "I'm ready."

Tyrell pulled the door open and Mia moved forward, her slow footsteps whispering against the stone floor. At the threshold, she paused—but she did not fall back.

Mia lifted her foot . . . and stepped into the hallway.

A shiver rippled through her, the only sign that she had crossed some invisible line. She braced herself, waiting for fear to clutch her, but even though her heart was pounding, all she felt was excitement.

She wasn't free. Not really. But she had stepped through a guarded door, and no one called her back.

A grin spread into place.

Fletcher, standing beside the door, gave her an answering smile.

Tyrell stepped out behind her, pulling the door closed. "Stay with the room," he ordered the guards. Then he started down the hall, leaving Mia to follow.

She did, the cool air of the corridor brushing her cheeks. She gazed at every wall, every torch, every window and stone—it was all new. There were only a few scattered tapestries, all of them more serviceable than artistic; the winters were harsh in Ryden, and the tapestries would help trap some warmth. The lack of décor wasn't surprising—Queen Iris was known for her hatred of art and excess. She valued practicality, and she had left her mark on this castle. It didn't stop Mia's enjoyment.

At the first staircase, she set her hand on the smooth stone rail. It felt ancient, and the subtle carvings bespoke a past ruler who must have appreciated artistry. The columns they passed were much the same; etchings Iris hadn't bothered to remove, but that stood out all the more now.

Tyrell walked beside her, pausing when she paused, never rushing her. Servants, guards, and several nobles passed by, all of them offering a deep bow to Tyrell and a curious look at Mia. They didn't attempt conversation, and Tyrell made no introductions.

Mia's sense of wonder extended through the windows they passed, showing new views of the world outside, but none of what she saw prepared her for the place Tyrell took her.

He came to a stop before a set of tall double doors in a deserted corridor. "No one will disturb us here. It's probably the least-utilized room in the castle, but I thought you would enjoy it." With that introduction, he pulled open the doors and Mia gasped, throwing her hands over her mouth.

The smell of dust, wood, leather, and paper wafted from within. The sight of towering shelves crowded with books were all she could see. Cobwebs glittered in the light that filtered through the dirty windows set along the back wall. It was a vast library, full of shadows and light and it whispered of being forgotten. The room was deep and mysterious, and undeniably grand.

She slipped into the room, feeling a thrill as she reached for the nearest shelf. Her fingertips ghosted over the leather spines, and her steps echoed in the vaulted room as she slowly walked the length of the bookcase. "Grayson used to bring me books," she whispered. "I thought I must have read all of them in the castle, but . . ."

No one could read all of these books. Not even if they had a dozen lifetimes.

"You can pick any you wish," Tyrell said, his voice drifting from the open doorway, revealing that he hadn't moved. He simply watched her.

Once, that would have chilled her. Now, she turned to him with a beaming smile. "Thank you for bringing me here."

He leaned against the doorjamb, his hands in his pockets, dark hair falling over his brow. "You can come anytime you wish. Just make sure you bring Fletcher, or invite me." The corner of his mouth dragged up. "I would never complain about seeing that smile of yours. Who knew a room full of dusty old books could make a person so happy?"

Mia laughed, though emotion thickened her throat as she moved around the shelf, walking deeper into the library. "This is the most beautiful room I've ever seen. It's a shame no one comes in. Books aren't meant to be ignored."

She wandered the aisles, fingering the spines as she went. She was aware of Tyrell drifting behind her, giving her space to explore, but keeping her in view. She pulled down several books, cradling them in a pile on one arm. The moment the stack wavered as she reached for yet another book, Tyrell wordlessly scooped the books into his own arms. Mia insisted she could carry them, but he only shrugged. "So can I. My entire afternoon is yours."

She bit her lower lip and his eyes dipped to her mouth.

Skin feeling too tight, she twisted back to the shelf. Fates, she didn't know how to act with him. He was a friend, nothing more. But she knew his feelings for her were growing, even though she'd been perfectly clear about how she felt.

"I've been raised to fight, and I don't give up. Not if it's a fight for something I want."

She thumbed through a book, not really seeing the text as she remembered his fervent words. "Do you like to read?" she asked.

"No. I've always preferred real experiences to sifting through pages."

"You're wrong, you know. About books. These pages can give you more experiences than you could ever fit into one lifetime. Sometimes, they're more real than what's around you."

"Pretty words, but books have never been a haven for me."

"Maybe they could be, if you'd let them. Do you have a favorite topic?"

A smile crept into place. "Moss has become a recent fascination of mine."

She rolled her eyes. "Please be serious."

"Oh, I am."

"Tyrell . . ."

He lifted one shoulder, carefully balancing the books he held. "I don't know what you want me to say. The only things I know are killing and the training of killers. Are there books about that?"

His answer caused a pang in her heart. She knew, of course, that Tyrell and Grayson had both been raised as their father's weapons. They hadn't spent much time with books—not compared to the other brothers, who had roles that demanded a more book-heavy education.

She remembered those early days with Grayson. He had been entranced by the stories she'd told him. One particular day, his eight-year-old brow had furrowed as he'd asked, "How do you know so many tales?"

Her parents had always told her stories before tucking her into bed, and her tutors had told her stories as well. She couldn't verbalize any of that, though—not when the mere thought of her life before this one strangled her. "Books," she'd finally answered Grayson. "I read books. And sometimes I make up my own stories. They have always been a love of mine—and an escape."

Standing in the library with Tyrell, Mia scanned the shelves around them, seeking something that would capture Tyrell's interest. Something that could be an escape for him . . .

Her eyes landed on a familiar spine. She grinned as she plucked it from the shelf. "I want you to read this."

He squinted at the title. "*Soren's High Sea Adventure.*"

"You'll love it. It's a story about a poor farmer who makes a bad bet and finds himself sailing the sea with a band of pirates. He has nothing but his quick wit and a talent for surviving all sorts of trouble."

He eyed the cover almost warily. "It sounds like something my mother would burn."

"All the more reason to read it." Mia stacked it on the pile. She remembered how much she and Grayson had loved this book as children. They'd read it several times together. Grayson's young face had stretched in a wide smile at Soren's antics. He'd loved how every misadventure ended positively—but often with a hilarious twist that would see Soren into some new kind of danger. Mia knew Tyrell wasn't Grayson, but she thought he might enjoy it, too.

"If I read this for you," Tyrell said, "will you consider doing something for me?"

Her eyes narrowed. "That depends."

"No need to look so suspicious." He shifted the weight in his arms. "There aren't many celebrations at the castle, but my father's birthday is in four weeks. I would be honored if you'd attend the feast with me."

Mia stilled. "I don't think that's a good idea."

"There's no reason for you to hide." His chin lowered, his eyes intent. "Peter knows about you, and others will find out. I would rather everyone in this castle had a chance to see you by my side. That will offer you protection."

Perhaps it would. But attending a party with Tyrell—aligning with him so publicly—felt like a betrayal to Grayson. And the thought of being around so many people, and coming face-to-face with King Henri after all these years? The man had loomed in so many of her nightmares. She hated him for all he'd done to her—and Grayson, and Tyrell, and everyone else he terrorized.

Her stomach knotted. "I don't know if I can."

"It's all right if you choose not to go," Tyrell said. "Just think about it."

She wouldn't be able to *stop* thinking about it.

Chapter 20

Clare

ELEVEN DAYS. THEY'D BEEN PRISONERS FOR eleven days, and the forest stretched endlessly around them. Most of the time Clare didn't know which direction they traveled, the woods were so confusing.

Her wrists seared with pain. The saltwater Salim had tortured her with nearly a week ago might have flushed out some of the infection, but new rope had been reapplied nearly at once, and the skin was once again raw, red, and oozing blood. Vera was the same, the two of them riding with shoulders slumped, stomachs growling, and throats burning for water.

Clare had not challenged Salim again. It seemed foolish to risk more torture when they needed to keep up their strength. But their meager strength was flagging, as was their hope.

Even if they had an opportunity to run, where would they go? Clare was utterly lost, and they had no food or water. Salim would follow them—find them. Any belief Clare had of being found was slowly dying. Perhaps no one had survived the ambush on the road. Some of Salim's men might have ridden after Serene and Imara, and killed them.

Whenever her fears would rise, Clare shoved them away, just like she pushed away her pain and grief at losing Bennick. If she didn't, she knew she would be lost.

The sun was just beginning to set when Salim raised a fist, calling a halt. None of the men dismounted as the leader spun his horse around and faced them. "Sedah is up ahead. Shall we sleep in real beds tonight?"

The mercenary pressed to Clare's back cheered along with the rest, making her jump.

Salim grinned at the enthusiastic response of his men, then turned to lead the way.

Clare's heart beat a little faster as the man behind her spurred their horse forward. She had never heard of Sedah, though she'd studied maps of Mortise with Ramus, her tutor back in Iden. She assumed Sedah must be a small village. Without large crowds, it would be hard for Salim to hide the fact that she and Vera were prisoners. This could be their best chance to get help—or escape. Hope fluttered in her chest, even as her gut twisted with nerves.

Sedah was indeed a small village. Nestled in the forest, the trees still thinned to give way to the scattered buildings. Fewer trees allowed Clare to see the first stars winking into existence in the sky above them.

Salim rode right to the front of a worn-looking inn and dismounted. The innkeeper was in the yard, and he quickly took in the group, lingering on Clare and Vera.

Salim clapped the man on the shoulder. "If you mind your business, Kes, I'll let you profit from mine. As always."

The innkeeper's tongue darted over his lips, his eyes lighting greedily, and Clare's hope shriveled. "You know there will be no trouble here, Salim." The man tossed a thumb toward a stable. "I've got space for your mounts in there, and a shed that locks if you need it for the girls."

"I prefer to keep them close," Salim said. "But thank you for your generosity."

The inn was much like those found in Devendra; the common room was crowded with chairs, tables, a fireplace that was probably only used in the coldest months. The differences came in the details. Mortisians were known for their artistic flair and love of color, and though the paint on the walls was faded and peeling, Clare could tell the blues and reds had once been bright. The staircase that led to an upper floor was carved with swirling designs. The chatter by the scattered patrons was in rapidly spoken Mortisian, creating a different sounding buzz of conversation. It sounded harsher, even though the accents were more rounded. And then there were the foreign scents from the kitchen. Sweet meats, spicy peppers, and sharp seasonings she didn't recognize. It was strange. They were not so far from the border, yet it was an entirely different world.

There were only a handful of patrons in the common room, and while they looked up when they entered, none raised an eyebrow at the two bound women being pushed to sit at a long table.

The innkeeper plunked down brown bowls of white rice onto the table, red and orange peppers diced and mixed in. The food was unfamiliar, but her stomach screamed for it.

Salim sat beside Clare and fiddled with the knot binding her hands. He freed one hand, leaving the other bound. He secured it to her chair leg. "Just to be safe," he said with a wink.

The position was uncomfortable, the tight rope forcing her to hunch forward a little, but she was too hungry to care. She snatched up the spoon that had been dropped by her bowl and began to shovel the food into her mouth. The peppers singed her tongue and the rice had a strange sweetness to it, but she barely stopped to taste it.

Across from her, Vera did the same. Tariq had tied her similarly to her chair, leaving one hand free to eat. Her hand visibly trembled, and Clare realized her own hand was also shaking. She didn't know if it was from the sudden rush of sensation, after being bound so long, or if it was because she was so eager to eat; they'd only been given water today.

Salim chuckled beside her. "I thought a princess would have better manners. But I suppose all Devendrans are animals."

The mercenaries laughed. Clare's cheeks warmed, but she ignored them and continued to eat.

The innkeeper brought drinks for everyone—except Clare and Vera, who Salim said *weren't thirsty*. Some of the tenseness left Clare's shoulders as the food began to settle in her belly. As wine and ale were passed around the table, the overall mood in the common room became lighter—and louder. The table was thumped as men told stories, and a few began to sing. Even Salim, seated beside her, seemed more relaxed than he had at any point in their journey.

Clare's thirst grew as she ate, and the spiciness of the peppers only made the sensation worse. Knowing water would not be forthcoming, she picked around the bright peppers, eating only the rice.

Salim noticed. "You don't care for the meal I gave you?"

Clare's fingers tightened around the spoon. There were many things she wanted to say, but she remembered all too well that he was not a man to be pushed. She couldn't let Vera be punished again. "The peppers are a little strong."

Tariq snorted mockingly from across the table. "Children eat these."

While the other men snickered, Salim frowned. "I hate to see you uncomfortable. Here—some ale will cool that burn."

Clare tensed as Salim lifted his tankard and dumped it over the top of her head. She gasped and spluttered, and the mercenaries roared with amusement.

Loose tendrils of hair were plastered to her forehead and neck, and her dress was soaked in sticky ale. Her chest rose and fell with heavy breaths. She blinked rapidly to get the ale out of her eyes and her free hand swept over her drenched face. Heat flushed her cheeks and tears leaked from the corners of her eyes.

Salim leaned in, his hot breath fanning her cheek. "You don't break as easily as I thought a princess would. But one thing is certain—you don't look much like a princess right now."

Clare's lungs felt too tight as Salim turned back to his meal. She trembled beside him—wet, dirty, and humiliated—ready to curl in on herself and release a flood of tears—or lash out.

Breathe.

It was Bennick's voice in her head. Calm and sure, just as he had always sounded when they trained.

In any fight, you need to remember to breathe. If you give into panic or fear, you're giving your opponent an advantage.

Even just the memory of those words did something to soothe the despair gripping her chest. Bennick might be gone, but she was still here, and so was Vera. Clare needed to remember that.

She took a few breaths, each one a little deeper and steadier than the last. Then she looked up, meeting Vera's concerned stare.

I'm all right, she tried to tell her without words.

Her friend was still pale, but she nodded slowly.

Salim and his men became lost in conversation, seeming to forget the two women. Clare had lost her appetite, so she searched the room. While many of the other patrons peeked at her and Vera, none of them said anything. Did anything. She wanted to think it was because they were just as evil as Salim and his men, or that they simply didn't care. But in some of those eyes she saw pity—and fear.

No help would come from them.

The main door opened and Clare watched two men enter. Though they wore common clothing, there was no missing the fact they were Devendran. This close to the border, it couldn't be too uncommon, despite rising tensions between the kingdoms. But they were no ordinary men. Clare recognized them, even if she couldn't recall their names. They were part of the palace guard, and they'd been supplementary guards for her since she'd left Iden.

Elation swept through her, the sharp relief making her eyes sting. Then terror bit down, hard.

Two men would not stand a chance against eight mercenaries.

Green eyes met hers, recognition flaring in the guard's gaze. He took her in, his jaw tensing. Then he looked pointedly away and murmured to the other soldier, the two of them moving to an empty table. They sat, and Clare's heart pounded as she tried to keep her gaze from them as they ordered drinks.

But it was too late. Salim had seen them.

Clare stiffened as he rose and strode over to their table, a thin smile on his face. "Hello, strangers," he said in Devendran. "What brings you to Sedah?"

The green-eyed soldier shared a quick look with his companion before he focused on Salim, his shoulders deliberately relaxing. "Had a bit of a dispute with a city guardsman in Stills. We're just looking for a place to earn a little coin."

"You won't find much opportunity for that in Sedah," Salim said. "Unless you're interested in a game of dice?"

"Afraid we don't have anything to wager," the other man said. "Just enough for these drinks." He lifted his tankard demonstratively.

"Ah. Hard times. It can be difficult to find work." Salim shook his head. "You should go to Afarah."

"Thank you for the advice."

"Oh," Salim blinked. "I suppose I misspoke. I meant you *should have* gone to Afarah. That way you might have survived the night."

The Devendrans tensed, but by the time they pushed to their feet, they were already surrounded by armed mercenaries.

The rest of the common room had gone eerily silent.

Clare's pulse thundered, fear gripping her as Salim stepped forward and casually relieved the soldiers of their weapons. "You know," he said conversationally. "I've always been able to spot a soldier. Your forced disinterest in the tied-up women only made it easier to see."

Green eyes narrowed as the soldier glared at Salim. "If you have any sense at all, you'll turn them over to us. You have no idea who is coming after you."

Salim only looked bored as he addressed his men. "Make them kneel."

"No!" Clare tried to stand, even though her bound hand wouldn't let her rise fully, but one of the men shoved her back into the hard chair. Despair and desperation twisted her voice. "Salim, don't!"

Salim ignored her as the soldiers were shoved to their knees. He spun one of the daggers he'd taken from the green-eyed soldier. "A fine blade," he complimented. "I think I'll keep it."

The knife flashed, and Clare and Vera both cried out as the first soldier fell, clutching his throat until he stilled against the floor in death.

The green-eyed soldier struggled against the hands that held him, his chest shuddering with furious breaths. But whatever he saw in Salim's face assured him he wasn't going to survive this, no matter how hard he fought. His gaze slashed to Clare and Vera. "They're coming," he said, his voice tense and urgent. "Sir Lines and Sir Grannard are coming—"

Salim's arm slashed out, and horrible gurgling filled the inn. Then a thump as the guard's body joined his fellow soldier on the floor.

Salim twisted around slowly, eyeing the knife that was coated in blood. His face was utterly relaxed in the lamplight—a horrible contrast to what he'd just done. "Truly, a fine blade," he remarked. He spotted Clare and noted the tears that ran freely down her face. The corner of his mouth lifted. He wandered over to where she sat, crouching so their eyes were level. "No one is going to save you, Princess," he said, his voice horribly soft. "And if they try, their fates will be the same as what you just saw."

Images flashed through her mind. Wilf and Venn, forced to kneel. Their throats cut as she watched.

173

"You should pray they don't come," Salim said. "Else their blood will be on your hands."

Without warning, he grabbed her free wrist, his fingers digging into the abused flesh.

Clare hissed in pain, and when he lifted the blood-streaked knife, she recoiled. Another man gripped her shoulders, pinning her back to the chair. She could do nothing as Salim ran the flat side of the blade over her palm, leaving a trail of blood that made her gut twist.

The mercenary leader's smile was dark and cruel. "*All* their deaths will be on your hands."

CHAPTER 21

WILF

"THEY'VE BEEN DEAD PROBABLY TWO DAYS," Venn said quietly.

Wilf eyed the two bodies. Devendran soldiers he'd sent ahead because he couldn't fully trust the Rose. The assassin had said Salim often stopped in the small village of Sedah, but Wilf hadn't wanted to abandon the trail completely and rush ahead in whatever direction the Rose told him to go. And now two of the men under his command were dead, their bodies left in the forest just outside of Sedah—directly on the trail they'd been carefully following. A taunt or a warning, it didn't matter—Wilf was infuriated either way. With himself. With Salim. Even the Rose.

He could feel Venn's frustration, which didn't help. He almost wished the younger soldier would curse him and his decision to take the careful path.

Venn looked up at him. "What now?"

Wilf stared at the dead bodies. Fates, this was all his fault. Just like it was his fault that Rachel had died. His wife had been caring for him. She'd gotten the pox from him. And the fates had deepened their cruelty when they hadn't taken his life, too, but made him live without her.

If he had listened to the Rose, they would have reached Sedah in time. Those soldiers wouldn't be dead. Clare and Vera would be with them now.

His hands fisted at his sides. "We need to bury them."

"And then?" Venn pressed.

Wilf faced him fully. "Are you willing to trust the Rose with this?"

Venn's eyes darted to the assassin, who was shackled across the trail from them. When he looked back, his jaw was set. "I would trust any demon right now if it meant saving Vera."

Wilf studied the younger man, his resolute stance, the hard lines of his face. Then he nodded. "We'll leave a couple of men to follow the trail, and if it leads somewhere they can send a runner to us. But we're going to Krid—right after we stop in Sedah."

Venn frowned. "Why bother going there?"

"Because if Clare and Vera were there, someone would have seen them. I want to know everything they can tell me."

Venn snorted. "I don't think the Mortisians will want to talk to us."

"I really don't care what they want," Wilf growled, already marching toward his horse.

Wilf and Venn entered Sedah's only inn, leaving the other soldiers and the Rose standing in the village street. It was after the
noonday meal, so the common room was mostly deserted. The
innkeeper was busy reorganizing his ales. He looked up at their
entrance, straightening sharply when he took in Wilf's towering
form.

"We have questions," Wilf said, his Mortisian a little rough. But
then, maybe his gravelly voice disguised that.

The innkeeper's eyes slid toward a side door, as if he truly considered bolting. "I want no trouble."

Venn placed a hand on the bar. "There won't be trouble if you
answer our questions."

The innkeeper swallowed, cutting a glance between them. "What
do you want to know?"

"A group of men led by a man named Salim passed through
here a couple of nights ago," Venn said. "They would have had two
women with them."

The innkeeper's shoulders fell a little. "I can't talk about that."

Wilf's hand was around the innkeeper's throat in the space of
a breath. He slammed the man back against the shelves of ale,
making jugs and bottles rattle. "You'll want to reconsider your
answer," he said, his tone low and hard.

The innkeeper gasped when he was released and rubbed at his
reddened throat. He leaned away from Wilf, his chest rising and
falling quickly as the words poured out. "Salim comes through
often enough. He and his men are a little rowdy, but always pay

well. They were here two nights ago."

"What of the women with them?" Venn asked tightly.

"They were bound. Didn't say much. They ate a little."

"Were they injured?" Venn demanded.

"No." The man swallowed harshly. "Just tired."

"We found two bodies just outside of town," Wilf said. "You know anything about them?"

"They were killed here. By Salim. It was a mess to clean up. And if you value your lives at all, you'll forget any sort of revenge. He's not a man to be crossed."

"Where—" Venn swallowed sharply, knuckles going white as his hands clenched. "Where did the women sleep?"

Ice froze Wilf's veins. He hadn't thought to ask, but if any of the mercenaries had touched Clare or Vera, he would tear their limbs off.

The innkeeper spoke in a rush, as if sensing a rise in that lethal rage. "They slept in one of the rooms upstairs."

Wilf ground his teeth. "Show us."

The innkeeper moved reluctantly, but he showed them up the narrow staircase. He was clearly a weak-willed man, easily bent with threat. No wonder a degenerate man like Salim frequented here— he was never challenged.

The first door on the landing was prodded open and Venn slipped in, his eyes tracking over every part of the room. Wilf kept his gaze on the Mortisian innkeeper, a silent challenge that kept the smaller man in place.

Venn suddenly dropped to a crouch, and his fingers brushed into one of the room's corners.

"What is it?" Wilf asked, impatience tightening his voice.

The younger man lifted a scrap of fabric, loose threads dangling over the edges. It had been caught on the edge of a blunted nail. His fingers smoothed over the worn material, and his shoulders rolled inward. "It's from Vera's dress," he whispered.

"You're sure?"

Venn's dark fingers curled, strangling the bit of fabric in his fist. "Yes."

Wilf let his hand settle around the hilt of his belted sword as he eyed the innkeeper. "Which way did they go? What was their destination?"

The man's tongue darted over his lips, and moisture beaded along his brow. "They went west," he said. "But I don't know their destination."

West.

Krid.

Wilf didn't bother with a farewell. He strode past the man and headed down the stairs, Venn right behind him.

CHAPTER 22

GRAYSON

"SER SIFA IS CHARMING," LIAM SAID DRYLY as they strolled down the crowded street. They had managed to sneak out of the castle after breakfast, and were headed to meet some of Liam's contacts. Grayson's eyes kept darting to the small purple flags that were hung out of seemingly every window. He'd overheard talk of a holiday approaching, but nothing more.

"I mean, I'm not surprised," his brother continued. "But when I attempted to talk to him after the council meeting, his lips actually peeled back from his teeth. He might be rabid." Liam glanced over at Grayson, finally noticing his curiosity with the flags. "Ah. Dawn of Eyrinthia. It's a two-week holiday in Mortise, marked with religious ceremonies, feasts, and festivals. There's always a huge ball at the palace on the last night."

Ryden had no holidays. The idea of a two-week celebration—the sheer excess of it—made Grayson's brow furrow. "Why?"

Liam shrugged. "Because they're Mortisians. They love any chance to celebrate."

"What are they celebrating, though?"

"Eyrinthia coming to the world." He glanced up at a long strand of small, fluttering purple flags that dangled overhead. "Their holy texts claim she wore a long purple dress when she first stepped foot here—in Duvan, of course. Mortisians wrote the accounts, so it only makes sense that they'd claim their goddess's favor."

Grayson frowned. "Eyrinthia isn't a goddess. It's just the name of our world."

"Many would disagree with you. But don't worry. The goddess doesn't exist in Ryden, so I'm sure she won't judge you for not knowing her name." He shoved his hands into his pockets. "Frankly, she's such a lofty deity that people don't really acknowledge her much anyway."

"Is she just in Mortisian religion?"

"There are some religions in Devendra and Zennor that claim her. As I said, though, she's far removed from her worshippers. She created the fates to rule for her." He lifted an eyebrow. "Laziness, or brilliance? I still haven't decided."

Something in Liam's tone made Grayson ask, "Do you believe in her?"

"No. If life experience has taught me anything, it's that no goddess watches over us."

That was hard to argue.

Liam sent him a look. "Still, a higher power is something we all need from time to time. Who else would we beg favors of, or blame when everything falls apart? Most people in Eyrinthia incur the fates. In Ryden, probably out of pure habit, and not any real belief that they'll help us. But there are some religious people who pray to Eyrinthia. Some believe the goddess's very essence runs through the blood of the Cassian family, which is why they wear the crown. But considering how cursed they seem to be, I feel like that's a lark. Maybe the Cassians agree, because they haven't been overly religious in years." He tossed Grayson a smile. "All the piousness aside, Dawn of Eyrinthia is a great time to be in Mortise. The food, the parties—you'll love it."

"Wonderful," Grayson muttered, sarcasm edging his tone. "More fish and more people."

His brother burst out a laugh. "I'll find you something to eat other than fish."

"Good luck." Fish, as made sense, was a staple in the coastal city of Duvan. Grayson had learned rapidly that he didn't enjoy it. The texture was odd, the taste even worse, and it didn't matter how it was prepared, whether it was with peppers that burned his tongue or spices that made his nose twitch. Eating it bland was foul, too. And everyone else seemed to love it—it was served at *every meal.*

"There are these delicious cinnamon orange buns with a sugary glaze," Liam said. "You would love them. I'm sure they'll be selling them everywhere during the celebrations."

It sounded like far too many flavors in one bun, but Grayson was glad his brother was in such a good mood. Curiosity had him speaking before he could overthink his words. "The woman you lost. Was she from Mortise?"

Everything about Liam changed. His smile dropped, the light from his eyes suddenly extinguished. "What makes you think that?" he asked in a stiff whisper.

182

Grayson silently cursed himself for saying anything. "You just seem to love Mortise. It made me curious if she was from here."

"I don't talk about her. Ever." His words were not a confession, but an order. "I can't. Not when her death hasn't been avenged yet. Maybe then . . ." A muscle jumped at his temple as his jaw tightened. "Maybe never."

"I'm sorry." The apology was more than just for bringing up such a painful topic. It was for the loss of her, too.

Not for the first time, Grayson considered what he would do if Henri killed Mia. It was a pain he wouldn't survive. He would murder his father, and that would be his final act.

Liam had lost the woman he loved, and though it had undeniably broken him, he wasn't rushing in for blind revenge. He was determined to utterly destroy Henri for what he'd done. He was going to destroy their family, so they could never hurt anyone again.

Liam was a better man than Grayson.

The rest of their walk to the warehouse district was made in silence. The air between them sang with a tension Grayson didn't know how to relieve, and Liam didn't seem to care to try.

They ducked into the whitewashed building that belonged to Rahim Nassar, a Mortisian merchant that Grayson had yet to meet. They were here to see Rahim's second in command, a man who went by the name of Neev Sal, though Liam called him Kazim.

A spy's life got complicated quickly, Grayson had learned.

Liam strode across the short entry and stopped at a long desk, where a thin man sat. With a few exchanged words, they were shown into a nearby office, where Kazim stood to greet them.

The Mortisian was tall and broad, clearly more suited to battle than books, despite the ledgers that spilled across his desk. His brown skin was marred with a few wrinkles around his eyes, and his dark hair was speckled with silver. A collection of daggers and knives weighed down his belt, and Grayson felt a grim satisfaction that the man eyed him carefully. A threat, clearly marked.

"You're late," Kazim said to Liam.

"Marginally." Grayson's brother strode toward the Mortisian, and the two men clasped arms. It wasn't the hard embrace of two long-lost friends, like the last time they'd met, yet the strength of their friendship wasn't in doubt.

For some reason, it irritated Grayson. Perhaps because it was a reminder that, while Liam seemed to know everything about him, Grayson still knew too little about his brother's many and varied lives.

Grayson glanced toward the other person in the room—Akiva. The young man was near Grayson's age, with dark hair and a slender build. He sat in one of the cushioned chairs near the desk, watching as Kazim greeted Liam. When he set aside the book he'd been reading, Grayson's attention was brought to the young man's hands. They were covered in scars. Pale lines traced over every part of them—even his fingers. It was miraculous he had any use of his hands with damage like that.

The moment Liam released Kazim, Akiva threw himself at Grayson's brother. Liam caught him with a grin. No hint of sadness, now. Only joy.

"Are you staying out of trouble?" Liam asked.

"Choosing my trouble wisely—as you taught me."

Liam chuckled, pulling back and ruffling Akiva's hair. The boy slapped his hand away, making Liam laugh.

Grayson swallowed. He'd never embraced his brothers. Never joked with them, or made them laugh. He wasn't sure why the thought hit him now.

Kazim was watching him. He forced his expression to remain neutral. "Kazim," he greeted.

"Saimon," the man grunted, using the false name Liam had assigned Grayson on their last visit.

He still wasn't entirely sure why Liam hadn't told them who Grayson was. When he'd asked before, Liam had brushed it off by saying they didn't need to know who he was. He was beginning to wonder if it was because Liam didn't want Grayson to truly be a part of them. They were more than Liam's friends—they were his self-declared family. A distinction Grayson clearly did *not* have.

Akiva shoved a hand through his hair as he surveyed Liam. "I'm glad you're all right. We heard about the trouble at the palace and assumed you were in the thick of it."

"There was a little skirmish in the library, but nothing to be worried about."

"Saimon kept you safe?" Kazim asked, his focus still on Grayson.

"Yes," Liam said smoothly. "He's a talented bodyguard."

"Do you need us to send someone after Sahvi?" Akiva asked, naming the drug master who had sold the olcain to Jamal. "We can kill him and make sure he stays dead this time."

"No," Liam said. "Sahvi can wait. I want you to switch your efforts to learning everything you can about the new council members. Talk to their servants, their business partners, childhood friends, family members—both estranged and close. I want to know everything about them. I'm especially curious about the newest member, Serai Razan Krayt. I want to know any history she has with the serjah and his bodyguard, Karim Safar."

Akiva nodded. "We'll begin today."

Kazim's attention finally shifted away from Grayson to land on Liam. "You asked me to keep an ear out if any assassins or criminals were employed within Mortise, and I recently heard Salim was hired to abduct someone near the Devendran border. Rumors say it's Princess Serene."

Grayson stiffened at the familiar name. The woman his father had sent him to assassinate. Desfan's future bride.

Liam, however, did not seem surprised. "I heard the same."

Kazim's dark eyebrows pulled together. "Do you want me to pursue it?"

"No. There's no need."

The man looked a little surprised, but he nodded. "Very well."

"There's another piece of news out of Zennor," Akiva said slowly. "Skyer has left the capitol."

Skyer. Grayson didn't know much about him. Carter had told him Skyer was betrothed to the Zennorian princess, Imara—the princess Grayson had been ordered to abduct so Peter could marry her.

It was clear the name *Skyer* meant something more to Liam, though.

His brother stiffened, his eyes darkening. "He was supposed to stay in Kedaah. He was speaking for the clans in Buhari's court."

"And then he left," Akiva added.

"Where did he go?" Liam demanded.

"We don't know yet," Kazim said. "I'll let you know as soon as I learn anything."

"Why does Skyer matter?" Grayson asked, his tone a little sharper than he'd intended.

Everyone looked at him, and he tried not to flush under their stares. Kazim frowned, and Akiva looked annoyed.

Liam's jaw tightened. "He's no one you need to be concerned with." He glanced at Akiva. "Why don't you show Saimon the warehouse? I need a moment with Kazim."

Akiva's annoyance was obvious as his fists clenched, but he did not argue. He didn't look at Grayson as he strode for the door, fully expecting him to follow.

Grayson thought about staying where he was—telling them exactly *who* he was and demanding to know what they were talking about. But if he was going to go toe-to-toe with his brother, he'd rather do it over something that actually mattered. Saving Mia, destroying his father—that was the ground he would fight for.

Frustration still bit at him as he pivoted on his heel and followed Akiva from the room. They bypassed the man sitting in the entry, mobbing straight for the warehouse. The smell of the sea clung to everything in the high, long space. Thick wooden beams held up the roof and crates, barrels, and large sacks were stacked everywhere.

They were in the middle of the vast room when Akiva turned on Grayson, his chin jutting out. "Who are you really?"

Grayson folded his arms over his chest. "You heard Liam. I'm his bodyguard."

"Liam never brings a bodyguard when he's meeting contacts. And he wouldn't bring a bodyguard here."

"Why?"

Akiva's eyes sharpened. "It's clear he doesn't trust you. If he did, you would know about Skyer."

Grayson's smile was thin and hard. "And yet he brought me here and told me your real identities."

"That hardly matters. Not when you don't know about Skyer."

"Perhaps you should be curious about what *I* know that *you* don't."

The young man scoffed. "Your jealousy is pathetically obvious."

"I'm not jealous of you."

"Of course not," he drawled. "You just don't like the fact that I know him better than you do."

Grayson's palm itched to hold a dagger, but he fought the urge to draw one of his knives.

Akiva leaned in, his tone dropping low even though they were alone in the warehouse. "I know Liam. He's a friend to many, but he only trusts a few. He hates everything to do with Ryden—where you're clearly from—and that makes me wonder just what he's using you for."

Grayson lowered his chin, his stare unblinking. "Perhaps you're the one feeling jealous."

The skin around Akiva's eyes tightened.

Before he could respond, Grayson took a deliberate step back. "I'm going to wait outside. But thank you for the tour, Akiva. It was . . . enlightening." He strode away, half-expecting him to follow.

He was a little disappointed when he didn't.

But then, Liam was irritated enough with Grayson. It probably wouldn't help if Grayson stabbed his friend.

———

Grayson's back was warmed by the whitewashed stone he leaned against as he waited for his brother to finish his business with Kazim. His irritability was climbing rapidly.

When Liam finally stepped out of Nassar's warehouse, Grayson's annoyance had reached his brother's own.

"Let's go," Liam said in a clipped voice, already striding up the street.

Grayson pushed off the building and followed, lengthening his steps until he walked at Liam's side.

Purple flags fluttered along the streets, a mocking reminder of the camaraderie Grayson had felt with his brother on their walk to the warehouse.

How drastically a morning could change.

Liam was silent as they walked, his gaze trained straight ahead. But Grayson was done with the silence. "Why did you even bring me here if you insist on leaving me in the dark?"

Liam shot him a look. "I brought you here because I'm trying to trust you. Sometimes you make that difficult."

"*I* make that difficult? You're the most distrusting person I've ever met."

"A trait that has kept me alive," Liam said, his voice brittle. "Forgive me if my habits are hard to break."

"As if trust comes easily to me."

"What about blind orders? Judging by your relationship with Father, you seem to have no problem with those."

Grayson's skin heated. He tried to ignore the insult, but an edge of anger entered his voice as he demanded, "Why won't you even tell them who I am?"

"Let it go. It doesn't matter."

"I think it does."

Liam glared. "I didn't have to bring you with me today. Doing so was a sign of good faith."

"Don't pretend you're doing me any favors," Grayson snapped. "You recruited me to be a traitor, but you don't share anything real with me. When I ask about your plan, all I get are vague answers. When are we going to *do* something? When are you going to trust me enough to tell me what your plan entails?"

"You're right. I don't trust you."

Grayson stopped beside the mouth of an alley. The streets in the warehouse district were surprisingly empty, though the voices of the workers echoed inside the buildings.

Every frustration Grayson had felt for the past several weeks rushed to the surface, and it took every bit of control he had to keep his voice low. "I know you don't trust me. But I don't trust you, either. How can I, when I see how easily you manipulate everyone around you? When I see you keeping secrets from everyone? You knew someone was hired to abduct Princess Serene, but you didn't tell anyone. Not Desfan, or me—why? What could you possibly gain by keeping such a thing to yourself? Did you *want* her to be abducted?" He shook his head. "And you're constantly cataloguing the vulnerabilities of everyone around you; I know you're doing the same thing to me. You know *everything* about me, and I know *nothing* about you. That's not exactly grounds for an even alliance."

His brother's jaw was tight. "I *do* know more about you than you know about me, and I know that doesn't feel fair. But there are things I'm not ready to share. Things I'll probably *never* share. That's who I am. Knowledge is my weapon, and how to use that to my advantage was beaten into me for years. Since I was twelve years old, I've been an active spy. Keeping secrets, collecting facts, noticing and exploiting weaknesses—that's what I was forced to do. Just like your ingrained reaction is to attack, mine is to reveal nothing. We might hate who our parents made us become, but we're both alive today because of the skills we have."

Liam leaned back, taking a slow breath before he continued

190

more levelly. "There are very few people I can rely on. My instincts are all I have. And my instincts are screaming that to tell you everything—reveal my entire hand—might ruin everything. I won't risk that. I've worked too hard, too long, to fail now. I will annihilate our family. I want you to stand with me. But I *can* do this without you. So. What will it be, Grayson? Will you choose to trust me? Or will you walk away? Whether you see it as a manipulation or not, I *am* Mia's best chance of freedom. What is that worth to you?"

Grayson stared at him, hands fisting at his sides. "I swore to help you, and I will. But can't you tell me *something*?"

"You can trust that I will always tell you exactly what you need to know, when you need to know it."

Grayson shook his head. "That's not good enough. Just tell me something—anything. Explain why you didn't tell me about Serene, or tell me who Skyer is to you and why you hate him. Fates, why won't you even tell me the name of the woman you loved?"

Liam shoved him into the alley, and Grayson was so surprised by the attack that he didn't react. His shoulders crashed painfully against the stone wall and Liam pushed up in Grayson's face. His nostrils flared as he breathed hard, his chest rising sharply. His tone was lethal as he said, "Mention her again and you won't live to regret it."

Grayson already had a knife in hand. It wavered in his grip, the tip a breath away from Liam's gut.

His brother didn't seem to notice. He merely glared before thrusting away from him.

Grayson slipped the dagger back into his belt, his eyes never leaving Liam as his brother retreated until his back hit the other wall of the alley.

Silence stretched between them, stiff and hot.

Finally, Liam's voice drifted across the alley. "I didn't tell Akiva and Kazim who you are because I wanted to protect you."

Grayson's brow furrowed. "How does that protect me?"

Liam looked away, toward the street. A muscle feathered along his jaw. "They would never trust you, if they knew you were my brother. They probably would have tried to kill you by now. They don't have a favorable opinion of the Kaelins."

Grayson snorted. "Does anyone?"

Liam gave a rueful huff. Then he exhaled slowly through his nose. "I'm trying, Grayson. I swear, I'm trying. But I need you to trust me a little while longer. Can you do that?"

Grayson tipped his head back against the alley wall. He knew what he wanted to say. But Mia's face flashed in his mind, and he closed his eyes, reigning in every frustration. "Fine."

What choice did he have?

CHAPTER 23

DESFAN

THE FIRST DAY OF FEASTING TO CELEBRATE the Dawn of Eyrinthia arrived, and Desfan was grateful for the break from meetings. There would be no trials or hearings during the holiday, and the council would not convene. While a few council members had left Duvan to visit family, most of them remained, inviting their families to visit the capitol. It was probably in an effort to make inroads with Desfan and other nobles of Duvan, but it certainly made the palace feel overrun. The laughter of young children and grandchildren filled the halls, and the sound tugged a nostalgic smile from Desfan. Once, he had run these corridors with his sisters, laughing and playing. It was good to have that energy in the palace again, even if it made his heart ache.

He knew it was too soon for Zadir to have found Gamble, but

he was desperate for news. He needed to know if one of his sisters was alive. The question haunted his every thought, even when he tried to push it aside.

Yahri's cane tapped the stone floor of the banquet hall as she ambled up beside him, pulling him from his thoughts. "You should be mingling more," she said, viewing the crowded banquet hall in her imperious way. "You need strong relationships with the newest members of the council, and you need to strengthen your ties to the older ones."

"A good idea," Desfan allowed. He lifted his glass of wine and took a sip. "Who appointed you as my chief advisor?"

"You did, when you reinstated me to the senior council seat." She nodded to his glass. "Go easy with the wine, but keep a glass in hand. It doesn't hurt to have others think you've indulged a little too much. They become less guarded."

"You're rather good at this."

"I've been around a while. I'm happy to teach you some useful strategies."

"Skills I would have learned if I'd stayed in Duvan, you mean?"

"I didn't say that." She peeked over at him. "But you did, so, yes."

He almost smiled. "Your lectures are so familiar, they're oddly comforting."

She rolled her eyes. "You were absent too long, Desfan—even before you went to sea. There are many things you need to learn now if you're going to keep up."

Yahri was an unlikely ally, and yet he was grateful for her. Her predictability, her long standing on the council, her opinions she didn't hesitate to share—all were assets. As a child, he'd thought her an ornery old crone. And while she might still be an ornery old crone, he had grown to respect her.

He leaned in, keeping his voice low so even Karim would not hear. "From now on, you need to be honest with me, Yahri. It's the only way this will work. You can never keep anything from me again. No matter how good you think your reasons are."

She met his stare easily. "You have my word, Serjah."

"Good." He pulled back, taking another sip of wine. "I think I'll take your advice and wander the room."

"Praise the fates," she drawled. "Miracles do happen."

Desfan chuckled, aware of Karim following him as he stepped deeper into the room. Conversations with multiple nobles took up his next hour; that's how long it took to cross the room. Most were brief interactions, but he could see that it made a difference. People smiled more widely after their conversation with him—new councilors, as well as old.

Fates, Yahri was good. He would do well to listen to her advice more often.

After making his way across the room, Desfan paused beside one of the towering pillars that led outside onto the wide balcony, taking a moment to survey the room. Not many years ago, he would retreat to the balcony to avoid boring parties. His father and various bodyguards had caught him there with several different girls and in several different compromising positions. His lips twitched at the flash of memories.

"She's avoiding us," Karim said beside him.

Desfan peeked at his friend. "Who?"

"Razan. She's been tracking us. When we moved across the room, she went the other direction, always keeping space between us."

With a little searching, Desfan spotted her. Razan was taller than most women in the room, and her long hair had been artfully piled atop her head, which only made her appear taller. She currently talked with several young men who watched her raptly.

"Maybe she's keeping her distance because she doesn't want to upset you," Desfan said.

Karim shot him an edged look. "If she didn't want to upset me, she shouldn't have come."

"Then perhaps she's avoiding us to irritate you."

His bodyguard huffed.

Razan's head tipped back as she laughed at something one of the young men had said.

Karim rolled his neck, but the tension clearly remained. He was focused on Razan. "I should look into anyone she's talking to. Just to make sure they're not a potential threat to you or the council."

"A good idea," Desfan said slowly. "You should pay special attention to the really handsome ones."

"Yes." Karim dipped his head once, his eyes still trained on her. Then he blinked and cranked his head toward Desfan, his face twisted in a fierce scowl. "I'm not jealous."

"I didn't say you were." He took a sip of wine, letting it roll over his tongue before he swallowed. "Maybe you're just feeling protective."

"Of her? Never. I'm merely trying to keep you alive. It is my job, you might recall." Karim snatched a glass of wine from a passing tray.

Desfan's eyebrows lifted. "You never drink while on duty."

"Shut up," his bodyguard snapped. His eyes narrowed when Razan touched a young man's arm. "Bloody fates," he muttered. He threw back his wine, drinking deeply.

Desfan fought a smile. "You still hate her, right?"

"Yes." Karim finished his wine and handed the empty glass to a servant. He eyed the full glasses on a tray nearby but didn't take another. As if to head off anything Desfan might say, Karim changed the subject. "Grayson and Liam seem at odds tonight."

"Really?" He'd seen the princes, of course. He'd even had a brief conversation with Liam, but he hadn't noticed anything amiss.

"Grayson normally shadows Liam, but he's not doing that tonight."

"You do like to keep an eye on them."

"Someone has to."

Desfan finally spotted Liam, talking with one of the new serais on the council. He couldn't see Grayson anywhere. "Where—?"

"Balcony behind us," Karim said without looking. "He seemed quite anxious for air."

Desfan gave his nearly empty glass to a passing servant before he turned to Karim. "Could you give me a moment with him?"

His bodyguard didn't look happy about it, but he jerked out a nod, and Desfan slipped around the pillar.

The air was much cooler on the vast balcony. Assorted potted plants were scattered across the wide space, creating a miniature garden with plenty of hidden alcoves for private conversations or couples to get lost in. The balcony was rimmed by a stone railing that overlooked the sea. The area was awash in moonlight, thousands of stars winking across the black night sky.

Desfan found Grayson near the edge, but the youngest prince of Ryden wasn't alone.

Even through the plant fronds, it was easy for Desfan to distinguish Arav Anoush and several of his friends. Desfan didn't know them well, though he'd met them several times throughout his life.

The pitch of Arav's voice told him he'd happened upon a tense situation, but Grayson's stare was unreadable as he regarded the other young man.

"It's a peace offering," Arav said, extending a glass of wine. "Just accept it."

"No thank you," Grayson said, his voice level.

Desfan tensed, ready to move around the plants and reveal himself, but someone else stepped from the shadows first.

Ranon Sifa shot Arav an irritated look. "Do you have a death wish? One of these times, the Black Hand might lose patience with you."

One of these times? Fates, Arav had cornered Grayson before? Desfan wanted to curse.

Arav straightened. "Ranon. Coming to the Rydenic prince's rescue again. You're making a habit of this."

"It's a far better habit than yours." Ranon switched from Rydenic to Mortisian, his words low and fast. "Did you put something in that wine? Fates, are you that idiotic? That could spark war—even if it's nothing truly dangerous. I know you want to impress everyone by baiting the Black Hand and making him look the fool, but *you're* the fool. And most definitely drunk. It's the only explanation for your stupidity tonight."

Arav scowled. "Don't tell me you're happy to have him here." He shoved a finger toward Grayson. "*All* Rydenic men are monsters—the Kaelins worst of all. They murdered half your family!"

Ranon's eyes narrowed. "Believe me, I haven't forgotten. Just as I'm sure you haven't forgotten your father's latest mistress is Rydenic."

Arav's fist flew toward Ranon's face, but the punch never landed. Grayson caught the throw in his gloved palm and he twisted Arav in the same motion, using the young man's momentum against him. In the space of a breath, he had Arav on his knees, his back to Grayson, his arm pinned so high it was almost to the nape of his neck.

Grayson leaned over Arav, his voice low and dark. "I keep hearing about Mortisian manners, but it seems to me your tactics at court are similar to Ryden's." He tightened his hold, and Arav released a pained gasp. "Except in Ryden, we actually follow through on our threats. So let me say this once. You approach me again, and I will make sure you regret it."

He didn't wait for a response—he just released Arav.

The young man's hands slapped the stone balcony as he caught himself. He shoved to his feet and whirled to face Grayson. His cheeks were flushed and he ground his teeth. For a split second, Desfan thought he would attack.

The Rydenic prince just watched him, his icy gray eyes unblinking.

Arav's nostrils flared. He straightened his kurta with a jerk, then stalked away in the direction Ranon had come. His friends hurried after him.

Ranon rubbed a hand over the back of his neck. "Thank you. I might have lost some teeth with that punch."

Grayson huffed a short breath. "There wasn't enough strength in his punch for that. And he was holding his fist incorrectly. If I hadn't absorbed the punch like I did, he might have broken some fingers."

"Too bad you didn't let him hit me, then." Ranon lifted the glass of wine that had once again been set aside. "You don't want this. Arav probably spit in it."

"I heard what you said to him. I may not speak Mortisian well, but I understand it fine."

Ranon's shoulders tensed. "I'm sure he didn't do anything to it,

I was just—"

"Oh, he put something in it." Grayson took the glass and held it up, turned toward the bright moonlight. "You can see the powder gathering at the bottom. It didn't absorb well in the wine. It was probably too grainy."

Ranon stared at him. Desfan felt a similar expression on his own face. "You knew he tried to poison you, and you said nothing?"

"I doubt it's anything lethal," Grayson said. "Probably something that would make me sick, or make me act like a fool in front of everyone."

"Still . . ." Ranon's words drifted as he watched Grayson move to a planter sitting on the railing.

The youngest prince of Ryden tipped the wine into the pot, his eyes going to Ranon. "I'm not willing to create conflict between our countries over something as irrelevant as Arav. What was it you called him . . . a *srik*?"

Desfan nearly choked on a laugh. That was *not* a word any tutor would have taught Grayson.

Ranon's mouth twitched. "Arav is the absolute definition of a *srik*." He shifted his weight, his eyes cutting to the ground. "I, ah . . . feel like I need to explain something, since you understood what we said."

"You don't have to say anything," Grayson said at once.

"But I want to." Ranon took a breath. "My uncle and his family were murdered several years ago. I was really young at the time, but I remember them well. I also remember how the news broke something inside my father. To be fair, I think it broke something in me, too. I was very close to my cousins. Especially Mia. She was near my same age, and she was like a sister to me . . ." He shook his head. "That's not really important. It's just, I don't talk about them much."

"I understand," Grayson said, his voice edged with an emotion Desfan couldn't name.

Ranon moved to the railing and reclined against it, his arms crossed over his chest. "There was never any real proof of who killed them, but it was a group of soldiers from Ryden. It had to be them. They'd been terrorizing the ser who was governing Shebar before the serjan sent my uncle there, and they tried to harass my uncle as well. People in Shebar saw my uncle stand up to them—and they killed his entire family for it."

"I'm sorry," Grayson said, his voice tight.

"None of it is your fault. You weren't there. You didn't take my uncle, aunt, or cousins away from me."

It may have been a weird play of the shadows, but it looked like Grayson flinched.

"I wish I could say my father felt the same," Ranon continued. "I'm sure he made your first meeting very unpleasant. I'm sorry for that."

Grayson said nothing for a short moment. Then, "I don't know what happened to your family that night. But I'm sorry for your loss."

"Thank you." Ranon shook his head. "Well, you've managed to have quite the party tonight."

Grayson cracked a smile. "Mortisian celebrations are rarely dull."

Ranon chuckled. "Perhaps not. Certainly not with Arav around."

"The *srik*."

Ranon laughed, and Desfan eased back, walking carefully back to the banquet hall.

Karim glanced over at him as he re-entered. "Where's Grayson?"

"He's fine," Desfan said, smiling a little.

CHAPTER 24

CLARE

CLARE UNDERSTOOD IMMEDIATELY WHY SALIM favored the city of Krid. It was dirty, smelly, and so crowded it was easy to get lost in. The roads were cramped, and the people seemed determined to ignore each other. She didn't see any city guard or patrol of any kind, and though there were many lamps and torches, the shadows stretched long and deep. The sandstone buildings towered on either side of every street, shops and homes strung together into a maze that swallowed them whole. Unfamiliar clothing, bright colors, and foods with new and intense smells combined to create an added feeling of isolation. The rolling Mortisian accent filled Clare's ears, making it all too clear that she was not among the familiar. Many windows displayed purple flags—symbols of a Mortisian religious holiday that Salim said began today.

From what Clare had seen of Mortise, it was hard to understand how they could believe in anything divine.

It had been five days since the two Devendran soldiers had been killed in Sedah, and Clare still had nightmares about their deaths. She knew it wasn't her fault they were dead, but it was hard not to feel guilty. Especially when she recalled the horrible feeling of their blood on her hands.

She and Vera clung to the reassurance that Wilf and Venn were coming, but now that they were in Krid, Clare couldn't help but feel their time had run out. Whoever had hired Salim would be meeting him in this city. They couldn't afford to wait for Wilf and Venn. If she and Vera didn't escape soon, they were as good as dead.

Salim led them into a run-down inn, secured a couple of rooms, then dragged Clare to sit beside him on a worn wooden bench at one of the common room tables. Vera and Tariq settled across from them, and Clare was alarmed to see how pale and exhausted her friend looked.

Food was carried to the table, and Salim didn't bother to untie their bound hands this time. The corner of his mouth twitched with amusement as he watched Clare struggle to eat and drink with tied wrists. If she hadn't been so hungry, she would have refused to serve as his entertainment, but she couldn't ignore the gnawing in her stomach.

The common room was packed with men and women this evening, and everyone was in a jovial mood due to the holiday. Their smiles seemed as cruel as Salim's as they celebrated, while Clare and Vera were obviously prisoners.

Underneath the ropes digging into her wrist was the silver

bracelet she had been allowed to keep. She had to shove away thoughts of Bennick whenever she looked at it, since he had given it to her. The disguised garrote was the only advantage she had, there just hadn't been an opportunity to use it.

"You seem deep in thought," Salim said.

Clare didn't have to fight to find Serene's voice as she said, "The man who hired you. Will he be meeting us here?"

Salim thumbed the handle on his tankard as he eyed her. "Not here exactly, but in Krid, yes. Why?"

"When?" she asked instead.

"So anxious to meet your end? Never fear, we gave ourselves plenty of time, so we have a few days before he comes." Salim leaned in, the ale on his breath fanning her face as he whispered, "Perhaps we can have a little fun before he arrives."

A shudder ripped through her, but she strove not to show her revulsion. "He didn't ask for my maid, so you can let her go."

"Haven't we had this discussion before?"

"You don't need her," Clare said. "You can let her go."

"I can also sell her," Salim said, his voice horribly casual. "There's always a market for a beautiful woman." He eyed Vera, who trembled.

Clare's gut hollowed. "You could ransom her."

Salim snorted. "No one would pay to ransom a servant."

"My father would. He knows what she means to me."

One thick eyebrow lifted. "What a generous father."

"You would receive more from him than the slavers."

The mercenary scratched his bearded chin. "But dealing in ransom is riskier than an easy sale. Friends and family ask questions, desire vengeance. Slavers don't."

Tariq spoke up. "If she's bound for the slavers, can I have her first?"

Salim shrugged. "I don't see why not. But not yet."

Clare's heart pounded. She was losing this argument, and Vera couldn't afford that. "Kidnapping a princess was a risk, but that didn't stop you."

"You *are* persistent, Princess."

"Please, Salim. I'll do anything."

His eyes traced over her face and a chill skated through her. "Anything?" he asked.

Clare refused to look away, despite the nerves fluttering in her gut. "Yes."

Vera leaned in, but Tariq pulled her back. He couldn't stop her frantic whisper, though. "Serene—don't."

Salim's gaze didn't leave Clare, though the corner of his mouth lifted at Vera's terrified words. "I do love your spirit. If only I had enough time to crush it completely."

Clare's fingers twitched on her lap, the only sign of distress she allowed.

Salim's eyes dropped to her mouth. "A kiss," he said. "I want a kiss, Princess."

The mercenaries gathered around the table leaned in, grins appearing.

Clare recognized the challenge. Knew he expected her to recoil or refuse, as she had in the past.

She only stiffened her spine, trying to ignore the rush of adrenaline that tightened her body. "If I do, you'll let her go?"

Salim's eyes widened a little. Then he smirked. "Kiss me, and I'll consider it."

"No," Vera said from across the table, her spine rigid.

Clare pulled in a slow breath, trying to ease the strain in her chest as she met Salim's stare. "All right."

The men at the table hooted and elbowed each other. Salim licked his lips, surprise and eagerness flashing in his eyes.

Vera made a pinched noise in her throat as Clare twisted on the bench toward Salim.

"Make it a good one," he said, his fingers brushing over her knee.

Bile rose in Clare's throat, but she swallowed it down. She lifted her bound hands. "Perhaps you should untie me, then."

The mercenaries chuckled, tossing out jeers that burned Clare's ears.

She expected Salim to refuse, but his fingers smoothed over the knots, his movements slow and deliberate. He watched her face, waited for her to flinch. But even though she could feel her cheeks heating, she didn't cringe away. Not even as the ropes fell to her lap and his fingertips lingered against her skin, a horribly gentle touch. Her abused wrists screamed in pain, the silver bracelet biting into the torn skin as he gradually tightened his grip, until he was manacling her recently freed wrists.

"I want you on my lap," he said, still watching for any sign that he had pushed her too far.

She gave him none, pulling her legs out from under the table and swiveling them to the other side of the bench.

Salim released her hands so he could grip her waist, his legs now straddling the bench. She lowered herself onto his knee, her back to the table.

She was still aware of every eye on her, especially Vera's.

Salim's fingers dug into her waist. "I've never been kissed by a princess before. Don't disappoint me."

Her hands shook a little as she set them on his wide shoulders.

She eased closer, her hands drifting back around his neck. As she leaned in, Salim ran his tongue over his teeth, his ale-soured breath spilling out. Clare smothered a cringe, her pulse hammering as her fingers brushed the ends of his dirty hair.

Before Salim's lips could touch hers, Clare's fingernail found the small catch on her bracelet. She tore out the garrote, ignoring the agonizing tug of the bracelet against her abused wrist.

She had the deadly wire wrapped around Salim's neck in an instant. His hands flew to the wire digging into his throat, so it was easy enough to spin off his lap and maneuver herself behind him. She tightened her grip as she went, nearly pulling him off the bench. His head and shoulders slammed into her front, and she held him there.

The men leapt to their feet as Salim choked, his fingers grappling with the wire in a useless attempt to tear it away from his skin.

"Don't come any closer," Clare snapped, jerking at the wire around Salim's neck. "If you do, I'll kill him."

The Mortisians stiffened, and she wasn't sure if it was her threat or Salim throwing out a hand that stopped them.

Tension sang in the air as Clare looked to Vera. Her friend had managed to leap away from the table, and there was a dagger in her hand. Tariq's, Clare assumed, since he clutched a bleeding hand while glaring at her.

The maid brandished the knife with her bound hands, her eyes locking with Clare's. "Let's go. Now."

Clare's eyes burned and her arms shook. Keeping Salim off-balance on the bench was taking all of her depleted strength. Adrenaline and desperation had leant her strength, but the endless days of near-starvation and abuse had taken a toll. Her hold would not last, and the moment she released Salim—dead or alive—the mercenaries would be on her.

It was a fates-blasted miracle they hadn't attacked her already. She assumed shock was what kept them so immobilized. But that wouldn't last.

She focused on Vera. "I can't go. But you need to run. *Now*."

Vera blinked rapidly, her lower lip quivering.

"Go!" Clare's unexpected shout made Vera jerk, but she bolted from the inn, the door banging loudly on the stone front as she ran into the night.

Tariq shoved to his feet, fuming as he stared after her.

The entire common room had gone silent, every eye on the drama unfolding in their midst.

Clare cinched the garrote tighter, making Salim gag and his legs kick under the table. Every eye snapped back to her, and Clare locked eyes with Tariq. "If you go after her, I'll kill him."

Tariq's eyes darkened, his nostrils flaring. "What's your plan, Princess?"

"I'll let him go once Vera—"

Salim threw a sharp elbow into her side. Clare gasped at the brutal blow and stumbled, her heart thudding as she struggled to keep Salim locked in position.

But that break in concentration had been enough. The mercenaries converged, and harsh hands dragged her away from Salim. The bracelet was ripped from her swollen wrist, cutting open several stinging sores that immediately started to bleed. She was pathetically easy to subdue.

Salim doubled over on the bench, dragging in rasping breaths as he grabbed at his neck, coughing harshly, his lungs heaving. Clare's body shook as she watched him slowly straighten, his head turning toward her.

His eyes were murderous, his jaw set, the bright red line across his throat bleeding a little. His voice was hoarse but uncompromising. "Sit her next to me."

Clare dug in her heels, but was yanked forward and slammed onto the bench beside him.

Around them, whispers had broken out, but after a few hard looks from the mercenaries, the other patrons slowly returned to their meals.

Salim lifted his tankard and took a long and careful drink, wincing as he swallowed. "Tariq. Find the maid and kill her."

Tariq strode for the door at once.

Tears pooled in Clare's eyes, hazing her vision. She didn't bother begging Salim for Vera's life. She knew it wouldn't do any good. Instead, she prayed to the fates that Vera could escape in the celebrating crowds—that she was already far enough away that Tariq wouldn't be able to find her.

Salim gingerly set his mug on the table, but he kept hold of the handle. His elbow brushed Clare's arm, crowding her. She could feel the vibration of his silent rage. She opened her mouth, but he cut her off with a quiet voice. "If you're wise, you will not speak right now."

Clare clasped her hands in her lap. She couldn't stop the tremble that rattled through her. She knew attacking Salim would bring punishment. She had comforted herself with the knowledge that he wouldn't kill her in retribution, but his fury was sharp.

He was not a man who wanted to look like a fool.

She didn't regret her actions, though. Not if this meant Vera lived.

Salim said nothing. He stared at his mug. Eyed the crowd. But he did not look at her.

Clare fought to still the shaking of her body as the minutes stretched and the room around them returned to normal. Boisterous laughter resumed, and someone even strummed a stringed instrument in the corner. But she knew that the delay was not mercy. Salim was merely drawing out this time to exacerbate the torture.

"Lay your hand on the table," he said at last.

Fear exploded inside her, but she set her unsteady hand on the table, pressing her palm against the worn wood in an effort to hide the involuntary quivering.

"Spread your fingers."

Her breaths came faster. "I—"

"Spread. Your. Fingers." Every word was a growl.

Clare complied, her hand shaking. Her terror was so prevalent it filled every part of her. She choked on it. She expected a knife. She expected to lose a finger, or perhaps all of them. It would not be the most sadistic thing this man had done in his life.

Instead of drawing a dagger, Salim traced the back of her hand with his roughened fingertips. "This hand was raised against me," he said softly. "I will not forgive that, Princess." His hauntingly gentle touch drifted up her fingers until his hand was lightly pressed against hers. His head ducked beside hers, his hot breath hitting her cheek and making her shiver. "I've killed men for less. I *want* to kill you. But I haven't come all this way to reach my client empty-handed." His hand began to lift away, his fingertips lingering against her skin.

Then he snagged hold of her smallest finger and wrenched it back.

Clare's scream split the air when bone snapped. She instinctively pulled away—but he gripped her broken finger, keeping her in place beside him. Sobs wracked her body, the shooting pain all-consuming.

Salim's voice was thin and dark. "I won't kill you. But I will make you regret this." To his men, he said, "Hold her still."

Hands grasped her shoulders and Salim grabbed her rope-burned wrist, keeping her hand against the table. His painful hold barely registered to her agonized senses, because his other hand slowly twisted her broken finger. Nausea punched through her along with a violent blast of agony. Sweat beaded her body and she shuddered, crying out.

"You attack me again," Salim whispered, "and I will not be so gentle."

"I won't," Clare rasped, her lungs heaving as tears rolled down her cheeks.

"I know." He latched onto her ring finger, and the snap of it breaking ripped through her along with an ear-piercing shriek.

Salim methodically broke every finger on her right hand. One shattering snap at a time, he broke her.

Clare was so absorbed by the excruciating pain, it became her entire world. She didn't fully realize he'd released her until he leaned back and took another drink of ale. Then his lips brushed against her temple.

She tried to shrink back, but couldn't—clawed hands still dug into her shoulders, holding her quaking body in place.

"Next time," Salim said. "I *will* kill you."

Pain splintered through her broken fingers, blinding her. Her hand twitched against the table, the crooked fingers already swelling. Loose strands of hair shivered in her eyes as she tried to control her tears, her chest rising and falling too quickly.

Salim's hand dipped into her pocket. She flinched as he drew out the tin soldier and rolled it between his fingers. The lamplight caught on the dented surface. Seeing him hold her last connection to Mark—to home—made her stomach drop.

"This means something to you," Salim said to her, his voice quiet. He tossed the toy soldier to one of his men. "Burn it."

A sob strangled in her throat, but before she could try to grab it with her good hand, Salim grasped her chin, yanking her to face him. "I hope you learned your lesson, Princess, because it came at a cost, and you gained nothing."

An hour later, curled into a ball in the corner of a room upstairs, Salim's words were proven true.

Buried in torturous waves of pain, she was barely aware of Tariq entering the room.

"Well?" Salim demanded.

Tariq smiled a little. "She's dead."

Clare broke completely.

Vera was dead. Which meant all of this had been for nothing.

Her hands were bound, the fingers on her right hand shooting with agony that was nothing more than an echo of the grief tearing through her chest.

Vera was dead.

Bennick was dead.

Eliot was dead.

And soon, Clare would be dead.

As the mercenaries settled in to sleep, Salim stepped up to her. He didn't give her a blanket, but he dropped something on the floor. It hit with a dull thunk. Nothing more than a hunk of metal, but she knew what it was.

All that remained of the tin soldier.

"You should keep him," Mark had told her, pressing the toy into her hand. *"He can keep you safe."*

Salim said nothing, just turned on his heel and strode for the nearest bed.

Clare didn't sleep. She hurt too much for that. All she could do was stare at the piece of twisted metal that symbolized everything she had lost as tears tracked down her face.

CHAPTER 25

WILF

KRID WAS A CESSPOOL. A *LARGE* CESSPOOL.

Wilf was no less determined to find Clare and Vera, but doubt crowded his mind as he shouldered through the clogged streets, leading his horse as he walked. They had followed Tamar Nadir's advice and were dressed as Devendran refugees. So far, it had kept them from drawing too much attention, though there had been several rude looks by some of the Mortisians they passed.

Venn strode beside him, not saying a word. That had become normal for him. He'd been uncharacteristically quiet since Vera and Clare had been taken. He was focused. Rigid. And, despite his attempts to look in control, Wilf could see that Venn was raw.

They reached the main square of the city, which was dominated by a huge fountain. There was a little more air to breathe here, since there was a little more space than on the overcrowded streets. Still, the square was lined with merchant stalls and haggling men and women. Purple flags were on display, and children ran and skipped around, laughing or thieving—sometimes both. Mangy dogs barked and weaved through the crowds, and scavenging birds skipped along the cobblestones, searching for discarded crumbs.

Venn stopped, a muscle ticking along his jaw. His long black hair was tied into a bun at the back of his head, but loose tendrils of hair stuck to his sweaty forehead. His tightly coiled muscles made him appear almost painfully alert. "We should split up."

Wilf frowned. "Why?"

Venn glanced to the Rose, who was shackled nearby, a guard on either arm. "He gave a list of inns and taverns Salim likes. I'll take some men and start searching each one while you take the Rose to the Black Scorpion."

It was the tavern Serene had sent reinforcements to. The soldiers should have arrived in Krid days before Wilf and Venn, because they had taken the more direct route on the road.

Wilf shook his head. "It's possible some of the inns have already been searched by the reinforcements. We need to coordinate with them first. There's a lot of ground to cover."

"Well," the Rose said, "I may have exaggerated the number of inns on the list."

The pounding water of the fountain nearly matched the roar in Wilf's ears as he twisted to face the assassin. "What?"

The Rose shrugged. "I made a list of real taverns and inns in Krid, and Salim has stayed at most of them. But he has three true favorites for conducting business. The Bloody Falcon, Briars, and The Mast."

A growl rumbled out of Venn. "Why not just tell us that in the beginning?"

"I didn't trust you. But you haven't killed me yet, so I'm willing to be truthful with you now."

Wilf wanted to strangle the Rose, but he somehow managed to settle his stance by focusing on Venn. "This is good. We'll be able to watch three locations easily enough."

"There's no point in going to any of them just yet," the assassin chimed in.

Venn shot the man a dark look. "Why not?"

The Rose squinted up at the afternoon sun. "Salim likes to conduct business in those taverns, but he won't room at any of them. He's cautious enough to stay other places until it's time to meet whoever hired him. But he does have connections with the innkeepers. If you go marching in there now, he'll find out and you'll risk scaring him off."

Wilf gritted his teeth. "Fine. We go to the Black Scorpion, find our reinforcements, and make a plan."

Venn looked ready to argue, but he only ground his teeth.

The Rose nodded to the other side of the square, since he had long ago grown tired of gesturing with his shackled hands. "The Black Scorpion is that way. Shall we?"

Wilf stepped up to the Rose. "If you're lying, I promise you'll live long enough to regret it."

The assassin's head tilted to the side. "As much as I admire a well-delivered threat, I assure you I'm not lying. I want to find Clare, too. She's my way to freedom."

Wilf wanted to punch the man in the face for using Clare's name. Instead, he practiced extreme discipline and turned away. "Let's move out," he said, striding away from the fountain. He'd only gone a few steps when he realized Venn wasn't following. He glanced over his shoulder. "Venn?"

The younger man still stood by the fountain, his eyes scanning the square, his shoulders tensed. When Wilf repeated his name, Venn glanced over.

"What is it?" he asked Venn.

"I don't know. I just . . ." His words drifted, and he spun in a full circle, his eyebrows drawn tightly together. He stepped onto the edge of the fountain's wide basin, allowing him to see over the crowd from his higher vantage.

Wilf opened his mouth to call him down when Venn suddenly froze. Then he heard it, too.

"*Venn!*"

He knew that voice.

Venn did as well. "Vera!" He whirled, searching the crowd with feverish intensity.

"Venn!" Her voice was closer now, and the younger bodyguard's head cranked to the left. Then he leaped off the fountain and dove into the crowd, shoving past everyone in his way.

Wilf was right behind him, and he knew the moment Venn caught sight of Vera because he stumbled. Then she slammed into him and his arms banded around her, clinging to her as fiercely as a dying man clings to life.

Their heads were ducked together, his face buried in her blonde hair, her arms thrown around his neck. She sobbed against him, and as Wilf drew closer, he could see the swollen welts around her wrists.

"You came," she gasped. "You came."

"Of course," Venn said, his voice threaded with steel, yet frayed with emotion. "I'll always come for you."

Her fingers dug into him, bunching his shirt as she shuddered against him.

Wilf scanned the crowd, but his spine stiffened when there was no sign of Clare. He turned toward the embracing couple. "Where is she?" he demanded. "Where is Clare?"

Vera looked up at him, her dirty face clearly showing the tracks from her tears, both new and old. Her cheeks were gaunt, her skin sunburned. "She's still with them," she said, a cry catching in her throat and stopping further words.

Wilf stepped closer. "Where? Tell me!"

"Wilf," Venn gritted out in warning, his arms tightening around Vera.

"No, it's all right." The maid struggled to choke back her tears. "I just—I've been so afraid. I didn't think I'd find you, but I'd hoped the main square might . . ." She pinched her eyes closed and visibly rallied. When her eyes opened, her words came out more evenly. "Clare is still with them. She helped me escape last night . . ." As she told them what had happened at the inn, Wilf had to bite his tongue to keep from cursing. Clare had taken a huge risk. A daring, but undeniably brave risk.

Venn held Vera's face in his hands, his thumbs brushing at her tears. "You did the right thing," he told her. "You had no choice but to run."

The girl trembled, and her voice cracked as she said, "I left her, Venn."

"You escaped," he argued. "You survived. That's what she wanted."

"Where is this inn?" Wilf barked.

Venn shot him a glare, but he wasn't in a mood to be gentle.

Vera didn't seem to mind his harsh urgency. "It's called the

Knoll," she said. "I haven't dared go back, but—"

"You don't have to," Venn cut in.

Wilf opened his mouth to protest, but the Rose spoke behind him. "I know where it is."

Vera's eyes widened, taking in the assassin for the first time. Even locked in chains and surrounded by soldiers, the Rose's presence clearly frightened her.

Venn kept one arm around Vera. "I'll stay with her. There's no point dragging her back there."

"There are too many mercenaries," Vera warned, her eyes darting between Wilf and Zilas.

"We have more men," Wilf assured her.

"I'll come with you."

"You need rest," Venn protested. "You—"

"I need to help Clare." Vera looked up at him, her throat flexing as she swallowed. "Please, just . . . don't leave me."

Venn's mouth formed a firm line, his hand locking on her waist. "No one will touch you," he vowed.

Wilf began walking. He could hear the others fall into step behind him, Venn murmuring to Vera, but his focus was elsewhere.

The Rose came up beside him, chains clinking, his guards on either side of him. "If we storm the inn, he'll only use Clare as a hostage. What will you do when he holds a blade to her throat?"

"I'll kill him."

The assassin snorted. "I think you're missing my point. We need to be smart."

"We need to end this," Wilf disagreed.

They reached the soldiers who had remained with their horses, and everyone mounted. Vera rode in front of Venn, and Wilf was half-convinced the young bodyguard would never let her go. Vera slumped against Venn's chest, her fatigue painfully obvious. Wilf tried to prepare himself to see the same gauntness in Clare, but the thought of her wrists torn and bloody, her cheeks sunken . . . it gutted him.

They made their way to the Knoll, and though Wilf itched with impatience, it didn't take long to reach the inn. Wilf swung down from his horse, and he didn't wait for the others to dismount as he strode through the front door. The common room was mostly-deserted, but his eyes still flashed over the tables. He wondered which one Clare had sat at, just last night.

He marched to the staircase, ignoring the innkeeper who called out angrily at him. As his boot landed on the first step, he heard Venn intercept the innkeeper, and by the time Wilf was at the top of the stairs with a dagger drawn, Venn called up to him, "First door on the left."

Wilf was aware of soldiers coming up behind him, but he ignored them as he shoved the door open. His eyes sliced over the room.

Rumpled beds. A small window. Rank chamber pots.

Deserted.

He let out a growl.

The Rose stood just inside the room, his guards close by. The assassin eyed the space. "Salim is paranoid. He doesn't stay in one place too long. He'll be in a different inn every night until he goes to do business with his client."

Vera edged into the room, Venn holding her hand. The girl's eyes fluttered around the space, finally settling on the corner.

Wilf followed her gaze, and he spotted an oddly-shaped bit of metal. He crouched, lifting it with a frown.

"Oh, fates," Vera whispered. "That's Clare's. Her tin soldier. It was a gift from her brother."

Wilf stared at the mangled tin in his palm. It had been melted beyond recognition, but he knew Vera was right. He'd only seen Clare hold the toy soldier a few times, but he knew she always carried it with her.

What did it mean that she'd left it? What had it done to her, to see it destroyed?

"This is my fault," Vera breathed.

When she swayed, Venn scooped her into his arms, one arm under her knees, the other behind her back. Her head fell against his chest, and Venn's expression tensed. "Wilf, we need to go. She needs a physician, and we gain nothing by staying here."

Wilf's fingers clenched over the melted tin.

Clare had been here. She'd needed him.

And, just like in Sedah, he had been too late.

Wilf watched as Venn tugged the door closed. "How is she?" he asked, his voice rumbling in the shadowed hallway of the Black Scorpion.

They had arrived a couple of hours ago, and while Venn had overseen Vera's visit with a physician, Wilf had been talking with the reinforcements Serene had sent. They were a mixture of Devendran soldiers and Mortisian guards from Serai Nadir's manor. They'd been here for two days, combing the inns and taverns the Rose had listed before they'd left the Nadir estate.

They hadn't found anything yet.

"She's sleeping." Venn's jaw stiffened as he leaned back against the wall beside the closed door. His arms crossed over his chest, his knuckles white. "Her wrists were rubbed raw. She's covered in bruises, and she's exhausted. They barely fed her. She says Clare was treated just as badly—worse, even."

Wilf turned away, the mangled tin soldier grasped in his fist.

The midday meal was upon them and the sounds of laughter and eating drifted up the stairs. It felt wrong in every way.

"I was just coming to tell you that we're heading out to check the three inns the Rose named," Wilf said. "I want you to stay with Vera. I'll leave two men with you."

Venn's forehead creased. "Vera told us Salim's client wouldn't arrive for a few days. If the Rose is right, then Salim won't be in those taverns until then. We probably won't find Clare tonight."

"I won't stop looking."

Venn bowed his head. "I'm worried too, Wilf."

"I know."

The younger man blew out his breath. "Do you think Bennick is alive?" The words were unexpected, but Venn immediately answered his own question. "He has to be." He scrubbed at his face, the heels of his hands pressing against closed eyes. "We have to find Clare. It will kill Bennick if we don't."

"I'll find her."

Venn said nothing for a while. When he did speak, his voice was soft. "Vera didn't tell me everything. She was too exhausted. But Salim . . . he's a sadist. He tortured them for no reason." His hands rolled to fists. "He needs to die."

Wilf pushed away from the wall, his voice a dark growl. "He will."

CHAPTER 26

DESFAN

DESFAN WAS BENT OVER PAPERWORK IN HIS father's office, and Karim read silently in the corner. The council may be taking a break from their duties during the holiday, but Desfan did not have that luxury. He did enjoy having fewer meetings, though.

A knock sounded, and Desfan glanced at the door. "Enter."

Liam stepped in. The Rydenic prince's usual smile was absent, though he did offer a slight bow. "Serjah Desfan, I'm sorry to interrupt."

"It's no trouble." Desfan gestured for Liam to sit in the chair across from him. "What can I help you with?"

"I'm afraid I just received word from our ship in the harbor," the prince said grimly. "The captain informed me of an incident

223

that happened last night. Some of the Rydenic sailors on shore leave were accosted by several Mortisians. They were beaten in the street, just outside a dockside tavern."

Desfan inwardly swore. The last thing he needed was a political incident with Ryden. "I'm so sorry."

"I appreciate that. The captain told me he's had his hands full trying to keep his men from retaliating. I thought we could devise a plan of action together."

"Of course. Were any names learned?"

"Of the Mortisians? No."

"That will make it nearly impossible for justice to be served. Perhaps we should announce that peace talks are beginning? That might appease people and release some of the tension."

"Or serve to encourage it." Liam rested his bearded chin on laced fingers, his elbows propped on the chair arms. "I've heard whispers that the Rose was hired to kill Princess Serene. If members of your own council would go so far to stop an alliance with Devendra, I'm not sure publicly entering peace talks with Mortise is a wise move for Ryden."

"That was a singular event, and those responsible are in prison."

"Still." Liam cocked his head. "I hope you can appreciate my caution."

"I do." Desfan leaned forward, his arms braced on his desk. "Perhaps you would feel more comfortable entering peace talks after my betrothal agreement is legalized? It would send a positive message for you and Grayson to be in attendance at the signing. I would like to have you both at my side."

The corner of Liam's mouth lifted. "It's an honor to be invited to such a historic event."

"It can be the official start of our peace talks, then," Desfan said, hoping for actual commitment.

Liam indulged him with a nod. "I think that timing will be excellent."

That was one victory, at least. "In the meantime, I think it would be wise to arrange Mortisian guards to escort your men when they wander Duvan. I don't want them to feel trapped, but I want to keep them safe."

"A kind offer. Thank you."

"I'll have something organized by tonight."

There was another knock on the door, and this time a guard stuck his head in. "Apologies for the interruption, Serjah, but Serai Tamar Nadir seeks an immediate audience with you."

It took Desfan a brief moment to place the name. When he did, he straightened in his chair. Serai Nadir lived near the border, and was the first Mortisian noble Serene would have stayed with. Perhaps she had news of Serene's progress. He rose, facing Liam with an apologetic look. "Was there anything else?"

"No, that should be all for now." Liam pushed up from the chair, clasping his hands behind his back. "Thank you again, Serjah, for sparing a moment."

"Of course."

The guard pushed the door wider so the Rydenic prince could slip out into the hall. Then Serai Nadir stepped into the room, half a dozen people following her inside. Two maids, and an assortment of guards that were Devendran, Mortisian, and even Zennorian.

Karim set his book aside—which he probably hadn't been reading since Liam entered the room—and stood, shooting a look to the guard at the door. The guard read the silent order, and remained in the room.

Desfan frowned, confusion rippling through him. "Serai Nadir, this is an unexpected visit."

The Mortisian noblewoman dropped into a curtsy, her expression serious. "I'm afraid there have been many unexpected things recently."

A pit yawned in his gut. "Has anything happened to Princess Serene?"

"Despite the attempts of many, she is safe."

Desfan opened his mouth to demand specifics, but he was distracted by the maid on Serai Nadir's right. She was part Zennorian, part Devendran, her skin a deep and beautiful brown. She had impeccable posture and sharp blue eyes that imperiously examined every inch of him, no hint of deference for who he was and no acknowledgement of her lower station.

He got the distinct impression he hadn't measured up to her expectations.

Her chin lifted and she took a small step toward him, putting her just forward of Serai Nadir. "I have many questions, Serjah Desfan," she said in Mortisian, her tone rich and direct. "I'm especially curious to know what you and Prince Liam Kaelin were discussing."

Desfan stared at her. It took his dull-witted brain far too many heartbeats to realize who he was looking at, never mind that he had never met her before. His cheeks warmed and he quickly bowed his head. "Princess Serene. I'm sorry I didn't know you at once."

She arched a perfectly sculpted eyebrow. "That *was* the point of the disguise."

The barb in her words caught him by surprise, but he managed to keep that from his expression. He came around the desk, noting that the two Devendran guards edged slightly closer to their princess. He tried to set them at ease by hanging back a step. "May I ask why a disguise was necessary?"

"I was the target of Mortisians one too many times," Serene said. "It's also why I'm here earlier than expected. I didn't particularly relish the thought of being attacked at every stop in Mortise. I do hope you'll offer my apologies to anyone I offended."

Desfan looked between Serene and Serai Nadir. "I—I'm sorry. What exactly happened?"

"I won't bore you with all the details," Serene said, "but I suppose my patience with Mortise ran thin when Ser Zephan, a member of your council, first hired mercenaries to kill me in Halbrook, and then orchestrated the prisoner exchange into a trap designed to kill me."

"Ser Zephan?" That made no sense. "I sent Ser Ashear to handle the exchange."

"Ser Ashear was murdered by Zephan. He also killed all the prisoners and replaced them with his own men and some Devendran rebels who sought to kill me."

"Serjah, I was there," Serai Nadir said. "I saw it happen."

Desfan reeled. He leaned back on his desk, his hands gripping the wooden edge. Ashear was dead. Zephan had betrayed them— no wonder he had not responded to any of Desfan's letters. And all those prisoners . . . "Fates," he breathed.

Serene's tone was even as she continued. "Though Devendra received no prisoners, I turned over the Mortisian prisoners to Serai Nadir, as she agreed to help them find their way home. I attempted to return Ser Zephan to you for a trial, but he was killed by Mortisian mercenaries when they ambushed my carriage."

Desfan felt the ball of lead in his stomach grow heavier. This was far worse than anything he'd imagined.

Serene's lips pressed together. Beautiful lips, it was true. He hardly dared think it, when she stared at him with such cool intensity. "I've lost many good men. The prisoners you promised were butchered. My life has been in peril from Mortise before I ever crossed into your country. I've had every reason to refuse this alliance, but I pressed on because I believed you had nothing to do with these attacks against me."

Even clothed as a servant, there was nothing deferential about the way Serene stood before him. She watched him unblinking, and in that moment nothing scared him more than the thought of marrying her.

Fates, she was still staring at him, and he needed to answer. "Princess Serene, I had nothing to do with any of these attempts against your life. I had no idea Ser Zephan had taken such violent steps to keep you from reaching Duvan, and I'm so sorry for the danger you were in, and for all the lives lost. The unrest in Mortise has been great."

Karim made a sound in his throat. A warning perhaps? As if Desfan could keep the truth from Serene when it would be so obvious; every person in the castle was still talking about all the new council members. And, with Ashear and Zephan dead, there were two new seats to fill. *Fates.*

The Devendran princess would hear all of Mortise's woes soon enough. It would be better to come from him. "Things have been unsettled here," Desfan began.

"And my journey hasn't been?" she asked.

"I didn't mean to imply that."

"Then what *are* you trying to imply?"

Desfan took a slow breath, but his skin still felt too tight as she eyed him. "I'm afraid I've had to make several arrests recently.

Half of my council were traitors to the crown, and . . ." His words trailed off.

Her gaze narrowed. "And what?"

He wracked his brain for the best way to say this. "I recently learned that several of them conspired against the alliance. More than that, they hired the Rose to kill you."

Silence cut through the room.

One of the princess's guards—a serious looking man with a very obvious scar cutting over his cheek—shifted closer to Serene.

"They're all in prison, of course," Desfan hurried to assure them.

Serene lifted an eyebrow. "Excellent news. Now I only have to worry about what the other half of your council has planned for me."

This was not going well.

Serene glanced at the other maid, and Desfan followed her look. He knew instantly this was another noblewoman in disguise. It was in the graceful way she stood. She had black hair, and though she shared similarities with Serene, she was shorter. Her skin was darker, and she had a gentler face—something quite welcome in this tense moment. She viewed him with something like apologetic sympathy.

"My cousin," Serene introduced them, waving her hand toward the beautiful woman. "Princess Imara Aimeth Buhari."

Desfan could at least muster a little grace for this royal greeting. He stepped forward and bowed. "Princess Imara, it's a pleasure to meet you."

Imara smiled gently, offering a graceful curtsy. "Serjah Desfan, it's an honor."

Serene seemed marginally less honored by his presence. Impatience thinned her voice. "Serjah Desfan, I would like to know why Prince Liam of Ryden was in a private audience with you. I heard that he and his brother Grayson had been invited to Mortise to potentially enter peace talks, but I want to know what you were discussing. Is it an alliance Devendra should be worried about?"

Desfan chafed at her tone, but he couldn't blame her for her irritation. "Prince Liam and I were merely discussing some issues regarding his ship in the harbor. He has resisted any entrance into peace talks, stating he would wait until your arrival."

"How considerate of him," Serene said dryly. "Do you really think Ryden wants peace?"

Desfan thought of Grayson. "I think some people in Ryden might. But certainly not all."

"Not exactly an encouraging response, but probably truthful." Her spine straightened. "I require a suite of rooms, and I'd like to be placed near Imara and Serai Nadir. She is one Mortisian I trust."

Desfan recognized the personal dig, but didn't let himself so much as blink. "I'll see to your accommodations at once. Will you be rested enough to join the court for a formal dinner tonight?"

Serene's eyes never left him, and Desfan had never felt so cornered. "I look forward to an official welcome to Mortise. We'll see if it's any better than the unofficial ones I've been subjected to thus far."

CHAPTER 27

SERENE

"HE'S VOLUNTEERED ADDITIONAL SECURITY for the hallway," Cardon said.

"Desfan?" Serene asked.

Cardon nodded, stepping up to the settee where she sat. "I believe you were right. Desfan isn't to blame for any of the attempts on your life. He reacted with honesty." A shadow entered her bodyguard's gaze. "It's the rest of his court I worry about."

Serene agreed, but she grunted. "I haven't decided how much I trust him yet."

"He's as handsome as they say," Imara said from beside her.

She frowned at her cousin. "His looks are the least of my concerns."

"That's because there's nothing to be concerned about. He's utterly dashing."

Serene rolled her eyes. "I'm more interested in his intelligence." Which was in question, after learning he'd only recently flushed out a handful of murderous traitors from his council.

"You were cruel to him," Imara said. "You barely gave him a chance to speak, and you kept pinning him in difficult positions."

"I was trying to catch him off-guard so I could better gauge him."

Imara shook her head. "Really, as far as forced marriages go, it could be much worse. He could be a decade older than you and turning gray."

She was very aware of Cardon watching them. Her cheeks warmed a little. "Imara, stop being ridiculous for a moment, if you can manage it." She focused on her guard. "Do you think we should tell Desfan about Clare?"

Cardon shook his head. "It would be best to keep quiet, I think. There's nothing he could do to help us at this point, and if—*when* Clare makes it to Duvan, we'll want to keep quiet about your having a decoy. Desfan may be told eventually, but we don't want anyone else to know."

Serene nodded, accepting Cardon's advice.

Fates, she wished she could wait to announce her presence in Duvan. She wanted to give Clare and Vera as much time as possible, in case Wilf and Venn hadn't found them yet. But if she delayed announcing her presence, she would risk news reaching Devendra that she'd been killed. Her father would react badly—not in grief for losing her, no doubt, but for the perceived betrayal of Mortise—and that could spark a war. Her rebels wouldn't respond well to news of her death, either.

No, she couldn't delay any longer. She had to trust that Wilf and Venn would secure Clare and Vera before news of Serene's arrival reached Salim and his mercenaries.

Imara's brow wrinkled. "Do you think the one who hired Salim might be one of the men Desfan imprisoned?"

Serene frowned. "I hadn't thought of that." If the mercenaries were at a meeting place and no one showed up to pay them . . . what would that mean for Clare and Vera?

"They'll be fine," Cardon said. "Wilf and Venn—they'll make sure of it." He took a step back. "I'm going to join Dirk outside. We want to speak with our borrowed guards about a few things." He retreated, crossing the spacious sitting lounge attached to Serene's suite. Once he was gone, the only sounds in the room drifted from the bedroom, where Bridget was busy unpacking.

"You're sullen today," Imara stated.

"I've got a headache."

"You've got a scowl on your face. And it's not just because of Clare and Vera."

That was true enough. She wasn't sure what she'd expected when she saw Desfan for the first time. Perhaps she'd wanted to feel something. Be impressed by him. See a confident diplomat, or that pirate they all claimed he was—someone who could help take down her father and brother.

After that brief meeting . . . Well, she doubted he would even be interested in her problems, when he clearly had so many of his own.

Imara patted her knee. "You can't judge him with one meeting."

Once again, her cousin proved how well she knew her. "You really are very astute."

233

"I know. My intuition has always been spot-on. And for what it's worth, I think you're lucky in your future husband."

The slight edge in Imara's voice snared all of Serene's attention. Her brow furrowed. "You know, we haven't discussed *your* betrothal."

Imara drew back a little. "Well, we've been fairly busy, with so many people trying to kill you."

"No one is trying to kill me right now," Serene pointed out. "Why don't you tell me about your future husband?"

"There's not much to tell." She smoothed a hand over her skirt, as if pressing out a wrinkle that wasn't there.

Serene's eyes narrowed. "You're avoiding the topic." Fates, Imara had been dodging questions about her betrothal since she'd met up with Serene. *Why?* "Do you hate him?"

Her cousin snorted. "Don't be so dramatic."

"Then tell me about him."

"Must you always be so intense about things?"

"It's my usual disposition, I'm afraid."

Imara released an impressive sigh. "Fine. His name is Eilan Skyer. He's twenty-five years old and the leader of the Kabu clan."

Shock rippled through her. "Kabu? They're the most hostile toward your family's rule."

"Sentiments can change."

Yet they rarely did when they ran so deep. And certainly not quickly. Serene frowned. "I never met Skyer while I was in Zennor."

"That's because he lives in the jungle." Imara crossed one knee over the other, her back straightening. Her expression was too smooth. "I'm really not sure what more there is to tell."

There was no fates-blasted way Serene would abandon this conversation now. "Twenty-five is young to be the leader of a tribe."

"He's a skilled warrior."

"You're avoiding again."

"I'm just not sure what you want to know."

"Everything."

The skin around Imara's eyes tightened. "Skyer's father led the Kabu before him. He challenged his father about two years ago and won the right to lead. And before you ask, he didn't kill his father. He exercised mercy and banished him instead, along with his mother and siblings."

Serene arched a brow. "He sounds delightful."

Imara ignored that. "He started talks with my father several months ago, and he's been the chief liaison with the other clans. He wants to work more closely with the monarchy so the clans can have a voice in court."

"So, he's a peace-seeking warrior?"

"Yes."

"And he overthrew his own father and banished his family?"

"That's what I said." Imara shook her head. "You know things are done differently in the clans."

That was true enough. Serene supposed she wasn't one to pass judgement, since she was actively mounting a rebellion against her father and brother—and she had no intentions of simply exiling them. Still. This was Imara's future husband. It didn't sit well. "Is he handsome?" she asked.

"He's ruggedly appealing."

"Somehow that seems lacking."

Imara rolled her eyes. "He's tall, broad-shouldered, and has dark eyes. He has khalmin tattoos inked all over his face and body in red, black, and silver to match the Kabu colors. They mark his station and his kills. His title is Warrior Sky Painter."

"Sky Painter? Is he a warrior artist, then?"

"You are far too literal, cousin."

"What exactly does his title mean, then?"

Imara sighed. "Deep in the jungle, the sky is not actually visible, so for the tribes, the sky is the canopy made by the trees. Skyer is known for painting the leaves with the blood of his enemies." The corner of her mouth raised fractionally. "Quite the legacy, isn't it?"

Serene's voice came out a little hard. "Your parents approve of this match?"

"Indeed. Mother thinks Skyer will be the perfect remedy for my more mischievous side." Though Imara smiled, Serene saw stiffness at the corners.

"I won't abide anyone changing you," she said firmly.

"Oh, he won't succeed," Imara assured her.

"How many times have you spoken with him?"

"Twice."

"Do you like him?"

"Do you like Desfan?" Imara threw back.

Serene frowned. "That's hardly fair. I don't know him yet."

Imara lifted one shoulder. "I don't know Skyer, either. I can't pass judgement yet."

"The fact that you keep calling him *Skyer* instead of *Eilan* has not escaped my notice."

"He's formal. He can be a bit dull, really."

"Considering everything you just told me about him, I would say Skyer is probably anything *but* dull."

Imara scoffed. "Wait until you have dinner with him."

"Oh, I can't wait."

The Zennorian princess shook her head. "You have nothing to be worried about, Serene. Do you really think my father would make me marry a horrible man?"

That was a good point. Serene admired and respected King Zaire Buhari. Her uncle was fair, brilliant, and kind. And he loved his family excessively.

Imara reached over and closed her hand around Serene's. She squeezed gently. "I promise you, I'm fine. We both knew that arranged marriages were in our futures, and I'm happy to serve Zennor. Peace with the clans is worth any cost."

"It's not worth your happiness."

Imara's smile was a little rueful. "And what of your happiness?"

"I thought you said Desfan was dashing?"

"Oh, he is. And I think he has every potential to make you very happy, if you'll let him."

Serene let out a long breath. "I suppose I was a little hostile, wasn't I?"

"It's fine to make a man squirm a little. But you may want to try a gentler approach at dinner. Speaking of, I should go and get ready. It's my debut in the Mortisian court, and I aim to impress."

Serene watched her cousin rise, and felt a tug in her heart. "I haven't thanked you."

Imara glanced over at her. "For what?"

"For being here. For staying with me, despite all the danger. It's easier being here, knowing I'm not alone."

Her cousin smiled, her dark eyes softening. "Of course. I wouldn't dream of being anywhere else."

Serene's lips curved in a returning smile. "You know, most people underestimate you because you're small and excessively pleasant."

"But you don't?"

"Never. You're quite masterful at manipulation, my dear."

Imara's eyes rounded. "What a thing to say!"

"You did con your way here, didn't you?"

Her rounded chin lifted. "I have an official letter from my father, you might recall."

Serene chuckled. "I suppose what I'm trying to say is that I know you can take care of yourself no matter where you are. Here in the Mortisian court or home with Skyer. I hope you know I do believe in you."

"I know. And I appreciate it." Imara's lips pressed together. "You *will* win the respect of Mortise, Serene." Her eyes twinkled. "And the love of that exceedingly handsome serjah."

Serene rolled her eyes. "You may go now."

Imara's laugh rang through the room as she left.

The Mortisian dining hall was a vast room with stone pillars along two walls that gave direct access to balconies overlooking the sea. Large iron candelabras lit with hundreds of candles hung from the vaulted ceiling, and a mezzanine ringed the room above them. It was a space for musicians and singers, their melodies drifting down to settle on the floor below.

The air was flooded with the scent of spicy meats and fragrant seasonings. Salty sea air carried in by the night breeze mingled with the expensive perfumes worn by the nobles who stood around the room. No one had taken their seats at the ridiculously long table that was laid with colorful cloths and set with glittering dishes. It would have been laughable to call this an intimate gathering, however—even if only one table was in use. It stretched the length of the room.

Conversation buzzed as clusters of brightly dressed nobles talked and sipped wine. Everyone seemed to be awaiting Desfan's appearance.

Serene stood with Imara, the two of them backed by their guards. Though the foreign atmosphere was intimidating, she kept her chin lifted and her diplomatic smile in place.

Imara wore a beautiful emerald gown cut in a Zennorian pattern that left her shoulders bare. The skirt—detailed with flowers in black thread—skimmed the floor.

Serene had chosen to wear Devendran blue, the dark color a definite statement among all the brightly dressed Mortisians. Bridget had piled her hair atop her head in a complicated bun, leaving some tendrils to curl around her face. She had taken care to weave in the widow's braid, so it would go unseen, as always.

Never unfelt, though.

She had always loved the story behind the widow's braid, though she'd never imagined she would wear one. Not until that awful night. She had only been sixteen, but her heart had been shattered. The devastation was not, perhaps, that which a widow would face. But it was enough.

Serene was not at all surprised when Prince Liam Kaelin spotted them right away and made his way over. The Rydenic prince was known to be a spy, probably with several identities. He was known as the Shadow of Ryden, and Serene had fantasized about capturing him and questioning him. She wondered if he knew the truth about what had happened to her mother—that Newlan had poisoned her. Perhaps he even knew about Clare being her decoy. She also wondered if he knew she was the leader of a rebellion. It was a secret she guarded closely. Only a handful of the rebel leaders even knew she was in charge. But if he knew, then he had the power to tear her down.

Liam drew to a stop before her and tipped his head respectfully. "Princess Serene Demoi and Princess Imara Buhari, I presume?"

"Indeed. And you are Prince Liam Kaelin?" Serene asked, pretending ignorance. After all, she'd seen him outside Desfan's office earlier today, but he didn't know that, as she'd been in disguise.

Unless he had spotted her then, too.

Fates blasted secrets. Unless they were her own, they were terribly inconvenient.

His smile widened just a little, making her wonder if she had actually fooled him at all. "You're quite correct. It truly is a pleasure to meet you both."

"The pleasure is ours."

Imara peeked past him. "And you must be Prince Grayson."

Serene followed Imara's gaze, spotting the young man standing behind his brother. She had been so focused on Liam, she hadn't noticed his shadow.

The infamous Black Hand.

He was striking, in a disturbing sort of way. His gray-eyed gaze was icy and critical, his mouth set in a line that bent toward the beginnings of a frown. He was only seventeen years old, and yet his reputation had spread through all of Eyrinthia. While Liam's features carried warmth in his tanned skin, pleasant smile, and brown eyes, Grayson was all darkness. He wore black clothes, including black boots and gloves. His dark hair was a little messy, the ends falling across his brow. His cheekbones were sharp, his face handsome except for the light scars that nicked over his skin. She couldn't read anything in his expression. While young in years, there was a hardness about him. He watched her like a predator, measuring every part of her in an evaluation she did not intend to fail. Still, there was a quiet and deadly air that screamed he could kill her before she could even blink.

The hairs on the back of her neck lifted as he continued to stare at her.

"It's so nice to meet you," Imara said, breaking the tense silence. She smiled and extended a hand, which Grayson eyed briefly before taking.

He touched his lips to her knuckles in a short, obligatory brush before pulling his hand away, his leather gloves creaking as his hands fell back to his sides. "It's a pleasure to meet you," he said, his voice low and deep.

From the corner of her eye, Serene saw Cardon watching Grayson carefully. He clearly viewed Grayson's lethal potential just as she had.

"You're both as stunning as the rumors say," Liam said with a charming smile.

"You're too kind," Serene said.

His smile tipped wider. "I only speak the truth."

That, Serene doubted.

A little fanfare from the musicians above them had them all turning to the main doors where Desfan stood.

He wore a scarlet kurta lined in black and gold. His brown eyes glittered in the candlelight and his dark hair curled beneath the rim of his shining gold crown. His shoulders were wide and strong, his stance firm and unyielding. She could see in him that mixture of rogue sailor and noble ruler. Strange, how all this time she had imagined those two parts of him would be opposing. In this moment, she could see how every part of him—the gambler, the pirate-hunter, the serjah—all came together to form Desfan Cassian.

He was undeniably attractive, and he grew even more so when he offered a half-smile and waved for everyone who had bowed to rise. And yet, even when he found her in the crowd, her heart pounded steadily on, unaffected by his attention.

He started toward her, his bodyguard close behind him, but he was almost immediately waylaid by a nobleman.

"I think they're afraid of us," Imara whispered, none too quietly.

Serene *had* noticed that no one else in the room had approached them.

The corner of Liam's mouth twitched. "I can't imagine they would be afraid of me. Or Grayson. It must be your beauty that intimidates them, Princess Imara."

Serene rolled her eyes, but Imara grinned. "You are quite the flatterer, Prince Liam."

"I believe," a new voice intruded, "they simply don't know what to make of royals from three kingdoms chatting so easily without a representative of their own in the group."

Serene watched the old Mortisian woman who relied heavily on her cane as she limped closer. Her face was heavily wrinkled, but there was a spark in her dark eyes that bespoke a feistiness Serene instantly liked.

Liam handled the introductions. "Princess Serene, Princess Imara, this is Serai Yahri. She holds the senior seat on the Mortisian council."

Yahri shot him a look. "Thank you, Prince Liam. But I assure you, I'm quite capable of speaking for myself."

"Of course." Liam tipped his head. "My apologies."

Yahri's gaze swiveled to the Black Hand, who had become a silent spectator. "Prince Grayson, I've not yet had the chance to thank you for saving my life in the library."

"No thanks are necessary," Grayson said, color touching his cheeks.

"I find the saving of my life to be a deeply meaningful thing," Yahri countered wryly. "Please, accept my thanks."

Grayson dipped his chin. "Very well."

Serene was suddenly very curious about *that* story. She would need to gather information quickly so she could learn the dynamics of the court—especially how Liam and Grayson fit into it.

Yahri turned to Serene. "Princess, I'm so pleased you arrived safely. The serjah relayed to me what happened at the prisoner exchange, as well as on the road with those mercenaries. On behalf of all Mortise, I wish to extend my deepest sympathy."

"Thank you. I appreciate that."

Imara shifted beside her, drawing Serene's attention to Tamar Nadir. The Mortisian noblewoman looked as beautiful as ever, her long dark hair spilling down her back, her pink sari draped over her willowy form. She did appear a little hesitant to approach them, but Imara waved her forward. "Please, you must join us," the Zennorian princess insisted.

Another round of introductions followed, and Serene didn't fail to notice the way Dirk watched Tamar—nor the way the Mortisian woman's eyes kept darting to him. On their journey to Duvan, Serene had found them traveling together often, talking quietly and exchanging smiles. Dirk was always the first to offer his hand when she stepped from the carriage, and he was always the last one she spoke to each night.

It warmed Serene's heart, though she would be lying if she didn't also feel a pang of longing. She darted a quick look at Cardon, but he was still watching Grayson.

Yahri straightened suddenly, looking beyond their group. "Razan! Do come here." She focused back on Serene and the others. "Most of the council left the city to celebrate the Dawn of Eyrinthia at home, but a few remain. Razan Krayt is one of them."

Serene did not miss the way Liam narrowed in on the beautiful young woman coming to join them. She looked to be in her early twenties, and she wore a sari similar in style to Tamar, but hers was a stunning turquoise that accentuated the warm tones of her brown skin and dark hair, which was piled onto her head and carefully held in place with ivory combs.

Razan Krayt curtsied gracefully to the royals. "It's an honor to meet you all, and to have you in Duvan."

"These are certainly historic times," Desfan said, appearing suddenly beside them. He greeted everyone individually, though his gaze lingered on Serene. "I'm sorry I wasn't here to meet you. I was waylaid."

"It's no matter," Serene said. "I can walk into a room on my own." Imara's slippered foot bounced against Serene's ankle beneath the cover of their skirts. Serene forced a smile as she viewed Desfan and added, "But I'm glad you're here now."

The serjah of Mortise smiled as well, and she wondered what was wrong with her. She needed to marry this man. Not just for peace between their kingdoms, but for his support in her rebellion. Besides, he was handsome. Flirting with him should not feel like a chore. And yet, all she could concentrate on was Cardon standing just behind her.

Liam turned toward Razan. "You're not from Duvan, are you?"

"No, I'm from Madihr. It's the largest city on the island of Dorma."

"I would love to hear all about it," Liam said with a charming half-smile. "And you."

There was a low grunt, and Serene's eyes shot to Desfan's body-guard. The man's eyes were narrowed on Liam, who remained oblivious.

Or was trying to appear that way.

Desfan cleared his throat. "Perhaps we should find our seats."

"I *am* starving," Imara said quickly, ever the peacemaker.

Desfan's smile was grateful. "Well, we can't have that." He of-fered his arm to Serene, and she took it. She was slightly sur-prised by the ripple of muscle she felt under his sleeve, though considering his past and all the rumors about him, she shouldn't have been shocked.

He led Serene toward the head of the table, their bodyguards and the others left to trail behind them. Serene kept her voice low as they walked. "Is there some disagreement between your bodyguard and Prince Liam that I should be aware of?"

Desfan sighed. "Let us hope not."

It wasn't a very descriptive answer, but she sensed it was gen-uine.

Fates, she had a lot to catch up on.

CHAPTER 28

GRAYSON

GRAYSON ENTERED ONE OF THE MANY ROYAL gardens on the palace grounds, his boots scuffing over the gravel path. They were only three days into the Dawn of Eyrinthia celebrations, and he was already weary of the feasts, parties, and assorted religious ceremonies. He participated when expected and kept to his rooms whenever he could. Desfan had sought him out twice for sparring, and Ranon had found him at every long dinner he attended.

Liam was avoiding him. So was Arav, which was a decided improvement.

The arrival of Princess Serene yesterday had caused a lot of talk at last night's feast. She and her cousin, Princess Imara, were clearly related, though Imara's skin was darker and her smile much more pleasant.

Grayson had already decided before leaving Ryden that he wouldn't abduct her as Peter had ordered, but even one meeting assured him he would never take her to marry his brother. She was far too kind. Peter would ruin her, and Kaelins had ruined enough as it was.

Wandering the garden in hopes of escaping his churning thoughts, the last thing he needed was to round the corner of a hedge and come face to face with Ser Sifa.

Ranon's father looked just as unpleasantly surprised to see the Rydenic prince.

Grayson's neck was stiff, but he offered a slight inclination of his head. A deferential kindness he didn't really feel, but decided he should offer anyway, considering the man was Mia's uncle. "Ser Sifa."

There was no nod of respect from Sifa. His spine steeled. "What are you doing here?"

Irritation clawed at Grayson, but he fought to keep his voice measured. "I'm taking a walk in the garden. It's allowed," he added, remembering Sifa's protest the first time they'd met in the palace art gallery.

Sifa's eyes narrowed, his bald head glinting in the sun. "You have no guards?"

"I don't really need them."

"No. I mean the serjah doesn't have you under guard?"

"Why would he? I'm not an enemy."

"You're *my* enemy." It seemed he might say more, but his jaw suddenly tightened as he forced some semblance of control. "As it happens, this saves me from writing you a letter. I want you to stay away from my son."

Grayson hadn't expected that. "Why?"

"Your imitation of friendship with him is a mockery of what you did to my family."

"I did nothing to your family." But that was a lie, wasn't it? He may not have helped kill Mia's family, but he was keeping her from them. Even now, by not telling Sifa that she was alive, he was stealing her from him.

"I don't want you near Ranon," the middle-aged man insisted, his tone firm. "You aren't welcome here. You or any of your kind."

"*My kind?*" Grayson's hands fisted at his sides. "I'm Rydenic. Not some inhuman animal."

"From where I stand, you're one and the same."

The muscles in his neck tensed, bracing for a fight he knew he shouldn't give in to.

The crunch of gravel made him glance away from Sifa, and he blinked in surprise to see Princess Imara.

His surprise grew tenfold when she very deliberately beamed at him. "There you are!" She crossed to him and threaded her arm through his. "I've been looking everywhere for you."

Grayson stared down at her. What in all the blasted fates was happening? Had she mistaken him for someone else?

Not likely. He didn't exactly blend in.

Imara looked to Sifa, her smile easy, her eyelashes fluttering a little. "I do hope you'll forgive me for interrupting, but Prince Grayson promised to show me around the garden."

Sifa's eyes darted between them, a vein throbbing in his forehead.

Imara didn't wait for a response. She flexed her grip on Grayson's arm. "Shall we?"

She didn't leave him a choice. She tugged him away, leaving

Sifa behind.

The princess retained her grip on Grayson's arm for several turns around the hedges before she finally released him. "Sorry about that," she said, taking a step back. "I hope I didn't startle you too much."

Grayson eyed her. "Why did you do that?"

"I heard the way he spoke to you. It wasn't right. My mother always said that women can stop more wars in a day than a man can start in a lifetime, all with a little diplomatic smile." She smiled then. "I'm Imara Buhari. We met briefly last night."

"I remember."

She was hard to forget. Despite her small size, she had a large presence, as well as a smile that was ever in place, yet seemed sincere.

"You don't really have to show me the gardens," she said. "But it would be nice if you did."

He didn't know how to respond to that. Or any of this, really. He'd never been approached by a young woman before. Most seemed to have enough sense of self-preservation to keep their distance.

Imara chuckled. "I think I've broken the Black Viper."

His forehead creased. "The Black Viper?"

She nodded. "It's what we call you in Zennor."

He had a Zennorian nickname. He wasn't sure why that seemed even stranger than this conversation, but it did.

The princess's head tilted to the side. "I've made you uncomfortable."

It wasn't a question, but he responded anyway. "No."

The corner of her mouth quirked. "Your words say one thing, but your tone says another. Not to mention your arm was tense as a bowstring when I touched you." Her eyes rounded a little. "Prince Grayson, do I make you *nervous?*"

"No." A bald-faced lie.

Still, she smiled. "Good. Between the two of us, I'd say you're the one to usually make others nervous."

He blinked.

She gave him a sort of wincing smile. "Sorry. I speak my mind too freely."

If it weren't so disconcerting, it might be refreshing. "It's all right," he said.

"It's a rather terrible habit in politics, unfortunately."

He cleared his throat. "Politics could stand to be a bit more straightforward."

"I agree completely!" Her head canted to the side. "You know, you're more charming than I thought you'd be. I think we'll be good friends."

Grayson nearly choked.

Imara only grinned.

His skin felt too tight. He glanced around for something to say—anything. "Where are your bodyguards?" Surely they would have something to say about her being so close to him.

"Oh, I slipped away from them hours ago."

Fates. If he'd wanted to abduct her, she would make it terribly easy for him. That was concerning, since Peter would probably send someone else after her, once Grayson returned without her.

Imara's smile was a little wry. "Sorry. I've been told that I can be overwhelming."

"It's fine."

She chuckled. "Clearly."

Grayson was saved from fumbling an answer as she spoke again.

"I suppose I've distressed you enough for one day." She dipped a brief curtsy. "I hope you have a pleasant afternoon, Prince Grayson. I look forward to our next meeting." Then she turned and swept away, her pink skirt gliding over the gravel path, leaving Grayson to stare after her, more than a little confused by what had just happened.

———◆———

Grayson left the garden behind soon after Imara disappeared. Thank the fates he didn't run into Sifa or anyone else. He had decided to spend the rest of the day in his room and was just approaching the guarded door when Liam stepped out of his own room. He stilled when he spotted Grayson.

The awkwardness between them was tangible. Grayson wondered what their Rydenic guards thought of it.

Liam cleared his throat. "I was hoping to find you."

"Really?" His brother's stiff stance said otherwise.

Liam ignored that. "Can we talk?"

Grayson didn't feel up for another conversation after Imara, but he dipped his chin. He pushed open his own door before Liam could offer his suite, and was aware of his brother trailing inside after him.

The sitting area was nearly an exact copy of Liam's room, but it felt more comfortable because it was *his* space.

"Do you mind if I pour a drink?" Liam asked.

"No." He watched his older brother move to a side table and prepare a drink from a decanter. It was more of that foul amber liquid, which Liam favored.

Once he'd taken a slow sip, Liam said, "You were right when you said I should share more of my plan with you. You have a right to know." He took another swallow, and Grayson tried to keep his expression neutral, though his heart beat a little faster.

His brother fingered the crystal tumbler in his hand, his eyes on the liquid inside. "Serene's early arrival was unexpected. But it made me realize that—even with variance—the timeline remains the same. The betrothal signing is still set for summer's end."

Grayson lifted his chin. "What exactly will we be doing?"

"I told you; we're going to start a war. Just not the one Father wants."

"I'm going to need more than that."

Liam's lips pressed into a line. "Father wants you to kill Serene in such a way that blame falls on Mortise. My plan is a little more . . . direct. At the betrothal signing, you will kill Serene very publicly, and everyone will know that Ryden is to blame. War will be inevitable—and not the war Father is prepared for."

Grayson's stomach dropped. "But . . ."

Liam lifted his free hand. "I know you don't want to be a killer. Fates know I don't want to be the spymaster of Ryden. But these are the best weapons we have, and I can't think of a more fitting way to destroy our father than to be exactly what he forced us to become."

Unease prickled across Grayson's skin. "If I kill Serene and everyone sees it, I'll be killed."

"No." He set aside his drink, the glass clinking against the wooden table. He stepped closer to Grayson, his voice low, his gaze bright. "I've thought of everything. I'll have men in the room to help secure our escape, and I've mapped out a series of exits we can take, in case any routes become blocked by guards. We'll board one of Rahim Nassar's ships with Akiva and Kazim. I've given orders for the Rydenic ship to sail at the same time, so if the Mortisians feel like giving chase, they'll pursue that ship. We'll be in southern Zennor in two weeks, and no one will ever find us. At that point, it will be safe for my man in Lenzen to act. He can free Mia, and in mere weeks you'll be reunited."

Grayson stared at his brother, but he wasn't really seeing Liam. He was seeing Mia. Her gentle smile. Her dark brown hair, falling in soft waves around her face. She was all that mattered. And yet . . .

His chest tightened. "I don't think killing Serene is necessary. If it's a war you want, why don't we just tell Desfan and Serene about Father's plan? We could join together in challenging Father."

Liam was already shaking his head. "That would never work. For one thing, they wouldn't believe us. They would assume we were manipulating them—no doubt on Father's orders. But more importantly, haven't you noticed that every blasted thing these royals do takes a ridiculously long time? They probably wouldn't be able to decide what color their forces should wear, and that would delay them from making any move. In the meantime, Father has plenty of spies that don't answer to me. They would tell him of our betrayal, and we would be killed—along with Mia—and then he would proceed to invade Mortise and Devendra."

"You don't know—"

"I've been plotting Father's downfall far longer than you," Liam interrupted firmly. "Trust me when I say this is the most efficient plan."

"I don't know if I can kill her." The words were out before Grayson could consider the wisdom in voicing them.

Liam's expression was a carefully held mask. "I'm trusting you, Grayson. It goes against every instinct I have, but I want you on my side. I need your total commitment. I'm afraid I can't leave this room with anything less."

"I don't want to kill her."

His bearded jaw stiffened. "There are many things in life we don't want to do. That hasn't stopped us from doing them."

"This is different."

"You're right. It *is* different. Because after we do this, we'll be free. Mia will be, too. And Father will be unable to come after us, because Ryden's forces will be overwhelmed by the combined might of Devendra, Mortise, and Zennor."

Grayson frowned. "Would they really all retaliate against Ryden for Serene's death?"

"Most likely. But I'm not leaving that up to chance. Which is why you're also going to kill Imara and Desfan."

His blood froze. "What?"

Liam set his hands on his hips. "Before I knew Imara would be here, I thought killing Serene would be enough to pull Zennor into retaliation against Ryden—her mother was a Buhari, after all, and King Zaire loves his niece. But the fates brought us Imara, and I will not lose this chance." He snorted. "To be honest, I feared how things might be different with so many new members of the council. But I've learned enough about them at this point that I feel confident about their unified response. When Desfan dies— and with Ryden to blame—the council will want revenge." His gaze sharpened. "I need you to focus on the three royals. My men and I will handle their guards, leaving you free to kill them. You're the fastest, and your reputation alone will spur fear. Word will quickly spread of what the Black Hand did, and three kingdoms will have a renewed hatred for Ryden."

And for me. Grayson's gut knotted.

How could he kill them? Desfan, who had somehow become his friend. Serene, a princess who had eyed him with distrust, but who didn't deserve such a dark fate. Imara, a young woman who barely knew Grayson, but had treated him with kindness.

All his life, he had been forced to be a monster. But this?

He shook his head slowly. "I can't do this."

Liam's hawk-like eyes narrowed. "You've killed before. What's different now?"

"This is murder."

"You're already a murderer."

The words were spoken evenly, but they pierced Grayson deeply.

"Father told me of his test," Liam continued. "You murdered an unarmed prisoner because Father told you to. You slit his throat and let him bleed out like an animal."

Sweat slicked his palms beneath his gloves. His stomach churned at the memory. "I didn't have a choice."

"Yes you did. Just as you have a choice now."

"This is completely different."

"Why? Because this time Mia isn't being threatened?"

Fire blazed through Grayson's blood. "Are you threatening her?"

"No." A shadow entered Liam's eyes. "I don't have to. She's living under constant threat. The only way for her to be safe is to be free of Father, and that can only happen if you trust me."

Grayson pushed to his feet and paced toward the nearest window. He could not form words. His hands shook as he gazed through the window. The city of Duvan sprawled below, and in the distance, the sea stretched to the far horizon.

His mind was inexplicably drawn to that moment on the street when he'd first arrived in Duvan; the little girl who had knocked into him had gaped at him in abject terror. The memory slammed into him, making it hard to breathe. That little girl's brown eyes had filled with horror as she stared up at him. It was an image that would never leave him.

Grayson did not want to be the stuff of nightmares.

If he assassinated Desfan, Serene, and Imara, that was exactly what he would be. And all of Eyrinthia would know it.

"This is Mia's best chance," Liam said quietly from behind him. "It's the only way for you to have her."

The strings of manipulation pulled, prickling the back of his neck. No matter the trust they'd begun to develop, Liam was still a Kaelin. Grayson felt that more now than ever.

He gritted his teeth, still facing the window. "Desfan is my friend."

"I know. That worked out far better than I could have hoped. He's already invited us to stand at his side at the signing. That wouldn't have happened without you."

Grayson's gut churned. From the beginning, Liam had encouraged his friendship with Desfan, all the while knowing that his plan was for Grayson to assassinate him.

He had underestimated his brother.

Glass scraped against wood as Liam retrieved his drink, sipping quietly behind Grayson. "Won't it be worth it?" he finally whispered. "Isn't our freedom—Mia's included—worth any cost? A final stain on our souls, but this would be the end of it, Grayson. We're so close. But I need you. I need you to tell me you can do this. That you *will* do it."

Grayson twisted to face his brother. "How does killing Desfan make sense? Who would lead Mortise to war?"

"Mortise isn't like any other kingdom. Cutting off the head of the snake won't leave them leaderless. Even though Desfan is the last Cassian, there will not be chaos. The laws are clear; in the event of a monarch's death with no heir apparent in line for the throne, the senior council member will take on the mantle of regent— that's Yahri. For one year, the crown won't be worn. It's a safeguard against anyone who might try to use assassination as a means to gain immediate power. During that year, the throne will be held by Yahri, and the country will be governed by council votes. And they will vote for war, Grayson. I'm sure of it."

He shook his head. "I think Desfan could be our ally, if we joined with him instead of—"

"Father forced me into politics and spying when I was barely old enough to walk," Liam interrupted curtly. "This is my area of expertise; the skills I've honed since childhood. Just like you were honed into Father's weapon. You don't enjoy killing, but it's what you're good at. It's what I need from you. What Mia's freedom requires."

His fingers burrowed into his gloved palms. "Are you saying you won't help her if I don't help you?"

"I'm stating fact. I *can't* help her if I don't have your help with this." His brother watched him a moment, and when he spoke again his voice was quiet. "I don't want to manipulate you into doing this. I'm not Father. Killing the royals must be your choice, or the plan will fail."

That feels like manipulation, Grayson thought. His face remained painfully smooth, totally closed off. He would not make the mistake of showing emotion around Liam again. He'd already trusted his brother too much.

He eyed Liam. "You want me to kill the royals. Is it your plan to abandon me here?"

"You truly think I'd do that?"

"It would be an easy solution. In the chaos, you could slip away. I'd be executed, and you would get your war against Father." And Mia would be caught in the middle.

Fates, why was she always in the middle?

Liam rolled his eyes. "I admit that was my original plan. But I decided long ago—back in Lenzen—that I wasn't capable of that. You're my brother, Grayson. The only Kaelin I desire to claim. I want you by my side, here and after. I won't betray you." His chin lowered, his stare intense. "Will you betray me?"

The question hung in the space between them. The air felt heavy, the room frozen. Grayson didn't think either one of them breathed.

In the end, Grayson gave the only answer he could. "No. I won't betray you."

Liam's shoulders loosened. "You won't regret it. Father will be destroyed, you will have Mia, and I . . ." He glanced past Grayson, eyeing some distant point through the window. His voice was soft as he finished. "I will finally know peace."

CHAPTER 29

MIA

HEAVY FOOTSTEPS ENTERED THE SITTING ROOM and Mia looked up from her painting to see Tyrell close the outer door.

"You're back early," she said, glancing toward the window where afternoon light filtered in.

"You haven't strained yourself?" he asked, concern in his voice.

She lowered her paintbrush, feeling only a slight ache in her side. "No. It's been lovely to paint." And she had so many things to capture. The library, in all its angles and lines. The stone banister on the staircase with its intricate and ancient etchings. She was even determined to capture the different views from Tyrell's windows.

"Just don't overdo it. Give yourself plenty of space to heal."

259

Tyrell lowered into a chair in the corner, studying her painting of the library doors, one of them cracked open. "You truly have a gift," he murmured. "Who knew there could be emotion in a door?"

Mia set aside her brush, snatching up a cloth to scrub some paint off her fingers. "How was your day?"

"Busy." Tyrell pushed a hand through his dark hair. His mouth opened, but words didn't come. Then he shook his head and said, "We had word from Grayson."

Mia stilled, her fingers still buried in the soiled cloth. Her heart was suddenly hammering. "Is he well?"

"Yes. The report was Liam's, but he said they're both settling well into the Mortisian court."

Surprise filtered through her initial shock. "Thank you for telling me." After months apart, it was a relief to hear anything about Grayson.

Tyrell shrugged one shoulder, but the motion was a little stiff. "According to Liam, Grayson is befriending the Mortisian prince."

Her eyes rounded, even as her breath caught. "The—serjah?"

Tyrell flicked a hand through the air. "Yes, whatever the Mortisian term is. I have to admit, I can't see Grayson befriending anyone."

"He's not who you think he is." Her defense of Grayson was uttered without thought. Truthfully, she was also surprised by the news. There was another emotion there as well, but she wasn't ready to examine it.

"If you'd like," Tyrell said slowly, "I can send a letter for you."

She blinked. "You could?"

He tipped his head. "I can't guarantee my father won't read it, and there's every chance Liam will intercept it. But if you want to write to Grayson . . ."

"Yes. Of course." Even if she was startled by the offer, she couldn't stop her rush of excitement. "I'll write him tonight."

Tyrell nodded, his expression inscrutable. "I'll send it in the morning." There was a brief silence, then, "I was wondering . . . did Grayson mention anything to you about our mother? Perhaps a meeting he might have had with her before he left? Or if she'd given him a task to complete in Mortise?"

A frown tugged at her mouth. "No. Why?"

"It's probably nothing . . ."

Anxiety tensed her shoulders. "What?"

"It was just strange. When my father shared the report with us, my mother was there. She said some things about Liam. Raised some . . . concerns."

"Is Grayson in danger?" The question was reflexive, but she already knew the answer. Grayson was about to become an assassin in an enemy kingdom. His only ally was his spymaster brother. If the spy turned against him . . .

"I don't know," Tyrell said, his words coming slowly—deliberately. "My mother made some comments about Liam's loyalty. She seemed to be questioning it. Father cut her off quickly, but I admit it unsettled me. My parents are usually united. That there is discord . . . It doesn't bode well."

"Do you think your father would hurt her?"

"No. But it made me wonder if she might have taken some action already."

Mia's fingers curled against her stained rag. "Do you think she asked Grayson to spy on Liam?"

Tyrell's eyes narrowed. "I think she would have asked him to do more than that."

The words caused dread to churn in her gut. Grayson was the strongest, most resilient person she knew. But if he had a secondary mission from his mother . . . If he was operating against Liam, what sort of danger was he in? What if he was acting against King Henri, even? If that was the case, there was no way this would end well for Grayson—or her.

"I'm sorry," Tyrell said. "I shouldn't have shared this with you."

"No. I'm glad you did."

He frowned. "I don't want you to worry."

It was far too late for that.

For so long, Mia had kept from drowning in her fears by ignoring everything that reminded her of home, the past, and the life she had lost. She had done a fair bit of that when it came to Grayson, too. She couldn't think about the danger he was always in. Couldn't imagine the things he was forced to do in his father's name. If she had, it would have torn her apart.

But now, she couldn't stop.

An image of Grayson came to mind—one she could have painted. He was surrounded by shadows and blades. He wouldn't be afraid, though. His face would be smooth, his gaze calculated, his jaw set against the danger surrounding him.

Grayson had spent the last nine years sacrificing everything to keep her safe. He was in Mortise now because of her. Surrounded by potential enemies and possibly torn between helping his mother or his father in their evil requests. He was getting close to the serjah, whether truly or through deception, and she wasn't sure which option caused her more anxiety.

It was her turn to save him.

The thought hit her hard, piercing deep into her chest.

She had spent half her life afraid, living in a cell. Unable to do much of anything. But she was out of that cell now. For the first time escape seemed possible. It was a terrifying prospect, but if she could reach Grayson, she could protect *him* for once. He wouldn't have to follow his father's orders, or his mother's. Because for the first time, she would be free. And if she wasn't under threat, they could both be free.

She would also be in Mortise. Home. That brought a swell of emotions she wasn't ready to untangle.

"I don't want you to worry about this," Tyrell said, breaking into her swirling thoughts. "That wasn't my intention. I just didn't want to hide anything from you."

Overwhelmed by too many considerations and fears, she had a hard time focusing on Tyrell's words. "Thank you," she finally managed, her heart pounding.

He frowned as he studied her. "Are you all right?"

"Yes."

It was most definitely a lie.

The next morning, Mia sealed her letter to Grayson as Rena Fletcher made the bed behind her. While Fletcher was always quiet, his wife was not. Rena was talkative and cheerful, with laughter lines spreading out from her eyes and mouth. She was a matronly woman who had quickly become more of a friend than a maid. She wasn't much taller than Mia, and her blonde hair was riddled with gray. She wore her long locks in a thick bun gathered at the nape of her neck, and though it felt odd to be waited on, Mia appreciated her companionship.

"Are you finished with any of these books?" Rena asked, waving a hand toward the stack towering beside the bed. "I can have them returned to the library."

"That's all right, I'm still reading them." The one on top of the pile was a book on mountaineering, which included basic survival skills, and detailed some of the hazards of traversing steep climbs.

Beneath it was a book containing maps of Ryden; the highways and towns between Lenzen and all borders. It had told her that there were three main choices for her escape: the sea to the west, Devendra to the southeast, and Mortise to the south.

As a retreat, the sea had a few distinct issues. There were the regular dangers, of course, but she would also need a way to pay for passage on a ship, and she had no coin. And without knowing what types of ships docked in Vyken—the closest port city—or how often they sailed, it could be a deadend for her even if she managed to steal some gold.

Devendra would be the least expected path, but the mountains were tall and Mia was nervous enough of getting lost in Ryden or Mortise—throwing another kingdom into the mix was daunting.

Mortise by land also held problems, since the mountains and forests were thick. She could easily become lost. And there would be a river to cross once she was in Mortise. Still, it seemed the safest option, though she wasn't sure what road would be best.

With summer coming to an early end in the north, there was already a bite in the night air. She would need to act sooner rather than later, though she wasn't ready yet. She wasn't fully healed from her stabbing, and she needed to surreptitiously gather supplies. She would also need to learn how to ride a horse. She'd been around the animals as a young child, and had even ridden a little—

with assistance from her parents. It had been too long ago, and she'd never truly been in control of the mount.

She needed to find her courage as well, because the thought of sneaking from the castle had her heart thumping painfully against her ribs, panic clawing her chest.

For Grayson, she would find the strength.

She stood up from the desk, letter in hand. *Grayson* was written on the front, though she wasn't sure how else Tyrell would need to address it in order for it to reach him in Duvan.

She hadn't known what to write; obviously, she couldn't share any of her concerns or plans. She had kept it simple—a brief update that she was living safely in the upper castle, and cautions for Grayson to be safe. And, of course, a reminder of how much she loved him.

She hoped it would reach him quickly. More than that, she hoped she wouldn't be far behind.

Mia stepped into the sitting room, eager to give Tyrell the letter over breakfast. She drew up short when she saw Peter standing at the window, Tyrell beside him.

The skin around Tyrell's eyes tightened. "Breakfast hasn't arrived yet."

What he didn't say was just as clear. *Go back into the bedroom.*

Her mouth dried and she slid back a step, but Peter pinned her in place with his sharp stare. "Ah, Mia. How wonderful to see you again. I admit, I've been disappointed each time I visit the training yard to observe Tyrell, and you're not there."

Mia's fingers tightened against her letter. "I'm afraid I spend my time in other ways."

"Like writing letters?" He nodded to the envelope in her hands. "Who is that for?"

"Her mother," Tyrell said.

"How mundane." Peter might have said more, but there was a knock on the door as servants arrived with breakfast trays. As they hurried to lay out the meal, Peter strolled to a cushioned chair and sat. "You don't mind if I join you?"

"Not at all." Tyrell darted a look at Mia. "Will you take yours in the bedroom as usual?"

He was trying to give her an escape from Peter, and she appreciated it. "Yes, I think—"

"Nonsense," Peter cut in, lifting a slab of bread and smothering it with butter. "Sit beside me."

A muscle in Tyrell's jaw ticked, but Mia knew there was nothing to be done. She moved to the chair beside Peter's and sat on the edge, the letter facedown in her lap.

Peter tore off a bite of the brown bread and chewed, then extended the piece toward her. "Care for a bite?"

Ignoring him, she reached for her own bread. Her stomach felt wooden, but spreading some butter and jam on the thick slice would give her hands something to do. Seeing the bowl of ucea berries made her think of Grayson; he didn't like the tart red berries, but he always brought some to her because she loved them. They reminded her of their first kiss—that first time he had admitted that he loved her.

The ache of missing him was a punch in her gut.

She ignored the berries and focused on preparing her bread.

Tyrell had taken the last available seat across from them, on the settee. He reached for the tea, his motions stiff.

"So, Mia. Where does your mother live?"

She glanced at Peter. She couldn't very well tell the truth—that her mother was dead. So, she lied. "Duvan."

"Were you raised in Mortise?" he asked. "If so, your Rydenic is very polished."

"I've lived in Ryden for many years."

"But surely you're a new arrival to Lenzen? I can't imagine you could have avoided my notice otherwise. I have a talent for finding beautiful things."

She barely repressed a shiver under his stare. She tried to keep her focus on the task of layering jam on her bread. "I've been in Lenzen for nine years."

"Really?" His surprise was genuine. "Your mother must miss you terribly." Without warning, he snatched the letter from her lap.

She nearly dropped her bread in her haste to stop him, but it was too late.

A smile slowly curved into place as he viewed the envelope. "Grayson? You've written a letter to *Grayson*?" Peter shot a look at Tyrell. "How interesting."

Tyrell's controlled expression revealed nothing. "That's not the word I would use."

"No, I would think not. But I must admit, things are making a great deal more sense." Peter fingered the edge of the letter, and Mia fought the urge to rip it from his hands. "Mia didn't include Grayson's title, which means theirs is a friendlier sort of relationship. Perhaps Mia was his *friend* before she became yours, Tyrell. You did leap to cover the truth of who the letter was for, which means you knew she was writing to him. And for some unknown reason, you're allowing it. As you've always been jealous of Grayson, it makes sense that you're trying to steal away that which was once his." He flashed a grin. "Or was I not supposed to tell her that is clearly your aim?"

Mia set down her bread, her jaw tight. "Give me back my letter."

Peter's head tipped to the side as he viewed her. "Clever girl. Ensnaring not one but two Kaelin princes. I admit, your prowess intrigues me." He flicked the letter at her.

She snatched it from the air, her pulse roaring in her ears.

Peter dropped his half-eaten bread back on the tray and stood, looking to Tyrell. "You've given me a much more fascinating visit than I could have dreamed. Thank you." He shot Mia a small smile. "Until we meet again."

The moment the door closed behind him, Tyrell dropped his teacup to the table with a rattle, his scowl severe.

"I'm sorry," Mia whispered, though she wasn't sure why she was apologizing. "I didn't know he was here."

"He came unexpectedly." Tyrell said tightly. "He wanted to let me know that Carter has accompanied our Mother on her annual trip to Rew. She always visits her childhood estate in the late summer to harvest anything she couldn't transplant from her father's poison garden."

It made a horrible sort of sense that Iris had grown up in a poison garden, but that wasn't what made Mia's brow furrow. "Why does it matter if Carter isn't here?"

"Because I must fulfill Carter's duties in his absence."

"But, you're already busy with your own—and Grayson's."

"It's fine. I'll just have to attend some boring meetings." He pushed to his feet. "I might be back late tonight." He glanced at the letter. "I can send that on my way to the training grounds."

"Oh. Thank you." Mia stood and handed him the letter, their fingertips brushing as he accepted it.

She rolled back on her heels, her cheeks warming. The morning had not gone as planned, and it was clear Tyrell wasn't in a good mood, but she tried to rally her thoughts. "I wanted to ask you something."

"Yes?" he asked, tucking the letter into his pocket.

She bit her lower lip. "I know you're incredibly busy, but I wondered if you might teach me to ride a horse."

His eyes darted to her, and a furrow grew between his brows. "Why?"

Her palms dampened with sweat; she forced herself to tell as much truth as possible. "It was something I enjoyed as a child. I never fully learned to ride on my own, but I would like to. Devon said the fresh air would be beneficial."

Tyrell's mouth tightened, his shoulders dropping a little. "I should have offered to take you outside sooner."

Guilt needled her. She hated that he felt sorry when she was the one manipulating him. "I didn't want to go out before. But I would enjoy it now."

"We'll talk to Devon, though I imagine he'll suggest keeping off a horse for a little while longer. We can go on a walk tonight, though, if you'd like."

Surprise ghosted through her. "Really?"

"Of course." The corner of his mouth twitched, chasing away his darker mood that had arrived with Peter. "A moonlit walk with you will give me something to look forward to. But as for the riding lessons, maybe we can strike a bargain?"

"What exactly did you have in mind?"

"No need to look so wary. Just promise that you'll come to the king's birthday feast with me."

Tyrell hadn't brought up the king's feast since first asking her to consider the idea of accompanying him. She had thought of little else at the time, but she'd become so preoccupied with planning her escape that Tyrell's invitation had completely fled her mind.

The thought of being surrounded by so many people—including the majority of the Kaelin family—had her chest tightening. But she needed those riding lessons, so she managed a nod. "Very well. If you teach me to ride, I'll go with you to the ball."

Tyrell smiled. "Excellent. We'll begin as soon as Devon says you're strong enough." He began to turn away but paused, his expression more serious as he eyed her. "I don't want you to feel like a prisoner, Mia. You can wander the castle and grounds as you'd like, so long as Fletcher or one of the other guards is with you."

"Thank you, Tyrell." And she was grateful, even though that flash of guilt remained. She struggled to ignore the whisper in her head that reminded her that Tyrell had tied his fate to hers. If she managed to escape, he would be punished. And he would no doubt come after her.

Fates, her plan would need to be good.

CHAPTER 30

BENNICK

RIDING A HORSE AT PUNISHING SPEEDS AFTER being run through three weeks before was not advisable. Bennick's entire body protested, but especially his side. His insides ached and his burns itched, aggravated by the sweat rolling down his body. The heat was intense in Mortise, even this far north. His once-white shirt clung to his body, and he'd wondered more than once if he had pushed himself too far and a fever was wracking him as punishment. But the other guards were just as sweat-soaked and flushed, so he didn't slow their relentless pace.

Jibar, the physician who had tended him for weeks, had kept his word. Bennick had made it onto a horse without doubling over from the pain, or falling on his face, so Jibar had let him go. He'd sent powders and medicines to help control the pain. "I know

271

you want to reach Clare," he'd said before Bennick left. "But just remember—she'll want you to reach her alive."

Bennick had tried to follow the man's advice on this mad dash to Krid. But as he steered his horse to a stop in front of the Black Scorpion, everything throbbed painfully. He delayed dismounting for a moment by taking in the building before him.

Serai Nadir had sent reinforcements to this inn, since Zilas had guessed Krid would be Salim's destination. Bennick knew there were a hundred different possibilities; Clare could be inside this inn right now, with Wilf and Venn; or they might have found her in the forest days ago, and had already started on their way to Du-van, sending a message to the reinforcements here. Inside that inn, he might even learn of her death.

His fingers clenched around the reins, and he had to force himself to breathe.

Fates, please let her be inside . . .

He dismounted carefully, moving as gingerly as possible. Pain still lanced his side, nearly doubling him over. He grasped the saddle for support, his boots firmly on the ground, his head ducked as he let out a slow breath through gritted teeth.

"Bennick?"

He looked over his shoulder to see Venn staring at him. His friend looked thoroughly shocked to see him, but that soon gave way to intense relief.

"Fates, you're alive!" Venn darted for him, and Bennick tensed.

But Venn caught himself before hauling Bennick in for an embrace. Instead, he set a hand on Bennick's shoulder and squeezed. "Are you all right? Should you be riding?"

"I'm fine," he said, the edge in his voice probably betraying the lie. He gripped Venn's arm. "Have you found them?"

Tension pulled at Venn's face, and his hold on Bennick tightened. "We have Vera. Clare helped her escape three days ago."

He heard what Venn didn't say, and his heart clenched. "Clare is still with them?"

Venn's eyes shadowed. "Yes."

Bennick forced his spine to straighten, one hand brushing over his aching side. "Do we know where she is?"

"She must still be in the city. The Rose has some ideas." Venn led the way into the inn. Bennick tried not to favor his side, but even though Jibar had declared his survival of the wound miraculous, his recovery was not yet complete. He didn't have his full strength, or his full mobility. Not for the first time, he felt a stab of fear. What would happen if he found Clare, but couldn't defend her?

He shoved that aside, blinking rapidly as his eyes adjusted from the midday sun outside to the filtered light of the common room. He followed Venn across the floor and up a narrow staircase that led to the upper rooms of the inn.

Venn pushed open one of the doors and entered a deserted room. "We've been staying here since finding Vera. We've been taking shifts to sleep."

"Where's Vera now?" Bennick asked.

"Resting in a room across the hall."

Bennick lowered himself onto the edge of a bed. He hated to show any weakness, but if he didn't sit, he was going to fall. His legs trembled, and he blamed it on the punishing ride. He forced his voice to remain even as he asked, "How is she?"

Venn shoved a hand over his head, his long dark hair in a loose ponytail. "She's recovering." He proceeded to tell Bennick everything—how they'd been reunited with Vera at a square in

Krid, and her escape from Salim. He shared Vera's account of being a prisoner, and though Bennick knew it wasn't every detail, it was enough to make him sick. The abuse Vera and Clare had suffered, the deliberate withholding of food and water—the way they had been mocked, and constantly bound. Bennick's heart stopped beating when Venn described in terse whispers what Vera had told him about a night by a campfire, where Salim had tortured them with saltwater on their bleeding wrists.

Venn's voice was low in the end. "I don't know what Salim would have done to punish Clare for attacking him, but . . . Fates, she was so brave to help Vera escape."

Bennick's hands fisted, his jaw so tight his teeth ached. Clare's bravery didn't surprise him. But it did terrify him. "Where's Wilf?" he asked.

"He's out with the Rose and a few other men. They're keeping an eye on three different taverns that the Rose has assured us are Salim's favorites. We hope to catch sight of them any day now; Vera was able to give us an idea of when Salim is set to meet his client, and it could be any night now."

"Does Vera know anything about who hired Salim?"

"No. She only mentioned that Salim was hired to bring Serene to him alive, so he could kill her himself." Venn's expression tightened. "There's something else I need to tell you. About Clare."

Every muscle tensed with dread. "What?"

Venn crossed his arms over his chest, his eyes grim. "She saw that sword go through you, Bennick. She thinks you're dead."

Venn insisted Bennick eat something. He ducked out of the room to fetch some food, giving Bennick a moment alone before he returned with a bowl of seasoned rice.

Bennick didn't taste any of it.

Clare thought he was dead. For weeks she had been enduring hell, and she hadn't even known he was coming for her.

It was such a small thing, yet it felt like everything.

Wilf returned while Bennick and Venn ate in the room. The large man's eyes went right to Bennick, and his gaze narrowed as he studied him. "You're all right?" he asked, his voice rougher than normal.

Bennick nodded. "I am, thanks to you. You saved my life, Wilf."

The older guard stepped forward, pulling him into a careful embrace.

Despite the surprising gentleness of his squeeze, Bennick still winced. He smothered that flash of pain when Wilf drew back, though.

The older guard gave a brief report of his time out in the city— no sightings of Salim or Clare at any of the inns—before he focused on Venn. "That physician was just outside. I think she's coming to check on Vera."

Venn stood at once. "I'll go meet her." He strode from the room, and as soon as the door closed, Wilf looked to Bennick.

"The boy can hardly stand to be away from her."

Bennick's throat felt too tight, so he only nodded. He was sitting on the bed once more, and he dragged a spoon through his rice, his stomach in knots.

"I'm sorry," Wilf said quietly. "I failed to find Clare, and I promised you I would."

"You tracked her to Krid." Bennick set the bowl of rice aside, fighting a grimace as pain rippled up from his side. "We'll find her."

There was no other option.

"After Vera found us, we went to the inn she'd escaped from. She found this in the corner of one of the rooms." Wilf reached into his pocket and drew out a small lump of metal.

Bennick's gut lurched as Wilf dropped it onto his palm.

"We think it's what's left of Clare's tin soldier," Wilf said quietly. "The one her brother gave her."

The twisted metal didn't resemble anything now. Still, Bennick knew it. There was a burn in his throat as he squeezed the ruined toy. He knew what it had meant to Clare. Only a cruel man would destroy something so harmless. It must have been another way for Salim to torture her. To punish her for attacking him and letting Vera escape.

He hated what it must have meant that Clare had left it behind. Fates, had she given up completely?

His fingers curled over the mangled tin.

I'm coming, he swore to her. *Just hold on a little longer.*

"We have men at all three taverns," Wilf said, rubbing a hand over his jaw. His beard was a mix of brown and silver, and it looked as unruly as it had in the first weeks after his wife had died. "Our men aren't going in, just watching from the alleys that surround the buildings. Even though they're hiding, we're rotating men; we don't want anyone to notice the same faces hovering around the same spot too long. If they see Clare, they'll send a runner to the other inns—and here—for reinforcements. The Rose thinks Briars is the most likely spot, but we really don't know." He grunted. "Then again, the assassin has been right so far."

"He's trying to save his own skin," Bennick said. He just hoped that lasted; he wouldn't be surprised if the assassin decided to steer them wrong in the end, just to watch Bennick lose Clare for good. His half-brother truly hated him.

He glanced at Wilf. "In case Zilas is telling the truth about Briars being Salim's favorite place, I want to be there tonight. And I want you with me." If his strength failed, he needed to know Wilf could reach Clare.

"And Venn?"

"He should stay with Vera. We'll need every other man at the inns, and he can protect her on his own." He swallowed. "I want to talk to the Rose."

Wilf's eyebrows pulled together. "Is that a good idea? He has a particular fascination with torturing you."

"I know. He's my half-brother."

Wilf stared at him. Blinked. Then he muttered a curse. "That makes sense, I suppose. The notes addressed to you. The taunting."

"I learned the truth after we captured him in Wexon," Bennick said. "Only a few people know."

"I don't blame you for keeping such a thing quiet. But you have to know that no one would think this reflects badly on you." Wilf's tone made it clear the blame was all on Commander Markam. "This complicates things, though."

"Complicated or not, I need to speak with Zilas."

Wilf nodded once. "Let's pay him a visit, then."

Bennick pushed to his feet, shoving aside the familiar flash of pain. He pocketed the ruined tin soldier and followed Wilf from the room.

In the narrow corridor, his eyes were drawn to the door across the hall as it opened. A middle-aged woman slipped out, and from her bag Bennick assumed she was the physician Wilf had mentioned earlier. She gave them a brief nod before moving for the stairs, leaving the door open. Beyond her, Bennick glimpsed Venn and Vera seated side by side on a bed. Venn's body was angled toward her, his head ducked. His words were low and his tone gentle.

The pang of jealousy hit Bennick hard, but he shoved it away. Venn was his best friend. His brother, in every way that mattered. He would not begrudge him this. And he was grateful Vera was safe.

He just needed Clare to be safe, too.

Venn glanced up, spotting them. He whispered quickly to Vera, who darted a look to Bennick. She remained on the bed, but she gave him a thin smile. His attention caught on the bandages around her wrists, though he still saw her sunburned skin and varied bruises.

He ached, knowing Clare had similar injuries that weren't being tended.

Venn stood, stepping into the hall and closing the door softly. "What's going on?" he asked.

"I need to speak to Zilas." Bennick nodded to Wilf. "I told him about his link to me."

Venn's gaze darted to Wilf, then he focused back on Bennick. "What more can the Rose tell us? He's already given us the three taverns."

"I have a plan to get Clare away from Salim—hopefully without a fight—but I'll need Zilas's help."

Curiosity rose in Venn's eyes, but he didn't ask for specifics as he led the way to a room at the end of the hall.

Zilas sat on one of the beds, and was just finishing his dinner. His two guards were also eating, though they rushed to stand when

Bennick and the others filed inside.

The assassin grinned slowly. "Markam. You lived."

Bennick kept his face smooth as he snagged a chair, spinning it around so he could sit facing the assassin. "I think you can do more to help us."

He lifted an eyebrow. "No friendly greeting? I thought royal bodyguards had manners."

"The only courtesy you're getting from me is your next breath."

The assassin set aside his empty bowl, his chains rattling. "I think your threats are improving. Brother."

Near the door, the two guards sucked in a breath. When Bennick didn't deny the Rose's claim, there was a low murmur—one that was cut off quickly, probably as a result of one of Wilf's glares.

The assassin quirked a smile. "Come to terms with the truth, have you?"

Bennick ignored that. "The bargain you made for your freedom dictates that you'll help me find Clare."

"True. But even if we find her, there's a great chance that I won't be walking away from this." Zilas eyed Wilf pointedly.

"The princess gave you her word."

"And royals never lie?" the assassin snorted. "We don't live in a fairy tale. I know my chances."

"If you do everything I ask, I give you my word I'll let you go."

"The word of a Markam means little to me. Father ingrained that in me long ago."

"You're dealing with me, not him."

Zilas scooted to the edge of the bed. Bennick didn't pull back, even when the assassin's boots landed on the floor, right in front of Bennick's. "You know I won't disappear forever," he said quietly. "Even if I decided to go back on my order to kill Serene—which would wound my professional pride—I can't ever let Clare go. Not when I know what she means to you. You must know that."

His words made Bennick acutely aware of the others in the room, and he wondered what Wilf, Venn, and the guards would make of them. But he said nothing. They sat there, mere breaths apart, staring at each other. Zilas watched to gauge any flicker of emotion. Any change in expres-sion.

Bennick didn't give him the satisfaction of reacting. "I know," he finally said. "Our fates are twined together." He forced a thin smile, the edge so sharp it entered his words. "But I'll be ready for you. *Brother*."

The corner of Zilas's mouth twitched. "I admire your confi-dence." He eased back a little, his posture relaxing. "What more do you want me to do, exactly? I already gave you the three inns Salim favors."

"I want you to accompany Wilf and me to Briars. You'll watch the tavern with us, and when Salim shows up—there, or one of the other taverns—I want you to approach him."

The assassin's eyes narrowed, his mind clearly racing. "Clever," he murmured. "You know I've hired him before. He'll be sur-prised to see me, but not suspicious about my sudden presence. He'll allow me to sit at his table—close to Clare."

"Yes. And I want you to offer him whatever coin is necessary for her."

Zilas's head tilted to the side. "It *would* be safer for her. Less messy for everyone, really. But not practical. You don't have en-ough coin on you for a princess's life—even a pretend one like Clare. Salim won't sell her to me."

"Then you'll stall him. Long enough for reinforcements to ar-rive, or for us, as your guards, to get into position. We'll grab Clare before they know what's happening."

"It's not a terrible idea," Zilas allowed.

"Will you do it?"

He lifted his chained hands. "These will have to be removed."

"The moment we see Salim. No sooner."

The assassin flashed a grin. "I must say, I'm impressed with your tactic—hide in plain sight by walking right up to Salim. You know, I employed a similar approach at the Paltrow's ball. I had the pleasure of dancing with Clare. You remember that, I'm sure. I managed to get close without raising any suspicions." He leaned in. "*Very* close."

The taunting was what Bennick had come to expect from the Rose, but that didn't mean he liked it. Still, he didn't rise to the bait. "You never actually agreed to my plan."

"I suppose I didn't." Zilas straightened on the bed. "Well, Salim is greedy enough to listen to me, even if he's about to wrap up another job. He thinks I'm the Rose's right hand."

"He doesn't know who you really are?" Venn asked.

His smile lengthened. "Few are so privileged." The double meaning was clear there. Most didn't know he was the infamous assassin—or the illegitimate son of Devendra's most powerful commander.

"Will you do it or not?" Bennick asked.

"Yes. I'll do it."

"Good." Bennick stood and stepped forward, his boots bumping into Zilas's. The assassin's neck craned back so their eyes could meet. "Betray us," he said warningly, "and I'll kill you."

The Rose smirked. "Understood."

An hour later, Bennick stood beside Wilf in a narrow alley, staring at the tavern across the street. Tension coiled in his shoulders and the wound in his side throbbed along with his pulse. He straightened as the door pushed open, but it was just a man stepping out and moving down the street, his hands in his pockets.

There had been no sign of Clare. He prayed to the fates this would be the place, that tonight would be the night. He needed to see her. Hold her. Know that she was all right.

Zilas, iron manacles still around his wrists, came to stand beside Bennick. "You won't lose your head the moment you see her, I hope."

Bennick tightened his jaw. "I won't ruin this. Be sure you don't."

The assassin's lips twitched. "I'll stick with the plan, Markam."

Bennick said nothing, done with the conversation.

Zilas, apparently, was not. "I'm glad you survived," he said, his voice low enough to stay between them.

Bennick snorted, his eyes still on the closed tavern door. "You expect me to believe that?"

"Yes. Because I don't speak from brotherly affection." He shifted his weight, the chains binding his hands clinking softly. "If you had died, I wouldn't have the pleasure of killing you someday. In front of our father. After I've killed Clare in front of you, of course."

Bennick glanced over at the assassin. "You're not really motivating me to let you go once this is over."

"Ah, but you'll honor your princess's word, won't you?" He huffed a low laugh. "Sometimes I wonder if you're really a Markam. You have an idiotic sense of honor. But then I see your eyes. They're *his* eyes."

Bennick twisted toward him fully, aware of Wilf and the other handful of soldiers watching them. They remained back, though Bennick still dropped his voice lower as he leveled Zilas with a hard stare. "I'm sorry he ruined your life. But being the son he chose to keep wasn't what you imagine. He was rarely in Iden. I barely saw him throughout my childhood. And—just like you—he was the hero I wanted to become. The man I would do anything to impress. I trained hours every day just so he would look at me the next time he deigned to come home. He didn't raise me. He didn't dote on me. Whatever fantasy you've got in your head, it's wrong."

"And yet he didn't abandon you," the Rose said tightly. "He didn't reject you. He *wanted* you. He *chose* you as his firstborn."

Bennick jerked his head toward Wilf. "That man over there? He did more to raise me than our father ever did. The commander abandoned you once, Zilas. He abandoned me repeatedly."

The assassin's hard laugh cracked in the night. "You want me to pity you? You, who lived in a castle and was never spat upon for being fatherless, or shunned for being poor? You never went hungry or cold. Father may have left you for months on end, but he never turned his back on you. Or your mother."

Bennick stiffened. "Don't bring her into this."

"Why not? It's her fault as well. She was a useless woman who couldn't please her husband, which made him rove the entire kingdom for what he needed."

Bennick's hand was around Zilas's throat in the next breath. He slammed the assassin back against the hard alley wall, the shudder of impact jarring up his arm. Bennick sensed Wilf wave the soldiers back, but his focus was entirely on Zilas. "My mother is not to blame for his sins. *Ever.*" His fingers clenched, emphasizing his words. "The harm he did to her is beyond what you can imagine."

"Is it?" Zilas's throat flexed as he swallowed, his words a little pinched and breathless. "Maybe I had to watch the same breaking in my own mother."

Bennick leaned in, their noses almost touching. "I'm sorry. Is that what you want me to say? I'm sorry for what you suffered. For what your mother suffered. But we're not the only ones with a terrible father. Nothing he did to you justifies your hatred of me, or your decision to become an assassin. Just as his sins are his own, so are yours. And if you come after me, or Clare, or my mother, I swear to the fates I will destroy you."

He released Zilas with a shove, and the assassin's shackled hands came up to his reddened throat. Bennick took a step back, sending a quick look to Wilf to assure him he was all right, even though his heart thudded painfully behind his ribs and his seared wounds stung.

He made it two steps before Zilas's quiet voice stopped him. "You may want to send your runners now."

Bennick shot a look over his shoulder. "What do you mean? Clare's not here."

Zilas tipped his head toward the tavern. "See that man sitting near the front window?"

Bennick followed Zilas's gaze and spotted a man who had been there for probably a quarter hour. "Yes."

"His name is Tariq. He's one of Salim's more trusted men. He will have been sent first as a scout to make sure the tavern is secure. Tariq's friend left a few moments ago—you saw him leave. He's gone to fetch Salim, who will be nearby with Clare. They'll arrive any moment."

Bennick's hands rolled to fists. "You've known all this time he was here. Why didn't you say something?"

Zilas's smile curved. "You were busy threatening me. Priorities, Captain."

His anger swelled, but he tried to clamp that down. Clearly, Zilas had been trying to throw him out of focus. Distract him. But why?

The truth slammed into him too late, and he bit out a curse. "You knew Salim would be here. The other taverns were a distraction—a way to divide our forces. You don't want us to succeed."

"Not at all. I would *love* for you to rescue Clare, if only so I have the opportunity to kill her later."

"Bennick," Wilf said, urgency making his voice thin and dark.

He pivoted away from Zilas and focused on the street, the clenching of his heart already telling him what he would see.

A cluster of shadows had arrived at the tavern, and near the front was the only one that mattered.

Clare.

In the darkness, it was impossible to see anything distinct, but he knew it was her. He would recognize her even if she were lost in a crowd of a hundred thousand. Something inside of her called to something inside of him. He was drawn toward her. Pulled forward an actual step, until Wilf grabbed his arm.

"Look," he ordered in a low breath.

Bennick's eyes searched the shadows. Her wrists were bound, her steps heavy as she was tugged forward by a hand wrapped around her arm. Then he spotted what Wilf had seen. Light from the glowing tavern window caught on the blade held against Clare's side.

Zilas's voice was low behind him. "I suppose you really do need me after all, unless you intend to risk her life. I'm the only chance you have of getting close and catching them off-guard."

Bennick couldn't tear his gaze from Clare. *Look at me,* he silently begged her. *I'm here. Turn around and see me.*

Clare didn't look anywhere but forward as the tavern door opened and the group of mercenaries crowded her inside.

Bennick shot a glare at Zilas, who merely raised his bound wrists. "Are you going to free me so we can save her, or are we going to stand here arguing?"

Bennick ground his teeth and shot a look at their runners. "Go. Bring all our reinforcements."

The men nodded and took off, running opposite directions.

Wilf stepped closer to Bennick, his voice dropping low. "He lied to us."

"I know. But we don't have time to make another plan." Bennick gestured, and one of Zilas's guards stepped forward with a key.

When the iron manacles were removed, Zilas let out a sigh and rubbed the red welts on his skin. He grinned at Bennick. "Shall we?"

He ignored the smug assassin, ignored the pain that flared in his side as he stepped into the street. He ignored the fact that Zilas had his own plan—whatever it was—and he could only hope they weren't being led into a trap of some kind. He tried to push back all of his anger and frustration, all the emotions Zilas had brought to the surface during their conversation—an intentional way of putting him off-balance?

In the end, it didn't matter. He ignored everything so he could focus on the one thing that *did* matter: Clare.

CHAPTER 31

CLARE

CLARE HAD BEEN SHUFFLED TO DIFFERENT INNS and taverns in Krid every day. She stopped paying attention to the names of the places—she walked where she was guided to walk, and sat wherever they pushed her. Her stomach ached with hunger and her head pounded with every labored heartbeat.

Salim had been distant with Clare since breaking her fingers two days ago. He seemed more than ready to be rid of her, barely looking at his handiwork. Her throbbing fingers were crooked and swollen, bruised in shades of black, purple, and blue.

Tonight as they walked the streets, Clare knew without being told that they were going to meet the man who had hired them. The man who wanted to kill Serene personally.

It was full dark and the streets were mostly deserted, but for the darting shadows of thieves, drunkards, and alley-dwellers. Hired women called out to them and music and laughter poured from crowded taverns lining the street. Each establishment appeared the same to Clare, but Salim led them purposefully into one on their right.

The common room bustled with activity. Eating, drinking, and trilling music filled the space, and the smells of food and sweaty bodies mingled sickeningly. Tariq sat near the window, but he joined them at a table toward the back of the room. He sat on the bench beside Clare, their arms brushing.

Clare jerked away, unwilling to have any contact with the man who had killed Vera.

Salim took a seat across from her, scowling at the scattered plates with bits of uneaten food on the table left by whoever had sat here before. He snapped for one of the serving maids to clean it up and bring fresh food and drink. Before she could take all the plates, he shoved one at Clare. "Enjoy your last meal," he said flatly.

Her stomach churned when she saw the half-eaten meal, shreds of meat still clinging to bone, but that didn't stop her from lifting each morsel to her mouth. She found every scrap on the plate. She was mindful of her broken fingers, but bumping them was inevitable since her hands were tied at the wrists. Lifting the mug proved even more painful, but her dry mouth demanded it.

"I hope you're killed slowly," Salim said.

Clare glanced at him, mug pressed between her palms. "I wish the same for you."

In the old days—before she'd strangled him with her garrote—he might have smiled. Now, he merely stared at her, his eyes hard.

288

"You will suffer a thousand tortures in the afterlife," Clare continued. "Just for what you did to Vera."

Salim set down his tankard, the back of his hand brushing over his mouth. "Given up on rescues, Princess? Now you've switched to uttering curses?"

"You'll be punished," she said, every nerve in her body sparking with hatred. "In this life or the next, you *will* be punished."

"If the fates will it. But the fates seem to favor me over you these days." He wrenched the mug from her without warning, purposefully knocking her broken fingers.

A cry ripped up her throat and she yanked her hands protectively to her chest.

Salim's lip curled—half smile, half snarl. "Do you even realize how far you've fallen, Princess? Your own father wouldn't recognize you."

Tariq chuckled along with the others.

Clare stared at her grease-stained hands. She refused to cry. Not in front of them. So she looked away, catching sight of a line of patrons heading toward the door. As they vanished into the night, someone new stepped in.

Everything inside her stilled. Her thoughts. Her heart.

The man standing in the doorway searched the room, and when his gaze landed on her, he froze, his eyes burning.

Glorious blue eyes.

Clare's lungs locked.

Impossible.

But . . . it was Bennick. He was here. Undeniably alive, and staring at her with an intensity that she felt all the way to her soul.

She blinked against a rush of tears, trying to take in every detail. He wore a loose shirt in a common Mortisian style. His dark-blond hair was unkempt, and his skin had bronzed in the sun. The planes of his face were hard as stone. Never once did his eyes waver from her.

He wasn't alone. Wilf walked in behind him, and . . . the Rose.

A chill gripped her, and her eyes flew back to Bennick.

His face remained hard and smooth, betraying nothing, but he shook his head fractionally in a silent warning.

"Fates," Salim muttered, his low voice making her jump.

Her pulse thundered, panic snaring her. Had she betrayed Bennick by staring? He and Wilf couldn't take on eight mercenaries. It was miracle enough Bennick was still breathing—surely he was in no condition to fight after being stabbed.

But Salim was not looking at Bennick. He was focused on the Rose.

The assassin smiled as he stepped up to their table. "Hello, Salim. Do you have a moment?"

Bennick and Wilf flanked the Rose as if they were his bodyguards. The moment felt unreal. Clare was half-convinced she was delirious.

The mercenaries at the table were wary, hands hanging near their sheathed weapons.

The Rose's smile remained unbroken, even though Salim's voice was hard. "I heard you left Mortise."

"I did. I'm back." He gestured to the table. "May I join you?"

Salim glanced at Clare. "I'm a little busy. Perhaps tomorrow?"

"This won't take long. And as always, my employer will make it worth your while."

Bennick kept darting glances at Clare from the corner of his eye, but he was more disciplined than her. She couldn't stop staring, though she knew she needed to—she couldn't risk betraying him to Salim. Still, even as she dragged her eyes away, her body shook.

Bennick was alive. He was *here.*

"I don't have long," Salim said. "I'm waiting for a client."

"So I assumed." The Rose spared Clare a quick look, his lips twitching. "She looks a little ragged, but still beautiful. Just like a princess."

Salim's eyes narrowed. "Perhaps we *should* talk." He waved away the mercenary seated beside him, allowing the Rose to take the spot. Then he eyed Bennick and Wilf. "It's not like you to bring guards."

"Sometimes I like to break pattern."

"Well, I'd prefer it if they took a step back. I think that would help us all relax."

"Of course." The Rose flicked his hand, and after a short but tense pause, Bennick and Wilf slid back a fraction. Clare noted the way Bennick favored his side, and concern rose sharply.

Salim smiled thinly. "But now they're blocking the walkway. Maybe they should find a table of their own?"

Clare swallowed hard as she watched Wilf touch Bennick's tense arm, and then the two of them backed away even further. One glare from Wilf and the occupants of the nearest table fled, and Wilf and Bennick lowered themselves into the abandoned chairs, angled toward the mercenaries.

"Much better," Salim said. "See? Now we all have space to breathe."

"May we begin our business, then?" The Rose tugged on his cuffs, straightening his sleeves with an air of total ease.

"Before I hear what your employer wants, I'm interested to know how you know *her.*" Salim jerked his chin toward Clare.

The Rose lowered his voice, though Clare still heard him clearly. "When one works for the Rose, one learns the faces of the elite. Abducting Princess Serene of Devendra—quite the job you've gotten yourself, Salim."

"I'd prefer not to discuss it. Client trust and all. You understand."

"Certainly. However, I'm interested in taking her off your hands."

He chuckled. "You know better than that. I promised to deliver her to my client, and I never fail to deliver."

"I'm sure I could offer enough to soothe your bruised reputation."

"Not this time."

Clare's heart pounded against her ribs. Her palms were slick with sweat and her attention slid back to Bennick. When he looked at her, his gaze was almost tangible. His blue eyes took in everything. Her ripped dress, stained with dirt, her oily, stringy hair, the obvious signs of hunger and fear, the crookedness of her broken fingers.

His nostrils flared, but he remained firmly where he was.

The Rose tapped the edge of the table. "Three hundred gold coins?"

Salim only laughed.

"Five hundred?"

"Any other time I might haggle with you, but you cannot match this price."

The Rose smiled, eyes flat. "It would make my employer very happy if you considered it."

Salim's wandering eye caught Bennick looking at Clare, and his thick eyebrows lowered. "I don't want trouble."

"Neither do we." The Rose said, shooting a look at Bennick.

Bennick's eyes shifted from Clare, his jaw rigid. He said nothing as he met Salim's steady gaze.

The mercenary's mouth slowly curved up. "I do believe this one's got a problem with me."

"He glares at everyone like that," the Rose said. "It's nothing personal."

A knot of tension grew in Clare's abdomen as Salim continued to watch Bennick. "So, he won't get upset if I do this?" He snatched hold of her broken fingers.

Clare cried out, unable to pull free of his crushing grip.

When Salim released her, silence reigned in the crowded room. Those who had not been aware of them before certainly were now.

Clare brought her tied hands to her chest, her broken fingers screaming as her breath rattled out of her, her vision sparking.

Salim's voice carried easily through the unnatural quiet. "Did that bother you?"

Curled in on herself, Clare cut a look to Bennick.

He stared at Salim, his mouth a thin line. His expression was utterly blank, but she could see his pulse jumping in his tensed neck. Every muscle in his body was tightly controlled.

He said nothing.

Salim shrugged. "Well, then I suppose I can do it again."

Clare flinched as he reached for her, and she saw Bennick's body jerk forward before he caught himself.

The Rose grabbed Salim's wrist. "Perhaps we can drop the theatrics? I'd prefer not to have an audience."

Salim looked pointedly at the assassin's hand encircling his own. Every mercenary at the table was ready to spring if Salim ordered an attack. Clare hardly dared breathe.

Then Salim sniffed and tugged his hand away. "Very well. Let's get down to business. But no more about *her*."

"As you wish." The Rose spread his hands. "I'm looking to hire your usual services for my employer. Nothing out of the ordinary."

"Where?" Salim's voice was clipped, but his posture had somewhat relaxed.

"Duvan. There's a spice merchant who needs his property thoroughly ransacked before his business partner is found dead; my employer has a client who has a very specific message he'd like to send."

Salim rubbed his chin. "I'll need three weeks to organize and travel."

"I can give you two."

He frowned slightly. "My fee?"

"It will be generous as ever. And I can include a little something extra if you're there on time."

"How much extra?"

The Rose leaned toward him. "Just a little something."

Salim's eyes widened. Clare didn't realize why at first, but she wasn't the only one to react slowly—the mercenaries had lowered their guard, and the Rose had taken advantage. Hidden by the edge of the table, he'd drawn a knife on Salim.

Bennick and Wilf sprang forward. The old warrior inserted himself behind Salim, his dagger at the mercenary's back and his sword aimed at another man, keeping him from rising to his leader's aid.

Tariq's hand clamped around Clare's elbow, but he froze when Bennick leveled his sword at his bobbing throat. "Let her go," he growled.

Tariq didn't move. Like everyone else at the table, he was frozen.

Salim seethed. "You've made a terrible mistake," he told the Rose.

"And you've made several." The assassin drew out a second dagger and flipped it in his hand. "This can go one of two ways. Easily, or with a good deal of blood. I have no preference. Do you?"

Salim only glared.

Clare could see Mortisians slipping out of the inn, anxious to escape before a fight broke out. As the door swung behind them, two disguised Devendran soldiers entered, weapons drawn. They must have been watching from outside, waiting for the right moment to reveal themselves. They reached the table and pointed their swords at the mercenaries, adding some balance to the numbers, though the mercenaries still outnumbered them.

Bennick kept the weapon trained on Tariq. "Release her. *Now.*"

Tariq scowled, but when Salim jerked out a nod, he uncurled his fingers.

Shaking, Clare pushed away from him and scrambled from the bench, lurching to Bennick's side. With her hands bound, she was unable to grab him, but his hand landed on her waist. He didn't pull her in for an embrace, but guided her to stand behind him. She pressed close to his tensed back, her heart hammering in her chest as she relished his warm touch. The solidness of him that she never thought she would feel again.

Bennick's fingers slid away from her too soon and returned to grip the hilt of his sword, both hands keeping it steady on Tariq.

"You're going to let us go," the Rose said, his tone conversational. "And I'm not going to kill you."

"You'll regret this," Salim sneered.

"Doubtful," the Rose said. Then his voice changed. "This is where I duck out."

Bennick's spine stiffened. Clare peered around his arm and saw the Rose's second knife resting against Wilf's gut.

CHAPTER 32

CLARE

"ZILAS," BENNICK GRITTED OUT. "WE HAD A DEAL."

The assassin smiled. "Yes. We did. But this is as far as I trust you." He found Clare and tipped his head. "I'll see you again soon enough, I'm sure. If Markam manages to keep you alive." He stood, one dagger still on Wilf, the other on Salim—no one could safely make a move to stop the Rose, pinned as they all were by weapons.

The assassin looked at Bennick. "I trust you'll make it out. You do seem to be a survivor." He kicked Salim in the back, knocking Wilf's dagger away and causing the tense hostage situation to suddenly end.

The mercenaries exploded into action, drawing their weapons.

Wilf growled and swung his blades, but Salim avoided the attack by shoving to his knees.

Bennick shuffled back, herding Clare toward the door while the two Devendran soldiers rushed to join the fight.

Clare glimpsed the Rose over Bennick's shoulder, bolting toward the back of the common room. He slipped through the door and out of sight.

Bennick leapt forward to meet a mercenary's strike, and without turning he yelled to Clare, "Run!"

She stumbled back, but couldn't make her limbs cooperate. Bennick fought Tariq, and Wilf battled two opponents at once. Her fingers were broken, and her wrists were tied, but she couldn't leave them.

She was sick of inaction.

Clare dove for the dagger sheathed at Bennick's waist. While he swung his sword at Tariq, she snatched the knife free of his belt with her good hand and sawed through the rope binding her wrists. The rope fell just in time for her to swipe the blade at a grasping hand.

The mercenary cried out as the dagger sliced over his palm, and he snatched away from her. Another man slipped around Bennick and tried to grab Clare's elbow. She ducked and whipped around, lifting her foot so she could slam her heel against the side of his knee, as Bennick had taught her.

The man howled and crumpled.

Clare glanced around the room. Wilf continued to battle multiple opponents, and Bennick's breathing was ragged as he parried blows from Tariq and another man at the same time. Bennick was visibly slower due to his injury, and even as Clare scanned the room she saw one of the Devendran soldiers go down, clutching the side of his neck with bloody fingers.

His fallen sword was too far for her to retrieve, not that she would have been able to wield it properly with her broken fingers. She gripped the dagger with her good hand, keeping her other hand close to her stomach as she stepped forward to defend Bennick's more vulnerable side.

She glared at a man who had edged around the fight, intending to strike Bennick at his weakest point. The man's knuckles went white around the hilt of his sword, and Clare rather liked that he hesitated. His eyes darted to the mercenary who cradled his bleeding hand, and the other Mortisian just now pushing off the floor and limping away from her.

Adrenaline pumped through her, pushing out her fatigue. Falling back into her training was both effortless and empowering.

The man flexed his grip on his sword, then he swung.

Clare dodged the strike and slashed the knife against his extended arm, tearing through the sleeve and digging into his flesh. He screamed and retracted his blade, cursed her, and struck again.

She leapt back, closer to Bennick, who was easing toward Wilf as he fought. To be fair, it didn't seem like Wilf needed help; the giant had knocked down two mercenaries. There were only a few still standing. Unfortunately, Salim was among them.

The man with the bleeding arm had not backed away. He edged further around Clare, so that her back was firmly to Bennick's as she faced her attacker. She was focused on the man's scowl, but from the corner of her eye she saw the limping mercenary had not vanished, either. He was approaching her from the side, even as his friend moved directly for her. She could not re-treat—if she slid away, Bennick would be left exposed.

She knew Bennick was aware of the danger, but there was nothing he could do—it seemed to be taking every bit of strength he had to fend off Tariq.

Wilf yelled something—Clare thought he must have also seen the danger she was in—but when both of the encroaching mercenaries attacked at once, Clare's training took over. Instinct overrode everything.

Her dagger stabbed into the limping man—the one closest to Bennick—and the blade sunk in to the hilt. Stabbing a man in the gut was a new experience for Clare, but she couldn't dwell on it. As he staggered back, he took her knife with him in his belly. Weaponless, she grabbed for his sword, which he held with slack fingers. She jerked it away from him, but when the weight was too much, she acted reflexively and grasped it with both hands.

Her broken fingers bumped the hilt, and the pain was instant. She cried out, and the sword fell, clattering to the ground. The other mercenary wrapped a hand around her upper arm, bruising her skin as he tugged her back against his chest. He hooked his arm around her neck, and she couldn't even attempt to pry his arm away from her throat—not with her broken fingers that still stabbed with agony.

He laid his sword over her stomach. "I'll kill her!" he yelled. "By the fates, I'll cut her open!"

Her breaths were little more than gasps. Her eyes stung and her fingers throbbed. She watched blearily as Wilf froze. His sword hung for a moment, then lowered.

Bennick grunted as he shoved away from Tariq. His blue gaze found Clare, and he immediately dropped his sword, his breath rattling harshly out of him.

In seconds, Wilf, Bennick, and the last Devendran soldier were forced to stand before Salim.

The mercenary leader plucked a dagger from his belt and twisted it over in his hands, eyeing the three Devendrans before him. "Kneel."

Images of the two murdered soldiers in Sedah flashed through Clare's mind. "No!"

Eyes flickered to her, but Salim remained fixed on the three men. "Kneel," he said again.

She would not watch Bennick die. *Not again.*

Clare jabbed her elbow into the gut of the Mortisian behind her. He grunted, but continued to hold her. She still managed to snatch the knife from his belt.

She pressed it against his side and he tensed.

"Salim," he said, shifting the sword he had resting against her stomach.

Clare glared at Salim. "I'll kill him," she said, her voice so dark it was nearly unrecognizable. "I'll kill him unless you let them go."

Salim glared right back. "Kill him, then."

The man under Clare's blade sucked in a breath.

She tightened her grip on the knife, refusing to look away from Salim. "Let them go. *Now.*"

"No."

In her periphery, she saw Bennick and Wilf stare at her. Bennick's lips were pressed tightly together. She could practically see him thinking, grasping for any way out.

By Salim's order, they were shoved to their knees. Wilf growled, and pain ghosted across Bennick's face as he was slammed down, hands crushing against his shoulders.

Clare's thoughts raced. If she remained frozen, she would see Bennick, Wilf, and the other soldier murdered. She couldn't physically help them—she needed to find something to exchange for their lives. But she didn't have anything to give Salim. She wasn't even Serene, she was just . . .

The idea struck hard, making her entire body seize. There were a hundred ways this could go wrong, but it was the only thing she could think to do. She ripped her eyes from Bennick. "Salim."

He glanced at her, irritation in his expression. "Yes, Princess?"

She swallowed. "There's something I should tell you, before your client arrives."

He tapped the flat side of his dagger against the edge of the table. "Oh?"

"No," Bennick said, his voice rough. "Don't say anything."

She ignored him, still focused on Salim. "I'm not Serene."

Wilf growled. Bennick hissed out a breath.

Salim's expression tightened. "You're lying."

She tried to shake her head, though the arm constricting her neck made the movement difficult. "I'm not lying. I'm not Princess Serene."

"Stop it." Bennick rounded on Salim, his glare so intense, so desperate, as if that could stop the rebel leader from hearing her words.

"I'm her decoy," Clare continued. "I was appointed by King New-lan. My name is Clare."

"She's lying," Bennick snapped.

Salim's attention swiveled between them, lingering on Clare.

She latched onto his indecision. "There have been times you wondered. I haven't reacted like you expected a princess would. Look, just—look at my hands. They're covered in scars because I used to work—"

"Serene, stop it," Bennick said, biting each word out. "This lie won't help."

302

Salim turned toward Clare. Bennick tensed as if to stand, but he was held firmly down. He ground his teeth as he watched Salim approach her.

Clare forced herself to meet his searching stare. She tried not to shake when he curled a hand around her arm and lifted the hand with the broken fingers—the one not holding the dagger against the mercenary's side.

Salim didn't touch her swollen fingers, but he examined them closely. The burns, the pale nicks and scars left behind from years of kitchen work were hidden by a layer of grime, but easy enough to pick out when told to look.

Salim's bearded jaw stiffened as he stared. His fingers around her arm tightened until she could feel her bones grate together.

Bennick saw her cringe. "Release her," he demanded.

Surprisingly, Salim did, though she remained flush against the man holding her.

Salim glanced around at his men, his pulse jumping in his neck. "Well?" Tariq asked.

Salim's words were low. "She's not the princess."

Murmurs rolled through the mercenaries.

Clare took a breath. "Salim—"

He backhanded her so hard even the man behind her stumbled. Clare lost her hold on the dagger, and it thunked to the floor. Her vision blurred, her cheek on fire from the heavy blow.

Bennick roared, and Wilf let out a bone-shaking bellow.

Hands wrapped around Clare's wrists and she was jerked forward until she slammed into a hard chest. She could feel a beard tickle her cheek, and she knew it was Salim who held her. She gasped, but couldn't squirm away from his tight hold.

"I could kill you," he growled. "I could kill you right now—"

"You need me!" she gasped.

"I have no use for a false princess."

"Yes, you do! Your client will be here any moment. You need me to be her if you want your payment."

Rage rumbled through him, but Salim didn't immediately snap her neck. A good sign.

Clare hurried to continue. "Let them go, and I'll be Serene again. I pretended for you, I can do the same for—"

Salim snatched hold of her smallest broken finger. She shrieked as he bent it back. Her legs buckled and she crashed to her knees.

"Stop!" Bennick yelled, his voice blistering with rage and fear.

Salim retained a grip on her finger as he hovered over her, his focus solely on her. "You'll be Serene or I'll kill you."

She forced herself to speak past the pain. "What good would a dead princess do you? If your employer walked through that door right now, I swear I'd tell him that you knowingly tried to trick him."

Salim snarled and applied more pressure to her finger.

Pain blinded her, but she could hear a struggle taking place. Wilf roared, men grunted in pain, and a body slammed against the floor.

"I'll cut out your tongue," Salim threatened.

Mouth dry, agony pinching her throat, she still managed to speak. "I'd—find a way—to tell him."

"What, write it down? I'll break *all* your fingers." He yanked harder.

Clare let out a sob when she felt her tortured finger snap again, in a new place.

Bennick's shouts rang in her ears, mixing with her own screams.

When pain no longer dominated everything, Clare blinked

through blurry eyes and saw that Wilf was sideways on the floor, pinned down by four mercenaries. One had his boot pressed against his cheek, forcing his face against the smooth wood of the floor. Bennick's frame was wracked with obvious pain. He was shaking, pinned in place by two mercenaries who had forced him to kneel.

Salim grabbed a fistful of Clare's hair, his knuckles digging into her skull. He retained his hold on her finger as he jerked her head up, forcing her to meet his gaze. "You will be Serene."

Her voice shook despite her best efforts. "Only if you let them go."

Their eyes were locked, nothing able to break them—not Bennick's yelled threats or Wilf's furious snarls. Though fear coursed through her, determination to save Bennick and Wilf burned hot.

The skin around Salim's eyes tightened. "I can't release them until you go with my client."

"Unacceptable. They go now."

Salim bristled. He shoved closer, their noses nearly touching. "I'll release them after you're gone and I have my payment. Not a moment sooner. If you refuse my offer, I'll kill them now."

She knew she'd pushed him as far as she could. She had no illusions that he would keep his side of the bargain. The moment she was gone, he would kill them. But she had no choice. This wasn't about securing their freedom; it was about buying them time so they could have a chance at escape.

"Very well," she agreed.

"*No.*" Bennick pulled against the men who held him, but to no avail.

Salim stepped away, tossing a glance at the men restraining the Devendrans. "Take them out back. Hold them there until my business is done."

"Wait." Clare swallowed. "I need a moment with them."

"No."

She set her mouth in a line. "You can keep watch. But you'll let me speak to them or I won't cooperate."

After a slight hesitation and a short nod from Salim, she was released.

Her heart pounded as she walked to Bennick and crouched in front of him. Her eyes trailed over his face, the flushed skin beaded with sweat, his skin tight with barely restrained emotion. A small cut near his eyebrow leaked blood, leaving a thin streak down his cheek.

Bennick's chest rose and fell too quickly, his arms pinioned behind him. He was captured and in pain, but there was nothing weak in his low voice. "I am *not* walking away from you."

Lifting her good hand, she touched his bristled cheek, stroking the unkempt roughness with just the tips of her fingers. He was warm, hard, and real. Emotion clawed her throat, and she pressed her palm against his strong jaw.

Every muscle in his body went rigid at the soft contact. His eyes sliced over her, and it took everything she had to keep back the tears that threatened.

He opened his mouth, but she cut him off. "I'll be fine. And you'll come after me." She had to trust he followed his own advice and kept a hidden blade somewhere. Wilf had to have one as well. She had to believe they would overpower the mercenaries before they were killed.

It was the only way she could let him go.

Their eyes were locked. She took a short breath. "I thought you were dead. I can't watch you die again."

A muscle in his cheek jumped. "And I can't lose you again."

She leaned in, setting her lips against his with the gentlest of pressures. Her lips lingered against his after the brief kiss. "You'll find me," she whispered.

A shudder rippled through him when she pulled back. Her hand fell from his face, landing on his kneeling leg. Something like panic swelled in his eyes as she turned to face Wilf. Emotion clogged her voice as she took in his familiar fierce expression. "Thank you," she said at last. "For coming for me."

"This isn't over," he said gruffly. "We'll find you," the hardened warrior promised.

Her stomach clenched—fates, what if they didn't escape? Last time she'd tried to help someone, Vera had died. Her grip on Bennick's leg tightened, and her words rasped with emotion. "Tell Venn I'm sorry. Vera . . ."

Wilf's brow furrowed. Then his eyes cleared. "She's alive. She found us days ago."

Clare shot a look at Bennick, who confirmed this with a nod, never taking his eyes off her.

"What?" Salim muttered. He turned on Tariq in an instant. "You said you killed her." When Tariq said nothing, Salim cursed. "You thought I'd never find out about your deception?"

Bennick's throat bobbed, distracting Clare from Salim's angry voice. Every line of his body was hard, his tension so obvious it was a wonder any bones hadn't snapped.

"Everything will be all right," she breathed, her words softened with a calm she didn't really feel, but hoped to give him.

"I'm sorry," he said, his eyes not leaving hers. "Clare, I'm so, so sorry."

She brushed a fingertip over the streak of blood on his face, keeping it from his eye. "This isn't your fault. I love you, Bennick."

He swallowed, and Clare prepared to stand, sensing Salim's mounting impatience. But before she could, Bennick jerked one arm free. He cupped her face with his calloused hand, his thumb swiping at the thin sheet of tears on her cheek. His blue eyes pierced hers. "I *will* find you."

She tugged in a breath and leaned into his palm, her eyes shuttering briefly. She never thought she'd feel his warm skin against hers again—never thought she'd smell him or hear his voice. In that split-second, she tried to take in everything about him—his warm scent, his strength, the sound of his breathing, the feel of his skin against hers.

"Stay alive," he pleaded softly. "Please just stay alive."

Salim's voice broke their illusion of privacy. "If they're still here when my client arrives, they're dead."

Clare planted a kiss on Bennick's palm, her eyes skirting over his face once more before she drew back. His chin tilted up when she stood, his gaze following her.

If the mercenaries hadn't levered Bennick to his feet, she didn't know if he would have moved. Wilf and the other soldier were also hauled up.

Salim surveyed them darkly. "If you give my men trouble, they'll kill you."

"I'll come back for you," Wilf told Salim, lethal promise living in his tone.

Bennick glared at Salim, adding to Wilf's threat with barely restrained violence in his voice. "You will regret ever touching her."

———◦◦◦———

Clare flinched as one of the mercenaries bound her wrists. Beyond them, Salim struck Tariq across the face, making the younger man's head jerk to the side.

"You not only allowed her to get away," Salim raged. "You thought to hide it from me?" He hit Tariq again, more sharply. Then he stepped back, his wide chest heaving. "I don't tolerate lies. You looked me in the eye and told me the girl was dead."

Tariq's nostrils flared, his temper barely restrained. "I didn't want to worry you. She could do nothing to us."

"She could have ruined us! If I hadn't insisted we move around, the girl could have led those soldiers right to our beds. And you said *nothing*!" Another backhanded strike against Tariq.

Clare winced, though she didn't feel sympathy for him.

Salim swore and paced away.

Tariq glared at his leader's back, his cheek burning scarlet.

Finally, Salim turned. "You won't get any part of the payment."

Tariq's face contorted. "You can't exclude me. Not after all I've done!"

"I can do anything I want. I could kill you for lying to me."

Clare struggled to ignore them. She didn't want to see or hear them. She wanted to close her eyes and see Bennick. *He was alive.* Though fear and anxiety still climbed through her, she felt true hope for the first time in weeks. She assumed Bennick and Wilf were waiting for a moment of laxity that would enable them to draw their hidden knives and attack. Or perhaps they were waiting for reinforcements? Venn had not come with them, yet he was clearly in Krid. Perhaps other soldiers were, as well? Maybe help was coming.

The common room was all but deserted at this point. The mercenaries who hadn't taken Bennick and Wilf to the back of the inn yard worked to drag out the dead bodies before the man who hired them arrived.

One of the mercenaries spoke suddenly. "What do we do when the client finds out the Devendran princess is still alive somewhere?"

"That will be his problem, not mine," Salim growled. "I was deceived." He sent Clare a withering look. If she couldn't still feel the comforting press of Bennick's hand against her cheek, she might have been more afraid. "If it weren't for *her*, I wouldn't have known the difference. We can't be blamed."

The front door creaked open, and Salim's mouth snapped shut.

The newcomer wore a hooded cloak, despite the heat that hung in the Mortisian summer night. He was broadly built, with stocky limbs. His clothes were worn—nothing like she had expected. She'd been prepared to see a nobleman, like Ser Zephan. A traitor to the crown with limitless resources and coin.

As he pushed back his hood, Clare saw that he was middle-aged. He had dark hair cropped short to his head, and no beard. His brown skin was weathered, as if he spent most of his time working out in the sun. He didn't seem the type of man to have the means of hiring a band of mercenaries to kidnap a foreign princess. Frankly, he didn't look like he had any reason to care about inter-kingdom politics.

"Salim, I assume?" he asked, his eyes almost wary.

The leader of the mercenaries frowned. "Who are you?"

"Latif," the man said, his eyes darting to Clare. "I was sent to collect a certain valuable."

Salim stepped forward, his hands braced on his hips. "Do you have proof of this?"

"Of course." Latif reached into his pocket and produced a sealed letter.

Salim took it, breaking the seal and then reading swiftly. When his head lifted, there was less tension in his shoulders. "You have the gold?"

"As promised," Latif assured, dropping a weighted purse into Salim's free hand. "Our mutual employer thanks you for a job well done." His eyes drifted to Clare, and there was a tightening in his jaw that stiffened Clare's spine.

"You may want this," Salim said, withdrawing the silver garrote bracelet from his pocket. "This is one of her well-known pieces. You'll want to keep it from her, though." He rubbed at the still-fading red line around his throat.

Latif took the bracelet, tucking it into his pocket. "I don't suppose you'd be interested in telling me why she's in such a roughened state?" His eyes dipped meaningfully to her swollen, crooked fingers.

"She's a feisty one." Salim shot Clare a look, as if daring her to say anything. "I've beaten all that out of her. You'll thank me."

Latif's eyes narrowed, but then he waved Clare forward. "Come."

Salim's eyes were digging into her skin. She knew that any attempt to resist could cost Bennick and Wilf their lives, so she lifted her chin and crossed the floor to stand in front of Latif.

"You will regret this," she said to him, her voice surprisingly steady.

The corner of his mouth lifted wryly. "I already do."

She frowned at his words, but she didn't ask for an explanation as he took her elbow and pulled her toward the door. She cast one last look at Salim, who slid his fingers over the coin purse while staring daggers at her.

Fear for Bennick, Wilf, and the other soldiers swelled inside her, but there was nothing she could do but keep up with Latif, who held her arm. He tugged her out into the night, leading her to the tavern's stable.

Should she scream Bennick's name? Would it put him in more danger, or give him the cue he'd been waiting for?

Indecision made her feet drag, and Latif noticed. "I'm afraid resisting will do little good, and we have a deadline."

Clare knew she was in no condition to fight him. Her hands were bound, half her fingers broken, and she was half-starved. Adrenaline was the only thing she had rushing through her. But if resisting him now meant being reunited with Bennick, she was more than willing to take the risk.

She allowed Latif to lead her into the stables, right up to a large stallion, which was already saddled. "You'll ride in front," Latif said.

He still held her arm, expecting her to step into the waiting stirrup.

Instead, she jabbed her elbow into his gut with all the force she could manage.

Latif choked and doubled over, releasing her in surprise.

Clare bolted for the stable door, ignoring the flashes of pain as her fingers were jostled, the aching in her head that spiked with every footfall.

She felt the warm air on her face, was in the process of taking the step that would take her outside, when she was tackled from behind.

Her head smacked the cobblestones, and everything dissolved.

CHAPTER 33

BENNICK

BENNICK'S KNEES DUG INTO THE HARD COBBLED alley behind Briars, and it took every bit of willpower he possessed not to reach for the hidden knife in his boot.

Wilf knelt across from him, his eyes hard with warning.

Bennick knew they needed to wait for their reinforcements to arrive. Unless Salim's four men attacked them, there was no point fighting now. Even if they managed to overpower them, they couldn't do anything to help Clare until they had help. Salim's guard was up. They needed the advantage of numbers.

Hurry, he silently begged the reinforcements.

Trapped behind the tavern as they were, he didn't know if Salim's client had arrived. What if he was there right now? He could see in his mind the coin changing hands. Clare being dragged out of the tavern's front door—or killed right there in the common room.

And he was trapped out here, with no good options.

But if Clare was gone already, then Salim would be here, giving the order for their deaths. Bennick knew Salim would never keep his promise to Clare. The moment she was gone, Salim was going to kill them.

And then there would be far too many mercenaries for Bennick and Wilf to fight.

Maybe they should act now . . .

Wilf's eyes narrowed, his jaw firm.

The silent call for patience was not one Bennick appreciated. He gritted his teeth, but he dipped his chin just a fraction, reassuring Wilf that he would wait.

He would do nothing to increase the danger to Clare.

He never should have trusted Zilas. The assassin had betrayed them. Not just when he turned a knife on Wilf and ruined their best chance of escape; he had also kept the truth from them. He'd known Salim would choose Briar's all along—he'd spotted Salim's man easily through the window and could have said something, but he'd forced them to divide their already limited forces into thirds, and then he'd triggered a fight to cover his own escape.

Bennick wasn't surprised that Zilas had acted in his own self-interest, but he was surprised that he'd allowed himself to trust the infamous assassin.

It was a mistake he would never make again.

Every second felt like an hour. Every breath seemed to last an eternity. His thoughts ran in endless circles, and all he could see was Clare. He was *so close*. He had touched her, and then she had been snatched away. If the reinforcements didn't arrive soon, she would be lost all over again. And this time, they would not have Zilas to guide them.

Boots scuffed the cobblestones, and Bennick's head jerked toward the sound. His gut fell.

It was Salim.

Which meant Clare was gone.

Loss and rage punched through Bennick.

"You're my last piece of business in Krid tonight," Salim said, as he and his men ambled forward. When he tugged out a knife, Bennick and Wilf moved as one, grabbing for their hidden blades.

Bennick's injury stabbed as he shoved to his feet, but even though the pain slowed him down, he still launched himself at the first man who reached for him.

Wilf fought with the ferocity of a bear, using his blade and his fist to drive back those who dove for him. Mercenaries fell to the ground with screams, clutching their injuries.

And then Bennick and Wilf were no longer alone. Devendran soldiers and Serai Nadir's guards came out of the darkness and swarmed the area. A few of Salim's men darted away, clearly measuring the fact that they were now the ones outnumbered.

Bennick locked eyes on Salim just as the Mortisian seemed to realize the same. His bearded face was twisted with rage, but his eyes showed a glimpse of fear. He twisted toward the back alley and ran.

Bennick tore after him, ignoring the fire in his side that screamed for him to stop. His feet pounded against the cobblestones and he pushed himself to run faster as Salim slipped into the shadows.

He would not lose him.

Salim rounded a corner, and Bennick was right behind him.

It was a dead end.

Salim's arms swung as he grated to a halt and spun to face Bennick.

Bennick breathed hard, his small knife clutched in his blood-streaked hand as he blocked Salim's only escape. "You've lost," he ground out. "Tell me where she is."

The ring of steel rasped in the darkness as the Mortisian drew his curved sword. "I've seen you favoring your side. You're not ready for this fight."

"After what you did to Clare, I'm going to enjoy killing you."

Salim gave a hard-edged smile. "You're the one who knelt at *my* mercy, remember?"

"Don't bother kneeling before mine," Bennick said. "I have no mercy for you."

Salim lunged, his sword swinging. Bennick pivoted and spun, dodging the blow and slashing out with his small knife. The blade sliced over Salim's arm—nothing fatal, only painful.

The mercenary's nostrils flared as he growled, his curved sword swinging for Bennick's gut.

Bennick jumped back, ducking to avoid another swing. He kicked the broken remains of a crate at Salim, who stumbled when the rotting wood pieces hit his legs.

The dance continued, rapid and fierce. The alley walls were close, making Salim's strikes hard to dodge. Salim's blade grazed Bennick's hand, and then his thigh, but Bennick barely registered the pain. Adrenaline poured through his body, pushing back everything except his need to make this man bleed for all he had done. To avenge every hurt Clare had suffered.

Clare.

Her name echoed in his head, a fist clenching in his gut. Every second this fight continued was another second she was being taken farther from him. If she was still alive at all.

A growl locked in his throat as he kicked out, his boot slamming into Salim's unprotected gut.

Pain ricocheted through him as his injured side felt every part of the blow. Even as Salim staggered back, hunched over his aching middle, Bennick doubled over—as if he had been the one to take the kick. Sweat dotted his forehead and slicked his palms.

Salim noticed his weakness and raised his sword—only to freeze in the next instant.

"It's over," Wilf rumbled.

Bennick looked over his shoulder, still not standing straight. Wilf was behind him, along with several other men.

Salim would not be able to fight his way through them. His shoulders stiffened, and he lowered his sword. "Let me go and I'll tell you everything I know."

Bennick straightened, breathing past the screaming pain in his side. "Where is Clare?"

Salim's eyes narrowed. "Gone. A man named Latif took her."

Bennick's fingers clenched around his knife. Gone. Not Dead. "This Latif," he ground out. "Is he the one who hired you?"

"No. I never learned my client's name, but it wasn't him. I met my employer only once, in Duvan, weeks ago. All I know is that he came from the palace."

"How do you know that?"

"Because I had one of my men follow him back to the palace. He was well dressed. Clearly not a guard or servant."

"And it wasn't the same man who came tonight?" Bennick pressed.

"No. He sent Latif to collect her. He had a letter—proof that he was sent by the man who hired me."

"I want to see that letter."

Salim's eyes narrowed. "I'll give it to you once you let me go."

Bennick ignored that. "Where was he taking her?"

"I don't know," he snapped. "My part of the job was done. But the longer you stand here interrogating me, the farther away they're getting."

"Describe Latif," Bennick ordered.

Salim did, adding that one of his men had seen the Mortisian's horse, which was brown with some black spots. "That's all I know," he finished.

Bennick eyed him, but quickly determined there was nothing more Salim could give him. He tucked his small knife in his belt.

Behind him, Wilf's voice was hard. "Bennick, you can't just—"

"Someone give me a sword," Bennick cut in.

Salim's lips peeled back from his teeth. "You promised to let me go if I told you what I knew!"

"I never made any such promise." Bennick held out his hand and one of the Devendran soldiers relinquished their blade.

Bennick gripped the hilt, swinging it once in front of him. His side protested, but he ignored that spark of pain. His focus was purely on Salim. "You can resist, and I will gladly kill you. Or you can lay down your sword and we'll escort you to the nearest city guard."

Those words were the hardest he had ever spoken, when his body vibrated with the need to kill this man.

Salim stared at him, no one speaking as they all waited to see what Salim would do.

When the man bent and lowered his sword to the ground,

Bennick felt a twinge of regret at his surrender.

Then, as Salim stood, he threw a small knife. Bennick spun to avoid it, but the blade still embedded in his upper arm. He gasped at the shock of pain and stumbled back.

Wilf dove around him, his fist catching Salim's face, making him fall back with a shout.

Wilf's voice was a furious storm, thunder rolling ominously through every word. "That man you just double-crossed is a far better one than I am." He slammed the heel of his boot against Salim's hand on the cobblestones, and the crack of bones breaking caused Bennick to flinch.

Salim howled.

Wilf drew his sword and aimed it at the mercenary's chest, his foot still planted on his hand.

"Wait!" Salim rasped. "I've got gold. I can pay for my life!"

"No you can't," Wilf said, his voice impassive. "You're worthless."

His sword flashed in the moonlight and Bennick felt nothing as the blade stabbed into Salim's heart.

The Mortisian gurgled, his body twitching. Then he stilled, going silent.

Bennick was numb as he plucked the knife from his arm, dropping it to the cobbled ground.

Wilf leaned over the dead body and rifled through the pockets until he found a crumpled paper. He carried it back to Bennick. "I won't apologize for killing him," he said.

Bennick said nothing, just took the letter and flipped it open. The Mortisian words took a moment for him to decipher.

Salim,
You will forgive me for declining to meet you in person.
Latif will bring her to me. So you know I sent him, I leave
you these words: fang and claw.
Our business is concluded.

There was no signature. No sign of who had written this. Just those two words—fang and claw; clearly a shared code.

Bennick folded the message and shoved it into his pocket. For now, it was a useless bit of paper, and he had other things he needed to focus on. "I want two men at every gate in this city. If you spot Clare or this man Latif, one soldier follows them while the other returns to the Black Scorpion. Wilf, I want you to talk to anyone who was in Briars or the stable, or anywhere nearby—see if you can learn anything."

"What about you?" Wilf asked.

Bennick's hands fisted at his sides. "I'm going to interrogate any of the men we captured. And then I'm sending Venn and Vera to Duvan. If Salim was telling the truth and whoever hired him is in a position of power at the palace, then Serene is in danger. She needs to be warned."

———————

They'd only captured three of Salim's men, and none of them knew a thing of use. When Bennick was done with them, he turned them over to some of Serai Nadir's men. He thought the city guard might take fellow Mortisians more seriously, so the mercenaries

would actually be imprisoned. Killing them would have been easier, but it hadn't felt right.

Bennick still felt nothing when he thought of Salim's death.
He'd *wanted* Salim to die, which was exactly why he'd held himself
back. Killing a cornered man was murder, and Bennick was a soldier. He had killed, but he wasn't a killer. He wasn't like Zilas.

But in that alley, for a moment, he had wanted to be.

Wilf quickly bound Bennick's bleeding arm, and they made
their way back to the Black Scorpion. They didn't speak; Wilf had
already reported that he'd learned nothing in his search around
Briars, though he'd spotted a small smear of blood on the floor of
the stable. Not enough to signify death, but Clare had probably
been hurt—perhaps knocked unconscious.

The mere thought made Bennick's blood run cold. Then boil.

Their only hope was that Latif would flee the city, and that a
gatekeeper would see them—and be willing to share that information—or that one of his men would have been in place soon
enough to spot them. Then they would at least have a direction
to go.

Venn and Vera were in the common room. Venn paced, and
Vera chewed on her thumbnail. She stood when she spotted Bennick and Wilf, her face falling. "Clare?"

Venn spun to face them.

Wilf answered tightly. "We almost had her. The Rose betrayed
us, and we lost her to a man named Latif. Salim is dead."

Vera sank back into her chair. Relief and grief warred across
her features.

Venn came forward, putting a comforting hand on her shoulder. His eyes locked with Bennick. "What's the plan?"

Bennick explained that he'd dispatched men to every city gate, and then he told them everything they knew about Latif and the mysterious man who had hired Salim in Duvan. He passed the folded letter to Venn. "I need you and Vera to leave at first light for Duvan. Take this with you. It's possible someone in Desfan's court will recognize the handwriting or make sense of the coded message. They might be able to identify the one responsible for this. That could keep Serene safe, and possibly lead us to Clare."

Venn nodded, already skimming the message. Memorizing it. He shoved it into his pocket. "Even if we can't find the one who wrote this, we can warn Serene about the potential threat in the palace. And let her know the Rose escaped."

"Thank you." Bennick rubbed at his aching temple. "I can only spare one or two men to go with you."

"No," Venn said. "You need all of them. You have no idea where Latif is taking Clare, or how many reinforcements he might have. Vera and I can make it alone."

Bennick dipped his head, his throat too tight for words. Up until this moment, he had been focused on the next step. And now there was no next step. All he could do was wait, and it was already strangling him.

Vera's voice was small. "Clare knows you're alive, Bennick. She knows you're coming for her."

The words were supposed to be comforting, but they caused the ache in his head to spike.

Yes, she knew he was coming, but that wouldn't protect her. And she'd already endured too much. He swallowed back the nausea that rolled through him at the memory of Clare's broken fingers. Her screams . . .

His hands shook, and he cleared his throat. "I need a moment." He strode past them all, headed to the back door of the inn.

In the narrow alley, he doubled his fist and slammed it into the brick wall of the building.

Agony burst across his knuckles as skin tore, but he ignored that. He hit the wall again. Once more. Then he sagged against it, pinching his burning eyes shut. That didn't stop the tears from leaking out.

The frustration, the fear, the hopelessness, the rage, the regret— it choked him.

They should have acted sooner. They shouldn't have waited for the reinforcements to help free them. He and Wilf should have drawn the knives from their boots immediately and reached Clare before she'd disappeared. Again.

He knew they hadn't had any other options. Knew that rushing back to face Salim would have been a mistake. They'd had no choice. The truth of that gutted him.

It was as if he were fates-cursed to keep losing her.

A hand on his shoulder made him twist to face Venn, who looked unusually solemn. The skin around his eyes tightened as he saw Bennick's tears. "I'm sorry," he whispered. "I know exactly what you're going through, because I went through it with Vera. She kept slipping through my fingers the whole time we were tracking them. It's pure torture."

Bennick leaned back against the wall, his shoulders stiffening against the stone. He swiped a hand over the wet trails that traced his face. "She was right there, Venn. I had her. If Zilas hadn't betrayed us . . ."

"I'm sorry," Venn repeated. "But you can't be stuck in the past right now. Clare needs you."

He spotted Wilf hovering near the inn's back door, watching them. He included both of his friends in his next words, spoken softly but firmly. "I love her."

Wilf's brow furrowed. "Is that supposed to surprise us?"

Venn snorted. "We're royal bodyguards. We're trained to notice subtleties, and you two weren't always subtle." He glanced at Wilf. "Was it Dirk who described Bennick's attempts at hiding his feelings from us as *adorable*?"

"I don't remember the word," Wilf said, "but it was Cardon who placed the bet that their first kiss would happen before we left Iden."

Bennick frowned. "Why didn't any of you say anything?"

Venn shrugged one shoulder. "It would have thrown off the bets. No interfereing—that was Dirk's rule."

Wilf huffed. "Did you think we were going to report you?"

"You could have." Strictly speaking, they still could.

"As if we'd turn you in," Venn said. "You're our captain. Our friend. And I've never seen you happier than when you're with Clare."

"Don't you worry that I'll lose focus? That I'll become distracted and put Serene at risk?"

"No," Wilf said.

Well, that was rather final.

Venn rolled back on his heels. "So . . . when was your first kiss? I'm just curious if I'll win this one."

Before Bennick could refuse to answer that, the door opened and Vera poked her head out, her eyes wide. "One of the men just returned. A gatekeeper saw Latif and Clare ride out through the west gate just over an hour ago."

Bennick was already moving.

CHAPTER 34

CLARE

THE SMELL OF SMOKE FILTERED THROUGH Clare's nostrils, and heat stung her face. She jerked into full-consciousness and scrambled back from the blinding flames, her heart slamming inside her chest.

It took several sharp breaths to realize she was not actually burning in a fire. She'd only been placed near a campfire. The encroaching darkness made the small fire appear larger. She stared at it, blinking quickly, blinking quickly, her head aching fiercely.

"How do you feel?"

Clare whirled, one hand fisting on the ground.

A middle-aged man with dark hair and no beard sat watching her. It took her a moment to recall who he was—Latif. The Mortisian who had taken her from Salim.

"Where are we?" she asked, her voice rough from disuse.

"In a forest, not far from Krid," Latif said.

She glanced around them, but the orange flames made the shadows around them look even darker. As she began to realize she wasn't in immediate danger, she finally noticed a stiffness in her right hand and looked down.

Her broken fingers had been straightened, carefully trimmed twigs serving as braces that were secured by twine. She eyed Latif, uncertainty surely marking her expression.

"I decided it would be a kindness to straighten them while you were already unconscious," he said.

She didn't know what to make of that. The fact that she wasn't bound, or currently being tormented, and that he seemed genuinely interested in caring for her injuries confused her. "Thank you," she said at last.

Latif crouched near the fire, checking on a pot of water. "Once the water's warm, I'll wash your wrists."

"Why?"

His brown eyes slid to her. "The wounds appear to be infected. The sooner we treat them, the better."

Clare tucked a strand of hair behind her ear, trying to search out something in the darkness. "How long was I unconscious?"

"A couple of hours." He added a couple of sticks to the fire. "Are you hungry?"

She hesitated, still wary about his unexpected kindness, but she couldn't help but nod. She was starving, especially after exerting so much energy fighting.

Latif fetched her bread and cheese from his saddlebags, which Clare bit into ravenously. When the food was gone, he handed her a water skin, which she summarily drained.

By then the water in the pot reached a boil, and then cooled slightly. Latif began the task of cleaning out the cuts and welts on her wrists. It was strangely intimate work, and Latif's gentleness was almost painful after the constant torture she'd endured.

To distract herself, Clare asked, "Why are you caring for me?"

He frowned, not looking up from his task. "Your wrists need care."

"Aren't you just taking me to my death?"

He grimaced, but did not refute her words. When he brushed the cloth against a particularly sore area, she hissed in pain.

"Sorry," he murmured.

She watched him a moment, completely at a loss. "I don't understand."

"Don't understand what?"

"Why care about healing me if you're just taking me to someone who wants to kill me?"

Latif's jaw flexed, but he remained silent.

Clare frowned. "Who would need so many men to hide behind? First Salim, and now you. Who is this person who is so desperate to kill me?"

"Perhaps we shouldn't talk about this." Latif unfurled the wet cloth and laid it on a nearby rock to dry.

There were a few things that might explain her sudden nerve, even after all she'd endured with Salim. It could have been because Latif was so completely opposite. It could have been the fact that she would probably never see Salim again, or that she'd finally fought back and that had felt good. Or perhaps it was because her hope had been restored; Bennick was alive, and so was Vera. She knew Bennick and Wilf would escape Salim, and that they would be looking for her.

She couldn't let herself think anything else.

"I want to know who hired you," she said. "I deserve to know who's so determined to see me dead."

Latif rummaged in his saddlebag and pulled out a jar of ointment. "This may sting at first."

She held out her wrist for him, mindful of the braces that made her right hand virtually immobile. He wordlessly dabbed the ointment over the red marks on her skin.

"You don't seem cruel," she said. "So why do you work for someone who wants to kill me? A person who would choose to hire someone like Salim?"

"I didn't have a choice," Latif said, not looking up at her.

"If you need coin, I can offer you as much as you're making. More."

He shook his head. "I can't be bribed. It's one of the reasons he chose me."

"Are you trying to be cryptic?"

His lips twitched—or perhaps it was a trick of the flickering fire. "No."

Suddenly, she remembered what he'd said back at the tavern, when he'd paid Salim. Clare had told him he would regret his actions. Latif had said, *I already do.*

"You can't be bribed because you weren't bought," she said slowly. "Is someone forcing you to do this?"

Latif glanced at her, but didn't answer.

She gritted her teeth. "There are some things Salim didn't tell you. My bodyguards caught up to us in Krid. They fought Salim."

"And yet they must have failed, because you remained a prisoner."

"They escaped. They'll come for me, and you won't win against them."

Once again, Latif said nothing.

Clare looked aside, toward his large brown horse tethered nearby. "So, you're taking me to the person who has blackmailed you somehow."

Nothing.

"Is he Mortisian, like you?"

Still nothing.

"Where exactly are we going? What city?"

He sighed.

It was a reaction, at least. She fired off more questions. "Which direction are we traveling? How long do you expect it to take? Do you abduct princesses often?"

Latif gave her a look that begged her to stop.

Clare leaned forward. "Answer one of those questions. Just one."

He lifted an eyebrow. "If I do, will you stop badgering me?"

"For tonight."

His mouth twisted, then he looked her in the eye. "The man who sent me here is not a Mortisian."

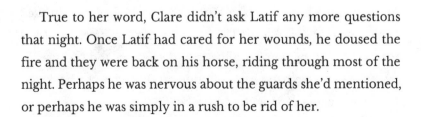

True to her word, Clare didn't ask Latif any more questions that night. Once Latif had cared for her wounds, he doused the fire and they were back on his horse, riding through most of the night. Perhaps he was nervous about the guards she'd mentioned, or perhaps he was simply in a rush to be rid of her.

Clare tried to stay awake, but she found herself dozing as they rode. When dawn broke, they steered off the road once more and slept for a couple of hours. Latif tied her ankle to his own, warning her he was a light sleeper. She had tested that, and he hadn't been lying; she'd barely moved, but his eyes had snapped open.

Then they were on the road once more.

Clare asked endless questions, though Latif remained mostly silent.

They passed several different riders and wagons, but Clare never dared call out. Not only did she doubt anyone would help her, she feared what Latif might do if someone tried to stand against him. He was a shorter man, but stocky. And he had many weapons on his body, including a curved sword strapped to his back. Everything about him, even the way he stood, marked him as a fighter.

She didn't want anyone else getting hurt because of her.

That didn't mean she was no longer searching for an opportunity to run. She was always alert. Unfortunately, Latif paid attention, and she knew with her broken fingers she didn't stand a chance against him if it came to a fight. And though he was feeding her regularly, she knew she wouldn't be able to outrun him.

While they rode, and in-between asking questions that Latif didn't answer, she mulled over what he'd revealed last night.

He had not been sent by a Mortisian, so who had orchestrated her abduction? King Henri? The Rydenic king could very well feel threatened by the coming alliance of Devendra and Mortise. In fact, King Newlan had been counting on that when he brokered the betrothal of his daughter to Desfan.

Or maybe Serene had made an enemy during her time in Zennor. It wasn't so difficult to imagine; the princess could be caustic. A Zennorian could have ordered this abduction in an act of revenge.

There was even the possibility that someone in Devendra had orchestrated Serene's kidnapping. Clare had seen firsthand how upset people were about the alliance. Some would go to any lengths to stop it.

For a brief moment, she even wondered if it could be linked to the princess's rebel activity. If someone had learned she was the leader of a rebellion against her father, they might very well be targeting her for that.

Or Latif could have been lying, and it *was* a Mortisian who had gone to all this trouble to kill Serene.

Fates, Clare's world had become a tangled, ugly mess.

For as long as she was a prisoner, she would attempt to learn all she could. She could then give that information to Serene. She may have declined to join Serene's rebels as a spy, but perhaps that had been a mistake. She was locked in the fight, whether she wanted to be or not.

They ate a simple lunch in the saddle, some dried meats and nuts. As soon as Clare finished, she resumed her questions. "If not a Mortisian, then who hired you? Who wants me gone? Are we headed to meet them? Are we headed to the coast, or Duvan?"

Latif waited for her to pause for breath before he said, "I would like to propose something. What if you ask me one question, and I will answer that question if I can, and then you won't ask me any other questions for the day."

"What about a question an hour?"

"No. One question a day, or none at all."

One answer was better than talking herself hoarse all day and getting nothing, so she nodded. "All right. Who wants me dead?"

"I cannot answer that."

She frowned. "Fine. Where are you taking me?"

"Shebar. It's a city on the coast. We'll ride to Tabakh, and then hire passage on a river barge. It will be our fastest course to Shebar, where we will board a ship that's waiting for us."

"A ship?" Clare bit back a surge of panic. It would be almost impossible for Bennick to find her on the sea. "Where are we going?"

Latif huffed. "I thought I had your promise?"

"You can't tell me we're headed for a ship without telling me the final destination. Are we going to Ryden or Zennor?"

"Neither."

Clare considered this. "So we're heading to another Mortisian port. Or one of the islands?"

Latif sighed. "This would be easier if you didn't talk so much."

"Perhaps I don't want to make this easy for you."

He snorted, shaking his head. "You are not what I expected."

"I've been dragged around your horrible country for weeks against my will. I'm not in a mood to be civil." It was becoming easier to sound like Serene, especially when she knew Salim could not hurt her anymore.

"How are your fingers?" Latif asked suddenly. "I have a little medicine for the pain, if you need it."

She glanced at her braced hand, the fingers still black and blue and throbbing. "They hurt, but I'd prefer not to take anything." She needed to stay alert.

"I *am* sorry for how you were treated."

"Thank you for tending to me," she said, a small sting in her words. "Before you take me to my death."

His exhale was heavy.

He said he was sorry, but that wouldn't stop him from delivering her to a man who would kill her. And yet, she sensed he really *was* sorry. And that was something she might be able to use to her advantage.

"Do you have a family?" she asked. "A wife? Children? Do they know you're doing this?"

Latif's voice was low. "I have no one."

"Well, I have a family." She thought of Thomas, who was only thirteen. Mark, who she had raised from infancy. Eliot, who had died in front of her mere weeks ago. "I have a family who loves me," she continued. "A family I love more than anything. They need me, Latif."

He stiffened behind her, but the only sound was the clopping of the horse's hooves.

She knew she couldn't tell him that she wasn't Serene—that could lead to a quicker death for her. But that didn't mean she couldn't try to make him see her as a person, and not just as the princess he'd been told to abduct. "I'm going to tell you about my little brother," she said, knowing he would never know that she wasn't talking about Prince Grandeur. "I'm going to tell you about a fire he started once, by accident . . ."

She told him story after story. And though Latif said nothing, she knew he had no choice but to listen.

CHAPTER 35

DESFAN

IT WAS LATE ENOUGH THAT KARIM HAD retired, so he could be ready to guard Desfan in the morning. Two bodyguards stood outside the office, waiting for Desfan to finally give up for the night.

Despite all the messages piled on the desk, there had been no word from Zadir. The pirate captain had been hunting Gamble for just over two weeks, and though Desfan knew a search like this would take time, he was impatient for news. He needed to know if Tahlyah or Meerah lived.

He finished writing a letter and signed his name, and then he set aside the quill and stretched his cramped fingers.

A light knock on the door had him looking up. Surprise flashed when Razan entered. "What by all the fates are you still doing up?" he asked.

"I could ask you the same." She nudged the door closed behind her. "I just finished walking the beach with Prince Liam."

Desfan stilled. "You were alone with him?"

Razan sank into a chair across from him. "I'm perfectly capable of taking care of myself, Desfan."

"I never said you couldn't. But Liam is—"

"A dangerous unknown," she interrupted smoothly. "Which is why I'm trying to get close to him."

"He's Ryden's spymaster. He's not going to tell you his secrets."

"Have a little faith in me." She tossed her long, curling hair over her shoulder. "I know he's not going to tell me everything. But he might let something slip if I'm around him enough."

"I don't think that's a good idea. Karim would agree."

She lifted one eyebrow. "I seriously doubt Karim would care if Liam put a knife between my ribs."

Desfan's brow furrowed. "The fact that you jumped to that scenario so quickly is troubling. Do you feel threatened by Liam?"

"No. And you're not denying that Karim wouldn't care."

Desfan sighed. "He would care, Razan."

She picked at a thread on her red and gold skirt. She was silent for a long moment before finally saying, "I'm doing this for you, Desfan. I need to redeem myself."

"You really don't."

"Regardless, I'm your friend and I want to help. Let me."

Knowing he couldn't stop her, he dipped his chin. "Fine. But you need to promise that you'll be careful."

"Of course. This isn't my first time dealing with dangerous men." Razan rested her elbows on the chair's overstuffed arms, her gaze direct. "The betrothal signing is set for summer's end, correct?"

"Yes. Although, truthfully, I wish we could just get on with it."

"Serene *is* very beautiful," she said.

"She is." And things between them were still stiff and awkward. But that was part of his reason for wanting to simply have it done. Perhaps it would push them past this limbo. If nothing else, it would at least open the door to peace talks with Ryden.

Razan's expression gentled. "You need to get to know her, and let her get to know you."

"We've spent time together."

"No. You've attended dinners and meetings together, and you gave her a tour of the palace. You're with her, but not actually spending time with her. You need to court her."

"I don't know how."

Razan laughed. "You're Desfan Cassian. You've been winning female hearts since you learned to smile."

He rolled his eyes. "That's a complete exaggeration. But regardless, it's different with her. She's going to be my *wife*. She's not just a girl I'm flirting with."

"This may be a revolutionary idea, but I believe a man can flirt with his wife."

He shot her a look. "Amusing."

She smiled. "You're charming, Desfan. Let her see that. Let her see *you*. Invite her somewhere special. Do something you enjoy. Share that with her, and I promise things will start to feel better between you."

"It's a good suggestion. Thank you."

"You're welcome."

He eyed her across the desk. "Perhaps you could take your

own advice with a certain bodyguard?"

She shook her head slowly, her small smile tinged with sadness. "I'm afraid some ships are destined to pass in the night." She pushed up from the chair. "Get some sleep, Desfan. And don't worry—I'll share anything I learn from Liam."

"Is there a reason you woke up and decided to take Princess Serene sailing today?" Karim asked, squinting up at the sun.

Desfan shrugged. "It sounded fun?"

Karim blinked, but didn't press.

They stood at the docks. Desfan had sent a message to Serene, inviting her to join him for a morning sail. He'd dragged Karim down to the harbor at first light to make all the necessary arrangements. Thankfully, as celebrations continued for the Dawn of Eyrinthia, there were plenty of docked ships, and it wasn't hard to find a captain who wanted to make some extra coin.

Everything was prepared. Now all he needed was for Serene to arrive. He had a passing thought that she might refuse. What if she didn't care for sailing? Maybe he should have presented her with a couple of activities. And what if she'd already made plans for the day? He knew she'd made appointments with dressmakers in Duvan, and she'd arranged several teas and lunches with the nobility, all with Serai Yahri's guidance. She wanted to get to know his court.

The court she would help him rule. As his wife.

He rubbed his sweating hands over his pants.

"I've never seen you so nervous," Karim said. "You look like you're headed for the gallows."

Desfan didn't appreciate the comparison. His future with Serene felt just as final as death.

Fates blast it, he was being overly dramatic. Though he'd given up his habit of taking olcain or any other drug years ago, he itched for something to numb his nervous edge.

Over the sounds of the awakening harbor, the clatter of an approaching carriage filled the air. Sailors and dockworkers turned to see the royal carriage roll to a stop. Desfan hurried forward so he could offer his hand to Serene.

The Devendran princess looked beautiful as always, with her hair in a thick, elaborate braid and a dusky purple dress suited for travel. She thanked him as he helped her down, and then she surveyed the bustling harbor. "Mortise is filled with early risers, it seems."

"Every day is a gift," Desfan said. "Never waste a morning." She eyed him a little strangely, and he cleared his throat self-consciously. "It's a Mortisian proverb."

"Ah." She stepped away, taking in the expansive view of the harbor.

Movement in the carriage drew Desfan's eye to Princess Imara. She looked a great deal like her cousin, though she was shorter and had a more pleasant smile. Her black hair was in a knot at the back of her head and she wore a light pink dress that contrasted beautifully with her dark skin.

She took Desfan's hand at once. "I hope you don't mind. Serene insisted I come along."

"Not at all." He lowered his voice. "In fact, I'm grateful you're here." He could use a buffering presence—especially one as charming as Imara.

The Zennorian princess offered a reassuring smile. "Serene can be a little frightening, but she's actually very wonderful."

"I appreciate the assurance."

Serene glanced back at them. "What are you two whispering about?"

"Nothing at all," Imara said brightly. She looked to the docked ships. "Which one is ours?"

Desfan pointed. "That one."

"Oh, it looks lovely." She clasped her hands together. "We should have invited Grayson."

Serene nearly stumbled—something that Desfan doubted the Devendran princess did often. Her head swung toward her cousin. "Why, by all the fates, would we have done that?"

"Because he's my friend," Imara said simply. "Admittedly, it's quite recent, and he doesn't really know it yet."

Desfan's lips twitched.

The skin around Serene's eyes tightened, but before she could say anything, Imara walked toward their ship, her two bodyguards trailing behind her.

Desfan extended an arm to Serene. "Shall we?"

She glanced at him before looping her arm in his, and then they followed after Imara. "I assume you've gotten to know the Kaelins during their stay," she said, her voice pitched low. "Do you think Grayson is safe?"

Desfan snorted. "You *have* seen him, haven't you?"

Serene pursed her lips. "I simply meant, is he a danger to Imara?"

"No. As strange as it may sound, he's become my friend as well. Now, as for Liam . . . I'm not sure how much I trust *him*."

"I heard you invited them to the betrothal signing."

Word certainly did travel. "Yes. Liam assures me we can begin peace talks with Ryden as soon as the betrothal is legalized."

"It will be interesting to see if that actually happens."

Desfan nodded.

They reached the gangplank and Serene tightened her hold on his arm as they ascended onto the deck of the ship.

Karim and Serene's two guards, Cardon and Dirk—Desfan had finally learned their names—followed behind them.

Once on board, the captain shouted orders to raise the anchor and free the sails.

Desfan led Serene and Imara to the ship's rail, where they would have the best view of the sea. He pointed out the palace, towering high above them on the cliffs, and told them of all the different types of ships that used the harbor.

Serene listened, Imara asked a lot of questions, and Duvan slowly began to slip away behind them as the ship moved into the sea.

Wind tugged at Desfan's hair and he couldn't stop himself from dragging in a long breath of salty air. Fates, he'd missed this. The swaying of the ship beneath him. The creak of the ropes and the ruffling of the sails. The heat of the sun on his face.

He hadn't realized he'd closed his eyes, but when he opened them, Serene had drifted away to better watch the city disappear behind them.

Imara remained beside him at the rail, and her smile was gentle. "You truly love the sea."

"I do," he admitted.

"You look more relaxed out here." She leaned one hip against the rail as she eyed him. "I like you, Cassian. And I usually have a sense for people. But there's something you need to know. If you ever hurt my cousin, I *will* murder you."

Desfan cracked a smile. "Duly noted."

"Good. Now, I know Serene isn't the easiest person to get to know, and I also understand how awkward an arranged marriage can be. So, I want to help you."

"You do?"

"I want Serene to be happy. And I already consider you a friend, so I'd like to see you happy as well." She dug in her pocket, then flipped a coin at him.

He caught it on instinct, his thumb running over the stamped surface. It was a phoenix, a legendary Zennorian bird. Seeing it pulled a smile from him—not that Imara would have known the significance to him.

"You're a gambler," Imara said. "So, we're going to make some wagers. If you carry on an actual conversation with Serene during this boat ride, you'll owe me that coin."

Desfan's brow furrowed. "Wait. Wouldn't the goal be for me to *keep* the coin?"

"Of course not. The goal is to get it back to me, so I can help create a new and very helpful bet. The real goal here is to win Serene's affection. Do please keep up."

The corner of his mouth lifted. "My apologies. I'm grateful for your help."

"Of course you are." Imara nodded down the rail, where Serene was talking to Dirk. "Tell her something about yourself that she doesn't know. It will prompt her to share as well."

Desfan pocketed the phoenix coin, feeling like it was a talisman. "Thank you, Princess Imara."

She patted his arm. "Please, just call me Imara. We're friends, after all."

He smiled at that. "You make friends quickly."

"It's a gift. Now, go." She shooed him away, and he obediently turned and made his way to Serene.

CHAPTER 36

SERENE

SERENE WATCHED AS DIRK'S CHEEKS REDDENED in response to her question. "Serai Nadir is a very kind woman," he said carefully.

"She is," Serene agreed. "But that's not what I asked. Do you care for her?"

Her oldest bodyguard scrubbed a hand over the back of his neck, his gaze on the horizon.

Serene had one hand on the ship's rail. Her stomach wasn't particularly enjoying the experience of sailing, so she was trying to distract herself by asking Dirk about Tamar Nadir.

The quiet man wasn't very forthcoming.

She took pity on him. "Tamar seems to think a great deal of you."

Dirk cleared his throat. "I believe we enjoy each other's company."

She smiled. "I'm happy for you, Dirk."

That seemed to ruffle him. "It's nothing as serious as all that."

"Do you want it to be serious?" When he didn't respond, she continued, "We're going to be living in Mortise. If you want to be with her, you can."

He eyed her, the wind teasing his graying hair. "Perhaps we should focus more on *your* courtship."

"Courtship? Do you admit you're courting Tamar, then?"

Dirk sighed. "You are incorrigible."

"Thank you."

He rolled his eyes. "There is plenty of time for me and Tamar. But your betrothal to Serjah Desfan is on the horizon. So. I'm going to back away so you can talk with him, and I want you to promise me you'll try to get to know him."

Serene glanced over her shoulder, and sure enough, Desfan was approaching.

She looked to Dirk with narrowed eyes. "We're not done talking about you and Tamar."

Dirk only smiled as he retreated.

Desfan came to stand beside her, only a small space between them. "Are you enjoying yourself?" he asked.

Serene ignored the slight squirming in her stomach as the boat swayed underfoot. "Yes. It's nice to be away from the chaos of the palace."

Desfan chuckled. "True."

Serene peeked over at him. His profile was strong, his nose long and proud, if slightly bent, and his angular jaw was covered in dark stubble. He was twenty years old, though there was a maturity to him she hadn't expected. But then, she knew all too well that loss aged a person. And fates knew Desfan's life had been filled with loss.

"I've never actually been on the sea," Serene admitted.

He looked to her. "Have you sailed at all?"

"A little, on Lambern Lake. And across the Ivern, to visit Zennor."

"Sailing the sea is a completely unique experience."

"It is," she agreed. "You probably grew up sailing these waters."

He nodded. "My family would sail often. And we took yearly trips to Dorma." Shadows entered his eyes, and she knew she'd triggered some dark memory. Hadn't his mother and sisters died on a return trip from Dorma?

She searched for something to say that might dispel the darkness haunting his eyes. "Something about the sea must call to you. After all, you chose to spend years on it."

"It wasn't really a choice in the beginning," he said. "When I was fifteen, my father sent me to sail on a patrol ship for a year to keep me out of trouble."

"Did it work?"

The corner of his mouth lifted, revealing a dimple in his cheek. "Not really. Trouble has a way of always finding me."

That half-grin caught her eye, and she was struck by how handsome he was. She was lucky, she knew. And yet the urge to search the deck for Cardon was strong. She knew he was near.

He was always near.

She deliberately kept her focus on Desfan. "I suppose when your year was up you decided to keep sailing."

He nodded. "I enjoyed it far too much to give it up. Helping people, making the sea safe . . . it gave me a purpose when I needed one."

"It must have been very hard for you to come home."

"It was." He looked at her. "And as you're well aware, I've had a difficult time finding my footing in court. I'm afraid I didn't prepare for becoming the leader of Mortise as I should have. I always thought I would have more time. But then my father fell ill, and in a single instant, I had to become regent."

"How is your father?"

"There have been slight improvements," Desfan said slowly. "He's still unconscious, and has occasional seizures. The physicians don't really understand his condition, so they're not sure how best to help him."

Above them, gulls cried and circled in the air.

"Perhaps I could write to the royal physician in Devendra," Serene said. "He may have some ideas. Only if you want me to, of course" she added quickly. "You could have your physicians draft a letter, and I can send it without reading it."

Desfan's brown eyes traced over her face. "Thank you, Serene. I would appreciate that very much."

She glanced away, feeling her cheeks warm. "It would be no trouble."

"Still, I'm grateful." He shifted his weight and looked out at the rippling water, going silent.

Serene eyed his profile, saw the breeze teasing his dark curls. His jaw was set, his gaze intent. She had never expected to love Desfan. Marrying him was something she needed to do in order to pave the way for her rebels to succeed against her father. She could have taken the evidence of her mother's murder to her uncle, and King Zaire would have attacked Devendra immediately. But while she knew she could count on her uncle's support, she didn't want all-out war. Devendra did not need to suffer more because of Newlan's sins. If she could make Desfan an ally, they could poise Mortise and Zennor against Devendra and force Newlan to abdicate. Even he could not be so arrogant as to believe he could stand against so many.

So Serene would marry Desfan. And though love may not be in their future, she could at least try to befriend him.

"I would love to hear more about your time at sea," she said.

His gaze shifted to her, his eyes clearing as the corner of his mouth lifted. "I'd love to tell you about it. The ship I sailed on was called the *Phoenix*."

"Phoenix," she echoed. "That's familiar."

"It's a legendary creature in Zennor. A bird who burns and rises from the ashes . . ."

The conversation ebbed and flowed, much like the water that carried their ship deeper into the sea.

Serene stared at James's note and rubbed her throbbing temple. Bridget had handed her the letter the moment she'd returned from sailing with Desfan. The code was easy enough to decipher; James needed to meet with her tonight, at midnight, at a tavern called the Raven's Wing near the docks of Duvan.

Getting there could prove difficult, as Cardon and Dirk were excessively protective, but sending Bridget in her stead was not an option. James was quite clear it needed to be Serene, and only her. This level of urgency could only mean something terrible had happened, and her mind raced with the possibilities. Had he learned something about Clare? Was it news from home? So many things could have gone wrong, but guessing was a waste of time and energy.

"Princess?"

Serene jumped, pressing the note against her desk even as she rose and twisted to face Cardon. "Yes?"

His eyes flicked over her—she knew she looked guilty, especially with her hand still behind her back.

She forced herself to let go of the note and lace her fingers in front of her. "Did you need something?" she asked, her voice calmer than before.

Cardon straightened into stricter attention. "I wanted you to know that Dirk requested the evening off. He wanted some time with Serai Nadir."

That made her smile. "How wonderful. I hope they have a pleasant evening."

Cardon rubbed a palm against the side of his thigh—a rare sign of nervous energy. "You seemed to have a good time with Serjah Desfan today."

Heat tickled her face. "Yes, I did."

His throat flexed. "Good. I'm glad to hear it." He glanced over her shoulder, his chin lifting. "I didn't screen any letters for you."

Her already thrumming heart beat faster. "Hmm?" She feigned momentary confusion, then plucked up James's note. "Oh, this? It came for Bridget. It's a harmless love note." The lie was easy enough to tell, since James had written it as such. It was a guise they'd used many times.

Cardon took a step closer. "She asked you to read it?"

Serene's cheeks heated, as often happened when Cardon got

too close. Knowing she needed an excuse for her blush, she said, "Bridget doesn't know I have it."

He lifted an eyebrow. Serene had wondered more than once if he'd gotten the habit from her, or if she had learned it from him. "Princess, that doesn't seem like you."

"You know very well that's exactly like me."

The edge of his mouth curved. He held out a hand. "May I?"

Resigned, Serene passed it to him.

Cardon read through the short note, his brow furrowing. "It's unsigned."

"Secret admirers tend to be *secretive*, Sir Brinhurst."

The corner of his mouth tugged down as he scanned the words. "Perhaps I should have a word with Bridget."

"Why?"

He eyed her over the note. "It's dangerous for her to become romantically attached to anyone in Mortise."

"And yet you're supportive of Dirk and Tamar?"

"That's different. Dirk is careful, and Serai Nadir has proved a friend. As your maid, Bridget needs to be wary of who she allows close."

"Bridget is a fine maid," Serene said defensively as she plucked the note from his fingers.

Cardon snorted. "Her taste in men is suspect."

Now it was her turn to arch a brow. "What makes you say that?"

"That note is the most poorly written love letter I've ever seen."

Serene set it on the desk, turning her back on him. "And just how much experience with love letters do you have?"

"More than you think, judging by your tone."

It took everything she had to sound disinterested. "As the receiver or giver?"

Cardon didn't answer. He slid in beside her, taking hold of the back of the chair. "Let me show you. Sit."

Her knees had begun to tremble, so sitting seemed the safest option.

Cardon's left hand remained on the chair as he reached for a sheet of clean paper. Serene wordlessly scooted the ink and quill closer to him.

"Now, the beginning is important," Cardon said. "Bridget's admirer said, *My Dear Bridget*."

"You find fault with that?"

"It's not how I would begin."

Serene folded her arms. "Do tell."

Cardon leaned down and lifted the quill, dipping it in the ink. He was so close she could feel his warmth. She became distracted by the clean smell of him and the way his jaw tightened as he wrote—his cheek was only a breath from her nose.

He eased back and Serene looked at what he'd written.

My Truest Love.

Under other circumstances, Serene might have laughed at such sentimentality coming from her rigid soldier. Not now. Not when he was still so close she could kiss him before he had a chance to react.

"What do you think?" he asked, his brown eyes sliding heavily over her profile.

She swallowed—a gulp that pulled her back from the edge of making a colossal mistake. She *would not* kiss him.

Still, her lips tingled as she imagined the scrape of his lightly stubbled jaw. "It's rather nice," she managed to say.

Cardon glanced at the note from James. *"From the first glance of the raven's wing until midnight, you are urgently in my thoughts."*

She gripped her elbows. "It's poetic."

Cardon ducked his head toward hers. "True poetry is simple. Honest." Serene watched the scar on his cheek as he set the quill to paper once more. She tried very hard to keep her breathing steady.

I think of you constantly.

Serene stared at those simple words, a flutter in her abdomen.

Without prompting, Cardon began revising the next lines, which were full of flattery—and the strategically placed message, *you must come yourself.*

Under Cardon's hand, the flowery praise became a simple statement: *You are the brightest part of my life.*

Serene kept her eyes on the page, even when he turned toward her. His mouth was near her temple. She could feel every warm exhale against her skin.

Why? Why would he do this? Was it the fates testing her resolve? If so, she refused to fail.

She cleared her throat. "You have many talents, Sir Brinhurst."

Cardon did not pull away from her. "Thank you, Princess."

She tapped a finger against the blank space left on the page. "Is your lover ever disappointed by the shortness of your letters?"

"I hope she would focus on what I say—not the things I don't."

Of all the fates-blasted treachery. This was the cruelest trick the man could play. He'd made it clear long ago how he felt about her. Why did he insist on torturing her when he knew full well how she felt about him?

She sealed her lips. Her body was stiff, but she couldn't relax. Not when he remained a breath away, watching her.

Finally, Cardon turned his head aside. "Of course, a love letter should always be signed."

Serene listened as the quill scratched the paper, heard the pauses as he dipped for more ink. At long last he slipped away from her, his fingertips brushing her shoulder as his hand dropped from the back of the chair. "I'll be right outside when you're ready to go to dinner."

He didn't wait for a response. His boots tread from the room, crossed measuredly over the empty sitting room, and finally left her entire suite behind.

Only then did Serene's eyes dip to the last lines he'd written.

I will fight forever to be at your side.

All my love.

Cardon

CHAPTER 37

SERENE

SERENE KEPT HER HEAD DOWN AS SHE approached the Raven's Wing. The tavern had a sagging roof, and was set so close to the harbor it was practically on the docks. The whole area felt different at night than it had this morning, with Desfan. To be fair, though, Serene was on the far end of the harbor, and it was visibly a part of the city's slums. The stench of rotting wood, fish, and sewage was thick. It was nearly midnight, and she almost couldn't believe she'd made it here so easily.

She'd snuck out of the palace a couple of hours ago, because she knew trying to leave at midnight would draw too much attention. Just after dinner, though? Plenty of palace staff and visitors would be making their way through the gates, making it easy to blend in.

With Dirk spending the evening with Tamar Nadir, Serene's biggest obstacle was slipping past Cardon. Luckily, he was adorably predictable. When Bridget had asked him for advice on the *secret admirer* she was exchanging letters with, Cardon was only too eager to follow her into another room. He would, no doubt, want to take the opportunity to assess the situation, and steer away any potential risk to Serene.

Everything else was fairly simple after that. Since her arrival in Duvan, Serene had made a point to keep people coming and going at all hours to repair her wardrobe, and any other trivial thing she could think of. And because each newcomer was screened before going *inside* the rooms, the guards were not concerned with anyone leaving.

Serene had donned a simple Mortisian dress that Bridget had acquired earlier from the palace laundry, and with a headscarf in place, the guards didn't see her face when she slouched past them. She mumbled a cursory goodnight in Mortisian, making her words curt but her accent rolling, like the servants she'd over-heard. The guards mumbled a reply reflexively back, and Serene disappeared around the corner.

Bridget had mapped out the servants' passages for her, and Serene had always had a head for memorization. She didn't have to double back even once to find her way unobtrusively into the darkened palace grounds, and she seamlessly joined the line of others making their way through the main gate.

Standing in front of the Raven's Wing now, Serene couldn't help but feel a flash of pride. Then again, getting back *inside* the palace would be the real trick. It would all come down to timing.

Out of habit, her fingers sought out the long dagger sheathed at her waist. It was hidden by her lightweight cloak, but the protection it offered helped her stride into the tavern without fear.

Despite the revolting locale and disgusting layer of scum covering every surface, the Raven's Wing seemed popular. Most patrons appeared to be—predictably—sailors and fishermen. Games of cards and dice occupied most of the tables, and the smell of strong ale saturated the air. The perfect place for strangers to ignore each other.

She was early, but James was already waiting. He looked travelworn, but still cleaner than any of the other men in the establishment. He'd claimed a table in the center of the room, as he preferred to conduct meetings in plain sight. He was convinced that shifty eyes always inspected corners first, and she supposed he was right. In a place this loud and chaotic, she knew they would be easily overlooked.

James stood when he spotted her. He didn't smile—another marker that things were dire.

She slid into a vacant chair across from him. "What a charming place you've found," she said lowly, attempting humor.

He settled back in his seat. "I like being near the docks. You hear more of the goings on."

"I'm relieved you didn't pick it for the smell. Have you learned anything about Clare?"

James shook his head, his eyes worried. "Nothing. I talked to someone who at least knows of a mercenary named Salim, but I couldn't learn anything concrete. We don't have many contacts in Mortise."

Serene's shoulders drooped. "Very well. Thank you for trying."

"I'll keep an ear out," he promised.

"Thank you." She took in a breath. "So. What's wrong?"

James settled his arms on the table as he leaned in. "We have two problems."

"Only two?"

"They're large enough." He tapped his thumb against the table's edge, a nervous habit. "You know that Prince Grandeur went to Lythe to inspect our military forces, as well as to take a stand against the rebels."

"Yes." Clare had passed along that information weeks ago, before they'd crossed into Mortise.

"Well, Grandeur has since been put in charge of Devendra's military."

"*What?*"

James nodded grimly. "My sources tell me that King Newlan wanted to demonstrate his faith in his son by dividing some of the monarchy's power."

Fates, this wasn't good. That kind of power in Grandeur's hands was dangerous. And chilling. Her brother had proven to be paranoid and impulsive—traits that seemed to grow worse over time.

This knowledge only made her more conscious of how important this rebellion was. Devendra would not survive with Grandeur at the helm. She could not let him become king.

She blew out her breath. "What's our other problem?"

James looked at her, his jaw hard. "Grandeur isn't just investigating rebel activity. He has organized something called *the Hunt.* If a person is even suspected of disloyalty, they're detained and tortured into making confessions. There's a lot we still don't know. I'm trying to learn more, but many of our rebels are disappearing—including key leaders." His eyes darkened. "The people are terrified, Serene. He's killing them. Rebels or not, it doesn't seem to matter to him. People are fleeing the kingdom in droves."

Fury snapped inside her. "This can't stand."

"What would you have us do?" James asked.

"Above all, be cautious." She bit her lip, trying to think. "We need more time. I can't make a move against Grandeur until I have a strong alliance with Desfan."

His brow furrowed. "Unfortunately, time is something we don't have."

Fates, but that was true. Serene pursed her lips. "I can't rush the wedding. But I can ask Desfan to move up the betrothal signing. He's anxious to enter peace talks with Ryden, so he may be amenable." Her heart stuttered a little at the thought of legalizing the betrothal sooner than expected, but she ignored it. "I can also write to my father. Perhaps he isn't aware of how brutal Grandeur is treating people."

"He knows exactly what your brother's doing, and he's not stopping him. Why would he? They're both terrified of another civil war."

A civil war was something Serene wanted desperately to avoid. Too many innocents would die.

"I'm sorry to make you come out here," James said. "I know it's not easy for you to sneak away. But I needed you to know what's happening in Devendra."

"You did the right thing," she told him. "I needed to hear this."

The time for hesitating was done.

Their meeting concluded minutes later, and then James slipped away. Serene would leave after a slight delay, just as a precaution.

She kept her eyes on the table, though she was aware of a game of cards turning heated in the corner. There were two different accents—Mortisian and Rydenic—and accusations of cheating littered the air.

Not interested in becoming part of a brawl, Serene stood. Others must have had the same idea, because the crowd was thick as she made her way toward the door.

She was nearly there when a strangled yell pierced the air, followed by the fleshy thud of a hard punch. Serene shot a look over her shoulder and saw the gaming table flip—and then chaos ensued. Chairs were thrown, bottles shattered, and bodies flew. The patrons around Serene turned into a frenzied crush, and elbows stabbed into Serene from all sides. She grunted at each blow, but steeled herself against the pain as she shouldered for the door.

A heavy body slammed into her from behind and she hit the floor hard, elbows and knees banging against the wooden floor. She couldn't breathe because of the crushing weight planted on top of her. She lay there, stunned, surrounded by the explosive sounds of the fight; the smack of knuckles striking flesh, shouts and curses from two different kingdoms, and the crack of tables and chairs being broken.

The man flattening her kicked off suddenly, sending an elbow into the back of her head. Her ears rang and her vision blurred as her chin hit the floor. She could feel blood welling to fill the cut.

That would not be easy to explain tomorrow.

Gritting her teeth, Serene scrambled to her feet—then ducked hurriedly to avoid a hurled chair. She hugged the wall and darted for the door. Her only goal was to make it out of the tavern without being further pummeled. When needed, she fell back on the lessons her bodyguards had taught her over the years—all ways to end a potential fight quickly. A kick between the legs. A quick jab to the throat.

"Soldiers coming!" someone yelled.

Fates. The last thing she needed was to be arrested for brawling in Duvan's slums. Cardon would never let her hear the end of it. Dirk would be utterly disappointed. And Desfan and his court would probably struggle between laughing at the absurdity of it all, or simply voiding the marriage alliance.

I'm sorry, she could almost hear Desfan say. *There can only be one reckless royal in Mortise, and I've already taken on that mantle.*

She sniggered, but instantly winced.

Perhaps that elbow to the head had done more damage than she'd thought. There was nothing funny about this.

She rushed for the door, finally pushing through the crowd. Once on the street, she bolted—but her run was short-lived. She smacked into a hard chest after only a few leaping steps.

Hands gripped her arms, steadying her, and Cardon's scar jumped in his cheek as he glared. "Of all the fates-blasted idiotic things you've done, this is legendary!"

"Soldiers," she rasped.

Cardon scowled, but he released one of her arms. "Come on," he snapped.

They sprinted away from the Raven's Wing and down a side street, cobblestones slick with something that smelled questionable. He never let go of her arm, even though they'd move faster if they were not anchored to each other.

She didn't complain.

After several minutes of running, Cardon hauled her to a stop. They stood in an alley, and Cardon scanned the dark windows and shadowed corners. Serene leaned back against the wall, fighting to regain her breath.

Cardon swiveled to face her. His grip on her wrist flexed. "Are you trying to get yourself killed?"

She bristled. "Of course not! And I was perfectly fine."

He thrust his face closer, their noses almost touching. "Do you have any idea what could have happened to you out here?"

"I took precautions."

"You didn't take *me*." His expression was severe, and his breaths came out forced. "What possessed you to leave the palace?" he asked, his voice rough. "What sort of stupidity drove you to sneak into the slums—*alone*—in the middle of the night? You could have been murdered, or a hundred other things!"

"You're overreacting," she began.

His glower silenced her. "I don't know what this is about—why you tricked me as you did—but I will never make the mistake of trusting you again."

He may as well have slapped her. Serene fisted her hands, her nails biting her palms. There was nothing she could say. Nothing she could tell him that he would accept. He wouldn't even believe the truth—not that she could tell him. For one thing, he'd probably have some choice things to say about her being the leader of a rebellion. For another, she would *never* put him in danger of being implicated in the treason she committed daily.

Serene glanced away, biting the inside of her cheek, desperate not to cry in front of him.

Silence stiffened the air between them. Gradually, his stranglehold on her arm loosened. "You're bleeding," he murmured.

She touched her chin reflexively. Her fingers came away sticky. "It's nothing."

Cardon's fingertips brushed her cheeks, tilting up her jaw. He examined the cut with hooded eyes and a thin mouth. "It's not too deep," he agreed. He produced a handkerchief and dabbed gently at the wound.

Serene's eyes flickered to his and then away, back and forth, the entire time. She noticed only now that he had taken the time to switch out his Devendran uniform for a Mortisian shirt, teal with loose sleeves.

"Are you hurt anywhere else?" he asked, holding the cloth to her chin.

"No."

He leveled a look at her.

"Just bruises," she assured him.

"Did you start the fight?"

She frowned, grimacing when the gesture pulled on her cut. "I did nothing of the sort. I was caught on the edge of it, nothing more."

"Are you going to tell me why you were there at all?"

"Didn't Bridget tell you?"

His hard expression didn't change. "I'd like to hear the truth from you."

Clever of him.

Wondering what Bridget would have told him, she cleared her throat. "I just needed to get out of the palace. It's stifling."

One eyebrow cocked. "You expect me to believe that?"

"It's the truth."

"If you were just out to wander, why did Bridget know exactly where you'd be?"

Drat. Her mind was not spinning lies as quickly or effectively as usual. Probably from the blow to her head. Or possibly because Cardon's hands still warmed her skin. "Very well. I was meeting someone."

His eyes narrowed. "Who?"

She sighed. "Someone I thought might have news about Clare."

Cardon had clearly not expected that. He stared at her a moment, then frowned. "Who?" he asked again.

"One of Serai Nadir's guards knew someone who has had dealings in the past with mercenaries."

"And you thought it wise to meet with such a person near the docks—alone—in the middle of the night?"

"It was the only way he would agree to meet."

He muttered a curse, but asked, "Did you learn anything?"

She blushed. "No. The man didn't come."

Cardon grunted, peeling the handkerchief away. "It could have been a trap."

"He didn't know I was the princess."

"Still." He busied himself folding the stained handkerchief, his focus on his meticulous work. "I apologize for losing my temper," he finally said, his voice muted. "My sole purpose is to keep you safe, and I can't protect you if I'm not with you." His brown eyes lifted, and for once they were completely unguarded. The open emotion was not easy to name, but desperation edged his words. "Please, Serene. Don't put me through this again."

Serene's breath stalled. He'd stopped using her name—at least in her presence—three years ago. She hadn't realized how much she'd missed hearing him say it.

But then his words hit, and her heart pounded. She couldn't

make any promises. Not that he'd expressly asked for one. No, this was worse. He was begging her, and she had no choice but to disappoint him.

Serene set her hand over his, still clutching the folded cloth. Her eyes fastened onto his gaze, her fingers tightening their hold. "I'm sorry. I never meant to worry you, Cardon."

The slight wrinkles around his eyes tightened. "I was more than worried."

"I know. And I'm sorry. It was my intention that you'd never know I was gone."

His forehead creased. "That is not reassuring, Princess."

"How *did* you find out?"

He slid back a step, tucking the handkerchief into his pocket. He indicated it was time for them to begin walking, and Serene was quick to fall into step beside him. "Bridget kept repeating herself. I thought at first she was too love-sick to notice her repeated compliments, but she kept glancing at the door. I realized she was a distraction, so I went to your room." He sent her an almost affronted look. "You didn't even fit pillows under your blankets."

"I didn't imagine you'd go into my bedroom, Sir Brinhurst."

He rolled his eyes. "It was rather easy to figure out that the man Bridget had been touting was fiction. She told a variety of lies, and I grew irritated. I asked to see her love note. Considering events, it was easy enough to decipher." He glanced over at her. "It was a summons. For you." His throat bobbed as he swallowed. "You lied to me."

"I knew you wouldn't let me go."

"Perhaps that should have told you something about the idiocy of your plan."

"I *did* make it all the way to the Raven's Wing without any trouble, you know."

"Again, not very reassuring. What was your plan for reentering the palace?"

"Princess Serene likes fruit brought to her rooms every morning at dawn. She can be quite picky about it." She smiled at him. "And you would have retired to your rooms by then, so fooling the guards at the door would have been easy enough. They don't know me as well as you do."

Cardon blinked. "You would have remained out in the city all night, waiting for dawn?"

"Yes."

He swore lowly, but there was no anger in his tone. Just exasperation. "Worrying over you has turned me gray before my time."

Serene glanced at his brown hair, somewhat lightened with silver at the temples. "You've a long way to go yet."

He muttered something under his breath, and then they walked in silence for a few minutes. Cardon prompted them to abandon a couple of streets where shadowed forms stood along building fronts. Even though he was tense beside her, Serene felt quite at ease.

When they neared the outer wall of the palace, Cardon halted in the shadow of a nobleman's estate. "We'll wait and enter at dawn, following your plan."

"I thought you disliked my plan."

"I disliked the thought of you out here on your own. The plan itself is good."

She pointedly ignored the thrill that jolted through her. "Is there really a need to sneak anymore?"

"Yes. It would be disastrous if Serjah Desfan—or any of the Mortisians—learned you were out in the streets unprotected."

"Nothing happened."

"Not true. You were hurt. And you slipped past me. After your betrothal is legalized, Serjah Desfan would be well within his rights to dismiss me over something like this."

Her heart seized. "But it wasn't your fault."

"I wasn't with you and you were hurt. It's entirely my fault."

"I tricked you."

He shook his head. "If the serjah believes I'm not fit to protect his future wife, dismissing me would be the only option."

"I wouldn't allow that, Cardon."

"You couldn't stop it."

Serene gritted her teeth. She had been making personal sacrifices her entire life. She'd made a heart-rending sacrifice to keep Cardon from leaving her three years ago. It was the worst kind of mockery that her marriage—her next largest sacrifice—could lead to losing the man she had given up so much to keep close.

Cardon sighed. "I'm sorry. I don't mean to hold that over you, only I . . . don't want to leave you." The admission seemed to cost him; the vulnerability of it certainly caught her by surprise. He glanced away. "We should find a place to sit. We still have a few hours before dawn."

Serene followed him wordlessly into a side street, knowing it would be a long wait. Any time she spent alone with Cardon was exquisite torture, because she couldn't do or say the things she longed to.

It was especially painful knowing she never would.

CHAPTER 38

BENNICK

THE DAYS WERE BECOMING A BLUR. RIDE HARD. Watch for evidence of a lone horse leaving the west road—follow that trail, and rejoin the road when it led nowhere. Stop at every town. Ask questions of everyone they saw.

Bennick was grateful for Serai Nadir's men, who were able to ask questions without resistance or cutting looks. When they asked travelers on the road if they'd seen a middle-aged man with a half-Devendran, half-Zennorian woman on a brown horse speckled black, they nodded and pointed.

From one small town to the next, Bennick chased after Clare. In the large city of Tabakh, the fates guided them to the riverside where they happened to find a man who had helped Latif book passage on a river barge to Shebar. And he confirmed that Clare was with him.

She was still alive.

Bennick clung to that as they waited impatiently for the next barge to depart. Traveling with the currents of the river would be faster than riding to Shebar, as they would have also had to go out of their way to reach the bridge that would cross over the river. To pay for passage they had to sell their horses, but that was all right—there wasn't room for them on the barge anyway.

Shebar was on the edge of Mortise, tucked near the Rydenic border. It was a large port, one where someone like Latif could easily disappear. All he needed was a ship, and he could take Clare anywhere—the islands, Ryden, Zennor, or somewhere else in Mortise.

If Bennick didn't find her in Shebar, there was every chance he would lose her forever.

He refused to let that happen.

After four days on the river, they reached Shebar. They asked around the river docks and learned nothing, so they set out for the sea docks. Ships creaked and bobbed in the water, towering vessels that flew a myriad of different flags, all of them belonging somewhere else in Eyrinthia.

As they waited their turn to speak with the dockmaster, Bennick glanced at the men grouped around him. Weariness etched their faces, and Bennick knew the strain of their rapid travel had worn them all thin. And yet they were still with him. Even Nadir's men, who did not owe him loyalty. They had fought beside each other, Devendran and Mortisian, all in an effort to save Clare. To keep the peace alive.

Bennick was reclining against a heavy barrel when the dockmaster approached. One of Nadir's men—a man called Fihtah—spoke with him.

Bennick was able to follow most of the conversation, but he was still grateful when Fihtah thanked the dockmaster, then translated for the Devendrans. "He said there was a storm that prevented any ships from leaving the past two days. He has not personally seen Latif, or anyone matching his description, but he said many people book passage on the ships. Because of the storms, it is safe to assume that Latif and Clare are still in the city—if Latif is, in fact, hoping to take her on a ship."

"Are there any records the dockmaster can check?" Bennick asked. "Any way to see if Latif bought passage?"

"He said that is up to each captain to track, and not all captains keep good records. Further, Latif may have used a false name. The dockmaster did say that four ships are set to sail tomorrow morning. One to Duvan, the second to Leeb—a Mortisian island—the third to Zoroya, in Zennor, and the last to Porynth, in Ryden. It's possible Latif booked passage on any of these."

"We could approach the ships," Wilf said. "Ask for their manifests."

Bennick wanted to do just that, but he needed to think like the captain he'd trained to be, not the terrified, desperate man he was. He couldn't let panic cloud his judgement. "If Latif is friends with the captain he's sailing with, asking questions could alert Latif and he might run. We need to hang back, but keep eyes on all four ships."

And if Clare and Latif never showed up . . . He would make a new plan then.

Wilf nodded, and Bennick asked Fihtah to learn where the four ships were anchored. The dockmaster found the information easily;

the one bound for Zennor was on the south side of the docks, but the other three were relatively close together on the north side. That would make them easier to watch.

Every day, every hour, every second Clare was gone was a painful stab in his heart. But he was getting close. He could feel it.

This time, he would not lose her.

CHAPTER 39

CLARE

CLARE SAT AT THE SMALL TABLE IN THE ROOM she and Latif had shared for the last two nights. They'd made it to Shebar, but storms in the city had kept them from meeting their ship. This morning dawned bright, however, and Clare knew she was out of time.

The past week with Latif had been a vastly different type of captivity. With Salim, every moment had been fear and torture. Conversely, Latif treated her with kindness. He made sure she had plenty to eat and drink. He respected her privacy, and when they stayed at an inn, he gave her the bed while he slept in a bedroll on the floor. Unfortunately, he was a light sleeper, and he always placed his bedroll in front of the locked door, so slipping past him wasn't an option. When they'd reached Tabakh, Latif had even bought her a new dress to replace her torn and dirtied one, along with a pair of new boots. He'd arranged a bath at the inn, and Clare finally felt clean. The dye was long gone from her skin, but even without layers of grime, her distant Zennorian heritage kept her looking enough like Serene to fool someone who had never met the princess. Besides, Latif had no reason to think she *wasn't* Serene. Not after all she'd been through.

Clare thought about telling him the truth—that she wasn't Serene. But Latif was clearly a desperate man, and whoever had blackmailed him was to be feared. Chances were great that Latif would still carry her to the man who wanted Serene dead, and the sort of man who hired Salim and conspired to kill an innocent princess would not hesitate to kill *her*—a mere decoy.

No, she would keep her secret for now.

While they traveled on the river barge, Latif taught her a Mortisian card game called Assassins to help pass the time. Clare didn't have much experience playing games, as she had spent most of her childhood working and taking care of her brothers, but Latif had assured her it was not a difficult game to learn. "It takes a little skill, but mostly luck," he said, shuffling the cards. "Can you bluff?"

"Lie?" She smiled a little. "I've gotten rather good at that."

As the days passed, Clare remained alert for a chance to escape, but there was nowhere to run on the river barge, or once they were secured in the inn bedroom. So she played cards and continued her efforts to get Latif to see her as a person. If he could see her as more than a prisoner, he might decide *not* to deliver her to her death.

Time for that was running out, though. Clare knew if they got on the ship, that would be the point of no return.

She held her cards in her good hand. Her broken fingers were slowly mending in the braces. They still ached, but the bruising and swelling had gone down considerably. Catching a glimpse of her wrist, she could see that scabs had formed around the deep rope cuts.

"You're quiet this morning," Latif said, studying his cards.

Clare eyed him. "When are we leaving for the ship?"

"Soon. But we have time for a couple more rounds."

"Where is the ship going?"

Latif said nothing.

"Do you really want to see me dead?" she asked softly.

His eyes pinched closed. "Princess, I have no choice."

"If you help me, I'll help you. No matter who your enemies are."

"You don't want my enemies."

"It seems I already have them."

His expression tensed. "You're right. So regardless of what I do, you're as good as dead."

She flinched.

Regret sparked in his eyes. "I'm sorry. I shouldn't have said that."

Clare laid her cards on the table. "I think I'm done playing."

Latif winced as if she'd struck him. She half-wished she had. Her attempts to befriend him had done nothing. He was still going to lead her to her death. What did it matter if his guilt was more apparent now? His cowardice was clearly stronger.

Because of her broken fingers, she couldn't braid her hair, so it fell loose around her face. She didn't bother pushing the dark strands back as Latif gathered their things and they left the room.

Latif kept hold of her arm as they walked the crowded street. Anxiety gripped her. She couldn't board a ship. At least at the moment, she only had one enemy—Latif. On a ship, she would be trapped.

She refused to be trapped again.

Latif had his bag slung over one shoulder as he threaded through the streets. Clare tried to keep her breathing even, her heartbeat steady. She would need the element of surprise when it came time to act.

The docks were chaotic, teeming with sailors, passengers, dock workers, and cargo. It would be easy to get lost in this crowd.

The anchored ships were huge and towering. She stared at the triple-masted ships and tried to imagine the sails unfurled. These were floating towns, not just ships like the barge she and Latif had traveled on. Hundreds of men could be housed in one. If that wasn't enough to make her feel small, her first view of the sea certainly did the job. It was vast. Unending.

She knew Bennick would tear Mortise apart looking for her, but if she got on a ship, he might never find her.

Clare made the pretense of tripping.

Latif grabbed her arm, steadying her. "Are you all right?"

"The laces on my boots," she said. "They're undone."

Latif glanced down, but her long skirt almost skimmed the street, so he couldn't see her boots. He loosed a sigh, glancing at her braced fingers before he released her arm and lowered to one knee.

Before he could see the laces were tight beneath her skirt, Clare shoved her knee up under his chin, knocking his head back.

He reared away with a curse and Clare bolted. She kept her injured hand close to her chest to avoid bumping it against anything as she ran.

Latif's shout was swallowed in the noise buffeting the docks, but she knew he'd be after her in seconds. Launching through the crowd, she weaved between people and crates, dodging her way back toward the main part of the city.

She hadn't gone far when a man stepped into her path. She tried to swerve around him, but their shoulders collided. The blow jarred her broken fingers, and Clare cried out.

The man snagged her arm, keeping her from spinning away. "Saw what you did to Latif," he said. "Not very polite."

She stiffened. His accent was clipped. Not the rounded Mortisian drawl she'd grown used to. His wasn't an accent she was familiar with, but she still knew it at once. He was from Ryden.

And he had said Latif's name.

Latif came up behind her and grasped her shoulder, tugging her around to face him. Spots of color dotted his cheeks and his eyes flashed angrily. "What was that for?"

Fury ripped through her, and Clare lifted her good hand to slap him.

He caught her wrist with his free hand, his frown hardening. "What's come over you?" he demanded.

She spat in his face.

The Rydenic sailor chuckled. "What a spirited princess Devendra has."

Latif used his shoulder to swipe at the spittle near his nose. He dragged Clare closer, but still lowered his voice. "Struggle again and I'll have no choice but to tie your hands."

"You lied," she growled. "You said we weren't going to Ryden."

Latif's jaw flexed as he ground his teeth. "We're not going to Ryden. Just to the border."

"As if that matters. What else did you lie about?"

He cursed under his breath and dragged her back the way they'd come, the Rydenic man trailing behind. He kept his voice quiet, just between the two of them. "Fighting won't help. These men are ruthless, but if you'll just trust me, I promise I won't let them hurt you."

Tremors shook her body. Latif's words meant nothing. She was as good as dead the moment she stepped onto a Rydenic ship. Revealing that she was a decoy would not save her life. In fact, the revelation might bring about her death sooner. Latif might kill her for fooling him.

They reached a long dock and crossed the length of it, stopping at the very end. The gangplank that led up onto the ship sat before her, and she dug in her heels.

"Don't be difficult," Latif said in her ear, true pleading in his tone. "Just get on the ship. There may be a way out of this for both of us, but you must trust me."

Clare twisted to look at him. "I can walk on my own," she said, her voice too level as she pointedly ignored his vague words of promise. Surely they were just a ruse to gain her obedience. Just as he had kept her distracted by his kindness, lies, and games.

Latif frowned. "I'm not—"

She elbowed him in the throat and Latif crumpled, choking. The Rydenic sailor snatched for her, but she ducked under his sweeping arm and slammed her elbow into his lower back, pitching him forward so he tripped over Latif.

Then she ran.

Men on the deck of the ship yelled, but there was no one on the dock to grab her. She ran toward shore, where she had a chance of disappearing if she could only vanish into the crowd.

She'd nearly reached the end of the dock when she heard someone yell her name.

Bennick.

She nearly stumbled as she whipped her head toward the sound, her heart exploding out of her chest when she spotted him on a parallel dock, the space too wide to jump. He was also running toward shore, where the docks would meet.

"Bennick!" she screamed.

He only ran faster, his arms pumping furiously as he stole looks at her. "Keep running!" he yelled. "Go!"

She redoubled her efforts, hearing the pounding footsteps behind her and the Rydenic shouts.

When she glanced back at Bennick, she saw he was no longer running alone. "Wilf!"

The large soldier glanced at her, still running at full speed.

Tears pricked her eyes to see him here, too. They were so close. So painfully close. And they were closing the gap quickly.

Wilf passed Bennick, who moved more slowly than normal—due to his injury, Clare was sure. Wilf plunged onto the crowded main dock, shoving his way toward the dock she was on.

"Clare!" Bennick shouted. It was her only warning.

Her vision blurred as she was tackled from behind. She hit the wooden dock hard, her shoulder and hip bruising. Her hands flashed out on instinct to catch her, and her braced hand slapped agonizingly against the dock.

She gasped breathlessly, shaking with pain even as she was harshly twisted onto her back. The Rydenic sailor who had jumped on top of her glared down, pinning her against the dock with his body. "Latif should have broken more than just your fingers," he snarled.

Clare shoved against him, knowing she only needed seconds. Bennick was here, and so was Wilf. They were running for her right now—

The Rydenic man grabbed her arm, slamming it against the wooden dock. Agony burst through her broken fingers. Her stomach lurched when she saw him double a fist.

"No—!"

He punched her splinted fingers and a scream tore from her throat, cutting off her words. Her body went rigid, all her struggles ceasing as every muscle seized.

He raised his fist for a second blow.

Wilf tore the man off of her, roaring as he attacked.

Clare rolled onto her side and wriggled away, gasping through her tears as she pushed into a seated position. With blurred vision she watched Wilf beat the man's face bloody, and beyond him she saw Latif stumble toward them, his skin pale.

In a haze of pain, Clare struggled to breathe. Nothing felt quite real about this moment, and she was desperate for this nightmare to end. Desperate for—

"Clare."

She twisted, still sitting on the dock, her broken fingers cradled against her chest. Her heart jumped as Bennick fell to his knees. He reached for her, his trembling hands framing her face as his blue eyes dragged over her, taking in every detail.

Then he pulled her against him. The hilt of his sword dug into her side, but she didn't care as he held her close. He tucked her head under his chin, his chest rising and falling rapidly against hers.

"You found me," she rasped, gripping his shirt with her good hand. The material was thin and loose compared to his usual uniform, but it smelled like him.

This was real. *He* was real.

Bennick's hands rubbed her arms, her back, smoothed over her unbound hair. He pressed his lips to her forehead, and then his stubbled cheek raked over her smooth skin as he buried his face in the curve of her neck.

Bennick's men rushed past them, forming a line of defense on the dock. A fight raged behind her, but she was safe. She was in Bennick's arms.

A sob caught in her throat, her chest tight with an overwhelming surge of emotion.

Bennick crushed her to him, and she realized they were both shaking. His forehead pressed against her neck, and one strong hand cupped the back of her head. His breathing hitched. She felt his tears on her skin, and she could feel her own tears streaking her face. She turned his head and kissed his temple. He shuddered against her, his arms pinning her more securely to his chest.

"You found me," she whispered again, her voice breaking.

He eased back, thumbing her tearstained cheek as he peered into her eyes. His crystal blue eyes had never been so bright, marked with a sheen of tears. "I will *always* find you."

She pressed her forehead to his, closing her eyes as she breathed him in.

His fingers traced over her cheeks. "Where are you hurt?"

"I'm fine." And she was, now that he was here.

"Bennick!"

They both looked up at Wilf's shout, and Clare's eyes widened when she saw Rydenic sailors pouring down the gangplank and rushing up the docks, swords drawn.

They were woefully outnumbered.

"We need to go!" Wilf yelled, already running toward them with their men.

Bennick pulled Clare to her feet, careful of jostling her right hand. She heard him hiss as they straightened, and she clutched his wrist. Her eyes darted to his injured side. "You're hurt."

Bennick's jaw stiffened. "I'm fine."

She frowned, but Wilf was beside them now, stopping her response. He grabbed hold of her shoulder, his eyes flashing with so many emotions. She knew that if they weren't on a dock, about to flee a small army of Rydenic men, he would have embraced her. "Stay close," he said.

She jerked out a nod.

Bennick pulled her forward, and Wilf called for their men to guard their retreat.

They made it only a few steps before freezing.

A row of Mortisian men stood at the mouth of the dock, blocking their escape. The man in front had a thick black beard and raised eyebrows. "It's not every day you see a dockside brawl," he said.

Everything halted. Even the Rydenic sailors stopped their chase.

Bennick was rigid beside her, but only for a moment. He slid his body in front of hers and Wilf shifted to guard her back.

Clare peeked around Bennick's arm and saw the bearded man eye them with something like amusement. "Who are you?" the man asked.

Bennick's voice was hard. "That's no concern of yours."

"Maybe. But maybe not." The man raised his chin, peering at Clare. "Are you in need of assistance, my dear?"

The heat and tension rolling off of Bennick was palpable. Clare cleared her throat so she could speak and hopefully stop the bearded man's stare. "I would like to leave this dock with my friends."

"You're not being held against your will, then?" the man pressed, shooting a look at Bennick.

"Not anymore."

Curiosity lined his weathered face.

"This isn't any of your business!" one of the Rydenic sailors called out, finally approaching.

Clare cringed, grateful Wilf stood behind her, shielding her from the hateful voice.

The bearded Mortisian crossed his arms, his eyes focused on a point beyond Clare. "Do you know who I am?"

Silence.

Clare noticed that even the chaos on shore had dimmed. They had gathered quite an audience.

She nearly jumped when Wilf boomed out, "No. Who are you?"

The bearded man cracked a grim sort of smile. "Syed Zadir."

Clare didn't know him, but the Rydenic cursing behind her indicated this was a man to be feared.

Syed Zadir focused back on Clare. "You were abducted, then?"

She hesitated, but saw no harm in answering. Staying on this man's good side seemed wise. "Yes."

"But you're among friends now?"

"I am."

"And it was these Rydenic ruffians who abducted you?"

"No, but he works with them." She looked behind her to search for Latif, but Wilf's wide form blocked her view. She looked back to Zadir. "He's a Mortisian. His name is Latif."

Zadir blinked. "Latif, you say?" A slow grin broke out on his face. "My dear, the fates have a sense of humor. It just so happens I'm looking for a man called Latif. Apparently, he also goes by the name of *Gamble*."

Bennick shifted slightly, drawing Zadir's eye. "Then it seems you have business with these men. Let us pass, and you can sort things out between you."

"And if I refuse to let you go?" Zadir asked.

Bennick drew his sword, the ring of steel oddly loud in the relative silence.

Zadir smiled. "Amusing. But I have twenty-five men behind me. You've got six. Think about that before you tell me how to do my business."

"We have no part in this," Bennick said, his voice firm.

"Ah, but clearly you do. Anything that concerns Gamble concerns me, so you're not going anywhere just yet. I need to know what business he had abducting the young lady."

Clare continued to grip Bennick's arm with her good hand. She flexed her hold, silently advising him to comply.

Bennick lowered his weapon, but didn't sheathe it.

Zadir wandered forward, his men falling into step behind him. He glanced back at the Rydenic men. "Unless you want a clash with Syed Zadir—which I assure you, you don't—then I suggest you get back on your ship and sail away. *Now*."

Clare watched—wide-eyed—as they slunk back to their ship. As they retreated, cutting whispers carried the word *pirate* clearly enough.

Clare felt the tension in Bennick spike, and her own pulse tripped.

"A pirate?" Wilf muttered under his breath.

Bennick shook his head slightly, his gaze trained on Zadir as he approached.

The man stopped several paces away, his head still craned around them. "You must be Latif. I've been looking everywhere for you."

Wilf shifted just enough that Clare could see Latif. He stood on the dock, pale and alone, his stocky frame tensed for a fight he clearly would not win. He glanced at Clare, and she thought she saw relief mingled with his fear. Could he be relieved she was safe? That seemed unlikely. But he certainly couldn't be relieved to be staring down Zadir and his men.

"Why have you been looking for me?" Latif asked Zadir.

"I was hired to bring you to Duvan. Using any means necessary, I might add." The bearded man's smile was firm. "Serjah Desfan wants a word with you."

Shock blasted through Clare. "Serjah Desfan?"

Zadir glanced at her. "The regent of Mortise. Heir to the throne. Maybe you've heard of him?"

"You're working for the serjah?" Bennick asked, sounding as shocked as Clare felt.

"Yes." He cocked his head. "What's it to you, Devendran?"

Bennick glanced at Wilf, then looked back at Zadir. "How much to book passage on your ship?"

Clare gaped at Bennick's back. She realized *why* he'd want to travel with a pirate—one under Desfan's employ, no less. They'd be safe enough, for they'd be the most dangerous ship on the water.

Still. There had to be safer ways of getting to Duvan.

"I don't take passengers," Zadir said. He glanced at Latif and shrugged. "Well. Not *willing* ones, anyway."

Some of his men chuckled.

"You'll want to take them," Latif said. "And you'll protect her with your life, if you want to earn a fortune." He nodded to Clare.

"That's Princess Serene. The serjah's future bride."

Bennick and Wilf both tensed.

Zadir's eyebrows shot up. He looked at Clare as if seeing her for the first time, and then he whistled lowly. "I do hope Desfan's got enough gold for this."

CHAPTER 40

BENNICK

BENNICK WATCHED AS CLARE WRAPPED HER arms around Wilf's middle, her cheek resting against his broad chest. "Thank you," she whispered.

Wilf rubbed a hand over her back. "I'm sorry it took so long."

Bennick balanced one hand on the deck railing. He couldn't pull his eyes from Clare. It was as if he needed to keep reaffirming that she was here. That she was safe.

The *Seafire* creaked as they sailed out of Shebar's port. Syed Zadir had told them it would take a week to reach Duvan. Bennick wasn't relaxing, though. Not while they were on a ship surrounded by pirates.

Wilf peeled away from Clare's embrace gently, overly cautious of her right hand.

Bennick's grip on the railing became strangling when he got a better view of her bruised and swollen fingers, locked in place with twine and sticks.

"I'm going to see if the captain will let me interrogate Latif," Wilf said. "We should find out what Mortisian hired him so we can identify him as soon as we reach the palace."

"Latif said he wasn't hired by a Mortisian," Clare said.

Wilf snorted. "He's a liar. Salim said the man who hired him was from the palace. And the letter Latif gave Salim is written in Mortisian."

Clare shook her head slowly. "I don't think he lied to me—about that, anyway. He said he wasn't hired by a Mortisian. Actually, he claimed he wasn't hired at all."

Bennick straightened. "What do you mean?"

She glanced at him. "He said he was blackmailed. His regret seemed real, so I believed him."

"Did you find out who was blackmailing him?" Wilf asked.

"No, but we were going to travel on a Rydenic ship to the northern edge of Mortise. That could mean something." Her lips thinned. "He spoke fearfully of his enemies. Whoever ordered him to take me . . . Latif was scared of him."

Bennick's mind leapt to the most powerful and terrifying person in Ryden—King Henri. Bennick knew enough about the Kaelin family to know any of them were capable of any atrocity.

"If it was someone important in Ryden," Clare said, "that could be enough to start a war. Even if it wasn't a royal."

"It *would* start a war," Wilf grunted. He shook his head and took a step back. "I'll see if I can confirm it."

"Try not to hurt him." Clare pursed her lips. "Latif may be an enemy, but he did show me kindness."

Wilf frowned, but he bowed his head in acknowledgement before walking away.

Clare turned to Bennick, the two of them now alone on this section of the deck. She stepped up to him, catching his hand with her good one.

He watched their fingers curl around each other. "Are you all right?" he asked softly.

She squeezed his hand. "I am now."

Her words warmed him, but he couldn't ignore the shadow crossing her face. "I know a little of what happened to you," he said quietly. "Vera told me some of the things Salim did."

Emotion flickered in her eyes—pain, fear—but just as quickly as they'd appeared, they vanished. Her gaze was shuttered as she met his stare. "I'm fine."

The remoteness in her face—her voice—were unlike her. Before he could press, she leaned in, lifting on her toes to set her lips to his.

He responded to her unexpected kiss, his free hand curving against her cheek. The heat of her skin scalded his palm. She was so soft, and yet so strong. Unbreakable, even after all the attempts to shatter her. He knew she wasn't completely all right—no one would be, after enduring what she had. But she'd fought on the docks. She'd made those men yell, and that's what had drawn Bennick's attention. If she hadn't resisted . . .

He tightened his hold on her. Even now, the ache of her absence still filled him. His heart thundered. His pulse rushed and his gut clenched.

She was here. She was in his arms. He had to keep telling himself that.

Clare finally eased back. Her beautiful blue eyes shone. "I still can't believe you're alive," she whispered. She pulled her hand from his and stroked his face. His cheek, his jaw. Her fingertips skirted over his lips.

He tried to kiss her again, but she kept her fingers against his mouth.

Her own lips twitched. "We really should be more careful. What would the pirates think if they saw?"

"I don't really care."

Clare half-smiled. "These pirates are Mortisian. I think they might take an interest if they see Serjah Desfan's intended kissing her bodyguard."

She had a point, fates blast it.

He wouldn't kiss her, then, but he couldn't move away. The ship dipped beneath them and Clare swayed. He steadied her, then gestured toward some nearby crates. "Why don't we sit and you can tell me everything?"

Once again, emotion ghosted in her eyes—there, then gone. But she walked with him to the crates. He began talking to her, hoping that would help set her at ease. He told her of Salim's death, and how they'd tracked her and Latif to Shebar.

When he was done, Clare told him what had happened to her after leaving Krid. Her tone was measured, and she spoke matter-of-factly. Hearing that Latif had not treated her brutally eased a knot in Bennick's gut, allowing him to breathe a little easier. But he still wondered about the things she wasn't telling him—especially about her time with Salim.

When she finished, he shifted his weight. His side slashed with pain, a punishing reminder that he had pushed his body too far. A grimace tore over his face, though he tried to smother it.

Clare's expression tightened with concern. "Are you all right? Did you strain your wound?" She reached for his shirt, but he gently stopped her hand.

"I'm fine," he said. He didn't want her to see the ugly burns.

He didn't want to see them.

The corners of her mouth fell. "That sword. It went all the way through you. It's a miracle you're alive. You should be recovering in bed. You shouldn't have been chasing after me."

"I had to find you." His fingers smoothed under her jaw, tipping her chin up so she would meet his gaze.

Her eyes filled slowly with tears. "I thought you were dead," she breathed, her voice thick.

"I'm right here." He placed a kiss on her forehead, holding her there for a long moment.

When he pulled back, she squeezed his hand. "How are you really? Please be honest."

He released a sigh. "There's pain, but it's manageable. I'm healing well enough." He thumbed the back of her good hand, eyeing the half-healed rope burns around her wrists. The sores and scabs. His jaw locked.

Perhaps to distract them both, he reached into his pocket and withdrew the misshapen piece of melted tin. It barely resembled the toy soldier Mark had once given her, but tears filled her eyes, and he knew she recognized it.

"Vera found it," he told her, his voice a little rougher than before. "Wilf gave it to me when I joined them."

She gingerly took it from him, her thumb brushing over the twisted metal before she wrapped it in her fist and pressed it to her lips. "Thank you, Bennick."

After a long moment of simply sitting beside each other, Clare tucked the melted soldier into her pocket and shifted beside him, fiddling with one of the sticks that braced a broken finger. It was crooked.

He silently eased her injured hand onto his knee and used both hands to gently straighten the stick and its binding tie.

Even being careful, Clare sucked in a breath as her smallest finger was bumped.

His movements stilled. He stared at those bruise-mottled fingers and imagined the pain they caused her. Her screams as they'd been broken. Too well he remembered when Salim had crushed them in front of him, and he hadn't been able to react. Couldn't tear Salim away from her, and then tear him apart.

"I'm healing," Clare said, giving him a pained smile. "Just like you. We'll be fine."

"I can't promise you won't be hurt again." Fates, he hated that. As the decoy, she would always be in danger.

She leaned in and set a brief kiss against his lightly bearded cheek. "Just promise you'll always find me. That's the only promise I need."

He curled some loose strands of hair behind her ear. "I will," he vowed. He wanted to say more. Say again how much he loved her. How much he'd missed her and worried about her. He wanted her to tell him every injury she'd received—every discomfort—so he could soothe them all.

In the end, he just kissed her, knowing the stacked crates shielded them from the crew. He had her back, and they could deal with anything else. Together.

She matched his slow intensity, meeting him kiss for kiss, touch for touch.

The waves rocked the ship, the distant hum of pirate voices in the air. But it was as if Bennick and Clare were the only ones on the ship.

The only ones on the entire sea.

CHAPTER 41

MIA

MIA WALKED TOWARD THE ROYAL STABLE, her heart beating a little too fast. Even though she'd been outside with Tyrell several times now, it had usually been in the evening, after he was done with his responsibilities. It felt different stepping out of the castle in daylight. Everything was more overwhelming. There were more people, more sounds, more bustling activity. The mountains seemed taller, the castle walls higher. She could see everything in vivid detail, and without Tyrell at her side she felt . . . nervous. Even though Fletcher was with her, it was as if—for the first time—Mia faced the world alone.

It was frightening, and exhilarating, and freeing, all at once.

Nobles nodded respectfully to her as they passed, making it

clear they knew she was associated with the Kaelins. None of them attempted a conversation, though, and Mia was perfectly fine with that. Soldiers who milled about the castle yard stepped respectfully around her, and no one told her she didn't belong. She would have perhaps breathed a little easier, but she was apprehensive about her first riding lesson. She'd been a child the last time she'd been on a horse, and she was uneasy to be near the large animals again. Still, she knew she would need to know how to ride if she was going to escape.

She entered the stable. A couple of boys mucked out stalls to her left, but other than a quick look at her, they focused on their chore. Tyrell was not inside. She assumed he'd been delayed at the training grounds, but she didn't doubt he would come. Even though she'd assured him she could ask a stable hand to teach her to ride, Tyrell had insisted on being her instructor.

Mia ran a hand down the front of her riding dress—a gift from Tyrell. The thick material offered some protection from the inevitable chafing. It was a deep green that made her dark brown hair seem even darker. She was sure it had been expensive, and the thought made the knot in her stomach twist.

She hated to betray him. And yet, what else could she do? For too long she'd been helpless in her cell, but now she had a chance to break free. To join Grayson in Duvan. Once she was no longer under King Henri's power, Grayson would be free, too. He wouldn't have to be an assassin, or get mixed up in any of the plots his family wove. She loved him enough to risk this. Even if it meant hurting Tyrell.

Fates forgive her . . .

Fletcher remained near the door, his nose wrinkling at the ripe smell of the stable. Mia fought the urge to cover her own mouth and nose, but she supposed she'd have to get used to the unpleasant aroma. She wandered down the center aisle of the stable, taking in the large horses that stared back at her.

A soft whinny made her turn, and a smile spread easily as she spotted the beautiful dark brown horse on her left. His long neck was craning to see her better, and his ears flicked as she moved closer. "Hello there," she murmured. "You won't bite me, will you?"

The horse chuffed.

The corner of her mouth lifted. "I suppose that could be a *yes*." Still, she hung back, not quite comfortable enough to go within biting distance. "I wonder what your name is?"

A memory surfaced. Another horse, another time.

Can I name him, Father?

A warm chuckle. *He already has a name . . . Ah, my dear one, don't cry. I'm sure he would love another one, especially from you.*

Mia swallowed hard and shook her head to clear the momentary fog. The emotions, though—those were harder to be rid of. Her throat was tight as she met the horse's soulful eyes. "Will you promise not to throw me? If you agree, I'll bring you an apple every day."

His head lowered, his black mane spilling over his long brow.

Carefully Mia extended a hand, letting the horse's nose dip the final distance. Her palm tingled at the contact, and she slowly slid her hand up the lighter stripe on his forehead. "You have a gentle soul, don't you?" she murmured, her lungs loosening as she took a step closer.

"Ah, milady?"

She turned toward the stable boy, her hand still on the horse. "Yes?"

The boy's eyes were wide as they darted between her and the

animal stabled behind her. "Th-that's the Black Hand's horse."

Her heart skipped. "Really?" She spun back to the horse, noting the size and power of him, even as she rubbed him gently. His large eyes watched her silently. Somehow, it fit that he was Grayson's. "He's beautiful," she said, knowing the stable boy lingered behind her.

The horse nosed her palm, tickling her skin with his whiskered lips. She chuckled as he tossed his head.

It was silly, perhaps, but being close to his horse helped her feel closer to Grayson. The pebble necklace was warm against her skin; she hadn't taken it off since Tyrell had returned it to her. It also kept Grayson close, but it wasn't enough.

Fates, she missed him. He had always been a light in her darkness. Her friend when she most needed one. She'd fallen in love with him so naturally, she wasn't even sure when it had happened. One day, one moment, he had smiled at her, and her heart had nearly burst in her chest.

She closed her eyes, her hand still brushing over the horse's soft hair. His steady, warm breaths grounded her, comforted her. It was a moment of peace. A reassureance that she was doing the right thing.

She sensed someone come up behind her, but she didn't turn, expecting it to be the stable boy.

It wasn't.

"So, not only did you enthrall Tyrell and Grayson, but you bewitched his horse as well?"

Mia twisted to face Peter, her spine bumping the gate on the horse's stall.

The corner of Peter's mouth twitched. "I must admit, when I saw a guard stationed at the door, I never dreamed it would be yours. He's a little feeble for the job, don't you think?"

Her skin crawled under his gaze. "I'm surprised he didn't follow you."

"No need to think him disloyal. I gave him very specific orders."

"You threatened him?"

Peter's eyes glinted. "Only a little."

Her heart clenched, but she spoke past her fear. "What do you want?"

"I'd hoped we could talk a little." His hands slipped into his pockets. "I've been investigating you, Mia. I learned that a physician has been seeing you because you were attacked—in the prison, no less. A conversation with my father illuminated things further."

The mere mention of the king who had imprisoned her shot a jolt of fear through her veins. "What did he tell you?"

Peter's smile spread slowly. "A great deal. He keeps few things from me."

Mia's mouth was dry, but she forced herself to say, "And yet he kept me from you all these years."

The prince's eyes narrowed. "Ah, she has some bite after all. I was beginning to wonder what Tyrell and Grayson saw in you."

A quick glance showed Mia that the stable boys had fled—not that she blamed them. She wished she could see Fletcher at the door, though. Or that Tyrell would walk in.

Peter took a step closer. "Does it feel strange to wander the castle grounds after being a prisoner for so many years?"

The horse behind her huffed a sharp breath, the rush of warm air stirring the curls that had slipped free of her long braid. It may have been ridiculous, but she felt less alone knowing the horse stood behind her. She stiffened her spine. "What do you want, Peter?"

"*Prince* Peter." His eyes were sharp, even though his smile remained firmly in place. "I doubt you'll give me what I want, but I suppose I can still ask. Tell me, Mia—to what end are you manipulating my brothers? I applaud your clearly effecttive methods, but while my father seems convinced you're nothing but a pawn, I see something else in you. To capture Grayson's interest and then Tyrell's—when they are both enemies—tells me you plot something. What exactly do you want from them?"

"Nothing." She refused to think of the maps in her room, the supplies she'd been gradually placing under her bed.

"Do you aim to pit them against each other?"

Her jaw tightened. "No."

"Too bad. That would have been amusing." Peter's head tilted as he studied her. "You can't convince me that you have actual feelings for them."

"I suppose it's impossible for you to believe that people might actually care for each other without ulterior motives. You've never had anyone truly care about you."

Peter laughed. "You think to wound me, but I assure you I'm only amused. Maybe that's why my brothers kept you around— you amuse them." The skin around his eyes tightened. "And yet, it's obvious you're driving Tyrell out of his mind. If it were possible, I'd think he had actual feelings for you."

"You think he's beyond feeling?"

"I know he is."

"Perhaps you're jealous."

"Jealous? Why by all the fates would I be jealous of my younger brothers? I'm more powerful and more cunning than both of them combined. I'll be their king one day."

"Only if they bow to you."

The prince's eyes narrowed, and a shiver raked down Mia's spine. "You're full of surprises, aren't you?" he whispered.

Before she could answer, Tyrell strode in. He took in the situation with a quick glance, and his features tightened. "Do you need something, Peter?"

"No." The oldest prince was already walking away, dismissing them both as if they were nothing.

Tyrell didn't take his eyes off his brother until he disappeared. Then he focused on Mia. "Are you all right?"

"Yes."

"What did he want?"

She blew out a shaky breath. "I think he just likes to hear himself talk."

Tyrell frowned. "He does. What exactly did he say?"

"Nothing very direct. I'm a puzzle to him. And I have a feeling he's the sort of person who likes to peel apart a puzzle until he understands it."

Tyrell's eyes clouded, but he didn't disagree with her assessment. The horse behind her snickered, drawing his attention. "Did they bring you to Grayson's horse?"

"No, we sort of found each other. Do you know his name?"

His brow furrowed. "We don't name our horses."

"Oh." She turned back to the horse, rubbing between his eyes. "We'll find your name," she promised him softly. When she peeked over at Tyrell, she found him watching her intently. Her cheeks warmed.

"Are you ready for your lesson?" Tyrell asked.

"Yes." She nodded to Grayson's horse. "Can I ride him?"

"He's a bit large for you," Tyrell said, eyeing the animal. "Per-

haps after you've gotten comfortable on something a little smaller."

Mia sighed, but deferred to him. With a last pat and a promise
to return, she left Grayson's horse and followed Tyrell.

CHAPTER 42

GRAYSON

GRAYSON'S BOOTS ECHOED WITH EVERY STEP through the upper halls of the palace. Afternoon sun filtered through the windows, highlighting tapestries and paintings that Grayson didn't actually see. He was alone, as he had once again dismissed his guards. It was entirely probable Liam knew where he was, however. He would not underestimate his brother again.

It had been nine days since Liam had shared the full details of his plan, and Grayson hadn't slept well since. His mind ached with his circling thoughts. Liam wanted him to kill Desfan, Serene, and Imara. To become the most public killer in Eyrinthia so the three southern kingdoms would turn against Ryden with a united front and destroy the Kaelin family.

If he did this, he would never be able to wash the blood from his hands, or the stain on his soul. He would be eternally hunted by everyone in every kingdom.

If he refused, he would lose his only ally—the one person who had the power to save Mia. Because Liam was set in his plan. He was convinced this was the most efficient way to destroy Henri Kaelin. If Grayson backed down, he was confident Liam would find someone else to do the job. Grayson would probably end up targeted as well, and if he died, Mia would have no one.

Not for the first time, he recalled the bottle of Ieannax in his room. The Poison Queen had foreseen Liam's betrayal and she'd given Grayson a mission: kill him.

Grayson could do that now. If he did, he wouldn't have to assassinate the three foreign royals. And yet, the thought of murdering his brother filled him with disgust. He needed to find another way forward. He just didn't know what that path was.

He rounded a corner and immediately wished he hadn't.

Princess Imara stood with her hands joined in front of her, her dark head tilted to the side as she examined a large oil portrait. Her back was to him, and he thought maybe he could retreat without being noticed.

He eased back a step, but her bodyguard's gaze shot to him.

The Zennorian princess noticed and turned. A smile curved her mouth. "Prince Grayson. How wonderful to see you again!"

He assumed her words to be a lie, though there was nothing in her open expression to support that. She looked genuinely pleased to see him; which hardly made sense.

Grayson bent his head in a polite, though slightly stiff, bow. "Princess Imara. I'm sorry to disturb you. I'll go."

"Oh no, please, it's no disruption. I'd enjoy your company."

He shifted his weight, the back of his neck warm. Being near Imara, especially in light of Liam's plan, was decidedly uncomfortable.

The Zennorian princess twisted back to the painting. "Isn't it marvelously done?"

Her bodyguard was still staring at him, and Grayson barely held back his sigh as he gave in and stepped forward. He took in the large portrait as he came to stand beside Imara.

The painting was fastened to the wall, but even if it had been sitting on the floor it would be taller than him. Captured on the canvas was a family. The youngest child was still practically an infant in her mother's arms, tucked up against the woman's chest. The father wore a gold crown and looked very much like Desfan, though slightly older. The serjan held a small but beaming girl on his knee with one hand, the other hand resting on his son's shoulder—a much younger Desfan. All three children were dark-haired and grinning, clearly close to the same age. The parents were smiling just as widely as the children. The artist had captured a family filled with love and joy—something Grayson had no experience with.

"How old do you think Desfan was then?" Imara asked. "Five?"

Grayson studied the boy in the painting, noting that the deep brown eyes had been captured perfectly, with just a touch of mischievousness. "Perhaps."

Imara chuckled. "Has he always been dashing, do you think?"

Grayson glanced at her profile. Was he supposed to have an answer for that?

Thankfully, Imara didn't wait for a response. "He looks very much like his father, doesn't he? But he has his mother's smile."

For all the details Liam had forced Grayson to memorize before arriving in Duvan, he hadn't learned anything specific about the royal family; only that Desfan's mother and sisters were dead.

Curiosity pulled at him, and he nodded to the portrait. "How did they die?"

"In a shipwreck," Imara said, her voice gentling. "Desfan was eleven, I believe. He and his father were here in Duvan at the time, or else they might have died, too."

Grayson studied the immortalized faces with new intensity. The painted smiles seemed frozen, now, the joy in the portrait shadowed with the reality of loss.

It was hard for Grayson to comprehend Desfan's pain. If the majority of *his* family died, Grayson would not mourn them. The only person he truly cared about was Mia. If he lost her . . .

"She's beautiful, isn't she?"

Grayson followed Imara's gaze to the seraijan, Desfan's mother. She was cradling the infant seraijah in her arms, her beaming face both regal and kind, her dark hair falling in graceful waves past her shoulders. She *was* beautiful. Even caught in paint, her brown eyes shone. She was the complete opposite of Grayson's mother. The woman in the painting looked more like Mia; there was an inherent kindness in her gaze that made it hard to look away.

"I'm sorry," Imara said suddenly, snagging Grayson's attention. "I didn't mean to keep you from anything."

Grayson pushed a gloved hand through his hair as he took a step back from the painting. "I should probably go."

Her head tilted to the side. "Where are you off to?"

A quick scan of her face showed only innocence. She was either an exceptional liar, or she wasn't trying to ferret out information.

He truly didn't know what to make of Imara Buhari.

She was still eyeing him questioningly, so he latched onto the first thing he could. "The training yard."

Imara's eyes brightened. "Sword fighting? How thrilling. Maybe I could join you?"

He felt himself blanch.

Imara laughed. "Oh fates, I only meant to watch. You look like I just asked you to duel!"

It was a uniquely terrifying prospect.

The princess's expression sparked suddenly. "I have a better idea. I heard some of the servants talking about a festival at the main market square. It won't last much longer, since Dawn of Eyrinthia is ending soon, and I'm *dying* to see everything. Would you come with me?"

Her bodyguard cleared his throat, but it sounded more like a warning grunt.

Imara rolled her eyes. "Relax, Kaz. You'll come as well." Then she focused back on Grayson. "Well?"

He scrubbed a hand over the back of his neck. "I don't know that you'll want to be seen in the market with me."

"Why not?"

He stared at her.

Realization dawned, softening her features. "Ah, because you're the Black Viper." She shrugged one shoulder and looped her arm through his. "Let them stare. I'm quite fond of making a scene."

———◆———

Without quite knowing how it happened, Grayson walked the streets of Duvan with Imara on his arm and her bodyguard shadowing close behind.

There was an uncomfortable twist in his gut and his cheeks felt too warm, though that could have been from the Mortisian summer heat.

Cooking meats sizzled, spicing the air with an array of exotic peppers and spices. Men and women called out wares, children laughed and raced around the large market square, and those now-familiar purple flags fluttered everywhere. Music drifted among the stalls and some men and women sang, eager for every coin dropped in their cup.

"It's more beautiful than I imagined," Imara said, her eyes a-light as she took everything in.

Grayson's view of things was decidedly different. The square was overcrowded, chaotic, and far too loud. Assassins and thieves alike would thrive in such an environment. He kept his gaze moving over the continually shifting crowd.

Imara's turquoise skirt swished against his leg as they walked, and she only released his arm when they reached a cart selling a variety of drinks. She chose one made from lemons and small red berries. She claimed it was tangy but sweet.

Grayson asked for water.

Imara watched him over the rim of her cup. "Are you sure you don't want to try this?"

"I'm sure." Just the smell made his mouth pinch.

She shrugged her narrow shoulders. She really was very short; her head barely reached his chest. After swallowing another sip, she said, "You're quiet."

"I don't have anything to say." Conversation was not a gift he possessed.

"That's all right. I have a hundred questions! Now, let's see . . . Is it true you made your first kill when you were three years old?"

Grayson choked on his water, coughing harshly as he whipped his head toward her. "What?"

"That's how the story goes in Zennor," she said easily. "The Black Viper learned the art of killing in the nursery—the way all Ryden children do—but he loved death more than the others. He killed his nursemaid when he was three and drank her blood, and he's never gotten enough of the taste since."

Grayson blinked at her. There were no words.

Her mouth twitched. "I'm assuming it's not true, then?"

He finally managed to find his voice. "No."

She bobbed her head. "After meeting you, I didn't think it could be true. You're not half as intimidating as your reputation."

That didn't exactly sound like a compliment.

Before he could make any response, Imara fired off her next question. "Is it true your mother has a poison garden?"

From the corner of his eye, he could see her bodyguard's hand on his knife. It had probably gone there at her last question, though Grayson had been too busy choking to notice. "She does," he confirmed.

"How interesting. My mother only embroiders."

Grayson snorted.

Imara grinned. "There! The Black Viper *can* laugh. Another rumor, utterly wrecked."

The princess's questions continued as they finished their drinks and returned their cups. They continued to wander the square, and though Grayson didn't relax his guard, he did grow more comfortable around Imara. She eventually pulled him toward a cart selling jewelry. There were some metal pieces, but the majority was crafted from shells and pearls. He didn't see any diamonds or precious gems, but they were still beautifully made.

"Oh, how gorgeous!" Imara scooped up a shell bracelet, asking the artisan about it.

Grayson's eyes wandered the cart and stalled on a simple necklace with a single rose-hued pearl. That was all it took for a memory to overtake him.

He had probably been twelve at the time, and Mia eleven. She had been humming as she read beside him, when suddenly she'd sprung up with a gasp.

Tension had locked every muscle in his body as he'd lurched to his feet, already positioning his body in front of hers, though he hadn't seen the threat.

She grasped his arm. "Grayson, we should have a ball!"

"A . . . ball?" His heart still hammered, his body not registering the fact that there was not, in fact, any danger.

"Yes! You know, with dancing and music? I could dress up!" She beamed at him, excitement shining in her eyes. "It would be so lovely. Please, can we have one?"

Grayson rubbed a hand over his thudding heart. "I don't know how to make one."

"It will be easy. Here, I'm sure I have a dress I can wear . . ." She moved for her trunk and dug around inside, finally pulling out a faded pink dress. "This is my prettiest one," she said. "You just need to imagine it's even more beautiful. That *I'm* beautiful. Can you imagine that?"

His heart raced, but for a new reason this time. "Yes," he said quietly, his throat a little dry. "I can imagine that."

Mia smiled. "Good." She jumped to her feet, the pink dress clutched in her hands. "Why don't you find your best clothes too, and when you get back, I'll be ready for our dance."

Dance? The concept was one he was familiar with, but he'd

never danced. Certainly not with Mia. She had always been comfortable touching him, even embracing him, but lately when she held his hand, it warmed him even more deeply. The thought of putting his hands on her waist while they swayed to music she hummed suddenly had him eager—and perhaps a little terrified.

His palms sweat as he left her cell and hurried to his room. He was too self-conscious to change into his court clothing in his room, so he carried the emerald and black uniform in a wadded up bundle to the prison, where he ducked into an empty holding room to quickly change.

He tried to ignore Fletcher's raised eyebrow as the guard admitted him into Mia's cell.

Grayson ground to a halt the moment he saw Mia.

She knelt before the open trunk, her back to him. The pale rose color of the dress made her brown hair look even darker. She'd twisted her long locks into a messy bun that spilled curls around her bare neck.

A quiet sniffle made his heart lurch. He took a step forward. "Mia?"

She shook her head, those loose curls shivering. "Don't look at me. None of this is right."

Grayson hesitated, but when she sniffed once more, he moved closer and sank to his knees beside her.

Her eyes were rimmed red from crying and her hands twisted in her lap. "I forgot the most important part," she breathed through her tears. "At a ball, a girl should wear a necklace." She flinched and ducked her head, one hand fluttering to her throat. "I had one," she whispered brokenly. "It was so important, but I lost it."

He had never seen her like this. Sometimes, the ghost of memories haunted her, but they were never more than shadows in her eyes. This pain? Her grief? He hated that it had been triggered somehow.

He grasped her hand, squeezing her fingers gently. "It's all right," he said quietly. "You don't need a necklace, Mia. You're beautiful."

She glanced over at him, and in the lamplight he could see the shiny trails of her tears. "My dress has a tear in the hem."

"It doesn't matter."

Her eyes traced over him, the corner of her mouth wavering up. "You look very handsome, Grayson."

His cheeks warmed. But it was the edge of sadness in her voice that made him grasp the hem of his green shirt.

Her eyes widened with understanding. "Grayson, no—"

There was a sharp rip, and he flashed her a smile. "There. Now we're perfectly matched."

It didn't matter if the servants told his parents and he was punished for damaging something so fine. Seeing the glitter in Mia's eyes was worth any price.

She surprised him by leaning in to press a kiss to his cheek.

The brief contact rocked him. His stomach clenched and heat blasted his face.

The corner of her mouth lifted as she drew back. "Thank you, Grayson. I'm ready for our dance now."

He hadn't been able to stop smiling. Not when he pulled her to her feet, or when his hands had cupped her waist. Not when her hands settled on his shoulders and she tugged him closer. Not when her humming filled the small room and her cheek rested against his chest.

It had taken him too long to give her a necklace. And the one he'd made with the pebble they'd first played with as children hardly counted as something fine. He wanted to give her this pearl necklace. It was the sort of beauty she deserved.

But then, he'd never given her what she deserved, had he? Freedom. A life away from him and his accursed family.

Instead, he had given her meal-sack dolls and pebble necklaces.

The pain of missing her hit him in the gut with the force of a boulder. Sixty-seven days, he'd been gone. Nine and a half weeks. Over two months without seeing her smile, hearing her laugh, feeling her touch.

An eternity.

"That's beautiful," Imara said, cutting into his thoughts. "Do you have someone at home to give it to?"

Grayson realized he was holding the pearl necklace. His face warmed as Imara and the craftsman stared at him. His initial reaction was to deny it. To protect Mia by refusing to even acknowledge her existence. But he wasn't in Ryden, surrounded by snakes who would strike at any perceived weakness.

Still, his shoulders felt too tight as he said, "Yes."

Imara's smile gentled. "She's a lucky young woman."

No. I'm the lucky one. They were words he couldn't voice, but he felt them deeply.

If he could save her and build them both a better life, then he would do anything he had to. No matter the cost.

———◆———

As soon as Grayson returned to the palace and parted ways with Imara, he sent a message for Desfan to meet him in the training yard. Then he sent for Liam.

While he waited for his brother to arrive, he opened one of his desk drawers and tucked away the pearl necklace he'd purchased for Mia.

Liam entered the room with long strides. "I hope we're not about to have an argument," he said, closing the door.

Grayson stood near the window, his hands clasped behind his back as he faced his brother. "I want to talk about your plan."

Liam sighed. "An argument it is, then."

"No. A proposition." He lengthened his spine. "I'm convinced that Desfan and the other royals will side with us. I believe if we confide in them, we can unite everyone against Father—without killing our potential allies. You and I don't have to be hated and feared, Liam. I don't want that for my future." His brow creased. "Which is why I'm going to tell Desfan everything."

Liam's expression didn't change, but Grayson didn't miss the slight flaring of his nostrils. "That would be a mistake."

"I disagree. That's why I asked him to meet me in the training yard in an hour. I know he'll be grateful when we tell him Father's plan, and he'll trust us because we're betraying—"

"No." Liam bristled. "You won't tell anyone. You will follow my plan."

"No," Grayson argued, his voice tightening. "I won't kill Desfan or the others."

"I don't think you understand." His brother's voice was low, his eyes locked on Grayson. "You will do exactly as I say, or you will regret it."

Grayson's eyes narrowed. "I'm not an assassin."

"You will be. Your refusal would be disastrous."

His shoulders stiffened. "Consider yourself in the middle of a disaster, then, because I won't help you kill them."

"Let me rephrase. Refusing to help me and revealing my plan to Desfan—or anyone—would be disastrous for Mia."

Grayson froze. He stared at Liam, hardly recognizing the hard glint in his brother's eyes. It rendered his gaze unfamiliar. Cold. Cruel. It made the hairs on the back of his neck rise.

Liam shook his head slowly. "I knew this might happen, though I prayed it would not. I didn't believe you were actually so weak-willed. I thought you would do anything to be free—for Mia to be free."

Grayson's fingers rolled to fists at his sides. "What are you talking about?"

"I gave you so many chances. I trusted you again and again, yet you choose to betray me? Now, when we're so close?" He snorted, the twist of his lips derisive. "I never should have tried to befriend you. Obviously, you're incapable of such a thing."

A growl ripped up Grayson's throat. "What about Mia?"

"You already know I have the unflinching loyalty of someone close to her, Grayson. Figure it out."

It only took Grayson the length of a breath to shove Liam against the wall. A knife was at his throat in the next instant.

Liam's eyes widened, shock freezing him.

Grayson leaned in, fury heating his skin. "I could kill you right now. One flick of my wrist, and you're dead."

His throat bobbed under the blade. His expression didn't reveal much, but the pulse in his neck quivered. "You *could* kill me," he said. "But if you do, Mia will die, too."

Grayson only pressed the dagger more firmly against Liam's flesh. Skin split, and a drop of blood welled to the surface. "That's an empty threat," he gritted out.

"It's not. If anything happens to me, there are orders in place. Mia will be killed."

His stomach wrenched, but he fought against a wave of panic. He kept his face a smooth mask, his voice even. "I can travel faster than your fastest messenger. I can reach her before any order you arranged can arrive."

"Wrong." Liam's jaw was stiff and blood dripped down his throat, but still he smiled. The expression looked horribly wrong. "I have a hawk, Grayson. How fast can you fly?"

His grip on the dagger clenched. "You're lying."

"No. I'm not."

Lead filled Grayson's veins. He swore his heart stopped. And then it was raging, pounding so fiercely it flared his terror. He knew birds were trained in the castle aerie. He knew Henri received messages from his spies that way, but . . .

Liam had prepared for this moment since the beginning. While he'd been befriending Grayson, he'd also put into place measures to control him. He had orchestrated Mia's death before ever leaving Ryden, just waiting for the moment Grayson might resist.

The realization shattered something deep inside him. Something his parents had tried to destroy a long time ago.

He never should have trusted Liam.

His brother's brown eyes were hard and unwavering. "I'm the Shadow of Ryden," he said quietly. "Did you expect anything less?"

Grayson ground his teeth. The dagger in his hand wavered, the blade cutting Liam just a little more. Then he stepped back, lowering the knife. His lungs weren't working right—his chest rose and fell, but each breath hurt.

Liam moved slowly, as if still wary of Grayson even though he had him tightly leashed. He fingered the cut on his throat, wincing. "You really would have killed me." He sounded faintly surprised.

Grayson strangled the dagger in his hand. His throat was too tight for words.

Liam eyed him. "I didn't want it to come to this. We could have been allies, but you made that impossible. So, I'll use you like Father uses you. It seems you can't understand much else."

Grayson's body vibrated. Fear clawed at him, along with a fury so deep it burned. Liam simply watched him. He knew Grayson was helpless. A warrior, unable to strike the one person he wanted to destroy most in this moment.

"Let me make things clear," Liam said. "If anything happens to me, Mia dies. If you fail to follow my orders, Mia dies. If you breathe a word of this to anyone—or in any way attempt to disrupt my plans—Mia dies. My contacts will know, and the message will be sent. You won't be able to stop it."

Grayson glared, but his gut churned. "Don't do this."

"You gave me no choice. I've worked too hard and too long to make this war a reality. I won't let you ruin this." Liam moved forward, stopping directly in front of him. "I can break you with a word. One word. *Mia.*" He scanned Grayson's face, searching for signs of mutiny.

Grayson was quite sure all Liam saw was hatred.

His brother took a step back and tugged at his cuffs, straightening them. "Don't worry. This arrangement of ours won't have to last long. Princess Serene requested that the betrothal signing be moved up. It will take place the morning after Eyrinthia's Ball."

A roaring filled Grayson's ears. The ball that marked the end of Eyrinthia's holiday was in two days.

"Oh, and don't bother looking for the Ieannax mother gave

you," Liam said. "I confiscated that a while ago." He strode for the door, deliberately turning his back to Grayson because he knew he wouldn't dare attack.

He was almost at the door when Grayson forced himself to speak. "Liam."

His brother turned back. "What?"

Grayson's voice was cold and dark, perfectly matching how he felt inside. "If anything happens to Mia, you're dead. It doesn't matter where you try to hide—I'll find you. You may be the Shadow of Ryden, but I'm the Black Hand."

Liam stared at him, that streak of blood still on his throat. Uncertainty flashed in his eyes, and then he fitted his mask into place. He lifted his chin. "Don't stay up here too long. You wouldn't want to keep Desfan waiting."

"Is something wrong?" Desfan asked.

They'd been sparring for nearly half an hour and both of them dripped with sweat. Desfan's shirt was off, the black tattoo over his heart rising and falling with each labored breath. It was the size of a man's palm and shaped like a sun, but Grayson had gotten close enough during their fights to see that the center was created by names twisting together. The names of his mother and sisters.

Fallen Cassians that he would soon join.

Grayson rolled his wrist, his sword spinning. He watched the late afternoon light glint off the blade. "No. Nothing is wrong."

"You seem a little . . . off."

"I'm fine."

Desfan's grip on his dual blades tightened. "I know we haven't been able to spar since Princess Serene arrived. I'm sorry about that."

"Don't worry about me."

Except when I come to kill you.

Desfan glanced around the yard. Karim was there, of course, standing just far enough away to give them space to spar. Grayson assumed he could still hear every word they exchanged.

Their usual audience had diminished, and the yard itself was uncharacteristically empty. Probably due to all the festivities going on.

"Do you miss home?" Desfan asked suddenly.

The back of his neck heated. "Yes." Because his home was Mia, and he was desperate to have her in his arms.

"I'll be sad to see you go," Desfan said. "Whenever that day comes."

Grayson was surprised by the words—and the truth ringing in them. "Your court will be relieved to see me gone."

So would Karim. The bodyguard was currently frowning at Grayson from his spot on the sidelines.

Desfan chuckled. "Probably true. But at least they've been so focused on giving you condescending looks that they've rather spared me their usual scorn."

He huffed. "I've one use, at least."

"You're a rather good sparring partner as well." Desfan's expression softened. "You've been a good friend to me, Grayson. I appreciate that. I lost most of mine when I left the sea."

Guilt soured in his gut. "I'm not a good friend."

"You could smile a bit more," Desfan said. "Perhaps laugh at my jokes. Make a few of your own. But nothing a little practice wouldn't fix."

Grayson glanced aside.

"There, see? That's a moment you could have smiled."

"Shall we begin another round?" he asked, hefting his sword.

The serjah frowned a little. "Very well." He adopted a defensive stance, raising his curved blades.

Grayson attacked.

The rapid back and forth of the fight, the sidesteps and whirls of their blades—all were more energized than ever before. Grayson didn't use his full skill, but he didn't reign in every blow.

Sweat beaded Desfan's forehead as he parried. The tension rolling off Karim from his vantage point several paces away was as overpowering as the afternoon heat. And still Grayson attacked, unrelenting.

When his sword almost clipped Desfan's shoulder—with the serjah barely managing to snatch himself back—Karim snarled and darted forward. "Enough!"

Desfan waved his friend back with one of his swords. "It's fine, Karim. We're fine." He glanced at Grayson, his shoulders tight. "What should I have done differently?"

"You need to be faster," Grayson said, tension coiling in his shoulders.

"I'm not as fast as you."

"Then you'll die."

Desfan stared at him, dark curls sticking to his sweaty brow. The confusion in his eyes was too much.

Grayson retreated a step, gripping his sword tightly. "I'm done." He glanced toward Karim—who, of course, glared back—and as he turned he caught a last look at Desfan. The serjan's frown was deep as he stared at Grayson, something like concern in his eyes. And wariness.

Good.

Grayson gritted his teeth and took a step away from them.

"Grayson."

He looked over his shoulder at Desfan, who studied him carefully.

The serjah said nothing for a moment, then, "Thank you."

His gratitude was worse than any cursing.

Grayson fled. As he reached the edge of the training yard, he saw Liam standing in a darkened archway watching him.

CHAPTER 43

CLARE

ZADIR HAD GIVEN HIS CABIN TO CLARE, since he deferred to her as Serjah Desfan's future bride. The room was simple, despite being the pirate captain's cabin. There was a small glass window, a lamp fitted to the wall above a simple bunk, and a wooden chair and small desk bolted to the floor near the door. Clare was most grateful for the bed, which gave her a place to give in to her exhaustion.

When morning came, Bennick entered the cabin carrying breakfast, and the two of them sat on the narrow bed, talking softly while they ate. This quiet moment was, in many ways, more surreal than the horrors she'd suffered with Salim.

As the meal wound down, Clare grew self-conscious. She hadn't washed her face or neck before Bennick arrived, and she wore the same dress Latif had purchased for her, the skirt creased with deep wrinkles from being tangled in sleep. Her hair, however, could not be ignored. It was a mass of tangles that she tried to pick free with one hand, but she soon gave up with a sigh.

Bennick brushed biscuit crumbs off his leg. "I can brush it and braid it for you."

Clare glanced at him. "You know how to braid hair?"

He shrugged. "It can't be too difficult. Teach me."

She shifted until her back was to him, and she melted when his fingers threaded through the long locks. She let out a sigh, her scalp prickling pleasantly as he explored her hair. She was so relaxed, speaking was difficult, but she managed to give him brief instructions.

Bennick's fingers stilled in her hair. "I don't have enough hands to do what you're saying."

Clare chuckled, offering her good hand to keep hold of one of the three separate ropes of hair. She talked him through it again, more slowly, but the simple braid took a good half-hour to complete. She almost began to wonder if he messed up just so he could hear her laugh. Or perhaps he simply enjoyed running his fingers through her hair.

She certainly enjoyed it.

When he finally reached the end of the braid, she brought it over her shoulder to see his work. "Very good, Captain Markam."

She sensed him lean closer. His breath warmed her skin, the only warning before he set a kiss against the nape of her neck. "You're an excellent teacher," he murmured.

Heat curled low in her belly, and it took a long moment for her pounding heart to calm.

Bennick rubbed a hand over her arm, prompting her to twist and face him. "I spoke to Zadir. He has a physician on board. If you're ready, I can send for him."

Clare glanced down at her braced hand. "All right."

The pirate's physician was an older man with a pronounced limp. His appearance was gruff, but his touch was gentle as he examined her wrists first. "These are healing quite nicely. I have some salve you can apply twice a day to speed it along, and it will help reduce scarring."

He studied her broken fingers next. "When were they broken?"

She thought hard. Time had blurred, especially while with Salim. "Nearly two weeks ago, I think."

"How were they broken? Smashed by an object?"

"No. Snapped." Her aching fingers tingled at the memory. She shoved away the pain and fear of that moment, as she'd been doing since her rescue. Pushing aside things she didn't want to acknowledge had become normal—her only way to survive without breaking.

Bennick watched her closely. He folded his arms over his chest, his jaw stiff.

The physician touched the knuckle on her first finger. The joint was tender, but the contact was not as painful as Clare had expected. "How soon were they braced after the injury?"

"A few days after." Clare swallowed. "Will I be able to move them once they heal?"

"I should think so. You'll want to keep the braces on for maybe three weeks or so. There will be stiffness, but it should go away with time." He leaned over her hand. "Your first finger is a little crooked. I'm going to straighten it."

Clare clenched her teeth as he undid the ties on the trimmed twigs splinting her finger. "This will hurt," he warned her. Then he yanked.

She gasped as something popped. Pain shot down her finger and up her arm. Her good hand clawed in her skirts, desperate for something to squeeze until the flash of pain faded. Suddenly Bennick was there, gripping her good hand, glaring at the physician.

The pirate didn't seem to notice. He reapplied the splint and tightened some of the other ties. As he left, he promised to send one of the ship's boys up with the salve and some powder to dull the pain, along with a wash basin and soap.

Finger still throbbing, Clare remained on the bed while Bennick closed the door on the man. "He could have given you something for the pain before," he muttered tersely.

"It's all right," Clare said, speaking more or less through her teeth.

Bennick frowned. "You're entirely too brave."

Clare almost smiled. "Why didn't you ask the physician about your injury?"

Bennick ran a hand through his dark-blond hair. "I'm fine."

"You've been favoring your side."

"I'm fine."

Clare pursed her lips. She wanted to press, but Bennick wasn't the only one dodging questions. He'd probed a little this morning over breakfast about her experiences with Salim, and when she had sidestepped them, he'd let her.

She supposed it was only fair to allow him to do the same.

Clare jerked awake with a gasp. It was the middle of the night and the cabin was dark, dim moonlight filtering in from the only window. Her heart thundered in her chest and sweat slicked her body.

She couldn't stop shaking. Gut-wrenching fear clutched her, making every breath too fast, too shallow. Even awake, the terror of the nightmare choked her. The shadows were thick and menacing—encroaching. Shards of ice dug into her spine, her panic spiking.

She fumbled to light the nearby lamp with one hand. Her broken fingers throbbed in their braces, and she wondered if she'd bumped them while thrashing in bed.

After several attempts, a glow finally warmed the space. Still, a shudder ripped through her as she sank back onto the bed, her back to the wall. Even with a lamp lighting the cabin, she still saw Salim's vile features; his curling lip and flashing eyes.

Clare drew up her trembling knees, holding them tight against her chest. Her jaw locked against a sob, and her eyes burned.

Knuckles rapped against the door. Her stomach dropped.

"Clare?" Bennick's voice was muffled, but she could hear his concern. He must have seen the light through the cracks around the door.

She wanted to tell him she was all right. More than that, she wanted to tell him that he should be sleeping, not standing guard. But if she opened her mouth, she knew her fragile hold on her tears would snap, and a cry would emerge.

Her silence seemed to increase Bennick's tension. "I'm coming in," he said tightly, a second before the door swung open. Through her blurred vision she saw him take in the sight of her. Curled against the wall in a rumpled bed, shaking as tears began to streak down her face.

He nudged the door closed and crossed to the bed without a word. He knelt beside her on the wrinkled quilt, gently folding her into his arms.

For so long, she had shoved everything back. Grief, pain, despair, panic, fear. Every emotion that had threatened to break her. The unrelenting desperation to not feel anything else had taken its toll.

It was as if her body—her soul—finally felt safe enough to lower every defense she had thrown up since her abduction. Now, she felt *everything*.

There was no pushing it away.

Her lungs heaved and a sob cracked out of her. She sank against Bennick, clutching his loose shirt in her good hand as she cried against his chest.

He held her in his lap, his back braced against the wall. One hand curled over the back of her head and the other smoothed up and down her spine. "You're safe," he whispered, his lips at her temple. "You're with me. You're safe."

She knew that. And still, she cried.

His bristled jaw skated across her temple as he tucked her close, his lips skimming her hair, her cheek, her neck. He stroked her loose braid, his long fingers massaging her scalp and then trailing down her back.

She didn't know how long she cried in his arms. How long he held her. But finally, the storm inside her began to calm.

As she sagged against him—completely spent—she could feel his stiffness. That's when she remembered his injury. She realized she gripped his shirt with a white-knuckled fist, and that she was pressing into the wound near his side.

Clare jerked away. She nearly slid off his lap, but his quick hands grasped her hips.

"I'm sorry," she choked.

"It's fine," he said too quickly.

Fresh tears bloomed in her eyes, but they fell more gently as she ran her fingers over the wrinkled material of his shirt. She fingered the hem, and Bennick's breathing sharpened. He didn't stop her when she slipped her hand beneath his shirt. Her fingertips brushed against smooth skin and hard muscle. Her hand drifted to his side, and finally she found the ridged scar.

Bennick stiffened.

She froze, but his expression wasn't pained. Just locked. He didn't want her to see the scars. As if he worried what she might think.

She never wanted him to feel that way. Never wanted him to think he needed to hide from her. Fates, neither of them should be hiding anymore. Not from each other.

She gently lifted the edge of his shirt, slowly revealing a swath of tanned skin. A stomach taut with rippling muscle. And then the light from the lamp caught the scar.

The wound looked torturous, a ragged mess of scarred flesh in varying degrees of red. The skin had been burned—seared in order to stop the bleeding. And she knew he had another one on his back.

She could only imagine the agony he had endured. The pain it still must cause him.

Her heart ached. New tears curved down her cheeks, dripping into the space between them. "Bennick . . ." Her throat closed tight with emotion.

A vein in his neck throbbed, his body rigid.

"I'm so sorry for this," she whispered, her fingers brushing along the edge of the scar. "I hate that you were so badly hurt. But you don't need to hide it from me. There isn't a part of you I don't love."

The lamp cast long shadows on his hard face, his eyes tortured. "I failed you."

"No. You saved me. You have always saved me." She dropped his shirt, letting it fall back over the scar. Then she wrapped her hand around the back of his neck and pulled him close, pressing her lips to his.

His breath caught, and her chest squeezed when his palms pressed against her back, bringing her closer.

When she angled the kiss, he met her easily, devouring her until they finally broke apart for breath.

She kept her forehead pressed against his as they both breathed raggedly. "I love you," she whispered. "And I trust you. Always. With everything. My life, my heart . . . You're mine, Bennick Markam. And I am yours."

He didn't speak, but his fingers tightened their hold and his mouth claimed hers again, one hand sliding up her back to cradle the nape of her neck. They lost themselves in the kiss, and for a moment Clare forgot everything that had happened before. Only this moment existed, and it was perfect.

Finally, they eased apart, his fingers threading through her good ones, his other hand cupping her waist, keeping her firmly on his lap. "Do you want to talk about it?" he asked quietly.

Her first instinct was to deflect. She didn't want him to see how vulnerable she felt. How damaged and afraid she was. She only wanted him to see the strength he'd praised her for. But she was done shouldering this alone. "It was a dream," she whispered. "A nightmare. About Salim."

Bennick's face tightened, bringing a threatening edge to his expression. "He's dead. He will never hurt you again."

Her throat constricted. "I know. But it felt so real. Like he was here."

Bennick's hand moved to cup her cheek, his thumb tracing over the trails left by her tears. "What can I do?"

Her unbroken fingers gripped his, keeping him close even though he hadn't moved. "Just stay with me."

"I'm not going anywhere," he assured her.

Silence stretched for a long moment, and Bennick's thumb coasted over her lower lip, smoothing away some of the tension there. "I've had nightmares, too," he admitted quietly.

Shock rippled through her. "You have?"

"Ever since you were taken." His pain was no longer masked, but fully there in his eyes.

Her heart fractured at the sight of his suffering. She squeezed his fingers, wishing she knew what to say to soothe him.

"Everything is still so fresh," he said, a muscle in his jaw jumping. "Even now, with you right here, I still feel the panic of losing you." He slowly twisted his grip so their fingers interlocked, their palms pressed together. "Sometimes I worry I'll always feel like this. That I won't ever be able to let you out of my sight without my heart stopping."

"I know what you mean. I came so close to losing you . . ." Emotion climbed her throat, but she forced the words out. "I

426

thought you were dead."

"I thought I'd lost you, too. A thousand different times I feared I wouldn't find you in time." His gaze fell and she watched as he lightly fingered the healing welts on her wrists. "I'm sorry for everything you suffered."

"It's not your fault."

His gaze lifted to meet hers. "I swear to you, I'll give my life before you're hurt again."

"No." She shook her head. "Don't promise me that. I've lost you once. I don't think I could survive it again."

His mouth curved into a thin smile. "You could. Your strength astounds me."

"I'm not strong. If I was, I wouldn't be so afraid."

"You're wrong. You're strong because—even though you're afraid—you're still here. You won't let anything stop you from doing what you feel is right. You've sacrificed so much for your family, for others. You let me in, even when it hurt." He pressed a sudden kiss to her cheek, the tip of his nose skimming her temple. "Every single thing you do is brave and strong."

The love in his eyes was so intense, she could never doubt it. She leaned in, kissing him slowly. There was less desperation now. This kiss was about reassureance. Comfort—seeking as well as giving. Her braced hand rested lightly against his chest, her good hand skimming over his bristled cheek, the curve along his jaw, and finally moving to wrap a lock of his dark-blond hair behind his ear. Bennick shivered and slipped his hand behind her neck, pulling her closer, his fingers tangling in her hair.

When they lifted apart, Clare wrapped her hand around his, her voice a little breathless as she said, "Thank you."

The corner of his mouth twitched. "Trust me when I say it was my pleasure."

Her cheeks warmed, but she smiled.

Bennick's smile dimmed slowly. His thumb glided over a faint scar on her first knuckle. An old burn, from her time as a kitchen maid in the castle. "There's something I need to tell you."

His tone made it clear this wasn't going to be good. Her stomach dropped.

He peeked up at her, still holding her hand. "We didn't catch the Rose when he escaped in Krid."

Anxiety flooded her. The assassin terrified her—especially since she knew the truth. He and Bennick shared blood. History. It meant the Rose would be back.

"I shouldn't have trusted him to help us rescue you," Bennick said.

Clare took her good hand away from his so she could press it to his cheek. The ball of her thumb stroked beneath his cheekbone, coaxing him to meet her gaze. "You did what you thought was best. You can't torture yourself with the past."

The skin around his eyes tensed. "But I should have known better. And he'll come after us, now. After you."

"We'll be on guard."

His jaw flexed beneath her palm. "I know there will be dangers when we reach Duvan. We have too many enemies for it to be otherwise. But I *will* keep you safe." He folded her into his arms, tucking her head under his chin. She could hear his heart beating within his chest, a steadying sound that slowly relaxed every muscle in her body. He was alive, and he was here.

She felt herself melting as the minutes passed, exhaustion creeping into her body. His back was to the wall, and gradually she slumped against him, sleep dragging at her.

She knew he was beyond tired, too. And that bothered her. "You shouldn't be standing guard at night," she murmured, already drifting into sleep. "Not when you're with me all day."

Bennick turned his head, laying his cheek against her hair. "I don't like to leave you."

"You can't keep watch over me all the time."

She felt his lips press against the top of her head, his callused fingertips brushing soothing circles on the inside of her wrist. "Wilf will relieve me at midnight," he whispered.

Wilf shouldn't be up half the night, either. She wanted to say as much, but she couldn't find her voice. Being in Bennick's arms, feeling his soft touch . . . it warmed every part of her. Her eyes fluttered closed.

And for the first time in a long time, Clare slept soundly.

CHAPTER 44

DESFAN

"IS THERE A REASON YOU'RE WEARING Devendran blue?" Karim asked.

Desfan had just stepped out of his dressing room and into the sitting room. He glanced down at the dark blue kurta, which was lined in gold. "It was Serene's idea. She's wearing red tonight." And they would both have accents of gold. A way to show the world they were united, and dedicated to peace. His bride-to-be had made the calculated suggestion at a feast the other night. Yahri had overheard and delighted in the idea.

It was a little intimidating to think that Serene and Yahri got on so well. In fact, it was terrifying.

Karim eyed him. "Are you sure you're all right with having the

betrothal signing tomorrow? It's weeks sooner than you expected."

"I'm sure." It was too late to call it off, anyway. They'd already
invited all of the council members and their spouses to attend,
along with a few select others. And there really was no point in
waiting. Serene had voiced several good reasons to hold the signing earlier, chief among them being that the sooner they legalized
their betrothal, the sooner they could enter peace talks with Ryden.
Which felt increasingly important, as lately things with Liam and
Grayson had felt a little . . . odd.

Desfan frowned slightly. "Do you think Grayson's all right? He
was quiet the other day." And he had never ended a sparring ses-
sion so abruptly.

"He's always quiet," Karim said. "Like a cobra waiting to strike."

Desfan rolled his eyes. "Hasn't he proven himself yet? He saved
my life in the library, you'll recall."

"One good deed doesn't make a saint."

"Come, Karim, you don't think he's as bad as all that."

His bodyguard arched a dark brow. "He's the fates-blasted
Black Hand."

"And my friend."

"I believe we've already covered your questionable choice in
friends." He crossed his arms over his chest. "Although, to be honest, Liam does worry me more. He's too affable."

"Agreed." Desfan ran his fingers through his hair, tossing a
quick look at the nearest mirror. "That's why Razan is getting close
to him."

Karim stilled.

Desfan winced, realizing his slip too late.

"What do you mean Razan is getting close to him?" Karim growled.

Desfan moved for the door. "Fates, we're going to be late—"

Karim snagged his arm and jerked him to a stop, his eyes narrowing. "Whatever scheme the two of you have thought up, I need to know about it. *Now.*"

He glanced down at Karim's white-knuckled hand, which encircled his arm. "You're going to bruise me."

Karim shook him a little.

Desfan huffed out a breath. "Fine. Razan came to me several days ago. She let me know that Liam had taken an interest in her, and she was letting him pursue her. She wanted to find out if he'd inadvertently tell her anything useful."

Karim's nostrils flared. "She's been spying on the *spymaster of Ryden?*"

"When *you* say it, it almost sounds bad."

His friend's grip clenched. "If he thinks she's trying to use him, he could kill her."

"You're overreacting. It's really not that dangerous—"

"He's the fates-blasted Shadow of Ryden," Karim snapped. "And he's a Kaelin—that alone makes him dangerous! It was iresponsible of you and Razan to do this."

"It wasn't my idea," Desfan protested.

"Like that matters? You could have ordered her to stop."

He barked out a laugh. "Order Razan? Have you *met* her?"

Karim released him, his nostrils flaring. "You're the serjah. She would listen to you. And if she didn't, then it might be a sign that she's planning to use you again."

"How?" He flipped up a staying hand when Karim's mouth opened. "No. You know what? I'm not going through this argument again. If you have a problem with Razan, then you go talk to her."

"Oh, I will."

Desfan blinked. Well, that hadn't exactly worked. "Huh. Really? I thought you were avoiding her."

"Clearly that was a mistake," he growled.

Desfan cocked his head. "Are you still insisting you don't love her?"

Karim snarled under his breath and marched for the door.

Strange, how reality picked certain moments to slap you upside the head with a jarring vision of your future.

That's what Desfan thought as he stood on the dance floor across from Princess Serene, the two of them exchanging bows before their first dance.

Her hand slipped into his, her other resting against his bicep. His hand cupped her waist, and he prayed to the fates that his palms wouldn't sweat.

She looked breathtaking in red. The scarlet color contrasted beautifully with her darkened skin, and the cut of the dress left her shoulders bare. Her dark hair was twisted and pinned perfectly against her head, though as they spun, he noticed several strands fall from their rigid perfection to brush against her cheeks. Her skirt, hemmed in gold, rippled around her, keeping him away despite the nearness the dance necessitated. He studied every aspect of her, his future wife, and yet could not feel any closer to actually knowing her.

And after tomorrow morning, there would be no going back.

Not that there was really a choice right now, either. The only way to peace was through marriage to this woman. A near stranger.

The crowd had left a wide berth for their serjah and his future bride. They were the only couple on the dance floor as the musicians in the balconies above them played, the strains of music echoing in the lofty ballroom.

They said nothing as they danced, and at the conclusion of the waltz, they parted with another smooth bow and curtsy. The crowd applauded.

A new song began, and Serene met his gaze. "We should dance again. It would be strange if we broke away while everyone is still watching."

He nodded, taking her in his arms again. As they began to move to the strains of music, other couples joined them on the floor.

"Your bodyguard seems tense tonight," Serene said, her voice low enough to stay between them. "Anything I should be aware of?"

"No. Karim is just a little preoccupied with a certain young woman."

"Serai Krayt?"

He blinked. "You're very observant."

"I pay attention."

That seemed an understatement, but Desfan inclined his head. "I believe Karim will want a few words with Razan when she arrives."

The Devendran princess raised an eyebrow. "This wouldn't have anything to do with her flirtations with Prince Liam?"

"You really miss nothing."

"To be fair, they weren't always subtle." A shrewd light entered her eyes. "Has she learned anything from Liam?"

"Not as of yet. But I'll keep you informed."

"I would appreciate that."

Desfan spun her, and as they returned to position, he flashed her a small smile. "You're a talented dancer."

She seemed surprised by the compliment, but she accepted it with a graceful smile. "You make a good dance partner."

When the song ended, Serene was first to take a step back. She curtsied smoothly. "Thank you, Your Highness."

He tipped his head in a polite bow. "It was my pleasure, Your Highness."

They parted, walking off the floor in opposite directions. Before Desfan could reach the edge of the crowd, someone called his name.

He turned and spotted Imara dancing with Grayson. The prince looked truly tortured, his expression strained.

"Desfan," Imara repeated. "You're not leaving the floor already?"

He shook his head. "Merely resting a moment." He stood at the edge, near where Imara and Grayson danced.

The seventeen-year-old prince had a soldier's grace, and he'd obviously received some instruction on how to dance. Still, each motion was stilted, unpracticed. That seemed odd, after sparring with him. But then, when Grayson Kaelin fought, that had his sole attention. At the moment, he kept scanning the ballroom. His apparent nervousness made Desfan's own nerves rise. Did Grayson sense trouble? Kiv Arcas had helped oversee tonight's security, since he'd recovered from the injury he'd received during the library attack. Arcas wasn't one to use guards sparingly, so surely there was nothing to fear.

Desfan did look for Karim, though, and he found him almost instantly. His bodyguard was standing nearby, his dark head ducked toward Razan. They were talking rapidly, their faces slowly flushing. Desfan noted the varied glances thrown their way, and he pasted a smile on his face as he approached them.

Clapping a hand on each of their shoulders, he kept his grin in place as he took in their startled expressions. "Things might go better if you at least move onto the dance floor," he said lowly. "People are staring."

"They'll stare more once I blacken his eye," Razan snapped.

Karim's chest rose with a heavy breath. "Razan, so help me, I will throw you over my shoulder right now."

Her eyes grew stormy. "You could try."

Desfan grabbed their hands and forced them together. "Get on that dance floor right now, or I'll arrest you both. And I'll make sure they put you in the same cell for the night."

Razan darted a look at him. "Arrest us for what?"

"Brawling."

She huffed a laugh. "As if you're one to talk."

Karim cursed, but his fingers curled around hers. "Come on." He tugged her toward the dance floor, though she dug in her heels.

"You're not serious?" she hissed.

Karim tucked his chin, ducking closer to her so she couldn't avoid his hard gaze. "I'm completely serious. So is Desfan. And the last thing I want to do tonight is sit in a cell with you, so we dance." He glanced back at Desfan. "Stay by Arcas."

Desfan nodded, but his friend was already pulling Razan onto the dance floor, just as a new song began.

When Karim tugged her into position, the newest councilwoman very purposefully stomped on his foot.

Karim's thick eyebrows smashed together, but he said nothing, just guided her into the first steps of the dance, and they were soon lost in the spinning couples.

Desfan's gaze wandered back to Imara and Grayson, who still stood close together, though they hadn't joined in this newest dance. It was painfully clear Grayson wanted to flee.

Desfan took pity on him and stepped forward, holding out a hand. "Princess Imara, might I steal you for a dance?"

Imara nodded, though she still tossed a smile to Grayson. "I hope we can dance again soon. You really are getting better."

Grayson mumbled some hollow-sounding thanks and retreated, bumping shoulders with one of the newly appointed councilmen in his haste to escape.

"He's so hard to read," Imara muttered.

"I usually can't tell what he's thinking," Desfan agreed. He took the princess into his arms and they wove deeper onto the floor, gliding with the other dancers.

"So," Imara said. "Serene told me you took her horseback riding on the beach the other day. She enjoyed it very much."

"Thank you for the suggestion."

She inclined her head, accepting his gratitude. "I believe it's time for another wager. Assuming, of course, you want to owe me the phoenix coin again."

Desfan quirked a smile. "Your help has been invaluable."

She grinned. "It usually is."

It was hard not to compare Imara and Serene. The cousins had similar features from afar, but up close they were entirely different. Imara was shorter, her face rounder and softer, her nose pert. Her dark brown eyes were deep, yet held surprising warmth. Her skin was a shade darker than Serene's and smooth as silk. Her black hair swam freely down her back, brushing the back of his hand, a slight wave to the dark locks. A faint smell of vanilla wafted from her, and the sweet scent loosened something inside his chest.

"Are you nervous about the betrothal signing tomorrow?" she asked.

"Would you think less of me if I said yes?"

"Not at all." Her expression softened. "Just because you're signing the betrothal doesn't mean you're suddenly married. You still have time to get to know each other better. And remember, you have me."

"I do appreciate your help."

Imara's brown eyes shined. "Serene is lucky to have you, Desfan. I hope you know that."

Before he could think of a reply, the waltz ended and a lively reel began. Desfan grinned. "I hope you're ready for this, Princess."

Imara's eyes widened at the fast tempo, but she gamely kept up with him as he pulled her through the rapid steps. A laugh burst out of her when Desfan nearly tripped on her skirt. She gripped his arms tightly to steady him, still laughing. "Are *you* ready?" she teased.

Her nearness stilled his breathing. The light in her eyes, the way her mouth curved upward—her beauty momentarily stunned him.

He shook himself and cracked a smile. "Keep up if you can."

Then they were moving again; spinning and jumping in time to the wildly-paced music. Everyone on the dance floor hooted and danced with gusto, and those who weren't dancing clapped loudly, keeping the beat and nearly drowning out the instruments.

When the song finally ended, Imara gasped out a laugh, her

cheeks flushed from the exuberant dancing. "How do you Mortisians keep up the energy for dancing all night when you throw in songs like that?"

"Lots of wine," he chuckled.

"That sounds wonderfully refreshing. Please, lead the way." She looped her arm in his and he guided her away from the other dancers.

They had just reached the edge of the dance floor when he spotted Serai Yahri standing beside Arcas. She looked horribly pale, and her mouth was set in a serious line.

Desfan moved toward her at once, Imara still gripping his arm. He waited to speak until they were close enough to avoid being heard over the music. "Yahri, what's wrong?"

The old woman's chin quivered. "It's your father."

Desfan's chest tightened. "Has he worsened?"

Yahri's eyes glazed with a sheen of tears. "He's dead."

CHAPTER 45

SERENE

'MAY I CUT IN?'

Serene glanced away from the Mortisian nobleman she was currently dancing with to see Amil Havim at her elbow.

She hadn't seen the Mortisian emissary since she'd left Iden. She knew he'd left soon after, rushing to Duvan in an attempt to sabotage the marriage alliance. Thank the fates Desfan hadn't listened.

Amil was tall, slender, and undeniably handsome. His expression was neutral, making it impossible for her to tell if he still blamed Devendra for his father's death. But just the fact that his charming smile was absent made her wary. In any of her interactions with Amil before Ser Havim's death, he had always smiled.

440

Serene's dance partner tipped his head and retreated, leaving Serene with no choice but to accept Amil's offered hand.

His grip was firm, but not painful as he guided her closer. His hand settled in the dip of her waist, and she couldn't help but flick a look beyond him.

Cardon and Dirk stood on the edge of the dance floor. Both looked concerned, though there was a barely leashed heat in Cardon's sharp eyes.

Serene focused back on Amil, trying to ignore the way her skin tingled under Cardon's gaze. "I was hoping we'd have an opportunity to speak," she said, her tone careful. "I'm sorry our paths haven't crossed sooner."

Once, this man had flirted with her. Now, he stared at her with no expression. "I must admit, I've been avoiding you."

"Why?"

"I think my reasons should be obvious." Amil led her expertly through the dance, his motions carefully controlled. The tightening of his jaw was the only sign of his tension.

Serene lowered her voice. "I'm sorry for what happened to your father. But you cannot blame Devendra—"

"Devendrans murdered him."

"They attacked all of us."

"And yet your father survived, and mine did not."

"It was a tragic accident—"

"No. His death was no accident." Amil's fingers clenched against her. "Your father failed to protect those within his own castle. By not keeping out his enemies, he showed weakness. Why should Mortise ally with a weak king?"

Pain sparked in her hand from his tight grip, adding to the unease that bloomed in her chest. She refused to show any of that, however, as she held Amil's stare. "The alliance is for our mutual benefit."

"Mortisians don't want this alliance."

"Have you discussed this with Desfan?"

Her knuckles groaned in relief as Amil's hold suddenly relaxed. His entire expression reverted to a neutral state.

Fates, but that was more unsettling than his ire.

"Yes," Amil said. "I've spoken with the serjah. He doesn't seem concerned."

"Perhaps you should trust him."

The corner of his mouth twitched. "Trust can be a fickle thing."

She frowned, feeling a chill skate across her skin. "Will you be at the signing tomorrow?"

"No. I would prefer not to see the beginning of the end of my country."

"Why did you approach me?" she asked bluntly. "Why ask for this dance?"

"I thought I might ask you to reconsider. Or at least convince you to keep the original date of the signing. There's no reason to rush."

"There's no reason to delay," she countered.

He shook his head. "People are talking. They wonder why you're rushing this. It's made them nervous."

"Does it make *you* nervous?"

The man's flat gaze went impossibly flatter. "Clearly I was mistaken. You cannot be reasoned with. Goodbye, Serene." He dropped her hand and fell back a step, offering a slight bow before striding off the floor.

She looked after him, standing on the dance floor alone as other couples continued to circle and sway. She felt the weight of a hundred eyes on her, and her cheeks slowly flushed. She glanced over the crowd, but she couldn't see Desfan, or Imara. A sea of strangers stared at her; Mortisians who disliked her, distrusted her, and didn't want her here. She was trapped in a foreign palace that would be her home, and she was living her last night of freedom. After tomorrow, she would be unbreakably bound to marry Desfan Cassian.

The roaring in her ears was a cacophony of sound; the thumping beats of her heart, the strains of too-loud music, and bursts of harsh laughter. Every one of her other senses were overloaded as well. The swirling colors that blurred with the dancers, the too-strong perfumes that burned her nostrils. Her lungs locked. She couldn't breathe.

The need to escape flooded her, stamping out all else. She spun on her heel, twisting her back to the dancers as she hurried for the nearest outer door. In her periphery she saw Dirk start forward, then hesitate. She knew why he hesitated.

This had happened before.

Serene hated balls. They all reminded her of her sixteenth birthday. This was the first time since that awful night she'd allowed herself to blatantly run away from one, though. And just like three years ago, Dirk didn't follow her because someone else already was.

Cardon cut through the crowd after her, just as he had three years ago.

She wondered if he thought about that long-ago night as he followed her now. If he remembered the Devendran waltz that had played. It had been one of her mother's favorites, and hearing it at her mandatory birthday celebration—even though her mother had died only three weeks before—caused a torrent of emotion to rip through her sixteen-year-old body. She'd fled the room, the song, the memories; and her heart had thrilled when Cardon, and only Cardon, had followed after her.

Serene could smell the ocean air as she approached the open door. The breeze made breathing possible, but she didn't stop. She stepped through the portal and onto the balcony. Hugging the castle wall was a stone staircase that descended into the darkness of the beach below. Guided only by the light of the moon, Serene ran down the steps, her skirt lifted high so she wouldn't trip.

She'd been desperate to escape all those years ago, too. Sixteen and heartbroken after losing her mother; distraught that adulthood was nearly upon her, despite her parents' mutual decision that her betrothal be put off until later; agonized that Cardon did not know how deeply she loved him. If only she could embrace him. If only he could stroke her hair and murmur assurances. If Cardon knew she loved him—if he loved her—then she could better shoulder her mother's death and the responsibilities that would begin to be hers.

She had been so naive.

"Princess."

Cardon's soft call sounded exactly the same as it had that night. Serene reached the bottom of the staircase and kept walking, ignoring him.

Three years ago, she'd stopped.

She would not make that mistake again.

Cardon let out a breath—she heard it even though he was at the top of the tall staircase—and then his boots thumped down after her.

She aimed for the switchback path that led down to the private royal beach.

"Princess, please."

"Please, Serene."

His voice was right behind her. She'd halted at his first call, and now she stood motionless.

Cardon's fingers brushed her arm, coaxing her to face him. It made her heart skid and nearly stop. She couldn't quite look at him, so she stared at his hand, so near her wrist. The garrote bracelet he'd given her for her fourteenth birthday shone in the moonlight. A thank-you gift for saving his life that day in the woods.

She had loved him since that day. Loved him so much it hurt.

Serene curled her fists, nails jabbing into her skin. The silver garrote was still on her wrist. It was the only part of Cardon she could claim. When she was younger and foolish, she had imagined that Cardon had given her the bracelet etched in vines purposefully, because of what vines symbolized in Zennor. Forever entwined; stronger together.

"You know I'm here for you, Serene. You can talk to me."

Serene stepped into the sand, and the grains slid into her slippers. She paused only long enough to rip them from her feet and toss them aside, and then she was moving again. She strode toward the grasping waves that stretched along the beach, only to be dragged back into the dark ocean.

Cardon was behind her, maintaining a short distance between them.

She wanted to face him. Wanted to throw her arms around his neck and sob, as she had done back then.

Her cheek scraped against his uniformed chest. His palms warmed her back, rubbing in soothing circles. She was in his arms, and it felt better than all of her imaginings.

Serene reached the edge of the waves. They rushed to her, but never touched her crimson skirt.

She tried so hard to let nothing touch her.

Cardon stopped five paces away. "Princess, what happened?"

She closed her eyes, hating the formality between them. She let the air tease the stray hairs framing her face, and she prayed for strength. "Leave me alone, Sir Brinhurst."

"I can't."

Her hands tightened to fists at her sides. "Please. I need to be alone."

"I won't leave you," he said, his voice pitched low. "I'm sorry."

"I'm sorry," he whispered, holding her with tenderness as he tried to calm her tears.

"I miss her," Serene managed to croak.

"I know. I'm so sorry for your loss."

"Is it something Amil said?" Cardon asked.

She shook her head, her back rigid.

"What can I do? How can I help?"

"You can't, Cardon."

The sand shifted under his boots as he stepped closer. His words were as halting as his movements. "You're rushing things with Serjah Desfan. Perhaps you should consider putting off the betrothal until you're ready."

She gripped her skirt in her fists. "I will never be ready. It's better to just be done with it."

Cardon said nothing. She ached to see his expression, but her pride wouldn't let her look.

He didn't know why she had to rush. He didn't know about Grandeur's appointment to royal military leader, or that Grandeur was torturing people—killing people. *Her* people. She had to act. And if she didn't have Cardon's love, it hardly mattered who she married.

Cardon's strong arms felt incredible wrapped around her. So right. And if she told him the truth, perhaps he would never let her go. The secret had burned within her since she was fourteen. She hadn't told a soul. But she had to tell someone. She had to tell him.

Her tears had slowed, and he led her to a stone bench sheltered by a weeping willow. It was the perfect moment.

"Cardon?"

He lifted his chin from her head and loosened his arms enough that he could peer down at her.

Her eyes slid to the scar on his cheek. She had not managed to save him from that mark, but they had saved each other. They were meant to be together. It didn't matter that he didn't have noble blood—he was the most noble man she knew. It didn't matter that she was young; she was mature enough to know her heart.

The words swelled in her chest. Up her throat. Past her lips. "Cardon, I love you."

His mouth quirked, his expression softening. "And I you, Serene."

Her heart soared. She smiled as she gazed into his expressive brown eyes. "I knew you did," she breathed. She cupped his chin and raised hers, moving in for a kiss.

She felt him freeze—felt him stop breathing—but she still pressed her lips to his.

His mouth was an exhilarating contrast of hard and soft. Silk and steel. Her lips parted over his, breathing him in.

Cardon jerked away, launching himself from the bench.

Serene's heart pounded in the sudden silence. Her empty hands hung in midair. Her cheeks grew pink as she watched his face turn flaming. "What? What did I do wrong?"

His hand scrubbed over his mouth. She thought she saw his arm

447

tremble. His eyes bored into hers, and his voice was hoarse. "Why did you do that?"

Her hands fell to her lap. "I . . . love you."

His hand dropped, hanging limp at his side. "Fates," he rasped.

She surged to her feet. "I love you. And you love me. You said so."

He looked sick. "No. Not like that. Never *like that."*

His words stabbed. Serene tried to ignore them, despite the twisting in her gut. "I love you, Cardon."

He ducked his head, the heels of his hands pressing into his eyes. "No. Serene, no. You've just lost your mother. You're upset. You don't know what you're saying."

"I've loved you since I was fourteen."

His whole body flinched, his hands still blocking his expression from her. "You're only a child," he said, voice thick.

"I'm sixteen."

"Exactly." His hands fell and he stared at her with such intensity it made her squirm. "You're sixteen. I'm . . . Fates, I'm an old man compared to you!"

"You're twenty-seven."

"Eleven years," he nearly choked. "I'm eleven years older than you."

"That hardly matters to me."

"It matters to me."

"You'll be missed inside," Cardon said quietly from behind her.

Serene watched moonlight flash against the rippling surface of the dark sea. Her scalp itched with all the pins piling her hair up. Her eyes were dry and scratchy. Her body quivered with too many emotions stacked inside her. She'd been pushing back her feelings for too many years. Her hold on them was cracking.

"Princess?" Cardon whispered.

"You're the princess, Serene. I could never love you in any other way

than that. I serve you. Protect you. That's all."

"I know there will be difficulties," she said stubbornly. "I'm not naive. But I know my father would let us be together."

Cardon blanched. "You must not speak of this foolishness to anyone."

Her eyes stung. "Foolishness?"

"That's what this is." He took another step back. "Princess, I don't love you. Not in that way. We must both forget this ever happened."

She grabbed his wrist and felt his muscles flex—a desire to pull away. She knew it was his iron will that held him there, not her slender fingers.

"Princess," he said slowly. "Please let me go."

"No. You have to listen to me. I love you, and I don't want to hide—"

"Serene, stop."

A tear curved around her cheek.

He glanced at the watery trail, and his jaw stiffened. "If you don't let me go—if you mention this ever again—I will resign."

Everything froze. Time. Her breath.

Her heart.

"Please don't do this, Cardon . . ."

His eyes sparked. "I swear it, Princess. If you utter a word of this to me again—to anyone—I will remove myself from your service forever. I will leave Iden. Do you understand?"

"Agreeing to marry Desfan is final," Cardon said, his voice barely audible above the rolling waves. "It cannot be reversed."

Heartbreak was the same, Serene thought, remembering the agony of that night. The finality of Cardon's words. The rigid promise in his burning eyes.

She had run from him, left him behind with tears rolling down her face.

And he had let her go.

"Many things in life are final," she said, her throat burning.

"I'll learn to cope."

"I don't want you to suffer marriage to a man you don't love."

"I've been doomed to that fate for a long time."

"Please look at me."

"I'd rather not."

"Why?"

Because he had broken her heart three years ago, and a little more every day since. And she was so pathetic in this that she still couldn't bear the thought of losing him; she would rather feel the pain of his rejection every day than never see him again. She couldn't look at him, because she couldn't say the words that would tear him away from her. And whenever she looked at him, she didn't want to say anything else.

I love you.

Her shoulders fell. "Why are you doing this to me?" she asked, her voice weak.

Cardon's breathing stilled.

"Why must you always torture me?" Back still toward him, Serene let out a brittle, breathy laugh. "Do you enjoy hurting me?"

"No. *Fates*, no." He took a step closer. "My only goal is to protect you. That's the reason for every action I take."

"That's why you don't want me to marry Desfan?"

A pause. "I want you to be happy."

She spun on him, grounded where she was at the water's edge. "I am a princess. I have everything, and nothing at the same time. My life isn't my own, no matter what I do. I will never be truly happy. Accept that, as I have."

The scar on his cheek twitched as his jaw clamped tight. "I cannot accept that."

"Then perhaps you should leave."

His eyes narrowed. "You want me to go?"

"Perhaps I want *you* to be happy."

"My happiness is dependent on yours."

Serene rolled her eyes. "What I really want is for you to stop saying things like that when you know perfectly well how I feel!"

Silence. Again.

She stared at him. He stared at her.

The waves rolled behind her, the only constant in this moment of emotional chaos.

Lines creased his forehead. "How *do* you feel, Serene?"

A chill raced through her. She rubbed her arms. "You know how I feel."

He shook his head. "No. I don't."

Did he *want* her to verbalize everything that had happened three years ago? Did he *want* to shame her, or make her feel that heartbreak all over again?

Cardon's eyes dug into hers, trapping her gaze. "Tell me how you feel."

Her breath hitched. "You are cruel."

His lips thinned. "I want honesty."

"My feelings for you are the most honest part of me. They've only grown since you forbid me to speak of them."

He grimaced. "You've hidden them well."

"I had to." She realized her face was wet. She swiped at the useless tears. "You would have left if I said anything."

"Serene—"

"You thought I was a child, feeling a child's love. You thought it would vanish. Well, it didn't."

He said nothing, only searched her face. As if he could not believe her.

She was sick of him not believing her. She ripped the pins from her hair.

The skin around his eyes tightened warily. "What are you doing?"

"That night," she said, not looking at him as she pulled her hair down, throwing the pins to the sand. "That night I ran from you, my heart was shattered. I realized I could never have you, but I refused to lose you completely. When I returned to my rooms, I did this." Her hair free, she snatched hold of the thin widow's braid. She stepped closer, holding it out for his inspection. "Do you know what this is?"

His eyes widened as recognition swept in.

She gripped the braid, her tears still spilling. "I have worn this braid ever since that night. I lost you. I'd lost my mother. This braid . . . It's for you, for her, and for myself. Because I had nothing else but me to rely on. After that night, I dedicated myself entirely to being the princess."

"I didn't know," he whispered. "I didn't realize . . . Fates, you were sixteen. You were vulnerable after your mother's death. You said nothing all this time . . ."

"I couldn't. You would have left me."

Cardon crossed the final space between them. The night breeze lifted strands of his brown hair as he set his hands on her bare shoulders, his fingers curling into her back. His face was pale and his chestnut eyes reflected silver moonlight. "I'm sorry for how I treated you that night. But you never listen to anyone. Threats don't touch you. I thought—if your feelings remained—you would have spoken, regardless of the consequences."

She gritted her teeth. "Losing you was a consequence I would not risk."

His thumbs stroked the tops of her shoulders and down her upper arms, his warmth cutting through the thin material of her sleeves. "You love me."

Her hands were balled fists at her sides. Her lips remained sealed. She did not dare speak.

"I would never leave you," he said, his eyes tracing her tear-stained face. "Because I love you."

Her heart slammed in her chest, but her face remained hard. "You're trying to trick me."

Pained amusement tightened his features. "No, I'm not."

"You told me you could never love me."

"You took me by surprise that night. You *were* a child, Serene. I didn't love you then—not like that. I didn't realize how I felt until you were eighteen and talk about your future husband began." His eyes pinned her, stopped her breath. "But I couldn't approach you, because it was wrong. Abominably wrong."

"Why?"

"I'm your protector, and you are my princess. I'm no more than a servant. I don't deserve you—have no right to love you as I do." His throat bobbed. "If anyone found out, I would be dismissed. Possibly executed. And you've said nothing since that night. I truly thought you didn't care for me anymore."

"So you said nothing because I said nothing?"

Cardon nodded once, the motion stiff.

"You've been trying to get me to speak first." Realization shot through her, burning away the irritation she felt. Her voice softened. "All the things you've been saying, the letter you wrote . . ."

"I meant every word," he assured her. "I love you, Serene."

Her fingertips lifted. She touched his jaw. The edge of his scar. The corner of his mouth. Then she kissed him. Tentatively at first, then with desperation, need pounding through her.

Her hands cradled his face as they stood in the sand, chest to chest, locked together. They must have taken a step back because the next wave from the sea washed over her feet, folding her skirt against Cardon's legs.

Her tears continued to fall, and his lips explored the salty wetness against her cheeks, always returning to press against her mouth. His thumb caressed her high cheekbone. His fingers twisted in her unbound hair. His palm warmed her skin, and the heat of his kisses heated everything inside her.

She had never hated anything more than she hated reality in that moment. It seeped into her consciousness, reminded her that she was all but betrothed. That her marriage to Desfan was a political move that many had already died for; something that could ultimately save thousands. It could preserve Devendra—from Ryden and her father. It would give her rebels a chance.

Loving Cardon would not help those people.

She loved him anyway.

Cardon's hands brushed her skin and his lips moved slowly, tenderly over her mouth. The thought of breaking away nearly broke her, but reality could not be ignored.

She dragged away from his lips, pressing one last kiss to his scarred cheek before pulling back.

Cardon blinked, breathing heavily. He didn't step away from her. His hands continued to cradle her cheeks. "Please say it. Say you love me."

Tears pooled in her eyes and heat splotched her face. "Cardon, I . . ."

"Please."

"It won't do any good. We can't be together. You know that."

His dark eyes burned, intense. "Say it anyway. Just once."

She knew her voice would crack, but she unburied the words and let them fly. "I love you, Cardon."

His eyes fluttered shut. The barest smile lifted his lips. But the severity of his stance did not change. He rested his forehead against hers. "We could leave," he said quietly.

She fingered the lining on his blue uniform. "We're both too driven by our duties." She bit her lip. "I must marry Desfan. If I don't, Devendra will suffer. But if you don't wish to stay . . ."

He cupped the back of her neck and eased away so he could search her face. "Leaving you is not an option. I may not be able to stand beside you, but I will always be at your back. I'll guard you with my life." His throat bobbed. "I will stand with you tomorrow at the betrothal signing. I will stand with you forever."

Serene closed her eyes. She didn't know if she was strong enough to have him by her side while she signed those papers. And yet, she wasn't sure she was strong enough to order him away.

"We could find moments together," she whispered. "After the wedding."

Sadness entered his eyes. "We are both too honorable for that."

His fingers had found her thin braid, and he toyed with it. His eyes grew distant as he looked out on the waves. "No one deserves you. Least of all me. And yet, no man will love you as much as I do."

She rested a hand against his chest. Her fingers trembled. "You're the only one I'll ever truly love."

Cardon set a gentle kiss against her brow. He whispered her name. Only her name, but the sound of it—the depth of it—filled her. Overflowed and consumed her. She drank in the love he gave with that single word, and she struggled to give him the same through looks and touch alone.

The waves continued to slide past them, wetting the bottom of her dress. It was their first and last moment out in the open, alone under the darkness of the night sky.

CHAPTER 46

GRAYSON

GRAYSON FLED THE DANCE FLOOR THE MOMENT Desfan rescued him from Imara. It was a unique torture to be surrounded by people, but unable to tell them the danger they were in. To look at Imara's smiling face as they danced and know that, tomorrow, he would be her enemy. To see Desfan eye him with concern, like a friend, when he had to kill him.

If he didn't, Mia would die.

The ache in his chest pierced deep, making it hard to breathe. There were a hundred knots in his gut that refused to loosen. And while everyone around him smiled and laughed, all he wanted to do was scream.

He'd nearly made it to the ballroom door when Liam blocked

457

his path. "Where are you going?" his brother asked, his voice low but his smile perfectly in place for anyone watching.

Grayson's entire body tensed. "I need some air."

Liam studied him a moment, his eyes sharp. "You still have much to learn about subterfuge, brother. You don't know how to disguise your mood to suit your needs. It's a skill you'll want to learn before we reach Zennor." He strode around Grayson, headed for Serai Razan—who looked to be in a heated conversation with Karim as they danced. Grayson wasn't sure why Liam had shown such an interest in Razan; whether he wanted to learn more about her, or perhaps use her to get at Karim. In the end, it didn't really matter.

Everything would change after tomorrow.

He felt someone watching him. A glance over his shoulder showed Ranon tracking him with a slight frown. He was caught in a cluster of young Mortisian nobles, but his concern was clear as he stared at Grayson, a furrow between his eyebrows.

Beyond Ranon was his father, Ser Sifa. He looked at Grayson with a glare.

You were right all along, Grayson thought. *I am the monster you should fear.*

He ducked out of the ballroom, leaving the noise, the chaos, and the people behind. If only he could outrun himself.

He thought about returning to his room, but that would only make him feel more caged. Yet he didn't want to leave the palace, in case Liam found out and grew suspicious. He couldn't give his brother any reason to send the order to kill Mia.

All day, he had fantasized about going to Rahim Nassar's warehouse. Finding Akiva and Kazim. He could force them to tell him where the hawks were. He could kill them, even—neutralize that threat to Mia, at least.

But the risk was too great. Liam had him cornered, and Grayson could see no way out. No matter how much it wrecked him, he knew what his choice tomorrow would be. What it *had* to be.

He would always choose Mia.

He prowled the shadowy corridors and tried to steady his breathing. He had no idea how much time had passed. An hour? Two? He was on one of the upper floors, but he could still hear the faint echo of music from the ballroom. His eyes had fully adjusted to the darkness, so when he rounded a corner and saw the large painting that dominated the wall, he knew exactly what it was. With just the glaze of moonlight filtering in from a window further down the hallway, he could see the outline of each member of the Cassian family, captured within a gilded frame.

A perfect family, before they'd been shattered. A mother and father, and their three beautiful children, painted with a love so vibrant it was hard for Grayson to look at their expressions.

It was equally hard to look away.

They were a ravaged family, about to be ravaged again—by him.

Grayson pressed his back against the wall opposite the painting, slowly sliding down to the floor. With legs bent and arms slung over his knees, he gazed at the portrait. Even dimly lit, the smiles were happy. The faces full of life. He doubted he had ever looked so innocent as a child. It was wrong that such innocence died while he and his corrupt family remained.

Time slipped past. The painted faces continued to smile, and Grayson's heart continued to constrict. Footsteps made his head turn.

Even in the darkness, he knew it was Desfan as soon as the serjah rounded the corner. His blue kurta was rumpled and his dark brown hair stood up in places—even now, he raked a hand through the curly locks. He halted when he spotted Grayson on the floor. "What are you doing?" he asked, his voice oddly worn.

Embarrassment flashed though Grayson and he shoved to his feet. "Nothing. I was just leaving."

Desfan didn't react. His shoulders were slumped, and instinct screamed that something was terribly wrong.

Grayson's eyes narrowed. "Where's Karim?" Desfan's body-guard was always close.

"I don't know," the serjah whispered. He sounded lost. Broken.

The hairs on Grayson's arms lifted. He took a tentative step forward. "Desfan, are you all right?"

The Mortisian man said nothing. He only moved closer to the portrait of his family. His hand shook a little as he fingered the edge of the frame. "I'm the last," he breathed.

Grayson was close enough that, even in the dim lighting, he could see Desfan's lower lip was swollen and there was a streak of blood. He'd bitten his lip until it bled.

"My father is dead," Desfan said. "I just saw his body."

For a wild moment, Grayson wondered if Liam had killed the serjan. But his brother had no reason to kill Desfan's father, and— if he had—surely he would have made Grayson do it.

"I'm alone," Desfan continued, his voice cracking. "They're all dead now." He stumbled back a step, his eyes on the painting, his hands sliding into his hair and lacing behind his head. "I can't do this," he rasped. "Fates, I can't—" A sob strangled his words and Desfan fell to his knees.

Grayson's heart pounded. He prayed for Karim to come running around the corner—for anyone else to come into view.

No one did.

Desfan's cries were the only sound in the corridor, and Grayson couldn't ignore him. He sank into a crouch beside the doubled-over serjah. His hand hovered over Desfan's trembling back, but he couldn't make himself touch him. Comfort him. Not when tomorrow would see them as enemies.

So he sat beside him while Desfan mourned his father's death; the loss of his entire family.

He didn't know how long they sat together. Minutes, or hours. Grayson said nothing while Desfan cried. He didn't say anything until Desfan's tears dried and he slowly raised his head, his eyes on the painting of his family.

"I'm sorry," Grayson whispered. The words were inadequate, but they were all he had.

"Thank you." Desfan's voice was hoarse. "For staying with me."

Grayson knew the words meant nothing. Not really. It wasn't as if Desfan had sought him out. It didn't mean they were friends. Still, the fact that Desfan was sharing this vulnerable moment with him made Grayson realize how desperately he wanted to be Desfan's friend.

They never would be, because tomorrow Grayson would kill him.

Shame made his cheeks burn.

Desfan exhaled slowly, swiping at his eyes. His voice was deeper than before. "There are so many things to arrange. I need to announce his death, prepare the pyre and the memorial, organize the period of mourning . . ." His throat flexed as he swallowed. "Plan the coronation."

Something like hope fluttered in Grayson's chest. "Will this postpone the betrothal signing?" Perhaps if he had more time, he could find a way to outsmart Liam.

Desfan shook his head. "No. I'll announce his death in the morning. At the signing. If only he could have held on a little longer." His gaze was on the portrait in front of them. "At least until we got word. Once we knew if she . . . And now he'll never know. *I* may never know . . ." His voice faded. When he glanced at Grayson, his eyes were filled with a grief no one should have to bear. "She might be alive."

Confusion rippled through him. "Who?"

"My sister." Desfan looked back at the painting, his voice haunted. "I don't know which one. I don't even know if it's true, but she could be out there. I don't know where. I don't know what she's had to endure, or what she must think of me for not coming after her sooner. But I didn't know. I swear, I didn't know until a month ago. Yahri told me. She knew all along. That's why my father collapsed. His ill-health combined with the shock of hearing one of his daughters might still be alive . . ." Desfan shook his head and glanced down.

Grayson followed his gaze and watched as the serjah slowly spun the obsidian ring on his finger.

"We searched for them," Desfan whispered. "As soon as we received word about the shipwreck, my father and I sailed to Dorma. We looked for their bodies, but the sea swallowed them. We never found them." His knuckles whited as his hands fisted against his knees. "I've been mourning them for nine years, but what if one of them is alive? I can't even imagine it. Tally would be seventeen."

Tally.

The familiar name jolted through him, and all he could see was Mia's beaming face as she'd cradled the doll he'd made for her out of a discarded meal-sack.

"Mia would be sixteen," Desfan whispered.

Everything in Grayson froze. "Mia?"

Desfan nodded, his eyes tracing the painted faces of his family. "We all had shortened names. I was Des. Tahlyah was Tally. Meerah was Mia." His palm rubbed over his heart. "I haven't said them out loud in so long. I can barely stand to think them."

There was a roaring in Grayson's ears as he stared at the painting. He looked at the seraijan, smiling so widely, her expression soft. Her beauty was undeniable, but that wasn't what made Grayson suck in a breath. No, it was the shape of her face. The curve of her cheeks. The slant of her nose. The light in her rich brown eyes. The way her dark, softly waving hair fell around her shoulders.

The infant girl in her arms.

No.

No, no, no, no . . .

Meerah Cassian would be sixteen.

Mia was sixteen.

Meerah Cassian had been lost at sea at the age of seven, nine years ago.

Mia had been imprisoned in Ryden when she was seven years old.

Nine years ago.

But no. It wasn't possible. Mia was a *Sifa*. There was proof. Liam had shown him the—

Liam. A man he clearly never should have trusted.

Grayson knew the genealogical record was real; Ser Sifa's rage came from the true loss of his family, and Ranon had even said Mia's name once. So there *had* been a Mia Sifa. Liam hadn't fabricated that. He'd probably even told Grayson a partial truth—

that he'd stumbled across the information while researching Sifa and the other members of the council.

But Mia Sifa was not *his* Mia. Grayson knew that for certain now, because he was staring at her likeness.

Just a few days ago, he'd looked at the seraijan's image and been reminded of Mia. He'd thought it had been because of her kind eyes. Perhaps the soft, warm features of a Mortisian woman, but no. He was staring at Mia's *mother*. And beside him on the floor was Mia's *brother*.

Serjah Desfan Cassian was Mia's brother.

Mia was a fates-blasted princess.

Grayson's thoughts spun, and his gut twisted. How had he been so blind? He should have known his father would only keep Mia if she was important—and not just as a way to manipulate Grayson.

Henri Kaelin knew the truth. He knew Mia's true identity. That she was the youngest seraijah of Mortise. It was the only explanation.

Did Liam know who she was, too? He had to. Didn't he? Or had he truly found her name in the Sifa's genealogy and assumed she was one and the same?

"Are you all right?"

Grayson's focus jerked to Desfan, and he was suddenly caught in his deep brown eyes. How had he not seen Mia in them? The resemblance was there. It was everywhere. Expressions he had seen in Desfan he could now recognize as echoes of Mia. They were brother and sister. The last of the Cassian family.

Desfan was the last living member of Mia's family, and Grayson had no choice but to kill him, or she would die.

"Grayson?" Concern pulled at the edges of Desfan's mouth. "Are you all right?"

Grayson's throat was dry, but he forced himself to swallow. "I'm fine."

It was one of the biggest lies he had ever told.

CHAPTER 47

GRAYSON

GRAYSON DIDN'T CLOSE HIS EYES THE ENTIRE night. The first half was spent sitting beside Desfan in the upper hallway, across from the royal family portrait. They had not talked much. Desfan mourned his father—his entire family—with near-silent tears while Grayson reeled from the shock that Mia was Princess Meerah Cassian. No—she was *Seraijah* Meerah Cassian, and that foreign title made everything feel even stranger.

Karim found them a few hours before dawn. He hurried around the corner, harried and pale. He cut right to Desfan and embraced his friend without a word, holding him fiercely as Desfan's tears began anew.

Grayson silently slipped away, eager to escape. But even as he fled to his rooms, he was not free of the truth.

The most inconsequential thoughts pierced him as he hurried through the palace. Mia had been born in this place. She had lived here. Learned to walk in these halls. She had laughed and played here. When he touched the handle to his bedroom door, he wondered if she had ever touched it, too.

He shoved into his room, sweat coating his skin. And yet he shivered as he dropped into the nearest chair, his hands gripping his head as he bent over, breathing too fast, too shallow.

Mia was Seraijah Meerah Cassian. She had known every comfort here. She had been surrounded by family. She'd enjoyed love, happiness, and security—before she'd known him.

His fingers curled, digging painfully into his scalp. Fates, Mia had walked the same beach he had; that would have been the very spot she'd envisioned when she'd asked him to walk in the sand. This warm palace had been her *home*.

She would have been raised on stories of Ryden, like all Mortisians. Taught to fear everyone from Ryden. Even though it had been years ago, she had probably heard stories of his brothers. Of him.

Her father had died tonight, and she didn't know. She couldn't mourn alongside her brother. If Liam had his way, Desfan would not have long to mourn, anyway. Mia would have no one, then. The grief Grayson had seen on Desfan's face—the haunted look that came from being the only survivor of a family—would be Mia's grief.

Perhaps Liam didn't know who she really was. If he did, surely he wouldn't kill her. She was too valuable. The thought came back to him several times, but he didn't go seek out his brother. Because in the end, it truly didn't matter if Liam knew the truth or not. His obsession with killing Desfan, Serene, and Imara would not be swayed. Grayson knew that he wouldn't divert his plan for anything. He would send the order to kill Mia if Grayson so much as hesitated.

He could not hesitate.

He was still sitting in the overstuffed chair when the sun rose, spilling light into the room. He only looked up when his door opened, and two men stepped inside.

The first was Kazim, Liam's contact who worked for Rahim Nassar. The second was Micah, one of Liam's bodyguards.

Kazim spoke first, his tone even, his eyes cold. "Saimon. Or should I say, *Prince Grayson*? Liam has entrusted me with the hawk. I'm to assure you that the message is ready, and that I'll be waiting in Liam's room. If you betray your brother or fail him in any way, the message will be sent, and the girl will die."

Grayson pushed to his feet. He had the satisfaction of seeing Kazim stiffen in what could have been fear, but it was a hollow thing. His skin felt too tight and nerves writhed in his stomach.

Micah spoke next. "Prince Liam has instructed me to be your bodyguard at the signing." He touched one of the blades belted at his waist and gave a slanted smile. "To be honest, I'm not sure what I'd prefer—your cooperation, or your resistance. It really would be my pleasure to kill the Black Hand. Your death would avenge many."

The man's taunts didn't matter. Nor did his threats. The only threat Grayson could see was the one directed at Mia, so he ignored them both and strode for the door.

Grayson paused beside Micah as the bodyguard showed his sword to the Mortisian guard at the door. For the treaty signing, each royal was allowed one bodyguard. The guards could have one sword, but no other weapons would be permitted in the room.

Grayson had several knives hidden on his body, and he assumed Liam and both of their bodyguards had the same. The Mortisian guards glanced them over, but didn't conduct a search. They just took the word of each person to walk through the door—as if all men were assumed to have honor and decency.

Liam's plan was horrifyingly perfect. This would be the best time and place to make such a strike. All the royals would be present, but with a minimal guard.

It would be a slaughter.

Liam led the way into the room, his bodyguard right behind him. Grayson followed, Micah a hulking presence at his back.

The room was moderately sized, with one large window at the back wall and a tall, circular table set before it on a rectangular dais. The remaining furniture was pushed up against the walls. Mortisian nobles were scattered around the room, though all were on this side of the table. Desfan stood beside Serene, behind the table, the two of them looking out at the gathered crowd.

Grayson's chest squeezed. The crown prince of Mortise looked as haggard as Grayson felt. He doubted either of them had slept.

All around the room, Mortisians were murmuring about Desfan, speculating as to why he looked so ill, so grave.

"It's the thought of marrying a Devendran," one woman whispered.

Grayson noticed that Serene looked just as solemn as Desfan, and she stood closer than she normally did. She had probably been informed about the serjan's death.

Princess Imara stood slightly behind her cousin. She also looked more solemn than usual, but she caught Grayson's eye and gave him a small smile.

He looked away, his jaw locked.

Liam gripped his elbow. "Remember what's at stake," he murmured. The only words Liam had spoken to him this morning.

Grayson forced a stiff nod, and his brother stepped away, his bodyguard following him to Serene's side. Her bodyguard was alert, at least; the Devendran soldier eyed Liam's approach with due wariness.

Micah eased closer to Grayson. "Move," he prompted, his whisper dark.

Grayson did. When he reached Desfan's side and the serjah looked at him, it was like being punched in the gut. Now that Grayson knew the truth, he could see Mia in him.

The serjah ghosted out a pained smile, his voice pitched low. "It looks as if you didn't sleep at all."

"I didn't."

"I'm sorry." He held out his hand. "Thank you for staying with me last night."

Grayson's palm sweat in his glove as he took Desfan's hand. He had no words. His throat bobbed as he swallowed hard.

The serjah's forehead creased, concern edging into his eyes.

"Your Highness." Liam outstretched his hand, his smile wide as he smoothly interrupted the tense moment. "Thank you again for allowing us to be here."

"Of course," Desfan said. He released Grayson's hand and shook Liam's. "Thank you for coming, and for bringing the hope of peace."

Grayson melted away, taking his position at Desfan's back. He

470

tried to keep his breaths even. He could feel Micah breathing easily directly behind him, and he wondered if he already had a dagger hidden in his hand. His back tensed, waiting for the deadly strike.

Mia. He needed to focus on Mia.

The double doors thudded closed, and two guards took up positions before them. A handful of servants milled about the room, serving light drinks to the councilmen and their spouses. Grayson wondered how many were in Liam's employ.

In the crowd, he spotted familiar faces from the Mortisian council. Ser Sifa, Ser Anoush, Serai Razan, Serai Yahri—they weren't Liam's targets. In fact, his brother didn't want the council harmed, if possible. He needed them to vote unanimously for war with Ryden. That didn't mean they were safe, though. Or that they weren't about to be the helpless witnesses of a massacre the likes of which Eyrinthia had never seen.

Royals from three kingdoms, killed in one brutal strike.

Serai Yahri stepped in front of the table, facing the crowded room. "Thank you all for gathering on this historic day. This betrothal signing marks a peaceful alliance between Devendra and Mortise, reliant on the marriage of Serjah Desfan Saernon Cassian and Princess Serene Aren Demoi. We are especially grateful to have the following royal witnesses: Princess Imara Aimeth Buhari of Zennor, Prince Liam Kell Kaelin of Ryden, and Prince Grayson Winn Kaelin of Ryden. Their presence shows a unity that our kingdoms have not known in centuries . . ."

Grayson felt Imara's eyes on him, burning his profile. He ignored the urge to turn. He stared at the tall table before Desfan, at the slice of parchment inked with small text stretched over the top. An elegant quill was perched in a stand beside the pot of ink.

The moment that treaty was signed, lives would end. *Grayson* would end them.

His heart pounded. *Fates forgive me . . .*

Serai Yahri cleared her throat, the guttural sound snagging Grayson's attention. "And now," she said, her eyes clouding. "We will be addressed by our serjah."

Desfan's posture was straight, his shoulders pushed back. Grayson imagined his expression was just as controlled. "Today marks a beginning as well as an ending," he said, his strong voice carrying through the room. "As is well known, my father, our beloved serjan, has been grievously ill. It is with a heavy heart that I announce his passing last night."

Eyes widened and faces paled. Muttering broke out.

Grayson felt Liam's eyes rake the side of his face. Perhaps his brother was not all-knowing, then. He hadn't known about the serjan's death, and now he wondered if Grayson had.

Let him wonder.

Desfan lifted his hand, and people quieted. "My father's rule was prosperous and fair. He was loved by his people and respected by his allies. His reign will never be forgotten."

The Mortisians chanted the last words back at him, low and somber. Several in the room visibly struggled to fight back tears.

"This treaty honors Serjan Saernon Cassian and the dreams he had for his people," Desfan continued. "Joining Mortise with the alliance that already exists between Devendra and Zennor makes all of our countries stronger." He lifted the quill. "To a future of peace."

No one said anything as he dipped the quill in ink and signed his name at the bottom of the document.

Grayson forced every muscle in his body to relax. He felt the

blade resting against his arm. He imagined snatching it free, envisioned it stabbing through flesh.

Desfan finished signing. He stepped aside and passed the quill
to Serene. Grayson thought he saw her hand tremble as she held
the quill, but she bent over the treaty and scratched her name beneath Desfan's.

Serai Yahri was the first to applaud, and the others in the
room—still clearly in shock over news of the serjan's death—
slowly began to clap as well.

Micah's breath was on Grayson's neck, hot and thin.

Desfan took Serene's hand and the applause grew louder.

Grayson whipped the knife from the sheath under his sleeve.
He flipped the blade in his palm and stabbed a killing stroke before anyone could react.

Desfan's muscled back flinched and he pivoted, still gripping
Serene's hand.

Grayson jerked the bloody knife out of Micah's gut, ignoring
the dying man's cry as he shoved Micah away with his shoulder.

Desfan's eyes darted to the bloody blade in Grayson's hand,
his face locked with horror.

A collective gasp sucked the air from the room. The first
screams came when Grayson kicked Desfan's hip, sending both
him and Serene staggering against the table. The bottle of ink
cracked against the stone floor, shattering.

But Serene was saved from Liam's swinging knife.

Liam snarled wordlessly at Grayson. His furious glare promised
retribution.

From the corner of his eye, Grayson saw Liam's bodyguard
pull his sword from Serene's bodyguard's back. The Devendran
man hadn't even been able to draw his weapon. He crashed to the

floor, bloody and shaking.

Serene's scream tore through the room.

Karim dove for Grayson with his long sword, slashing at him and forcing him away from Desfan, who was crouched on the ground, clutching Serene to his side as she continued to cry out and reach for her fallen guard.

Grayson stooped and snatched Micah's sword, still gripping the bloody dagger in his left hand. He brought up his newly acquired sword and blocked Karim's angry blows, sweat beading on his forehead as he tried not to damage Desfan's bodyguard.

"Stop," he snapped. "I'm trying to help!"

Karim only growled and struck with more intensity.

Shouts stabbed through the crowd. Liam's men ordered Mortisians to their knees. Women and men sobbed for their lives.

The two guards by the door had drawn their swords, but remained blocking the door. Grayson thought he heard the echoes of a fight in the corridor; probably more of Liam's men, converging with the Mortisian guards stationed outside the doors.

Karim's blade sliced Grayson's upper arm, leaving a burning cut. He ground his teeth and brought his focus back to Karim. His mind continued to race, searching for a way out. Mia's time was counting down. The moment his betrayal reached Kazim, the message to kill Mia would be sent.

He needed to reach Kazim. *Now.*

Liam yelled, and Grayson's eyes shot to his brother. The Kaelin prince stumbled back from Imara's hulking guard, a hand clamped over a wound on his arm. The bodyguard raised his sword, but Liam's guard rushed in, defending him.

Imara pressed herself deeper into the corner, her eyes wide and terrified.

Grayson cursed and switched to the offensive. He beat Karim back with each strike until finally their blades clashed and locked. "Stay with Desfan," he growled over their crossed swords. He twisted and ducked under Karim's arm so he could slam his elbow into Karim's side.

The Mortisian man stumbled with a grunt, his eyes flashing with pain and fury.

Imara's scream turned Grayson's blood to ice. He spun to see Liam's bodyguard poised to stab the Zennorian princess with his long sword.

Grayson dove forward, and Imara's scream leaped octaves when Grayson's blade plunged through her would-be killer, speckling her with blood.

The Ryden guard crumpled and Grayson yanked back his sword, his eyes darting over Imara.

Shivers wracked her petite body as she huddled in the corner. She gazed up at Grayson with terror and dread, her dark hands braced against the stone wall. Her chin trembled and tears dashed over her round cheeks.

Grayson swallowed thickly. He wanted to explain. Apologize. The fear in her eyes—fear of *him*—assured him that an eternity would hardly be enough time to regain her trust. He had saved her, but he was the Black Viper. He'd started the carnage by killing the first man. It didn't matter if the man had been from Ryden.

Grayson could see it in Imara's eyes—he had just confirmed every story that had ever been told about him.

"Grayson!" Liam howled, his voice thick with a thousand curses.

"Stay back," Grayson hissed at Imara, and then he whirled to survey the room.

Chaos reigned. Serene sobbed over her bodyguard, who shuddered and gasped on the floor, blood pooling around him. Desfan crouched next to her, his eyes boring into Grayson, accusation and betrayal thick in them. Karim tore after Liam, but he was met with resistance as Liam's men—dressed as servants—leapt to defend their leader with long knives drawn. There were at least a dozen of Liam's men between Grayson and the double doors.

His father had trained him for worse odds.

Grayson spun his blade and dove into the fray. He cut down his enemies, let the practiced motions of fighting keep him from panicking. He ducked, parried, stabbed, and dragged his sword back. He killed in perfect rhythm. His enemies paled when they saw him approach. Some ran from him. His cold ferocity—the ease and grace with which he killed—terrified *him*. He did not count the men he killed as he made his way to the double doors.

Mortisian nobles struggled out of his way, though they weren't his targets. He stabbed both guards at the door before glancing back, his chest heaving.

Imara was where he'd left her in the back corner of the room. Serene and Desfan were still behind the table, though it looked like Yahri and Serai Razan had joined them. Karim had finally reached Liam, and with a single blow he knocked Liam's dagger from his hand.

There was nothing more Grayson could do here. He needed to reach Kazim before he learned of Grayson's betrayal. With how loudly everyone was screaming, it wouldn't take long.

Grayson wrenched open the doors, prepared to cut his way through the rest of Liam's men.

Shock jolted him when he saw bodies littering the hallway. A cluster of Mortisian guards stood in the center of the devastation. Two uniformed Devendran guards were with them. Grayson rec-

476

ognized the man in front as one of Serene's main bodyguards.

The scar on his cheek throbbed, his eyes deadly. He lifted his sword, blocking Grayson's path. "Lower your weapons," he commanded.

His grip on his sword and dagger clenched. If Liam's forces had already failed out here, had Kazim sent the message?

Please, no . . .

"Let me pass," Grayson said, breathless.

The soldiers edged closer to Serene's bodyguard; even the Mortisians were following his silent lead.

The Devendran leveled his sword at Grayson. "Surrender and step aside," he barked.

Grayson didn't move. "Let me go." *Please.*

The other Devendran soldier had edged closer to the doors. "Cardon," he said tightly, "I don't see the princess."

The scarred guard—Cardon—did not take his eyes off Grayson. His glare was the blackest Grayson had ever seen. "What have you done?"

He didn't have time for this. *Mia* didn't have time. He lunged at the Devendran, his sword raised.

Cardon slapped Grayson's blade away with his own, his skill ringing with every blow he landed. Still, Grayson blocked each attack, maneuvering around Cardon so he could have a clear retreat down the hall.

In his periphery, he saw the Mortisian soldiers rushing into the room, hurrying to defend Desfan. But the threat was past. Karim had subdued Liam. The royals were safe. *Mia* was the one in danger now, but no one would listen to him.

Grayson didn't want to kill Cardon, but the man fought with a force almost as barbaric as Tyrell. If Grayson didn't find an easy out soon, he would have no choice but to kill him.

The opportunity never came.

Grayson was struck from behind, a blow so staggering he stumbled, nearly dropping his sword. Something—a hilt, he imagined—had been knocked against his temple. Blood rushed in a river down the side of his neck. His vision sparked and sound distorted. He didn't realize he'd fallen to his knees until Karim came into view, towering over him.

"Please," Grayson rasped, his head spinning, bile burning in his throat. "Mia."

Karim's face could have been cut from stone. "I *will* kill you for this," he vowed.

Another blow to his head ended everything.

CHAPTER 48

SERENE

DIRK WAS DEAD, BUT SERENE STILL PRESSED HER hands to the wound in his unmoving chest. The blade had pierced through him, driven through his back in a brutal attack. Blood pooled on the floor, covering her hands and skirt. She could not stop shaking.

"It's over," Desfan said quietly, his hand on her shoulder.

She blinked up at him, uncomprehending, her fingers curled against Dirk's chest. Each thud of her heart brought a different thought.

Her fault. This morning, she'd asked Dirk to come instead of Cardon.

An attack. The two Ryden princes had tried to kill every person in this room.

Dirk was dead. What would she tell Serai Nadir?

Dirk had been her protector since her birth. Now he was gone.

Cardon. This could have been Cardon.

Relief and guilt throbbed through her, making her wince. Cardon was alive, but Dirk was dead, and it was her fault.

"Serene?" Desfan's voice was gentle. "Serene, he's gone."

"I'll stay with her."

Serene looked up.

Cardon stood there, his hands hanging at his sides.

Desfan squeezed Serene's shoulder as he rose. "I must see to the damage." The serjah sounded almost as numb as Serene felt. But at least he had the ability to move. He paced away toward some of his gathered soldiers and Cardon took his place, kneeling at her side. His mouth twisted in a grimace as he took in Dirk's body. Then he looked to her.

He scooped a lock of dangling hair from her eyes and curled it behind her ear. "You can let go of him," he whispered.

Her hand trembled against the wound. "He didn't have a chance," she managed to say. "They struck from behind."

Cardon laid a hand on her back, his fingers long and warm. She hadn't realized how cold she was. "I stopped Prince Grayson," he said. "He was attempting to flee."

Hatred slashed through her, heating her blood. "Did you kill him?"

"No. Karim knocked him unconscious. He wanted both Liam and Grayson alive for questioning."

"They deserve to die," she said, only mildly disturbed by the fervor in her whisper.

"Dirk will have justice," Cardon assured her. He glanced around.

"Imara is in shock."

Imara sat in the corner of the room, her arms wrapped around herself, her eyes staring at nothing. Serai Razan knelt before her, talking gently.

Fates. If something had happened to Imara, it would have been Serene's fault, too. She wouldn't have been here if not for her.

A shudder wracked her, and Cardon pressed his hand more firmly against her back. "Are you hurt?" he asked, a catch in his voice.

She shook her head. "No."

"Thank the fates," he breathed.

She peered up at him. "How did you get here so quickly?"

His throat flexed as he swallowed. "When Dirk told me you'd asked him to replace me at the signing, I didn't protest. But I wasn't going to leave you completely. We stationed ourselves around the corner from the doors, just in case. A group of men attacked the guards. It was lucky we were there, or the guards would have been overpowered."

"I'm sorry," Serene whispered. A tear leaked from the corner of her eye.

Cardon rubbed the tear away with his fingertips. "This is not your fault. Dirk gave his life to protect yours. That is the best death a bodyguard could have." His mouth tightened. "Let's get you out of here." He wrapped his hands around her wrists and all but pried her away from Dirk's body.

Her fingers dripped blood. Her sleeves were streaked with it. Only now did she fully realize the wetness of it. Crimson slicked her palms and edged her fingernails. Dirk's sightless eyes stared up at her, his blood soaking through to her knees.

She gulped back vomit and pinched her eyes closed.

481

Cardon slipped his hands under her arms and urged her to her feet. He kept an arm around her waist, the other gripping her nearest elbow as she glanced around the room. Most of the nobles had left. The few that remained appeared to be injured with Mortisian guards hunched over them. Low crying and moans writhed through the room.

Desfan was surrounded by members of his council. Ser Anoush was speaking to him. "This cannot go unpunished. The council would back you if you were to declare immediate war on Ryden."

Another council member—Ser Sifa—glowered. "Yes. Send their bloody heads to their father." He darted a look at Serene, cringing at the blood on her hands. "I imagine Devendra and Zennor would both support you in war."

"We cannot act with undue haste," Serai Yahri warned.

Desfan opened his mouth, but Karim re-entered the room, snaring his attention. The Mortisian bodyguard fumed as he strode toward them. "They've been locked up," he reported. "Liam isn't saying anything and Grayson is still unconscious."

Cardon moved as if to pull Serene away. She dug in her heels, silently demanding to stay. He sighed, but didn't force her.

Desfan looked at his bodyguard. "The men who fought with them?"

"Dead, captured, or escaped." Karim was visibly seething. "I have no idea how they managed to find so many friends. Most were Mortisian."

"Liam is a master spy," Serene said. "And Grayson is a walking nightmare. They could have rallied anyone to their cause. This should not have been a surprise."

Desfan rubbed a hand over his forehead.

Ser Sifa grunted. "The princess is right. They never should have been allowed so much freedom. They would have murdered us all if Karim hadn't responded so quickly. Did you see the Black Hand? He killed so many—"

"Grayson saved my life."

Everyone turned to Imara, standing with Razan at her side.

"What?" Desfan asked.

Imara wet her lips and spoke again. "Grayson saved me. He killed the Rydenic soldier that tried to kill me."

"He attacked me," Karim argued. "He knocked Desfan to the ground. He would have killed him if I hadn't stepped in."

"I know what I saw. He defended me." Imara looked to Serene, as if for corroboration.

Serene shook her head. "I only saw him sweep through the room, killing everything that came against him."

Impatience now lined Imara's tone. "Yes, but he killed his own bodyguard."

Everyone darted a look at each other.

Imara frowned. "You wouldn't have seen, Serene—he was behind you. You as well, Desfan." She looked at Serai Yahri. "What did you see?"

The old woman blinked. "I don't know. It happened so fast..."

"He attacked me in the hall," Cardon said.

"And Desfan," Karim reminded them, his voice tight.

"He was trying to run," Cardon added. "He was obviously guilty. The desperation to escape was clear on his face."

Imara pursed her lips. She looked like she might argue more, but Desfan spoke. "Karim, search their rooms. Perhaps we'll learn something. If there's a Rydenic man still breathing in this castle, imprison him immediately. Send word to the docks for the Rydenic ship to be seized. I want all the sailors held there and interrogated."

Karim bowed. "As you wish."

Desfan glanced between Imara and Serene. "I suggest we retire to our rooms for the rest of the day. I'll send for both of you when we can better discuss what actions to take."

Serene wanted to demand the heads of both Rydenic princes now, but she knew Desfan was thinking more clearly than she was. They needed to get to the bottom of what had happened today. They needed to decide if this meant war.

Then they could kill Liam and Grayson Kaelin.

CHAPTER 49

CLARE

BENNICK HAD JUST FINISHED BRAIDING CLARE'S hair for the morning when there was a heavy knock on the door. When Bennick opened the portal, Clare's eyes widened as Captain Zadir stalked in, followed closely by a scowling Wilf.

Zadir tipped his head toward Clare, then focused on Bennick. "I would appreciate it very much if you would keep *him*," he tossed a thumb over his shoulder, indicating Wilf, "away from my prisoner. He's making my guards skittish."

"I have questions for him," Wilf growled. "Just let me ask them and then I'll leave your guards alone."

"No." Zadir prodded a finger against Wilf's wide chest. "As I've told you every day since you got on my ship, you're not talking

485

with him until I've turned him over to Desfan and collected my payment. I don't quite trust you not to snap his neck."

"Would you trust me with him?" Clare asked.

Zadir twisted toward her, one eyebrow lifting. "A princess running her own interrogation?"

She drew on the image of Serene, letting the princess's confidence fill her and straighten her shoulders. "Why not? The man abducted me. Obviously, I have questions."

"I don't think that's a good idea," Bennick said.

"He can't hurt me," Clare reasoned. "And I think he'll be more likely to talk with me than any of you."

Bennick frowned.

Zadir's mouth twitched. "If I may be so bold, I think you and Desfan will get along well. Frankly, I look forward to seeing him keep up with you." He shook his head. "That aside, I don't know how Desfan would feel if I let you interrogate his prisoner without him."

Wilf turned to the captain. "Did the serjah know Latif was interested in Serene?"

Now the pirate frowned. "When Desfan hired me, there was no mention of the princess in association with Gamble. He didn't even know the sailor's real name." He smirked. "Of course, it only took me a week to learn that."

Clare drew up to her full height. "As Desfan's future bride, I would like to see Latif."

Zadir scratched at his beard, debating. "Oh, very well." He glanced between Bennick and Wilf. "If either of you so much as blackens his eye, you'll be in the brig, too." He sent a smile toward Clare. "Of course if the princess wants to hit him, she can. I don't believe in standing in a woman's way."

486

The brig was located on the lower decks of the ship. There were two barred cells, and only one was occupied. Latif sat on a wooden bench, head tipped against the bars. He glanced up at the sound of their approach and when he saw Clare, he stood.

"How have you been treated?" she asked, coming to a stop before his cell. Bennick and Wilf stood on either side of her. Zadir hung back, a silent spectator.

"Well enough," Latif said. He kept focused on her. "I'm glad you're safe, Princess."

"I want to know who you were working for," Clare said, telling herself that she needed to be firm in order to get answers. "Was it King Henri?"

Latif drew back a little. "No."

"But you *are* working for someone in Ryden."

He let out a heavy sigh. "Yes."

"One of the princes?" she pressed.

"Yes."

Wilf growled low in his throat. "Are you really going to make us waste time guessing?"

"It's not easy to talk about this." Latif's eyebrows drew together. "I've been haunted by a mistake I made nearly ten years ago. No one knows the full truth of what I did. No one but Prince Liam Kaelin."

"He's the middle prince," Bennick said.

"The one known for spying," Zadir added. "I'm not big on politics, but I do like to keep track of the dangerous ones."

"Prince Liam is the one who told you to kill me?" Clare asked Latif, wanting to be clear.

"Yes." The skin around his eyes tightened. "Never let him get hold of your secrets. Once he has them, he'll never let you go." He shook his head. "I tried to do the right thing. About a year ago, I decided I could no longer ignore my sins. I made my way to Duvan and requested an audience with Serjan Saernon."

The pirate captain stepped forward. "This doesn't sound like something Desfan would want talked about."

"I deserve to know the truth," Clare argued.

Zadir didn't protest further. In fact, he looked just as interested in Latif's story.

"I first met one of the serjan's most trusted advisors, Serai Yahri," Latif said. "I told her I'd overheard some sailors talking about the shipwreck that killed the royals—that they said one of the seraijahs survived."

Clare's eyes widened. "One of the seraijahs survived the shipwreck?"

"Impossible," Bennick said. "She would have been found. Who were these men you overheard?"

"Fictions," Latif said. "Even when my guilt compelled me to go to Serjan Saernon, I didn't have the courage to tell the actual truth." His eyes found Clare. "I was on the ship that rescued the girl. I was younger then, and foolish. I'd fallen in with some very bad men and I . . . well, that doesn't matter. I was the one to pull the girl from the water, where she'd half-drowned in the storm. As soon as we hauled her up, she told us who she was, trusting that we'd take her home. Instead, the captain of the ship—a greedy demon of a man who's been dead some five years now—decided to sell her."

Clare sucked in a breath. Bennick and Wilf both stiffened. From the corner of her eye, she saw Zadir's face darken.

Latif raked a hand through his graying hair. "The captain didn't want to deal with Serjan Saernon directly, so he took her to King Henri instead."

Disgust curdled in Clare's stomach. "And you let him."

"I didn't stop him." His tongue darted over his lips, misery in his eyes. "I wish I had."

Wilf muttered a curse.

Fates, that poor little girl . . .

Zadir growled. "Desfan is going to kill you when he finds out." To be fair, it sounded like Zadir might kill Latif himself. His revulsion and rage was clear.

"Is she still alive?" Bennick asked, his fists balled tight. He looked ready to march to Ryden right now and rescue the stolen seraijah.

"I don't know," Latif said. "I kept waiting to hear word of King Henri bargaining with the serjan, even long after I left that ship behind for good. When nothing happened, I tried to forget it all. I was a coward. But finally, I couldn't stomach the guilt anymore."

"So you went to the serjan, but even then you didn't tell him everything," Wilf grunted. "A coward still."

Latif winced. "You're right. I *am* a coward. That night, I gave them my old ship name—Gamble—and told my story to Serjan Saernon and Serai Yahri. The serjan, he . . . collapsed. He has not yet recovered."

"His illness," Clare murmured. "It was brought on by the shock. To learn his daughter might be alive after so many years."

"Serai Yahri convinced me it would be best to remain quiet. She said she would look into the rumors while the serjan healed.

I was given coin for my silence and sent on my way. I didn't know what else to do." His shoulders slumped. "I went to the nearest tavern and I drank. For days, I drank all the gold I'd been given. That's where Prince Liam found me, though of course I didn't know who he was at the time. He called himself by another name, pretending to be Mortisian. His accent was flawless. He wanted to know what had me drinking so much, and I was so wracked with guilt, I confessed everything. The entire story, including my part in it.

"Before I realized it, this stranger knew my darkest secret, and it was too late. He had the power to destroy me. So when he told me to keep my mouth shut and my head ducked, I obeyed. He told me to stay close to Duvan, but out of sight. I was too afraid to run. Some say Prince Liam is a demon. That he can walk the shadows and find you anywhere. And he did find me again, about three weeks ago. He gave me a letter and said to remember the code phrase *fang and claw* and he told me to go to Krid and meet Salim. I was to take Princess Serene off his hands before the real client could arrive."

"Wait." Bennick held up a hand. "Prince Liam didn't hire Salim?"

"No. From what I gathered, he was simply taking advantage of the situation. My orders were to take her from Salim before the client could, and kill her at the Rydenic border. Liam even arranged a ship." He shook his head. "I didn't think I had a choice. Liam would have told the serjah that I'd abducted his sister, and I would be killed." He glanced at Clare. "Prince Liam told me to make sure your death looked like King Henri was to blame."

"He was trying to frame his father?" Zadir scratched at his beard, his frown deep. "Well, that's interesting."

Clare still reeled from the thought of that small girl, abducted years ago, who might still be alive. What atrocities had that girl suffered? Clare could not bear to imagine how she would feel if such a thing had happened to one of her siblings. When Serjah Desfan learned this, he would surely be furious—and very possibly kill Latif.

Bennick turned to Zadir. "Is this why you were after him? Did Desfan find out what Latif did?"

Zadir looked like he might not answer, but then he shrugged. "The serjah gave me no specifics. Just that I was to find Gamble and drag him back to Duvan. I assume Serai Yahri, who was recently arrested along with half of his council, told him the story. Once he knows Gamble's true involvement in things, though . . ."

Latif's voice was surprisingly soft, his eyes on Clare, face pale. "I am terrified of Prince Liam, make no mistake. But I would not have gone through with killing you. We had no choice but to board the ship he arranged, but I decided to run with you as soon as we landed at the border. I would have helped you escape."

She thought she believed him, though she supposed she would never know for sure.

CHAPTER 50

MIA

"YOU'RE GOING TO LOOK SO BEAUTIFUL!" Rena Fletcher said, kneeling before Mia. She was bent over the hem of a gown she was currently pinning. The dress was undergoing its final alterations before the king's upcoming birthday.

Mia ran her hands over the smooth material, still shocked by the silkiness beneath her fingers. The pink material was more beautiful than anything she'd worn in years. The design was relatively simple, but elegant. The fabric alone marked the gown as expensive. She hadn't worn a dress so fine since her childhood, and it felt oddly wrong.

Rena glanced up at her. "Do you like it?"

"It's a very lovely dress."

The older woman must have heard something in Mia's tone, because she paused in her work to meet her gaze. "It suits you, my dear."

Mia fiddled with one sleeve. "I suppose it doesn't feel quite real."

Rena smiled gently. "Ah. That, I understand." She went back to her pins. "Sometimes I think I'll wake up and have to return to the castle laundry."

"Was it very hard work?"

"Yes. I hear your previous caretaker isn't taking too well to the change."

Mia's eyes widened. "Mama is working in the laundry?"

"It was that or the street. According to whispers I've heard, she may still end up there. She's quite lazy."

Mama was indeed that. The middle-aged woman who had been Mia's chief caretaker had also been a drunkard, and she'd never really cared for Mia at all. She'd hit her just as often as Papa had, when Mia was younger. Once Grayson was firmly in her life, the beatings had stopped.

Well, they'd truly ended once she'd stopped talking about her former life. It was still difficult to think of her past without her lungs tightening, her heart clenching, and sweat slicking her palms. It was an ingrained reaction. Thoughts of home meant pain—both emotional and physical.

"How long did you work in the laundry?" Mia asked, needing a distraction.

"Nearly my whole life." Rena shot her a short smile. "I can't be upset about it, though. I wouldn't have met Alun, otherwise. I was fifteen when I first saw him. He was here, training to be a soldier."

"Fletcher wasn't always a prison guard, then?"

Rena shook her graying head, sticking another pin in the hem with deft fingers. "There aren't many professions for young men in Ryden. Farming and soldiering are really the only options, and Alun couldn't find work as a farmer. So he came to Lenzen. We met during his training, but then he was sent to defend the border against Devendra." She eased back, her eyes misting in memory. "His letters . . . Fates, they were so bleak. Killing wasn't something he could stomach. But after a year, he managed reassignment to the castle as a guard, and after another year, we married. Then we had our son."

Intrigued by this new glimpse of her long-time guard, Mia cracked a smile. "He never told me he had a wife and son."

Rena's smile was thin. "He's a quiet man. Especially when it comes to Thane." Her lips pursed. "Our son died a long time ago, defending the border."

Sorrow swirled through Mia. "I'm so sorry."

"Thank you." Rena lifted another pin, going back to her work. "He was only sixteen. Alun and I worked so hard to find him another profession, but he was determined to be a soldier like his father."

A short knock on the bedroom door interrupted their conversation, and Devon peeked in. The physician's eyes brightened at the sight of Mia. "You look lovely!"

"Thank you." Her brow furrowed. "Did we have an appointment?"

"No, I was just nearby and thought I'd stop in. How are you feeling? I want to make sure the riding lessons haven't proved too strenuous."

"No." In fact, they'd become the thing Mia looked forward to most. Tyrell wasn't able to assist her every day, but Mia had proven to be a fast learner when it came to horses, and she was quite over her fear of the large creatures.

Of course, as the king's birthday loomed, she had to wonder if the trade had been worth it. Her stomach jumped unpleasantly every time she thought about attending the large feast. Even with Tyrell at her side, she would be facing a room full of strangers, as well as Peter and King Henri.

Her heartbeat kicked up, and she knew she needed to stop thinking about it.

Devon must have followed her thoughts, though, because his smile ticked a little higher as he said, "Perhaps you're not quite healed enough for the king's feast?"

"Would you tell Tyrell that?" Mia asked, only half-joking.

"I could," he said. "But the riding lessons would have to stop, and I have a feeling the prince might supersede me and force you back to full bed-rest."

She exhaled slowly. "I suppose I have no choice, then. I can't believe I agreed to go."

Rena chuckled. "You'll be the most beautiful girl there."

"I'd rather no one noticed me."

"As you've managed to gain the attention of two Rydenic princes, I'm afraid that's quite an impossible wish."

Mia groaned. "Does everyone in the castle know about me?"

"News has traveled well and fast," Devon chimed in. "Apparently, the nobles arriving for the ball are quite intrigued by the *mysterious Mortisian* who is mingling with Kaelin princes."

"I've heard the same," Rena confirmed.

Mia didn't know if Peter was the cause of the rumors, or if word had simply spread as she'd moved about the castle and grounds. Regardless, her skin suddenly felt too hot. "Devon, do you have something that might make me just sick enough to avoid the feast?"

The physician laughed with Rena, but Mia was becoming increasingly serious.

Rena took pity on her and changed the subject. "Have you gotten a reply from Prince Grayson yet?"

"No." While her letter would have made it to Duvan by now, she knew it was probably too soon to receive a reply. She was anxious to hear from him, though.

Fletcher stepped into the room, a small tin in his hand. "More pins, as requested." He handed it to his wife, the sleeve on his arm pulling back to reveal deep red scratches on his wrist.

Rena grasped his hand. "What's this?"

Fletcher tugged away, shaking down his sleeve. "Nothing."

Rena shot him a worried look. "It looks like some animal mauled you."

"It's nothing," he repeated firmly. "I was just in the castle aerie, and one of the bird's clawed me."

His wife frowned. "What were you doing in the aerie?"

"Just a quick assignment. It's nothing."

Mia winced. "Those scratches look deep."

"Would you like me to take a look?" Devon offered.

Fletcher shook his head, his ears reddening as he rubbed his wrist. "I don't need any fuss."

"You should take better care of yourself, then," Rena muttered.

The old guard grunted, even as Devon chuckled.

Mia felt a slow smile spread. There were few people in the world she trusted, and she was grateful to have so many of them with her.

CHAPTER 51

GRAYSON

"ARE YOU HIDING SOMETHING?" MIA'S *eight-year-old voice was filled with curiosity. The excitement in her brown eyes made Grayson's cheeks warm.*

He halted just inside her cell. The guard—Fletcher—closed the door behind him. There was no going back now. His throat went dry at the thought.

Mia sat on the floor, two stones clutched in her small hands. Yesterday when they'd played, the rocks had been playful dogs. The day before, they'd been racing horses.

Mia scrunched her small nose at him. "You're hiding something. Behind your back."

He shifted on his feet, pinned under her stare.

His new friend stood, her hands brushing the dirt from her gray skirt. She seemed oblivious to his unease—as she always seemed to be. "Is it a treat?" she asked.

He should have brought her something from the kitchens. Even though she complained that the cake had no icing or fruit filling, she always licked every crumb from her fingers.

Mia clasped her hands. "Oh, Grayson, please show me what it is!"

His narrow nine-year-old shoulders tensed. "You'll laugh."

"I will not." Her lips tugged into a smile, though.

As uncomfortable as she often made him—from her drawling accent to her propensity to constantly grab his hand—Mia was the only one with whom he ever felt truly happy. She was his escape from his brothers' torments, the place he could run to avoid his mother's painful lessons and his father's disappointed glares.

Mia crossed over to him. "You brought it, so you must want me to see it," she reasoned.

Dread swelled inside him, but Grayson knew he could not win against her. Jaw stiffening, he showed her what he'd made.

It was supposed to be a doll. It was really an empty meal sack he'd stolen from the kitchens. He'd rolled and tucked the rough sack, tying bits of twine to give shape to a too-small head and bulging arms. The rest of the folded sack was left draping, like a dress. He'd drawn a face on it, but because of his lack of practice, the doll's smile was crooked. He'd tried to make the eyes the same size and shape, but one dot always seemed bigger. He'd kept adding to the smallest one until both eyes were gaping, taking up too much of the face.

The left one was still bigger.

Grayson cringed as Mia stared. She didn't reach for the doll, and he wished he could tear it to pieces. He stared at the ugly thing rather than watch Mia's frozen face.

Finally, he heard her thick swallow. "You made this?"

He jerked out a nod.

One of her small hands stretched out, tentatively touching the doll's arm. He felt the need to state the obvious. "It's ugly."

"She's perfect," Mia whispered. "Grayson . . ." She fingered the back of one of his hands. His grip on the doll tightened. "I lost all my dolls."

"I know." She'd told him so, and he'd wanted to give her a doll. He wanted her to be happy. Like she made him happy.

Mia stroked her fingertips down the doll's shapeless dress. "You made her for me?"

"Yes."

She threw her arms around him, trapping his arms and the doll between them. He tensed, his thin body vibrating against her constricting hold. He swallowed hard, forcing himself not to shove her away. This was Mia holding him—not his brothers. She wasn't going to hurt him.

"Thank you," she said against his chest. "Thank you!" She pulled back abruptly, cooing an apology to the doll. She scooped the lifeless thing from his hands and cradled it tenderly in her arms, bouncing it as if it were a real baby. "Tally," she said, smiling up at Grayson. He thought he saw tears in her eyes. "I'll call her Tally."

She took his hand and pulled him deeper into the room, telling him that he must help get Tally ready for bed.

While Mia murmured a lullaby to the doll, Grayson's lips eased into a smile.

He knew he was dreaming—locked in a memory—just as he knew what would happen to that doll. He would burn it on his father's orders, and Mia's face would stream with tears.

Caught between sleeping and waking, Grayson knew that he had failed Mia yet again. Only this time, *she* would be the one who burned.

Grayson woke slowly. His cheek and chest were flush with the stone floor. His head throbbed and he couldn't see anything, even with his eyes stretched wide. Chains dragged on his wrists as he shifted his numb body.

For the first time since entering Mortise, he was cold.

The clinking of chains grated through the silence as he struggled to sit. He knew he was in a cell, even if he couldn't see it around him. Thoughts still sluggish, Grayson slid his hands over the smooth, slightly rippled stone floor. It had clearly been worn down by prisoners for countless years, and the feeling of being trapped made his stomach plunge.

Following the chains on his wrists, he found he was near a wall. He slumped a shoulder against it, feeling the tug of more chains and shackles around his ankles. Anchored to the wall, it seemed he only had enough mobility to lay on the floor, or stand beside the wall.

His gloves were gone, as were his boots. He knew without searching that every hidden knife was gone as well. His black shirt must have been torn in the search, because it sagged, baring half of his scarred chest.

He dug the heels of his hands into his eyes, shackles dragging on his wrists. He grimaced at the pounding in his head. Karim had hit him hard—

Mia.

The hawk.

Panic punched through him, bringing him fully awake.

How long had he been unconscious? Was he truly too late to stop the hawk from flying?

Desfan. He needed to talk to Desfan. Tell him about Mia. Surely, if he knew that Mia was his sister, he would do anything to stop that hawk—to help her.

"Is anyone there?" Grayson called out, his voice cracking.

There was no response.

Pulse kicking faster, he pushed his hoarse voice louder. "Hello? Anyone? Please, I need to speak to Desfan!"

Nothing.

Fates blast it, where were the guards? "Please! I need Desfan!" He grabbed the chains bolted to his wrists and beat them against the floor, making as much noise as he could. Pain blasted over his knuckles as he misjudged and they struck the unforgiving stone. Gritting his teeth, he kept hitting the chains against the floor. "Desfan!"

Someone had to hear him. *Please don't let it be too late . . .*

"*Desfan!*"

"Would you shut up?"

Grayson's head cranked to the left. He couldn't see anything in the blackness, but he could hear the rustle of movement—something heavy dragging across the stone floor, the rattle of chains.

He didn't need his sight to know who was there.

His fingers curled, hatred seizing him. "Liam."

His brother huffed a terse breath. "It seems we're both still breathing, despite your betrayal. Probably not for long, though."

Grayson shoved aside every heated response that burned his tongue. Because right now, only one thing mattered. "Was the message sent?"

Silence.

Fury and fear ripped through Grayson, heating his veins. *"Was the message sent?"*

In the wake of his shouting, all he could hear was the pounding of his heart. Then, "Yes."

Agony pierced him, cutting through the center of his chest. Grayson slumped back against the wall, his lungs too tight to fully expand.

It was too late.

Even if another message was sent, it wouldn't stop the first one. He didn't know how long it would take a hawk to reach Liam's man in Lenzen—a week? Less? It had taken him four weeks to travel to Duvan—two weeks on the Rydenic highways, and two more on the water.

Even if he left right now on the fastest ship and rode horses into the ground, he would never reach Mia in time.

"Who is it?" Grayson whispered, tension steeling his soft words.

"Does it really matter?" Liam asked, his voice just as quiet and every bit as hard.

No. It didn't matter. Because there were few people who knew of her existence, and if Liam's man was close to her, there weren't many candidates.

Fletcher, the day guard. Devon, the physician. A handful of night guards. It could be any of them, or someone else entirely.

"You should have listened to me," Liam said. "All of this could have been so different if you'd just listened to me."

Grayson's fingers curled into fists. His knuckles stung, sticky with blood from scraping the floor, but that was nothing compared to the pain ripping through his heart. "You lied to me," he gritted out. "She's not Mia Sifa."

There was a brief silence, and he wondered what expression his spymaster brother wore. Surprise? Condescension? Glee? Or was his face composed in the smooth mask of a man capable of hiding every secret in Eyrinthia?

Finally, Liam spoke. "Is *that* what did it?" Curiosity lifted his tone, but Grayson could hear the undercurrent of anger. "You learned the truth about her, and suddenly you couldn't stand to kill her brother?"

The blithely offered truth clenched his gut. "So it's true. She's Meerah Cassian."

"I wasn't sure what she'd told you," Liam said thinly. "But after some carefully placed conversations, you started to trust me and I knew you had no idea who she was. It seemed a gift from the fates that you didn't know; there was no need to further complicate your mission."

"Why did you tell me she was Mia Sifa?"

"Because I needed to galvanize you." Chains clinked dully as Liam shifted his position. "You were hesitant to join me, and I needed you fully committed. While researching Ser Sifa, I came upon the genealogy, and poor Mia Sifa's story was too perfect. She was born the same year as Meerah, and she had the seraijah's shortened name, as many girls her age did. Royal names are popular in Mortise. Fates, I only had to alter her death date by a year to coincide with the same year you met your Mia, and the forgery was easy enough. It was fates-blasted perfect. And when you heard the story, it did exactly what I needed it to—it brought you to me. After all your hesitating, you were finally ready to take a stand against Father."

"How long have you known the truth about Mia?"

"About a year."

Grayson's breath stalled. *A fates-blasted year?*

"Knowledge always comes in useful," Liam continued quietly. "You just need to be patient. Keep your secrets until the right moment. It's something Father taught me well."

"Were you ever going to tell me the truth?"

"No. There was no need."

Grayson ground his teeth. "You're every bit the monster Father is."

Liam cracked out a harsh laugh. "If you think that, then you haven't known the full evil of our father. Everything I've done has been in an effort to stop him."

"You lied to me. *Used* me."

"Then you betrayed me and we both lost. I hope you're pleased with yourself."

"If Mia dies, I *will* kill you," Grayson vowed.

Liam snorted. "Not if the Mortisians kill us first."

Desperation and pain twisted together, punching a hole through his chest. Grayson lifted the chains and began whipping them against the floor again, wincing at the sound as it cut through his abused skull.

Liam groaned. "Not this again . . ."

"Desfan!"

"He's not going to hear you. And he's certainly not going to save you. You not only betrayed me, but all the kingdoms. He won't forgive you for that."

Grayson ignored his brother, still hitting the floor with the rattling chains, still calling out for Desfan.

Time was impossible to measure, but his cramping stomach told him it had been at least a full day since his arrest. Would Desfan just leave them here to rot? That didn't seem right. It wasn't a logical move, and Desfan was intelligent. He would have them questioned.

Where was he, then? What was he waiting for?

After what must have been hours, the sound of footsteps echoed somewhere above him. A door slammed. More footsteps, descending and drawing nearer.

Grayson tugged at his chains with new fervor, ignoring the bite of blisters and the hard edges of the shackles cutting into his wrists. He all but threw the chains against the floor, raw knuckles hitting the stone in his haste. "Please! I need to speak to Desfan. It's important!"

The footsteps came nearer. Another door opened, and the dim glow of light melted the shadows.

Prison bars took shape before him; the solid wall behind him was the only real wall he had. In front of him and on either side, he was fenced in by iron bars. They were set less than a handbreadth apart from each other, impossible to squeeze through. His cell was probably five paces deep and three wide—a constricting box that seemed to be pressing him in, now that he knew how confined the space was.

Liam was in a neighboring cell on his left, the two of them separated by bars. He sat with his back against the wall and his knees drawn up, his arms folded across them. His eyes gleamed in the growing light, quietly feral. A panther, caged but not broken.

Grayson swallowed and pushed to his feet, stepping as close to the barred door as the chains allowed. They trapped him in the middle of the small cell.

The light made him squint, but he could see the shadowy figures of four people halt before the cells.

Grayson hadn't realized he'd stopped calling out until one of the guards grunted. "Finally lost your voice, Rydenic filth?"

Grayson's eyes shot to the man standing directly in front of his cell. He held a torch, and the brightness of the light made it impossible to see his face.

"I hope you haven't lost your voice," the man continued darkly. "I want to hear all your screams."

"Please," Grayson rasped, his voice weak after hours of shouting. "I need to see Desfan."

The soldier holding the torch barked out a hard laugh.

Grayson clenched his hands to fists. He forced himself to speak firmly, despite the cracks in his voice. "He'll want to see me."

"We're here for a different reason." The man with the torch jerked his head in a silent order. One of the men stepped forward and unlocked Liam's cell.

Grayson's heart pounded. He glanced at his brother, who had not moved. If his breaths hadn't been so measured, Grayson might have thought Liam was made of stone.

While Liam's cell was invaded by two men, the guard with the keys moved to Grayson's door.

The man with the torch spoke, his voice rippling with anger. "Good men died yesterday. You murdered them."

Grayson said nothing. He knew what was coming. He squared his shoulders, not taking a step back when the other men stepped into his cell.

He heard a fist smack against flesh off to his left. Liam barely grunted, but the rain of blows continued. Kicks. Punches. Curses.

Grayson met the eyes of the soldier who had unlocked his door. The man's chin had lowered as he glared. "My best friend is dead," he spat.

"I'm sorry," Grayson said evenly. "But I didn't kill him."

The man struck. Grayson didn't fight back, knowing that would only prolong the beating. It would not get him any closer to Desfan, which meant it would not help Mia. He would endure it, as he had endured everything in his life.

But it hurt.

The other soldier set aside the torch and joined in. They knocked Grayson to the ground, and continued kicking him. He raised his arms to protect his head, but the chains restricted his movements. A boot caught under his right eye and he saw sparks of light. Tears streamed and he did all he could to keep another from catching his scarred face.

The beating lasted several eternal minutes before the men left—cursing and spitting on him as they strode away.

Grayson heard Liam's ragged breathing, but neither of them spoke, even after the Mortisian soldiers left them in the dark.

CHAPTER 52

DESFAN

'I KNOW WHAT I SAW," IMARA INSISTED FIRMLY.

Desfan sat at the head of the long table, watching the Zennorian princess argue with her cousin who sat across from her. His head ached. Another night of little sleep had left its mark—not to mention the events of the past two days. His father's death, the betrothal signing, the unexpected and brutal attack by Ryden.

By Grayson.

Imara's expression was fierce as she pressed her palms against the table. "Grayson saved my life. The only people he attacked were our enemies."

Serene's mouth twisted. "You don't know that. You weren't watching him the whole time. And you can't think he's innocent.

508

He brought weapons into that room. He fought Karim and Cardon. He tried to run!"

"He probably thought we would throw him in prison without listening to him," Imara snapped. She took a breath and twisted toward Desfan. "You've sparred with Grayson. You know his skill. Could he have killed you yesterday?"

Desfan swallowed. "Yes."

Easily.

It made the space between his shoulder blades itch.

Imara nodded once, her eyes sharp with determination. "And yet he didn't kill either of you, even though your backs were turned to him."

"That doesn't mean he didn't betray us," Serene said cuttingly.

"You're right," Imara admitted. "But he could also be our friend."

Desfan grimaced at her words. He hadn't realized how vulnerable he'd made himself until yesterday, when Grayson had kicked him to the ground. Fates, the Rydenic prince wasn't his friend. Friends didn't turn on you without any warning or explanation.

Imara looked at him pointedly. "We won't know his intentions until we talk to him."

He let out a sigh. Imara was right. But he didn't think he was capable of facing Grayson. Not yet, at least. "There is much to be done, but I'll be sure both Liam and Grayson are questioned soon. They will give us answers."

Imara stilled. "What kind of questioning?"

"The brutal kind, I hope," Serene grunted.

Imara stared at Desfan, horror in her eyes. "You're going to *torture* them?"

He fingered the edge of the table. "We need answers. Once we learn whatever we can of King Henri's plans, we can begin making our own. I don't think it would be premature for both of you to write to your fathers, informing them of the situation and the attempts on our lives."

Imara frowned. "I won't allow Grayson to be tortured. I can't believe you would, either, Desfan."

"What other choice do I have?" *He gave me none*, he nearly added.

"You could talk to him," Imara said, as if it would be that simple. "Or let me."

"No," Serene said. "You're not going anywhere near that monster."

Imara's eyes narrowed. "You don't command me, Serene. And I would appreciate it if you would stop insulting the person who saved my life."

"I'm only trying to protect you," Serene countered.

"Well, stop." Imara twisted to face Desfan. "Will you let me talk to him?"

He was saved from having to answer when the door opened and Serai Yahri entered.

The old woman looked haggard today. Worn. But her eyes were clear as she stopped at the foot of the table and stared down the length of it at Desfan. "I'm sorry to interrupt, but I'm afraid we have a problem."

Desfan stifled a groan as he leaned forward. "What now?"

"The announcement of the serjan's death hit the city at the same time the news of the assassination attempts. Rumors spawned that Ryden was responsible for your father's death as well as the attack made against you and the visiting princesses. The people are infuriated. They loved your father, and they've turned violent against anyone from Ryden. Rydenic merchants have been murdered in the street. Women and children who have lived here peaceably all their lives have been stoned or beaten. The Rydenic ship in the harbor was torched, nearly taking out another row of ships. Most of the Rydenic soldiers were able to abandon the ship, and now they're lost somewhere in the city." Yahri's grip on her cane tightened. "We need to stop the violence before Duvan becomes a battlefield."

Desfan glanced toward the sunny window, unable to fully comprehend the evils happening in those streets. *His* streets.

He couldn't think about the coronation. The serjan's crown that would soon weigh down his head.

He took a breath. "Yahri, do you have any suggestions?"

"You need to make a public announcement," the councilwoman said at once. "The people need to see you. They need the truth of your father's death from you, and they need to see that you are alive and well. They need hope. We'll spread the word that you will address them tomorrow afternoon. That will give time for everyone to know, as well as prepare all the details for the serjan's pyre and your coronation."

"And our enemies?" Serene asked. "What if they try something at the announcement?"

"We'll secure a perimeter on the street," Yahri said. "And there will be plenty of guards around Desfan."

"I don't mind the risk if you think it will help protect people," Desfan said.

"I believe it will. Panic and fear make people do unspeakable things." Yahri pursed her lips.

"What?" Desfan asked, wanting to hear the rest of her thoughts.

The councilwoman looked between all three royals. "I know war has been the primary discussion here. But I don't think this is the best time for it. We need stability first. Without a crowned monarch, things will feel much more uncertain. Wait for the two weeks of mourning, and the two weeks of celebration. Put aside all talk of war until after the coronation."

Serene didn't look overly pleased, but she nodded her agreement. "It will give our letters time to reach Devendra and Zennor," she said, glancing at Imara. "Replies might already be on their way at that point."

Desfan stood. "Yahri, see to it that notices are sent out to the people about my address tomorrow. Also, summon the council. I would like their input on the situation in the city, and the events of yesterday. I'll meet with them in two hours."

Yahri nodded and retreated.

"And what about Grayson?" Imara asked.

"I don't have time to interrogate him yet, but I will as soon as I can."

Imara's lips pressed into a line. "I want to see him."

"No. Not without me." He didn't know if he would ever be ready, but at least for now he had plenty of other fires that needed his attention first.

He glanced between Serene and Imara. "I would value both of your opinions at the council meeting."

Imara seemed ready to argue more about Grayson, but Serene stood. "We would love to help in any way we can, Desfan."

CHAPTER 53

GRAYSON

GRAYSON'S HUNGER WASN'T EXACTLY PAINFUL anymore, which told him it had been days since his arrest. He'd been given water, but even that came sparingly.

The emptiness in his gut and the weakness in his limbs reminded him of a time his father had forced him and Tyrell to fast for three days before dueling. The whole court had been invited to watch the spectacle in the training yard. Grayson had been fifteen at the time, Tyrell sixteen.

The sword in Grayson's hand had felt a hundred times heavier than normal. He was dizzy. Light-headed. His swings were not so careful or precise, and neither were Tyrell's. When both were flecked with cuts, stumbling with fatigue and dehydration, King Henri ordered food and water to be brought to the field. Grayson and Tyrell were forced to eat and drink everything put before them, and then the fight resumed.

Grayson was the first to fall to his knees retching, everything he'd consumed coming up at once. Tyrell smacked the flat of his blade against Grayson's head, nicking his ear and knocking him unconscious.

He'd woken a few moments later, covered in his own vomit, to find Tyrell declared the victor. It was one of the only times Tyrell had bested him since Grayson was thirteen.

Even hours later, Grayson's hands still shook. When he'd made his way to Mia that afternoon, she'd cradled his head in her lap and stroked her fingers through his hair. She continued to hold him even when he heaved into a bucket.

He felt like throwing up when the Mortisian soldiers returned. Covered in blood and bruises from his last beating, he didn't look forward to another.

His cell door swung open, and he hissed a pained breath as rough hands dragged his throbbing body to his feet. His shackles remained on his wrists, but he was freed from the chains mounted to the wall and the manacles around his ankles. The flickering torchlight made his eyes water. Well, the one that wasn't swollen shut.

Liam, he noticed, remained untouched, his cell door firmly locked.

Grayson stumbled as he was dragged out of the cell and into the narrow corridor. Dizziness rushed through him and his vision swam—from hunger, nausea, or pain, he didn't know.

There was a soldier on each arm, supporting more of his weight than he liked. He abhorred feeling weak. His scalp prickled as they pulled him up staircases and through doorways, climbing higher and higher in the castle prison until they reached a deserted room. The glowing lamp on the small table revealed a space larger than his cell, with solid stone walls on every side. They pushed him against the far wall and shoved his bound arms up, securing him to short chains that kept his back against the stone and his shackled wrists above his head. Numbness began to creep into his arms almost immediately from the raised position.

He knew what was coming. The beating in his cell had been about vengeance, but this would be an actual interrogation.

He was about to be tortured.

His body vibrated, a combination of panic and desperation. Taking a slow breath muted some of the agony along his cracked ribs as his lungs expanded, but he still winced. "I'll answer any questions," he said, his voice rough. "But I need to speak with Desfan—"

A fist slammed into his face and he bit his tongue.

"Shut up," one of the guards sneered. "You're in no position to make demands. The serjah ordered this."

Grayson's heart pounded against his chest and his head sliced with pain, a headache that flared with every beat of his heart. He tried to steel himself for the coming pain. His cold mask was in place—though probably not as impressive as usual, with dried blood streaking his swollen face—when the door opened.

He stiffened in shock.

Imara stood in the doorway, her expression hard. "Out," she ordered, striding into the interrogation room. Despite her small stature, she easily dominated the room.

One of the Mortisian guards frowned. "That wasn't in our orders."

"Your orders were to follow my instructions. You brought him here, and now I want you to get out." Imara's eyes darted over

515

Grayson's battered body. Her mouth thinned.

"Princess, it would be dangerous for you to—"

"He's chained to the wall," she said, the words almost dry. But there was an undercurrent of fury that coursed just below the surface. "Now, unless you wish to take this up with Serjah Desfan, after he issued me a letter of permission . . ." She trailed off, her eyebrows raised.

The lead guard's expression tightened. "We'll be just outside."

Imara waited to roll her eyes until the men had shuffled past her, but the brief show of levity vanished from her expression when she met Grayson's gaze.

The door closed, and Imara crossed her arms over her middle, worry in her voice as she asked, "Are you all right?"

He stared at her. He couldn't fathom what she was doing here—without her guards. And why would Desfan have sent her to interrogate him?

"I suppose that's a stupid question," Imara murmured, her jaw tightening as she once again viewed his injuries. Regret flashed in her eyes. "I had no idea they would do this. I'm so sorry."

He finally found his voice, though it cracked. "What are you doing here?"

"I thought you'd be grateful."

He was. Relief threaded through him, but confusion won out. "I didn't expect to see you. I didn't think that . . ."

Her expression softened, her shoulders dropping a little. "You saved my life. I'm trying to return the favor, but I need your help. Serene is livid. Desfan is, too, as is the entire Mortisian court. You need to explain everything that happened so I can plead your case."

He shook his head. "I need to speak with Desfan first."

"He doesn't want to see you right now, so talk to me." Her knuckles whitened as she gripped her elbows. "I know you saved my life. You chose to betray your brother and sided with us. So why did you try to run?"

Grayson shifted, and the shackles on his wrists rattled. There was also a stabbing in his side, but he tried to ignore that. It was probably only a sprained rib. "What I tell you can't reach anyone but Desfan. Will you promise to keep this secret?"

She looked uneasy, but she nodded. "You have my word."

Though he knew she was perhaps the only ally he had in the entire kingdom, he still hesitated. After keeping Mia a secret for so long, it felt wrong to speak about her.

But if he kept silent now, he might not be able to save her.

He took a breath, his body tensing. "I would have told you and Desfan sooner of my brother's plans, but I couldn't. He threatened me."

Imara's forehead creased. "We could have protected you."

"No, he didn't threaten *me*. He threatened someone in Ryden. Someone I care deeply for. Liam threatened to have her killed."

"Her?" Imara blinked. "Is this the girl you bought that pearl necklace for?"

He nodded. "She's a prisoner of my father's."

A furrow grew between her dark brows. "You care about one of your father's prisoners?"

"Yes. For most of my life, we've been friends."

Imara eyed him, faint distaste touching her features. "And yet you never helped free her?"

"I couldn't. You don't know my father."

Imara suddenly paled. "Wait. For most of your life? How long has she been a prisoner?"

"Nine years."

"Fates," she breathed, looking sick.

"I've tried to protect her." Yet he knew he'd failed so many times. The truth of that had never seemed so stark. Grayson grit his teeth, his stomach cramping. "I couldn't let Liam kill you or Desfan. Or Serene. And now Mia might die."

"But we caught Liam."

Grayson shook his head. "He ordered a message to be sent with a hawk if anything at the signing went wrong. There's nothing I can do to stop that message now."

"I know you're afraid for her," Imara said. "But this is good. Once Desfan knows the truth—that you saved our lives in the only way you could—he won't punish you." She took a step closer, her tone full of comfort. "And perhaps the message won't make it."

He winced, his heart seizing. As soon as he told Imara who Mia was, there would be no going back. "I need you to tell Desfan about her," he said, his voice too quiet.

"I will," she said at once. "Of course. Maybe there's something he can—"

"Mia is his sister."

Imara stared. Blinked. Then the emotions flickered over her face. Shock. Disbelief. "Impossible," she whispered. "His sisters died at sea."

"Nine years ago," he said. "The same time Mia was imprisoned."

She shook her head slowly. "Grayson, this will only make Desfan angry. I know you hope to gain his favor, but this isn't the way."

His short laugh choked him. "I know. But she *is* Meerah Cassian."

Imara rubbed at her arms, slowly shaking her head. "If you're wrong . . ."

"I'm not wrong."

The Zennorian princess searched him with intensity. "I know

you're not trying to hurt Desfan by giving him false hopes about his sister. I can see that you believe Mia is his sister, but . . ."

"Believe me. She is."

It would be so much easier if she wasn't. But then, when had life ever been easy?

Imara sighed. "You'd better compile your evidence, then. And it had better be compelling, or Desfan is going to kill you."

CHAPTER 54

DESFAN

IMARA STEPPED INTO HIS OFFICE WITHOUT knocking. "Desfan, I need a word."

He frowned when she pressed the door closed. "I'm rather busy at the moment." He knew she would not be dissuaded, but he wished she would have given him a bit more time before harassing him about visiting Grayson. *Again.*

For the past three days he had been focused on memorial arrangements for his father, calming the chaos in the city streets, and assuaging the fears of his court. He hadn't had time to question Liam and Grayson, and he thought it wouldn't hurt to let them sit in their cells and wonder about their fates. It might make them more willing to talk.

Imara glanced at Karim in the corner, then she faced Desfan, her shoulders squared. "I went to see Grayson."

Her words didn't make sense at first. Desfan lowered his quill, his lungs feeling too tight. "You did what?"

She clasped her hands, her chin lifting defiantly. "I went to see him."

"How did you get to him?" Karim asked, his voice a little sharp. "The guards have orders not to let anyone in."

"We're straying from the point," Imara said, dodging the question.

Desfan eyed her. The Zennorian princess was very different from Serene—he'd realized that almost instantly. Their similarities, he'd thought, only showed in their appearance, but apparently they had other things in common. Like stubbornness, and the ability to drive him a bit mad. "I thought we agreed to go together," he said, striving for calm.

Imara's eyebrows pulled together. "You kept delaying, and I couldn't wait any longer."

"Didn't you think it might be dangerous for you to visit the prison alone?"

"Did you know your men beat him?" she shot back.

Desfan stilled, though his pulse rushed faster. The images that leaped to mind made him feel sick. He wasn't sure why; Grayson had been the one to betray *him*.

"No," he said at last. "I didn't know. I'll look into what happened."

"He looks like he can barely stand," Imara said, pain in her gaze. "He hasn't been given any food and barely any water. He was your friend, Desfan. How could you abandon him to that?"

Fates, he'd had no idea. He'd told the guards to keep Liam and

Grayson away from other prisoners, but he hadn't given orders to deprive them of food.

"Grayson Kaelin is no friend," Karim said, cutting into his thoughts. "Not to either of you."

Imara kept her focus on Desfan. "He betrayed his brother for you."

"He betrayed me, Imara. *Us.*"

"No, he didn't. And you're a fool to keep insisting that he did when you have no evidence."

Karim scowled, but Desfan spoke before his friend could. "I *was* a fool, but only because I trusted him. He gained my confidence so he and his brother could be at the betrothal signing. Any friendship between us was a lie."

"You're wrong.," Imara said. "He saved me. He saved all of us. Without him, it would have been a massacre."

Desfan rubbed a hand over his forehead. "Imara, I know you want to believe that—"

"Why don't *you* believe it? Why are you being so fates-blasted stubborn? You're an idiot!"

His arm dropped and he stared at her.

Heat flushed her cheeks and indignation burned in her eyes. "Grayson didn't betray you. You're punishing him because of what his brother did, but that's wrong, and I know you're better than that." She sighed heavily, her shoulders dropping. "I know you just lost your father, and I'm sorry. But Grayson doesn't deserve this."

He took a slow breath, pinching his eyes shut.

There was a moment of stillness. Silence.

"Why didn't he tell me?" Desfan finally asked, opening his eyes. "If he truly didn't betray me, then why didn't he tell me what his brother planned?"

A shadow crossed Imara's face. "He was protecting someone. A girl, back in Ryden. Liam would have had her killed if Grayson said anything."

"A girl?"

"A young woman." Imara let her arms drop to her sides, and the skin around her eyes tightened. "Grayson insisted that I tell you . . ."

"Tell me what?"

She hesitated. "Promise me you won't do anything rash."

"Why would I?"

"Do I have your promise?"

Confusion bled through him. "Very well," he agreed. "I won't do anything rash."

Imara smoothed down her blue skirt. "The girl in Ryden . . . Her name is Mia."

Desfan froze, the familiar name hitting like a blow.

But Imara wasn't done. Her expression solemn, she added, "Grayson insists that she is Meerah. Your sister."

Desfan charged into the holding room. He ignored the flash of guilt he felt at Grayson's appearance—slumped against the wall, the chains the only thing holding him up. His face was bruised and swollen, smeared with dried blood.

Desfan ignored everything except the rushing in his ears, the pounding in his head.

Imara ran behind him, still in the corridor, calling for him to wait. He'd even left Karim behind.

Desfan grabbed Grayson's abused jaw and forced their eyes to meet. "Tell me everything," he gritted out. "Tell me *everything* about Mia or I swear I'll kill you."

Grayson's throat flexed as he swallowed, surprise flashing in his gray eyes. "You believe me?"

A growl grated up from Desfan's chest. "*Where is she?*"

Karim darted into the room. "Des, be careful."

Imara was right behind him, her hands outstretched. "Don't hurt him!"

Desfan continued to glare at Grayson. "I learned weeks ago that one of my sisters might be alive."

Imara sucked in a breath.

"A rumor claimed one of my sisters was dragged from the water after the shipwreck. That she was abducted. I haven't heard anything else, until now." He tightened his hold on Grayson's jaw. "Tell me what you know. *Now.*"

"She's in Lenzen," Grayson said, his voice hoarse. "In my father's dungeon. I swear I didn't know she was your sister. She never told me who she was."

Desfan's entire body clenched. "You've spoken with her?" But of course he had.

Still, Grayson's simple answer rocked him. "Yes."

His jaw locked, his lungs burning. Too many emotions gripped him, but one thought reigned.

His sister was alive. Truly alive.

"Desfan," Karim said, stepping closer. "He could be lying."

"I'm not," Grayson insisted.

"Why didn't you say anything?" Desfan snarled. He knew he was hurting Grayson, bruising his swollen skin and forcing his head back against the wall. He couldn't let go, though. This was his con-nection to Meerah.

"I didn't realize who she was until the night of the ball," Grayson said. "While looking at the portrait."

Desfan was immediately hit with the grief that had buried him that night. His father's sudden death. Seeing his body. Stumbling down a hallway and finding Grayson. He remembered his conver-sation with the Rydenic prince, as they'd sat before the portrait of his family. The way Grayson had gone silent. Desfan hadn't thought anything of it—Grayson was always quiet.

But now he knew why.

He ground his teeth. "So knowing she was my sister—that changed your mind about slaughtering us all?"

Grayson's shoulders tensed. "I didn't ever want to hurt any of you, but Liam threatened me. He said if I betrayed him, he would have Mia killed."

Desfan flinched. The thought of losing his sister now, after everything . . .

"I didn't think I had a choice," Grayson said. "But when I realized who she was, I knew I couldn't go along with Liam's plan."

"Why didn't you say anything?" he demanded. "We were in that corridor for hours! Why didn't you tell me?"

"Liam has eyes and ears everywhere. I couldn't risk Mia by say-ing or doing anything that might make him suspicious."

Desfan glared, too many emotions pulsing through him to speak.

Beside him, Karim folded his arms, his impressive glower aimed at the Rydenic prince. "How do you know this Mia is the seraijah?"

"She's been a prisoner for nine years," Grayson said. One eye was swollen shut, but the other was focused on Desfan. "That matches when you lost your sister. She has brown eyes—just like yours—and she closely resembles your mother. She's sixteen."

Karim frowned. "These could all be coincidences."

"I gave her a doll when she was eight years old," Grayson said. "She named it Tally."

Desfan reared back. His hands trembled, his heart beating faster.

"She loves to paint and draw," Grayson continued. "And she loves to sing—especially Mortisian lullabies. She rarely talked about her time before—the life she'd lost—but she told me her mother used to sing to her every night, and her father would tell her stories."

Desfan sucked in a breath. "Mia."

"Des." Karim's voice was hard. "He could be manipulating you."

Desfan stood only inches from the prince in chains, and the truth was plain in Grayson's expression. Every part of Desfan echoed with the same conviction.

Mia was alive, and she was a prisoner in Ryden.

"Tell him about the hawk," Imara whispered.

Grayson suddenly looked ten years older.

Desfan's stomach dropped. "What hawk?"

"Liam ordered a hawk to be sent to Ryden if I failed him at the signing." Grayson swallowed hard. "The message calls for Mia's death."

Desfan felt the color drain from his face. "No."

"Why do you think I fought so hard to get out of the signing?" Grayson said, clearly misunderstanding Desfan's denial. Frustration edged his words. "I wasn't trying to escape—I was trying to stop the hawk from being released."

"You killed innocent people," Karim growled. "You're a fates-blasted murderer."

"I only killed your enemies," Grayson shot back. "If I'd wanted to kill you, Karim, you'd be dead."

Karim glowered, his face turning red.

Desfan's hands rolled to fists at his sides. "Was the message sent?"

Grayson's face hardened. "Yes."

Desfan rounded on Karim. "Bring Liam here."

"There's nothing he can do," Grayson said. "We need to focus on Mia now, not him."

Karim glanced to Desfan, awaiting his order.

Fates blast it, he hated that Grayson was right. His nostrils flared. "Fine."

Karim settled his stance, his chin lifting as he eyed Grayson. "This doesn't make sense. If your father had Meerah all this time, why didn't he ever make any demands? The serjan would have given anything for his daughter's return. King Henri would have known this."

"I don't know my father's mind. He likes to hold on to a person's weaknesses. It's possible he has a larger plan, or maybe he just wanted to keep her close in case an opportunity arose to use her against Mortise."

Desfan dragged a hand through his hair, but he froze when Imara asked cautiously, "How *is* Mia? After being a prisoner for so long . . ."

Desfan's fingers clenched in his hair, both desperate and terrified to hear the answer.

Grayson stiffened. "She's fine. Perfect."

"I didn't mean anything negative against her," Imara said quickly. "I only wondered if she's well."

His throat flexed as he swallowed. "I've tried to protect her, give her everything I could, but . . ."

She had suffered. That's what Grayson wasn't saying.

All Desfan could see was his seven-year-old sister, her bright brown eyes and eager smile. To imagine her in a dark cell in Ryden for nine years . . . it made him physically ill.

"You love her," Imara whispered.

Desfan glanced at her. Of course he loved . . .

She was looking at Grayson.

The Rydenic prince dipped his chin, no apology in his voice as he said, "I do."

Desfan's whole world slanted. "You . . . what?"

Grayson stood as straight as the chains allowed. "I love her."

"No." Desfan couldn't say anything else, so he repeated more firmly, "*No.*"

Grayson took a breath. "Desfan—"

He'd landed a punch before Imara could gasp.

The back of Grayson's head slammed into the wall, blood oozing from a reopened cut on his lip. The Rydenic prince didn't curse him, though. Only turned his head and met Desfan's livid gaze.

His knuckles smarted, but the pain was worth it. "If you've hurt her in any way," Desfan growled, "I swear by the fates I'll tear you apart."

Grayson's chin lowered, dark strands of hair spilling over his brow. "I would cut my own throat first."

The vehemence in his voice was unmistakably sincere, but that only made Desfan's blood boil hotter. "You're sick," he growled. "You took advantage of her. Fates rot you—"

"Stop it!" Imara cut in. "Desfan, this argument doesn't matter. *Meerah* does."

That penetrated the fury that flooded him. Desfan took a step back, his jaw working.

Imara faced Grayson, her arms folding over her chest. "There's something I don't understand. You keep saying that it was Liam's plan, but wasn't it your father's?"

Grayson shook his head. "Our father sent us here under the guise of peace to get close to Princess Serene. We were to kill her after the betrothal was legalized and frame Mortise for her death. He wanted Devendra and Mortise to go to war and weaken each other, so he could sweep in and conquer both kingdoms."

"Did he have any plans for Zennor?" Imara asked.

Grayson hesitated. "Not at this time. But my brother, Peter, ordered me to abduct you and bring you back to Ryden to be his bride."

Imara's eyes flew wide. "Oh."

Karim muttered a string of Mortisian curses.

Desfan's skin heated. "Your family is pure evil."

Grayson huffed a short breath. "Agreed. I was never going to go through with that, though," he said, his eyes finding Imara. "I'm only telling you now so you'll be on guard, in case he sends someone else."

Imara nodded slowly, still looking a little shaken. "Thank you. I appreciate that."

"What was Liam's plan?" Karim asked.

"He wanted all the kingdoms to unite against Ryden. He wants to see our father destroyed." Grayson snorted. "I agree with his sentiment, just not the method."

Desfan shook his head. As fascinating—albeit disturbing—as it was to glimpse the inner workings of Kaelin minds, he didn't care about politics right now. Not while his sister was a captive of the most twisted family in Eyrinthia. "Tell me exactly where Meerah is," he said to Grayson. "Every detail."

The prince licked his cracked lips. "You can't rescue her."

Desfan's vision hazed red. "If you don't cooperate—"

"You can't march on Lenzen with an army," Grayson overrode him. "My father would cut you down before you ever got close."

"Then I'll take a small group of men."

"You won't make it into the castle."

"You won't be going at all," Karim said tightly.

Desfan's spine stiffened. He turned on his friend, opening his mouth to argue, but Imara cut him off.

"Karim's right." She laid a hand on Desfan's arm, a comforting touch that helped rein in some of his raging impulses. "You are to be crowned serjan," she reminded softly. "You can't leave right now. The people need you."

Desfan's jaw clenched. "I can't entrust my sister's life to anyone else. I have to go."

"No," Karim said, his tone hard. "*I'm* going." His thick eyebrows pulled together, intensity living in his gaze. "I'll bring her back to you, Des. On my life, I swear it."

"You would never reach her," Grayson said. "It's a fool's mission."

"I'm *not* abandoning my sister," Desfan bit out.

"I'm not asking you to." Grayson straightened, though it must have pained his battered body. "I'm the only one who can walk into that castle, right into her cell. I can get her out, and I swear that I'll bring her back to Mortise."

Karim growled low in his throat. "You think we'll just let you go free?"

"Yes," the prince said. "Because I'm the only one who can save her."

Karim angled closer to Desfan. "He'll never come back. Why would he? He should be executed for his crimes. The people will demand it. He knows this. He'll run back to his father and escape the punishment he deserves."

"I *will* come back," Grayson promised, frustration edging his words. "Hang me if you want, but only after I've saved her."

"We're not going to hang you," Imara said. When Desfan didn't immediately rise to echo her, she scowled at him. "You *really* intend to kill him after all he's done for you? For Meerah?" She shook her head, throwing up her hands. "I don't even know why he's still in chains!"

"Because he's a liar and a betrayer," Karim stated flatly.

Imara turned her scowl on him.

Grayson hadn't looked away from Desfan. "Please. Let me save her."

Fates blast it, he was considering it, wasn't he? But could he really trust Grayson Kaelin—who had already betrayed him once—to rescue his sister? He was the Black Hand. His fates-blasted father had been the one to imprison Mia. And even if Grayson escaped with her, how could Desfan trust him to bring her back to Duvan?

He could send Karim. His best friend's vow was no lie—he would die for Meerah. But how could he send him into the cobra's nest when they had no idea what awaited him there?

For Grayson, it wasn't an impenetrable fortress with countless enemy soldiers to dodge. The castle was his home. He knew it—could navigate it with ease. He could reach Meerah without causing alarm. And if anyone could walk out of there with her, it was Grayson.

It would be the safest path for Meerah.

Desfan ground his teeth. "If you return without completing your father's mission, how do you know you'll be received with open arms?"

"My father's arms are never open, but I can survive whatever punishment he wants to deliver for failing him. He won't kill me. And when he's done, I'll be able to get Mia out." Grayson's forehead creased. "My father will be furious if I return without Liam. He expressly ordered me to keep him safe."

"Now you want us to release Liam?" Karim bristled at the mere thought.

"No," Grayson said quickly. "He needs to be here. I would suggest not killing him, though. He has a considerable amount of knowledge, and since my father values that, Liam could be an important bargaining piece someday."

"Why not bargain now?" Desfan asked. "Liam for Meerah?"

Grayson shook his head. "My father would never give her up—not unless the terms were his. He's been saving her for a reason, and he'd kill her before letting someone else use her. It's the way he is." His head tilted to the side, his expression growing speculative. "I might have an ally in my mother. She asked me to kill Liam, so I'll tell her I have."

Karim muttered another curse. "A family of demons."

Grayson didn't disagree.

"Your mother wanted you to kill your brother? Her *son*?" Imara shook her head, her eyes wide. "I can't imagine . . ."

None of them had a response for her unfinished thought.

Desfan tried to ignore the sinking in his gut. "Are you truly my sister's best chance?"

"I'm her *only* chance," Grayson said. "I won't count on my mother's help, but even without an ally, I *will* free Mia."

"You'd have an ally if you took me," Imara said. "Your brother, Peter; he would reward you somehow, wouldn't he?"

Both Grayson and Desfan flinched. "No," the Rydenic prince

said firmly. "I'm not taking you anywhere near Ryden."

"I don't need your father declaring war on me," Desfan added to her. He couldn't imagine letting Imara go to Ryden. The mere thought had stopped his heart.

She frowned slightly, though hesitant relief glowed in her eyes. "All right," she said, looking between him and Grayson. "If you're sure it wouldn't help."

Karim's frown was deep, his thoughts clearly racing. "Liam's hawk is days ahead of us. There's nothing we can do about that, but we can't waste any more time. If we're sending him, we need to do so quickly."

Desfan nodded. "I'll get a list of ships from the harbormaster. We'll pick whichever one is fastest."

"It can't be a military vessel or a royal ship," Grayson said. "Those would draw too many questions in Vyken."

The cell door pushed open without warning. Desfan turned to see Kiv Arcas stride into the room. "Apologies," he said, clearly addressing Desfan, though his eyes darted around the room. "I have an urgent message for you, Serjah."

What now? Desfan could only take so many problems at a time. Still, he waved the kiv forward and took the folded note. The seal was a simple round of wax, easily cracked.

Desfan,

I look forward to my payment for one Mortisian named Gamble — also known as Latif — and a reward for the safe return of your future bride, Princess Serene.

Come see me at the harbor at your earliest convenience,

Syed Zadir

Several emotions swirled through him, but confusion swam to the top. His brow furrowed. "Serene . . .?"

Karim frowned. "What is it?"

Desfan shook his head. "It's from Syed Zadir."

"The *pirate*?" The corner of Imara's mouth lifted. "Fates, you know the most interesting people."

Karim grunted.

Desfan focused back on the letter. "I don't understand. He says he has Serene with him at the harbor."

Imara's breath hitched. "What?" She snatched the letter from him, her eyes raking the page. Then—"Yes!" Her happy cry made Desfan jump, and when she gripped his arm he didn't understand the joy brightening her face. "Oh fates, she's alive! It has to be her. Serene must be told at once!"

"What are you talking about?" He glanced at the letter. "Who is *he* talking about?"

Imara's grin stretched wider, and tears gathered in her eyes. "Clare," she burst out. "Clare is alive!"

CHAPTER 55

CLARE

CLARE STOOD AT THE RAIL OF THE *SEAFIRE*, Wilf beside her. The sun dipped low in the sky, nearly gone, but there was enough light to study Duvan. It was a colorful city, sprawling and impressive as it wrapped around the harbor and climbed up from the beach. The palace built on the edge of the southern cliff seemed larger than the castle in Iden, and the stone was of a warmer, lighter color than any found in Devendra.

"Have you ever been to Duvan?" Clare asked Wilf.

"No. I was only ever stationed near the border, so I never ventured far into Mortise." He peered over the rail, down at the docks. Men and women milled around the shipyard, but the crowds were thinning along with the daylight.

Clare fiddled with the silver bracelet on her wrist.

"Don't be nervous," Wilf said.

"I'm not." But that was a lie. This ship had been a haven, and leaving it to re-enter the world of politics and danger was not an appealing thought. She knew she would never forget the terror and pain she'd endured while in Salim's hands, but she also knew she would move on from this. That the fear would not be a part of her forever.

Especially with Bennick at her side.

He would make a fair lady-in-waiting, Clare had decided. Every morning on the ship, he'd carried in her breakfast and gently applied the ointments to her healing wounds. He'd also become quite adept at washing and braiding her hair. The mere memory of his fingers combing through the long waves made warmth rush through her, tightening her body. And when he would crouch to tie her boots, she hadn't stopped her good hand from getting lost in his hair. He would glance up, and the half-grin on his face was one she would remember forever.

She didn't want to return to reality. She didn't want these precious, healing moments with Bennick to end. Still, it would be wonderful to see Vera again, and to be reunited with Imara, Serene, and the other bodyguards.

Bennick crossed the deck toward them, a deep furrow between his eyebrows. "I asked Zadir for a little more detail about his message to the serjah," he said, his voice low. "He told Desfan that Serene is on board."

"That could stir some questions, since Serene has hopefully been in Duvan for weeks," Clare said.

Wilf grunted. "Desfan would have learned sooner or later that Serene has a decoy. Let's just hope he has enough sense not to make a scene and let the whole world learn about Clare."

"Is Desfan coming here, then?" she asked.

Bennick rubbed the back of his neck. "Yes. Zadir doesn't want us disembarking until he arrives."

"What will happen to Latif?"

"Why are you so concerned about him?" Wilf asked.

She folded her arms, careful of her braced fingers. "He was kind to me. I don't want to see him hurt."

"He's in Desfan's hands now," Bennick said.

Clare decided she would ask Serene to speak for Latif, if the need arose. The man had made mistakes, but he had also shown her kindness. Clare could do the same.

There was not much to prepare for their departure. Clare had next to nothing, and Bennick and Wilf did not have many things either. The Devendran soldiers and Serai Nadir's men joined them on deck, a small huddle amid the pirates who went about their nightly duties while others were absorbed by card games as they waited.

The wait for Serjah Desfan was not long.

In the deepening darkness, Clare watched a heavily guarded carriage pull to a stop at the docks. The door swung open, and a long line of passengers filed out. Clare had obviously never seen the serjah before, but she knew Desfan instantly. He was tall, handsome, and carried himself with confidence. She did not study him for long, though; Imara and Serene were right behind him, with Cardon in the rear.

Zadir greeted them with arms spread wide as they reached the deck. "Welcome to my kingdom, Serjah! The *Seafire* welcomes you."

Desfan's eyes darted to Clare. He surveyed her with curious

intensity, but her view of his study was interrupted when Imara darted forward, throwing her arms around Clare in a fierce embrace. "Thank the fates you're here," the Zennorian princess gasped.

A hand touched Clare's back and she peeked over her shoulder, still locked in Imara's arms. Serene stood there, tears glinting in her eyes. "I'm so glad you're safe," the princess whispered.

Clare offered a smile, moisture sliding down her cheeks. "I'm glad you are, too."

Beyond Serene, she noticed Captain Zadir watching them, a speculative look in his eye.

Fates, she and Serene were standing side by side. Even though Clare looked a little ragged, the similarities between them would be striking—especially to someone as observant as the pirate captain.

Zadir noticed Clare staring. He gave her a small, reassuring smile.

Serene rubbed a hand over Clare's back, drawing her attention. "I'm so relieved you're here. We've been so worried."

Clare's gaze met Cardon's and he gave her a warm smile, though his eyes lingered on her braced hand.

She swallowed hard, searching all the faces on the deck. Disappointment swept in when she didn't see her best friend. Bennick had assured her Vera was safe, but Clare needed to see that with her own eyes before it felt real. "Are Vera and Venn at the palace?" she asked.

Serene stilled. "They're not with you?"

Anxiety spilled into Clare's gut. "No." She glanced to Bennick, whose face had gone hard.

"Clare and Vera were separated," he explained shortly. "I sent Venn and Vera here from Krid while Wilf and I went after Clare. They should have arrived by now."

Fear clutched Clare's heart. "Where could they be?"

Cardon, Bennick, and Wilf exchanged looks. "I'm sure they'll arrive soon," Bennick finally said, but his expression was tense.

"I can send men to look for them," Desfan offered.

"I'm afraid I don't do searches on land," Zadir said. "You'll have to find someone else."

The serjah eyed the pirate. "Actually, I have another job for you."

Zadir whistled. "You're lining my pockets so quickly, it's just like stealing. But perhaps you can pay me for Gamble and the safe delivery of your future bride, first."

"You'll get your payment, and you can name your price for this next job, but I need you immediately."

"Any price? Well, that's all it takes to grab my attention." The pirate set his hands on his hips, his feet spread wide. "What have you got in mind?"

"How quickly can you make it to Ryden?"

Zadir shrugged. "Depends on the winds."

"Two weeks?" the serjah guessed.

Zadir laughed. "A decent ship can make the journey in two. Mine is the best, and built for speed. I can make it in twelve days. Faster, if the fates bless us with good winds."

"Can you be ready to sail by morning?"

The captain scratched at his beard. "My men won't love that, but as you're being so generous with the compensation . . ." He grinned. "Morning it is."

For the first time, Clare noticed who else was missing. Her forehead creased. "Where is Dirk?"

Dirk's death was a blow. Clare had not been as close to him as Serene's other bodyguards, but he had always been kind to her, and she had loved the gentle peace he'd brought to their group. She mourned his loss deeply, and she wished she could do something to assuage the shock and grief Bennick clearly felt.

Serjah Desfan had given Dirk a place of burial in a corner of the royal gardens. The custom in Mortise was to burn bodies, but he had apparently approached Serene with the burial plan before she had to ask. Imara described the gravesite—with palm trees that stretched overhead and vibrant, colorful flowers spread around. It sounded peaceful. Beautiful.

It still didn't feel right, though. Clare had had enough experience with death to know it never got easier. Losing someone you loved . . . it always left a mark.

Because Venn and Vera had not arrived yet—Clare had to believe they still would—Bennick explained what had happened in Krid; that the Rose had escaped, and that whoever had hired Salim was from the palace—probably a noble.

"We should ask Liam what he knows about the one who hired Salim," Cardon said. "Even if he was only taking advantage of the situation, he must know something. How else could he have known where Salim would be?"

"I'll confer with Desfan tomorrow," Serene said. "He can give us access to Liam, and he might even be able to make sense of that code phrase, if it had ties to one of the Mortisian nobles."

It was entirely possible there wasn't a clue to be found in *fang*

540

and claw; they may have simply been two words plucked from thin air. But if they could lead to the identity of the man who'd hired Salim, Clare was certain Serene would be able to figure it out.

Imara took the lead in explaining what had happened in Mortise: the serjan's sudden death, the imprisonment of the two Rydenic princes, and everything known about the long-thought-dead seraijah, Meerah Cassian—something that Desfan was not publicizing until she was safely recovered. When Imara told of Grayson's mission to Ryden, Clare realized why Desfan had hired Zadir's ship.

"Can he really be trusted to go free?" Bennick asked.

"That remains to be seen," Serene said stiffly.

Imara's lips pressed into a thin line. "Grayson was only trying to protect Meerah. He can be trusted. He'll return with her, and if Desfan has any sense he'll celebrate Grayson as a hero rather than throw him in prison."

"The Mortisian nobles won't agree," Serene said. "Grayson should have betrayed his brother sooner if he truly intended to help. He could be manipulating Desfan even now—and you, dear cousin—and this may be the last we ever see of him."

Imara's eyes narrowed. "He isn't the one who killed Dirk."

Serene's mouth tightened. "No. But if he would have come forward, Dirk's death might have been prevented."

Imara did not argue this, and soon the bodyguards retreated from the room, leaving Clare, Imara, and Serene alone in the princess's suite. They spent half the night exchanging stories, and, though tired, Clare was content to remain awake. She was safe among friends again.

After Imara finally retired to her room, Serene faced Clare alone.

"I want to apologize for what you went through."

"You don't need to."

"I do. It should have been me suffering those atrocities."

"I don't blame you, Serene."

The princess sighed. "Perhaps you should."

Before Clare could respond, Serene stood and moved for a desk against the far wall. She rifled in the drawer for a moment before returning with a handful of letters. "These arrived for you—from your brothers."

Clare's heart skipped as she took the letters. Emotion swelled in her throat as she saw Mark and Thomas's familiar handwriting. She shot Serene a quick smile. "Thank you."

Serene nodded, and Clare noticed a smaller letter still in her hands.

"What's that?" she asked.

"Also for you. From *my* brother. I opened it, since I didn't know when you would return." Her eyes grew troubled. "Grandeur was put in charge of the Devendran military, so I've been extra wary."

Clare set her brothers' messages on her lap and took the new letter from the princess, her pulse jumping as she unfolded it. "Grandeur was put in charge of the military?"

"Yes." Serene's lips pursed, her eyes dipping purposefully to the letter.

Clare scanned the carefully written words.

Miss Ellington,

I'm disappointed that I haven't heard from you, when I know so much must be happening in

Mortise. I am left to believe you no longer have an interest in our relationship. That is truly unfortunate.

Crown Prince Grandeur Demoi

Fates. After all that had happened, Clare had almost forgotten that she'd been pretending to be a spy for Grandeur. He thought she was spying on Serene when in reality, she was a spy *for* Serene. She'd originally confided in Serene when she'd overheard Grandeur and a man talking in one of the castle gardens in Iden. They'd discussed threatening her younger brothers, if motivation was needed for her to turn against Serene.

Now, looking at this letter, with its subtly threatening tone . . . A tremble rippled down her spine. She looked up at Serene. "Did he just threaten my brothers?"

The princess frowned. "I don't think so. My impression is that he's angry, and he's trying to scare you into sending him a reply." Serene met her gaze. "Your brothers are safe, Clare. My father has guards watching them, and I have some of my rebels keeping an eye on them as well."

The reassurances helped Clare breathe a little easier, but nerves still danced inside her. "Would you like me to respond to him?"

"No. Let him wonder a while longer."

"He wasn't careful in sending this message," Clare said, scanning the words again. "He must have known it could have been opened at any stage—especially if anyone was curious as to why the prince would write to one of the princess's maids."

"I can't decide if his paranoia has grown so bad that he was careless without thought, or if this was calculated. Maybe he wanted me to discover this, so I would question you, or attack you." Serene shook her head. "Regardless, after so long without word from you, I don't think he trusts you anymore."

"I was a little too busy being a captive to write him letters." Clare handed the note back to the princess. If she kept it, she would only read it again—and worry.

My brothers are safe. Besides, if Grandeur was going to threaten them, she suspected he would do it bluntly. That would make it easier to get her cooperation.

Serene looked thoughtful. "What if your brothers came here?"

Clare shot her a look. "What?"

The princess lifted one shoulder. "I don't believe they're in danger from Grandeur, but if you would feel better having them here, I could make arrangements."

Clare's first instinct was to say no. Mortise was dangerous—the journey alone would be long and perilous. But they wouldn't be targeted; not like she had been. And though she didn't want to take them from all they knew, she couldn't deny her eagerness to have them close. Here, she could be with them. Care for them. Be a part of their lives. And if war came to Eyrinthia, she could protect them.

She eyed Serene. "Would King Newlan allow them to come?"

"I can annoy my father enough to convince him of nearly anything. And if he refuses, well . . . I *have* rebelled before." The princess tilted her head to the side. "This is the least I can do for you. If you want them here, I'll make it happen."

She stared at Serene for a long moment. Her thoughts raced, but she knew what she wanted. What she needed. "I would like them here—if King Newlan and Serjah Desfan will allow it."

"I'll write to my father tonight." Serene gestured to Clare's letters. "I'll leave you to read those and get some rest. I don't want you to worry about anything right now except healing."

"I suppose I'll have plenty of time to rest." Clare lifted her braced fingers. "I can't be your decoy until these are off."

She would have plenty of time to adjust to Mortise—and prepare to introduce her brothers to this new kingdom.

CHAPTER 56

GRAYSON

GRAYSON HAD NOT LEFT THE INTERROGATION room since Desfan and the others had rushed out to the harbor. Kiv Arcas had released Grayson from his chains on Desfan's orders, and he'd also brought food and water, along with a small jar of ointment for his various cuts and bruises.

Grayson paced the holding room, his tension steadily building as time stretched. He was desperate to begin his journey to Mia. To distract himself and work the stiffness from his sore body, he forced himself through a familiar exercise routine.

He stopped abruptly when the door opened, revealing Karim. The bodyguard's expression was hard, making his disgust for Grayson perfectly clear. "We found a ship to take you to Ryden," he said shortly. "It leaves in the morning."

Grayson wanted to leave now, but he understood that the ship might need some time for preparations. He also didn't want to anger Karim or Desfan with further requests; it was a fates-blasted miracle they were letting him leave to save Mia. He didn't want to press his luck. "Thank you," he said.

"Don't thank me." Karim's eyes darkened. "I don't like you, and I don't like this. If you do anything to harm Desfan or Meerah, I will end you." With that, he strode from the room.

Grayson had no idea what hour it was, but he let himself slump into the corner—facing the closed door—and he tried to sleep. He needed the strength and healing it would give him, but his rest was plagued by nightmares.

It was a relief when the door opened, signaling morning. He pushed up from the floor, his one eye still painfully swollen as he faced the soldier who carried in a breakfast tray, light from the hallway torches spilling into the room. The guard dropped the tray on the table with a careless clatter, his eyes shooting daggers at Grayson. His hatred was all too clear, but it was his swollen knuckles that convinced Grayson this was one of the men who had beaten him and Liam.

The guard's nostrils flared, but before he could speak, Imara swept in, a bag slung over her shoulder. Grayson recognized it as his own.

He glanced past her, but—as he'd come to expect—there was no bodyguard trailing her. He frowned. "How do you always slip past your guards?"

"Ah. The question they ask themselves every day." Imara flashed a smile, but instantly winced as she drew closer. "Fates, your face still looks terrible."

It felt terrible, but he ignored that. "You really shouldn't sneak away from your guards."

"Because your brother might send someone to abduct me?" she asked.

"Yes." And for a thousand other reasons. Imara was far too trusting—and reckless. She'd befriended *him*, for fates' sake.

Imara ignored him, sending a quick glance to the Mortisian guard. "You may wait outside."

The man didn't look happy about it, but he stalked from the room. That's when Grayson saw a hardened-looking Zennorian guard hovering in the shadowed corridor.

Grayson frowned. "You could have told me your bodyguard was out there."

Imara grinned. "But you were so sweet to worry about me." She used the heel of her shoe to nudge the door closed, and then she stepped up to Grayson, handing him the bag. "I wasn't sure if you'd want a servant packing your bag, so I just threw some things inside. You'll want to change into a fresh set of clothes, and I can see about a wash basin for you. You have a few minutes before we need to go to the harbor."

"Thank you." He set the bag on the table beside the breakfast tray. "And thank you for believing in me."

"Of course. You're my friend, Grayson." Her words were simple, and wholly sincere.

Her guileless kindness reminded him of Mia. Fates, but some people were too good for this world.

"You should eat," Imara said, nodding to the tray.

He felt too anxious to eat, but he picked at the tray's offerings of pastries, bread, cheese, and fruit. Not usual prison fare.

Imara had no doubt had a hand in that.

"I never asked how you managed to get to me," he said, slipping a grape into his mouth. "I would have assumed no one was allowed close, except for Desfan."

Her lips crept into a smile. "I keep expecting Desfan to ask me again, too. Let's just say I have many talents." She reached for his bag and withdrew a letter. "Here."

Grayson wiped his fingers on his pants before taking it; he thought he recognized the seal as Desfan's, and his brow furrowed. "What's this?"

She wiggled her eyebrows. "One of my talents."

He frowned, his fingers tightening against the stiff envelope. "Imara, what is this?"

"Your way out. It's addressed to the captain of your ship—a pirate, of all things." She rolled her eyes. "Mortise." Then she tapped the letter. "It's written in an exact copy of Desfan's hand. It took me all night, I'll have you know. Anyway, it's an order for you to be released at the port of your choosing, once Meerah has been rescued."

He stared at her, dumbfounded. There were so many things wrong with this, he didn't know where to start. "Forgery is a serious crime."

"Don't turn me in, then." Her tone dropped, even though they were alone. "You can't come back here, Grayson. The Mortisian council is calling for your head, and Liam's. Truth be told, Serene is too. After you've saved Meerah, you can give this letter to Captain Zadir and he'll let you off wherever you like. He'll bring her safely to Duvan."

"No. I promised to bring her back to Desfan, and I will." He would also never abandon Mia—especially with pirates. He held out the letter.

Imara frowned, not taking it. "You're being stubborn."

The corner of his mouth twitched. "I'm grateful to you, Imara. No one has ever done anything like this for me. But I can't accept this."

Her jaw tightened. "You'll be imprisoned the moment you return."

He lifted one shoulder, still proffering the letter. "I would never leave Mia. I couldn't."

Imara exhaled. "Fine. But you may as well keep it, in case you change your mind."

"I can't. If my father found this, he'd know I was plotting against him."

She sighed, but took back the letter. She fingered the rigid corners, her eyes downcast. "Why didn't you tell me you had orders to abduct me?"

He blinked at the sudden question. "What?"

"Yesterday, when we were alone. Why didn't you say something?"

His forehead wrinkled. "I wasn't going to take you to Peter. There was no point in mentioning it."

"You didn't want to frighten me." When he didn't argue, she bit her lip. "Were you also protecting me when you said my presence wouldn't help? Because I'll go, if you think it will give you and Meerah a better chance."

"There's no sense in you risking yourself. Besides," he tried for a lighter tone, "without you here to calm Desfan, he'll be more likely to kill me when I get back."

She rolled her eyes, muttering something in Zennorian. It didn't sound complimentary, though Grayson wasn't sure if the condemnation was for him, Desfan, or all men.

His lips twitched, but seriousness lived in his words as he said, "Imara, I would *never* place you within reach of my family. Not for anything. There are very few people I . . . care about." The words were hard to say, but they were true.

Imara's face softened. "Meerah is very fortunate. So am I." She placed a hand on his arm. "One day, Desfan will realize it, too."

Grayson was beginning to think he wouldn't see Desfan before leaving Duvan. Imara was the only familiar face with him as he left the prison and was escorted to a waiting carriage. He took one last look at the palace behind him, noting the tan-hued stone, towering columns, open corridors and walkways. The blatant majesty was still foreign, even though he'd been here for several weeks. And yet, he uttered a silent prayer to the fates that he would see it again, with Mia at his side. Death might be coming for him, but as long as he could return Mia safely home, he could face whatever the fates decided.

The carriage took him and Imara—and a handful of guards— to the edge of the docks. Before Grayson could shoulder his bag, the door was pulled open, revealing Desfan. His dark hair was ruffled by the breeze coming off the sea, and dark circles lived under his eyes.

Karim stood behind him, but before Grayson could look further, Desfan spoke. "I want a moment alone with him, please."

His words were directed at Imara, but Grayson felt the ice in them.

Imara hopped out of the carriage, shooting a warning look at

Desfan before he climbed inside, shutting the door with a small but punctuating snap. He sat across from Grayson, the tension in the dim carriage stretching the air between them. Anxiety tightened Grayson's shoulders, but he refused to look away from Desfan's intense gaze.

The serjah spoke in Rydenic, as if he was determined that Grayson understand him perfectly. "The only reason I'm letting you go is for her sake. My sister means more to me than anything else in Eyrinthia. If you try to take her away from me, there is nowhere you'll be able to hide." Threat lived in his deep voice, but there was a vulnerability edging his words that clenched something in Grayson's gut.

"I promise I'll bring her back to you," he said, also in Rydenic. "I would give my life for hers."

A muscle in Desfan's jaw ticked. Clearly, he had some strong feelings about Grayson's devotion to his sister. He glanced down, twisting the obsidian ring on his finger. "When you reach her . . ." He cleared his throat, his tone rougher than before. "Tell her I love her."

"I will. But soon you'll be able to tell her yourself."

Desfan didn't say anything, just gave Grayson a look that spoke a thousand lethal promises and an equal amount of pleas. The moment was raw and charged. It ended abruptly when Desfan opened the door and pushed out of the carriage.

Grayson followed, his hand fisted around his bag. He didn't have his black gloves, since Imara hadn't packed them, but, strangely, he didn't feel the usual need to hide his scars. He wasn't sure why, but he didn't take the time to dwell on it as he stepped onto the cobbled road. He shot Imara a brief, reassuring smile. It eased her frown somewhat, though she came to walk beside him as they followed Desfan and Karim onto the docks.

Standing beside a hulking ship was a heavily bearded Mortisian who eyed Grayson with unbridled interest. "So, this is the Black Hand. Well, Prince of Ryden, it looks like you're going to be under my rule for the next few weeks. What do you have to say about that?"

"As long as you get me to Ryden as quickly as possible, we won't have a problem."

Zadir's eyebrows lifted. "Desfan, I'm surprised you're not friends with this one. He's as arrogant as you are."

Grayson shot Desfan a look, but the serjah pointedly ignored him as he faced the pirate. "You have his weapons?"

"Yes, Karim brought them earlier," Zadir said.

"Good. Don't give them to him until you land in Ryden."

"If he gives you any trouble," Karim added, "throw him in the brig. He's still a prisoner of Mortise."

Imara slipped her arm around Grayson's, linking their elbows. The action drew Desfan's attention, and the skin around his eyes tightened.

"None of this is necessary," Imara said. She looked to the captain. "Grayson knows what he's doing, and what's at stake. You should listen to him."

"I'll follow Desfan's orders," Zadir said.

Imara twisted to face Grayson, surprising him when she pulled him into an embrace. He'd only ever been hugged by Mia, but he realized he didn't mind Imara's touch. It was actually pleasant, except for the clouded stare Desfan pinned him with.

"Please be careful," Imara whispered.

Grayson nodded. "I will be."

Desfan watched them. It looked like he might say something,

and Grayson wished he would. Or that he could find his own words. He wanted to apologize for his betrayal. He wanted to assure Desfan that their friendship had been real, before he'd ruined it. He wanted to assure Desfan that he would get Mia, and he would bring her home.

But the serjah turned on his heel and strode away, and Grayson did not call him back.

CHAPTER 57

MIA

MIA EYED HERSELF IN THE TALL MIRROR Rena had insisted be brought in. The king's birthday had finally arrived, and Mia was wearing a dress fit for a storybook princess.

The deep pink gown nearly glowed in the lamplight, and the way the skirt flowed to the floor was almost liquid. The sleeves were off the shoulder and ended at the middle of her forearms. The dress wasn't elaborately decorated, but it was beautiful in its simplicity. Her dark hair spilled around her face, though Rena intended to pin it into a loose bun, leaving strands to curl against her cheeks. She had a dark pink shading on her lips, something she'd never worn in her life, and some dusky powders brushed onto her eyelids.

Staring at the young woman in the glass, Mia saw a stranger. A young woman who might have been, if fate had dealt her a different hand. Her life had not been ball gowns and elegance. But it hadn't just been darkness and misery, either.

She'd had Grayson.

She touched the small pebble hanging around her neck. She refused to take it off, even though Rena had shown her several different necklaces she could choose from.

There was a tightness in her chest. It had been there for a while now. She wasn't sure if it was the beginning of a panic, or if it was a side-effect of her sleepless nights. A cold fear had begun twisting in her gut. It whispered of danger, though she wasn't sure if it was for herself, or for Grayson.

She'd been worrying about him a lot lately, because laying her plans for escape were taking longer than expected. And she had yet to get a response from the letter she'd sent him.

Just hold on, she pleaded silently. *Stay safe. I'm coming.*

She tried not to think about where he was. The halls he walked. The people he saw.

Desfan.

The name, even unspoken, was like a blow. Her throat cinched, halting her breath. It had been so long since she'd allowed herself to even think his name.

Grayson had said it, before he left. If ever she had wanted to tell him the truth, it had been in that moment, when he'd told her where he was going. Who he would see. But like always, panic had swept in, overtaking everything.

Desfan.

She could see her brother's wide smile, too big for his young face. She thought of his high-pitched laugh, his made-up games.

The way he would tug at her hair whenever she got frustrated, and he wanted to make her smile. She remembered hours spent on the beach, making palaces in the sand and playing in the waves.

Thinking of him brought other memories.

Her sister, giggling behind her hand at a feast. Her parents, watching the three children dance together at a ball. Her mother's rich singing. Her father's booming voice as he told them stories before bed; even after a busy day, he had nearly always done that.

Tears stung her eyes as she stared at her reflection. The years had changed her so deeply, and in so many ways. It made her wonder how different Desfan would be now, from the boy in her memories. She wondered what her father would look like—how he would look at her, if he knew what she'd done that night, so many years ago.

Shoving aside the wave of guilt before it could swallow her, Mia closed her eyes and tried to breathe. She pushed back the memories. It was the only way she would get through the king's feast.

It was the only way she'd managed to get through the last several years of her life.

"Mia?" Tyrell called from the other side of the bedroom door. "May I come in?"

She twisted away from the mirror and cleared her throat, desperate to keep her emotions tethered. "Yes."

Tyrell stepped into the room, halting instantly when his eyes landed on her. His perusal was slow. Deliberate. And when his gaze finally met hers, Mia's cheeks were flushed.

She fingered her skirt. "It's too elegant."

"It pales in comparison to you."

Mia huffed a weak laugh, one hand going to her hair. "I'm not even finished. Rena left to get some hairpins."

Tyrell's focus didn't waver. "You're beautiful, Mia. You always have been, no matter what you wear or how your hair is done."

She shuffled her bare feet, self-conscious under his scrutiny. "You look nice."

It was an understatement. In his emerald and black uniform, his wide shoulders and tall frame were perfectly pronounced. His dark hair had been swept back from his face, but several stubborn strands fell over his brow. His angular jaw was clean-shaven, and the smell of his soap added a slight spice to his natural outdoorsy scent.

Once, he had terrified her. Terrorized her. And now, somehow, he was her friend. A friend she would betray in order to escape the castle and reach Grayson.

Her stomach rolled over.

Tyrell's hand dipped into his pocket. "I wanted to give you this." He held out a small black box, a red ribbon tied carefully around it.

Mia took it slowly. "You shouldn't have. You've given me enough."

"I wanted to." Color touched his prominent cheekbones. "Open it."

She tugged at the end of the silky ribbon, undoing the careful bow. Tyrell took the freed ribbon, pocketing it as he watched her lift the lid.

She froze. "Tyrell . . ."

Nestled in the small box was the black queen from his Stratagem set. The beautifully flawed one, from the first set he'd carved.

She glanced up at him. "But, your set won't be complete."

"I'll carve a new one," he said. His throat bobbed. "If you don't like it, I can find something else—"

"No. I love it." She tipped it free of the box and the small piece of painted wood rolled onto her palm. She ran her thumb over the many ridges and grooves. "Thank you."

When she glanced up at him, his eyes were riveted on her pebble necklace. "I suppose I wanted you to carry a piece of me, too."

The plaintive quality in his otherwise deep and strong voice tugged at her heart. Mia stepped closer, cupping his cheek. "I'll treasure this always. Just as I treasure our friendship."

Beneath her palm, a muscle in his jaw jumped. "I know you love him," he said quietly. "But people change, Mia."

Her hand fell away. "Grayson will always love me."

"But will you always love him?" Tyrell leaned in. "In the time that he's been gone, you've changed. He's not the only person in your life, now. You don't have to choose him—you could choose me. Don't you think Grayson would allow you that choice?"

"He would." Grayson would sacrifice anything for her happiness. He would do anything she asked him. It was a staggering and sometimes terrifying weight, knowing the power she held over him. She pursed her lips, her heart aching as she studied Tyrell. "I don't want to hurt you. That's the last thing I want to do. But I will always choose him."

Pain flared in Tyrell's eyes before he managed to fit a mask over his features. His fingertips brushed her chin, the line of her jaw, finally scooping back long, curling tendrils of her hair and tucking them behind her ear. "I won't stop trying to change your mind," he whispered. A knuckle dragged down her rounded cheek and a shiver caught her.

She took a step back, her skin feeling too warm, too tight.

Tyrell's hand fell, and he took a step back as well. "I'll wait outside to escort you. Whenever you're ready."

There was a deeper meaning there, but neither of them acknowledged it. He simply turned and left, closing the door softly behind him.

Rena finished Mia's hair and declared her ready. With promises to return after the feast to help her change, the older woman wished her luck and left.

Mia gave herself one last look in the mirror, one last deep breath, before she walked into the sitting room.

She nearly stumbled when she saw Peter standing in the center of the room. A quick glance showed Tyrell was gone.

Peter's eyes raked over her, his eyebrows lifting. "You continue to surprise me. You look beautiful."

Between her anxiety and the emotionally charged conversation with Tyrell earlier, Mia was not in the mood. "What do you want?"

"I wanted to wish you luck. This is your first official foray into Ryden's elite circle, and I would hate for you to trip." His smile said he would like nothing more than for her to make a fool of herself.

Her spine straightened. "Do you know what I think?"

"No, but I assume you're about to enlighten me."

"I think you can't stand to see anyone be happier than yourself. Especially your brothers. You're the oldest. The crown prince. And yet you're so weak compared to them."

Peter's smile tightened. "I must admit, I find it amusing how staunchly you defend them, considering what monsters they are."

"*You're* the monster. You find joy in controlling and torturing everyone around you."

"I'm not the only Kaelin who indulges in a little control." He plucked out an envelope from his pocket and waved it gently in the air. "I believe this belongs to you."

Mia's breathing thinned. She moved forward slowly, the voluminous skirt suddenly dragging heavily against her legs. She took the letter he held out, already knowing what she would see.

Written in her own hand, Grayson's name stared back at her. Her heart clenched in an invisible fist.

"I found it in Tyrell's desk," Peter said. "It was already open."

Mia turned the envelope over and saw the broken seal. Her fingers tightened, crinkling the paper. "I don't understand."

"Really? You seemed so intelligent." Peter nodded to the letter. "Tyrell never sent that, even though he told you he did. It's really not surprising. He's always been jealous of Grayson—always coveted what was his. Everything from a shiny new dagger to our father's recognition. Tyrell has been lying to you, Mia. Manipulating you. Maybe it's because he really thinks he wants you. Or maybe he just doesn't want Grayson to have you." He took a step back, his smile firmly in place. "I do hope you'll sit near me tonight. The entertainment will be fantastic." With that, he strode from the room, leaving Mia alone with the letter in her hand and tears stinging her eyes.

Her lungs were locked; impossibly frozen. It was like the beginning of a panic, but the sheer terror was missing. Instead, there was hurt. Betrayal. And, undeniably, anger.

Those emotions were burning her from the inside out when Tyrell entered the room. His head was down as he tugged at his cuffs, striding comfortably forward. "Sorry, Peter asked me to make a quick inspection of the guards before the feast. Are you ready?" He glanced up and stilled.

Mia lifted the letter, trying to ignore the subtle vibrating as her hand shook. "Why did you tell me you sent this?"

Tyrell's face revealed nothing. Even his eyes were shielded.

"You lied to me," she said, her voice thready with tension. "You told me you sent this to Grayson, but you didn't."

The skin around his eyes tightened. "You looked through my desk?"

"No. Peter gave it to me."

Thunderclouds overtook his gaze. "That snake."

"He is a snake," Mia agreed. "But so are you."

Hurt flared in his eyes before he managed to lock down his expression. "I meant to send it—"

"You *read* it."

"I had to make sure you didn't say anything dangerous, just in case my father got his hands on it."

Her fingers clenched on the letter. "That doesn't explain why you didn't send it. Why you lied to me."

His shoulders tensed. "I didn't lie—"

"*Yes you did!*" Her chest rose and fell sharply. Staring at him, seeing the harsh lines on his face, she flashed back to all the times she had been manipulated. Employed as a weapon. Fates. How many times would she be used by a Kaelin? Henri, Peter, Tyrell—they were all the same. All of them tried to wield her like a knife—use her to hurt someone else, or be what they wanted. To them, she was nothing more than an object. A thing to be used. Years of abuse and misuse slammed into her, and her heart cracked. "I trusted you. I can't believe I trusted you."

Tyrell's jaw flexed. "I meant to send it. I almost did, a hundred different times."

"Then why didn't you?"

"I don't know."

"You don't know?" Mia edged out a hard, disbelieving laugh. "You don't know why you repeatedly lied to me—"

"I didn't want to share you with him!"

She reared back at the venom in his words.

Tyrell glared, but his fierce look did nothing to diminish the desperation edging his tone. "Every time I read those words you wrote for him, I wanted them to be for *me*. I want you, Mia, and I won't apologize for that. That stupid letter was a constant reminder that—even in another kingdom—I'm still competing against him. It's not fair. He's had you for years. It's *my* turn. Not his!"

Mia stared at him, her heart hammering. Slowly, she shook her head. "I can't believe I ever thought you were my friend."

Tyrell's hands rolled into fists at his sides. "I'm sorry," he gritted out. "Is that what you want me to say? I made a mistake."

"This wasn't a mistake. It was a choice."

"Mia—"

"I'm not some possession you can claim," she cut in. "I'm not some *thing* you can manipulate in order to hurt Grayson."

"I never said you were!" He stepped forward, reaching for her.

She flinched back on instinct.

He ground to a halt, letting his hand fist, and then drop. His face flushed. "I'm not going to hurt you. Fates—how could you think that?"

"You've done it before."

He stiffened. "I would never hurt you, Mia. Never again."

"You won't," she agreed shortly. "I won't let you." She strode for the door.

Tyrell snagged her elbow, halting her. "Where are you going?"

"Away from you."

He muttered a curse. "What about the feast?"

"I'm not going." She tugged at her arm, but his grip didn't loosen.

"Don't do this," he said tightly. "Don't walk away."

"You haven't given me another option. I can't trust you anymore." Fates only knew what else he'd been lying about.

His eyes narrowed. "I told you I would fight for you, and that's what I've done—in the only way I know how. I love you, Mia."

Her stomach twisted. "This isn't love. It's the furthest thing from love."

Hurt flashed in his eyes. "I've tried to give you everything. A new life. Freedom."

"This isn't freedom. All you did was give me a bigger cage."

Tyrell released her as if burned. He fell back a step and shoved a hand through his dark hair. His expression was shocked. Then anger settled in. "What else do you want from me? I've given you more than Grayson ever has, and yet you still think he's better than me."

"Grayson has never lied to me," Mia snapped. "He's never deliberately tried to hurt me—"

"I wasn't trying to hurt you!"

"But you did!" That was the horrible truth, she realized. The betrayal, the anger—it was a thousand times worse because he *had* hurt her. She had trusted Tyrell. Befriended him. Seen a softer side of him. She had let him in, and he had hurt her.

So little in her life was in her control, but in this moment, she had a choice.

She walked away.

Tyrell's fingers closed around her wrist. "Mia—"

She acted without thought. Grayson had taught her how to break such a hold, and in a few precise movements she was free. Her wrist dully throbbed as Tyrell stared at her, stunned. There was an unspoken plea in his eyes, and his hurt was undeniable.

Her stomach clenched. "Don't follow me."

His body was as rigid as the stone around them, and the torches outlined his face starkly. "The only thing I'm guilty of is caring about you too much."

She didn't respond. She grasped the handle and jerked the door open.

Fletcher straightened in the corridor, his eyes taking her in, then darting past her. The other stationed guards looked just as unsettled.

Mia focused on Fletcher. "I don't care where we go, but I will not stay here another night." She didn't wait for him to lead the way; she marched down the hall, her gown trailing over the cold stone floor.

She half-expected Tyrell to follow her, or order the guards to drag her back.

None of that happened.

Within moments she was alone with Fletcher in the corridor, the letter to Grayson still clutched in her shaking hand. She probably would have kept marching all night, but the old guard touched her arm, steering her toward a closed door.

"This will be a safe place for you," he said, reaching into his pocket and withdrawing a brass key.

When the door swung open, stale air hit her face. It was a darkened bedroom, the suite noticeably smaller than Tyrell's. There was no sitting room, just some armchairs set before a cold fireplace. A large four-post bed stood on the right side of the room. To the left, a dressing table, empty wash stand, and a shuttered closet.

Heavy drapes were tugged over the windows, making the shadowy space feel even darker.

"This is Grayson's room," Fletcher said. "He gave me the key before he left."

Shock rippled through her, but she stepped inside. By the light of the lantern clutched in Fletcher's hand, she could see that everything in the room was neat and tidy. Everything was put away, making the room feel almost empty. There were no obvious personal touches, no art or tapestries. And yet, stepping into Grayson's space was everything she thought it would be. There was peace here. Stillness. Calm.

She stepped to the bed and trailed her fingers over the quilt. The familiar scent of leather, pine, and woodsy spice filled her nose, and an ache gaped inside her chest, threatening to swallow her. His absence stretched until it was nearly colorless—an unending separation that was a void she didn't know how to fill. Couldn't fill, without him.

"I'll send a message to Rena. She'll bring your things." Light flared as Fletcher lit the lamp on the desk

Mia twisted to face him. "Thank you."

The old guard swallowed, rubbing at the scratches on his wrist. Fates, they hadn't healed yet? Or were those fresh? She was distracted by the steel in Fletcher's voice. "Don't thank me."

She frowned. "Why not? You've always taken care of me."

"I've never done anything for you. I've been a bystander. Nothing more."

"That's not true. You've been my guard and my friend." She gestured around them. "You brought me here, where I didn't even know I needed to be. Thank you."

He shook his gray head, his ears burning. He reached into his pocket once more, this time drawing out a letter. "Grayson asked me to give this to you if he didn't return from Mortise."

Ice froze her veins. "Is he—?"

"I've not heard anything," Fletcher said in a rush. "I just thought that, whatever words he wrote, you may need them now." The moment she took it from him, he retreated a step. "I'll be just outside."

Unable to form words, she simply nodded.

When the door clicked closed behind him, Mia moved to Grayson's desk and lowered herself into his chair. Her fingertips coasted over the worn surface of the desk, imagining Grayson's hands doing the same. Then she opened his letter, tipping it toward the lamp so every carefully written word was illuminated.

Mia,

You know I'm not gifted at expressing my thoughts. Luckily, you've always been able to read my every one. Please know that leaving you is the hardest thing I have ever done. If I could, I would take you with me. I would protect you with every drop of my blood. If I could.

Know that I fought with everything in me to return to you. Know that I loved you, Mia. I loved you so much, I sometimes thought the weight of it would break me. You have always been the light in my darkness. You kept me from be-

coming what I feared. You allowed me to love you. More than that, you loved me in return. That is the greatest gift I have ever been given. Thank you.

In all those stories you told me when we were children, your favorite part was always the ending. The moment when everything came together and everyone was happy. I wanted to give you that. I wanted to give us a happy ending. But even though I'm gone, your story isn't over. You will get your happy ending. I swear it.

I prepared everything I could. I have given Fletcher coin and instructions for your safety. He's promised to help you escape, since I no longer can.

Writing these words, knowing that you might someday read them—I'm sorry. That's the only thing I can think to say. I'm sorry, Mia. For so many things, I'm sorry.

The only thing I fear in death is losing you. Fates, I don't want to leave you. But if I'm not given a choice, then at least I'll know this final message will reach you.

No words could ever express how completely I love you. No letter could ever carry the depth of my feelings, but it can at least bear this truth: I love you, Mia. Forever.

Grayson

CHAPTER 58

GRAYSON

GRAYSON GRIPPED THE SHIP'S RAIL AND STROVE for deep, cleansing breaths. The obligatory retching was accomplished for the morning. He hoped it would be over for the entire day, though he doubted he would be so lucky.

He truly hated sailing.

"You're leaving a thick trail of vomit behind us," a deep voice boomed out.

Grayson peeked over his shoulder and saw Zadir amble toward him, walking the rocking deck like he'd been born on the water. Perhaps he had. The heavily bearded pirate hadn't spoken more than a dozen words to Grayson since they'd left Duvan three days ago.

No one had spoken to him, not that he'd made any efforts to be friendly. He'd been shown a hammock belowdecks and ordered not to touch anything. Though bruises and aches lingered from his beating by the Mortisian guards, he was mostly healed. His eye was no longer swollen, though he still had some deep purple bruising on his eyelid. He wished he had access to his sword or daggers so he could stretch his sore muscles with some practice. And not go mad from inaction.

He spent most of his time on deck, staring at the waves and wishing the ship could travel faster. And, of course, quite a bit of time was dedicated to throwing up or fighting the urge.

Zadir came up beside him. "The infamous Prince Grayson Kaelin, reduced to a green-faced spewer who hangs over the side of my ship. Tragic."

"At least I do it over the side."

The pirate laughed. "True. So. Is it like this every time you sail?"

"I don't do well on the water."

"Hmm. I suppose you've never considered piracy, then?"

Grayson blinked. "No."

Zadir smiled and leaned against the rail, his arms crossed over his wide chest. "I'd never hire you, of course. Even without the retching."

Grayson eyed the captain, who looked totally at ease. "Is there something you wanted?"

Zadir lifted a bushy eyebrow. "Do I need a reason to stand around my own ship?"

He frowned. "No. It's just . . ."

"Oh, have you been feeling a bit ignored? Not used to that, I'd imagine. Well, Your Highness, Desfan gave me no special orders about your royal treatment."

"I'm not complaining."

"Well, I am. I think it's time you contributed." He nodded to Grayson's hands, which—without his gloves—were visibly scarred. But that wasn't what Zadir was looking at. "You're strong," he said. "Strong enough for mending sails. That's something you can do in between flinging out your guts." He clapped Grayson's shoulder, and he barely refrained from flinching away from the unexpected contact. "I'll introduce you to Swallow, the sailmaster."

Grayson knew nothing about mending sails, but he figured that was a moot point. Besides, it would give him something to concentrate on.

He wished he'd fought the point three hours later. His fingers had been pierced by the thick needle so many times they were swollen.

"Try not to bleed on the sails," Swallow sighed. He was a thin man with a long nose that twitched whenever he looked at Grayson. He had graying hair, but he looked fit despite his age, and his fingers tugged the needle through the sail without pause.

One pirate snorted at another beside him. "He can't even handle a needle. What a swordsman."

Grayson didn't know the names of these other pirates, and he had no desire to learn them.

It wasn't until daylight began fading that Zadir strolled by. "How's he doing?"

Swallow glanced at Grayson, his nose wrinkling. "Not bad."

Grayson couldn't hide his surprise. After all of Swallow's critiques, he'd expected insults.

Zadir huffed, but his beard couldn't hide his smile. "Well, if things in Ryden don't work out, maybe the Black Hand can start a new life making ball gowns."

Several of the pirates sniggered.

Zadir's eyes sparked with amusement. "Well, Spewer, you excel at retching and you're tolerable when it comes to stitching. I want to see how you fare in a fight."

Grayson arched a brow. "Desfan told you not to give me a weapon until we reach Ryden."

The captain shrugged. "I'm a pirate. I live to break rules. Besides, my men could do with a little entertainment."

Grayson flexed his cramped fingers. He knew he should probably refuse, but he wanted to lose himself in a fight. "I'll try not to damage your crew."

Zadir grinned. "I can't say they'll promise the same." He turned and bellowed for a set of daggers to be brought out, and then he called forward five men.

Swallow spoke quietly at Grayson's side. "You better be half as good as the rumors say, or you'll be lucky if you limp away from this."

Grayson eyed the men Zadir had chosen. They were all larger than him, but that would make them slower. And even if they had the benefit of not feeling nauseous or unsteady on the ship, Grayson hardly needed that advantage to win. He glanced at Swallow. "I'm not worried."

The sailmaster's large nose twitched, but he didn't reply.

Grayson took the two daggers handed to him. He tested their weight and balance as he watched a ring of spectators form a sparring circle with Zadir at the center.

"The fight goes until one fighter surrenders or falls unconscious." The captain smiled a little. "Or if I call the match. Blood is expected, but no killing."

When the captain waved only one of the five men forward,

Grayson nearly snorted.

His first opponent had also been working on the sails, and he'd found several opportunities to insult Grayson. He stepped forward with swaggering confidence, two daggers gripped in his hands. "Spewer, huh? Let's see if I can't give you a new name. Bleeder, maybe? Or Weeper?"

Spectators snickered, but Grayson said nothing.

The pirate made a show of slicing the air with one of his blades, and the watching pirates called out suggestions of how best to make the Rydenic prince cry.

After a useless delay meant to destabilize him with fear, the man finally attacked.

Grayson caught the descending knife with his own, deflected the other knife with a cut to the right, side-stepped, then drove his knee into the man's stomach. A deliberate shove tossed him face first to the deck.

The pirate hit the deck with hands splayed, his daggers bouncing away. He scrambled to twist around, his eyes wide with shock.

Grayson took a step back, flipping his blades once. "Don't worry, I won't take *Weeper*. It suits you."

Some of the pirates hooted, obviously feeling more loyalty to humor than their shipmate. Many looked at Grayson with mixtures of awe and unease. Zadir stood at the forefront, his teeth glinting in his black beard.

The man Grayson would now call Weeper cursed soundly. Even as he limped to his feet, the cursing continued. "Fates-blasted demon—how did you move so fast?"

"Practice." Grayson used one of his knives to gesture at the man's stomach. "And I don't carry that."

More laughter from the pirates.

Weeper ground his teeth. "I want to go again."

"Later," Zadir called. "I want to see how our newest recruit fares. Gale!"

Gale was a thickly built man, but not overweight. Grayson had seen him frequently because his hammock was next to Grayson's. Out of all his opponents, Gale seemed the most challenging. His arms were thick, but there didn't seem to be a spare bit of fat on him. He looked to be in his early twenties, and he had a pale scar that sliced through his eyebrow.

The crowd struck up bets now that they'd seen what Grayson was capable of. He didn't feel the least bit intimidated when the majority still bet against him.

Gale sank into a ready stance, his daggers close to his body as he poised for attack. Instinct told Grayson Gale wouldn't strike first, so he rushed forward, his blades swiping toward the pirate's left side—his less dominant side, according to the foot he led with and how he angled himself before a fight.

The clash of knives rang out. The shock of the blocked blow rippled up Grayson's arm. He swung his other blade, but that was met as well. Gale attempted to land a kick to Grayson's knee, but he dodged the boot and slammed his elbow into Gale's upper arm, bruising his flesh.

Gale grunted, but didn't retreat. He obviously understood the importance of sticking close in a knife fight.

They caught each other's blades with the edges of their own, locked in a fierce struggle. Gale was good. One of the best knife fighters Grayson had ever faced. Still, it only took a minute before Grayson jammed the base of one hilt against Gale's right wrist. He hit the sensitive inner point and Gale cursed as he dropped the blade. He tried to raise his remaining knife, but Grayson kept it pinned down with his own, then thrust his other dagger up against Gale's throat.

Men hollered and cheered.

Gale glared, his chest heaving.

Grayson twitched out a smile, breathing hard himself. The thrill of fighting filled him, calmed him. During a fight, he was in control. It was a feeling he craved, especially now.

Gale said nothing as he shoved away from Grayson and stalked into the crowd, shouldering through the spectators as he made his escape.

Grayson ignored the sweat beading on his neck and rolling down his back. He pivoted to face Zadir and cocked one eyebrow. "Next?"

Weeper begged for another chance, but Zadir waved the impatient man away and called for the next. When Grayson summarily beat him, Zadir waved the last two opponents to face Grayson together. It was not so much a challenge as just a different kind of fight. Grayson altered his tactics and still won quickly, disarming the first man and mock stabbing the other in the side.

He gained only a few bruises and several blistering looks from the defeated men and their friends. As the crowd broke apart, Swallow gave Grayson an approving nod.

Zadir came forward and clapped Grayson's shoulder. "Not bad, Spewer."

He handed the knives back hilt first. "Thank you for the diversion."

"You realize you made some enemies today?" Zadir asked.

"That's nothing new for me."

The captain chuckled. "I do respect your attitude, boy. You fear nothing."

He feared plenty. He just couldn't show his fear. Ever. He'd been trained not to.

Zadir strode away with the knives, calling over his shoulder, "I'd still never hire you."

CHAPTER 59

MIA

MIA HAD NOT LEFT GRAYSON'S ROOM SINCE her fight with Tyrell five days ago. She didn't want to see him. And not just because she was still upset with him.

"I can't believe I ever thought you were my friend."

Recalling those words she'd thrown at him made her wince. Tyrell *had* lied to her, that was true. But she had been lying to him, too. Using him to facilitate her escape, knowing full well that he would be punished once she was gone. She had tried to push that aside, tried to focus on the fact that she wasn't risking this escape just for her sake, but because, for once, she needed to protect Grayson.

Perhaps it was different—less intentionally hurtful than what

Tyrell had done in not sending Grayson's letter. Regardless, she couldn't shrug away her guilt.

She was reminded of a time soon after she'd met Grayson. They'd both been young, not wholly sure of each other. She still struggled to speak his language, and she didn't understand why an eight-year-old boy carried such stiffness, even as they played.

She'd been so desperate for a friend that, when he'd abruptly straightened to leave one day, she had grabbed his wrist.

He'd jerked away from her. His eyes had gone dark, and his body tensed as he recoiled.

Her empty hand stung, along with her heated cheeks. "I'm sorry," she whispered, close to tears. Fates, had she just scared away her only friend?

Grayson had stared at her with the watchfulness of a predatory animal. But no, that wasn't right. He wasn't preparing to attack.

He was waiting for *her* to attack.

He had been so abused, he hadn't known how to react to her clinging touch. He had perceived it as a threat.

The haunted look on Grayson's face, that wariness—Tyrell had looked the same when she'd lashed out at him. The two brothers were horribly alike in that. Neither of them had known kindness. Gentleness. They didn't always know how to react, and sometimes they reacted badly.

Perhaps she had reacted badly, too. Tyrell's lies had only hurt so much because she'd come to care for him. He was her friend— even if he had lied to her.

Even if she planned to leave him.

Too many emotions crowded her. She wasn't ready to face him, so she hid in Grayson's room. Sitting at his desk, the glow of the lamp chasing away the immediate shadows, Mia studied the map of Ryden. Rena had brought all of her books, clothes, and painting supplies, though of course she didn't know about the blankets and non-perishable foods she'd been hiding under Tyrell's bed. Hopefully, he wouldn't discover them, either. She would need to find some way to reach them.

She needed to leave. Her urgency had only increased since Fletcher had given her Grayson's letter. The words he'd written, thinking he might die, had hit her hard.

She would not let him die in Mortise.

Grayson is befriending the Mortisian prince.

The report, so flippantly given by Tyrell weeks ago still plagued her. Grayson and her brother, together. It was such an impossibility; she couldn't imagine it. And she feared why Grayson would be getting close to Desfan. To kill him?

She needed to be in Duvan. *Now.*

She had the supplies, though they weren't as accessible as she would wish. She knew how to ride now, and though she wanted Grayson's horse, she would take any she could get. She had picked a route—to cross the mountains into Mortise—and she had studied the maps until they were burned into her mind. Devon had declared her fully recovered from her stabbing. All she had left to decide was how to get out of the castle.

She'd thought she might convince Tyrell to take her for a day trip outside of Lenzen, and that she might be able to slip away while riding. That was not feasible, now. Not only because of their fight, but also because she knew she couldn't use him in that way. Not after the guilt she already felt cutting into her gut.

She could ask for Fletcher's aid. Would he help her, though? Would she really expect him to take such a risk, when she knew it would not just be him who paid the price, but Rena as well?

No. She would have to figure out a way to slip out of the castle on her own. And it had to be an infallible plan, because she would only get one opportunity. If she was caught, she would be back in her cell forever.

Or killed.

Mia closed the book, rubbing her hand over the leather cover. She was already dressed for bed. Rena had even turned down the blankets before she'd left, probably an hour ago now. She had led Fletcher away, leaving a night guard in his place.

Mia frowned as she thought of her old guard. Fletcher had been acting strangely the last few days. Distant. A little jumpy, even. And he kept rubbing those red scratches on his wrist. Were they not healing? Or were those fresh marks?

Mia shook her head. Too many mysteries. She needed sleep, so she could focus on the puzzle that needed her attention the most—how to escape the castle.

Tomorrow, she needed to leave the safe haven of Grayson's room. She needed to see just how much freedom she still had, now that she wasn't with Tyrell anymore. Hopefully, she would be permitted to wander the castle so she could find the best way out.

She tested the bolt on the door, even though she remembered Fletcher locking it as he left. She wasn't trapped, since she could flip the lock on this side, but she felt better knowing no one else could get in.

She blew out the lamp and padded softly to the bed. Buried in the blankets, she breathed deeply to capture every bit of Grayson's lingering scent. In the darkness, she could almost imagine he was with her.

She was just sinking into sleep when she heard a small click.

She frowned against her pillow, not opening her heavy eyes. Had she imagined it?

Then came a whispering sweep, a barely-there creak.

The door, slowly opening.

Ice shot through her, waking her fully. Her gaze snapped to the doorway, and there was just enough light from the torch in the hall to illuminate the shadowy form of a tall man slipping into the room.

Fletcher? He had the only key. But why was he here?

Tension coiled Mia's shoulders as she forced herself not to move. She wasn't even sure why she was feigning sleep, when she should just call out to him. But instinct kept her still. She eyed the dagger on the bedside table. She'd found it in Grayson's things, and had kept it close.

Her pulse roared when she saw the shadow of a second man at the door, a third shadow trailing behind. This one was shorter and wider, and the slightly labored breathing gave away her identity before she whispered, "I've got the gag."

Mama.

Confusion spiked, but fear cut through everything else. Mia lurched up in the bed. She snatched her pillow and threw it at the closest man. He hissed, falling back in surprise.

Mia grabbed for the dagger beside the bed. Her fingers managed to wrap around the cold hilt a second before one of the men snared her arm.

Dropping the knife into her free hand, Mia slashed at his middle. He bucked away, dropping her in his effort to avoid the sweep of the blade.

Mia screamed, praying someone would hear her. But Grayson had clearly chosen a room as far away from the rest of his family as possible. Fates, where was the night guard?

"Shut her up!" Mama hissed.

The first man dove onto the bed behind her, and her legs tangled in the sheets as she tried to whirl on him.

He moved faster, locking his arms around her chest and pinning her arms to her sides. "Get the knife!" he grunted, even as she struggled against him.

The other man gripped her fingers so fast and so hard, Mia's shout tore with pain.

He pried the knife from her hands, the fragile bones in her hand aching. He threw the dagger aside and it clattered over the floor. He held down her legs, and with a few harsh movements, Mia was pinned to the bed by both men, with Mama leaning over her.

"Hold the wretch still!"

Mia threw her head back against the mattress, still screaming for help when Mama shoved the rough cloth between her lips. The gag dug painfully into the sides of her mouth as Mama tied it roughly behind her head, strands of hair getting painfully tangled in the harsh knot.

Mama's face was cast in shadow, but Mia could feel the woman's glare. "Stop fighting. It's useless."

Mia ignored her. She bucked and struggled, though it hardly did any good. Her wrists were roughly bound, the coarse rope cutting into her skin. She was hauled to the edge of the bed and when she kicked, her ankles were snagged in a bruising hold a second before Mama's slap landed on her cheek.

Mia's face burned, pain radiating from the unexpected strike.

Mama's voice rasped with fury. "You're the reason my life fell apart—the reason my husband is dead. Trust me when I say it would be my pleasure to kill you."

"You said we'd get payment for her live delivery," one of the men snapped.

"If the brat doesn't behave, I don't care about the coin." Mama's shadowy arm waved toward the door. "Hurry! The path won't be clear for long."

One of the men held Mia from behind, half-lifting her. Her bare feet slapped against the cold floor and one of his arms wrapped around her chest, squeezing her until she was breathless. Panic speared through her as she was dragged into the corridor.

The torch guttering further down the hall provided plenty of light for her to see the night guard's dead body. Her stomach heaved.

Mama dropped a brass key on the guard's unmoving chest, and Mia went cold.

That was Fletcher's key.

Everything slammed into place, brutal and undeniable. Fletcher's strange behavior, his inability to look her in the eye—the fact that he'd given Mama this key.

Fletcher had betrayed her. He wasn't here, but he was a part of this.

She was going to be sick.

"Hurry," Mama hissed again.

Mia's eyes burned. She didn't understand why Fletcher had betrayed her, or why Mama was abducting her. But she did know that if she was carried out of here tonight by these people, she might never be found again.

I fought with everything in me. The words were Grayson's, written in the letter meant to be his final words, but now they were hers. She would keep fighting, even if she could not win.

She dug in her heels and shoved against the man who held her.

He grunted, nearly stumbling. Galvanized, she dropped in his loosened arms and threw an elbow between his legs.

He howled, releasing her as he doubled over.

Mia used her bound hands to bat away the second man's grasping hand, and she followed that with a kick to his knee.

The leg buckled and he stumbled, but he didn't fall. She had only used that move before with boots; she hadn't kicked hard enough with her bare feet.

The man tackled her, his bristled cheek scraping against her own as his body slammed against hers.

The back of her head flared with pain from hitting the stone floor. Fear flooded her from being pinned by his merciless weight. But even with her hands bound and the breath knocked out of her, she clawed at his arms, his face—any part of him she could reach.

And then his hands were around her throat, cutting off her air.

Her eyes flared wide and her heels kicked off the floor as she tried to dislodge him. But he sat firmly on her chest, crushing her lungs even as he strangled her.

His face was twisted with rage, and bleeding from several deep scratches. Over his shoulder, Mama talked urgently. Mia couldn't hear her words, due to the rushing in her ears. Every thud of her heart was heavy, and the gaps between the beats stretched longer, and longer. The coldness of the stones beneath her seeped through her nightgown and settled deep in her bones.

Her vision darkened at the edges, narrowing to the man's hateful eyes. Her muscles twitched weakly. Her feet stopped moving. Her throat was crushed. Her heart wasn't beating anymore.

I'm sorry, Grayson. I'm sorry.

There was an animalistic roar.

The crushing hold on her throat was suddenly gone and Mia's head lolled on the floor, her lungs burning as air seared into her body. Her shadowed vision came back in a flash, and she saw Tyrell.

His clothes were disheveled, his dark hair a mess. Fury etched his face in harsh lines as he lifted his dagger and buried it in the chest of the man who'd been strangling her.

Mama screamed.

The other man rushed toward Tyrell, but the Rydenic prince caught him, one hand wrapped around his neck, the other sinking the bloody knife into his heart.

Soldiers arrived, and one of them grabbed Mama.

Tyrell dropped to his knees beside Mia, breathing heavily as he leaned over her. "Mia? Mia!"

His pale face blurred as her eyes welled with tears. Everything felt strangely distant. Sluggish.

Tyrell's fingers trembled as he worked the knot of the gag. When he tossed the cloth away, his hands settled against her cheeks. He had just killed two men without hesitation, but now, looking at her, fear was in his gaze. "Mia? Fates blast it, say something!"

Her throat was too ravaged for words, but she grasped his fingers with her bound hands and squeezed.

Tyrell ducked his head and muttered a string of fierce curses. When his gaze lifted, his eyes glittered with unshed tears. "I thought I'd lost you."

The world was in sharper focus now, and Mia felt flashes of pain as the bruises across her body made themselves known. Her heart thudded painfully against her ribs, and even breathing hurt.

Tyrell's fingers brushed over her abused throat, and his jaw clenched. He moved his focus to the binding on her wrists. He used a knife to cut her free, and then—still seated on the floor—he pulled her into his arms.

She leaned against him, curling into his chest for warmth and comfort. "Thank you," she breathed, her voice hoarse as she blinked back tears.

He only held her tighter.

"Is she all right?"

The familiar voice made her gut clench. She pushed back from Tyrell, just enough to see Fletcher. He stood in the flickering torchlight, his cheeks gaunt, his eyes shadowed. "You," she rasped.

Pain cut into his face. "I can explain."

Tyrell shoved to his feet, pulling Mia with him. One arm remained around her, keeping her protectively close to his side, as he faced Fletcher. "You will explain everything," the prince demanded of the old guard. "*Now.*"

"I can't," Fletcher said, misery coloring his words.

Tyrell stiffened. "The only reason you're not dead right now is because I want answers," he seethed. "You knew about the attack on Mia before it happened, but you waited to get me until it was underway. She could have been killed!"

"The key," Mia managed to say, her throat burning. "You gave—her the key."

Fletcher's face crumpled. "I'm sorry. I'm under strict orders not to speak of this."

"Whose orders?" Tyrell growled.

"The king's."

Mia blinked.

Tyrell seemed just as surprised. "What does my father have to do with any of this?"

"Everything," Fletcher said.

Tension spiraled between the two men.

Mia couldn't comprehend any of it. All she knew was that her lungs were growing tighter, and her breathing hitched and rasped.

Fletcher's eyes narrowed on her, concern lining his face. "Are you having a panic?"

Tyrell's arm tightened around her. "Mia?"

"I—I'm—fine." She wasn't. Her breath was coming in short pants, and all she could see were the bodies in the hallway.

Tyrell followed her gaze, then glared at Fletcher. "Don't try to run." Without warning, he swept Mia into his arms and marched into Grayson's room, leaving the corridor and bodies behind. "Where are your salts?" he asked her.

"Your—room."

Tyrell barked for one of the soldiers to fetch them. While the young man hurried off, Tyrell set Mia on the edge of the bed. He crouched before her, squeezing her hands in his. "You're safe. Just breathe."

She tried, but the panic already gripped her lungs in a ruthless vice. Her safe haven had been violated. She'd nearly been murdered. Fletcher had betrayed her. Tyrell had saved her—killed for her.

This night had been a nightmare, and it wasn't over.

Someone lit the lamp on Grayson's desk, flooding the room with light. It did nothing to dispel the shadows in Tyrell's eyes as he watched her struggle to breathe.

Near the door, Fletcher hovered. Mama was there as well, held in place by two guards.

Finally, the guard returned with her salts, and Tyrell snatched the jar from him. He twisted off the lid and held it under her nose.

The calming lavender scent loosened the tension in her chest.

Slowly, it steadied her breathing. Steadied *her*.

The panic gradually rolled away, leaving her exhausted but able to breathe. She nudged the salts away and Tyrell set the jar aside, his gaze intent. "Are you all right?"

"Yes." The word sounded mangled. Her throat ached from being crushed, and she wondered how long that would take to heal.

"Where are you hurt?" Tyrell asked, his voice stiff.

"I'm fine."

The skin around his eyes tightened at the sound of her ragged words, as did the grip on her shoulder. "I'll send for Devon."

She didn't have the voice to protest. She watched as yet another guard darted away for the physician, and then her eyes drifted to Fletcher, who still stood just inside Grayson's room, watching her.

Tyrell looked over his shoulder, pinning Fletcher with a look. "I want answers. *Now*."

The older man's throat bobbed as he swallowed. "You'll get them, Your Highness. The king is on his way."

CHAPTER 60

MIA

WHEN KING HENRI KAELIN STRODE INTO THE room, Mia's gut clenched. He was inarguably handsome, his jaw angular and his beard neatly trimmed. His hair was brown, but lined with silver—that was new. His eyes, however, were the same as she remembered; a horribly flat brown, until he smiled. Then they glinted with an evil light.

The last time Mia had seen him, she'd been eight years old and he'd ordered Grayson to burn her doll. She had not been able to stop shaking.

Now, years later, she still trembled at the sight of him.

Tyrell stood to face his father, though he remained near Mia. "What is the meaning of this?" His demand was softly spoken, but his tone didn't match.

King Henri glanced over his shoulder into the hall. "Fletcher, I believe I told you to make sure the traitors were kept alive, yet I see bodies."

"I killed them," Tyrell said, before Fletcher could open his mouth.

Henri looked to his son. "Didn't Fletcher pass along my orders when he fetched you?"

"He did."

The king lifted an eyebrow. "Then why are they dead?"

"My blade slipped."

"Right into their hearts?"

Tyrell's hands fisted at his sides. "Yes."

Henri's lips pursed. "I see." His eyes skipped over Mia and settled on Mama. "Bring her forward."

Mama whimpered as the soldiers dragged her before the king, their hold uncompromising as they forced her to kneel.

"You may speak," Henri said, his voice deceptively calm.

Mama's body shook. "Please, Sire, none of this was my plan. It was my husband."

"A man who is conveniently dead." The kneeling woman flinched, and Mia couldn't help but feel a stab of pity for her. Henri's dark eyes were hard as he viewed Mama. "I know about the message. Someone wrote you with the order to steal what is mine. Who are you working for?"

"I don't know!" Mama clasped her hands, tears thick in her voice. "Please, Your Majesty, you must believe me! My husband said someone approached him. I don't know who. Just that communication would come to us through the hawks and we would be asked to take the girl to Vyken in exchange for a fortune."

Tyrell's already tightly coiled body stiffened further.

Henri's tone was a shade darker than before. "Who asked you to do this?"

"I don't know," Mama said. "I never got a name."

"So your plan was to take my prisoner to Vyken and, what? Hope you happened to find the buyer?"

"I-I was desperate. Confused. I'm sorry!"

"You're only sorry you were caught." Henri glanced to Fletcher, who stood silently watching this exchange. "Fletcher noticed your frequent trips to the aerie. He knew you had no purpose there, so he was naturally curious. And then he discovered the message addressed to your husband—the order to take my prisoner away. Naturally, he brought it to me at once." Henri smiled a little at Mama, though the sharp edge stole any warmth. "I could have brought you in then, but I was curious. I wanted to see who else might be involved, and what the plan would be. I wanted confirmation of your treason."

Mama's fear was tangible—as was her desperation. "Please, I've told you all I know. My husband never trusted me with all the details. He made the arrangements!"

"I believe you." Henri tipped his head, and one of the soldiers lifted his sword. Tyrell slid in front of Mia, blocking her view.

She still heard Mama's scream. Heard the horrible slice of the blade as it cut into her body and tore back out. Her last rattling breath as she slumped to the floor.

"Clear out this mess," Henri ordered.

Mama's body was dragged away, and Mia put a hand over her mouth, her gut twisting.

Tyrell was horribly stiff, his focus on his father. "You knew there was a possible threat against her, and you didn't tell me?"

"As I said, I was curious how things would play out. I knew their plan was to abduct her, not kill her. She wasn't in any real danger."

Tyrell's mind was clearly racing. "So when Fletcher brought you the note, you made him put it back."

Henri dipped his head. "I needed the traitor to act, so it was the only due course."

"Fletcher gave that woman the key to this room?" Tyrell asked, his words edged.

"No," the king said. "I simply had him start the rumor that he had a key, and where he kept it. The servants gossiping took care of the rest. We didn't know when the strike would happen, but when Fletcher realized the woman had stolen the key, we knew it would be tonight. He alerted me, and then he hung back—as ordered. He went to you when the time was right."

Mia peeked around Tyrell, finding Fletcher. The old man darted her a look, apology in his gaze.

"Fletcher," Henri said, stealing the man's attention. "You no longer need to monitor the hawks. Now that I know the aerie master has no stake in this, I'll have him look for any additional messages addressed to the girl's former caretakers. It seems that's our only lead at this time." His eyes slid to Mia, and it was the first time he'd looked directly at her.

Meeting his stare was the most terrifying thing she had ever done, but she did not let herself look away.

The corner of his mouth lifted, and a chill raked her. "I would like to speak with the girl, now. Alone."

Everyone moved obediently for the door—except Tyrell.

Henri eyed his son. "You will wait in the hall, or I'll ensure you never step foot in the same room as her again."

Tyrell's shoulders went rigid, but he didn't budge.

Mia touched his nearest hand, her voice a low murmur. "Go."

He shot her a look over his shoulder, and his gaze was intense. But—finally—he moved for the door.

As he passed his father, they shared a look, and though Mia didn't understand the unspoken message, her stomach knotted.

The door closed, and Mia slowly stood. She refused to sit in King Henri's presence. But she was grateful for the space that remained between them. Hopefully, it would hide the fact that her knees trembled beneath her nightgown.

The king's head tilted to the side as he studied her, and she wished she was at least fully dressed. It was hard to feel any amount of strength while barefoot.

"You've grown," he finally said. "I hadn't realized how much, even when I saw you lying in Tyrell's bed."

She knew he referred to a visit after Papa had attacked her. She had been unconscious at the time, but she thought she'd heard him speak.

She didn't respond to his words, just waited. Somehow her spine remained straight, despite the fear swirling inside her.

"You were such a small thing when you first arrived." Henri stepped toward the desk, and her heart lurched as he fingered the edge of the book of maps. She prayed he wouldn't lift the cover and guess what she planned. "I'm not sure if you remember," he said. "You were so young."

Her chin lifted slightly. Her choked throat hurt, and her words came out weak and scratchy as she said, "I remember."

She had been hauled into the throne room. Flickering torches offered the only light, because it was the middle of the night. The vaulted room had many shadows, but it was easy to see the space was nearly deserted. A handful of guards stood near the throne, and all of Mia's weariness vanished when she spotted the large man seated on the throne.

"Help!" she'd cried out, instantly turning to the powerful man for aid. He had a crown, like her father. Surely he could save her from the bad men who refused to take her home. She yanked against the rough hands that held her. "You must help me!" she begged the man on the throne. "Please!"

She was close enough now to see his mouth quirk. "My Mortisian isn't very good," he said in the trade language, addressing the men who held her. "But she sounds quite desperate."

"She's a brat," one of the sailors behind her said. "But a royal one."

"Have you any proof?" the king asked.

The man holding Mia gave her seven-year-old body a shake. "Tell King Henri your name," he ordered in Mortisian.

Mia blinked away tears, the salty taste reminding her of the sea that had tried to swallow her. Her dress was torn and her hair disheveled, but she craned her neck, staring up at the king who towered above her on his throne. "I am Meerah Jemma Cassian, and you must help me. My father will be so worried!"

"Oh, I'm sure." Henri focused back on the men. "I hope you realize I'll require a little more proof than that. You could have taught any waif to tell me a name and shed pretty tears."

One of the men stepped forward, a bit of cloth wadded in his fist. He handed it to a guard, who in turn passed it over to Henri.

Mia's gut churned as she saw him unfurl the royal standard. It had flown proudly on the ship, and it had snared on part of the wreckage Mia had clung to as she awaited rescue.

King Henri had smiled at Mia then, and a shiver slid down her spine.

His voice now brought Mia back to this moment, standing in

Grayson's bedroom. "You were such an outspoken thing. You demanded that I deliver you home. You promised that your father would pay any price. Do you remember?"

Mia said nothing, only stared at him and fought the memories that threatened to overwhelm her. The way her heart had hammered that night. The screams that had torn her throat as she'd been thrown into a dark cell. The tears that had choked her as she'd cried for her father to save her.

Henri turned his back on the book of maps, his gaze thoughtful as he studied her. "Of course, that changed. Within a year of your imprisonment, I barely recognized you anymore. The outspoken little girl was gone. Of course, when Grayson burned that filthy doll he'd made for you, I recognized you when you screamed and begged."

Revulsion and something startlingly like hatred rushed through her, making her fists clench. "What do you want?" she rasped, forcing the words through her raw throat.

Henri smiled a little. "I suppose I'm just delighting in your transformation. You've become beautiful. Perhaps that's why Tyrell and Grayson are so bewitched by you. I must say, that has worked in favor of my plan for you."

She ground her teeth. "What plan? All you did was hide me away for years."

Henri folded his arms across his wide chest. "You know, the way Grayson has always shielded you, I was under the impression that you were weak."

She forced a grim smile, though it was small and tight. "You didn't answer my question."

His mouth twisted. "No, I didn't."

The hairs on the back of her neck lifted, but she struggled to ignore that. "You couldn't have planned for Grayson and me to meet."

"True," the king allowed. "That was a happy accident."

"Why did you lie to him, then? Why did you tell him I was here solely to motivate him?"

"It kept him in his place." Henri's head tipped to the side. "And I'm not the only one who's lied to him, am I?"

Mia didn't answer, because he was right. All these years, and not once had she told him the truth.

But Meerah Jemma Cassian didn't exist anymore. Not really. She'd been broken, one beating at a time, until only Mia remained.

Letting go of the past, losing herself—it was the only way she'd survived.

Henri reclined against the desk, his arms still crossed. "Grayson was weak before he met you. I allowed his attachment because, finally, he was trying to please me. You were a crutch I thought he would outgrow. Instead, he only seemed to need you more." His head tilted to the side, and his eyes seemed to absorb her. "I should thank you. Grayson would never have reached his full potential without you. You made him the ultimate killer—the perfect weapon."

The pang in Mia's chest hurt more than she would ever let this man see. She fought to keep her expression hard, though she thought he must have seen some cracks, because amusement crossed his face.

He shook his head. "I have studied manipulation all my life, but you . . . you have a gift. The way you've bent Grayson to your will astounds me. And now you've done it to Tyrell." He chuckled. "I sent him to you, knowing that—once Grayson returned—he would be tortured with the idea of all those hours you two would have spent alone. Imagine my surprise when Tyrell began to change in his attitude toward you. I didn't realize the full force of his infatuation until he killed your caretaker and asked me to allow you to remain in the upper castle. That he would tie his fate to yours?" Henri clapped slowly, his gaze glowing in the orange lamplight. "I'm impressed with your skill. It seems you and I have more in common than I thought."

"I'm nothing like you," she cracked out.

"But aren't you?" His gaze grew more serious. "Tyrell has not defied me in years, and yet he wouldn't have left this room if you hadn't given the order. You have captured two fine warriors, girl. What will you do with them? Order them to kill me?"

"I would never use them as you do."

"Believe that if you'd like."

Mia's eyes narrowed. "Why did you grant Tyrell's request? What do you have to gain by letting me out of my cell?"

Henri paced away from her. "Do you know why I've always pitted my sons against each other? It gives them less time to think about turning on me. Grayson and Tyrell have always been particularly fierce rivals. I must admit, it amuses me that they both want you."

"This was about more than just your amusement."

"True. It will be good for Grayson to doubt his standing with me. He'll wonder why I granted Tyrell's request for your freedom so easily. Perhaps it will keep Grayson from foolish threats in the future." He rubbed at his throat, and the action seemed unconscious. "It's also beneficial for him to doubt himself—and you." He eyed her. "Yes, this will serve me well in the next stage of my plan."

"Which is?"

He eased out a smile. "You have become so much more than I ever thought possible. You will bring about the fall of Mortise, and Grayson and Tyrell will never fight harder for me, because only one of them will be able to win the prize. With how ensnared Tyrell is now . . ." His chin dipped, the shadows altering menacingly on his face. "I think Grayson may have to learn to operate without his crutch."

With that, the king of Ryden strode from the room, leaving Mia standing there with ice in her veins and a tremor in her heart.

<hr />

"I'm sorry," Fletcher said quietly.

The old guard had returned to the room after King Henri had left. Tyrell, Devon, and Rena had entered with him.

Tyrell glared at the guard, speaking before Mia could. "Why didn't you come to me with that message from the hawk?"

The old man's shoulders tensed at the prince's brittle tone. "I thought the king could do more to protect Mia. And once I was sworn to secrecy, I couldn't risk betraying him." His eyes darted to Rena, who sat beside Mia on the edge of Grayson's bed. The older woman's arm was wrapped comfortingly around Mia's shoulders.

Devon had finished his inspection of her, and though she had bruising around her throat, he said the damage would heal in time. Tyrell had looked over the man's shoulder the whole time, his stance rigid.

Fletcher looked utterly miserable as he looked to Mia now. "I'm so sorry."

Mia shook her head. "You did what you had to do. And you did protect me. You brought Tyrell."

Fletcher didn't look fully convinced.

Tyrell looked furious. "You're dismissed from her service. You and your wife."

"No," Mia said. Her voice was raw, but she spoke as strongly as she could. "I don't want Fletcher or Rena to leave."

Tyrell's features tightened, but he didn't argue. Standing in Grayson's room with his white shirt untucked and his hair disheveled, he looked younger than he ever had. For the first time, Mia noticed that his feet were bare. "Do you want to stay here?" he asked her.

Please come back with me. Those were the words he didn't say, but they were clear in his eyes.

"I want to stay here," she said quietly.

His throat flexed as he swallowed hard. His voice came out rougher than before. "I'll remain outside your door tonight. No one will touch you."

"You don't have to—"

"Trust me, I do." His heavy tone brooked no argument.

Rena offered to stay the night with Mia, but she declined the offer. After everything that had happened tonight, and her conversation with the king, she wanted to be alone.

Devon left one of his lavender candles with her, and a promise that he would return in the morning. Fletcher and Rena left hand in hand, and then Mia was alone with Tyrell.

In the silence, he asked stiffly, "Did my father hurt you?"

"No." Not entirely the truth, but Henri had never laid a hand on her.

Tyrell's eyes narrowed, but he didn't press. "Is there anything you need?"

"No. But you really don't need to guard me."

"This is my fault."

Her brow furrowed. "How is this your fault?"

"If I hadn't destroyed your trust, you would have been in my room. No one would have dared attempt this."

She shook her head. "You don't know that."

His eyes shadowed. "If I'd sent that blasted letter, you wouldn't have left. I know that, Mia—we both do." His jaw set, and he took a step back. "I'll be outside if you need anything."

There was a lump in her burning throat as she watched him go, but she did not call him back.

CHAPTER 61

DESFAN

DESFAN SAT IN THE SAND, HIS KNEES PULLED UP to his chest as he stared across the rippling blue-green sea. Sunset glowed in the distance, painting the sky in dusky pink, purple, and orange. Karim had remained at the foot of the trail to keep everyone away from the private stretch of beach.

This was the first moment of privacy Desfan had stolen in three weeks. He'd been in meetings for much of that time, of course, and there were feasts, conversations, and interrogations to be conducted. So far, he hadn't been able to determine who'd hired Salim; all of the arrested council members had been questioned, but no one was volunteering anything. Kiv Arcas was conducting a search through their records and correspondence, but that would take months.

And in the midst of all the demands being made of Desfan as he prepared to take the throne, he found his thoughts drifting. Days and events had blurred since his father's death, though he remembered that same fog of disbelief after his mother and sisters had died.

But Meerah is alive.

The truth slammed into him all over again. He didn't know if the shock would ever stop rocking him. His sister was *alive*.

When he'd stood beside the pyre and watched the serjan's wrapped body burn, he had made his father a promise he would bleed to keep.

When I have her back, I'll never let her go. I won't let her be hurt. Never again.

The smoke from the pyre had spiraled higher, before being dragged on a current of air toward the sea.

I'm sorry I wasn't a better son. I swear, I will be better.

He knew he would never be as loved by the people as his father had been. But he would do everything in his power to hold Mortise together. To protect his country from every enemy, within and without.

Not for the first time, his thoughts strayed to Grayson. It terrified him that he was relying on an enemy for something so vital and precious as saving his sister. But his instincts screamed that Grayson truly would do anything for Mia. Even if his devotion sparked rage and disgust in Desfan, he knew Grayson would protect her. It was the one reassurance he had in all this chaos.

Arms locked around his drawn up legs, Desfan eyed the frothy waves that rushed up the beach.

How many picnics had the Cassians enjoyed on this stretch of sand? How many times had his sisters tackled him, tickling him until he begged for mercy? It was here that he'd tried to teach Mia to swim. He'd stood in the swelling waves, gripping her hips as she struggled to stay afloat. It was here that Tally had confided her fear of spiders; she'd pleaded with him to stop teasing her with them, and he had swiftly agreed. This was where he'd taken his first steps, according to his mother. And it was here that he had collapsed, weeping, after the combined memorial for his mother and sisters. His father had found him, sat beside him, and stroked a hand over Desfan's shaking back. They'd said nothing, only suffered their own hurt silently together.

Desfan bowed his head, the wind tugging through his curly hair and weaving the salty scent of the sea through the air. A question had been spiraling through his mind the past couple of days, but for the first time, he had a moment to actually explore it.

What if Meerah hated him?

She had plenty to blame him for. For not finding her sooner. For not looking hard enough. For giving up. For leaving their father to bear the weight of ruling alone, until it had killed him. What if she didn't want anything to do with him?

"May I join you?"

Desfan's head lifted, and he saw Imara approach. Her dress was a calming mix of deep blue and ivory, and her skirt billowed in the breeze. She gave him a gentle smile, and the sight of it quickened the beats of his heart. He wasn't sure how she'd convinced Karim to let her pass, but then, he rather doubted anyone could resist such a force as Imara Buhari.

She stood beside him, waiting for an answer. He cleared his throat. "Yes, of course."

Her brown eyes softened and she settled next to him in the sand, brushing her long skirt down before wrapping her arms around her knees, mimicking his posture. "I've been looking all over for you. I wanted to know how you're doing."

Her kindness was not a surprise. Desfan clearly remembered how she'd stood beside him in the ballroom when Yahri had told him about his father's death.

Shock had held him immobile. Stolen his breath, his thoughts.

Imara's hand had wrapped around his. "Would you like me to come with you?" she'd asked softly. "To see his body?"

Music swirled around them, laughter and conversation booming. He was in the middle of a celebration, and he needed to go see his father's body. How did that make sense?

Imara squeezed his fingers. "Should I come with you?" she asked again. "Or I can find Serene, if you'd prefer to have her with you."

"No." Desfan cleared his throat—forced himself to think. "No, that won't be necessary. You should stay here. I don't want to cause a scene." He wasn't sure why that seemed important. No one was looking at him. No one knew what had just happened.

Imara had nodded, but the worry in her eyes, the pain . . . it had followed him out of that room.

Sitting on the beach now, Imara eyed him. "Things have been so busy, we haven't had a moment to talk."

That was true. The palace had been chaotic since the serjan's death. The massacre at the treaty signing had left Desfan scrambling to assuage grief in those who had lost loved ones, as well as fighting his own fury to better calm the members of his court who howled for vengeance. Learning the truth about Meerah, and sending Grayson after her. And then of course there had been his father's pyre and memorial to arrange, and the feasts of mourning, as well as the feasts of celebration. It was hard to believe he would be crowned serjan in one week.

"I'm fine," Desfan said.

Imara said nothing for a moment. Then, "I ran into Razan Krayt on my way here. I like her."

He almost smiled. "So do I."

"Karim doesn't."

"He likes her too well, actually."

"Ah." The corner of Imara's mouth lifted. "Well, that explains some things. Anyway, Razan was in a conversation with Ser Sifa."

"Is he still demanding the heads of Liam and Grayson?"

"Yes."

Desfan hadn't told anyone outside of Imara, Serene, and Yahri that he had sent Grayson to Ryden. As far as anyone else in Duvan knew, both Rydenic princes were securely imprisoned. Desfan had no doubt it would create serious fractures within the council, once the truth came out. But he and Yahri agreed that the secrecy would keep Meerah safer, so fates rot everyone else.

Imara shifted her weight. "I should probably apologize."

Desfan arched a dark brow. "For what?"

"Well, while I was looking for you, I checked your father's memorial."

There would be many memorials for the serjah that artists would take years to create, but Desfan knew the one she meant. A simple stone marker in the Cassian mausoleum. It sat beside a marker for Seraijan Farah Cassian, as well as one for Tahlyah and one for Meerah.

He would need to have Meerah's removed, once she returned. That was an arrangement he would be happy to take care of.

"There was quite a large crowd of nobles gathered," Imara continued. "I told them to leave."

He blinked. "You did?"

"Yes. That memorial is for you, not them. If you wanted to be there, I didn't want you having to fight a crowd."

"Thank you," he said, a little stunned by her thoughtfulness.

She winced a little. "Perhaps don't thank me. I may have insulted them a bit."

A short laugh escaped him. "Frankly, I would have enjoyed seeing that."

"Well," she smiled, "it's probably best you weren't there. This way you can pat their hands in sympathy when they tell you how rude that Zennorian princess is."

"I'm sure you had more grace than I did when I came back to be regent."

"I doubt that. I was quite *ungracious*."

Desfan chuckled. "Well, at least your behavior was deliberate. I had no idea why I received so many wide-eyed looks every time I opened my mouth. I'd just come back from sea, so I supposed I talked louder than I needed to, but still. I was confused. Finally, Yahri pulled me aside and told me I needed to stop swearing so much."

Amusement sparked in her eyes. "The nobles didn't appreciate your sailor's vocabulary?"

"It *was* quite extensive."

She giggled. "It's a pity Yahri wasn't impressed."

"Oh, she was impressed. Just also appalled."

Imara watched him with a small smile. "You miss sailing."

"I do."

"Perhaps when things settle, you can take a trip. Visit one of the islands."

He nodded, even as he wondered if things would ever settle.

Imara nudged his shoulder with her own. "Is there anything

in particular you're thinking about out here?"

"Meerah." The answer slid out of him, no thought to try and shield the vulnerability in his voice. The fear.

Imara pursed her lips. "Grayson will bring her back. It's obvious how much he cares for her. And for you."

His brow furrowed. "Our friendship wasn't real."

"You're wrong." He glanced at her and she lifted her eyebrows. "Well, you are. And I think you know it. Liam was a fake—Grayson was sincere."

Stated so directly, he couldn't deny she was right. Every smile Liam had given Desfan—every word he'd said—had been layered. Grayson's eyes grew shuttered sometimes, and his expression was often guarded, but when Desfan thought of the moments they'd spent sparring or talking, he knew Grayson had been genuine.

"Everything he did, he did to protect Meerah," Imara reminded him gently.

"I know. I'm just having a hard time forgiving him."

Imara laid her cheek against her bent knees and stared at his profile. "May I be blunt?"

"Are you ever anything else?"

She snorted. "My parents certainly tried to keep me perfectly princess-like, but I'm not Serene."

"No." She certainly was not. His eyes caught a tendril of dark hair teasing her cheek. His fingers itched to swipe it back.

Imara's smile slowly faded, her expression growing serious. "Is it possible you keep blaming Grayson because you've spent so long blaming yourself?"

His skin prickled. Fates, it was like she'd picked through his thoughts—knew exactly what he'd been thinking before she arrived.

Imara lifted her head. "I think you've been blaming yourself for a lot of things, for a very long time. Irrationally, of course. It probably feels like a relief having someone else to blame."

His eyes traced the side of her face—the swell of her round cheek, the soft curve of her jaw, the loose strands of black hair glancing off her chin. Her full lips.

He tore his gaze away. "I don't know. Maybe."

The ebb and flow of the waves rushed and faded, filling the silence as the sun slowly disappeared from view.

"After everything that happened to your family, weren't you afraid to sail?" Imara asked suddenly, her voice soft.

"Yes," he admitted. "Terrified, actually. But I grew to love it."

"So you've always been brave, then." Her eyes grew distant. "When I was seven or eight, a couple of my sisters and I thought it would be amusing for me to hide in a small cupboard so I could jump out and scare the maids. We snuck out after we'd already been tucked into bed, and I waited in the cupboard while they left to get the maids. But no one came. I began to panic. I was alone in the dark and cramped space, and there was no handle. I couldn't get out. I screamed for help, but no one heard me. They'd gone to bed already. I was in there all night, petrified. I kept hearing things. Ghosts, I thought. I could hardly breathe. My sisters forgot all about me, not remembering until I was late to breakfast." She peeked at Desfan, her mouth curving. "I know this isn't anything like what you've been through. But I've been terrified of small places and the dark ever since. You were just a child when you suffered so much, but you faced your fears. You even found peace and meaning on the sea that had stolen so much from you. That's the sort of bravery that will make you a good monarch. A *great* monarch."

That thread of hair was teasing her cheek again. Desfan moved without thinking, brushing it back with his fingertips and folding it around her ear. His knuckles skimmed the warm skin of her jaw before he dropped his hand. Their gazes locked, but only for a moment. Imara was quick to glance away.

Desfan let his tingling hand press into the warm and grainy sand between them. He cleared his throat. "You make me sound far too good. My father sent me to the sea because I was out of control. I'd abandoned my responsibilities."

"You've embraced them now," Imara pointed out.

"I wouldn't say *embraced.*"

She flashed a smile. "Still. I'm proud of you, and I know your family would be, too."

He rubbed the back of his neck. "I disappointed my father in so many ways. If I'd been home these past years, maybe he wouldn't have been in such poor health. Perhaps he wouldn't have been so overwhelmed by the rumors about Meerah."

Imara's hand curved over his knee, halting his breath. "Every single person can look backwards and ask *what if* or *maybe,* but those questions don't do any good in the past. They belong in the future, where they can actually shape our lives and do more than needlessly torment us."

His eyes slid over her face, his heart skittering in his chest. He was hyper-aware of where she touched him. "Serene may be considered an impressive diplomat, but you are a sage."

Imara chuckled, retracting her hand. "Hopefully not an old ugly one."

Desfan's stupid heart was still skipping. "Definitely not."

"That's a relief." She shifted beside him, momentarily leaning closer as she tucked her legs beside her. He caught the scent of her hair—warm and soft, with an edge of spice—and then she pulled back, tossing him a smile.

Distantly, he realized his knuckles still tingled from touching her a minute ago.

"You really will make a good serjan, Desfan." A new emotion entered her eyes, somewhat dimming the light in her gaze. "Serene is very lucky. And you are, too. Once she's more integrated in your court, she'll help you keep those nobles in line."

"Like you did today?" He shouldn't have said the words. They made him sound oddly desperate.

"She'll do a much better job. Your people will come to respect her. Love her. Just as you will." Her throat constricted as she swallowed, her eyes on the sea.

Desfan said nothing, and the moment to speak passed. Imara asked him about Meerah, what she had been like as a child, and he answered her questions.

Time passed, and even though Desfan and Imara never moved closer together, they did not shift even a breath apart.

CHAPTER 62

GRAYSON

GRAYSON BELTED ON HIS KNIVES AND SLID one small blade into each boot. He strapped his sword to his back, cinching the harness over one shoulder and around his chest, hilt angled over the left shoulder for easy access. He finally felt like himself, the familiar weight of weapons settling him.

Once he had his basic weapons in place, he flipped the clasps of the box waiting on the table. The poisoned daggers were pristine, with glinting steel blades and matching blue hilts, padded carefully in dark velvet. Grayson lifted them and wrapped them in leather, placing them—and the vial of accompanying poison—in his pack. Then he turned to face the open door of Zadir's cabin.

Captain Zadir blocked the exit, his arms folded over his chest, his black beard obscuring his expression. "You look quite menacing, Spewer. Just like the adventure tales; a one-man army intent on invading a fates-cursed castle to rescue a stolen seraijah."

The corner of Grayson's mouth twitched. "I'm not exactly a heroic knight in armor."

"No," Zadir agreed. "More like a nightmarish assassin. But that's just fine. Your father deserves a good nightmare." The pirate straightened. "Well, I suppose this is goodbye."

"I'll see you in Porynth," Grayson said, shouldering his pack.

"If you survive."

"I will."

Zadir smiled. "Your optimism is admirable. In four weeks, then, we'll meet at Porynth."

Grayson tightened his grip on the bag. "I may need longer than that."

"You said you could travel fast."

"I can get to Lenzen in ten days, but I won't be able to move as quickly with Mia." After years of imprisonment, she wouldn't have the stamina necessary for a cutting dash across Ryden. They wouldn't make good time, and they would be fugitives. That was why they couldn't ride back here, to Vyken—the road was too public.

"I won't wait forever in port for a dead man," Zadir told him, not unkindly. "We agreed on four weeks."

"Desfan's paying you enough to stay at least five."

The pirate nodded. "Fair point. For Cassian's sake, I'll give you five weeks."

Grayson hoped it would be enough. If he and Mia arrived too late, they could very well find themselves trapped against the sea, with Henri's soldiers at their backs.

As he left the ship, no one said a word. He hadn't expected farewells, though. Only a few crew members seemed to pay him any sort of attention: Swallow, the sailmaster, who critiqued his stitching; Weeper, who sneered a lot and tried to goad Grayson into another fight; and Gale, who did not speak to Grayson at all, merely glared from his near-constant spot in Grayson's periphery.

If Grayson made it back to the *Seafire*, he might have to worry about the enemies he'd made. Though, if Weeper and Gale were the only enemies he had to deal with in the future, he'd call himself fates-blessed.

Grayson left the harbor and demanded a horse at the first military outpost he found in the city. Once he was recognized as the Black Hand, soldiers leaped to assist him. They looked quite relieved when Grayson turned down the offer of an escort to Lenzen.

Traveling with anyone else would only slow him down.

He rode hard, galloping across the distance to the next town, and then the next. At each outpost he demanded a fresh horse. He pushed himself and the animals past the point of endurance, stopping to rest only when his pace started to lag or he began swaying in the saddle. He snatched a couple hours of sleep when his body demanded it, and then he was on his way again. His relentless pace devoured the leagues between him and Mia, though nowhere near fast enough.

I'm coming, Mia. I'm coming.

Lenzen sprawled over the northern hills of Ryden, the largest city in the kingdom. The trees in the surrounding mountains had begun to turn orange, yellow, and red, the crisp air hailing the quick change of seasons. In the cold north of Ryden, fall never lasted long.

Grayson's heart thudded in his chest. He had left Lenzen over three months ago. Every day he'd been away, he'd longed to be back with Mia. And now, finally, the castle was in sight. The solidly-built keep towered over the city, seated on top of a tall hill. Built of dark stone harvested from the northern mountains, the castle was a menacing fortress.

Fates willing, this would be the last time he'd ever have to return here.

He nudged his horse forward, riding quickly through the city. People crowded the streets, though they were quick to dodge away from him the moment they recognized him. With every recoil, Grayson felt his mask slipping more firmly into place.

He rode through the castle gate and stopped before the solid front doors. He dropped from the saddle and tossed the reins to a soldier who had hurried forward. Then he strode up the castle steps and shoved inside.

The pull to veer left and seek out the dungeons was nearly irresistible, but when a guard informed Grayson that his family was at a private dinner, he knew that was where he needed to go first. Mia would have to wait a little longer.

The dining room was small and undecorated, except for the Kaelin standard on the wall—an emerald banner with two black serpents twisted around a longsword, poised to strike with venomous fangs over the hilt. Several torches guttered in brackets along the wall and three iron-cast candelabras were centered on the long wooden table, illuminating the faces of Grayson's family.

King Henri sat at the head of the table, his eyes full of surprise at Grayson's unannounced entrance. Peter sat on his right, frowning deeply. Iris was on the king's left, her delicate eyebrows arched. Carter sat beside the queen, hurriedly swallowing his mouthful of potatoes. Tyrell stared at him, his face inscrutable, but his shoulders tense.

Dinners with all of them present were rare; usually they were called by Henri or Iris, if either of them had a report to share or orders to give. As it was the end of summer, Grayson wondered if it was due to his mother's annual trip to Rew. She would have recently returned.

Grayson stopped at the foot of the table.

Henri's eyes flicked to the open door. "Leave us," he ordered the lingering guard. The door thumped shut and the king focused on Grayson. "Where is Liam?"

"Dead."

Silence.

Grayson dared a glance at his mother.

She was smiling thinly, a wineglass in hand, her eyes shining in the candlelight.

Henri's face darkened as he stared at Grayson. His jaw audibly cracked. "Explain."

Grayson did, following the plan he'd made with Desfan. He told Henri that Liam had decided to betray Ryden and unite the three kingdoms against the Kaelins. How Grayson had tried every argument, but Liam would not be swayed. How Liam had taken matters into his own hands at the treaty signing and been stabbed by a Mortisian guard. How Grayson had been unable to complete his mission of killing Serene, due to Liam's treason.

He had briefly considered telling his father that he'd assassinated Serene, just to avoid some of the king's rage, but Grayson couldn't afford to be caught in a lie.

His father's face grew tighter with every word Grayson spoke. When he finished, the king's voice was thin and sharp. "So, you failed me utterly."

"I returned to Lenzen with all haste to tell you what happened," Grayson said, striving to keep his tone even. "Liam betrayed you. You shouldn't mourn his death."

Henri's eyes flashed. "He was a valuable asset. No one else knows all of his contacts. The network of information he established has been lost to us. Traitor or not, you should have brought him back."

"He got himself killed," Grayson argued. "My priority was returning to you."

"And yet you did nothing that I asked!" The king's fist hit the table, rattling dishes. His face was twisted in a snarl. "Liam is dead, the princess of Devendra still breathes, and there is no war between Devendra and Mortise!"

Grayson tensed at his father's fury, but he didn't let any emotion cross his face. He'd known Henri would be livid, and he could take any abuse leveled at him.

Fates knew he was used to it.

"Why did Liam seek to betray me?" Henri demanded. "What were his reasons?"

"He said he didn't want to be ruled by you any longer."

Henri shoved back from the table, the chair legs grating loudly against the stone floor as he stood.

Grayson's heart skidded in his chest. Perhaps he should have given Henri another reason for Liam's treason. Something that wouldn't sound quite so defiant.

Or perhaps he should have marked his tone.

The other Kaelins watched in silence as Henri rounded the table, his gait measured as he moved toward Grayson. He didn't stop until they were eye-to-eye, their boots almost touching.

Grayson's spine was stiff, his lungs tight as he met his father's gaze. He refused to step back.

Fury vibrated his father's frame. "I could *kill* you," he hissed. "For your cowardice in fleeing while your brother died. For your weakness in failing to kill a single princess. I could gut you where you stand for failing me."

Grayson's eyes narrowed. "We both know you won't." He couldn't afford to lose two sons.

Henri's nostrils flared. "You dare speak to me like that?"

He clamped down his anger, his resistance—forced himself to take a breath. Now was not the time to challenge his father. "What's done is done," he finally said. "You need to make a new plan."

"This plan was perfect," Henri snapped. "You ruined it!"

"Liam ruined it," he countered. "You underestimated your son. You need to decide what you're going to—"

Henri snatched the knife beside Carter's plate and slashed for Grayson's face.

The attack was unexpected from his usually calculating father, but the shock barely registered as instinct kicked in.

Grayson jerked back, even as he snatched his father's wrist. He was stronger than Henri, but the king was standing too close— the blade missed his eye and cheek, but cut into his jaw. The knife hit bone, jolting Grayson with agony. He hissed, wrenching his head aside, but the motion only dragged more of his jaw against the blade.

Strangling Henri's wrist, he thrust his hand away, forcing the king back a step. He tightened his hold on his father, a fierce jab of his thumb forcing Henri's fingers to snap open. The knife dropped with a clatter against the stone floor, the reverberations ringing through the silent dining hall.

Grayson's free hand flashed to the dagger at his belt as he glared at his father, his eyes burning with pain and fury, every instinct screaming to draw his knife. To retaliate. To kill.

Henri's eyes widened. The rage that had overtaken him was still in evidence in the harsh lines carved on his face, but the anger was frozen as he stared at Grayson. Fear flickered in his gaze, and Grayson relished that show of weakness—that flash of terror. Knowing he had put it there filled him with a pleasure that should probably disturb him.

His heart pounded, adrenaline sparking every nerve. Fiery pain scorched his jaw, and droplets of blood rolled down the side of his neck. His hand clenched painfully tight around the hilt of his belted knife.

It would be so easy to kill his father. Henri was a skilled fighter, but he was no match for the Black Hand. He had brutally forced Grayson to become the most lethal weapon in Eyrinthia, and there was a certain kind of justice in the fact that Grayson could be the one to end him. Here. Now.

His eyes were on Henri, but he was aware of the rest of his family. His brothers stood around the table, their hands on their knives. If Grayson drew his blade, they would attack—they might even succeed in killing him, but not before Henri was bleeding out on the floor. His mother remained in her seat, watching raptly. In her alert gray eyes, Grayson caught a gleam of curious fascination.

Grayson had frozen the entire room with one move. His family was trapped in this moment as they waited to see what he would do next.

Every torture Henri had ever inflicted on Grayson ran through his mind. Most had been indirect—orders Henri had given, the pain administered by others. But every agonizing second of his life could be traced back to this man. The one who had sired him. The one who had taken Grayson and broken him—*ruined* him— so he could mold him into *this*. A heartless weapon.

Every threat he had ever leveled at Mia—every pain he had inflicted upon her—Grayson felt them all in this moment, and he craved his father's death with an intensity that staggered him.

But if he killed Henri now, he would die. One of his brothers would kill him, or call for the guards to do it. He would never see Mia again. He wouldn't escape Ryden with her. He wouldn't return her home, to Desfan.

Eyes locked on his father, Grayson slowly—deliberately— released his knife without drawing it. He uncurled his grip on Henri's wrist one finger at a time and forced his hand to drop. Forced his chin to lower. He ignored the blood still running from his throbbing jaw as he looked directly into his father's eyes and repeated the words he'd spoken before. "You underestimated your son. What are you going to do now?"

Henri's chest rose and fell, his hands fisted at his sides. The underlying challenge in Grayson's words was something the king could answer, or ignore.

Tension strangled the air in the room.

Then Henri took a step back—the first retreat Grayson had ever seen his father make. The hatred that flashed in his eyes was not unexpected.

The king pivoted on his heel, striding toward the double doors at the back of the room. "Peter," he barked. "My study—now.

620

Tyrell and Carter, take Grayson to a cell."

Peter shot Grayson a look, openly unsettled as he followed Henri.

Iris slowly rose from her chair and trailed after them. Grayson didn't know if she would prove to be an ally or not, even though she assumed he'd killed Liam for her. His mother was nearly impossible to predict.

Tyrell and Carter stepped forward, and the wariness on their faces gave Grayson some measure of satisfaction. He kept his expression carefully blank as he tried to ignore the aching cut that stretched over his jaw and the blood seeping beneath his collar.

He didn't give them any reason to touch him—he led the way from the room.

CHAPTER 63

GRAYSON

TYRELL AND CARTER ESCORTED GRAYSON to one of the rooms in the upper prison, usually reserved for torture so Henri didn't have to deal with too many stairs to witness the cruelty. A prison guard set a flickering torch into a bracket on the wall, revealing the nearly empty space. There was a bucket in one corner, and a pile of chains in the other.

The slice along Grayson's jaw throbbed, but the blood was already drying, leaving itchy paths to curve down the right side of his neck.

They took his weapons—even the hidden ones—and then Carter moved for the door. When he noticed that Tyrell lingered in the cell, he hesitated. "Aren't you coming?"

"In a moment," Tyrell said, his eyes on Grayson.

Carter frowned. "I don't think Father wants us to speak to him."

"I won't be long." Tyrell sent Carter a look. "Go."

Carter bristled. He was older, but weaker—at least physically. Grayson viewed his second eldest brother as a poisonous snake; no one would see him in the shadows until he struck, and by then the venom would already be delivering death.

Carter wasn't one to fight head-on, though, so he marched out of the cell, and Tyrell closed the door.

Grayson's fingers twitched at his sides. He wished he had his weapons as he faced his older brother. There was only a year between them, which had probably made their rivalry all the more intense. Henri had always forced them to attack each other, and sometimes it felt like fate itself had decreed them to be enemies.

The low snap of the torch was the only sound in the cell.

Fates, he needed to see her. He needed to know she'd survived whatever threat Liam's hawk would have brought.

His desperation made it slightly easier to ask Tyrell—one of the only people in the castle who knew she existed—the question he burned to know. "How is she?" He tried to ignore how the cut along his jaw dragged at his mouth, making each word sound heavier.

Tyrell's face tightened, making it clear he knew exactly who Grayson meant. He had tortured her on Henri's orders, and since Grayson had beaten him into unconsciousness in retaliation, Tyrell couldn't have forgotten her. "She's well enough," he finally said. "For now."

Grayson's eyes narrowed. "You're threatening her?"

His dark eyebrows pulled together. "No, but Father will punish her because of you. You lost him his spymaster, and you failed to kill Serene. You all but attacked him just now. He could kill

Mia, he's so furious."

Grayson's spine stiffened. Now that he knew the truth about Mia, he knew Henri would never kill her. Everything he'd told Grayson—that Mia was just some girl he had found to help motivate Grayson to fight—had been a lie. But that didn't mean Henri wouldn't hurt her.

Grayson had almost convinced himself that he would take the brunt of his father's punishment—not Mia. He couldn't afford to doubt that now. His father's anger was fierce, but surely he would deem it punishment enough that Mia would never go free. "He'll focus his anger on me," Grayson finally said.

Tyrell's jaw ticked. "Pray that he does."

His words hardly made sense. A frown tugged at Grayson's mouth. "Why do you care?"

His brother glanced away. "Much has happened since you left."

Unease filtered through Grayson, tensing every muscle in his body. "What do you mean? What happened?"

Anger snapped in Tyrell's gaze. "Before you left for Mortise, you snuck into father's room and held a knife to his throat. Did you really think he wouldn't punish you for that?"

Grayson's hand fisted. He could still feel the blade sliding through his hand as his father watched, a pool of blood on the desk. "He *did* punish me."

Tyrell snorted. "Whatever he did, it wasn't the only part of your punishment. He told me of your demand—that I'd never be allowed near Mia again. That told him *exactly* what would hurt you the most."

An icy ball of dread rolled in his gut. "He sent you to her while I was gone?"

"Yes."

In an instant, Grayson had Tyrell's throat in his hand. He shoved his brother against the nearest stone wall, his blood seething. "What did you do?" he hissed. "Did you hurt her?"

Tyrell bared his teeth, the guttering torchlight cutting shadows over his angular face. "No."

"You're lying." His heart banged against his ribs, threatening to burst out of his chest. "What did you do to her?"

"*Nothing*. He ordered me to visit her regularly while you were gone. That's all."

"Why?"

Tyrell's features tightened. "To torture us all."

Grayson's vision hazed red. The thought of Mia alone in her cell with Tyrell—not once, but repeatedly—made his grip around his brother's throat clench.

Tyrell's nostrils flared. "Release me," he gritted out hoarsely. "Or I'll make you."

Grayson relished the idea of a fight. It would release his anger, fear, and frustration. But he needed to save his strength. And if he killed his brother, he might never know what he'd done to Mia.

He could always kill him later.

He shoved away from Tyrell, but he kept his brother in his sight as Tyrell peeled slowly away from the wall.

The silence between them was brittle.

"She'll want to see you," Tyrell finally said, his eyes remote and his voice thin. "Should I bring her?"

Grayson stared at his brother. Nothing about his offer made sense. Mia was locked in a cell—she wasn't allowed out. And why would *Tyrell* try to show Grayson a kindness?

"She's been given some freedom," his brother explained shortly. "She's been staying in your room upstairs. I can bring her here—

or I can keep her out of Father's sight, and we can hope his anger will distract him enough that he won't think to hurt her."

Grayson's mind spun. He was missing vital information, that much was clear. What had happened here in his absence?

"Well?" Tyrell asked, his voice hard. "Do you want me to bring her?"

"No," Grayson said. The words were a knife in his gut, but he refused to let his selfishness endanger her.

Tyrell jerked out a nod. His boots scuffed the floor as he shifted his weight. For a moment, it seemed like he might say something, but in the end he simply left the cell, shutting and locking the door behind him.

The torch sputtered, but kept burning. Even still, Grayson felt thoroughly in the dark.

———⋅•◉•⋅———

It had been an hour at least, and Grayson hadn't stopped pacing his cell. He dreaded his father's imminent punishment, but the sooner it was done, the sooner he could get out of here.

The sooner he could see Mia.

He didn't understand anything Tyrell had said. That his father had broken his promise and ordered Tyrell to visit Mia was not hard to believe—King Henri only ever did what he wanted—but Grayson couldn't understand the purpose. To torture him, clearly. And fates, did it torture him.

What had those visits been like? He could only too well imagine Mia's fear. Had she had any panics? What had Tyrell done or said?

And why had Henri granted Mia some freedom? To think that she was staying in his room right now . . . he couldn't comprehend Henri's reason for allowing such a thing. Trying to figure it out was driving him insane.

As one hour bled into two, staying level-headed grew more difficult—especially knowing Mia was so close, but impossibly out of his reach.

When a key grated into the lock, Grayson was undeniably relieved—even if it was just his father coming to punish him.

He pivoted to face the opening door. Light from the corridor poured in and Grayson squinted, unable to see anything but bursting light.

He heard a sharp intake of breath, and every muscle in his body tightened. He knew who would speak even before he heard her voice.

"Grayson!"

Mia slammed into him. His arms closed around her in pure reflex. Her arms went around his neck in a fierce embrace, and she buried her head in the curve of his neck. Her soft hair brushed his cheek, and her heart pounded against his chest. The scent of her—jasmine and a hint of lavender—filled his lungs.

He was with her. After so long, he was finally with her. Finally, he could breathe again.

When Mia pulled back, he very nearly didn't let her go. But he was desperate to see her face, and now that his vision had adjusted to the harsher light, he drank in her features. Fates, she was beautiful. Every curve of her rounded face, every wave of dark hair that tumbled in soft curls around her shoulders. Her warm brown eyes studied him with stark intensity, and at first he didn't understand the horror rising on her face.

She lifted trembling fingers to the edge of his throbbing jaw. "Who did this to you?" Her voice shook, but not solely with pain. Anger and a raw thread of vengeance bled into her words.

He couldn't stop staring at her, and when he spoke, it wasn't in answer to her question. It was the only word he could manage to utter in this moment—her name. "Mia." He hardly knew his own roughened voice, he was so breathless from the sight of her.

Her fingers tightened against his jaw, and then she pressed her lips to his. The gentle kiss warmed every part of him. He felt her tears against his face as she placed kisses along his cheek, his temple, and his forehead, being mindful of his injury. And then her arms were around his neck and she gripped him tightly again. "Fates, I can't believe you're back."

A boot scuffed against stone, and Grayson's gaze snapped to Tyrell, who stood in the corridor watching them. His eyes were shielded, but the muscle pulsing in his jaw spoke volumes.

Grayson tightened his hold on Mia, but she eased back, her hands shifting to his chest as she glanced over her shoulder to follow his gaze. "Can you please fetch Devon?" she asked.

Grayson tensed to hear her address his brother, but Tyrell's answer was quick and even. "No. My father won't allow that."

She pursed her lips. "Can you at least bring me something so I can tend him?"

Tyrell darted a look to Grayson, but he jerked out a nod and left. Confusion rippled through Grayson as the door closed and the lock snapped back into place.

He looked to Mia to ask her what was going on with Tyrell, but he was distracted by her intense stare. "I can't believe you're here," she whispered. "Tyrell said you didn't want me to come, but I had to see you."

Grayson couldn't stop staring. Her face was one he knew better than his own, and yet it was strange to see her with new eyes. Eyes that knew the truth. She was so unmistakably Cassian. Her eyes were Desfan's exact shade of brown. Their hair was the same dark hue, both curling around their faces.

The truth hit him all over again. This was Seraijah Meerah Cassian. Desfan's sister. Grayson's born enemy. She was no longer simply *Mia*. *His* Mia.

In truth, she never had been.

Mia swallowed, one thumb sliding over his cheekbone. "How badly are you hurt?"

"I'm fine." His physical well-being was nothing compared to the emotional pain currently rending his insides. He was going to save her, only to lose her. But he couldn't dwell on that right now. Not if he was going to get her back home. He would have the rest of his life to mourn the loss of her.

Which may not prove very long, if Desfan hanged him.

Her fingertips ghosted along his cut jaw, distracting him. "Did your father do this?"

"I disappointed him." But that hardly mattered right now. There was an unexpected burn in his eyes as he drank in every part of her. "Fates, I missed you."

She pushed out a wavering smile, her eyes wet. "I missed you, too." She cupped the back of his neck with both hands and drew him down for another kiss, this one more intense than before. Her lips dragged over his with a desperation he fully understood. He let himself forget everything for a glorious moment, putting everything he had into kissing her. The hollow ache he'd felt during their separation slowly lessened as his world resettled.

The cut along his jaw stung, but he ignored the flashes of pain as he turned his head, his mouth slanting over hers in a new angle. Her palms curved down his neck, fell over his shoulders, then her fingers wound around the loose material of his shirt, the heel of one hand resting above his thudding heart. Even when their mouths fell apart so they could breathe she remained close, clinging to him.

He could feel the heat of her blush against his cheek, feel the wavering breaths skimming his neck. When she eased away, Grayson ducked closer, his nose brushing her cheek as he stole another kiss.

She braced her hands against his chest and viewed him with a searching gaze. "I can't believe you're really here. That you're back."

"I promised I'd come back."

"I know, but I didn't expect you yet." A frown tugged at her mouth. "Why did your father throw you in here? Tyrell said he was angry with you, but he didn't tell me why."

"I failed in my mission."

Her question shocked him. The fact that she knew what his father had sent him to Mortise to do, even though Grayson had never told her . . .

Her visits with Tyrell. Perhaps he had told Mia the truth.

He expected to see at least a hint of judgment in her eyes, or even revulsion. But there was none. He cleared his throat. "No, I . . . couldn't kill her."

A thin smile curved her lips. "I'm glad. Though I'm sorry he hurt you."

"He's angry about more than that. I told him Liam is dead."

"He is?"

"No." Grayson shook his head. None of this mattered right now. "It's a long story, and I promise I'll tell you, but . . ." He pulled in a breath. He would probably never be ready for this conversation, but she deserved to know. "Mia . . . I know who you are."

Five words. Five simple, earth-shattering words.

Mia stared at him, frozen. She wasn't even breathing.

His voice was a whisper, and he refused to acknowledge the ache in his voice. "You're Meerah Cassian. The youngest seraijah of Mortise."

She rolled back on her heels, her hands falling away from his chest. She visibly reeled, and her face paled.

Fates, he shouldn't have thrown the truth at her like that. "Mia—"

"How?" Her demand was softly spoken, but firmer than he'd expected.

He swallowed. "It took me a long time to realize the truth. Too long. I should have put it together sooner, but you *are* her."

Mia folded her arms over her middle, tightly gripping her elbows.

He ached to wrap her in his arms, but he sensed she needed space. It killed him, but he would give her that.

He would give her anything.

"Desfan and I—we made a plan," he explained. "I'm here to take you home."

"Home?" she echoed.

"To Duvan. A ship will be waiting for us in Porynth. It's a port city in Ryden, about a three-week journey from here."

Tears swam in her eyes, and something about her expression seemed lost. "You . . . know?"

Seeing her shock, her vulnerability . . . it hurt him. He tried to gentle his voice. "Yes, Mia. Meerah." Her real name felt wrong on his tongue—sounded strange to his ears.

She peered up at him, and he hated the pain in her eyes. "I'm sorry," she breathed. "I'm sorry I didn't tell you. I—"

The lock groaned, warning them a second before the door swung inward. Grayson wrapped an arm around her even as she twisted to face the door.

Tyrell's boots scuffed the worn stones as he entered, a small bowl of water in one hand and a rag in the other. His eyebrows were drawn low and tight, and Grayson didn't like the way his attention lingered on Mia. "Did you want these or not?"

Grayson tensed, but the rough words seemed to snap Mia into action. She slipped away from Grayson and took the bowl and cloth, facing Tyrell without any sign of fear or hesitancy.

"Thank you," she said.

Tyrell's mouth tightened. "I can wait outside for you."

"I'm not leaving."

"You can't stay here." Tyrell shot a look to Grayson, silently re-questing support.

He didn't ever want to agree with Tyrell about anything, but his brother was right. Mia shouldn't stay. He met Tyrell's gaze over Mia's head. "Just give us another moment."

"No." Mia's grip on the bowl turned her knuckles white. She looked back at Grayson, her jaw set. "I'm not leaving you."

"You don't want to be here when our father comes," Tyrell said.

Mia's eyes narrowed. "If he's going to punish me, there's nowhere I can hide. I'm staying with Grayson."

Tyrell muttered something under his breath as he stalked out of the room, closing the door with more force than necessary.

Mia faced Grayson, her expression hard. "Don't argue with me."

Any other time, he might have. But he simply stared at her, con-fused by everything that had just happened. The way she'd spoken to Tyrell ... that was not normal.

Mia had always been quiet around others. With him, her courage was as much a part of her as her kindness. As a child, she'd even been bossy at times, but it had always been when they were alone. Her wariness around those who might hurt her—Papa, Mama, Henri—all of that made sense to him.

What he had just seen didn't make any sense. Not just in Mia, but in Tyrell's reaction as well. Something had changed between them while he was away, and he was scrambling to figure out what.

"Come sit closer to the light," Mia said, kneeling with the bowl of water under the flickering torch.

Grayson obeyed, sinking to his knees in front of her. Tension kept his spine rigid as she wet a corner of the rag in the bowl. "Tyrell told me he was ordered to visit you," he said.

She nodded, her face smooth as she began dabbing at his cut. Her focus was clearly on her task, but she still answered his unspoken question. "He came quite often. He never hurt me, though." Her lips pursed, and he wondered if there was more she wasn't saying.

He'd been gone for months. Of course there was more.

"What did he do?" he asked.

"Nothing." Her brow creased as she dipped the rag back into the bowl, tinging the water pink. "At first it was unnerving. We argued. He watched me paint. We played cards. He was as upset about it as I was, I think."

His mouth was horribly dry. "But that changed?"

She peeked up at him, her expression unusually guarded. "Yes."

His stomach twisted.

Mia went back to cleaning the cut on his jaw. "Tyrell became my friend. Or at least, we *were* friends. I don't know anymore."

She shook her head. "Fates, none of this matters."

Grayson grasped her hand, pulling it from his aching cut. His eyes searched hers. "You can tell me anything."

She swallowed. "I know. But I don't think I'm ready to talk about this."

That hurt, but he refused to let her see that. He merely nodded. "Whenever you want to talk, I'm here."

"Thank you." Her thumb brushed against his skin, and then she tugged her hand away and resumed her quiet work. Silence reigned for a few moments before she whispered, "You saw Desfan?"

His shoulders loosened a little. "Yes. He . . ." Well, he wasn't really a friend anymore, was he? "He loves you. He asked me to tell you that."

Mia closed her eyes, looking almost . . . pained. "M-My father. Did you see him?"

His heart cracked. "No, I never saw him. He . . ."

Her eyes slowly opened, and the light in them was dulled. "He's dead, isn't he?"

"Yes." Fates, how he wished he could change that for her.

Tears swam but didn't spill as she asked, "When did he die? Was it a long time ago?"

Grayson shook his head. "No, it was only a few weeks ago."

"Oh." Her voice was quiet. Distant. She looked down, focusing too hard on her task of wetting a new corner of the rag.

"I'm sorry," he whispered. When she said nothing, he continued softly, "The night he died, I found Desfan in a corridor . . ."

He told her everything. About the painting, the things Desfan had said that had finally helped Grayson see the truth about Mia. He told her about Liam and his threats, and how Grayson had betrayed him anyway.

Mia had listened without saying anything, but at that, she sucked in a breath. "Mama." Seeing his confusion, she hurried to explain.

His chest tightened as she told him about Mama's attempt to abduct her. That Tyrell had saved her came as a shock, but his eyes only widened further when Mia added that Papa had died weeks before.

"Papa attacked me," she explained. She touched her stomach, the action seemingly unconscious. "He was in one of his drunken tempers, and he stabbed me."

Grayson stiffened. "He what?"

"I'm all right," she said quickly. "Tyrell came. He killed Papa, and he carried me upstairs to his room. Devon reached me in time. I'm fully healed now."

Grayson's tension didn't dissipate, however. Mia answered his questions, describing her injury and recovery, and he felt grudging gratitude for his brother. He didn't understand Tyrell—and whatever had happened between him and Mia made Grayson tense—but he *had* protected Mia. He would always be grateful for that.

Although he almost wished Tyrell hadn't killed Papa. He would have preferred to have done that himself.

By the time they finished telling each other the most important things that had happened in their time apart, Mia was done cleaning his cut. It still felt painfully raw, but without ointment or needle and thread, there was nothing else to be done.

She set the rag and bowl aside, the water a swirling pink. "I wonder why Liam's order was for Mama to take me, rather than kill me."

Grayson had been wondering the same thing. "He knew who

you were. While he needed to threaten your death in order to control me, it does make sense that he wouldn't want you dead." She was too important.

She would always be the most important part of his life, but he hated that others saw her as a thing to be used. Liam, his father—men like them would always covet her for who she was: the long lost seraijah of Mortise.

"I'm not surprised Liam bought Mama and Papa's loyalty so easily," Mia said.

Her caretakers had always been greedy, terrible people. Grayson's fists clenched. *Someone close to her*, Liam had said. Those awful people had spent nine years overseeing her life, living adjacent to her cell. Physically, no one else had better access. Grayson had simply taken Liam's words to mean someone Mia would trust.

Thank the fates Fletcher had been vigilant. If Mia had been taken, Grayson might have lost her forever.

But no. He never would have stopped searching for her.

Liam had been cruel to let him believe that the hawk carried orders for Mia's death, rather than her abduction. But then, no Kaelin was truly kind, especially to those who betrayed them. He just hated that he'd misjudged Liam so terribly. How had he ever believed their friendship was real?

"Mama is dead, too," Mia said suddenly. "Your father ordered her death."

Every nerve drew taut. "My father was there?"

"Yes." She explained how Fletcher had gone to the king with his concerns, and had been ordered to let things play out.

Grayson wanted to strangle his father for the danger he'd put Mia in. He was equally upset by the idea of Henri being in the same room as her.

Mia met his gaze, her voice quiet. "I truly am sorry I never told you the truth. About who I am."

"It's all right."

She shook her head. "I should have said something. Especially when you told me you were leaving for Duvan. I tried—I promise, I did. I just couldn't make the words come."

He knew how she'd been beaten during her first year of imprisonment. A scared child, hurt every time she talked about her home. Her past. His stomach churned, his hands aching to protect her against the pain she'd already survived. "You don't have to apologize. You did nothing wrong."

"But if you'd known . . ."

Grayson shook his head. "I don't think it would have changed anything."

"Of course it would have changed things."

"How? I would have still had to go, leaving you behind. I would have listened to Liam's every promise, because he would have been the only alternative to following my father's orders." He wouldn't have wanted to hurt Desfan, but he hadn't wanted that in the first place. The more he thought about it, the surer he was. "Knowing the truth from the beginning wouldn't have changed anything."

Mia still looked doubtful, but she didn't argue. So many thoughts and emotions swirled in her eyes, and he knew she wasn't ready to voice all her thoughts. He held back his questions, even though they burned inside of him.

"How did my father die?" she finally asked.

Grayson fought his instinct to shield her from the truth, and it made his words heavy. "He collapsed about a year ago. No one knew why at the time, but Desfan recently learned it was because of a rumor he heard. A rumor that you were alive. The shock was too much for him."

Grief shone in her eyes. "I don't understand. How could a shock—no matter how severe—have made him collapse?"

"I don't know all the details, but apparently his health was failing before his collapse." The guilt that crossed her features made him squeeze her hand. "This isn't your fault."

Mia glanced away, her throat visibly constricting as she struggled with her emotions. "It's my fault Tally died." Her words were soft, yet ragged. A pain compounded by years.

Grayson cupped her cheek, gently forcing her to look at him. "It was a shipwreck, Mia. There's nothing you could have done. It's a fates-blasted miracle you survived." A miracle he would never stop thanking the fates for. He could not imagine his life without her.

A muscle in her jaw jumped against his palm. "You don't understand. I'm the reason Tally didn't survive. I killed her."

His first reaction was to brush aside her perceived guilt. There was no way Mia had killed her sister, no matter what she thought. But he knew that wouldn't help her, so he gentled his voice. "Tell me what happened."

She looked down, and he let his fingers slide into her hair as she breathed in slowly. "Everything about that night . . . I remember it all. The rain that whipped so hard through the air it stung my face. The violent flashes of lighting. The booming roar of thunder. The fear that clutched me so hard I couldn't breathe. The shouts of the sailors as they tried to bring in the sails. The terror on my mother's face. The terrible crack of the ship as it shattered beneath my feet. The taste of seawater as it poured into my mouth." She swallowed. "I don't know what happened to my mother. I could hear her screaming as I was swallowed by the water, ripped away from her. It was so dark, and the sea churned. I didn't even know which direction to swim." She paused. "There were bodies in the water. Dead bodies. They stared at me . . ."

Grayson gathered her into his arms and pressed his lips against the top of her head. Everything inside him ached for what she'd endured. "I'm here," he murmured. "You're safe."

She burrowed into him, clinging to his loose shirt. "Something bumped me. I nearly screamed, thinking it was one of those bodies. But it was Tally. She grabbed my hand. When she started swimming, I kicked with her. I trusted that she knew where to go." Emotion clawed her throat, but she didn't stop. The words were pouring from her—a dam cracked open, spilling everything now that the wall of silence had been broken. "Someone grabbed me around the waist. A sailor. He hauled me toward the surface. I don't know why he didn't grab us both. Maybe he was injured, and could only grab one of us? Maybe he didn't see her in the darkness? Maybe he thought I was smaller, and needed help first? I don't know, but I held Tally's hand, and she was pulled up with us. For a moment. But her hand started to slip. I still see her eyes . . . the fear in them. Her fingers slipped through mine." She shuddered against him, her words pinched as she said, "If I'd held on just a little longer, she would have been with me. She would have lived. But I let go."

Grayson's heart ached as he cradled her to his chest, her body hitching with ragged sobs. "That wasn't your fault," he breathed against her hair. "You didn't let go. You were being pulled away."

"I watched her sink," Mia gasped, shaking with the force of her tears. "I was the last person to look into her eyes. She was so afraid. My sister was terrified, and I left her." She pushed back enough to look at him, and in the flickering torchlight, her face was twisted with pain. "How am I supposed to face Desfan when it's my fault

Tally died?"

Grayson palmed her wet cheeks, dropping his chin so their eyes were level. "Desfan won't blame you, Mia. I promise you, he won't. Because you're not to blame. You did nothing wrong."

A tremor wracked her shoulders as she sucked in a shuddering breath. "Why couldn't I just hold on?"

Grayson tugged her back into the shelter of his arms as she cried. Every tear cut him like a blade. That she had felt this guilt and pain for years and had never said a word? It killed him. He wanted to take it all from her. Bear it for her. But he couldn't. He couldn't change her past, or his own.

So, while she relived her darkest memory, he held her. Because there was nothing else he could do.

Eventually, her tears ran out and her shoulders stopped shaking. But she didn't pull away from him as she whispered, "I sent him back for her. As soon as we broke the surface, I told him to go back. He settled me on a piece of wreckage and told me to hold on. He dove into the water . . . but he didn't come back. He died, too. I sent him away, and he died."

"It's not your fault," he whispered again. "None of it."

She didn't respond, but he knew she didn't believe him.

He hoped one day she would. Until then, he would spend every day showing her that it was a blessing she had survived that night— not a reason for guilt.

CHAPTER 64

CLARE

THEY HAD BEEN IN DUVAN FOR ABOUT A month, and Clare had come to learn that nothing in Mortise was done simply. The mourning period for Serjan Saernon Cassian lasted two weeks and was filled with religious ceremonies, time set aside for reflection, and endless feasts with poets who recited Mortisian history—specifically Saernon Cassian's greatest acts. Renowned singers filled the palace halls with their mournful ballads and heartfelt tributes to their lost monarch. Every day brought new visitors to stay at the castle, and servants bustled with the increased activity, rushing to ready more rooms and food.

After the official mourning period, there were two weeks of celebration. Of the previous serjan's life, but also of Desfan Cassian,

641

the man who would be crowned serjan at the conclusion of this joyful period. According to Serene and Imara, the feasts became more boisterous, filled with an anticipatory excitement for Desfan's ascension to the throne. Serene was inundated with invitations to teas and walks in the gardens, as the nobles of Mortise were eager to rub elbows with their future seraijan.

Clare could only imagine how busy Desfan was. She felt sorry for him. She remembered too well the grief she'd felt after losing her father, and then her mother. But she hadn't been able to break down. Her mother was gone, but there were clothes to be washed, meals to prepare, and frightened siblings to look after. Mark had only been a baby. Personal mourning had been pushed aside, and she thought that Desfan was in a similar situation. Only instead of a household to oversee, he had an entire kingdom.

She did not envy him.

Clare had only seen the serjah in brief glimpses, since her still-healing fingers had kept her from playing the decoy. She was finally able to remove the braces in time for the final celebratory feast before Desfan's coronation. She could still feel an ache in the places her fingers had snapped, especially if she did anything too strenuous or intricate. Still, she'd fully expected to take Serene's place at the large feast—until Serene had insisted on being present.

"I'm still making important connections within the Mortisian court," the princess had argued. "There will be a great deal of conversation tonight, and I don't want to miss it."

Bennick had reviewed the security and, after discussing it with Wilf and Cardon, they'd determined the threat of an attack at the feast to be minimal. After all, there had been weeks of feasts with no unrest, and the coronation tomorrow would be much more public. An attack during the crowning ceremony would also make

642

a more impressive statement if any enemies were planning to strike—which was why Clare would be taking Serene's place there.

Tonight, Clare watched as Serene swept out of the room, headed to the vast dining room on the main floor of the palace. Without Dirk or Venn, the royal guard was understaffed. Bennick was clearly torn, since it would be best to have three guards on Serene at the opulent feast, but that would leave the room guarded with only their Devendran palace guards.

Imara offered to leave one of her royal bodyguards at the suite, and that convinced Bennick. His eyes were still serious as he viewed Clare and Bridget. "Stay in the room."

Clare nodded. It was an easy promise to make, as there was no reason to leave.

Once the others had left for the feast, Bridget settled into a chair and worked on mending one of the princess's dresses. Clare lifted a book of Mortisian poetry. She'd used it these past weeks to brush up on her studies, and she was once again grateful for her unexpected talent when it came to learning languages.

She was, admittedly, trying to distract herself. Several things weighed on her mind.

Venn and Vera were still missing. Desfan and Serene had sent men to search for them, but there had been no word yet. They were a month overdue, and Clare had no idea where they could be—or if they were even alive. The not knowing was agony.

She had also not forgotten Prince Grandeur's letter, or the subtle threat in his words. Even though Serene had persuaded her to not worry overmuch, she was still uneasy when she thought about it.

The only thing that assuaged those fears was to think of Thomas and Mark coming to live with her in Duvan. She'd written to them

weeks ago, advising them—and their caretaker, Mistress Keller—
that arrangements were being made. Serene had not received a
response from Newlan yet, but she expected one any day now. If
they didn't hear from him soon, Serene said they would proceed
without him.

Being separated from her brothers had been the hardest part
of being the decoy. The thought of having them with her again—
especially after losing Eliot—brought Clare a peace she hadn't felt
in a long time.

A knock on the door interrupted her thoughts. One of the
Devendran guards—a man named Davis—stuck his head in, his
eyes falling on her. "Miss Ellington, I'm sorry to intrude. I have a
Mortisian prison guard here. He says he has a message for the princess. I've told him that she's at the feast, but he wants to leave the
message with one of the princess's maids."

Brow furrowing, Clare rose from her chair. "Let him in."

Davis pushed the door open further, his gaze predictably wary
as he watched the Mortisian guard step inside.

The foreign man was wholly respectful as he tipped his head to
her, a simple maid. "My apologies," he said in the trade language.
"I'm stationed in the prison, and it's not often that I can slip away."

"It's no trouble, I'm happy to take the message. Who is it from?"

"A man named Latif," the Mortisian guard said.

Clare hadn't had an opportunity to visit Latif yet, though she'd
asked Serene to speak to Desfan on the Mortisian's behalf. Clare
knew the serjah had been too preoccupied to decide Latif's fate,
however.

"He's one of the prisoners on my floor," the guard continued.
"He said he needed me to take an urgent message to Princess Serene." His cheeks reddened a little. "I wouldn't normally worry

about delivering a prisoner's message, but he was quite insistent, and it was just cryptic enough that I . . . Well, these are strange times. If there is a real threat, I need to report it."

More confused than ever, Clare tightened her grip on the book. "What is his message?"

"He said . . . *The one to fear is here.*"

The hairs on her arms rose. "That's all he said?"

Behind his beard, the Mortisian guard looked a little sheepish. "It's probably nothing at all. But he wouldn't explain himself. He wants to talk to the princess. I know she's at the feast, but I thought perhaps he would talk to you, as one of her maids."

Davis—who had remained close—frowned. "*The one to fear is here*," he repeated. "It sounds to me like nothing more than shadowy words from a man desperate for an audience."

"Perhaps." The Mortisian guard glanced back at Clare. "He's usually quite calm, but he was agitated when I went down to start my shift. It was odd. I wouldn't ask this of you at all, but with the coronation tomorrow, I need to make sure there's no real danger."

"Of course." Clare set aside the book. "I'll come at once."

"Wait." Davis stepped forward, his hand out. "Captain Markam expressly said you were to stay here." He, like the other palace guards with them, had not known about Clare being the decoy when she'd left Iden. But even though the secret was closely guarded, their guards were so few now, they knew the truth. Davis's concern went beyond that, though; he'd been one of the men to help rescue her in Shebar. His over-protectiveness warmed her.

The Mortisian set his fist over his heart. "My oath, the maid will be safe with me."

Davis eyed the man, but Clare spoke before he could. "We need to know if there is any threat for tomorrow." *Or tonight*, she thought, her pulse skipping. What if Bennick and the others were in danger right now?

Davis must have read the determination on her face, because he sighed. "I'm coming as well." He looked to Bridget. "Remain in the room."

The red-headed maid nodded brusquely. "Be careful," she added.

Clare offered quick assurance, and then she followed the Mortisian guard out. Davis fell into step behind her, leaving two guards to watch the room. As they walked down the deserted corridors, her scalp prickled. The emptiness and silence in the corridors felt wrong, when she knew the palace was so full of people. But everyone of import was in the dining hall, leaving the rest of the halls strangely deserted.

Their footsteps echoed loudly against the worn stone, and with the Mortisian guard leading them, they took a direct path to the prison. Descending the long staircase forced a shiver through Clare's body. Maybe she should get a message to Bennick. Ask him to come with her . . .

But no. He was busy, and if Latif was aware of a threat, there was no time to delay.

Besides, she needed to prove to herself that she could do something as simple as walk into a heavily guarded prison without Bennick at her side. Her time with Salim had not broken her.

She wouldn't let it.

Steeling her spine, she followed the Mortisian guard deeper into the prison. He nodded to several of his fellow guards stationed at specific junctures.

"The guard down here seems thin," Guardsman Davis noted.

The Mortisian guard nodded. "We switch to a minimal guard in the prison during major palace events."

Davis said nothing, but Clare could feel his unease. It brushed against her skin, tightening something in her gut that she tried to ignore.

They reached Latif's floor and turned left in the torch-lit hall. The Mortisian guard led them to a cell located about halfway down the deserted corridor and produced a set of keys. With the soft grate of the lock disengaging, he pushed open the door.

Clare stepped closer, glimpsing Latif inside. He seemed caught in the middle of pacing, his untouched dinner tray set aside on his bed. His brown skin was unusually pale, and when he saw Clare, his gaze skated over her simple dress. "I need to speak to the princess," he said. "Not one of her maids."

"I can get a message to the princess," Clare said.

Latif's eyes narrowed as he took her in again, more carefully this time.

Her heartbeat stuttered. Would he recognize her?

"Your message was cryptic," Davis said, his voice commanding. "What do you actually want to tell us?"

Latif's attention skipped from Clare to Davis. "Princess Serene must be told that Liam Kaelin is imprisoned here."

Davis snorted. "Is that all?"

Clare felt the tension that had coiled in her shoulders loosen. "We're aware."

Latif blinked. "You know?" He glanced at them all, agitation obvious in his edged voice. "Fates, don't you understand? You must do something!"

Clare took a step into the cell. "It's all right. He's under heavy guard. He can't hurt anyone."

Latif huffed a short breath, shaking his head quickly. "You don't understand. This is *Liam Kaelin*."

"I assure you, he's not a threat," Clare insisted.

"He's in a cell, just like you," Davis added.

Latif's tongue darted over his lips, fear evident in his eyes. "That won't matter. He's the Shadow of Ryden. No prison can hold him. He should be moved immediately. Some other place, more secure."

"There is no place more secure," the Mortisian guard said from the hall. "Besides, he has been here for weeks and nothing has happened."

Sweat beaded along Latif's hairline. "I didn't know he was here. I heard some guards talking today, I—" He shook his head, cutting off his own thought. "You must move him."

The Mortisian guard angled toward Clare, his cheeks reddening. "I'm sorry, Miss Ellington. I'm afraid I wasted your time—"

"You aren't listening to me," Latif cut in. "You can't cage a shadow." His eyes went back to Clare, intensity tightening his face. "You must tell Serene. You need to—"

A harsh thunk and a strangled gasp jerked Clare around. The Mortisian guard's eyes were wide and his hands clutched at his neck—where a crossbow bolt was lodged.

Davis cursed and shoved Clare more fully into Latif's cell. "Stay in—" A bolt struck Davis's chest as he tried to turn, his sword half out of its scabbard.

Clare cried out even as she ran for Davis, intent on dragging him into the cell. If they could just close the door, they could have some shelter from the attack. "Help me!"

Latif dropped into a crouch beside Davis, but instead of helping Clare grab the downed soldier, he grasped the dying man's sword and dragged it free of its sheath.

Clare's breath hitched. "What are you doing?"

A shadow fell over them, and when Clare blinked up at the man standing in the doorway, her stomach dropped. *Impossible* ...

His face was so unexpected, all she could do was stare as he lowered his crossbow, the corner of his mouth curving upward. "The fates are smiling on me tonight. I thought I'd have to come looking for you, Clare."

His voice—painfully familiar, though she'd only heard it a handful of times—sent shock blasting through her. The last time he'd said her name, he had been screaming it on a field outside of Stills, just after the prisoner exchange had gone so terribly wrong.

Just after Eliot had been killed.

"Michael." Fear knifed her gut as she met the deadened eyes of her brother's best friend. It was wholly obvious that the Devendran rebel still blamed her for Eliot's death.

That horrible smile still twisted Michael's face, even as he turned to Latif. "Your freedom is here, prisoner."

Distantly, Clare could hear other cell doors opening. Hoots and cheers, some men barking orders she couldn't quite make out.

"If you wish to join us, get your orders at the stairs," Michael continued to Latif. "Or you can leave—it doesn't matter to us." His piercing focus shifted back to Clare as he drew a long knife at his hip, his smile hiking cruelly. "This one is mine."

CHAPTER 65

DESFAN

LAUGHTER ECHOED IN THE BANQUET HALL, and the spiced scents of seasoned meat and peppered rice permeated the air. Desfan sat at the head table, a wineglass dangling in his hand. The seat on his right was empty, since Serene was making her way around the room during the lull between courses. She truly was a gifted diplomat. Her Mortisian was excellent, and she conversed easily with the nobility. She also listened, which Desfan thought might be the reason some nobles walked away from their meetings with a surprised sort of smile on their faces. Her guards stood near, their gazes alert though they managed to look relaxed.

Imara sat on his left, and Desfan knew the moment she leaned in. Not because her warm vanilla scent became stronger, though

650

it did. No, he knew she eased closer because he had become increasingly aware of any space between them.

Wrong.

The thought was a punch to his gut. But it didn't stop his breath from hitching when her arm brushed his.

"I think it's time for another wager," she said, her voice easily covered by the musicians who played music in the mezzanine that wrapped around the upper part of the vaulted room.

Desfan turned to her. She had a golden circlet weaved into her hair, which was piled elaborately upon her head. It revealed her slender neck, adding the illusion of height to her petite form. Her dress was a vibrant purple, one shoulder bared while the other was draped in a diaphanous spill of lighter purple fabric that crossed over her chest and flowed down her arm.

He was staring. He shook himself, feeling the weight of his crown. A crown he would exchange tomorrow for a far heavier one. "What do you propose?" he asked.

After swallowing a sip of wine, Imara shot him a mischievous smile. "I don't have anything specific in mind, but I think you should start by walking the room with Serene, rather than simply staring after her."

Heat bloomed across his cheeks. "I'm not sure she wants me with her. She's trying to show the court her autonomy."

"I understand her need to be seen as an individual, but isn't it equally important that they see your unity?"

"Perhaps." His grip on his wineglass tightened. "I think she's still angry with me."

"For letting Grayson go?"

Desfan dipped his head. "She wanted a trial immediately." She'd wanted justice for Sir Arklowe, and he didn't blame her for that.

But saving Meerah had been far more important. He thought Serene understood that; she just didn't trust Grayson to return.

"You did the right thing," Imara said. "If anyone can bring Meerah home, it's Grayson."

Before Desfan could respond, a piercing snap and a fleshy thud echoed in the room. A horrible scream stole all the air from the banquet hall, only to be overpowered by the snick and twang of more crossbow bolts shooting from the mezzanine and into the crowd. Shouts and cries almost immediately drowned out the sound of more bolts being fired.

Desfan didn't think.

He tackled Imara, his chair toppling in the process. The Zennorian princess gasped as they both hit the floor, but he didn't pause. Careful not to crush her, he rolled them both under the table for the meager shelter it offered.

A rising tide of screams turned his blood to ice. The musicians had stopped. Had they been the first to die, or had they been the attackers all along? The mezzanine afforded an excellent view of the room. Which made him wonder why he and Imara were still breathing. Wouldn't they have been the first targets?

Darts hammered into the table above them and Imara's nails bit into his wrist. Desfan kept her locked in his arms as others bumped against them, all of them seeking cover in the tight space. An elbow caught Desfan's temple and he grunted at the flash of pain, but he didn't let go of Imara. The red tablecloth fluttered almost to the floor, blocking most of the view of the room.

"Desfan is dead!"

The shout went up, first with one voice, then repeated by a dozen more. Desfan was not overly concerned. First, it was an obvious lie. Second, that first voice had belonged to Karim.

Fates bless his best friend—he was a quick thinker. Desfan really should pay him more.

Unfortunately, the assault didn't cease at the shouted announcement of Desfan's death. Darts were still being loosed into the crowd, shot from long-range crossbows, and Desfan's people were dying. These assassins weren't just interested in killing Desfan, then. Were they after Serene and Imara as well, or simply anyone who breathed?

Imara's eyes were wide—panicked. "Did you see Serene?"

"No." He searched around them, peering under the tablecloth's edge, but it was all confusion. Bodies squirmed and bucked against each other, seeking safety. He saw some nobles kicking their peers, forcing them out from under the table in order to assure themselves the safest position.

Sickened, Desfan pulled Imara's back more securely against his chest. He could almost feel the weight of her fear pressing against him. Oddly, it only strengthened his resolve to push down his own fear.

Keeping her safe in the shelter of his arms, Desfan deflected many of the unwitting blows sent their way as people scrambled beneath the table. He had to trust that his soldiers were doing all they could to reach the balconies and stop the crossbow attack before his entire court was decimated.

He tried not to think of why Karim had not joined them yet. He refused to believe his friend was dead, though dread curled in his gut.

"There!" Imara said suddenly. "Serene!"

Desfan peeked under the tablecloth, following Imara's jabbing finger. He saw the Devendran princess huddled beside a chair, one of her bodyguards—the one with the scar on his cheek—draped over her, using his own body as a shield against the raining darts. Desfan couldn't see the other two bodyguards who had been beside her earlier.

"Cardon!" Imara yelled. "Serene!"

"There's no room under the table," Desfan told her.

"We have to help them. We—" She broke off with a scream as a heavy body slammed onto the table above them, rattling dishes.

Others around them also panicked, lashing out at each other in their fear. Desfan hunched over Imara's smaller body, taking a kick to his shoulder that would have otherwise hit the side of her head. He grunted, but didn't shift away from her. His heart hammered against her back, his jaw stiff.

Imara clutched his arm in a stranglehold, as if he were her lifeline.

Perhaps it was Desfan's imagination, but he thought he heard fewer snapping crossbows. He wasn't sure what that meant. Were the attackers dying, or simply drawing swords and descending to the floor? The screams in the room created a near-constant roar, the more piercing screams of death coming far too frequently.

Glancing over his shoulder, Desfan spotted Serene from beneath the hem of the tablecloth, still crouched beside the chair with Sir Brinhurst at her back. Captain Markam knelt there as well now, yelling instructions that Desfan couldn't quite hear.

As he watched, Serene was hauled to her feet and shielded by her three bodyguards, all of them rushing out of his line of sight. Knowing that Captain Markam would have had a better vantage to assess the situation, Desfan knew the risk they took in running across the room must be worth it. And while the implications of that terrified him, he knew he would do well to follow suit.

Ducking his head so his mouth was at Imara's ear, he said,

"We need to get out of here. We're going to move to the head of the table, then run for the servants' passage against the back wall. All right?"

She nodded her head with a jerk, her soft black hair brushing his cheek. Her gold crown was small and entwined with her hair, but it still caught his attention.

He would not let it catch the attention of anyone else. Being as gentle as possible while still moving quickly, he plucked out pins and threaded his fingers in her soft locks, prying the crown free. He dropped it to the floor, and before he could grab his own crown, Imara snatched it off as well.

She looked up at him, fear and determination mingling in her gaze. With her hair a rioting mess around her face, she looked beautifully fierce. "Ready?" she asked him.

He nodded, his heart thudding against his ribs. "Don't let go of me."

"I won't," she promised, squeezing his hand.

They crawled toward the end of the table, Desfan doing his best to protect Imara from the flailing bodies around them. Crouched over her smaller form, it took a considerable amount of time to wriggle past the frightened nobility. Finally, they reached the end of the table. Desfan peered under the tablecloth, but all he saw were running feet and the less fortunate fallen bodies, stuck with darts.

A hand suddenly wrapped around Desfan's ankle and he jumped, banging his head on the table. Imara let out a half-scream as they both turned to see Karim, crouched just under the table's edge. "What are you doing?" his bodyguard demanded.

Desfan swallowed through the rush of relief. Karim was alive. "We need to get out of here. I saw Serene's guards rush her out of the room."

Karim clearly followed Desfan's thoughts. "It's not just an attack from above, then."

"The attackers will reach the table soon," Desfan predicted.

Karim grimaced, favoring his leg.

"You're injured," Imara gasped.

Desfan spotted the dart sticking in his friend's thigh.

"I'm fine," Karim grunted. He looked to Desfan. "You need to take Princess Imara and hide."

"Karim!"

They all twisted to see Razan wriggle her way under the table. Her face was pale as she carefully grasped Karim's leg, studying the bolt in it. "You're losing a lot of blood."

"It's nothing." Karim gritted his teeth, sweat beading on his brow. "You need to run with Desfan."

Razan's dark eyebrows smashed together. "I'm not leaving you."

Karim cursed. "Will you listen to me for once, you fates-blasted woman?"

She ignored him, her gaze cutting to Desfan as she tugged one of Karim's belted knives free. "I'll stay with Karim."

Desfan knew there would be no changing her mind. There was also no time to argue; he needed to get Imara to safety—now. He leveled Razan with a firm look. "Stay alive." He looked to Karim. "Both of you."

Karim rose to his knees, blatantly ignoring the fact he had a crossbow bolt buried in his leg. Razan's hand on his arm steadied him as he gripped his sword, and his eyes met Desfan's. "I'll keep them off you as long as I can, but don't you dare die."

Emotion thickened Desfan's throat, but he flashed one of his characteristic half-smiles. "I wouldn't dream of disappointing you, Karim."

His bodyguard muttered under his breath.

Desfan grabbed Imara, tugging her in front of him so he could shelter her better. "Stay close," he told her. "Run, but don't lose me."

"Don't worry," Imara said, patting his hand with fingers that trembled only a little. "I won't leave you behind."

His mouth quirked, and he had the sudden urge to kiss her. Reining in that reckless impulse, he clutched Imara's arm and the two of them shot out from under the table.

The crowd was a colorful blur, each person rushing for safety, all of them seemingly convinced their best chance of survival rested in the opposite direction. They crashed into each other, dragged each other down, used each other as shields; Desfan tried to block out the sights, his only purpose now to get Imara to the servants' passage. He would worry about what remained of his court later.

He heard Karim shout, and he threw a look over his shoulder. His bodyguard was locked in a fierce sword fight. He was protecting Desfan, even now—as he always had. And Razan crouched behind him with her dagger, guarding his back.

Imara veered sharply to the left to avoid a fallen body, and Desfan barely managed to follow her.

They'd nearly reached the servants' passage when a man barreled into them. Desfan lost his grip on Imara and they fell apart, both of them knocked to the floor.

Desfan blinked, his shoulder bruised from hitting the hard stone. A man stood over him, and as he came into focus, Desfan's eyes flew wide. "Jamal?"

The former councilman was supposed to be in prison, yet Omar Jamal towered above him. Once, Desfan had thought the youngest councilman to be an ally. But the traitor had been a drug master, bringing olcain into Duvan and making an obscene profit. He'd been behind the plot to hire the Rose to kill Serene, and he had blackmailed Yahri and others on the council. He'd also tried to kill Desfan before his arrest.

Jamal was thinner, his time in prison clearly leaving its mark. His clothes were dirty, his beard unkempt, and his oily hair hung in limp strands around his face. His grim smile—edged with hate— was terrifying.

"You stole everything from me." The traitor lifted a sword. "It's only fair I return the favor."

Confusion wracked Desfan—how was Jamal here?—but there wasn't time to figure it out. The sword stabbed toward him and Desfan rolled, the edge of the blade grazing his side, but mostly missing him. He kicked at the traitor's knee, knocking it out from under him. Jamal stumbled, but didn't fall. Swinging the blade, he came at Desfan again.

Desfan had just enough time to kick the sword aside before he shoved to his feet, hands itching for the dual blades sitting in his room.

If he lived long enough to become serjan, he'd insist that swords could be worn to feasts.

He grabbed the small dagger belted at his side and sank into a defensive crouch. He could see Imara from the corner of his eye, and he spoke to her, his focus still on Jamal. "Go, Imara."

She hesitated, and Jamal chuckled. "Others always fight your battles, don't they, Serjah? Your bodyguard. Old women like Yahri. And now a Zennorian."

Desfan's eyes slid briefly to Imara. "*Go.*"

She swallowed hard, but thankfully darted away.

Desfan turned his attention back to Jamal, the two of them slowly circling each other.

The crossbow bolts no longer seemed to be flying, but the chaos in the room was undimmed. Fights had broken out across the space, and though the itch between Desfan's shoulder blades made him think someone was watching him, his focus was on the threat in front of him. "How did you get out of prison?" he asked.

"With a little help from another enemy of yours," Jamal said, his voice casual, his hold on the sword white-knuckled. He was holding it with both hands; he was weakened after his imprisonment.

Desfan could use that.

"I have so many enemies," Desfan said, stepping carefully over a fallen body, his gaze riveted on Jamal. "You'll have to be more specific."

"I'm afraid I don't know who orchestrated this," Jamal said. "My cell was opened and I was told I could flee, or I could stay and wreak havoc on you." He grinned, revealing stained teeth. "I'm pleased to say that most of your prisoners chose the latter."

Fates.

Desfan's heart kicked in his chest, but he tried not to let his panic show. "I'm not sure what it is that makes people want to kill me."

One of Jamal's eyebrows lifted. "Have you *met* you?"

He snorted. "You wound me."

"Not yet."

Desfan's grip on his knife flexed. "Many have tried to kill me, Jamal. Obviously none have succeeded. Surrender now, and you'll live."

Jamal growled and lunged. Desfan spun to avoid the strike, his dagger slashing at the former councilman. Jamal raised his arm, taking the cut across his forearm. He grunted and swung again at

Desfan.

Jamal had some skill with a blade, but he was reckless and desperate, and the sword was already visibly dragging at his arms. Desfan dodged each strike, wearing him out until his sword drooped.

Jamal would be too slow to bring it up again if Desfan struck now.

He gritted his teeth. "Last chance, Jamal. Surrender, or you'll leave me no choice."

Jamal's answer was an attempted thrust of his sword, and Desfan sidestepped, lifting his dagger—

A sword shoved through Jamal's chest from behind and the man's eyes rounded as he jerked. Blood dribbled from the corner of his mouth, pain and confusion twisting his face as he crumpled.

Behind him stood Amil Havim, breathing hard.

"Amil." Desfan blinked back surprise. "Thank you."

The nobleman's eyes flicked up from Jamal's body, his bloody sword still clutched tightly in his hands. Fury burned in his gaze, and Desfan's pulse faltered. "He gave me no choice," Amil said, his voice edged in darkness. "You're *mine* to kill. That was my only order."

The scene slanted, and Desfan struggled to make sense of it. "What are you talking about?"

Amil's lips pulled into a thin smile. "Are you really surprised? You sent my father to Devendra and he died—and you wouldn't do anything to avenge him. I will never support you."

Desfan's mind spun as he slid back a step from Amil's gradual advance. "*You* planned this attack?"

"Your father's death left me no choice. I won't let you be serjan." He shook his head. "Before that became inevitable, I'd planned to punish you simply by wrecking the marriage alliance. I tried to take my revenge against Serene at the same time, but that failed. I hired the best mercenaries in Mortise, and yet she still showed up in Duvan—even sooner than expected."

Desfan sucked in a breath. "You hired Salim to kill Serene."

"Well, I hired him to *abduct* her. I wanted to kill her myself. But considering how everything turned out, I wouldn't recommend hiring Salim. He's not as good as he thinks." Amil slowly rotated his wrist, spinning his blade in a perfectly controlled circle. Jamal's blood sprinkled the floor, and Amil's gold ring caught the light, flashing the engraving of a lion.

Fang and claw.

The code words Desfan had been asked to investigate. He'd been so focused on the traitors he'd arrested, he hadn't thought about Amil—or the Havim family symbol.

Amil glanced at the chaos around them. "You did this, you know. By believing peace with Devendra was possible. By sending my father to the slaughter. By not listening to me. Even as we speak, your prison is emptying, your court is dying, and your treasury is being raided." His lips quirked. "But then, you won't have to worry about any of that. I'll kill you, and then I'll find Serene and kill her. With both of you dead, I think we can consider the peace thoroughly wrecked. Don't you agree?"

"Amil, this is madness. You're destroying Mortise—"

"*You* did this," he hissed. "I told you that allying with Devendra would be a mistake. You didn't listen." He lifted the blood-streaked sword. "As long as I breathe, you will never be serjan."

"I suppose you leave me no choice, then." Desfan attacked, but he underestimateed Amil's speed. The man whipped away, dodging the blow and then striking out with a roar, his longsword slicing toward Desfan's neck.

Desfan ducked and pivoted, diving for Jamal's prone body. If he could just get his sword—

Imara was there, kneeling beside Jamal's body, his sword in her hands. The hilt was extended to Desfan, the blade flat on her palms. Her eyes were wide, locked on a place behind him.

Desfan grabbed the hilt, sweeping it up with care not to nick Imara's soft skin. He swung around, the blade cutting through the air.

Amil barely snatched himself back in time, and then their swords clanged together. Desfan clenched his jaw at the jarring impact that he felt to his bones. Their swords slid apart with a rasping hiss and Desfan dropped his dagger, needing both hands to meet Amil's strong blows. He parried another hit, grinding his teeth as he struck out.

Their blades hit and glanced off each other, the two of them spinning around the floor in a deadly dance, stepping over fallen bodies as screams still echoed through the room. Amil fought with a mix of fluid grace and cold hard rage. Desfan hadn't fought with a longsword in a long time, and he mentally cursed himself for not practicing. But his sparring with Grayson had taught him the importance of a fast strike, so he hammered Amil with blow after blow.

After a particularly strong hit that vibrated all the way up Desfan's arms, he shoved Amil back and kicked him in the stomach.

Amil's heel caught on a prone body and he staggered, then crashed onto his back.

Desfan jumped forward, the tip of his blade coming to rest on Amil's heaving chest.

Imara stomped on the nobleman's wrist, keeping his sword pinned to the floor.

Desfan's chest rose and fell with heavy breaths as he cut a look to the Zennorian princess to make sure she was unharmed. "You didn't run."

She grinned, her hair hanging loose around her flushed face. "You're welcome."

He huffed a short laugh, his attention turning back to Amil. His blood froze when he saw the small knife glint in Amil's hand.

"No!" Imara cried.

But Amil wasn't striking at Desfan—he was too far away. No, Amil rolled inward, his knife plunging for Imara's stomach.

She reared back at the same time Desfan shoved his blade into Amil's heart, but the dagger sank into Imara's leg above the knee, going in deep.

Her shriek of pain nearly blinded Desfan.

He dropped his sword and caught her, aware of Amil shuddering with his last breath.

Imara collapsed against Desfan's chest, sweat streaking her face, her shaking hands gripping his arms. Her eyes were riveted on the short hilt that stuck out of her leg.

Bile heated Desfan's throat. Fates, it was so deep it must have hit bone.

Imara's breaths were short and pained, her hold on him crushing. "G-get it out."

Blood seeped from the wound, slowly soaking her skirt. He hesitated to remove it. What if it made the bleeding worse? But they couldn't just stand here, waiting for help. People were still fighting— dying. He needed to get Imara out of here, and carrying her with a knife embedded in her leg could do even more damage.

Taking the only option in front of him, he grabbed the hilt and tugged it free.

Her scream rang in his ears.

He threw the blade away, his palm burning. There was no time to make a bandage. They needed to run. He balled up a handful of her skirt and pressed it against the bleeding wound, even as he lifted her in his arms. Fates, but she was small. And as she sagged against him, he feared she was losing blood far quicker than he'd thought.

"Put pressure on it," he ordered.

Imara's hand moved weakly, but she did as he said.

He ran for the servants' passage. Her breaths stuttered shallowly against his throat, her head against his shoulder. "Hold on," he begged her. "Just hold on."

Her frayed breathing was her only answer.

Plunging into the narrow hallway, he prayed no enemies waited inside.

CHAPTER 66

CLARE

CLARE'S HANDS WERE ON DAVIS'S CHEST AS she felt the last breath leave his body. As he stilled, grief tore through her, punching momentarily through her fear. The Mortisian guard was also lying prone in the hallway.

How quickly things had spun out of control.

"Go," Michael Byers repeated to Latif.

"What will you do with her?" Latif asked, eyeing the knife in Michael's hand.

"That's not your concern. Leave." When Latif didn't move, Michael's eyes narrowed. "*Now.*"

Latif glanced down at Clare.

Her heart thudded in her chest, her fingers wet with Davis's blood. Her eyes pleaded for Latif's help. He didn't know who she was—he'd only known her as Serene, and she was not dressed as the princess right now.

Latif swallowed, his gaze moving back to Michael. His grip on the sword flexed—and then his eyes narrowed.

Behind Michael was another Devendran. He was obviously a fellow rebel, though both were dressed as Mortisian guards. "What's taking so long?" the newcomer asked, impatience thinning his voice.

Michael's stare didn't leave Latif, but his words were for the man behind him. "We may have a new recruit." He jerked his chin to the floor. "Lose the sword and join my friend in the corridor." He lifted his knife. "Or you can become an issue."

Clare's pulse roared in her ears as she watched Latif's expression clear. He straightened, and then the sword dropped from his hand. The rattling *clank* on the floor reverberated through Clare's bones.

"I don't want any trouble," Latif said, raising his hands as he eased past her and Michael and joined the other rebel in the hall.

Michael eyed him the entire time he moved, then he focused on his friend. "Clear out the next floor. I'll join you soon." His attention drifted back to Clare. "Miss Ellington and I need to have a little chat."

Still on her knees beside Davis's body, Clare watched Latif and the Devendran rebel walk away, their boots clipping against the stone walls.

Latif leaving her shouldn't cut into her chest like it did, but her lungs felt too tight as she was left alone with Michael. Having him loom over her raised every hair on her body, but if she remained crouched, she would have better access to the knife strapped to her calf. She just needed to wait until his friend was far enough away that a shout wouldn't draw him back. If she could surprise Michael with a fast strike, she could stab him and run.

Bennick's voice was in her head. *You do whatever it takes to stay alive.*

Looking up at Michael, she could see the haunted edge in his eyes. The traces of grief that lined his face. She had seen him flash a charming smile before, but his expression now was warped by loathing.

"I knew I'd find you tonight," he said, his voice low and deep. "I just didn't think it would happen down here. I assumed you'd be impersonating Serene, or hiding in her rooms."

Clare's fists were so tight, the ghosting breaks along her fingers ached. She forced them to unclench, forced herself to speak through the fear that clawed her. "Why are the rebels freeing Mortisian criminals?"

Michael slowly twisted the knife in his hand, the long-bladed dagger catching in the flickering torchlight. His face was cast in shadow, making the angles sharper. Harsher. And yet his voice was chillingly cool. "Even enemies can become allies, as long as they have a common enemy to fight."

"I would have thought you'd had enough of allying with Mortisians, after what happened to Eliot."

His eyes narrowed. "You're the reason he's dead."

"No. Your stupid desire for war is what got Eliot killed. You're the one that convinced him to join the rebels, weren't you?" It was a guess, but it was clear Michael blamed himself in some way. That was why he was so vicious in his desire to blame *her;* it was far easier to blame someone else.

Rage sparked in his hard gaze. "You know nothing."

"But I do know that you allied with Mortisians. Ironic, since that's exactly what you're fighting against. You still want to stop the alliance, I assume?" She shifted a little as she goaded him, letting her hand drop closer to the hem of her skirt. The knife belted to her calf was small, but it was her best chance.

"Yes," Michael said. "I want the alliance to fail. But more than that, I want to see the life fade from your eyes."

The intensity of his hatred burned her skin, but she refused to cower. "So you volunteered to come to Duvan?"

"Yes. Because I knew you'd be here." He pointed the knife at her. "Stand up. Back against the wall."

Clare itched to grab her knife, but his was already out. Without a distraction, he would reach her first. Slowly, her eyes never leaving his, she pushed to her feet and stepped back.

Michael stayed in the doorway, but even though the distance between them increased, she only felt more cornered.

She tried to keep her voice quiet. Reasonable. "I know you're upset, but Eliot wouldn't want—"

"Don't say his name, Clare. You'll only make me angry."

A shudder wracked her body at his even tone, but she wouldn't allow herself to look away from him. "He was my brother," she whispered. "I loved him. You act as if I'm the one who killed him, but I didn't."

"Didn't you?" Michael's jaw cracked as he ground his teeth, his grip on the knife clenching. "You were in a position to help us succeed, but instead you forced Eliot to choose you at the prisoner exchange. You made him feel so guilty about putting you in danger that he abandoned the cause—gave his life—for you."

"I did nothing. He made his choice."

Michael was on her in an instant, one hand pinning her shoulder to the wall, the other holding the knife to her throat. He leaned in close, fury blistering his voice. "You may have convinced yourself of that, but you won't convince me."

She cursed herself for getting distracted. Now she had no hope of retrieving the knife. And with his blade at her neck, she didn't dare try to fight him.

"I'll avenge his death." Michael ground out. "I'll kill you, and then I'll fight until my dying breath to see Mortise ruined and King Newlan dead. Mortisians slaughtered my family—my neighbors and friends. But it was a border skirmish, and did Newlan ever make Saernon pay? No. It was all forgotten in the interest of *maintaining the truce*, but the truce was already broken." His grip on her shoulder clenched painfully. "Newlan betrayed us to the Mortisians. So now we betray him."

"The prisoners," Clare whispered, finally understanding. "You want a larger army. You're recruiting criminals of Mortise to fight against Serjah Desfan. To create trouble for him."

"Not exactly." The corner of his mouth lifted. "Make trouble for the surviving Mortisian nobility? Yes. But Desfan Cassian won't need to worry about the repercussions."

Clare's stomach dropped. "You're here to kill him."

"And Serene," Michael said. "There will be no marriage alliance once they're dead." The knife nicked her throat and she winced. He leaned closer, his breath heating her face and making her cringe. "We're bringing Mortise to its knees, Clare. We're doing what Newlan was too cowardly to do. We're going to destroy them." He pulled back only to place the tip of the dagger under her chin. "I will finish what we started. For Eliot."

Desperation made her voice hoarse. "He wouldn't have wanted this. He gave his life for me. You're not thinking—" Clare gasped as the blade sliced into her skin.

Before the cut could become deadly, Michael was shoved aside.

Clare grasped her bleeding throat as Latif plunged a sword into Michael's chest, forcing the rebel up against the wall.

Michael gurgled, his eyes wide. His knife clattered to the stone floor as he slumped down the wall and crumpled to the floor. His body shuddered once, then went still.

Latif jerked the sword free and looked at Clare. "Sorry. Wrestling away this sword took a little longer than anticipated."

Clare stared at him, adrenaline shaking through her body. "You came back."

Latif frowned. "I'm sorry you thought I'd abandoned you. But I won't stand silent among evil men ever again."

She looked down at Michael's body. The growing patch of blood under his still body made her ill.

"He would have killed you," Latif said. "I had no choice."

"Thank you. You saved my life." She glanced at him. "Did you hear any of what he said?"

"A little." He stepped toward her, angling his head toward the cut. "Is it deep?"

"No." She swallowed, the motion convulsive. "Why did you come back?"

He tightened his grip on the sword. "I'm afraid I didn't quite recognize you at first. But you *are* Princess Serene, aren't you?"

She shook her head slowly. "I'm the one you knew as Serene, but my name is Clare. I'm the princess's decoy."

"A decoy?" Latif stared. "But . . . all that time with Salim . . ."

"He couldn't know the truth." Clare shifted forward a step, grasping his hand. "I'll explain, but later. We need to warn everyone. Freeing prisoners is only part of this attack. They're going to kill Desfan and Serene."

Questions clearly burned in Latif's eyes, but he wordlessly led the way out of the cell, sword in hand.

Clare followed, carefully stepping around Davis's body and that of the Mortisian guard. Sorrow gripped her, but she would mourn them later.

There were still lives she might be able to save.

Latif and Clare walked cautiously but quickly down the corridor, headed for the stairs. Clare took out her hidden knife as they moved. Clutching the short blade made her feel marginally safer as they climbed the main staircase that led to the prison's upper hall.

Latif took the first step into the main corridor, and Clare nearly ran into him when he came to an abrupt halt. Clare peeked around his arm.

A man a couple of years older than her stood in their path. He looked quite harmless at first glance—completely at ease, and undeniably handsome, despite the rumpled clothes and untrimmed brown beard that marked him as one of the escaped prisoners. A few other men were gathered behind him—rebels, dressed as guards.

Latif seemed rooted to the floor, his gaze stuck on the bearded man. He was rigid. Afraid, Clare realized with a stab of dread.

The prisoner stared right back, a smile slowly widening into place. "Latif. Of all the surprises this day has held, I never would have expected you to be one of them." His voice was deep, and he spoke perfect Mortisian. Clare had never seen Prince Liam Kaelin, but she was quite certain that's who now grinned at them.

"Latif strolling through prison halls with Princess Serene dressed as a servant. Regardless of the whys, this does open up a realm of possibilities." Liam took a leisurely step toward them, though the rebels hung back.

Clare couldn't believe that Liam had made the assumption that she was Serene—but then, as a spymaster, he was probably good at memorizing faces and seeing through disguises. Even if, in this case, there was no disguise.

Liam continued to speak as he approached. "I was rather disappointed when you showed up in Duvan, Princess. When I learned that Amil Havim had hired Salim to capture you, I sent Latif to intercept you in Krid. Of course, you weren't there—you were already here."

Clare's thoughts spun. "Amil hired Salim?" The emissary who had once been friendly to Serene—too friendly, at times—had hated her so much in the end that he had wanted to kill her?

"Yes," Liam said. "I make it my business to know the grudges and dealings of everyone around me. Amil's grief twisted into a white-hot anger. It wouldn't have served my purposes for Amil to kill you, though—I needed Ryden to be blamed. So, I stole some of Amil's correspondence, learned his code words for Salim, and contacted someone I knew would not dare betray me. Not when I hold his secrets." He tipped his head toward Latif, brown locks of dirty hair sliding over his brow. "I'll admit, I didn't expect Amil to be capable of allying with Devendran rebels and organizing all this."

Clare's heart thudded against her ribs as she stared at the Rydenic prince. "*You* didn't orchestrate this?"

Liam cracked a hard smile. "No. And from the look on your face, it seems we both underestimated Amil Havim. But I'm more than willing to adapt and take advantage of this chance to escape. And, really, it's quite fortuitous we all ended up together, isn't it? Almost as if the fates willed it."

Latif trembled beside her.

Ice slivered through Clare's veins as Liam studied her. "It does seem like a night for surprises," he said quietly. "I didn't realize you liked to play the spy. Ghosting through the dungeons on your own . . . Perhaps we're more alike than I thought."

"No," she said, forcing her voice to remain strong like Serene's. "I don't think we're much alike at all."

Latif glanced between them. "What do you intend to do?" he asked the prince.

"I'm a free man now," Liam said. "My options are nearly endless. Though I do have a few select tasks to wrap up." He tilted his head, calculative eyes on Clare. "I'd planned to have you killed at the Rydenic border, but I'm nothing if not flexible. Latif." He nodded toward Clare. "Kill her."

CHAPTER 67

BENNICK

BENNICK LED SERENE'S RETREAT THROUGH THE shadowed corridor. Wilf walked beside him, leaving Cardon to walk behind Serene, protecting her back. Free of the dining hall, they were able to move more quickly now, though they didn't drop their guard. There were still escaped prisoners and terrified Mortisians scrambling for safety. Bennick saw only a handful of Mortisian guards fighting for order.

Fates, this was a full-on disaster. It seemed as if soldiers had been targeted just as much as the nobles—perhaps more so. It was a smart move; with the soldiers diminished, these criminals would have free reign and could take their time with the nobles who still breathed.

674

A part of Bennick wondered if it would be safer to take Serene out of the palace, but her room would be easily defensible. And he needed to reach Clare.

The further they got from the main hallways, the quieter their route became. Until they reached one of the final crossroads on their path to Serene's rooms.

Sharp cries of pain mixed cruelly with triumphant shouts caused Bennick's footsteps to falter. The sounds came from further down a corridor he hadn't ventured down before.

Cardon frowned. "That's the treasury, I think."

Wilf muttered a curse. "It's a three-pronged attack. They're after Desfan's court, his prisoners, and his gold."

"But who is *they*?" Serene asked. "Who could orchestrate this?"

None of them had an answer.

When they reached the princess's suite, the two soldiers standing guard looked utterly shaken. "We heard shouting. What's happening?"

"An attack," Bennick said shortly, following Serene into the sitting room. A quick scan of the space showed Bridget, but no one else. The sinking in his gut told him Clare wasn't in the back bedrooms. "Where's Clare?" he demanded of Bridget.

The princess's senior maid was pale. "She left with Guardsman Davis at least a quarter hour ago."

Fates blast it—he hadn't even registered that Davis was missing from the hall, he'd been so anxious to get Serene inside.

"Where did she go?" Wilf asked, his customary growl roughening his words.

"The prison. A Mortisian guard came and said a prisoner had an urgent message for the princess. He would only talk to her. The guard thought a princess's maid might suffice."

Latif. Bennick would bet anything on it.

Then it hit him, and terror locked every muscle in his body.

The escaped prisoners. The prison would be a battleground.

"Wilf," he barked, but the old soldier was already moving for the hall. Bennick twisted to Cardon, who stood with a hand wrapped around Serene's arm. "Lock this room down," he ordered curtly. "No one comes or goes until the fighting is over."

Cardon gave a firm nod, and Bennick knew Serene was in safe hands.

He tore after Wilf, wincing a little as he pushed his body. The wounds in his side ached dully, but he would not let that stop him.

Wilf slowed when they reached the main door of the prison, and Bennick followed suit. There were no guards stationed in the hall, and the door was not latched.

It was too quiet. Silent, in fact. Was the fighting already done? His blood chilled at the thought.

Sword drawn, Wilf prodded the door fully open and slid into the cooler corridor. They kept to the shadowed walls, and did not have to go far before Bennick heard voices. A moment later he saw a group of people standing near the wide descending staircase.

Clare drew his eye first. She stood beside Latif, the stairs at their backs and a group of men blocking their way forward.

There was a little blood on Clare's throat, but she appeared otherwise unharmed. One of the men spoke to her, but Bennick was far enough back he couldn't make out the words.

He counted the men between him and Clare—six.

Wilf hissed softly. "Prince Liam."

Bennick's eyes narrowed on the man in front. He hadn't seen the Rydenic prince, but he trusted Wilf. Though it was unspoken, Bennick and Wilf both knew they had to do what they could to secure him alive.

Prince Liam's voice rose suddenly. "Kill her now, or I'll kill you both."

Bennick tensed, quickly gesturing toward the men he would take down. Wilf nodded, their plan silently set.

His eyes fell back on Clare, who was looking at Latif. The fear etched into her tight expression froze Bennick for a split-second.

A fatal mistake.

Bennick watched—horrorstruck—as Latif grabbed Clare's arm and shoved a dagger into her side. Her strangled cry pierced the stone walls, and she gaped at her attacker.

"*No!*" The word tore from Bennick. Desperation wrenched him forward and out of the shadows. "Clare!"

Her head jerked toward him, but he lost sight of her as their enemies spun to face them, their swords lifting.

Wilf let out a bellow and slammed into the first wave of attackers, his sword flying in a vicious dance that left few standing.

Bennick's pulse was like thunder in his ears, and as he swung his sword to battle the blades coming for him, he forced himself to concentrate on the fight.

She wasn't dead. He could still save her. The wound didn't have to be fatal. Fates, if he'd survived being run through, she could survive this. She was the strongest person he knew.

Fates, don't let her die!

The fight was harder than it should have been. He didn't have the flexibility he'd had before his injury, but he put everything he had into each swing of his blade, making up for his shortcomings with pure determination. Finally, he broke through the knot of enemies, though he remained several paces away from Clare.

He was aware of Wilf diving to intercept an attacker who

planned to take advantage of Bennick's distraction, but all Bennick could see was Clare. She knelt on the ground, sinking to lie on her side even as he watched. Her eyes locked with his. The hilt of the dagger was still visible, her arm against her side, blocking the extent of the damage from his view.

Liam and Latif were locked in a brutal fight, but Liam got in a staggering blow when he stabbed his elbow into Latif's gut. While Latif stumbled back, Liam turned on Clare with a growl, slamming a boot into her unguarded stomach.

She screeched as she was shoved down the stairs. She rolled, dropping out of sight.

Bennick nearly lost his grip on his sword. "*Clare!*"

Latif tackled Liam, the two of them now grappling on the floor. Bennick darted past them, though he swore he'd be back to finish off whoever won their death match.

Clare was sprawled several steps down, head turned away from him.

She was not moving.

Bennick leaped down the steps, ignoring the flaring pain in his side as his old wounds stretched. Nothing mattered except reaching her—saving her.

He crouched on the stairs beside her, settling a shaking hand against her forehead. He brushed back her hair, gasping her name.

She stared up at him, her eyes wide. Then she blinked and let out a small groan. "Ow."

Bennick gripped her shoulder, his other hand drifting toward the hilt buried between her arm and side. "Hold still. You'll be all right."

She pulled in a shuddering breath. "I'm sorry," she whispered. Then she moved her arm, and the knife clattered to the stone floor.

The blade was clean.

Bennick stared, his lungs locked. There was no blood on her dress. The material was oddly frayed, but . . . His heart kicked against his ribs, heat flashing through him along with disbelief. "He didn't stab you."

She shook her head. "For a moment, I thought he had. But do you remember what you taught me during my first lesson? Sometimes the best way to stay alive is to play dead. I guess Latif knew that trick, too."

Relief flooded him. He dragged her into a fierce embrace, squeezing her so tightly to his chest that he could barely breathe. With her head tucked beneath his chin, her body warm and perfect against his, he prayed for his heartbeat to steady.

She was alive.

He couldn't speak, so he simply held her, until finally she eased back. He scanned her face. "Are you sure you're all right? You weren't hurt falling down the stairs?"

"Just a little bruised." She gripped his forearm. "Is everyone all right? Serene?"

"We're all fine."

Clare closed her eyes, tension leaking from her body as she exhaled. "Thank the fates."

Bennick helped her to her feet, stooping to retrieve his sword and the fallen dagger before leading the way up the stone staircase. His rigid muscles relaxed slightly when he found Wilf had subdued the rest of their enemies. He stood over-seeing Latif as the man bound Liam's wrists behind him with a belt.

Clare released Bennick to embrace Wilf, then she turned to Latif. "Thank you. You've saved my life twice today."

The Mortisian eyed her. "Let's hope there won't be an occasion for a third."

Wilf grunted.

Bennick faced the older bodyguard. "I want you and Latif to secure Prince Liam in a cell. Keep watch until more guards arrive."

Wilf nodded, and Bennick led Clare out of the dungeon.

CHAPTER 68

DESFAN

"I HOPE AMIL WAS LYING ABOUT MY TREASURY being robbed,"
Desfan said, his tone musing.

Imara chuckled weakly, exhaustion lining the sound. "Indeed.
What's a monarch without his gold?"

They were hiding in the pantry just off the kitchens. It was a
little closer to the banquet hall than he wanted to be, but Imara had
been losing too much blood. She had needed immediate care, and
he couldn't afford getting locked in another battle. So, the nearby
pantry had won as their best option. They'd gone undetected for
what had to have been a half hour now.

There had been no servants when they entered. They'd probably fled when they heard the screams.

He held a dagger in one hand and he kept an eye on the make-

681

shift bandage he'd wrapped around Imara's leg. The blood hadn't seeped through the newest layer—yet.

Tension still coiled in his shoulders, and he didn't know how long they should stay hidden before trying to reach a physician. For now, he was just trying to keep Imara awake. "Overall, how would you rate your experience in Mortise?" he asked.

Imara tipped her head to rest against the wall, looking tired but still managing a thin smile. "The entertainment at the feasts is a little too involved for my tastes."

He huffed a short laugh. "Your father would hang me if he knew the half of it."

"Probably. Or at least raise the trade tax. He's fiercely protective." She closed her eyes, her voice drifting lower. "He's a wonderful father. But he's an even better king. Sometimes I . . ."

"What?"

She shrugged weakly. "For him, duty to the crown is more important than anything else." Her eyelids peeled back, her deep brown eyes searching his gaze. "How much would you sacrifice for your kingdom, Desfan?"

He glanced away, eyeing the closed door of the pantry. He'd given up his past when he left his life at sea to become regent. In a way, he'd given up his future when he agreed to marry Serene. He'd endured attacks—both physical and political—at every turn. What *hadn't* he given for his people?

"Everything," he finally said. "I would sacrifice everything."

Imara did not answer immediately. When she did, her voice was soft. "You will make an incredible serjan."

Confused by her solemn tone, Desfan reminded her, "You've said that before."

The corner of her mouth lifted. "I meant it then, too."

Desfan's eyes lingered on her lips. "Why didn't you run?" he asked softly.

"I told you I wouldn't leave you."

"You saved my life."

Her eyes sparkled. "I know."

Desfan had so many reasons to remain exactly where he was. But reason didn't have a place in this intimate moment. He ignored everything but the pounding of his heart as he dipped his chin and set his mouth against her soft lips, the fingertips of one hand holding her chin in place.

The kiss was gentle and slow, and though Imara froze at the first brush of their mouths, she warmed almost at once. Her fingers slid over his cheek, keeping him close as their mouths melded together.

After a few eternal seconds, Desfan lifted away. His fingers lingered against her skin, and her hand still cradled his jaw. They both breathed deeply, and when their eyes locked, a pressure built inside his chest.

Imara's lips parted, preparing to speak.

The pantry door banged opened. "Desfan!"

Imara jerked away, and Desfan's empty hand burned. He twisted to see Karim limp into the pantry, Razan just behind him, along with a handful of guards.

Desfan scrambled to his feet, his cheeks feeling too warm. "You're alive."

"Thank the fates you're still breathing," Karim muttered. A makeshift bandage on his leg was splotched with blood, the pink material matching Razan's dress.

It was her eyes that darted to Imara. "Are you all right, Your Highness?"

"I could use a physician," Imara said, sounding just a little breathless. Desfan's lips tingled.

Razan patted Karim's arm. "He needs one, too. We can all go together."

"Is the palace secure?" Desfan asked.

Karim rubbed his forehead, expelling a heavy breath. "We think so, though we're patrolling the halls and searching every room. It's still uncertain who was behind this attack, and we're definitely not past the fallout."

"It was Amil," Desfan said.

"Havim?" Karim blinked in surprise. "Is he dead?"

"Yes."

Karim's mouth thinned. "Good."

"At least the castle is still standing," Imara said from her spot on the floor.

"True," Razan nodded. "And many of the prisoners were recovered—Prince Liam included."

Well, that was a fates-blasted mercy.

"What about Serene?" Imara asked.

"She's safe," Karim assured her. "We've received word from her guards that they made it to her rooms unscathed. She's worried about you, though. I'll let her know and she can meet us at the physician's ward."

"And what of Desfan's treasury?" Imara asked.

Karim grimaced. "It was not untouched."

Desfan sheathed his knife with a sigh. "Paying for the coronation might be a bit difficult now."

"At least you still have enough of a court to form an audience," Razan pointed out.

His mouth quirked. "There is that."

He crouched beside Imara, but she held up a quick hand. "I think I can walk."

"That's good." Desfan gave her a smile as he lifted her in his arms. "I'm pretty sure I can carry you, though."

Karim limped back into the kitchen, and Desfan didn't miss Razan's steadying grip on his arm. Or the fact that Karim didn't shrug off her touch.

Imara wrapped an arm around Desfan's neck, drawing his attention. "I'll say this for Mortise," she said quietly. "Their future serjan is extremely helpful."

Desfan tightened his hold on her. So close to him, she was all he could see. All he could feel.

Fates, what was he doing? He was promised to her *cousin*. She was promised to someone else, too.

Something low in his gut clenched, and he had to drag his gaze from her lips. He forced himself to flash a flippant smile, even though his heart pounded. "Perhaps that somewhat redeems your experience here?"

"Yes," Imara said, her deep brown eyes locked on his. "He certainly does."

CHAPTER 69

GRAYSON

"THANK YOU FOR THE LETTER," MIA SAID SOFTLY.

Grayson looked over at her. They were sitting side by side, their backs against the rear wall of the cell. The torch was still burning, but they'd been alone for hours now. "Letter?"

The corner of her mouth lifted. "The one you wrote in case something happened to you in Mortise. Fletcher gave it to me a few weeks ago. He thought your words would help me, and they did."

His cheeks warmed a little, knowing she'd read his last words, but he pressed a kiss to her temple. "I'm glad it helped."

Mia wrapped her arm around his and leaned her head against

his shoulder. "I'm sorry."

He blinked. "For what?"

"For everything you've had to suffer, but mostly for everything you've been forced to do because of me. I know how much you've been hurt all these years, and I know that much of the blame rests on me—"

"Mia." He waited until she looked up at him before continuing. "I have never blamed you."

She pursed her lips. "I don't know how that can be."

He shook his head. "Everything my family has done is their fault, and theirs alone. I love you, Mia. I don't want to think of where I'd be without you."

She looked at him steadily, easily reading his mind. "You would never be like them."

He wasn't so sure, but he appreciated her faith.

Voices on the other side of the door had him uncoiling from the floor. He would have moved to stand in front of Mia, but she gripped his hand, placing herself firmly at his side.

The door swung open, and King Henri walked in. Peter was just behind him, with Tyrell and Carter filtering in last.

Grayson didn't miss the worried look Tyrell shot at Mia. He also caught Peter's lip curling upward as he viewed Grayson, anticipation in his gaze.

A bad sign.

"I've thought long and hard about what you've said, Grayson," Henri said, his deep voice resonating against the stone walls. "My anger remains strong. You failed to kill Princess Serene, and you failed to bring Liam home, traitor or no. But I won't throw away your talents, not after all the work I've put into you. With Liam gone, there is an even greater need for all of my sons to be at my side. War is coming. So, I'll forget your failure for the greater good of Ryden." He paused meaningfully. "*I'll forget*, but I won't allow you to *ever* forget."

Grayson didn't know when his emotionless mask had shifted into place. The moment the door opened? All he knew was that the mask had frozen over his expression, hiding the panic rising in him.

Henri jerked his chin at Carter, a silent command. Carter lifted a glass vial filled with something white. Grayson's eyes narrowed on it, running all his mother's poisons through his mind.

"What is that?" Mia asked, her fingers clenching around Grayson's.

Henri's eyes flicked to her. "A reminder. Grayson can choose who will wear it."

The contents of the bottle shifted as Carter tipped it, revealing it was a powder, not a liquid. Realization punched into Grayson, making him stiffen. He knew it, because it had been used against him before. His fingers still carried the scars.

He swallowed back a wave of nausea, but he didn't hesitate. "Me. Not her."

Henri's eyes were hard as steel. "You'll prove your choice by not fighting it. If you attempt to remove it before it has run its course, she will receive the same."

Grayson learned firsthand how long that would be. His mother had made sure of it. "I understand."

Mia glanced between them, anxiety tightening her voice. "Grayson . . ."

He didn't look at her. "She doesn't have to be here. I won't fight."

"For her sake, I'm glad to hear it." Henri waved his hand, and Carter handed the bottle to Tyrell, who had jerked on a pair of thick gloves.

Grayson tugged his hand, but Mia's grip was strangling. He glanced at her. "Let go."

"No." Mia glared at Tyrell. "What are you going to do?"

He stared back at her, his face a mask that perfectly matched Grayson's. "Move aside, Mia."

Her eyes darted between all of them. "What's going on?"

"Carter," Henri ordered levelly.

Carter grabbed her, hauling her away even as she squirmed in his grasp. "No, let go—*Grayson*!"

He made sure Carter wasn't hurting her, but then he looked away and focused on his breathing. He tried to ignore everything in the room, especially Mia's frantic screams as Carter held her in the corner. He kept his eyes on the bottle Tyrell held.

"Kneel," Henri commanded.

Grayson did, watching Tyrell, who now towered over him. His brother stared right back, a muscle in his cheek jumping at an especially loud cry from Mia.

A half hour. That's all Grayson had to focus on surviving. Just a half hour, then the pain would begin to fade. If he made it through this, Mia would not be hurt.

If this was the price required to protect her, he would pay it a thousand times.

"Every time you see it," Henri said, "you will remember me. Fail me again, and you won't experience my mercy."

Tyrell uncorked the bottle and grasped a handful of Grayson's hair.

Grayson's stomach lurched. Fates. It was going on his *face*.

He pressed his fists against the floor, hoping no one would see how much his hands shook.

Tyrell tilted Grayson's head to the side, upturning his cheek.

"The other side," Henri said, speaking over Mia. She was crying now, struggling to break free of Carter's locked embrace. "Pour it into the cut on his jaw."

Tyrell hesitated. Grayson almost wondered if he'd imagined it, because a split-second later he was moving, twisting Grayson's head around. Still, Grayson wondered if—impossibly—Tyrell had been trying to help him by keeping the Flames Breath away from the fresh wound.

King Henri looked on silently from his place in the center of the room. Beside him, Peter smiled, his eyes alight with excitement.

Tyrell kept a firm grip on Grayson's hair, but he didn't restrain him further.

He didn't need to. Grayson would not fight this.

The vial was emptied across the exposed cut that sliced across his jaw. The burning started upon contact, the bite of it sharper than he'd remembered. Grayson ground his teeth against a snarl. His flesh was being eaten by the acidic Flames Breath—seared until it felt like his skin was bubbling. Melting.

"Rub it in," Henri said dispassionately.

Tyrell dropped the vial and rubbed the powder deeper into the cut, the leather glove stiff.

Grayson jerked and ground his teeth against the flare of pain as the fine powder seared inside him. It might have been his imagination, but it seemed Tyrell wasn't pushing as hard as he could have. He also moved slowly, as if he was trying to keep the powder from spreading up onto his cheek.

The pain was nearly blinding.

Tyrell finally finished and released his hold. Grayson doubled over, his fingers digging into the stone floor so he wouldn't grab his face. He couldn't bite back a scream as his skin burned, but he didn't thrash against the torture. Even when Mia sobbed his name, he didn't fight.

But he would.

His fingers bit harder into the stones beneath him, clawing so deep they bled. He felt his father's stare and he forced his chin to lift. His whole body shook as he met Henri's gaze, and it was clear the king thought he'd won.

He was wrong.

His father had forced him to become a monster. The Black Hand. The Scourge of Ryden.

It was time for Henri to be afraid of the demon he'd created.

CHAPTER 70

CLARE

NEARLY AN HOUR AFTER CLARE AND BENNICK had returned to the princess's suite, word arrived that Serjah Desfan had survived the attack. Imara had as well, though she'd been injured. While the message made it clear the wound wasn't life-threatening, Serene insisted on going at once to see her cousin. Cardon escorted her with a few other guards, leaving Bennick with Clare alone inside the princess's sitting room.

"I'm fine," Clare told him yet again, even as he made her take a seat on the long settee. "I could have gone to see Imara."

"Indulge me." Bennick sat beside her, his gaze intent. "Please."

She sighed. "When you look at me like that, it's impossible to argue with you."

The corner of his mouth lifted. "That's good to know." His eyes narrowed in on the shallow cut that stung high on her throat. His fingertips brushed her skin, skimming along the edge of the mark. "Michael?" he asked tightly.

She had told him everything that'd happened in the prison, including Michael's surprise appearance—and the harsh things he'd said. "Yes." She met Bennick's gaze, and she felt a haze of tears. "I know I'm not responsible for Eliot's death, but . . . fates, I miss him."

Bennick cupped the side of her face, his thumb skating over her cheek. "He made some terrible choices, but I will always be grateful that his last choice was to save you."

Clare smiled a little, but it wavered. "There's so much I never got to say to him. So many things I'll never know. I barely knew him in the end."

"He loved you. That's what you need to remember. Let the rest of it go." Bennick's words were so simple. So perfect.

Clare leaned in, placing a soft kiss against his cheek. "Thank you."

He tugged her close, his bristled jaw grazing her temple as his head ducked beside hers. "Things will be easier once Mark and Thomas are here," he whispered.

She had to agree. Still . . . "Do you think I made the right choice? Will they be safe here?"

Bennick rubbed a hand against her spine. Resting against his chest as she was, she felt every beat of his heart. "It would have been too dangerous to bring them with us, but now . . . Despite the dangers in Mortise, I can't help but think they'll be safer near us."

"Just not *too* near." Clare sighed. She would still be the decoy, and she needed to protect her brothers from that knowledge—and the accompanying danger.

"I wonder if the coronation will be delayed," Bennick murmured. "This attack was brutal."

She hadn't thought of that. "I suppose it will be up to Desfan to decide."

He tightened his hold on her. He took a breath to respond, but before he could, a knock on the door sounded.

"Captain Markam?" a guard called through the door.

Bennick pulled back from her and stood, straightening his uniform. "Enter," he called out.

The door pushed open and a Devendran guard stuck his head inside. "Captain, sorry to interrupt, but we just received a letter from Commander Markam."

Bennick's brow grew lined as he stepped forward to retrieve the missive from his father. "Thank you."

The guard bowed and retreated, and Bennick studied the envelope. He frowned. "It's addressed to you."

Surprise rippled through her. She moved to Bennick's side, her skirt whispering over the carpeted floor. She took the letter, her hand trembling a little as she did so.

It didn't make sense. Why would Bennick's father be writing to *her*?

She cracked the wax seal, not sure why unease swirled in her gut.

Not until she read the carefully scripted words.

Miss Ellington,

I regret to inform you of an unfortunate

incident. It has been my task to check in with your brothers during your absence. On my most recent visit, I learned there had been a fire in Lower Iden. It destroyed most of the homes on your street—including yours. I'm afraid your brothers and their caretaker were inside, and there were no survivors.

I have begun an investigation into the fire's origins, and will keep you informed. I offer my condolences for your loss.

Commander Markam

THE STORY CONTINUES IN
ROYAL REBEL
BOOK 4 OF THE FATE OF EYRINTHIA SERIES

GLOSSARY

AFARAH *(ah-FAHR-ah)* A city in Mortise.

AKIVA *(ah-KEE-vah)* One of Liam's Mortisian contacts. Alias: Zeph.

AMIL HAVIM *(uh-MEEL hah-VEEM)* A Mortisian nobleman who served in Devendra with his father as an emissary of peace. Due to his father's murder in Devendra, he no longer supports the alliance.

ANOUSH *(ah-NOOSH)* A newly appointed member of the Mortisian council. Father to Arav. Full name: Ramit Anoush.

ARAV ANOUSH *(AH-ruhv ah-NOOSH)* A Mortisian nobleman. Son of Ser Anoush, a newly appointed member of the Mortisian council.

ARCAS *(AR-kus)* A kiv in the Mortisian city guard. Full name: Manusch Arcas.

AREN BUHARI DEMOI *(eh-RUHN boo-HAR-ee de-MOY)* The late queen of Devendra, mother to Serene and Grandeur. Was married to Newlan Demoi. Sister to Zaire Buhari, king of Zennor.

ASHEAR *(uh-SHEER)* A former member of the Mortisian council. Deceased. Full name: Duman Ashear.

BENNICK MARKAM *(BEN-ick MARK-ahm)* Captain of Serene's bodyguards. Commander Markam's son. In love with Clare Ellington.

BRIDGET *(BRI-jeht)* The senior maid for Serene.

CARDON BRINHURST *(CAR-den BRIN-herst)* One of Serene's body-guards. He has a distinctive scar on his cheek.

CARTER THELIN KAELIN *(CAR-tr THEL-in KAY-lin)* The second prince of Ryden and a close follower of Peter's. Also a dutiful pupil of his mother's.

CLARE ELLINGTON *(CLAIR EL-ing-tun)* The decoy for Serene. Former maid in the castle kitchen. Sister to Eliot, Thomas, and Mark Ellington. In love with Bennick Markam.

COMMANDER DENNITH MARKAM *(DEN-ith MARK-ahm)* A high-ranking Devendran commander. Father to Bennick and married to Gweneth Markam.

DAWN OF EYRINTHIA A two-week holiday in Mortise celebrating Eyrinthia, proclaimed goddess of the world and creator of the fates.

DESFAN SAERNON CASSIAN *(DES-fawn SAIR-non CAS-ee-uhn)* The heir to the Mortisian throne and currently serving as regent due to his father's illness. His official title is *serjah*.

DEVENDRA *(duh-VEN-druh)* One of the kingdoms of Eyrinthia, ruled by the Demoi family.

DEVENDRAN *(duh-VEN-drun)* Relating to the kingdom of Devendra or its people.

DEVON *(DEV-uhn)* A physician who works in the Rydenic castle.

DIRK ARKLOWE *(DIRK ARK-low)* One of Serene's bodyguards. He is the oldest of the guards and has protected the princess since her birth.

DOLBAR PASS *(DOHL-bar PASS)* A mountain pass that connects Ryden and Devendra.

DORMA *(DOHR-muh)* The largest Mortisian island.

DUVAN *(DOO-vahn)* The capital city of Mortise.

ELIOT ELLINGTON *(EL-ee-uht EL-ing-tun)* Clare's older brother. He was a Devendran city guardsman who rebelled against King Newlan. Also known as Eliot Slaton. (Slaton was his mother's surname.) Deceased.

EYRINTHIA *(air-INTH-ee-uh)* The name of the known world. The four kingdoms of Eyrinthia are Devendra, Mortise, Ryden, and Zennor. In Mortise (and select religions in Devendra and Zennor) Eyrinthia is also the name of a goddess.

FARAH CASSIAN *(FAIR-uh CAS-ee-uhn)* Desfan's mother, the late seraijan of Mortise.

FLAMES BREATH A powder that causes extremely painful burns.

FLETCHER *(FLEH-chr)* Mia's day guard. Full name: Alun Fletcher.

GALE A pirate aboard the *Seafire*.

GRANDEUR NEWLAN DEMOI *(GRAN-jer NEW-luhn de-MOY)* The crown prince of Devendra and heir to the throne. Serene's younger brother.

GAMBLE A Mortisian sailor who overheard a rumor that one of

the seraijahs might have survived the shipwreck nine years ago.

GRAYSON WINN KAELIN *(GRAY-suhn WIN KAY-lin)* The young-est prince of Ryden. He is the enforcer of his father's laws. Also known as the Black Hand.

GWENETH MARKAM *(GWEH-neth MARK-ahm)* Bennick's mother. She is married to Commander Dennith Markam.

HENRI KAELIN *(HEN-ree KAY-lin)* The king of Ryden. He is mar-ried to Iris Kaelin, and they have five sons.

IDEN *(EYE-den)* The capital city of Devendra.

IEANNAX *(EYE-ahn-ax)* A rare poison that delivers painless death. Originates from Zennor.

IMARA AIMETH BUHARI *(ih-MAR-uh AY-meth boo-HAR-ee)* The third Zennorian princess and daughter of Zaire Buhari. She is Serene's cousin.

IRIS KAELIN *(EYE-ruhs KAY-lin)* The queen of Ryden. She is mar-ried to Henri Kaelin, and they have five sons. Also known as the Poison Queen.

IVAR CARRIGAN *(EYE-vaar CARE-i-guhn)* King Newlan's cousin. He led a failed uprising in Devendra ten years ago. Alive; current location unknown.

IVERN *(EYE-vern)* A river that separates Zennor from the other kingdoms.

IVONNE SMALLWOOD *(ee-VOHN SMAHL-wood)* A former maid of

Serene's and older sister to Vera. Deceased.

JAHZARA *(jah-ZAR-uh)* A Zennorian noblewoman and Peter's mistress.

JAMAL *(jah-MAHL)* A former member of the Mortisian council. Recently arrested for treason and other crimes. Full name: Omar Jamal.

JAMES *(JAIMZ)* A Devendran commoner who is a friend to Serene and serves as one of her leading rebels.

KARIM SAFAR *(kah-REEM sa-FAR)* Desfan's bodyguard, as well as his best friend.

KAZIM *(kah-ZEEM)* One of Liam's Mortisian contacts. Alias: Neev Sal.

KEDAAH *(ke-DAH)* The capital city of Zennor.

KIV *(KIV)* (rhymes with *give*) A Mortisian military title, similar to the rank of captain.

KRID *(KRID)* A city in Mortise.

LAMBERN *(LAM-burn)* A lake located in Devendra.

LATIF *(lah-TEEF)* A Mortisian man with many secrets. He assists with the abduction of Clare.

LEEB *(LEEB)* A Mortisian island.

LENZEN *(LEN-zuhn)* The capital city of Ryden.

LIAM KELL KAELIN (*LEE-um KEL KAY-lin*) The third prince of Ryden. He is the spymaster for his father. Also known as the Shadow of Ryden.

MAMA One of Mia's former caretakers.

MARK ELLINGTON (*MARK EL-ing-tun*) The youngest of Clare's brothers. She has raised him since his birth.

MEERAH JEMA CASSIAN (*MEER-uh JEH-muh CAS-ee-uhn*) Desfan's youngest sister, one of the late seraijahs of Mortise.

MIA (*MEE-ah*) The young woman who loves Grayson. She has been a prisoner in Ryden for several years.

MICHAEL BYERS (*MY-cull BY-urz*) A former Devendran city guardsman and a current rebel intent on killing Serene and King Newlan. Best friend to Eliot Ellington.

MORTISE (*mor-TEES*) (rhymes with *geese*) One of the kingdoms of Eyrinthia, ruled by the Cassian family.

MORTISIAN (*mor-TEE-shun*) Relating to the kingdom of Mortise or its people.

NEWLAN DEMOI (*NEW-luhn de-MOY*) The king of Devendra, father to Serene and Grandeur. Was married to the late queen of Devendra, Aren Buhari Demoi. Cousin to Ivar Carrigan, who led a rebellion against him ten years ago.

OLCAIN (*OHL-cain*) A highly addictive drug that originates from Zennor.

ORI (*OR-ee*) A Mortisian street urchin who works with the infamous pirate Syed Zadir.

PAPA One of Mia's former caretakers. Deceased.

PETER HENRI KAELIN (*PEE-tr HEN-ree KAY-lin*) The heir to the throne of Ryden and the oldest Kaelin brother.

PORYNTH (*por-INTH*) A port city in Ryden.

RAHIM NASSAR (*rah-HEEM nah-SAR*) A Mortisian merchant and suspected smuggler.

RANON SIFA (*rah-NON SEE-fah*) A Mortisian nobleman. Son of Ser Sifa, a newly appointed member of the Mortisian council.

RAZAN KRAYT (*RAA-zan KRAYT*) A Mortisian noblewoman. She has a complicated past with Desfan and Karim, which is detailed in the novella *Fire and Ash*.

RENA FLETCHER (*RAIN-uh FLEH-chr*) Wife to Alun Fletcher. She serves as Mia's maid.

REW (*ROO)* A small city in Ryden.

RYDEN (*RYE-den*) One of the kingdoms of Eyrinthia, ruled by the Kaelin family.

RYDENIC (*rye-DEN-ick*) Relating to the kingdom of Ryden or its people.

SAERNON JARON CASSIAN *(SAIR-non JAIR-uhn CAS-ee-uhn)* The ruler of Mortise and Desfan's father. Currently incapacitated by illness. Official title is *serjan*.

SAHVI (*SAW-vee*) A Zennorian drug master.

SALIM (*sah-LEEM*) A Mortisian man who leads an infamous group of sadistic mercenaries.

SEAFIRE The ship of the infamous Mortisian pirate Syed Zadir.

SEDAH (*SEH-dah*) A small village in Mortise.

SER (*SAIR*) The Mortisian term for *lord*; title used to address noble males.

SERAI (*SAIR-ay*) The Mortisian term for *lady*; title used to address noble females.

SERAIJAH (*sair-AY-zjaw*) The Mortisian term for *princess*.

SERAIJAN (*sair-AY-zjawn*) The Mortisian term for *queen*.

SERENE AREN DEMOI (*ser-EEN EH-ruhn de-MOY*) The princess of Devendra. She is Newlan's firstborn but not in line for the throne, because in Devendra women cannot rule.

SERJAH (*SAIR-zjaw*) The Mortisian term for *prince*.

SERJAN (*SAIR-zjawn*) The Mortisian term for *king*.

SHEBAR (*sheh-BAAR*) A port city in Mortise.

SIFA (*SEE-fah*) A newly appointed member of the Mortisian council. Father to Ranon. Full name: Abeil Sifa.

SKYER (*SKY-ur*) The leader of the Kabu clan in Zennor. He is betrothed to Imara. Also known as *Sky Painter*.

SWALLOW A pirate aboard the *Seafire*.

SYALLA (*sy-AL-uh*) A pain-causing potion that is often applied to blades. Generally used in Ryden.

TABAKH (*tah-BAWK*) A city in Mortise.

TAHLYAH FARAH CASSIAN (*TAHL-yah FAIR-uh CAS-ee-uhn*) Desfan's younger sister, one of the late seraijahs of Mortise.

TAMAR NADIR (*tah-MAR nah-DEER*) A Mortisian noblewoman who lives near the Devendran border. A great supporter for peace between Mortise and Devendra.

TARIQ (*tah-REEK*) A Mortisian criminal, and one of the highest-ranking members of Salim's mercenaries.

THE ROSE The most feared assassin in Eyrinthia. He always leaves a rose with his victims. His real name is Zilas. He is the illegitimate son of Commander Markam and half-brother to Ben-nick.

THOMAS ELLINGTON (*TAH-mus EL-ing-tun*) Clare's younger brother.

TYRELL ZEV KAELIN (*ty-REL ZEHV KAY-lin*) The second youngest prince of Ryden. Grayson's closest rival. He oversees the training of Ryden's soldiers.

VENN GRANNARD (*VEN GRAN-ard*) One of Serene's bodyguards and Bennick's best friend. He is half Zennorian; his father was a Devendran soldier who died when Venn was young.

VERA SMALLWOOD (*VER-ah SMAHL-wood*) One of Serene's maids.

Younger sister to Ivonne and friend to Clare.

VYKEN (*VY-ken*) The main port city of Ryden.

WEEPER A pirate aboard the *Seafire*.

WHISTLER A pirate aboard the *Seafire*.

WIDOW'S BRAID A Zennorian custom for widows to mark the stages of mourning.

WILFORD LINES (*WIL-ford LINES*) One of Serene's bodyguards. Former captain of Grandeur's bodyguards, before being demoted. He nearly died from the pox five years ago. The same illness killed his wife, Rachel.

YAHRI (*YAH-ree*) The senior member of the Mortisian council. Full name: Amna Yahri.

ZADIR (*zah-DEER*) A Mortisian pirate captain. Full name: Syed Zadir. Also known as Crush.

ZAIRE BUHARI (*ZAIR boo-HAR-ee*) The king of Zennor. Imara's father and Serene's uncle. Brother to the late Aren Buhari Demoi.

ZENNOR (*ZEN-or*) One of the kingdoms of Eyrinthia, ruled by the Buhari family.

ZENNORIAN (*zen-OR-ee-un*) Relating to the kingdom of Zennor or its people.

ZEPHAN (*ZEF-uhn*) A traitor and former member of the Mortisian council. Deceased. Full name: Ganem Zephan.

ZILAS (*ZY-luhs*) Illigitamate son of Commander Markam, half-brother to Bennick. He is also The Rose, the most infamous assassin in Eyrinthia.

ZOROYA (*zo-ROY-uh*) The main port city of Zennor.

ACKNOWLEDGEMENTS

As always, I need to give a huge thank you to my family. You are all so supportive, and I'm so grateful to have you in my life!

Thank you to my incredible beta readers who helped shape this book into something so epic. I appreciated all the conversations, re-reads, and the encouraging words when I needed them most. Kimberly Frost, Rebecca McKinnon, Laurie Ford, Cynthia Ford, and Anna Brown. Thank you!

Thanks to my amazing proofreaders and early readers, who are literal angels! Marlene Frost, Crystal Frost, Stephanie Blue, Elyce Edwards, Michalla Holt, Amelia White, Jonnie Morgart, and Amy Cardon. Bless you all!

Finally, thank YOU for picking up this book and loving these characters. Thank you for spreading the word and bringing more readers to Eyrinthia, and for sharing this journey with me. Your enthusiasm and love helps to keep me going!

If you liked this book, please consider leaving a review!
It truly makes a WORLD of difference.
Thank you!

WANT TO SEE DESFAN AND KARIM BECOME FRIENDS?
CURIOUS ABOUT HOW THEY MET RAZAN?
CHECK OUT THE NOVELLA, FIRE & ASH!

HEATHER FROST

FIRE & ASH

A FATE OF EYRINTHIA NOVELLA

A FIFTEEN-YEAR-OLD DESFAN CAN GET INTO
A LOT OF TROUBLE . . .

FIRST THE FLAMES . . .

When Desfan Cassian, the future ruler of Mortise, skips his fifteenth birthday celebration so he can gamble in the slums, he knows his father won't be pleased. Then again, the serjan hasn't been happy with him in years. And while Desfan anticipates a reprimand for his latest transgression, he doesn't expect to be thrown out of the palace and exiled onto a patrol ship for the next year.

THEN FROM THE ASHES . . .

Furious to be trapped on the same sea that stole his family four years ago, Desfan is fully prepared to hate his new life. After all, the *Phoenix* is run by a strict captain, and Desfan's annoying new bodyguard, Karim, is his constant shadow. But when Des-fan learns that a group of dangerous pirates may have been behind the deaths of his mother and sisters, he's suddenly com-mitted to hunting down the truth—no matter the risk.

HE WILL RISE.

ABOUT THE AUTHOR

Heather Frost writes YA fiction and she has a soft spot for tortured characters, breath-stealing romance, and happy endings. She is the author of the Seers trilogy and the Fate of Eyrinithia series. Two of her books have been Whitney Award Finalists, and both *Royal Decoy* and *Royal Spy* were Swoony Award Finalists. She has a BS in Creative Writing and a minor in Folklore, which means she got to read fairy tales and ghost stories and call it homework.

When she's not writing, Heather likes to read, travel, and re-watch The Lord of the Rings. She lives in a beautiful valley surrounded by towering mountains in northern Utah.

To learn more about Heather and her books, visit her website: www.HeatherFrost.com.